J.McCOY
DOUBLE-BLIND

BOOK TWO: GILDED TOWER

aethonbooks.com

ALSO IN SERIES

CHAPTER ONE

<Quest Received>
Quest: Helpline
Primary Objective — Locate Sae.
Secondary Objective — ???
Personal Objective — Remain unidentified by other Users.
Threat Level: Low
EXP GAIN (S)
Time Limit: ???
Reward: ???

The quest objective was so vague it was almost nonexistent. To the point that I wondered if the nonspecific nature was some sort of mind game. The objective simply called for locating the target, alive or dead, and the rest of the text gave nothing away. Contrasting this quest with Jinny's, there was no allusion to a positive outcome—implied or otherwise.

It could just be coincidence. But if the system was self-aware and malicious, keeping the description limited following the deceptive bundle of horseshit that was "Light In the Darkness" would be a decent method for catching my eye.

If anything, it felt like I'd made the right call, waiting until after the Transposition to read it. I was in a better headspace now than I had been at the time, though I was still obsessing over every little detail in the text.

Even though it was cryptic, there were a few things that stood out. It explicitly stated the threat level was low. From my experience, if a quest was either complex or exceedingly difficult, the system would typically tag it with a "???" threat level. Granted, low didn't always mean easy—my early quest in the hospital could have easily proved fatal if it went wrong. But it probably meant this wouldn't be a complex quest. The fact it wasn't a chain supported that theory in tandem.

If I wasn't wheelchair bound, I might feel better about the possibility of having to retake the trial.

On some level, I knew what I was really doing. I was distracting myself. From the very real possibility that Sae was gone.

Any doubt remaining in my mind had evaporated once the Transposition started. Whatever was happening, it wasn't about correcting or fixing us, as the Overseer implied. It was a meat grinder, pushing us head first through motorized blades, intending to use whatever survived the process to some unknown purpose.

And I held little hope for a meat grinder's mercy.

"Rice cake?" Our driver shoved the open mouth of a cylindrical plastic bag toward me and wiggled it, so the wrinkled plastic seemed to wave. I took the opportunity to study Kinsley's henchman, Steinbeck. That was how he'd introduced himself, last name and nothing else. He was sporting a military crewcut, black cargo pants, and a gray t-shirt that seemed vastly uncomfortable with the bulging shoulder muscles that rippled as he moved, threatening to shred the shirt at any given moment.

"No."

"Cap?" He twisted his arm to aim the bag at Kinsley, wiggling it again, all the while never looking away from the road.

"Later. Save me a few." Kinsley shook her head. She looked similarly stressed, though likely for different reasons. Her eyes were glazed over and she was navigating system screens furiously, probably messaging.

"Ten-four." Steinbeck feigned a lazy, two-finger salute and returned his attention to the road. I didn't like involving outsiders in something this personal. Not to mention, it was the one timeline discrepancy that could still trip me up. We'd fed him a line about my friends being overdue after telling me about the trial, that they'd disappeared before the Transposition started and I wanted to check on them after. It still felt like an unnecessary risk, but Kinsley either trusted the man or had enough leverage on him to vouch for his short-term loyalty. Considering how she handled me, there was a good chance of a contract being involved.

"Problem?" I muttered under my breath to Kinsley.

"Negotiating with other merchants for market access."

"I respect the hustle, but is that really what you need to focus on right now?" I asked. There were half a dozen things off the top of my head that seemed more important.

Kinsley's expression soured. "Once the Transposition ended, automatic restocking stopped completely."

I took a drink of one of the tall glass potions and fought down a gag as the thick, acrid fluid worked its way down my throat and into my stomach, a process I could vividly feel all the way down. Something about what she'd said suddenly clicked. "They handed us the means of production, and now the training wheels are coming off."

"Right," Kinsley said, only half paying attention. "And I'm working on getting the vocations we need. Armorers, Smiths, Alchemists, and so on, but that'll take time. Countless people are still hiding out due to how heavy-handed the guilds were early on. So, there's a shortage. Anything I put up on the store is getting bought up immediately. A few extra merchants would go a long way to fill the stopgap. Enter the Merchants' Coalition—a couple chucklefucks that figured out the position I'm in and have every intention of holding me over a barrel until I agree to their terms."

"Their terms that bad?" I asked.

"Highway robbery." Kinsley huffed back in her seat. "I offered 20%, prepared to negotiate down to 10. They countered with 2%, final offer."

"When did that happen?"

"This morning."

"So, you've been arguing with them since then?" I asked.

Kinsley nodded. "They won't budge. And they keep talking down to me."

"It's a power play. They insulted you with their terms and they know it. This is about testing how much shit you'll put up with."

"Then what am I supposed to do?"

I thought on that for a moment. "Cut all contact. Keep pursuing other merchants, regardless of how good their selection is and how useful of an add they would be. Don't respond to anything the coalition sends you, don't say anything to them for the rest of the day. You have to show you're willing to walk away from the table."

Kinsley sighed, visibly struggling to accept the idea. "I'll think about it.

"We're here," Steinbeck called from the front.

———

After some debate and argument, Kinsley had agreed to stay in the car, leaving Steinbeck to escort me. Reason being, he could easily throw me over his shoulder and escape if the monsters in the tunnel had repopulated. Factor protecting Kinsley into that equation and the odds became much more questionable.

Steinbeck had changed into his gear as we descended, a full-on suit of armor with two bronze-colored, scythe-shaped swords crisscrossed on his back. He'd easily picked me up, wheelchair and all, navigating the stairs, and dropped into the train tunnel as effortlessly as if he'd been carrying a box of clothes. He snacked on a bag of Goldfish as he wheeled me down the tunnel with one hand.

"Do you ever stop eating?" I asked. It was meant to be a joke but came out more harshly than intended.

"Not when I can help it," Steinbeck admitted. "Ain't much in life that isn't improved by a full stomach. Or sharing." He held the bag out to me again. "Come on, that growling in your gut is gonna ring the dinner bell for any monster down here."

I shook my head, appreciating on some level that the man was distracting me. "I'll eat something after."

"Had a few squadmates like you, once upon a time. Usually the first ones to lose their lunch when we got into combat. Nauseous types, you understand. The thing we all sort of collectively figured out? If you're gonna puke, you're gonna puke. Full or empty, makes no difference. So, the question is, Matthias, do you want to taste bile and acid when you puke? Or that light snack you indulged a second time around?"

I bit back a smartass remark as we passed a section of wall that showed a small patch of red blood I was intimately familiar with. The place I'd sat for so long after regaining consciousness, the blood from bashing the back of my head against the wall over and over, trying to summon the strength to get up.

"Fine. Give them."

"That's the spirit." Steinbeck grinned and dropped the bag in my lap. He spoke again, after I'd shoved two tasteless handfuls into my mouth. "Could be wrong, but if I were to make a door for a trial, it'd look something like that."

Up ahead was the ornate door. And twenty feet from it was the slab of cement Jinny had died on. Just like before, there wasn't a single trace of her. My jaw tightened. The suits were thorough. They'd erased any evidence. For all but a small handful of people, it would be as if she'd never existed in the first place.

"Gotta be," I agreed, reaching down toward the wheels. "I'll take it from here, Steinbeck."

"You sure?"

"Yeah. Just going to open the door and call in after them. I won't go in."

Steinbeck studied the door, then looked back at me. "And if you open the door and some monster decides to give you a Columbian necktie before I can cross the distance?"

"Then you can tell the guild leader I refused your help out of stubbornness."

Unsurprisingly, Steinbeck wouldn't to go back to the entrance of the tunnel. But he agreed to stand thirty yards back and placed a pair of earbuds in his ears of his own volition. He must have raised the volume significantly, because I could hear snippets of something orchestral and bombastic.

There was a hollow emptiness in my chest as I grabbed the handle of the door. Some part of me expected to find her there immediately, lying dead on the floor, worked over by monsters and whatever else the trial had repopulated with.

Bracing myself, I threw the door open, finding nothing. Unless the format had changed, I knew the initial room opened up after a length of hallway. The hallway was still gray and mottled with chitin material. Beyond the hallway, I could see just enough of the first room to pick out the reflection of green torches on dark water. Something scurried away just out of sight, leaving ripples in the dark water.

The trial hadn't changed much. It was impossible to say if that was a good thing or a bad one for a person who'd retreated inside.

"Sae. It's Matt. Came back for you, like I promised." My voice echoed off the walls back toward me. I turned one ear toward the hallway, listening intently.

No answer. Just the smallest ripple in the water.

I kept talking. "You, uh, missed some things. Nick is still alive. The suits took him, left me in the tunnel. I regained consciousness just in time for the Transposition. It was a hard day. Harder than any I can remember. We lost some people."

What was I doing? It was painfully obvious Sae wasn't there. Either dead or just... gone. I grabbed the handrims and prepared to leave. Then, unbidden, the words began to flow again.

"You, uh, want to hear a joke?" I chuckled, putting a hand on my forehead. "This probably won't surprise you, but I'm a loner. Always have been. It's easiest for me to operate that way. So, going into the Transposition solo should have been a return to form. Me, on my own, trying to contribute as much as I could." I leaned my head back and looked at the ceiling. "Only this time, things got... really dark. And desperate. And painful. I had to make some decisions that are gonna stick with me for the rest of my life. And—here comes the joke—all I could think about, during the worst moments, was how much I missed having all of you at my side. People willing to share the burden. Friends I could rely on—maybe for the first time ever. I know it's stupid. Outside of Nick, I didn't know you or Jinny long enough to call you that. But the more I consider it, the more likely it seems we were headed that way." My voice cracked at the end, sounding pathetic as it echoed off the walls.

Before the suits ruined everything.

I crossed my arms over my aching gut and leaned forward in the chair.

"I keep thinking about stupid shit. Like the four of us training. Running dungeons together and eating barbecue or pizza at Nick's after. Trivia nights. Maybe that makes me an idiot, I don't know."

It's hard to say how long I waited for an answer. Seconds, minutes, all blended as I accepted the reality.

Sae was never coming back.

"I'll be out of commission for a few more days. But when I'm back on my feet, I'll get a group together to run the trial for a more thorough search. I know it's pointless, that you're probably gone. But that doesn't matter. I have to know for sure."

I wiped my face and spun the wheelchair around slowly, cursing myself for the weakness I'd shown, even if no one had been there to see it. The pain I was feeling was a result of my foolishness. My hubris in believing that things could be different. Ignoring my carefully curated rules and allowing my mental armor to soften.

Never again, Matt—

"I'm still here."

The voice that emanated from the doorway and interrupted me mid-thought was faint, barely more than a whisper. Before I could turn back, Sae whispered again, more fervent than before.

"Don't look."

CHAPTER TWO

"Okay. I have my back to you." I looked out over the grounds my first team had been decimated on, seeing each of the suits present in my mind's eye. Other than a few inevitable glances, I'd been doing my best to avoid it. Now, I was forced to fully take it in. To remember and relieve every moment of what had happened.

Beyond the tracks, Steinbeck had caught the movement and began to pull his earbuds out. I signaled for him to stay where he was and he got the message, shrugging and replacing the bud.

Somehow, I'd managed not to turn around. For all I knew, there was some monster mimicking her voice, luring me into dropping my guard. It was something in her voice that stopped me. The Sae I knew had been a proud person—bordering on arrogant at times. When she'd spoken—if it was her—the last two words, "Don't look," had been suffused with so much shame and pathos she'd sounded like someone else entirely. I'd been so convinced she was dead, just seeing her would have made all the difference when it came to silencing doubt. It felt like some ancient Greek or biblical parable, where the simple act of looking would cost me everything.

Still. "Don't look." Why wouldn't she want me to look?

If it were me and I'd been trapped in a dank, fetid dungeon for over a day, very little would stop me from racing out the moment the door opened. Gray-hair said he had no idea what happened to a User if they stayed in the area during a trial collapse. Only that he wasn't sure whether they could survive.

Joshua Denbrough came to me again, his flayed arm reaching up from the floor of flesh.

There were a million different possibilities between alive and dead. Each uglier than the last.

To add to the complexity, this sort of situation was not my strength. Interrogation, intimidation, manipulation, and shock tactics came easily. Gently coaxing a scared and possibly injured person into doing something I wanted, with no leverage to speak of, was entirely uncomfortable. While I understood the basics, it would be too easy to slip back into old habits.

Should I use Cruel Lens?

Something floated to the surface of my mind. An image of walking through middle-school corridors looking for my sister, eventually finding her stowed away in her locker, unwilling to come out. It would have been easier to force her. But I didn't. I'd been uncharacteristically patient, enunciating carefully in front of the vent so she could see and hear me. Eventually, I'd said the right thing and she'd come out on her own. An aspect that hadn't seemed important to me at the time, but Iris had taken me aside to thank me for later.

This was different. Sae was an adult and my sister was a child. But **<Cruel Lens>** was a bludgeon. Maybe a more subtle version of that passive approach I'd taken with Iris was the better course.

"Is Jinny really dead?" Sae asked. "I cracked the door to look out, once. Her body was gone."

"Yes. I did everything I could, but she's gone. Got her User core and hid it, just in case there's a chance we can bring her back."

"Do you think that's really possible?" Sae asked.

I hesitated, then answered. "Probably not."

"She was the best of us, I think," Sae replied. She sounded more distant than before, as if she was drifting away.

"What do we do now?" I asked, mindful to keep my voice low and gentle.

There was a long, painful silence before Sae spoke. "You showed up, like you said you would. Promise fulfilled. Now leave."

I ignored the knee-jerk dismissal. If she'd really wanted me to leave, all she had to do was stay silent in the first place. "Are you hurt?"

"No."

"We didn't bring much in. How are you doing on food?"

"I'm fine, Matt... there's plenty to eat." There was a hint of revulsion in her voice. I ignored it and all the horrible implications carried with it.

"That's not what I was asking. Anyway, some businesses are opening up again, courtesy of Selve circulation hitting the public." I reached in my inventory and pulled out a bag marked with golden arches. "Had to drive all the way to Northside, but I got you something." I held the bag out to the side and wiggled it.

"My favorite," Sae said dryly. "How do I get the feeling you already knew that?"

I shrugged, opting for honesty. "Observation is my strong suit. People watching's part of that. I'm not some freak, I don't usually notice diet, but you stuck out a bit. Every few weeks, you'd ditch the perfectly composed salad and whip out a quarter pounder in the cafeteria while your friends acted like you were killing the cow in front of them."

"God. What a stalker." The accusation was a weak jab by her standards.

"Is it really stalking if I do it to everyone?"

"Who knows," Sae said.

"Want it or not?" I asked, realizing I sounded like a grumpier version of Steinbeck.

"I could eat," She confirmed, a bit too quickly.

I considered the current situation. My wheelchair was blocking the door open and I was holding the bag in one hand. "Sae, hand to god I'm not fucking with you here, but I don't know how to get this to you. That black water's still on the ground and will bleed through the bag and ruin the food if I just put it down behind me. I'd check to see if there's anywhere to place it, but I can't turn around."

"Just hold it there."

Simultaneously, I sent a message to Steinbeck.

<**Matt:** Get behind something. Don't react or draw your weapons, regardless of what you see.>

Had to hand it to his professionalism. Steinbeck didn't blink or ask questions. I watched as he read the message, then immediately dropped into a crouch behind a cement pylon. A small hand mirror appeared to the side of the pylon, pointed toward the doorway.

I held the bag out further from my side. Suddenly, there was a presence behind me, unlike anything I'd ever felt. A quick blur of motion flashed by the fringes of my extended periphery, and the bag was gone.

Something about the exchange shook me. I'd never heard her footsteps in the water. She was there, for one moment, then gone. Across the tracks, the mirror was still hovering on the same place. Only now it was vibrating somewhat, as if the hand holding it was shaking.

<**Steinbeck:** We need to leave. Now.>
<**Matt:** Fuck off if you'd like. I'm staying.>
<**Steinbeck:** You didn't see it.>
<**Matt:** I don't care.>

There was a rustling noise from further back in the hallway, followed by a gagging sound. "Ugh. Pickles."

"Guess I'm a bad stalker."

"Sorry. It's good, Matt. Really... really good." There was a muted noise that could have been a stifled sob.

The exchange hadn't been quite as simple as it seemed. I'd positioned myself outside the doorway, intentionally holding the bag a few inches from the entrance. Sae had simply taken it instead of asking me to move the bag inside the doorway. I had no way of knowing if there was some psychological restriction or system fuckery binding her to the trial, but I now had confirmation that there was no physical barrier keeping her from leaving.

Still, we were at an impasse. Sae was completely withdrawn into herself, either unable or unwilling to volunteer more information.

"I'll leave you alone, if that's what you really want. But I have to ask. Why won't you just come back with me? The suits are gone. It's safe now."

"Nothing is safe anymore. And even if it was, there's nowhere for me to go, Helpline," Sae whispered. "My mom and dad—they barely tolerated me before. If I went back to them like this, they'd never forgive me."

Nick's place was unoccupied since the kidnapping, but seeing as how it was likely still on the suits' radar, that was probably a bad idea. My lip curled in irritation at the idea of Sae's parents turning her away in a moment of need.

"Fuck 'em. I have a whole goddamn region of people who owe me. The least they can do is help find a place for you."

"I don't want anyone to see me like this."

"We can—"

"No. We can't. You don't understand." She raised her voice until it was a strangled cry. "You can't possibly get what it's like."

"Then tell me. I want to understand."

She struggled through it, voice breaking. "I waited... my entire life. To not look at myself in the mirror and hate what I saw. For my reflection to match the person I am inside. Slowly suffocating over a lifetime of living in someone else's skin. And finally—finally, I got the chance to be who I wanted to be. I could breathe."

Several things clicked into place. Least of which, the reason Sae felt so uncomfortable with the idea of going home.

"I knew from the moment I saw my title that the system was cruel. And I was right. It's all gone. Everything I fought so hard for. And now... I'm suffocating again."

It took everything I had to temper the rage growing within me. Just like with Astrid and Astria, the system seemed to enjoy doing this. Taking people's worst fears and throwing them in their faces.

"You're right. I can't begin to imagine what it's like." I tapped my fingers on the armrest. "But I'll tell you this, Sae. I'm living evidence that the system can be beaten. I managed to stop an event that should have been inevitable. It's neither perfect, nor infallible. We just have to find the loophole."

"You really believe that, Helpline?"

I nodded. "I'm not promising a fix. Or that whatever's happened can be reversed. There's no way to know for sure. But there's a chance. And if there's a way, we'll find it."

"I want them to hurt." Her voice was raw. "The people who killed Jinny and kidnapped Nick. I want them to feel what we felt."

"Now *that*?" I smiled coldly. "That I *can* guarantee. The wheels are already in motion. They'll pay for what they did. One way or another. But for the best chance of that happening, I need you in my corner."

"I'm not an idiot. I know you're manipulating me."

"Guilty as charged. That doesn't make it any less true."

"Jinny won't be the last person we lose," Sae said. Her voice trembled. "And from what little you've said, it sounds like you just went through hell. People stumbling over each other, squabbling over pieces of this shit-city. What are you even fighting for?"

I considered that. In reality, there were more than a few times I nearly gave up. What kept me going was the same line of thought that struck me in the beginning. "When was the last time you watched the news or pulled it up on your phone before the dome came down?"

"I don't remember."

"Me neither," I admitted. "And I think it's because we all learned to stop caring. Apathy as a defense mechanism. The people in charge never gave a fuck about us. Things rarely changed, and when they did, it was either too slow or directly to our detriment. But now, *everything* is changing. And there's not a room packed with out-of-touch fossils driving that transformation. It's us. Yes, there's opposition, both human and otherwise, and an agenda beyond our capacity to understand. Yet, for the first time, we have the power to affect that change."

My thoughts went to the Allfather and the unique role I'd been entrusted with.

"I don't know how it'll shake out. Realistically, whatever we end up with could be far worse than what we had in the first place. But even if it drags us into the dark, I think we have to do everything we can to guide that change."

"You might be delusional," Sae groused.

"Entirely possible. Haven't taken my meds for like three days," I half-joked. **<Born Nihilist>** did an excellent job warding off my more harrowing symptoms, but I had no idea if it worked as a long-term replacement. When she didn't laugh, I lowered my voice and prompted her. "Come back with me, Sae?"

"Okay." Her voice was closer. She was standing right behind me.

Slowly, I turned around, affirming over and over again how necessary it was to not visibly react, no matter how bad it was.

My mind didn't process the image correctly, at first. It almost looked like she was wearing a black diving suit, complemented by strange, stalagmite-ish shaped spikes of dark face paint around her chin and jaw. Her face and hair were largely the same, but the entire surface of her eyes was dark red, with an almost octagonal pattern. Two appendages extended from the sides of her mouth, similar to mandibles.

It was only then, when I realized they *were* mandibles, that I realized the black bodysuit wasn't armor. It was carapace, or chitin. She'd been changed in accordance with the theme of the trial. I looked down and found that, along with an extra joint, her legs were unnaturally thin and seemed to naturally bend backward now.

"How bad is it?" Sae asked. Despite her fierce exterior, she looked uncharacteristically fragile, like the wrong word could easily blow her away. "I couldn't see everything, in the water. Just bits and pieces. Jesus Christ, Helpline, your face is frozen like it's stuck that way. Fuck. Just say it... I'm hideous... right?

I wanted to tell her she was beautiful, but when she finally got a good look at herself, she'd probably assume I'd lied. She wasn't monstrous, as I'd feared. Just foreign, and different, and difficult to describe. But we're always our own worst critics, and what she saw in the mirror would be vastly different from my impression.

"Not at all. You're still you. Still the friend who kicked this trial's ass with me." I pushed myself out of the chair, grunting from the pain and exertion. Then, I reached out a hand. When she took it, I pulled her out of the trial hall into me and hugged her gently. She clung tightly back, sobbing a handful of times before she fell silent.

"Welcome back."

CHAPTER THREE

The apartment was more or less the same as how I left it. Save a stack of oddly warped hammers in the corner.

"Doing inventory?" I questioned Kinsley, pointing to the stack.

"Nope." Kinsley closed the dimensional door, glancing at Sae, then back to me warily. She crossed the room, picking up a hammer with a handle that literally curved in on itself like a pig's tail. "Not really the quality I look for. How the hell did they get here?"

"Maintenance or housekeeping?" I guessed, glancing toward the kitchen, confused. "The stools are gone too."

I shook my head, returning my focus to the matter at hand.

Contingencies. That was the name of the game now.

I hadn't forgotten what happened the last time things were going well. I'd been caught off guard and blindsided. Every second of inaction would cost me. If I wanted to keep the people important to me safe, I needed to move quickly and definitively.

There were more than a few action items on the docket.

"When you said you had support, I thought you were exaggerating. Nice digs, Helpline." Sae looked around, rubbing her arms furiously.

"I hooked him up," Kinsley said.

"God, it's freezing in here. And my stomach is killing me." Sae stuck a thumb at Kinsley, "Who's Oshkosh B'gosh?"

Kinsley almost choked on her tongue. *"Bitch—"*

"*—Kinsley,*" I interjected, rubbing my forehead, "is the leader of the Merchants' Guild. She's also the founder of the system site. That's how we know each other. Kinsley needed a way to sell her wares safely, Mom had the technical know-how and savvy to make it happen. First to the top of shit mountain."

Sae's jaw dropped. "She's a guild leader?"

"Got something to say?" Kinsley bristled.

Sae processed that, then stuck a finger at my face. "You knew her before you ran into us. That's how your gear was so good. During the trial, despite being lower level, you were still shrugging shit off that was bodying me." She gave Kinsley an approving nod. "Your stuff is quality."

"Oh. Uh, thanks." Kinsley looked pleased, the blustering anger vanishing as quickly as it had appeared.

"You know, for a Keebler elf."

"Look here, cun—"

"—Sae," I cut in loudly, giving Kinsley a warning glare, then lowered my voice. "Full transparency. Kinsley and I are going to have a conversation. It involves you. I know you're dealing with something traumatic, so if you want to give me the benefit of the doubt that I'll advocate for you, you're welcome to bow out and I can bring you up to speed later."

Sae considered that, then glanced down at herself. A shadow of distaste crossed her expression. "It's tempting. But if I wanted to hide away from everything, I would have stayed in the trial. Before that, though, I really, *really* need a shower."

It was easy to forget she'd been stewing in muck for two days because the rest of her appearance was so distracting. Still, her hair was visibly matted, and what skin she had was smeared with grime. I felt like an idiot. "Of course. Head toward the front door, take a right down the hall. The second door on the left is a guest room with its own bathroom. Room's yours until we find you a place."

"Got it." Sae headed back toward the bathroom, then slowed. "Are you sure it's okay? Me staying here?"

"It's the least I can do." I waved her on. When she'd disappeared around the corner, I lowered my voice. "Maintenance took down the mirror, right?"

"Both of them," Kinsley confirmed. "The standing one is in the storage closet. And they uninstalled the bathroom mirror. It's gone. She seems fine, though. Tougher than you made her sound. I'd be a mess in her shoes."

Kinsley was right. Sae *seemed* fine. Seemed being the operative word. Trauma manifested differently for different people. Some stewed in it, processed for weeks or even months before they returned to normal life. Others put off the processing for just as long, instead fixating on moving forward. I'd put money on Sae being in the latter camp. Which meant it would hit her eventually.

"We need to be careful." I shook my head grimly. "Thanks to the

Transposition, most people in this city have had some sort of harrowing experience with monsters. A lot of the population is apt to shoot first and ask questions later."

"You're worried about a Frankenstein situation."

"Frankenstein was the creator—it doesn't matter. Yes. In short, I want her in this building if possible. With daily care if we can manage it. I have no ideas what complications this new form carries with it, but if it lines up with the usual system fuckery, she may have specific needs."

I pointed the remote toward the shutters and pressed the button. Or, at least I thought I did. The fireplace roared to life.

I scanned the remote and pressed the correct button again. A small vacuum robot emerged from its housing on the wall. It bumped into my footrest, then pivoted and zoomed away. "It was V2, right?"

"No. W2. Like "W" for windows. Apparently, the app was way more intuitive—are you sure you're alright?" Kinsley glanced from the windows to me, concerned.

Not the sort of mistake I made often. Tentatively, I prodded the protrusion of flesh on the back of my head, where it bounced off the cement when I fell. I'd had a concussion when the meteor struck. This would be my second. "Don't hesitate to check me, if you sense that I'm off."

"Do you feel off?"

"I feel fine, but that's not always how brain injuries work. You had my back with Ellison this morning." An old fear bubbled up from my gut. "This thing with Sae. Choosing where she's living, the mirrors. Am I being too controlling?"

Kinsley thought about that. Long enough that I had to respect her for it. She was taking the question seriously. "No. So long as you're being genuine when you're giving her the option to decline. And considering what she just went through, I think she probably appreciates having someone call the shots for now." She raised an eyebrow suspiciously. "And... you're not using suggestion—"

"I'm not. The only time I'd even use that on an ally is when they're in danger, or they missed something critical."

"'Critical' leaves a lot to interpretation."

I grimaced. "Look, there's—"

The door to my bedroom was thrown open and banged loudly against the doorstop. Kinsley shrieked and I nearly toppled the wheelchair.

Iris was standing in the doorway, two malformed hammers held at her side. Her face was bright red and she was visibly fuming, more worked up than I'd ever seen her before. To my absolute shock, she actually shouted. "Ugh—these stupid hammers!"

I glanced at Kinsley to see if she had any clue what Iris was talking about. She looked as flabbergasted as I was.

"Hey, Iris." I gave her a half-wave, then leaned to the side for a better view of my room.

The anger disappeared from my sister's face. She dropped the hammers, ran across the room, and tackled me. "You're not a vegetable!"

I grunted and patted her head. "Definitely not. Though I might as well be rooted to this chair. Uh. What's with the hammers?" I asked, signing simultaneously.

Iris scowled. Her hands were a blur. "This ability is annoying. They tell me, Oh, You Can Make Whatever You Can Draw. Only no, they leave out the fine print until after a painstakingly detailed sketch of a sword that there are pre-requisites and I actually can't just make whatever. Apparently, I need my own tools and workspace first. To make it even dumber, I don't actually use the tools, just need to be in their vicinity. So fine, I require a forge. But I have no idea how to draw a forge, so maybe it's better to start with something small and simple, like a hammer."

My head spun. Ability. My sister is a User.

Kinsley was leafing through an invisible screen excitedly. "Iris — Trance Forger, Level 2. Holy shit. You won the lottery. In more ways than one." She smiled wickedly. "We should renegotiate your contract."

I held out a hand in annoyance. "Keep your greedy fingers away from my sister while we figure this out. Also, since when did you understand ASL?"

"I took a translator feat." Kinsley shrugged. "Seemed like a worth-while investment, considering what we're going for."

Iris placed a sketchbook in my lap, followed by a hammer. Considering the mess of failures in the corner, I was guessing it was the best one. I picked it up, studying it. It looked right, but the distribution was all wrong. The head was uncharacteristically light in both color and mass. "Okay. So, it looks almost perfect in terms of appearance. Seems like weight is the issue, even though you got the proportions more or less correct." Something about the grain caught my eye. "This wood. Did—did you make the handle out of Ellison's baseball bat?"

"I needed equivalent materials. The magic reforms it once the blue-print is done."

I handed the hammer to Kinsley and she took it, tapping a painted nail on the uncharacteristically light hammerhead. **<Ordinator's Emulation>** told me she was using some sort of skill, though the glowing red ring around her pupil made that mostly unnecessary. "Aluminum. That's why you're having balance issues. If only you knew a kindly merchant who would be happy to provide both workspace and unlimited materials for a nominal percentage..."

"Would you?!" Iris wrapped her arms around Kinsley's neck, squeezing her tightly until the merchant made choking noises.

Kinsley looked uncomfortable with the sudden contact, then seemed to smile and accept it. She glanced at me.

"If you fleece my sister, I will hurt you," I mouthed.

The merchant snorted but nonetheless gently pushed Iris away. "We'll figure out terms later. Lemme get in contact with the landlord for now, and we'll get you a space and some basic materials to get started."

"Is that okay?" Iris looked at me with full-power puppy-dog eyes.

"Fine." I put my hand on my forehead. "Just don't bite off more than you can chew. And ask for help sooner rather than later. Furthermore, if you're going to take this seriously, we should probably get you an easel and better art supplies."

Iris's resulting victory dance looked more like a series of muscle spasms than an actual dance. Which, of course, was when Sae emerged from the hallway, towel wrapped around her hair. Now that it was washed, the spiny carapace fitted to her form glimmered, almost reflective. She looked at the two girls, then to me. "The Keebler elves are multiplying."

My heart went into my throat. If I'd thought about it, I would have warned Iris ahead of time. But I was still barely keeping up with everything that was happening. Kinsley and I both looked at Iris, who'd stopped stock-still. She was studying Sae, as if entirely unsure of what to make of her.

Please don't freak out.

I hurriedly pulled up the UI, trying to head off any shocked reaction with a brief message. Before I could send it, Iris spoke. "Hi. Did you get that armor from Kinsley's shop?"

"*Iris,*" I hissed.

"Uh. No. It was a drop," Sae said, looking visibly relieved. "From a dungeon."

Iris glanced at me. "Is your armor that cool?"

"I'm a new User. I just have the basics."

But Iris wasn't even paying attention to me anymore. Instead, she scampered around Sae, sizing her up. "Can I sketch you? For armor ideas. My future employer will pay you for it."

"Say what now?" Kinsley blinked.

Suppressing a snicker at how the tables had turned on Kinsley, I shot Sae a message.

<**Matt:** Feel free to turn her down. She just gets manic sometimes.>

<**Sae:** Actually, it's okay. She didn't run away screaming at least. I appreciate you looking out for me. Guessing the mirror didn't just grow legs and walk away. But avoiding my appearance is just going to bite me in the ass. Maybe seeing a sketch of myself first would actually help.>

I inclined my head.

Sae bent down and poked Iris' cheek. "So cute. Matt must be adopted. You can sketch me later, after the three of us have a discussion."

"Actually, put a pin in that." Kinsley's expression was all business as she skimmed an invisible screen. "The Adventurers' Guild and region reps are in the lobby." She looked up from the message. "Before I tell them to head to the conference room, have you reviewed the Transposition options for the region?"

"No." There wasn't time.

"I can stall," Kinsley offered.

Delaying would ensure I was well-informed, but people were probably already growing anxious. The last thing I wanted to do was squander the goodwill I had and start things off on the wrong foot, again. "Sae, are you good here for a few hours?"

"Don't inconvenience yourself on my account," Sae stretched. "Just gotta get a cup of coffee and pose on the couch."

I wheeled myself toward the door. "Tell them we're on our way, Kinsley. I'll cram in the elevator."

CHAPTER FOUR

<Region Interface>
<Region 14>
<Characteristics: Educated. Central Location. High User Population.>
<Affluence: Silver>
<Alignment: Neutral>
<Core: Undeveloped>
<Flauros Bind: Strong>
<Incursion Chance: High>
<Vulnerability: High>
<Luminaries: 4>
<Allied Regions: N/A>
<Patron Deity: N/A>
<Settlement Policy: Case-by-Case>
<Ranking: 14 of 20>
<Beneficiary: N/A
<Low-Grade Transposition Available>

The usual vein stuck out on my forehead.

There wasn't nearly enough information to draw from here. Apparently, Region 14 had a high vulnerability, but there was literally no explanation as to what that meant, what the underlying reasons were, or how to fix it. I hypothesized that Flauros Bind and Incursion Chance were probably correlated somehow. If we had a strong connection to the Flauros realm, that likely meant dungeons and trials would be much more common in this region—thus monsters were more likely to break free and attack.

No clue what luminaries were, apart from the vague hunch that they were most likely individuals. Core and the significance of ranking was also lost on me. Something about the number of regions was bothering me, now that I saw the total of twenty, but I made a mental note to return to that when I wasn't in a time crunch.

I reached out and blindly pressed several more buttons on the elevator, slowing our descent.

"What, again?" Kinsley squawked. "Why didn't we just make them wait before we got in the elevator?"

"Excuse me for expecting this interface to be intuitive," I muttered, scanning more text.

While the region having no patron deity was good for me, it was probably bad for everyone else and the region in general. I had no idea how one went about getting a deific patron, but even if I knew, the Allfather of Chaos was out. It would be too obvious of a giveaway, and the last time I'd spoken to him, he'd made it clear he was weakened and dying. Limited use. Nychta was a better choice, but only relatively. I knew nothing about her, which made even considering the option dangerous.

Better to leave that for now.

<Transposition Electives>
<Balanced Stakes>: Quests assigned in the region become far more common and rewarding. However, the time limits are reduced, and penalties for failures grow significantly more severe.
Increases: Flauros Bond, Vulnerability, Potential Core Development.
Decreases: Security.
Restricts Settlement Policy to Proportional.

I furrowed my brow and reread the description. In a perfect world, this would have been the immediate pick regardless of the other options. Quests were by and large the best way to rack up experience, and having more of them meant faster growth. Anything that put us that far ahead was worth a look.

However, the penalty aspect severely tainted it. I knew from personal experience that quests weren't always fair. Or achievable, for that matter. The only reason I hadn't failed most of mine was thanks to extended or unspecified time limits. If those time limits became more severe and we weren't perfectly organized to handle it, people would start failing more quests—or rush in unprepared and die trying to complete them, costing us a User and a penalty. It'd be all too easy to spiral.

<Dark Lord's Descent>: The region flourishes. Materials rare in other regions become bountiful, along with rare monsters and items. A random

ungifted is uplifted to the Dark Lord class. All benefits remain if the Dark Lord is vanquished.
Increases: Affluence, Flauros Bond, Security, Potential Core Development, Luminary Propagation.
Decreases: Alignment, Vulnerability, Incursion Chance.

Everything about the option set off alarm bells. When it came to increases and decreases, there was practically no downside save alignment, which was obscure in contrast to the clearly defined gains. All we had to do was allow a dangerous User into our midst, with the implication that we could face no consequences if we dealt with them early on.

Nick scared the hell out of me, and in terms of ranking, he was only a Knight. I would rather not see what a Dark Lord was capable of.

It was an almost automatic no.

<Resource Paradox>: A precious resource is discovered to be bountiful within the region. Acquiring and processing it will take considerable effort, but the rewards for doing so are exponential. So much so that other regions may take notice.
Increases: Affluence (Significant), Vulnerability, Flauros Bind, Incursion Chance, Potential Core Development.
Decreases: Security, Luminary Propagation.

Another legitimate option I didn't trust. Mainly because it was leaving a lot of shit out. The implied downside was that we'd be so wealthy it would cause trouble from other regions. But what it was actually invoking was a phenomenon known as the resource curse, which had far more downsides than the option inferred. There are countless examples of this. Just off the top of my head, Nigeria and Angola both rank incredibly high on the list of oil-producing countries, yet their currency value and GDP per capita are astronomically low.

With Selve being a universal currency, the currency deflation issue wouldn't necessarily apply to us. But developmental slow and industrial pigeonholing would, along with external region interference once they discovered what we had. It was hard to say if the pros outweighed the cons.

I pinched the bridge of my nose.

Jesus fuck, I'm not an economist, give me a break here.

"First day and you're already scaring the tenants," Kinsley commented in amusement.

The elevator had opened on a lower floor. An old man with a cane waited outside the doors, staring back at me.

"There's plenty of room," I offered absent-mindedly, still mentally running through the region options.

The man shook his head, wispy white hairs from a barely there combover floating before they settled back down. "No, no. I'll get the next one, son. You're him, right?" Tentatively, he reached in his pocket.

I immediately reached down to my back and partially withdrew my crossbow, prepared to activate **<Page's Quickdraw.>**

The old man withdrew a golden oblong object with trembling hands, gave an obvious backswing, and tossed it to me. Adrenaline washed through me, and I nearly threw myself from the wheelchair to dodge it before **<Born Nihilist>** interfered.

He's obviously not a threat.

I caught the object at the last second. It was somewhat shaped like a UFO, so reflective I could see the deep bags under my eyes.

<Item: Charm of Recall>
Craft Level: Masterwork
Description: The result of the purest inspiration and deft technique. This small piece of unknown metal allows the User to roll back a single feat and refunding their expended points. Once the process is complete, the charm will disintegrate.
Item Class: Rare

By the time I looked up from the description, the doors were already closing. "Wait—"

The doors closed, leaving me with the image of the old man waving with a twinkle in his eye. Annoyed by the abruptness with which the exchange had ended, I leaned back in my chair. The red ring around Kinsley's eye faded and her mouth dropped open.

"That's—"

"Incredibly valuable," I finished.

"I've seen crafted items before. But never a masterwork," Kinsley mused. I passed the item to her and she studied it. "This is pristine. Crafted items almost always look shoddier than system created counterparts. Maybe that's because most vocational Users are still getting started."

"The system seems slow in general to assign vocations unless you start with them," I agreed. "I was supposed to get a vocation with my chain quest for helping you."

"You were?"

"Yup. Still hasn't happened. Look him up later?"

"Already on it," Kinsley nodded. "No way I'm passing up any crafters at this point, let alone one who can make something like this. If he's not already attached to a guild, I'll snag him."

Still split between the region options, I rattled them off to Kinsley. I was tempted to screw with the wording of **<Dark Lord's Descent>** to poison the well and push them away from it, but Tyler would be present. Working around his truth ability was difficult enough without sprinkling in more lies.

Kinsley transcribed the "Region Options" into a message to be sent to anyone present.

"Before we get in there, do you have a preference?" I asked.

With a sigh, Kinsley skimmed the text again. "I'm leaning toward **<Balanced Stakes.>** Split between that and **<Resource Paradox.>** You?"

"Narrowed it down to the same two, but leaning toward the opposite. Anything else?"

She let out a long grumbling noise. "I'm worried the others may push for **<Dark Lord's Descent.>** The other two options create short-term problems and hurdles with big payoffs if we can stick the landing. Organization and production. Descent offers a lot of short-term gain with a long-term concern. If you don't have any experience with them, it's impossible to know how dangerous these 'special' classes are. We're familiar with that issue, but they may not be. And we can't exactly explain why."

"Right."

The elevator doors opened on the first floor. The lobby was covered in dark-marble flooring and pillars and scattered with multiple couches and tables for impromptu discussions and get-togethers. I wheeled myself out, Kinsley walking slightly ahead. It was eerily silent.

When I surveyed the atrium, I realized why. Everyone was looking in our direction. "Great," I groused quietly, "you really are famous."

"Maybe check again before you blame it all on me," Kinsley half-skipped, moving ahead. Sure enough, the assortment of eyes didn't follow her. They weren't watching Kinsley.

They were watching me.

A few people approached to voice appreciation. Others followed with gifts, a handful of potions, and Selve. I found myself on the receiving end of multiple handshakes.

"Weird. This is really weird," I whispered to Kinsley.

"I've never seen you so uncomfortable before," Kinsley snickered.

"Allow me," a male voice said from behind me. Someone took the handles off my wheelchair and began to push me in the direction Kinsley was walking. Like the old man, they probably didn't mean any harm. But I still felt my anxiety climbing to a peak. It didn't stop until Kinsley, reading something I'd let slip through, thanked the man pushing the wheelchair and took over, maneuvering me toward one of several conference rooms.

"That wasn't just discomfort," Kinsley said, the levity in her voice gone.

"I'm fine."

"You weren't fine. Ask for help if you need it, idiot."

Never been good at asking for help.

Kinsley opened the door and revealed the conference room. It looked more at home in a corporate office than an apartment. A long brown table with rounded edges was surrounded by rolling office chairs. The far end of the room was crowned by a projector screen, the projector itself hung in the center ceiling and powered down.

Sara and Tyler stood as we entered, all smiles. Tyler was dressed in business attire—a simple suit that looked off the shelf but fitted. Sara was wearing armor that looked more fantastical in nature, but the hint of regalia in the silver chain accents on the flowing garment still gave it a dressed-up air.

"There he is," Tyler boomed, "the conquering hero."

Sara's smile was genuine, but more reserved. "Glad we're finally meeting in better circumstances."

My heart jumped into my throat for just a moment before I realized she was referring to the meeting at the region barrier and, before that, the open forum. "Sorry we're late."

Tyler shook his head. "Considering the circumstances, you have nothing to apologize for. And you aren't even the last to arrive."

As if on cue, the door behind us swung open. A man entered with a leather folio under his arm. The Rolex on his wrist glinted in the soft office light, accenting his light-blue suit and tie. The suit was so high-end I didn't recognize it. Maybe because I was too fixated on his face.

A strong jawline that jutted outward. A hundred-dollar haircut. Stubble maintained at the perfect length. Eyes that saw everything and considered it beneath him.

It'd been almost five years, and aside from the gray streaks in his sideburns, he hadn't aged a day.

Aaron Verner. Daphne's asshole father. Probably a suit. And worst of all, the man who'd played a key role in my mother's indictment. "Matthias?" he said, in a perfect simulation of surprise.

"What—what are you doing here?" I asked, dumbstruck.

"I'm the region representative." Aaron grinned and held out a hand.

CHAPTER FIVE

Kinsley tensed at my side. I was confident I wasn't showing anything on my face, but she'd seen me go blank like this before. After briefly considering switching to **<Cruel Lens>**, I thought better of it. I wasn't sure I could maintain my composure without my default title.

If you said the word "enemy," Aaron's smug face would usually be the first association in my mind. He was rarely at the estate when I visited Daphne, but when he was, he'd been kind. Eager to play the father figure and give advice. The faux parental aspect was strange, but I put up with it because his lessons were fascinating to me, fundamentally different from anything my parents and therapists had taught me.

In my mind, he'd occupied the same space as Estrada. A valued adviser with no parallel. Which is why the betrayal cut so deeply.

Aaron had tried to hang the entire Quad Sigma clusterfuck on my mother's neck. Accused her of misusing company resources to create what the news at the time called the most dangerous black market in the history of the internet, solely of her own volition. Thankfully, the DA wasn't an idiot and offered to knock down the charges against her from what could have easily been life in prison in exchange for her cooperation if she testified against her former boss and associates.

A few of them went down. Low-security bids for a handful of years—I think the highest was three. But save a lifetime ban on trading equities and six years of probation, Aaron got off scot-free, all his gray money undoubtedly secured in the Caymans.

It's stupid, but I used to fantasize about hacking him, wiping out his savings, ruining his life. The idea eventually led to a two-month stint, during which I discovered I had no talent for computer science or programming, let alone hacking.

Aaron slowly let his hand drop, grin diminishing to an apologetic half-smile. "Of course. I saw the video before I came here. It wasn't the best quality. You looked familiar, but I didn't put it together until now."

Was that even possible? Maybe. But I fucking doubted it.

"Do we have a problem?" Tyler looked between us, concerned.

"No problem." Aaron shook his head. "Matthias and I have some history. I wasn't always a lawyer. A lifetime ago, I ran the hedge fund and his mother was one of our employees." He glanced at Tyler. "I'm not certain how much you know about finance, but hedge funds generally operate in something of a legal gray area. As such, they present a juicy target for overeager prosecutors looking for another notch on their belt. Most of the charges were dropped."

Because you sold out your associates. Including my mother.

"... clear overreach on their part—but ultimately, it was my firm. My responsibility. It would be totally reasonable if he resented me for the part I played." Aaron frowned, all sympathy and regret. "If you'd prefer, I can recuse myself. Pull another representative from the City Council. They may not be as familiar as I am with the area. But it's more important that things run smoothly."

"They let you practice law?" I asked, genuinely shocked.

Aaron smiled. "Life's little ironies. My firm is just down the street, and I live on the other side of the region. I was trapped in here with the rest of the ungifted during the Transposition. Same shelter as Lizette."

When I didn't react, he explained. "Tyler's wife."

I tried to ignore the fact that by fortifying the region, I'd unintentionally saved Aaron's life. There were things that didn't make sense that took precedence. I'd assumed for as long as I knew of them that Aaron was a high-up in the suits' hierarchy. Daphne's presence was too strong of a connection, and I was certain I'd overheard one of the mooks tell Daphne her father would be pleased that first night in the alley.

But if that was true, what the hell was he doing here, in a region that had missed the fortification deadline? They had a surplus of Lux in Region 3, and I doubted that was all they had. If they wanted to avoid suspicion, they would have just waited until late into the Transposition to fortify.

So, what did that mean? Was it possible there was some sort of power struggle within the suits? Had they left him to die as a part of some internal coup?

"Do you want to move forward with the meeting, Matt?" Sara interjected. "Or roll the dice with another member of the City Council?"

Kinsley nudged me.

I shook my head slowly, then stuck out my hand. "No reason to hold on to pre-system baggage, right?"

I had no doubts that whoever Aaron selected would be firmly in his pocket. And at the end of the day, I'd much rather deal with the source than a proxy. As unpleasant as that source might be.

Aaron returned my handshake with both hands, his megawatt smile returning full force. "I'm so glad you feel that way, Matthias."

"I go by Matt these days." I wheeled the chair backward and slid into the table, resting my arms across it. "And now that I feel completely underdressed, why don't we get started." I signaled for Kinsley to send the message containing the developmental options for the region.

All three of them pulled up their UI, reviewing the options. I went over it as well. A message appeared.

<**Tyler:** Are you under duress? If you need me to act on your behalf, I can fabricate a reason to pull another council member.>

I glanced up from my reading. Tyler caught my eye and gave me a reassuring nod. In the aftermath of the Transposition, I'd forgotten how much I liked the man.

<**Matt:** It's complicated. But it's better that he stays. I'll fill you in later.>
<**Tyler:** Understood.>

The suits were going to find out one way or another. They knew I had a connection to Daphne. It was possible sending Aaron in particular was a straightforward flex, letting me know that regardless of where I went, they were still watching. But it felt more complicated than that. Plus, when it came time to broach the topic with the Adventurers' Guild, Tyler was going to fly off the handle when he discovered how brazenly they'd stuck a thumb in his eye.

"Tough," Aaron commented, looking around the room. "None of these options are shoo-ins."

"<**Dark Lord's Descent**>—for one thing, it's too long, so let's just call it DLD—looks promising," Sara said, still engrossed in her reading. "If we make Region 14 our primary base of operations going forward, a single User shouldn't be much of an issue."

You say that because the only special class you've dealt with ran away and jumped in a car.

"You've never dealt with a special class," Aaron said.

I stared at him, gobsmacked, as he paraphrased the exact point I'd considered.

"And you have?" Tyler asked.

"No, but I hear things." Aaron leaned back in his chair, his hands steepled. "The Ordinator is the big one we all know about, thanks to that little dog and pony show the Overseer put on. But he isn't the only one. And from the reports I've heard, these fucks hit hard. Maybe you get an idiot who runs out in the street, screaming he's the Dark Lord, and the problem takes care of itself. Maybe you don't. It's a total roll of the dice, and I don't like betting when I don't know the odds. Don't get me wrong, I think consolidating the Adventurers' Guild here is still a good move. Fourteen lacks a guild, so it's free real estate. And we could certainly use the protection."

"I'm inclined to agree. Vetoing that option." Kinsley swiveled back and forth in her chair, glancing at me for confirmation.

"Same," I added.

What world did I slip into?

"There's already too much we don't know," I continued, "adding another variable would be unnecessarily dangerous. Fourteen didn't fortify in time, so every option is going to have a drawback. There are too many benefits for the special class not to be a significant threat."

"I like the way you think." Aaron pointed at me.

Die in a fire.

Tyler nodded, "I agree that the risks are too high. We're in accordance then."

"Then that leaves us with two options," Sara skimmed through the invisible text.

Tyler and Kinsley both made strong arguments for **<Balanced Stakes>**, positing that if we had a system in place with Users prepared to assist with any quest that had dire consequences, or was about to be failed, we could mitigate any potential spiral.

Aaron and Sara both argued for **<Resource Paradox>**. Aaron seemed to consider the resource curse a total myth, and even if it wasn't, argued that it was most damaging to nascent countries and we were too developed to be affected. I pushed back, stating that by the standards of this new world, we were underdeveloped. Something Aaron vehemently disagreed with. Sara was less concerned with that, more uncomfortable with the idea of increased penalties for quests, guessing any system we put into place would be easily overwhelmed if the time limits were as unforgiving as the option implied.

Which, of course, left me as the swing vote.

CHAPTER SIX

I felt all four of them staring at me. Aaron was still leaning back in his chair, completely relaxed. Either he was fine with both, or whatever outcome he wanted was assured. We'd had arguments before, more for the sport of it than actually engagement with whatever the topic was. None of them particularly heated or high-stakes, but he won more than he lost. Seventy-thirty in his favor. Occasionally, I'd realize after that he'd maneuvered me into taking a position that seemed reasonable at first, but one he knew to be ultimately indefensible.

If anyone was a shoo-in to beat me at my own game, it was Aaron.

I fidgeted with **\<Broken Legacy\>** absent-mindedly under the table, letting it fall and then bidding it back to my hand. Laying whatever extraneous elements led to Aaron being trapped in a doomed region aside, I had to assume he was involved with the suits and that he still held some power.

At some point, I'd work through the minutia to see if there was anything I could use. Preferably after my Necromancer gambit bore fruit and I'd gleaned more information in general.

For now, I needed to make sure he didn't get whatever he wanted from the region. And what he wanted wasn't necessarily the **\<Resource Paradox\>**. If he hadn't trotted out the regretful apology right out the gate and I got the feeling he legitimately didn't remember me, that would be different. But he'd lampshaded our previous relationship. Hung it out there for everyone to see. There were too many possible mind games for me to narrow down which one he was playing.

I needed to shake up the room.

"I didn't ask for any of this when I meddled with the region. Had no idea the sort of responsibility and spotlight it would bring."

"Saved," Sara said quietly.

"What?" I asked.

"Look around. You didn't meddle. You saved the region," Sara insisted. "That being said, if you'd prefer to let us drive the ship, no one would blame you for it."

"And the opposite?"

"Pardon?" Sara asked.

"If I said fuck voting, the system established me as region owner, I'm going with **<Dark Lord Descends>**."

"Matt?" Kinsley stared at me.

Out of the corner of my eye, I saw Aaron smirk. It was small, almost a micro-expression, but it was there. Sara and Tyler both looked at each other, and Sara gave him an almost imperceptible nod.

Tyler rested his big arms on the table and the wood beneath creaked. "This vote is mainly a formality. Like Sara said, you saved this region and nearly paid for it with your life. If you chose a Transposition elective that directly harmed the region, the Adventurers' Guild would need to withdraw support and possibly interfere. However, none of the options you've presented directly harm the region. DLD is concerning long-term but causes no direct harm. So if you decide to go your own way, I see no issue."

Eloquent. Reasonable. One-hundred percent rehearsed. They'd discussed the possibility I'd go off-script before they'd even walked in the room.

I crossed my arms, rubbing my thumb against my bicep. It was a movement that used to be my tell. Not bicep necessarily, thigh, face, and index finger were all common mutations of the same giveaway. I'd picked my bicep because I needed something visible and above the table, something Aaron would see. His eyes flicked down toward my arm then bounced back up, face utterly neutral.

"Just curious. I have no intention of going that route. But I'm of two minds. I was committed to **<Balanced Stakes>** before I walked into the room. The resource curse is nothing to fuck with. Nonetheless, Aaron and Sara both made good points. Both the Merchants' Guild and the Adventurers' Guild have a positive reputation coming out of the Transposition and are growing exponentially. We might be able to handle it."

"As much as I appreciate your ability to overlook personal biases, you should go with your gut." Aaron shook his head. "I'm just a lawyer, not a professor of socio economics or political science."

Right.

"Kinsley was selling Girl Scout cookies out of the back of a minivan before we met. And I'm a high-school student. None of us should be in the position to call these shots, yet here we all are. Tyler. The Adventurers' Guild consolidating in this region a sure thing?"

Tyler's lips tightened. "Yes. Most of our current territory is spread out and contested, which caused issues during the Transposition. Consolidating is our best bet for now, then slowly establishing forward-operating bases near allied groups."

"Good, we'll need the firepower." I rubbed my bicep again. "Buckle up, ladies and gentlemen, we're about to break the resource curse."

Aaron didn't react. But for the rest of the meeting, he sat up straighter.

———

"That's it for me. I'd love to stay and chat, but I have to report to the City Council." My once-mentor gathered his documents. Then fastened the top button of his suit jacket and readjusted his tie with a practiced motion. "Whenever the local government decides to get off its ass and actually do something, they'll appreciate that you heeded my guidance."

I waved him off, parroting words he'd so often said to me. "Happy to listen."

His smile grew wider. "Look at us. Maintaining civility in the face of the apocalypse. A cut above as always, Matthias." He paused at the door and turned back to me. "You're in an advantageous position now. A place where you can finally use that mind of yours to its fullest potential. If you have time, swing by my office. I've missed our talks."

My lip curled. "If I find the time."

"Ciao." Aaron waved as he left, his Rolex band clinking with the motion.

<Kinsley: You said you were leaning that way before. But I get the feeling you chose it for an entirely different reason than whatever you thought of on the elevator.>
<Matt: I'm reasonably certain that Aaron's a suit.>
<Kinsley: WHAT.>
<Matt: I'll fill you in later. What's more important is that he left with the impression I was lying about picking <Resource Paradox> and intend to choose <Dark Lord's Descent> without informing the others.>
<Kinsley: I didn't get that impression at all.>
<Matt: Neither did Tyler or Sara. That was the point.>
<Kinsley: Oh. OH. DLD does something similar to <Resource Paradox>. Only more and in greater volume, without lowering the security of the region. It'll take him a while to realize you were bluffing and just did exactly what you said. Or would that be a reverse bluff? My head hurts.>

<**Matt:** Plus, I'm betting they'll want to get their hands on the Dark
Lord.>

The more of the suits' time and resources I could waste, the better.

Somewhere in the back of my mind, I heard a distinctively feminine
chuckle.

During our text exchange, Kinsley crossed the room and shook Tyler's
and Sara's hand. "I know this is a sore point, but it needs to be said.
Thanks for leaving Myrddin out of that conversation. He was a monster
for what he did, but I doubt he'll be an ongoing threat."

Tyler's smile was strained. "You weren't there. If he decides to come
after us out of some twisted sense of revenge, trust me, that would be a
serious problem. No need to drag your reputation over a hypothetical,
however. Considering the good your guild did. There were probably too
many witnesses to suppress the information completely, so it may still
spread, but we won't be the ones spreading it."

Sara nudged him. Tyler gave her a tired look, then continued. "We're
still investigating. Unfortunately, our focus is split between that incident
and whatever happened to Region 6."

Everyone looked distinctly uncomfortable at the mention of the quar-
antined region.

Tyler continued. "Myrddin killed three of my men and lied about it
being self-defense. That much is ironclad. However, from some initial
inquiries, there are elements that don't entirely line up. Gossip around the
three dead members that paints a less than generous picture of their character. It's possible there's more to the story than a robbery gone bad." He
sighed. "Do you have a way to contact him?"

<**Ordinator's Emulation**> flashed.
<**Matt:** Polygraph skill's up. Be truthful and keep your answer short.>

A bead of sweat appeared on Kinsley's hairline. "Yes. There's no guarantee he'll answer though. He tended to keep me in the dark even before
the clusterfuck."

Tyler nodded, apparently unbothered by whatever it was he saw. No
sabotage of his ability this time. It made sense. And confirmed that
whoever—or whatever—had screwed with his title ability during our
altercation had crossed a line. The deities could break the rules—it had
happened more than a few times at this point—but they didn't have free
rein. Even they were beholden to the system to some extent.

"If he does get back to you," Tyler said, "tell him we want to talk. No
setup. No bullshit. Man to man, at a place of his choosing."

My instincts said trap. It was the third time in an hour I was tempted to switch titles. **<Jaded Eye>** or **<Cruel Lens>** would have been worth their weight in gold for this discussion—but the pain from both my healing injuries and my seething stomach from the witch's potion was already a constantly needling distraction. Coupling that with the way I kept jumping at loud noises and forgetting things, swapping away from **<Born Nihilist>** seemed like a terrible idea at the moment.

"I'll let you know if Myrddin returns my messages," Kinsley said.

"When are you planning to lock in the region option?" Sara asked, watching me curiously.

I blinked. "As soon as this meeting is over. No reason to delay, really. There's no timer, but the system doesn't clearly state any of its rules, so the sooner the better."

Sara looked to Tyler.

"We're done here." Tyler nodded.

Sara stood. "Let's go outside then. You can lock it in and see what happens."

"Could be glaringly obvious," Tyler said, "Region 4 was overrun with machinery and mechanisms, for example. Could be almost imperceptible. Still, I am curious."

"Why not."

I wheeled myself out of the office and through the lobby, trying to ignore the blatant stares and whispers as the others followed alongside me. The double doors slid open and wind rushed in, the scent of smoke and blood lingering on the outside air.

Nervously, I pulled up the region interface.

<Transposition Staging: Resource Paradox.>
<Confirm?>
<Y | N>

I confirmed the prompt.

CHAPTER SEVEN

Region 14 was simultaneously spectacular and minimalistic. The entrance to the—no, my—apartment complex looked more like the entrance to a high-end hotel or downtown bank building. The buildings nearby were dozens of stories tall, and save for the occasionally recognizable logo, it was impossible to tell if they were now-defunct office buildings or residential.

The timer ticked down from five minutes.

"And you're sure we shouldn't bother with an announcement?" I asked.

"What if one of the buildings comes down?" Kinsley added nervously.

Sara shrugged. Despite her casual air, the tip of her foot tapped rapidly against the cement. "So far, nothing like that has happened. Everyone's aware that rapid changes may occur. They saw what happened to Region 13."

"What happened with Region 13?" I asked, more than a little annoyed with how much I'd missed in a single day.

"It was grim." Tyler sighed. "The civilians tore each other to pieces, and they still barely filled the receptacle in time. Then things got... weird. Really weird. Surprised the girl—" Sara elbowed Tyler. He rubbed his side, giving Kinsley a sheepish look. "—guild leader didn't fill you in."

I glared at Kinsley, who suddenly appeared completely invested in something on the other side of the street. It was obvious that Kinsley wasn't just being practical—she wanted to live here. She'd been pushing for it since I'd awakened. "I'm sure she had her reasons. How weird are we talking?"

"I'll show you." Sara stepped out into the street and pointed down it with her one good arm. The reflective glass of a nearby building was blocking my view. I wheeled myself down the ramp for a better look.

I breathed out in a hiss.

Up to a certain point, it was like any other downtown street. Cars parked next to meters, a food truck, and people going about their daily lives. There were far more vendors than was common for this part of town, their stalls strangely medieval looking in a way that didn't really match the setting. People were wearing armor and robes in the open now, which gave the strange feeling that we were adjacent to some sort of massive fantasy convention.

Around a dozen blocks away, it stopped. The midday light ceased as deep shadows overtook what I assumed to be Region 13, as if the sun itself had abandoned it. There were silhouettes barely visible at this distance, tiny specks of people—or things shaped like people, milling about.

"What the hell?" I muttered.

"We don't know," Sara said, still transfixed on the darkness. "From what we've seen, none of the surviving civilians are under visible duress. But they don't seem interested in leaving their region or even talking."

"A few of ours were on the scene," Tyler said regretfully. "But... most walked away at the peak of the violence. Watching something like what happened there and being unable to do anything—well, you can see how that'd be difficult. Can't say that I blame them."

"Most?"

A shadow flitted over Tyler's face. "Yes. Owen. A boy not much older than you. Our only surviving member from Region 13. He had family there."

"Past tense."

"Yes," Tyler confirmed. "He stayed until the end. Supposedly, the last thing he heard before the lights went out was a voice."

"The Overseer? Or something else."

"Different voice. No one's heard from the Overseer yet," Sara said.

"According to his report, there was a gap of time between when the receptacle was filled and the... result. Probably whoever owned the region making their decision. The voice announced, 'the prophet has been chosen.' Blackout hit immediately after," Tyler finished.

"Great. Not foreboding at all." I wanted to go look. Investigate. But that wasn't going to happen while I was still stuck in this chair.

"We sent a scout." Sara chewed her lip. "She was supposed to check in."

"Let me guess," I said drolly, "you haven't heard from her."

"Still giving her some time," Tyler said, "She's good at what she does. Might just be waiting for a good time to come up for air."

"Of the twenty regions, 13 and 6 are the biggest question marks."

Kinsley finally joined the conversation, though she wouldn't meet my eye. "Dungeons are popping up all over 5, but the monsters are contained. Region 15 seems to be doubling down on being some sort of trading and crafting hub. And the others are still either figuring it out, or being cagey about what they have."

"Region 3?" I asked, my voice cold. It wasn't so much that they were poaching Lux. As desperate as the event was, some degree of strife and conflict was understandable, even justifiable. It was that they continued to do so even after their receptacle was filled.

And, you know, the whole killing Users for cores thing didn't really work in their favor either.

"Totally isolationist. Hostile to anyone not local to the region. Which means we have no idea what they have or don't have."

Fantastic. Even if I decided to throw this all away and go home, I'd still have a problem neighbor.

I eyed something else. A construction crew at the end of the street and several open-backed trucks. "Are they putting up a barrier? What if 13 sees that as an act of aggression?"

"A lot of the regions are throwing up walls and checkpoints," Kinsley confirmed. "What we're doing is nothing out of the ordinary. Region 5's the big exception. They seem to want Users to come there in droves. As many as they can get. They're charging for dungeon entry, but not nearly as much as they could be. Still figuring out the angle."

I thought about the information I had and came to a decision. "Get me in a room with Owen."

"He's traumatized. Borderline catatonic," Sara said. "I'm not convinced he has any more useful information than what he's told us."

"Maybe. But it can't hurt. If you make it happen, he'll talk to me." I grimaced. "Whatever the next event is, we need to be ready for it. That means strengthening our positions on all fronts. And ensuring that what happened in Region 6 isn't going to spread. Being proactive is the name of the game, from this point onward. If they don't give us enough information to prepare for whatever's coming, fuck it. We'll prepare for everything."

There was an odd reaction, and I realized I'd erred. I looked around, suddenly self-conscious. "It's... been a rough week. I've gotten used to calling shots without any real regard to hierarchy."

After a pause, Tyler rested a hand on my shoulder. "Kinsley says you're her primary advisor. And that she owes much of the success of the Merchants' Guild to you. And given that your guild not only took a pay cut to help the entire city, but also managed to fortify your region and save this one?" He shrugged. "I'm prepared to seriously consider any advice you might have."

The nagging puzzle piece finally fell into place. What I'd been missing this entire time. "There are twenty regions. But at the beginning of the event, the Overseer said only sixteen needed to be fortified."

"We noticed that too," Sara said. "As far as we can tell, every region had a receptacle. Haven't made sense of it yet."

"I see." I rested my head on my palm. Whatever the reason for the discrepancy, it wasn't a mistake on the Overseer's part. Either the system had plans for the four regions that didn't have to be fortified, in which case it was strange they didn't just gloss over that in the announcements. Or four of the regions had achieved some sort of clemency before the event began. And it was a total hunch, but I had a strong feeling that wherever the suits resided was probably one of those regions. "Not a fan of the way they're dividing us. Or the timing."

"Same here. Hopefully we'll know more in a few days," Tyler said.

My wheelchair jostled as Iris arrived at my side, landing with both feet. Only after did she seem to notice the group that had formed, and her smile lessened somewhat.

"You called?" she signed.

I checked the timer. Less than a minute remained. "Yup. Something might be happening soon. Figured you'd want to see. Where's Mom and Ellison?"

The double doors behind me *wooshed,* and I turned to see my mother step out from Iris's wake. She looked glass-eyed and bleary, as if she'd just woken from a deep sleep.

"He's not coming," I asked Iris. More statement than question.

"Haven't seen him since this morning," Iris confirmed.

She scrambled carefully up on my lap, eyes almost comically wide as her head swiveled back and forth.

"Sister?" I heard Sara whisper to Kinsley. Kinsley murmured an affirmative.

The first thing I noticed was a shift in temperature. It was almost always hot, but this was different. More humid somehow.

A single green sprout emerged from the crack in the sidewalk before me. Dozens more followed suit, thin green fingers scrambling for purchase. There was a resounding crack as the sidewalk itself shattered.

Someone grabbed the handles of my wheelchair and yanked me backward before it tipped over. When I looked back, something gnarled and brown was emerging from the concrete, widening the hole as it grew.

People avoided the sidewalks and roads as more greenery emerged, wrapping itself around anything nearby—cars, meters, and drains. The unending orchard of trees sprouted gray-blue leaves and golden blossoms as they reached their apex of twenty to thirty feet.

I caught a flash of movement from above and looked up. Behind a nearby skyscraper, a massive trunk, expansive in diameter, extended above the building and up into the clouds.

Iris stared up at it in wonder.

Countless car alarms were going off, all at mixed intervals. Civilians and Users alike had stopped running from the chaos and were gawking at the scene, unsure what to make of it.

"Ho-lee shit." Tyler said.

"It's beautiful," My mother whispered.

"Going to be a bitch to commute." Sara approached the tree that sprouted from the concrete before us. She poked it once. Then tentatively reached up to a thin, low-hanging branch, testing it. Eventually, she lifted her entire body in a one-handed pull-up, then dropped and landed with a grunt. "It's strong."

I blinked. Regardless of how sturdy the tree was, there should have been some movement. But the branch hadn't budged. Whatever I'd expected—metal deep in the earth, some sort of oil analogue perhaps—it hadn't been this. Not even close.

"Iris!" My sister dropped from my lap before I could stop her, approaching the tree as Sara had. Sara reached out to grab her, but Iris ducked away, giving the woman an apologetic smile. Before any of us could intervene, Iris touched the tree. Her palm was flush to the wood, her face a mask of concentration.

<Ordinator's Emulation> ticked in the back of my mind.

CHAPTER EIGHT

A small nova of near-transparent energy erupted around Iris. The display was as impressive as it was highly visible. I moved forward, trying to break line of sight. Kinsley beat me there, accompanied by two members of Roderick's lodge I'd previously taken as unaffiliated Users.

Quick on the uptake, Tyler barked out a verbal command and Sara, along with a couple other Adventurers' Guild members following in their wake, filled out the wall. Before I could even shout, any view of my sister was blocked by a wall of bodies. I approached and two people parted, letting me through.

"Iris, what the fuck are you doing?" I hissed, and immediately regretted the outburst. My sister knew there was danger—everyone did at this point—but she didn't know the face of it. Not yet. Thankfully, she wasn't able to hear me. Her face was a mask of concentration, bordering on a frown.

"What's wrong?" I tried again, calmer than before.

Iris started to finger spell in ASL, then grew frustrated and spoke out loud. "I thought it would make a nice handle for my hammer. But it's more difficult than absorbing regular metal. Almost like the wood itself is fighting me." She swiveled toward me, a horrified expression on her face. "Does that mean it's alive?"

I shrugged, glancing around to make sure our human barricade was still intact. "Probably. It's a tree. Hard to say more than that. Not like we can ask it."

To my surprise—and embarrassment—Iris did exactly that. "I'm sorry. I tried to take from you without asking permission."

Someone snickered, and I felt my cheeks growing red with embarrassment.

Still totally focused, Iris cocked her head. "Oh. I see. You don't like the idea of being a hammer. What would you like to be then?"

A single branch pointing east stirred, as if by a gust of wind. Even though I knew from Sara's demonstration that the branches were far too sturdy for that. Iris looked in the direction the branch was pointing. "You want to help hold back the dark? I don't know what that means."

"Region 13," Sara realized, glancing toward the neighboring region. It was firmly obscured from view now that we were effectively entrenched in a forest, but the blackness on the horizon was still visible.

"How would it even do that? Hold back the dark? It's a fuckin' tree." Kinsley scratched her head. A thin branch lashed out and smacked against the back of her neck. She jumped straight up with a shriek, then glared at the tree. "Don't make me get a lighter, stumpy."

I considered what Tyler had said about the regions erecting walls and a thought occurred to me. "Does it want to contribute materials to our defenses?"

Iris relayed the message. There was a tinkling of leaves that sounded suspiciously like an affirmative.

"Small problem. I want to help," Iris chuckled nervously. "But I don't have the necessary tools. And I could get other materials to make them, but if you're as strong as you say, I'm not sure they'd work on you."

A branch shifted again, this time pointing to a smaller sapling with a trunk that was a lighter shade of gray.

Iris started to head toward it. I caught her shoulder, considered the fact that we had an audience, and looked at Tyler. "Give us a minute?"

Tyler nodded, and the group dispersed as Iris stepped away from the tree.

"*What?*" she signed.

"*I don't want you involved with this. Not so directly.*"

Iris's eyes narrowed. "*Why?*"

"*Because it makes you a target,*" I signed, my hands moving in sharp motions. "*This isn't something to take lightly. There are people out there who want your abilities and aren't above kidnapping a little girl to get their hands on them.*"

"*And you controlling a region doesn't already make me a target?*" Iris responded, a streak of rebellion in her eyes.

"*That's... different.*"

"*It is dangerous, Iris,*" Kinsley said, backing me up. "*More dangerous than you can imagine. People took me and hurt me just for being a merchant.*"

Iris made a wide sweep with her arm, staring both of us down. "Everything is dangerous. The world is scarier than it ever was, and that's saying a lot." She stuck a finger at me. "I love you. And I know you've kept us safe. And I understand how hard it's been. But this is probably why Ellison has been so standoffish lately. You can't protect us from everything."

Anger built in my gut. Iris was just riding the high that came from being a User. She felt optimistic and elated at the possibilities, the same way I'd been before that first experience with a bounty brought that crashing down.

I reached out with **<Suggestion>**, pushing past her mental defenses—

And found that Iris was terrified. There was so much fear that it was a miracle she wasn't a hyperventilating heap curled up on the ground.

The only thing keeping her going was a determination so strong it was almost blinding.

It took me a minute to get it.

Iris had never been useless. But in the context of a crisis, she'd always played third chair to me and Ellison. Generally out of the way, supporting and observing. It was just the nature of how things had fallen into place. Ellison was far more comfortable taking risks and putting himself in difficult positions. Iris was clever, but prone to anxiety and panic.

I'd never really considered how that must have felt. Watching your family struggle—fight to survive—and feeling like your contribution was next to nothing.

Reading people was my strength, but there's always blind spots for the ones we love.

Her fear was probably heightened, considering everything we'd been through. She'd never complained or broken down. But there were times in the past, when things were hardest, where her cheery disposition had come off as artificial.

Was the ray of sunshine act a facade?

Has she always been afraid?

I withdrew **<Suggestion>** immediately, somewhat nauseous at how close I'd come to breaking my own rule. Kinsley was watching us, unsure of how to proceed.

"Sidebar?" My mother's voice. The scent of tequila reached my nose. Just a trace, rather than the stink that came from a legitimate bender.

I broke eye contact with Iris and nodded.

"That doesn't smell like gin," I groused, once we were out of earshot.

"Don't do that."

"Do what?"

"Launch a preemptive strike because you know you're not going to like what I'm going to say." My mother gave me a knowing look.

I rolled my eyes. "Fine."

"You're smothering them."

I clenched the air in frustration. "It's not about control."

"—It's about protecting them. I'm familiar with the concept. Tried my hand at it once upon a time, if you remember. How well did that turn out?"

I blinked. Partially because I *didn't* remember. She'd been a decent mother until we'd lost Dad, then everything had gone to shit. But my memories of that time were patchy at best.

"Even though I had your best interests at heart, you hated me for it. That's when I learned I couldn't force you to do anything." Mom reached out toward a low-hanging branch, touching the edge of a gray-blue leaf. It left a line of red on her fingertip. She winced and pressed the wound against her waistband. "They're both getting older. Even if it's the best thing for them, you can only advise and hope they listen. If you take a hardline stance, they'll just get better at hiding whatever it is they want to do."

I bit back a cruel response. There was a vulnerability in my mother's expression that told me she knew exactly how hypocritical it was that she was giving this advice. How badly she'd fallen short.

"Okay," I said.

She tilted her head, as if not quite believing what she'd heard. "What?"

"You might be right."

———

Iris had already started making tools by the time I returned to the group. She stuck a hammer-shaped object behind her back. Kinsley stood next to her, looking just as nervous.

"I told her it'd be fine to make a few tools. Just to test the materials," Kinsley said.

"Let me see." I held out a hand. Iris tentatively placed the handle in my palm. There were issues with the design. Bark formed the handle, which would probably still chip off too easily, even if the wood itself was devilishly strong. But the weight was well-balanced, and the head of the hammer looked solid. I thumped it against the metal frame of my wheelchair and was surprised when it left a dent. The hammerhead was completely unmarked from the impact, no scuffs or imprints.

"Not bad at all."

"And check this out." Kinsley held out a small twig, placing a metal zippo beneath it. She flicked the wheel and the spark ignited into flame. The light-colored twig colored red around the flame but didn't catch fire.

"It's not flammable?" I raised an eyebrow.

"It's called Wraithwood, according to my identification skill. Stronger and more enchantable than Ebonscale—of course I had no idea what that was, but after a cursory search on the store, it seems to be a material commonly used in high-level armor and weapons. No idea how well it'll hold an edge, but I figure we'll need to test it anyway." Kinsley trailed off, seeming to realize we'd left key business unresolved.

<**Kinsley:** I know it's not my business. But she really seems to want this. We could set her up with a protective detail.>

The sound of an engine grew closer. One of the trucks that had been working on a barrier at the end of the street had stopped, the vehicle stopped at a crooked line of trees blocking the road. The driver—a man in a hard hat and reflective vest—stepped out, swearing like a sailor.

"Who's in charge here?"

Tyler, lingering nearby, left his group to speak to the man. "Everything alright?"

"Pretty far from alright, to be frank. Care to tell me how me and my guys are supposed to work with a god-damn forest in the way? Not even sure we could get the truck out now."

My first thought was that he could simply recall the truck to his inventory. But I wasn't certain how that worked if it wasn't a system-assigned vehicle. I was the only one who could inventory my bike, for example. Anyone else would have to steal it the hard way.

"We're working on a solution," Tyler held both hands out placatingly, glancing back toward us.

"Well, work faster," the man grumbled. "We were supposed to get this thing up in a week. Around the entire region. That was already gonna be difficult without the great outdoors fuckin up supply lines. What's up with that anyway?"

"Can you do it?" I asked Iris.

"Do... what?" Iris asked hesitantly.

"Help the construction crew get barriers up. Checkpoints. Observation towers."

"I'm not very high level." Iris put her hands behind her back. "But as long as the designs are simple, yeah, I think so. The barriers at least." She was being guarded, worried I'd snatch the wind from her sails.

I pinched the top of my nose. "If you get a weird feeling. Like there's someone around you don't recognize, or if you feel like you're being watched. Anything. Message me and Kinsley immediately. We're also going to get some people to watch your back—ow."

"Thanks, brother." Iris released me from her stranglehold and bounded toward Tyler and the construction crew leader.

\<Quest Received\>
\<Quest: A Steady Hand\>**

I hoped I wouldn't regret this.

CHAPTER NINE

<Quest Received>
Quest: A Steady Hand
<Quest Received>
Primary Objective — Ensure Region 14's Survival
Secondary Objective I — Establish Short-Term Defenses
Secondary Objective II — Establish Trade and Alliances with other Regions
Secondary Objective III — Uncover the Region Luminaries (1 of 4)
Secondary Objective IV — Discover the Secret of the Wraithwood
Secondary Objective V — ???
Personal Objective — Remain unidentified by other Users.
Threat Level: ???
EXP GAIN (L)
Time Limit: Before the Transposition Event
Reward: Class Specific Boon.

The rest of the day passed quickly. But there were some growing pains. At first, the construction crew was clearly irritated, both by having to redo sections of the region barrier and by Iris's presence. Like the rest of my family, Iris wasn't used to mincing words. If there was a problem, she'd comment on it immediately. She was clear and up front about what she wanted, and that rankled them.

After the initial negotiation, tension climbed so high there were multiple times I thought I'd need to intervene, doctor's warning be damned.

Thankfully, that was unnecessary.

Because Iris's personal debut left an *impact*.

Iris spent a lot of time on a sketch for the barriers. Made sure there were supports in the correct places along with other functionality, thanks to Gideon Fenberry, an NPC architect who lived in our building.

"It's not very pretty," Iris said, studying her drawing. She seemed to be growing more comfortable speaking aloud. There was a pencil smudge on her chin, and her hair had grown frizzy with the heat.

"Doesn't have to be," I replied nonchalantly, still studying the details of the most recent quest I'd received. The secondary luminary objective caught my eye.

"Normally, I'd loathe the apathy toward creativity," Gideon said, shooting me a curious side eye. "But considering the scale of this project, your brother is correct."

He was a bit shorter than average, maybe a half-inch shorter than me if I were to guess, and a bit stuffy. His blue office shirt was wrinkled but still tucked into his chinos. Large glasses framed his round face, and I had a feeling they were prescription. The only noteworthy element of his apparel were the vibrant magenta, yellow, and cyan vertically segmented suspenders.

Iris placed her hand on a nearby felled tree and muttered under her breath.

"Looky there. Our mascot's communing with nature again." One of the many men in orange vests milling around snickered.

"That helps, thanks." Iris patted the tree in appreciation and picked up her pencil, then began to draw excitedly.

I glanced over her shoulder. No one had managed to recreate Iris's ability to communicate with the trees. My guess was that it had something to do with her class, and that her connection to the materials themselves were heightened.

"Can you—" Iris started to sign, then stopped and spoke aloud to the man who had just cracked a joke. "Can you help gather leaves?"

"For... what?" The man looked at her like she was losing her mind.

I was worried. Iris didn't deal with conflict well. With this degree of hostility and pushback, I wouldn't have been surprised if she shrank into herself. But whether it was due to the urgency of the situation, or just plain determination on Iris's part, she didn't back down.

"For materials," Iris said. "They dampen magic. Magic Users—along with artillery spells—are the biggest threat to us, according to Users I've talked to."

And by Users, she was referring primarily to me.

Iris continued, "If we integrate the leaves into the wood itself, it should go a long way toward protecting us."

"And if one of those Wizards can fly?" the man challenged. "Don't know if you've noticed, but there are people just flitting around up there."

Iris glanced at me.

"We'll cross that bridge when we come to it," I mouthed. There weren't many fliers. Only a half-dozen or so in the sky at any given time. It came without saying that we'd need other defenses. This was barebones. A foundation for everything that would come after. I didn't like that the regions were all walling themselves off.

Iris's smile dampened. She pointed to the eternal darkness of Region 13, now less than a block away. "Do you see anyone flying over there?"

The man's expression soured. "Well, no."

"Then let's just worry about getting the walls up, and we'll deal with the fringe issues later."

"Hey, Martinez. Didn't you have a landscaping thing? Half-pint wants help gathering leaves."

"It was a rental company, you cretin," Martinez said. He was laying in the back of the truck, hat pulled down over his eyes.

"Yeah yeah."

"The more people help, the faster this will go," Iris said, probably missing some crosstalk.

Unsurprisingly, the man's lip curled. He crossed his arms and set his feet, unmoving. His companions were less direct in their misgivings but still made no effort to start gathering leaves.

I sighed and grabbed a nearby bag. "How many do you need?"

Iris glanced at me, then the forest that had cropped up behind us. "A thousand, give or take."

"Total?" I asked, surprised by the number.

"Per section. More or less depending on the length," Iris said, clearly concerned for my well-being. "But, Matt, you should rest."

"Nah." I coughed, deep and painful, then turned to the side and spit blood and phlegm onto the ground. I could feel the workers watching uneasily as I thoroughly ignored them. "So, what? I just pick them off the ground?"

"No, they wouldn't like that. The Wraithwoods. Just ask them. They'll understand, even if they can't talk to you directly. It's up to each tree how much they'd like to contribute, if anything," Iris said hesitantly. I could tell she was about to try to talk me out of it, so I immediately turned and wheeled myself to the nearest tree. The obliterated road was littered with roots and detritus, and I probably made a pitiful sight, maneuvering my wheelchair across the treacherous terrain.

Doing my best to hide how silly I felt, I reached out and knocked on the trunk. "I need leaves for the wall."

A single gray-blue leaf detached itself from the tree and drifted slowly toward me. Remembering how my mother cut her finger against a leaf's edge, I quickly withdrew one of the sturdier bags I'd used to hold Lux during the trial and held it open. Without prompting, a dozen more leaves detached themselves and drifted into the bag.

With well over a hundred leaves in hand, I moved on to the next tree. And the next. Before long, I saw Gideon standing nearby, holding up a leather satchel. He gave me an encouraging nod.

"Careful!" I heard Iris shout. She wasn't talking to me. Rather, one of the construction crew. The one with the attitude was still standing back, but several of them had followed my lead, unwilling to let the boy in the wheelchair show them up.

Before long, we had more than enough for the first section and many more after that. Iris knelt in front of the materials, a bead of sweat on her forehead. She looked back at me and I nodded, gesturing for her to go for it.

White light emitted from Iris's palms. Someone gasped.

The wall wasn't constructed piece by piece, the way you'd assume. Rather, a thin gray veneer of wood stretched up skyward until it stopped, around three stories tall. Then, it thickened. Support beams extended from the wood itself, in a near perfect copy of what Iris had sketched. Small sliding sections that hid a portcullis assembled themselves. Slowly, the leaves rose from their various bags. They were oval naturally, and shed their stems as they drifted toward the wall. Iris arranged them layer by layer on top of each other, until the entire section of wall was covered. With the way they were arranged, the wall looked almost scaled in nature.

I reached up and tried to pry a leaf loose. It was like attempting to pull a metal pole out of concrete. When I tried again, I noticed the other leaves seemed to compress, locking the one I was tugging in place.

That was a minor relief. No one would be stripping the metaphorical copper out of our walls.

Iris stood slowly, surveying her work with a distant smile.

I ruffled her hair. "Good job, kiddo."

That was all it took to throw the construction crew into action. With the first section in place, they seemed to recognize how much time Iris could save them and intended to capitalize on the advantage.

By evening's end, the district was completely enclosed, with gated entrances on all four sides. I would have preferred having a few towers in place, but Iris was asleep on my lap, dead to the world. She'd gone nearly all day, only pausing for a nap halfway through when her mana was low.

I shrugged. There were nearby buildings we could use as lookouts in the interim. And considering how quickly the construction had gone, this was more than a win already.

"She is very talented," Gideon said. He'd offered to push my wheel-chair, and despite my previous feelings of weirdness about that, I was too tired to say no.

Iris stirred against my chest, curling up tighter. I patted her head. "She's always been clever." *They both are.* Unbidden, my thoughts turned to Ellison.

"More than just clever," Gideon said enthusiastically. "Generally, in my profession, people tend to lean one of two ways. Artistic or pragmatic. Both are necessary, in varying degrees. But most skew one way or another. Your sister seems to understand the balance. Even when she was experimenting. Another good sign. If even half of my students were so gifted." He shook his head.

"You were a teacher?"

"Part-time at Columbia, when wasn't overloaded with work," Gideon affirmed.

"Hell of a commute."

"Not really. I had a summer home there." His expression clouded. "Though I suppose my days of teaching are behind me."

I glanced down at my sister. "Everything is changing. We have plenty of existing infrastructure that's obsolete."

"Yes." Gideon's mouth pulled downward. "I have ideas. Ways to rectify and salvage what we have, improve it. But the City Council seems more interested in sitting on its hands and bracing for whatever comes next than rebuilding."

I wondered, absentmindedly, if I was being baited. Then dismissed the notion. Gideon was smart, not above getting his hands dirty, and most importantly—patient with Iris. If he'd been more like Miles, I'd be far more suspicious and hesitant to bite. But he seemed too socially awkward to be manipulating me intentionally. And even if he was, he clearly knew what he was talking about.

I sighed. "You affiliated?"

He blinked. "I'm accredited."

"Do you have a guild?"

"Oh. No."

Before I could talk myself out of it, I pulled up Kinsley's contact card and sent it to Gideon. "Reach out to her. Message, not voice. She's swamped right now. Tell her Matt recommended you for membership, and explain what you can offer."

"And what... is it that I'm offering?" Gideon asked, his eyebrow furrowed. "You know I'm not a User."

"Here's what I'm thinking. You've seen what Iris can do. Take on my sister as an apprentice. Teach her at a college level." Before he could argue, I held up a hand. "She's not stupid. Anything foundational you can think of, she's probably already learned. Keep in mind you likely won't be her only teacher and manage the workload accordingly. In return, she helps with improvements you want to make around the region, as long as Kinsley green-lights whatever it is you have in mind."

"Quick point of order." Gideon cleared his throat. "This is *the* Kinsley, is it not?"

"Yes. Unless there's another guild leader by that name I'm not aware of.

"Is there any contract?" Gideon asked, his eyes narrowing.

Ah. He'd been to the open forum, or at least had interactions with a guild like the Local Relief Effort. Explained why he still hadn't joined up with anyone.

"No contract. I'll leave pay negotiations to you and her." I waved him off. There were too many irons in the fire to try to manage things at a micro level. I'd trust Kinsley to handle the recruitment. And more importantly, to get one of her mercenaries to investigate Gideon.

Even if he seemed well-meaning and wasn't triggering any red flags, there was no world where I trusted my sister to an outsider without due diligence.

/////

By the time I returned to my penthouse, I was spent. Between the physical exhaustion that came with being injured and the hell of drinking the recovery potions, it was hard to keep my eyes open. Sae was nowhere to be seen. Her guest room door was locked shut, no light emitting from beneath the doorframe. Probably asleep. She'd be just as exhausted as me, if not more so.

And she wasn't the only one.

Mom was passed out on the couch. Ellison had kicked open a recliner and fallen asleep watching a movie with the volume muted. He opened one eye to look at me as I came in.

I gave him a half-wave and the eye closed, as if he'd only woken to confirm that nothing was amiss.

Gently, I placed Iris down on the love seat perpendicular to the couch my mother was sleeping on, and pulled a plush blanket from the hallway closet to drape over her. She didn't stir at all, further confirming my suspicion that she'd pushed herself too hard.

When I thought about it, I found that my reticence to live here had diminished. Iris's walls likely had something to do with it. I made a mental note to talk to the building super in the morning. From what Kinsley said, there were plenty of available rooms, and the building owner seemed ecstatic to dole them out to us. I'd need to talk to them, whoever they were, sooner rather than later.

We'd lived cramped together in an apartment for too long already.

Now that we had options, they deserved their space. Iris would probably still live with Mom. That was the best case for both of them. My sister would be able to keep an eye on Mom and tell me if her issues started becoming problems again. And she wouldn't be alone.

Ellison was a different story. I wanted him completely separate, on a different floor. I'd thought about it comprehensively. The elevator required a keycard, which meant it'd be easy to track his comings and goings. He'd still have access to us, but we'd know he was coming— whether he wanted us to or not. I'd need to be careful how I spun it when I told him. He was more keyed in to how I thought than most people, so I wanted to at least take the night to come up with a plan. With that in mind, I sent him a message.

<**Matt:** Talk in the morning. Just bang on my door when you're awake.>

Either he'd be there or he wouldn't. Hopefully, our relationship wasn't that far gone.

Sae—well, I wasn't sure what to do with Sae. Eventually, I wanted the penthouse to myself. It would be easier to handle everything—as both Matt and Myrddin—without anyone else tracking my comings and goings. But I wasn't going to put that over her well-being. She'd been through hell. As long as she was in hiding, her social interaction was limited to me, Kinsley, and my family. Other than our initial discussion, I had no idea where she was at, in terms of headspace. And as Kinsley had so recently reminded me, isolation could be a hell of its own.

I crawled onto the hospital bed in my room, feeling profoundly on the back foot. From the moment I woke up, it felt like I'd been managing people and delegating, which wasn't my forte. Hopefully, Kinsley would be able to take more of a leading role as time went on and everything settled. With that in mind, I finished what was left of the recovery potion, gagging at the taste.

Idly, I pulled up my character sheet. There hadn't been any changes. I still wouldn't know how much the augmented stats altered my abilities until I could let loose.

One down, one to go.

Speaking of which. I had two levels to distribute. I'd yet to bother with them, considering everything else that was going on. Now that there wasn't an immediately impending crisis, there was no reason not to take my time and consider my options carefully. I read through the Ordinator feats first, noting anything that looked promising, then through the Page feats. There was an improved version of <**Page's Quickdraw**> that looked promising, along with some general-purpose feats that would help in the short term.

I navigated to the dropdown—and stopped.

<Ordinator>
<Page>
<Pending^>

It suddenly clicked. I was offered a class for completing the receptacle in Region 14. I'd assumed that offer would simply be null, due to the nature of my subterfuge. But there it was. I focused on the carrot and text began to scroll.

<System Notification: A new class cannot be selected with unresolved advancement. Please allocate all available stat points before entering the Null.>

CHAPTER TEN

<System Notification: A new class cannot be selected with unresolved advancement. Please allocate all available stat points before entering the Null.>

Interesting. The system specified that I needed to distribute stat points, leaving feat points unmentioned. That wasn't an accident. I knew from experience it was possible to bank the feat points and use them later—normally a terrible idea, considering the stakes. There wasn't really any excuse for not using everything I had at my disposal at any given time. But in this case, I could safely level and save the feat points in case I unlocked anything worth pursuing.

I swapped my local identity to Myrddin to simplify things for the level.

Matt
Level 12 Ordinator
Identity: Myrddin, Level 10 ???
Strength: 6
Toughness: 6
Agility: 18+
Intelligence: 16+
Perception: 8
Will: 14
Companionship: 1
Active Title: Born Nihilist
Feats: Double-Blind, Ordinator's Guile I, Ordinator's Emulation, Stealth I,

Awareness I, Harrowing Anticipation, Page's Quickdraw, Vindictive,
Squelch.
Skills: Probability Cascade, LVL 3. Suggestion, LVL 18. One-handed, LVL
16. Negotiation, LVL 11. Unsparing Fang (Emulated), Level 10.
Summons: Audrey — Flowerfang Hybrid, Bond LVL 3. Talia — Revenant
Wolf, Bond LVL 4
Selve: 112,000 (-100 per week)
Skill Points Available: 6. Feat points available: 4.

The amount of Selve didn't line up. I'd been around that number
before, but I'd spent nearly half of it on the motorcycle and a shitton on
healing and curative items. I leafed through my notifications and found
the explanation.

<**System Notification:** Guild Leader Kinsley has awarded you
S50,000.>
<**Listed Reason:** Event Performance.>

Huh. Kinsley hadn't mentioned it. Not even to grouse about it.
Considering her miserly nature, I had to wonder how much she'd made
on the event itself. Probably a killing.

Dismissing the anomaly, I returned to my listed stats. And frowned.
I'd been mainlining agility and intelligence, but they were both
augmented now. Improvement before augmentation had been significant
in an incremental way. There was no question I was a capable of maneu-
vers I wouldn't have dreamed of before. I absolutely thought faster on my
feet, and was far less vulnerable to the mental spirals that had plagued
my adolescence and teenage years.

Both agility and intelligence had served me well. Whether growth
from here was incremental or exponential, the choice should have been
clear.

If it wasn't for the adaptive dungeon.

I wanted to clear the dungeon's fifth level before engaging the suits.
Completing the long-standing quest would likely net an additional level.
There was no way of knowing how involved or compromised I would be
after the meeting, and I wanted as much firepower as I could get my
hands on before entering the lion's den.

My safest bet would be boosting intelligence and agility further.

But the real gamble, with the greatest reward, was the lithid.

Before I could chase that train of thought further, I had to check something first. Groaning, I grabbed the railings of the medical bed and bore
down, sweat beading on my forehead as pain racked through me. It was
far worse than any previous instance of summoning. The plucking feeling

went beyond skin deep, and it felt as if my very organs were being strummed. I nearly stopped the process.

A mist of shadow formed the dark silhouette of a wolf in the corner.

"You were not supposed to use magic, human," Talia growled.

I panted, struggling to catch my breath. A bead of sweat dripped down my forehead. "No choice. Had to risk it." An incongruity stood out. "How would you even know that?"

The wolf panned the room, taking in her new surroundings. "A new ability. Or something along those lines. I am still sightless in the void, but sounds and voices make their way to my ears. From what I gathered, you retrieved our pack member. Is she well?"

Further confirmation that I was making the right call. There was no way I could hide this from her.

"As good as she could be, considering."

"That is a relief. And cannot have been easy, considering your state. Thank you." Talia approached the bed and lowered her neck, pressing the crown of her head into my hand. Her fur was surprisingly soft. I was suddenly paralyzed, not knowing what to do. She'd likely take any reciprocation as demeaning.

"Don't thank me yet," I said quietly.

Talia pulled away and took a step backward. "Explain."

"You still want the suits, right?"

Teeth glinted in the darkness. "Naturally. They struck me down without cause and decimated a smaller pack that posed no threat to them. I loathe them nearly as much as the wretch."

I winced, suddenly grateful the room was dark enough to hide it. "I agree. Beyond what they did, their methods are unconscionable. They can't be allowed to monopolize power on a greater scale."

"Yes."

"And we agree that we should leverage every possible advantage to make that happen?"

"On that, we are in accord," her voice reticent. By now, she probably sensed the catch but still hadn't connected the dots.

"I've been considering this for a while," I said, speaking quickly, "Keep in mind, it's impossible to say for sure. The sample size is too small."

"Speak plainly, human."

I'd done everything I could to frame the conversation. Now it was up to Talia. "I've killed multiple monsters outside of the dungeon and received nothing but standard drops. Given that, I'm guessing, because of the nature of my class, the adaptive dungeon has a higher chance of dropping monster cores."

"No," Talia said immediately, a low growl in her throat.

I held up a hand, "Just hear me out. We're talking like this because I value you. Highly. Too much to spring this on you out of nowhere. You pulled my ass out of the fire multiple times. I'm honestly not sure I would have made it through the trial if it wasn't for you, doubly so for the Transposition event."

"Then *listen* to me when I tell you that a lithid is not to be trifled with!" Talia shouted. "Their kind thrives on pain. Delights in suffering. Acquiring one would be an exercise in self-destruction."

"Not a summon." I shook my head. "Not like you or Audrey. Not even close. From what you've said, it's too evil for that. It would be nothing more than a tool. A weapon to be unleashed on our enemies and dismissed as soon as its work is done."

Her silhouette quivered. "It tormented me for days. But it felt like an eternity."

"You saw the suits, Talia." I tried to redirect her to the big picture. "You know how powerful they are. Didn't you agree we needed every advantage we could get?"

"If you are correct and follow this path, I will not follow. You will have to compel me for *anything,*" Talia seethed.

I laid my head back on my pillow. "Which is why we're talking about this now. If you decide this path is untenable, I'll discard the core."

After a moment, she stopped shaking. "Could you do it? What you're asking of me?"

I considered that. If it was my mother, or Iris, or Ellison who died. "Absolutely. It wouldn't be easy. But it would be my first course."

"Your... first?" Her voice cracked.

"Revenge is a distraction."

"Yes. You've said that before."

"I didn't have time to explain what I meant." I pushed myself up in a sitting position and studied her. "There are lines that can't be uncrossed. These lines are universal, translated across every society, sophisticated or undeveloped. You don't maim or torture unnecessarily. You don't attack your enemy's family or loved ones if they're uninvolved. And you don't hurt children."

"And if they do it anyway?" Talia growled.

"Then it gets ugly. Suddenly, you're unburdened by civility, unencumbered by rules. There's a certain freedom in that. Maybe you use that justification to get a little dark, or gruesome. But I think there's a better way."

"If you say *forgiveness*—"

"No." I shook my head. Aaron's face popped up in my mind. "Not even close. It's better, I think, to use them. Ingratiate yourself. Get close enough that they eventually become dependent on you. Exploit them for every benefit and advantage they can offer. Create weaknesses and undermine them in the shadows. And when they start to panic, inevitably overextending in a feeble attempt to cling to their waning power? All you have to do is watch them fall."

Talia slowly sat down. "At times you frighten me, pup."

"That doesn't change the fact that I'm in your corner, Talia. Always."

"And when this group is gone?" Talia prompted. Her eye gleamed in darkness.

"Assuming any of this actually happens? Pull the trigger whenever you want. The only way this works without creating resentment between us is if I give you the option to veto. Unconditionally."

She looked away, scuffing the carpet with her paw. "There... is sense to your argument. Still. As hard as it is to admit. This is... difficult. For me."

I thought about what I knew about Talia. What I knew about wolves. Even with how the cliched "alpha/beta" hierarchy had been thoroughly debunked at this point, dominance was important to them. Talia herself embodied that, refusing to take anything that resembled an order unless it was framed as a suggestion. There were some elements of her personality that made me think of her as a Viking at times. The warrior spirit.

"Take your time." I smiled wider than normal, letting a growl into my voice. "In the interim, let me ask you another question. How often have you had the opportunity to destroy your enemy twice?"

Talia's head slowly swiveled toward me. Her teeth glittered in the darkness. She chuckled. "This would be the first."

———

I slotted four points into willpower, praying that would be enough to meet the requirements for controlling the lithid. In truth, it was only a short-term gamble. If it didn't work out, I'd be prepared for whatever high-level summon came next. The remaining two points went into intelligence and agility, respectively. Leveling was less painful than usual with willpower as the primary focus—and of course, I'd locked it in one level at a time.

My vision faded as darkness took me.

<System Message: User. Are you there?>

CHAPTER ELEVEN

The void was all around me. Nothingness. No sensation, no sense of weight or distance.

Black.

It was strange to be here again. Back where it all started.

If I relaxed my mind, it was almost like everything that had come to pass was a fever dream, and I was reset to the frantic moments after the meteor. In reality, it wasn't the same. The overload of panic and existential terror was entirely absent.

I'd gotten used to it. Accepting the unknown was almost automatic.

The text loomed in front of me, magnified several times larger than what I'd grown accustomed to on the system overlay.

<System Message: User. Are you there?>

When I went to select the only option, I was surprised to find the text field empty. Before, the options had all been selected for me. They'd all been answers I likely would have selected if I was being completely and totally honest with both the questions and myself, but generally things I never would have admitted to. Other Users had similar experiences.

Maybe that was meant to be a safeguard. There was no way I'd have taken it seriously enough to answer honestly the first time around.

Given the lack of mouth, I didn't speak so much as focus my thoughts on the text. "Yes."

<Welcome, User.>

I waited.

<Are Are Are Are Are Are Are Are Are AreAreAreAreAreAreAreAreAr-
erarerareraerarearearearearearearearearear-
aerearearearearearearearearearearearearearearearearearearearearea—>

The window snapped shut. Confusion formed the beginnings of alarm as it became clear something was wrong. This was either a malfunction or something worse.

"Hello?"

There was no response. The silence dragged out long enough for my alarm to turn to dread. If something went fundamentally wrong, did that mean I was stuck here? Forever catatonic in my bed.

Suddenly, the text reappeared.

<Are you having fun yet?>

"No."

<Too bad. Good thing I am. When our mutual friend informed me how her boon might restrict your ability to consult a consecrator in the Null, she seemed to find it nothing more than an amusement. No imagination, that one.>

A quiet anger swept over me. Apparently, the old saying held true. Three people could keep a secret if two of them were dead. Even in the realm of gods. And I was getting really fucking tired of deific interference.

More importantly, I needed to know if Nychta had intentionally set me up to fail.

"And what, if I may ask, would have happened without this intercession?"

<Hm. What to say? I could tell you that you'd be trapped in here forever. Turn you against her before she even manages to sink a single talon into you. But I suppose she and I *are* friends... of a sort. In answer to your question, the session would have timed out and you'd be returned to your body, with no penalty or benefit.>

"If I'm filling in the gaps correctly, the gods use the Null to grant classes to mortals?"

<Got it in one! Lesser gods, usually. Though, I'm sure you've realized there's always exceptions.>

He was including himself in that, of course. Letting me know he wasn't a lesser god without saying it.

Something crucial occurred to me. When I'd spoken to the Allfather at the shrine of elevation, his message text had been capitalized. The same held true for my initial venture into this place, after the meteor, and when I'd awoken the Ordinator's summoner variant. It was just a guess, but a grounded one. The Allfather had been my proctor the first time around and continued to directly oversee anything to do with my advancement as an Ordinator.

"How do we proceed?" I asked.

<You're not going to ask who I am? Plead for me to keep your secret?>

The vein above my brow would have popped out, if I had a forehead to speak of.

"First, I'm assuming if you wanted me to know who you were, you would have told me. Your associates—"

<Ew.>

I sighed. "The *other* gods haven't been shy when it came to introductions. Figured that came with the territory. Secondly, I'm pretty sure you want something. Nychta emphasized that I'm marked. I'm assuming when she told you about me—even though I really wish she hadn't—she did so with confidence you'd keep it to yourself. Not that I have any clue what any of you actually want. Or expect for this to be my last deific house call."

<Almost. But you've got something backward.>
:)

The symbol appeared on its own, floating toward me in the void before dissipating to nothing. Something flashed through my mind. An image in the hotel lobby of the same symbol emblazoned on a metal backplate behind the reception desk.

"Nychta didn't tell you about me. You told her."

<Sigh. I was going to give you something really nasty if you missed the connection. Pity. Oh well, on to business.>

"Business?"

<I'm your consecrator. This position is generally far below me, but

I'm not completely irresponsible. I volunteered to get into this space. So, it's time to do the work.>

While the entity talked to itself, I spoke again. "Are you willing to tell me anything about the game? Or my brother's class?"

The text paused. <Of course not. That would violate the consecrator's vow.>

I sighed. "Figured—"

<It would be completely unprofessional if I told a supplicant, for example, that a person they asked me about has backing from an individual that scares the absolute hell out of *me*. And that's saying something.>

A cold chill went through me. "And if you were being so unspeakably unprofessional, what would you advise the supplicant to do with this information?"

<Tread carefully. Honestly, they'd be better off disowning them and losing their contact card. You can always get another brother. Everyone's doing it these days.>

Behind the babbling text, I sensed a grain of truth. It was dubious. This entity wasn't my friend and had already admitted they weren't above lying for their own amusement. But the already significant concern I felt for Ellison had grown exponentially.

<No. No. No. No—*Miner?* They were going to present Miner as one of your options. Blech.>

"I mean, I'm not opposed to a resource-gathering class."

<Well I am. God, so boring. No imagination there. What do they have in the restricted—Oh? This isn't—OH. Heh. Hahaha. HAHAHAHAHA...>

A wall of laughter scrolled, long and excessive. If I had a body, there was no question I'd be in cold sweats right about now. When the text returned, it was all business.

<Let's begin.>

<Are you a Raven or a Hawk?>

I hesitated. On the surface, it looked the same as the sheep and wolf question from the first go around. Only, it wasn't. Hawks were generally fiercely solitary and territorial. By contrast, ravens weren't nearly as passive as sheep. They weren't necessarily birds of prey, but in addition to scavenging, they did hunt. Sometimes alone, sometimes cooperatively. And their cleverness was well documented.

"Raven."

<Should judicial action aim for punishment or reformation?>

Good. A softball.

There was a common undercurrent of thought that more severe penalties worked as a deterrent for criminals. If I remembered correctly, this wasn't the case. Surprisingly, it did almost nothing to reduce recidivism, either. It just made people more likely to commit additional crimes to cover it up. If the penalty for robbing someone is already horrific, you're much better off just killing them after to reduce the chances of being caught.

"Reformation."

<Far in the future, a man is in a terrible car accident. Along with several crushed organs, his arms and legs are pulverized beyond repair. After the initial surgeries, the doctors discover old fragments from the accident scattered throughout the man's body have infected the surrounding muscles and skin. They replace the damaged limbs with cybernetics and grafted skin, and regrow the muscle with a mix of stem and animal cells. Now. Given the extent of his injuries and invasiveness of the replacements, is this still the same man?>

I wanted to roll my eyes. "Really? We're doing Theseus?"

<Invalid answer. Please try again.>

Another philosophical problem with a twist. The unaltered version didn't refer to man at all, rather whether a ship that had all its components replaced over time was the same ship. There wasn't a correct answer to the paradox. This version was further complicated because the question made no reference to the man's brain. No notable damage or otherwise. And with the brain being key to who we are, it was entirely valid to argue he was the same.

I changed my answer at the last moment. "No. He's not the same."

\<Why? Your answer is locked in, this is just to satiate my curiosity.\>

It was a struggle to put it into words. "My reasoning has nothing to do with the replacements from the surgery. And there's no mention of brain damage. But his mind won't be the same. Trauma and hardship always catalyze change. Good or bad. And after an accident of that severity, grieving over what he lost, and undergoing treatments and exhaustive physical therapy? I can't imagine anyone would come out unaltered."

\<Interesting. Well, this will be fun. Our time's up, Ordinator. See you in the betting pool!\>

Before I could respond, the darkness faded and I jolted upright in bed.

\<System Message: Congratulations. You have awakened the Aries Cluster.\>
\<Between the confluence of your answers in the Null and your titles, you have unlocked a secondary class.\>
\<System Notification: You have unlocked King's Ranger as a secondary class. Do you wish to proceed?\>

CHAPTER TWELVE

The sun bathed my bedroom in orange hues as I reviewed the options for King's Ranger. I tried to focus on the positives.

It appeared to be a mostly ranged class.

As a secondary, it integrated cleanly with Ordinator and was tied to my true level, which meant I didn't have to worry about it lagging behind in level like my Page class.

It was usable as an additional identity, if I wanted to go that route.

There were options that served as shortcuts for mastering other weapons, which solved my problem of constantly falling back on a crossbow.

All things considered, it really could have been worse.

Still, I kept coming back to the same repetitive thought. Nychta's friend was an asshole.

Unlike both the Ordinator and Page class, King's Ranger personified the one element I'd wanted to avoid from the start. It was flashy as hell. There were trick shots, massive attacks that drained almost all mana to utilize, even some options for drawing aggression.

More problematic was that the name wasn't for show.

King's Ranger. Emphasis on *King*. There were feats like **<Fealty>** that gave bonuses to acting on the King's orders. **<Steadfast>** granted a massive power boost for coming to their defense. The potential connection to that Court the suits were pursuing wasn't lost on me.

I supposed it helped to some extent in terms of providing an additional cover. It would be easy to spin as an alternate reason for seeking the suits out. But I didn't like the idea of being beholden to anyone. Especially when I had no idea who they were. With luck, the class being my secondary would diminish whatever pull the "King" might have with his entourage.

There were two acquisitions that came with the class. **<Bow Journeyman>** and **<Acclimation>**, a skill and feat respectively. Because of the nature of hand crossbows and the clunkiness of their larger counterparts, I'd been limited on range from the start. It was possible to inflict serious damage at considerable range with **<Probability Cascade>** and its counterpart, but it was unreliable by definition as a method of attack. Being able to pepper targets at range while my summons ran interference, then swap to my crossbow for anything that broke mid-range range was far closer to ideal than the way I'd been haphazardly throwing myself into fights.

It would help differentiate me in social settings as well. Using the same weapons regardless of identity was going to bite me in the ass eventually. If I wanted to distance Matt the Page from the Myrddin persona, it would be easy enough to have the bow as Matt's primary weapon. Bow and saber for Matt, knives and crossbows for Myrddin.

<Acclimation> was a little more questionable, in terms of benefit.

According to the description, it buffed navigation and mobility in familiar environments. I'd lived in or adjacent to cities all my life, so I was most likely to see that benefit in urban environments. Which was a serious boon—if the skill itself wasn't a joke. No way to know until I tested it.

All that in mind, I used all but one of my feat points to purchase **<Bow Adept>**, which upgraded the **<Bow Journeyman>** skill. It was the first time I'd seen a feat directly affect a skill. I couldn't help but wonder if this was the sort of flexibility the direct combat-oriented classes had access to from the start.

I glanced at the time. Just past seven. As antsy as I was to talk to Ellison, waking him up and dragging him off somewhere was the perfect way to start this off wrong. I just... needed to be patient. With that in mind, I bought a small training bow and a padded target.

<Kinsley: Negotiations are going well. People have been noticing how quickly we're building. Got a few merchants from that group of fuckers I mentioned. Not sure what made the difference, but you were right, walking away from the table made a difference. Tired as hell. Gonna be dead to the world for a while, so VC if there's an emergency.**>**

Still working her ass off. No surprise there.

<Mom: I've been monitoring the intranet. Expected a million things to pop up after the market went live and people figured out how to access it,

but there's almost nothing. There was something interesting though. A partially made site that, I think, was meant to be a replacement for SMS after the cell towers went down. Guessing they abandoned it when the system-integrated messaging went live.>

<Mom: It gave me an idea. What if we set up a discussion board? We could have sub-forums for crafting, dungeon sightings, people looking for groups, and User abilities and theory crafting. It won't take long to make.>

I cocked my head, considering the possibility. It was an excellent idea. Not to mention, it would give Mom a project to work on to distract herself, decreasing the chances of a backslide.

The problem was the potential for misuse. Scams, misinformation, or worse, a streamlined method for Necromancers or similarly incentivized Users to lure others into a trap.

<Matt: Sounds solid. Just wait to go live with it until we have safeguards in place.>

My last unread message was from Sae. It'd come in later than the others, close to four in the morning.

<Sae: Is there anything I can do to help?>

I wasn't certain how to answer. The purely pragmatic answer was no. Given what she'd been through and what she was dealing with, any help she could offer was likely to be unreliable at best. But she'd never struck me as particularly proactive before. When we'd formed our short-lived party, Sae seemed happy to let Nick and Jinny operate as co-leaders and went with the flow of whatever was put before her.

Which made this departure from the norm concerning.

<Matt: Plenty. What would you like to do?>

I winced after sending it, hoping she wouldn't notice the flagrant attempt to stall. Our main hurdle was her inability to go out, well, pretty much anywhere. There was a very real possibility that anyone who saw Sae would misidentify her as a monster and act—or rather, overreact—accordingly.

After a few more moments, I reached out to Iris.

<Matt: Hey. I know you're still getting a grip on your power and your

plate is already full, so feel free to disregard this if you don't have the time. That being said, my friend Sae is in a bad spot. You're not stupid, I know you probably realized that what she said about her armor being a dungeon drop wasn't true. Good job taking that in stride, by the way. Anyway. What we need is some way of making it look more like armor. It doesn't have to be functional, though that would be a future goal.>

A notification pinged, notifying me that the bow and target had arrived. I eased myself out of the bed and into the wheelchair to place the target on the far side of the room, next to the walk-in closet. I took a position across from it and took a few minutes to study the bow. It wasn't particularly sturdy and had a light pull. Which was fine. It was meant for training, after all.

I nocked an arrow, noticing how smoothly it locked into place, and, taking in a quick breath, drew the string to my chin and released.

The arrow whizzed through the air, landing with a thump in the third ring of the target.

Interesting.

<Unsparing Fang> had taken an adjustment period to get used to, and even now, there were still times it felt unnatural and unwieldy. Every time I used a crossbow had me wishing for a Glock instead. But with <Bow Adept> my movements were instinctive and intuitive, like I'd been doing it all my life.

The result wasn't perfect, however. I took a few more practice shots and realized the problem. Horizontally, the arrows were well centered. My issue was vertical. I was compensating too much for drop, still adjusting for distance like I was using a crossbow.

Keeping that at the forefront of my mind, I tried again.

One arrow landed in a perfect bullseye.

Encouraged, I tried to replicate it and failed. Still, every shot I fired after landed in a tight grouping within the center ring. It'd take some work, especially when I added more range into the mix—the entire reason I was considering a bow.

I tore myself away from it after an hour of practice. Ellison had a strict internal clock that woke him at eight every morning, regardless of how much sleep he'd had. It was well past that now, and he still hadn't responded. He was either avoiding me or wanted me to come to him.

Fine. If that's how he wanted to play it.

I opened my door to find Iris swaying on her feet outside the guest room door, rubbing sleep out of her eyes. She was still wearing the same clothes from the previous day.

"Where's your brother?" I asked.

"Woke me when he left," Iris yawned. "Said he was gonna go talk to Kinsley about something."

This early?

I clamped down on the beginnings of alarm and fired a message to Kinsley, checking to see if Ellison was there. The anxiety grew more significant when she didn't answer immediately. Maybe Ellison had fed Iris a line of bullshit and Kinsley was still asleep, but I wasn't willing to leave it up to chance. Kinsley was my Achilles. The foundation of everything we were building and working toward. Few people knew that, but with his involvement up to this point, Ellison could easily put it together.

If he was working to undercut me, he would absolutely start with Kinsley.

The gruesome aftermath from the cathedral played on repeat in my mind.

"Gotta go. You need anything?"

Iris shook her head, stifling another yawn. "Nu' uh. Just gonna talk to Sae."

Dammit. If it wasn't for the Ellison issue, I'd ease Iris into this, frame it so Sae understood what we were trying to do. Still. Out of all of us, Iris was the most empathetic. Which was probably why she'd moved my request to the top of her list.

I'd just have to trust her. "Thanks, kiddo."

Iris knocked on Sae's door as I passed her, exiting the penthouse into the hallway.

CHAPTER THIRTEEN

My panic faded somewhat as I reached Kinsley's door. There was music playing within, barely audible with the soundproofing, and the scent of cooking reached my nose. That was strange. As far as I knew, neither Ellison nor Kinsley were any good in the kitchen. Ellison was terrified to even toast his sandwiches after an incident where he almost set the apartment on fire.

I banged on the door. When there was no answer, I banged again.

The electric deadbolt unlatched and a smiling, dark-skinned woman opened the door.

I blinked. "Abuelita?"

Estrada lightly swatted at me. "For the last time, Matthias. I'm not that old."

"What's the historical justification for hitting a guy in a wheelchair again?" I straightened my hair, watching her with amusement. My once-professor looked different. Closer to how I remembered her from our office hours, when she was still teaching.

"Chitón" Estrada shook her head.

Whatever I'd been expecting to find, it certainly wasn't this. "What are you doing here?"

Before she could answer, Kinsley yelled from deep in the apartment. "Is that Matt?"

Estrada twisted in place to answer. "Yes."

"Good, maybe he can help solve this *clusterfuck*."

"Doubt it." Another voice. My brother.

"Swearing, niña." Estrada challenged loudly. In all the time I'd known her, I'd never heard her raise her voice.

"Uh. Sorry." Kinsley sounded genuinely chagrined. Which was even stranger.

Well, from the sound of it, Ellison hadn't done anything drastic. I'd been so prepared for the worst that dealing with anything less felt like a relief.

"What's happening?" I asked in a low voice as Estrada let me in.

"I'm cooking. And your brother and Kinsley are negotiating."

Before I could ask the obvious question, I saw them. Ellison and Kinsley were sitting across from each other. Ellison looked irritated. What really took me back was Kinsley. Her typical grumpy disposition was gone, replaced with a dead-eyed stare and neutral expression.

"Bringing him into this isn't going to help." Ellison sighed.

"I can't know what's going to help if you don't tell me what you want." Kinsley steepled her fingers under her chin.

"You can't give me what I want."

I scanned the room, considering how to approach this. They'd clearly reached an impasse. Jumping directly in just after arriving would make Ellison feel cornered, like we were ganging up on him.

"Miss my message?" I asked Kinsley.

She glanced at me and sighed. "Kind of in the middle of something."

I noticed Estrada's family photo on the table. When I glanced toward the kitchen, she was still milling about, steam rising above the stove. "Estrada's living with you? How did that happen?"

"Oh." Kinsley lost the dead-eyed expression for a moment, suddenly nervous. "Guess you haven't looked at the roster lately. Before shit hit the fan, I may have told her a little bit about my situation and she basically gave me a crash course in economics. Pretty much became a consultant in everything but name, so it was only fair to make it official. Estrada's in the Merchants' Guild now."

Irritating as it was that she hadn't consulted me on that decision, it was probably the right call. Since it seemed more and more likely we were consolidating here, I'd want Estrada in our region anyway. Granted, I would have tried to do it less directly and kept her insulated and uninvolved with the guild, but I appreciated that Kinsley had recognized her value and put her on the payroll.

"See?" Ellison leaned back on his hands, smirking. "The Merchants' Guild is growing by the day. You can handle losing one person. It's not like I'm helping anyway."

Kinsley's dead-eyed expression snapped back into place. She focused on Ellison, unblinking. "Yes. I don't need you. And the Merchants' Guild would survive your absence. That doesn't mean I don't want you in it. You're a founding member. More than that, you think fast on your feet, and the information you gathered at the open forum formed the founda-

tion for the alliances we're building today. Which is why I'm willing to
revisit your contract and adjust it within reason. If you want more to do,
I'm willing to work with you on that as well. Things are entirely different
than they were a week ago. Not being able to contribute now means
nothing when the world could flip itself on its head tomorrow."

I couldn't help but be impressed with how much Kinsley had
improved. There was no trace of the desperation that plagued her during
our negotiation for the dungeon key. On an average person—hell, even a
shrewd person—it would have worked. But I knew from years of experience that you couldn't take a hardline approach with Ellison. He'd just
egg you on and stop taking the conversation seriously.

Right on cue, Ellison scratched his chin. "But if the state of things is *so*
volatile, what if the world flips itself back? I'll just be useless again."

Kinsley cheeks reddened. "You—"

"Look, I'm going to save you a lot of air. Nothing you say will convince
me. There's no magic words that will suddenly make me want to stay.
There's nothing you can offer me. We're done, kid." Ellison leered.

The taunt worked. Kinsley puffed herself up, about to bite down on
the kid comment, which was undoubtedly what Ellison wanted.

"Enough." I looked between them. Neither met my gaze. "Ellison.
Let's take a walk."

"Roll, you mean?" Ellison tried.

I ignored it. "Come on. I want breakfast."

———

Sam's, the restaurant that branched off from the lobby downstairs, was
apparently a spinoff of Nick and Sam's, an upscale steakhouse in downtown. I'd never been, but it had enough of a reputation that I'd been
hearing about it for as long as I could remember. Sam's seemed to have
largely copied the original's aesthetic.

The expansive dining area was bordered with a barrage of modern art
with price tags in the thousands. Above us, the ceiling curved upward,
opening in a large circle where a crystal chandelier hung as the only
source of light.

Most people came here for lunch or dinner. It wasn't really a breakfast
place, though the menu could have convinced anyone to the contrary.

Ellison stared at me, daring me to say something, probably looking for
an excuse to bow out early.

With moderate effort, I held my silence.

"This is riveting, really," Ellison tried.

I said nothing.

The sounds of the kitchen and the couple whispering in the corner booth were the only noises present. Ellison ordered Bananas Foster Belgian Waffles. I wanted eggs—but after my daily dose of recovery potion, I wasn't sure I trusted my stomach to handle an omelet, let alone an omelet with duck confit, whatever the hell that was.

Our waitress—a blonde woman with kind eyes—recommended their breakfast soufflé. Again, I had no idea what to expect, but she seemed to think it would satisfy my egg request.

When our orders came, Ellison's was precisely what it said on the tin. Belgian waffles with fancy quartered bananas. Then the waitress slid my plate in front of me. And all I could think was how it looked like a giant yellow cupcake, sans frosting.

Ellison clapped a hand over his mouth. I thanked the waitress. He waited until she walked away to burst into laughter.

"What?"

"Your... reaction. You looked genuinely stumped."

I tilted the plate up toward him wryly, noting how it wobbled. "This look like eggs to you?"

"No." Ellison wiped his eyes. "What even is that?"

Unable to help myself, I poked it with my fork. "It's, uh, bouncy."

My brother doubled over with laughter. For a moment, the jaded person I'd grown accustomed to faded away. I remembered teaching him how to ride a bike. How determined he'd been to make it happen on his own, despite falling, over and over again. I remembered our nights of talking about pointless shit, like Marvel movies and anime power-rankings.

At some point along the line, we'd lost that. And I couldn't for the life of me remember when.

Silence returned as we dug into our breakfast. It turned out, the waitress had picked perfectly. The soufflé was definitely made of eggs, but it felt fluffier and lighter somehow. The only other ingredients were bits of sun-dried tomato and herbs. With the lack of strain on my stomach, I devoured it, completely unaware of how hungry I was.

I leaned back slowly, fully sated, and studied my brother. He'd torn through his waffles just as quickly.

"Did you ever think we'd be here?"

Ellison set his fork down. "Trapped in a dome indefinitely, surrounded by people with powers—"

"—Not... that. I mean, eating at a place like this."

"Oh. God. For as long as I can remember, Burger King was luxury. Kind of hard to imagine a life beyond white-bread sandwiches and pizza pockets, to be honest," Ellison said, studying the remains of his plate. Then he looked up. "Did you?"

"Not really." I hesitated. "Not for a long time, anyway. With your ages, the timeline didn't really track. As it was, I'd have to land one hell of a job to supplement you and Iris's college funds." I looked around again. "Maybe after. Once we all made it through, we could come to places like this."

Ellison scooted the lone banana around his plate. "You are being... tactically vulnerable. Hoping a healthy dose of nostalgia will change my mind."

"I know I can't change your mind."

He stuck the fork at me. "Then what's the point of this."

"I wanted to eat breakfast with my brother. And... I guess I want to know why."

"Why what?"

"Why you're doing this now." I shook my head. "Sure. We clash. And there have been times when I've been too heavy-handed, or shot down your ideas. But I've always had your best interests at heart. Always encouraged you to explore and discover what drives you, despite our circumstances."

"You have." Ellison nodded slowly. The agreement threw me. I'd expected him to immediately push back.

"What I can't understand is the timing. We built something. All of us. You, me, Iris. Even Mom. And now that it's all coming together, you want out. Why?"

For a moment, I thought Ellison might leave. Push back his chair and walk out the door, never to be seen again. Instead, he relaxed, shifting in his seat. "Do you remember when I got suspended?"

"Vaguely."

"Really?" He raised an eyebrow. "Because it's one of my most vivid memories. Right up there with the trial and the funeral. I got busted for letting a friend mooch off me during a midterm. He got a failing grade, and I got suspended for a week. Do you remember what you said to me?"

I did. But I wanted to hear what he remembered. "That was a long time ago."

Ellison smiled to himself. "I thought you'd be furious. You weren't even angry that I'd let a friend cheat. Just disappointed that I'd taken the risk. After that, you told me I should always put myself first. Always. That's a weird thing for a kid to hear, you know? Totally counter to every-thing we're taught. Sharing, compassion, rainbows, and fucking butterflies."

The first shred of guilt I'd felt in years lanced through me. "Surviving was day-to-day, back then."

Ellison held up a hand. "I'm not contesting that. Anyway. Because it was so uncommon, the advice fascinated me. I cautiously took it to heart, and after a while, realized you were right. Nothing in the real world reflected the lessons Dad taught us. People who share get taken advantage of. Compassion is just a tool others use to feel better about themselves."

"Dad couldn't possibly know what was in store—"

"He lied to us." Ellison's distant gaze slid to me. "And so did you. The longer I watched you, the harder I clung to your philosophy, the more I realized it. You're a hypocrite, Matt. And after I realized that, it was all I could see. The tear in the projector screen. And the more I saw it, the more I started to hate you."

I fell deep into **<Born Nihilist>** and banished emotion, letting the words wash over me. "That doesn't make any sense."

Ellison shook his head. "First, you put your life on the line to save a region that has nothing to do with us. Then you woke up, beat to hell and in a wheelchair. And the first thing you do? Bring some broken girl home. She can't even leave her room, and when she does, it's like she's scared the walls will swallow her. There's no endgame in it. You just did it because she was your friend or something. And those are just the most recent examples. You've never practiced what you preach."

I bowed my head low. "You have *no* idea what you're talking about."

Ellison threw his hands in the air. "Maybe I don't. Could be this is all part of Matt's master plan. But if that's true, it's yet another example of you keeping me in the dark. I'm done."

"What about your sister. Mom. Are you done with them too?"

For the first time, Ellison hesitated. It lasted a fraction of a second, but it was there. "Yeah. I am. Until recently, Mom's been nothing more than a burden. Iris is too naive."

It was obvious what he was doing now. He was angling for a clean break. One so severe it could never be mended.

I held my head up and looked at him. Really looked. He squirmed under my gaze. "I know you're trying to twist the knife. Make this conversation irreversible. It's not. We can go back, Ellison. To before we sat down at this table. Before you asked Kinsley to void your contract. It'll be like nothing ever happened. I'll bury it."

Ellison put a hand to his mouth, then slowly lowered it down to the table. "That's not an option, Matt."

My eyes stung. I didn't want to do this. But I had to know. "You know what bothers me, about your whole philosophy? The philosophy you say I gave you? And maybe I did. I don't know."

"What now?"

I seethed. "If I was out there, during the Transposition? If I was a User? I would have run myself ragged trying to protect all of you. There's nothing that could have stopped me from fighting, no cost too high. Maybe that makes me a hypocrite, but who gives a fuck. It's a hill I'd be happy to die on. But *you?*" I glared at him. "Someone following the path you're on? I get the feeling they wouldn't raise a fucking finger to help anyone. Family included. They'd still go out there, of course. To get theirs. Because that's all that fucking matters, *right?*"

If he had no idea what I was talking about, it would have sounded like hypothetical raving. But the truth was written all over his face. A wave of rage that surged from nowhere, shattering his apathy. There it was. Final confirmation Ellison was a User. For a moment, I thought he might leap over the table and strangle me.

"Ready for the—" I jolted at the sound of our waitress's voice. She looked between the two of us, her eyes wide. "I'll come back."

"It's fine." I took the bill and flipped it open. It looked remarkably similar to Kinsley's original invoices, before we'd ironed out the store. I signed my name and left a tip. There was a squiggle of text on the upper-right-hand side of the receipt. I focused on it. "Tara... Strickland. Why'd she write down her name?"

"Probably for you to add her as a friend."

"But... why?"

Ellison gave me a dry look. Then pointed to where the waitress had dotted the "I" in Strickland with a heart. "She likes you, idiot. You probably saved her cat, or grandma, or something."

"Oh." Now I could never come back here.

"I'm guessing you want me gone," Ellison said. He'd turned sideways in his seat to stare at the nearby wall, his veneer of apathy completely reformed.

I shook my head. "You're my brother, Ellison. That hasn't changed. Go talk to Kinsley. She's cooled down by now. She'll find you a place somewhere in the building."

"Some distance would probably be better. It'd be awkward if I keep running into you all after... this." He made a vague gesture between us.

"I'll let her know."

"Great."

"Good."

I couldn't bring myself to look at him. "For once, I need you to take what I'm saying at face value. This isn't a gambit, or bait, or a guilt trip. Whatever angle you're working, I genuinely hope it goes well for you. But if you get in too deep, you can always call me. I will always be here for you. The door never closes."

"Just... stop." Ellison pushed his chair out and stood. "Hell, you should be celebrating. I'm finally out of your hair."

With that, he shoved his hands in his pockets and walked away.

I waited there for a long time after he left.

CHAPTER FOURTEEN

Ellison made his choice. He's an enemy now. Same as the rest.

I shook my head. That was wrong. Not only was Ellison young, he'd just been through one of the biggest societal upheavals in the last century. If not the biggest. Anyone would be confused. Reevaluating what you once held as fact and using that as foundation for challenging old thinking was a natural part of learning.

Even if that's true, it doesn't excuse what he did. You can say with relative confidence that he was the User at the cathedral. Yet, no noteworthy contributions to the receptacle before you made your last drop, right before the buzzer. He had every intention of letting you all die.

There had to be a reason. Something I was overlooking. Considering how he was already halfway out the door before we'd talked, I'd avoided confronting Ellison on his User status directly, reasoning it would only push him further away. As it was, that was only a partial success. My brother had chosen to remain in the building, unready to strike out on his own yet.

Still, that was probably temporary.

Ellison ignored both nuance and context and latched on to the most selfish, self-serving aspect of what you taught him and ran with it. Then he followed it to its logical conclusion, with no budgeting for wiggle room or gray areas. You've spent plenty of time ruminating on the far-reaching aspects of your philosophy. You know exactly where it leads.

"Shut up," I hissed, laying back on the couch and placing a hand on my forehead. There was no one left to witness my frustration. It'd taken a large chunk of the morning and afternoon to get my family settled. As expected, Iris and Mom had opted to live together. I'd spoken to them separately to ensure that was what they both wanted. They were still taking up two apartments at the end of the hall—Iris was using the adjacent room for a future workshop. According to Kinsley, Ellison chose an apartment on the seventh floor, content with the tradeoff of reduced square footage in favor of distance.

The only place we were likely to run into each other now was the lobby.

Maybe that's for the best. If you need to deal with him, it'll be easier—

"Shut up!" I shouted at no one in particular, then immediately felt stupid. Sae was still in the guest room. Iris said their initial meeting was productive, giving her plenty of ideas for how to improve Sae's situation, but I hadn't seen Sae herself since yesterday.

<Born Nihilist> could go fuck itself. Even if I wasn't overlooking anything and the reality was exactly as it appeared, there was no reality where I "dealt" with Ellison preemptively. Perhaps he wasn't an ally anymore, but he was still my brother. The only way I'd ever consider that line of thought was if he posed a clear and direct threat to the rest of my family. As it was, he was just selfish.

And, frankly, not nearly as rational and pragmatic as he believed himself to be. There were plenty of holes in what he was putting forward. If he was truly that cold and calculating, what he'd done made little sense. Even if the situation was the worst case and he was actively working against us. The smarter move would have been to ingratiate himself with both the Merchants' and Adventurers' guild. He was already positioned for it. Which made the justification to shut himself off from the resources of both over notions of philosophy, hypocrisy, and pride a borderline idiotic call.

And whatever else he was, my brother wasn't stupid. Either it was an emotional decision, or there was another a reason.

Tired of spinning my wheels and coming up empty, I glanced over to a pile of boxes next to the door. I'd been explicitly forbidden from helping with the moving process. Instead, Kinsley sent some of her mercenaries over to help Mom and Iris pack up the apartment, and they had stopped by afterward to drop off most of the things from my room.

With a sigh, I started going through the boxes. One was mostly clothes. I didn't have a lot of variety when it came to wardrobe. Generally jeans, unbranded t-shirts, and hoodies. As I unpacked, my mind began to wander in another direction.

King's Ranger wasn't exactly an ideal fit, even beyond the fact that it implied the King was a real User who would potentially hold sway over me. The immediate issue was one of stats. From the feats I'd reviewed, it prioritized agility, strength, and intelligence, in that order. It would have been worse if Nychta's "ally" had assigned me a class with strength as the primary focus, like a variant of Knight or Barbarian. But current circumstances still called for reevaluating my leveling strategy if I intended to use a bow at long distance. Heavy draw weight was crucial to both range and penetration. At my current strength, I could probably manage to draw and fire an average compound bow. But the bows I'd seen both in Kinsley's store and in the wild were exclusively recurve. Even the training bow I bought took significantly more effort to draw than I expected.

It went without saying that the higher-quality, harder-hitting bows would likely have a strength prerequisite along with agility.

Which rankled. If Ordinator was better rounded, I would have no issue using King's Ranger like I'd been using Page. Cherry-picking feats with no requirements that augmented and iterated on my current fighting style, and ignoring anything that was tertiary or unsuited. An additional pool to draw from when it suited me.

But if the Overseer was to be believed, the Ordinator class wouldn't reach its full potential until far later. Which made it necessary to lean on King's Ranger in the interim.

Why couldn't it be a mage class?

Anything with magic focus would have taken care of my range issue. I could have kept leveling intelligence as my primary stat. Thanks to my experience in the Null, I was going to have to find a way to work around the conflicting goals of two classes that didn't work particularly well together.

I opened another box and found it stacked to the top with test prep and study materials. Most of the notebooks were full of half-awake scribblings and bullet-points, only a few of them blank or partially filled. I kept the mostly blank notebooks and tossed the others, along with my prep-books. It felt strange discarding items I'd once valued so highly, but there was no point in keeping relics of a bygone era. They served no purpose now.

There was a high-pitched series of clinks, like marbles mashing together. I reached below the textbooks, searching for the source, and pulled out a brown drawstring bag. It was full of multi-sided dice, all the same variation of dark-blue, black, and red.

My thoughts immediately went to Daphne. Our afternoons of *Fifth Edition Dungeons and Dragons* that eventually came to a bitter end. If all went well with the suits, I'd be seeing her soon.

Strange to think about.

I withdrew a crimson twenty-sided die with silver lettering. Back when I'd played regularly, it was always the dice I used for overly difficult skill-checks or perilous combat situations. Daph called it the "Oh-Shit dice" and made a point of calling it out every time I fished it out of the bag.

It wasn't superstition, exactly. The reason the dice seemed to roll better than the rest was simple. The sample size of a few rolls per session was too small. If I rolled it enough, it'd roll the same as any other dice.

Still, after a few sessions, I'd subconsciously started to rely on it.

As I fiddled with the dice, rolling it around in my palm, something occurred to me.

<Probability Spiral> increased the chances of a certain variable working in my favor. It was a reliable way of creating windows of opportunity and using the surrounding environment to get an edge, and creating unexpected obstacles for any opponent. Without fully realizing it, I'd been using <Probability Cascade> the same way I learned to use its predecessor. Casting it once in hopes of achieving a specific result. The description was too vague. But the name itself—cascade in lieu of spiral—seemed to imply something more.

I held up the dice and studied it. I'd start with something simple to rule out what the skill was capable of.

Give me a twenty.

Taking a deep breath, I emptied my mind and began to lower the dice toward my kitchen counter with the silver one facing up. This was the control test. If I didn't drop it and set it firmly on the counter, it shouldn't be possible to achieve the goal I wanted. Better to rule out the impossible first, before I started testing in earnest.

"Whatcha doin, Helpline?" Sae asked.

I jumped in my seat, sending the dice flying. Sae had crossed into the kitchen to talk to me. She'd spoken just before entering awareness's range and made absolutely no sound before that. The shower and night's rest had gone a long way toward improving her bedraggled appearance, though the red compound eyes were still off-putting.

Sae reached up and caught the dice out of the air without turning her head. Then placed it back down on the table and slid it across the counter.

I caught it beneath my hand, my brow immediately furrowing at the timing.

No fucking way.

Slowly, I removed my hand and revealed a silver twenty.

That shouldn't have worked. Too many moving parts, and I had no idea Sae was there. The only time I ever tried something remotely similar, it nearly knocked me out, and all the arrow had to do was hit the target. Not land in a highly specific manner.

"Nice." Sae raised an eyebrow. "Can we retroactively say I was rolling to talk you into raising the thermostat?"

I bit back a catty response on the table etiquette of calling out what you were rolling for before you actually rolled and used the penthouse remote to bump the temperature five degrees higher. "Done."

"No banter?" Sae's face fell. "Please tell me you're not abstaining from your usual assholery out of pity."

I shook my head, "Nope. I'm abstaining from assholery because I want something."

"Oh. Well... I did come out here to try to make myself useful, especially considering everything you're doing for me. Iris is far too nice, by the way. Guess I'm game." Sae shrugged, then her eyes narrowed. "As long as it's not too weird."

I thought about it. As an exception to my "remain unidentified as an Ordinator clause," Kinsley would have been ideal. But she was busy, and I relied on her too much as it was. As the only standing member of my original group, Sae already knew my cover story of receiving User status after the Transposition event was bullshit, and that, in truth, I'd been a User long before that. And from the footage the Overseer had shown, Ordinators varied drastically. Even factoring for the possibility that more information came out, it was unlikely she'd be able to connect the dots. There were too many classes and abilities to make that logical jump. Still, I'd need to be careful.

"Matt?" Sae tried again.

I made a decision and stuck the dice bag in my pocket. "Come on. Grab a notepad and pen from the box."

CHAPTER FIFTEEN

Before I explained anything, I wanted to make sure I could back it up. I called Doctor Ansari first and asked if it was alright to use minor abilities. <Ordinator's Guile> significantly reduced the amount of mana required to use anything on the probability tree, so I figured it wouldn't hurt.

She muttered something disparaging, but eventually relented after I promised to do nothing physically taxing, stop if I got short of breath, and agreed with her requirement to "stay in the damn wheelchair." When I asked if there were any early indicators beyond shortness of breath to look for, the response was, "Sudden unspeakable pain, followed by loss of consciousness." After that, she hung up.

Dr. Ansari *really* didn't like me.

We sat around the coffee table. Sae listened as I described "Ranger's Fortune," outlining <Probability Cascade> as clearly as I could without calling it by name. She clearly didn't believe me at first. I understood why. As paradoxical as it seemed, magic required little faith. Most of it was obvious, the cause and effect easily apparent. What I was describing was far more abstract.

"We've all been under a lot of stress, Helpline," Sae said, cutting my explanation off. "And with the system throwing all these fantasy elements and powers into the mix—"

"You think I'm losing it," I said dryly.

"I didn't say that," Sae answered quickly, glancing away. "But weren't vivid dreams one of the side effects of the recovery potions you're taking?"

I'd warned Sae earlier because I didn't want her to panic if she heard me screaming. Still, I could understand why that was working against me now.

"Pick a number between one and twenty."

Sae raised an eyebrow. "Between? So, I can't pick one or twenty?"

I shrugged. "Whatever you want. Just figured you'd want to go for something less common."

"Fine. Thirteen," Sae said.

I held up the twenty-sided dice and prepared to roll, picturing the number in my mind.

"Wait." Sae took the drawstring bag and pulled out a black twenty-sided die. It matched the unnaturally dark chitin that covered most of her body. "Use this instead."

"Why?" I was curious to hear her reasoning.

"I instinctively picked a number without really thinking about it. It's possible you forced that choice somehow. Subtly suggested it."

That was surprisingly paranoid coming from her. "You think I'd do that?" I asked.

"No, dumbass." Sae rolled her eyes. "If the point is to prove something, it helps to eliminate any doubts I might have before we start."

"Fair enough." I took the dice from her hand and paused, glancing over conspiratorially. "What if that's the loaded dice, and I arranged it this way because I knew you'd request a substitution?"

Sae gave me an even stare. "Don't be a dick."

"Fine."

I pictured the result I wanted. Unlike before, I actually rolled the dice, giving my power plenty of time to work. It came to a stop, spinning on a corner before it came up on thirteen.

Sae blinked. "Okay. Kinda creepy, but still possible."

With a smirk, I rolled the dice again. And again. On the third result, Sae stopped me and rolled the dice herself. When she came up with a seven and one, she glared at me as if I'd sabotaged her somehow. "I'm still swapping your dice."

"That's fine."

Sae pulled three twenty-sided dice with different coloring from the bag and handed them to me. "Go again."

She meant for me to roll them one at a time. I had something a little different in mind. So far, I hadn't strained myself at all. I could afford to push a little more. Focusing in, I imagined the result. While red and blue dice would land normally on the table, the gray dice would settle on one and skitter toward her. Whether she caught it or it fell to the carpet, it would still land on the desired number. This was the first time I'd tried for a split result, contingent on what might happen.

The blue and red dice landed together, jettisoning the gray dice toward Sae.

Sae caught it in a chitin fist. "Redo?"

I shook my head. "No need."

Sae opened her hand and drew in a breath. She looked up and muttered, as if calculating something.

"Not sure what the exact chances of that are, but—"

"One in sixty-four million." Sae grinned. "If life ever goes back to normal, Helpline? We are so going to the horse races."

———

Testing took most of the day. Sae seemed genuinely excited about the possibilities of my power and helped think up ways to test its limits. I'd described the many ways I'd used **<Probability Spiral>** couched as hypotheticals, and Sae shook her head.

"You know what your problem is?" Sae asked.

"Which one?"

"Lack of creativity." She fell back on the recliner, snapping her notebook shut. "Obviously, you've got a lot going for you with this. The potential is borderline bullshit. But you're too practical. Tripping, fucking with car engines, interrupting attacks. It's so one-note." She made a winding motion with her hand, "Like, you're so obsessed with getting from point A to point B, you automatically pick the most efficient route."

"Isn't that... ideal?" I cocked my head.

"If you want people to figure your shit out, sure."

I stayed very still.

Sae gave me a frustrated look. "It's not hard to put together. One of the first things Nick told us about you was that you're very private and tend to hold your cards close to the chest. So far, that's accurate. I don't care why you were lying to the others about being an NPC before the Transposition, that's none of my business—though I'll admit, I am curious. But it goes without saying that you wouldn't want other people to know about this power." She studied her hands and her expression further soured. "Since that first scuffle, I've wanted a rematch. I've thought about how to fight you. And knowing you have this ability thoroughly changes any strategy I had. Of course you'd want to hide it."

Feeling like we were drifting into uncomfortable territory, I asked a leading question. "What did you mean, people figuring my shit out?"

Sae held up a finger. "One. You can only screw with someone the same way so many times before they wise up. If I trip once, I'm a clumsy idiot. If I trip twice, consecutively? Something's up." She extended a second finger. "If I tend to fall all over myself when the same User is around, you bet your ass I'm going to be looking hard in their direction. The same goes for vehicle malfunctions, or missing when I know I'd usually hit."

I realized Sae was touching on a serious blind spot. I had a tendency to fall back on what worked under pressure. Thus far, I'd been relatively anonymous, so employing the same strategies over and over hadn't done much harm. The conflict with the Adventurers' Guild and my upcoming infiltration into the Suits had made that thoroughly unviable.

With enough attention to detail, even if they didn't understand how, it wouldn't be hard for someone to figure out what I was doing and how to mitigate the damage.

"I'm not confident how to counter that," I admitted.

"Yeah." Sae chewed her lip. "I've been racking my brain while we've been testing."

"Oh?"

"I think it's a question of extremes. Using your power subtly most of the time, so low-key it's almost impossible to detect. Then, when push comes to shove, and you have to go big, and you have to do something visible, making it look like something else entirely."

I leaned forward, resting my chin on my hands. "Like another ability."

Sae grinned. "From an entirely different class. Think about it. We're talking about a skill that makes something with one-in-six-million odds an everyday occurrence. You could confuse the hell out of anyone trying to get a handle on you."

Or terrify them.

A simple example was telekinesis. Regardless of whether telekinetic magic existed, it would be trivially easy to make people think I had it. I'd been avoiding using gestures ever since I realized they were unnecessary in an attempt to hide my ability. Playing it up instead was an interesting idea, and only the tip of the iceberg. I'd have to dig deep and come up with a portfolio, but there was plenty I could do in theory to imitate elemental magic, or advanced melee combat skills.

Sae's phone beeped. She glanced at it, then at the light fixture above the table. "That's time. Want to try the if-thens?"

Above us, a half-dozen dice were balanced on their edges on the light fixture. The first if-then was my idea. I wanted to see if I could get **<Probability Cascade>** to activate under specific conditions. First, I made the trigger holding a hand beneath the dice for two seconds or longer. When that worked for both of us, I specified Sae. The dice remained fixed for me, only toppling when Sae held out her hand.

Next, Sae suggested we test how long the command lasted. I cast the ability, trying to keep my mana use even. She'd placed a die on the fixture roughly every half-hour for the last four hours.

I held up a glass, walking from left to right. One by one, they clinked into the glass, until I reached the last dice, the first we'd put up.

I shook the glass beneath it in case my depth perception was off. "I guess that's it."

"You *cannot* tell me you're disappointed right now." Sae stared at me, slack-jawed.

"Not... exactly." But I'd be happier if there was some way to confirm that the time limit was tied to the ability's level. Its earlier iteration had nothing like this, so there was no way to know for sure.

"Three and a half hours is *fantastic*. There's so much you can do with that." Sae stood and stretched up to grab the errant dice. The movement lengthened her chitinous body in a manner that looked off, somehow. She clenched her fists in excitement. "Not to mention, you're not even breaking a sweat. Holy shit. I want to see how this would work in combat. We've gotta get back out there."

I held my breath, expecting at any moment for her to realize what she said and take it back. Getting the recovery potions down had been brutal, but I was on schedule to finish the second potion tonight. Meaning, if she was willing, I could take her to the adaptive dungeon with me. Not to fight the lithid, of course—considering what Talia said the creature was capable of, that'd be a terrible idea—but maybe to revisit the earlier floors to test Sae's abilities and ensure I got a level out of it. I had a feeling the dungeon would recalibrate for a party of two.

But that would mean throwing Sae into a combat situation she might not be ready for.

"Is that what you want?" I asked.

The excitement petered out of her expression and her hands slowly lowered to her sides. "I can't slow down, Helpline. Every time I'm alone and the lights are off, I'm back in the trial. With the whispering walls and that fetid water soaking into me. Reliving every mistake over and over. I have to *do* something. I have to move."

That I could relate to, even though the rest of her situation was so far off. I ran through it in my mind, considering the possibility. "You realize that's not sustainable."

Sae glanced down. "I know. But it's what I need right now. Iris said she'd have something that would work temporarily by late tonight."

"I'll be back on my feet tomorrow. If Iris pulls through—keep in mind, she's new to this—we'll find a place to spar and see if you're up to it—" I stopped mid-sentence as a message rolled in.

<Kinsley: You watching this?>
<Matt: No. What's happening?>
<Kinsley: Get your ass over here. The Overseer's announcement is going live.>
<Matt: On my way.>

"What's up?" Sae asked.

I glanced at her, my expression hardening. "We'll talk more later. It's time to see how the assholes behind the scenes are going to spin this."

CHAPTER SIXTEEN

After double-checking to make sure the hallway was clear, I made my way to Kinsley's apartment.

Kinsley led us in, Sae trailing behind. In normal circumstances, I would have introduced her to my old teacher. But Estrada was completely focused on the TV, her normal congenial manner nowhere to be found. Instead, she was sitting forward in the recliner, peering at the image with unmitigated focus.

On its own, this wasn't completely out of the ordinary. She often acted this way when a student asked a particularly difficult question. The kindly grandmother qualities disappeared when she called on her full intellect.

"Niña, did you suspend the market for the next hour?"

Kinsley swiped an invisible screen away. "It's done. Put up a "down for maintenance" message so people didn't freak out."

"Good. That should ward off at least the initial panic buying."

"Can't leave it down for too long," Steinbeck said. He was leaning on the kitchen counter, eyes glued to the TV. "If people think their only source of commerce is unreliable, demand will grow exponentially."

"I am aware," Estrada snapped. Finally, she seemed to notice us. Her eyes flicked to Sae, then immediately back to the TV. "Come in, Matthias and company. The monster is showing its face."

Sae hesitated. She didn't look particularly comfortable, confronted with a new person—I could understand why. Kinsley and Iris were both kids, naturally disarming. She sat down on the far end of the loveseat opposite of Estrada.

On the television, the Overseer was speaking. He looked much the same as before. His body was perilously thin, with limbs that were little more than twigs, though it was impossible to gauge his actual size. Something about his body language seemed different from before. His pose was the same, but he was drooping somewhat.

"—And so ends the first Transposition." His tone was flatter and more irritable than before. "Even with a shortened time limit, most of you performed admirably. Despite some unexpected irregularities."

An image flashed, a barricade of red-and-blue lights surrounding a squad of police and riot shields. Most of them were unrecognizable, though I recognized Yulia, the woman at the Dallas Police Department recruiting table that was talking to Iris at the open forum. She was near the middle of the huddle.

Hundreds of goblins rushed toward them with clubs and rudimentary swords, while taller variants waited at the back, taking potshots with slings and bows.

It was a bad match up for the goblins. In a formation that looked more like a spartan phalanx than a modern police tactic, Users with pikes, spears, and long swords paired with the police in SWAT gear and riot shields, waiting until the goblins clustered up to the point they were almost immobilized to strike.

"Jesus." Sae poked me, still transfixed on the images. "Was it like this everywhere?"

I shook my head. "No. Inner-city got hit the hardest. But I didn't know it was this bad. How'd they even manage to gather anything?"

"From what I've heard, certain humanoid monsters were dropping Lux," Kinsley said, grabbing a seat across from Sae. "No idea if the bastards dropped it naturally or picked it up at some point. Either way, the drop rate was so low the average User probably wouldn't see one."

As goblin bodies piled up at the shield wall, they seemed to realize—a bit too late—that they needed to change tact. A goblin with red face paint raised a cudgel and shouted something inaudible, and most of the throng followed him to the far-left edge of the phalanx.

Yulia turned back and yelled to someone off-screen. A series of rapid reports rang out, tearing through the ranged goblins on the backline. The attack wasn't as horrific as it should have been—instead of dropping the goblins immediately, the impacts were reduced to the same effect as being hit with a frozen paintball, disorienting the goblins and knocking them down at best. Suddenly, the left side of the Phalanx parted, allowing two Users—one with a giant mace, another with a double-sided axe—through, easily laying waste to the bunched-up attackers. When they began to pull back, Yulia leaped over the shield wall, spear glowing a vibrant red as she drove the cluster of goblins against the barricade of police cruisers in a barrage of attacks so quick they blurred together, pinning them against the cruisers while the heavy hitters continued to decimate the goblins.

Interesting. There was clear disciplined strategy at work, the phalanx, utilizing NPCs with firearms with User attacks.

The scene switched, showing members of the Adventurers' Guild working together to bring down one of the giants I'd spotted near the city center. Tyler and a handful of other bruisers hacked away at the giant's legs, while more mobile Users attacked from range and set traps, dodging in and out as the giant tried to swat at them. Sara scaled the giant—her dismembered arm replaced with a glowing yellow prosthesis—using her whip to accelerate the process. When she reached the giant's shoulders, she danced around its shoulders and neck, lashing out at its eyes, doing whatever she could to blind it. Eventually, it fell to its knees and toppled.

"Coordination worthy of celebration," the Overseer crooned. "But not all of you were cooperating quite so smoothly."

The next scene was a stark contrast. Two massive groups of Users that rushed at each other on a five-lane road, forming colliding walls of violence. It could have easily been a LARP, or a reenactment of some kind, before the moment of collision. The impact was almost palpable through the screen, as flesh collided with flesh.

As far as I could tell, they had no way of differentiating friend from foe. There were multiple instances of friendly fire. A bedraggled man with wild eyes was stabbing another man on the ground repeatedly. Someone tackled him. A mage, who held a wand to his face and seared him until he was almost unrecognizable. The mage stood to his feet, swaying slightly, then stood stock-still as he studied a sword jutting out of his chest.

I looked over to Kinsley. "The hell happened there?"

Kinsley chewed her lip. "Given the area, it looks like it could have been 19 and 20? No idea why they're fighting."

A familiar image came into focus. Our siege of the storage center in Region 3. I felt some relief, as most of the attention was centered on the conflict outside the facility. That relief shifted into unease as I witnessed exactly how brutal the diversion had been. The assholes in Region 3 had streamed out at first, trying to overwhelm us with numbers. Astrid launched artillery spells at the encroaching force, aiming at their periphery, trying to do enough damage that she couldn't be ignored but avoiding the sort of center mass hit that could have easily wiped out Users whose defense wasn't up to snuff.

Still, it wasn't perfect. A glowing artillery blast landed a bit too close to the group, severing the leg of a nearby User, who collapsed to the ground. Another fell next to him, his eyes open.

Dead before he hit the ground.

A User screamed in rage and rushed at Astrid. Bob darted out from the median and tripped him with a bow before he could attack her shield, driving the end of the bow into the man's head. A bit too hard, as blood trickled from the man's ear.

The "camera" panned toward the building and began to move toward it. Recognizing the direction it was headed, I held my breath, gripping the handles of my wheelchair tightly. It passed through a blacked-out window and into a hallway, where Miles and I were working in tandem to take down the Users in the entryway.

I breathed out quietly as I saw myself, garroting a User. My proportions were off, but more importantly, it looked like I was standing in deep shadow, even though—considering the overhead light—I should have been completely visible. Miles made exactly the impression you'd expect. He looked like an action hero from a bygone age, managing to smoothly dodge attacks and put his targets down with the minimal force needed.

The Overseer continued on, detailing the achievements and shortcomings of several regions. Eventually, he shifted gears.

"Many of you took initiative. Put your lives on the line to protect the ungifted." The Overseer narrated. "But there are always cowards."

It cut away from the previous scene and showed a crowded receptacle. A handful of Users in starter gear stood around, fear written on their faces, diminishing somewhat as a more proactive group made a deposit and immediately left.

"For those of you who chose to do nothing? Who blindly allowed others to carry the weight, ignorant of their toil? Well. Let us state this simply to ensure you understand. Everything you're about to see, is entirely your fault." The Overseer pointed toward the camera.

What followed was footage interspersed from Region 13 and 17, the regions that had failed to fill their receptacles. I'd only caught flashes of the chaos in Region 13. Now, viewing it in its entirety made me sick to my stomach. Gangs of people kicked in doors, dragging others out and executing them like livestock.

"It's almost too obvious. The way they're using tragedy to radicalize any remaining bystanders," Estrada said, her voice laden with detached interest.

"And exacerbating the tensions between new and experienced Users." I shook my head. "Anyone who wasn't a User before the Transposition is going to get lumped in with the people who stayed passive, unless they have someone respectable to vouch for them."

Estrada looked away from the carnage on screen, locking eyes with me. "This is pure propaganda. A calculated process of creating division among the masses, when division will hurt us most."

Despite trusting her judgement, I hoped she was wrong. Because if

Estrada was correct, the Overseer still had another avenue to drive that division home.

The footage cut off mid-scream, eerily silent without the cacophony of background noise. Slowly, the Overseer leaned forward. With the way he was positioned, the jagged smile on his mask was almost crookedly apologetic.

"What we are about to show you should not have been allowed to happen. It occurred outside the natural order. It is the natural result of a warning unheeded."

I braced myself for the inevitable, as the blood-red landscape of Region 6 filled the screen.

CHAPTER SEVENTEEN

Steinbeck let out a low whistle from the back of the room.

"What *is* that?" Sae whispered.

"Gehenna," Estrada murmured.

"Are those things... people?" Kinsley's face was pale.

There's a lot of ugly in the world. Shootings. Genocide. Apartheid. The list goes on and on. At first, it's nearly impossible to look away. Our minds need logic, some sort of pattern to follow. So, at first, we stare the horror in the face and search for the reason it exists.

Eventually, the reality becomes clear. There is no reason. It simply is. And dwelling on it only harms our state of mind. Eroding our worldview, digging talons of anxiety into our psyche.

The prospect of looking away becomes too tantalizing to ignore. To forget. To allow ourselves to be desensitized.

I didn't want to shut this out. I could see the shambling figures in my peripheral, the endless expanse of crimson.

So, why was it so difficult to look?

"You were warned of the cancer in your midst," the Overseer crooned. "It wasn't subtle. We showed you what would come to pass. This is the cost of your inaction."

The view of Region 6 was a slow, sweeping panorama. It settled on a black dot, surrounded by red. Slowly, the recording zoomed in, the black dot gaining more distinct, human-like qualities. His features were cast in silhouette, almost indistinguishable beyond being human. My heart caught in my throat as I recognized the moment the Overseer was showing. My foolish display of defiance.

If you mess this up?

If you fail to take me off the board early, and I gain even a fraction of the power of those Ordinators in the footage you showed?

I'll find you.

The figure tilted his head up toward the sky. Any moment now, I'd remove my mask.

"One hundred and seventy-four thousand lives. Ended pointlessly, for the sake of nothing more than hubris."

I braced myself as the recording zoomed in closer. With only one potion left, I could be back on my feet in less than twelve hours. I'd need Kinsley's sanctuary. Hell, we both would. This was bad, worse than I'd feared. The number of people I could rely on was about to shrink to low single digits, maybe less, if they bought everything the Overseer was saying.

Onscreen, I reached up slowly toward my mask.

Then the recording cut away.

Why? They had me, dead to rights.

"Neither gifted nor ungifted was spared from his wrath. The Ordinator lingered, afterward. Sullying what was already defiled."

They showed the silhouetted figure striding among the dead, picking up cores from the ground.

"For those of you unaware, there is a small chance that, upon death, a gifted or ungifted may drop a core. This core is of little monetary value. But it is not worthless. To some, it might be more precious than anything left in this world. They contain a portion of the person's very soul."

Of course, they were careful to edit out any footage that showed the twisted remnants of Region 6 moving said cores, or the tainted receptacle.

But that wasn't the only element they were avoiding.

I watched myself reach out toward something. My memories of that moment were scattered, but I'd used both Talia and Audrey to speed up the process. Again, the footage cut away.

I covered my mouth, hiding a predatory smile.

So, that's it. You can't show my summons. More importantly, you can't show me without the mask. That's one of your rules, isn't it? And not one you can play fast and loose with. You can tell people I exist. Stoke their fear. But you can't land the killing blow. That must be infuriating.

An unnatural calm settled over me. I closed the chat message I'd intended to send to Kinsley the moment my face was shown and glanced over at her. She was shivering, fear written across her expression. Her shivering crescendoed to full-blown shaking as the scene changed again, showing a silhouetted figure facing off against the Adventurers' Guild, making no effort to hide the connection.

<Matt: It's okay, Kinsley. This works to our advantage.>

<**Kinsley:** How the fuck can you say that? I heard you on the call. You were terrified of making the wrong choice. And now they're fucking lying about it. Making people think you're a monster.>

Word would spread quickly. Vernon had probably already told the suits my name. If they were as connected as I expected them to be, it wouldn't be hard for them to make the connection. And with the Overseer implying to the entire dome that I held the power to wipe out an entire region, the likelihood of my recruitment had just skyrocketed.

But all of that would be for naught if Kinsley cracked.

<**Matt:** Myrddin's the monster. We're the only two people in the world who know the truth. Anything else is just conjecture and speculation.>

Slowly, Kinsley's shaking slowed until she was utterly still. Her fear was gone, but the rage in her face remained.

<**Kinsley:** This won't go unanswered.>
<**Matt:** Be patient. For now, we play the long game.>

"The Ordinator must be purged. Unfortunately, we must abide by the restrictions of the system. And this all we can speak on this matter. But we urge you. Make haste. The longer you delay, the more his power grows."

"Anyone working out a plan to take this asshole down?" Sae asked. Her expression was grim.

"Be careful not to lose focus on what's important," Estrada said. She looked somewhat disturbed from watching the broadcast, but there was steel in her voice. "We established that we were being shown propaganda. That hasn't changed. Whether the Ordinator did what they are accusing him of is not set in stone. They did not show him attacking the region directly, only salvaging from the aftermath. And even if he is responsible, he was not the one to put a city into chaos, forcing people into conflict with countless innocent lives hanging in the balance. Regardless of the veracity of their claims, it is likely they are using him as a scapegoat."

"He doesn't seem like the kind of threat we can ignore," Sae insisted.

"Our plate's a little full. And I'm still wrapping my head around everything else," I answered honestly. "But after this, there will be plenty of factions out for justice. We'll cooperate with them as much as we can."

"Yeah," Kinsley agreed quietly. "At the very least, we need answers. To make sure what happened to Region 6 doesn't happen again."

The Overseer continued in the background. "To end on something of a lighter note. We cannot disclose the exact ranking, as the victor of this event received something priceless for their efforts. That being said, Regions 3, 5, and 15 were the first to gather enough Illuminating Lux to fortify their areas of operation, and thus were rewarded handsomely for their excellence."

Excellence. What a joke. I knew next to nothing about the other two, but Region 3 had been hoarding Lux and preying on Users that drifted into their territory. Whoever the victor was, I hoped it wasn't them.

The Overseer leaned back on his crystal throne. "With that, the first Transposition event comes to a close. You might be tempted to recuperate, grieve those you lost. Enjoy the spoils of your victory. We strongly advise against this notion. Continue to hone yourselves. Make the most of the gifts you've been given. Because this reprieve is only temporary. And the next event could be right around the corner."

There was a collective silence that pervaded the room as the television turned to static.

Steinbeck broke it. "Son of a bitch needs to eat a sandwich."

Kinsley snorted. "That's your answer to everything."

"Respectfully, ma'am? If you put me in a padded room and starve me 'till I look like that guy, I'd probably come out a sadistic motherfucker too."

"This goes a bit beyond hangry, Steinbeck."

Sae joined in. "And what's with tuxedo? Who wears a tuxedo anymore?"

"Maybe the cosmic horror store was out of suits in his size." Steinbeck shrugged.

"If only that bowtie was a little tighter..." Kinsley trailed off, swiping through an invisible menu. Her smirk disappeared.

"Problem?" I asked.

"Adventurers' Guild." Kinsley's mouth moved silently as she read through the message. "Looks like a mass message to essential members and other guild leaders. Calling for an emergency meeting in two hours. Vague on any details apart from the topic being a joint threat."

It wasn't hard to guess what they planned to talk about. I glanced over at the open window. The sun had set, and the last vestiges of gold and orange were fading fast. I'd planned to get plenty of rest for my venture into the adaptive dungeon tomorrow.

It looked like that wasn't happening.

————

All told, as we filed into the plush bleacher seating at the ground floor of one of the larger rooms of the conference hall, I wasn't particularly worried. There were already dozens of people around us, with more entering by the minute. Being here meant we were still in the circle of trust. Above suspicion, at least for the moment.

As long as we were coolheaded and kept our stories straight, this would be nothing more than another uncomfortable bump in the road to our goals.

Or at least, that's what I thought. Before a familiar face took a seat beside me.

Expensive cologne assailed my nose as the man leaned over me to extend a hand to Kinsley. "From what I've heard, congratulations are in order. This is your region now, right?"

"Oh," Kinsley blinked, and returned the handshake. "We did, uh—"

"Miles," he said, giving her his megawatt smile.

Fuck.

Miles settled into the seat beside my wheelchair and peered at me. "Sorry, the last few days have been chaos. Have we met?"

CHAPTER EIGHTEEN

"Not that I remember?" I gave Kinsley a questioning look, struggling to stay indifferent despite the rising internal panic.

Why the fuck was Miles here? He had no direct connection to the Adventurers' Guild, at least as far as I knew. It was possible he was one of the people they'd talked to, as part of their investigation. But it felt like more than that.

"Matt, this is Miles. He assisted with the raid on Region 3," Kinsley said quickly, eyes darting back and forth. She probably felt ambushed. Couldn't blame her, really, as I felt similarly. Him being here, choosing a seat next to us? None of it was coincidence. The question was whether this was a coordinated attack or a fishing expedition.

We'd had ample time to get our stories straight over the last few days. If it was just a question of sticking to them, that wouldn't be a problem. But this was Miles, someone I knew from experience who had a hell of an eye for detail.

Doing my best Nick impression, I gave Miles a rueful smile and shook his hand. "Ah. From what I've heard, you did us trapped civvies a serious favor. They were kidnapping Users from Region 2, right?"

Miles waved away the compliment, his eyes twinkling. "Nah. All I did was take down some mercenaries. Your guildmate did most of the heavy lifting." Instead of drilling down on that, like I expected, Miles was suddenly distracted, glancing across the room, lighthearted expression dimming. I followed his gaze to where a group of people were finding their seats. I didn't recognize any of them individually, but their corporate call-center aesthetic immediately called to mind the recruiting table at the open forum, luring people in with barbecue.

"LRE." I leaned toward Kinsley. "Surprised the Adventurers' Guild was willing to pull them into this. Whatever this is."

"That's not even the bottom of the barrel. Look three rows below them." Miles was careful not to point, or even look directly at them. I followed suit. The group was dressed in all black and seemed to have adopted something of a Viking aesthetic, complete with blue face paint.

"Aesir." Kinsley scowled.

"What's their deal?" I asked.

"Mostly ex-cons. Supposedly targeting and robbing Users from the jump," Miles said, his voice cold and analytical. For the moment, the veil of congeniality faded away and I could see the hardened operator. "Nothing definitive though. Just rumors. Probably why they weren't blacklisted. Say," he leaned toward me innocently, "you're the boy who lived, right?"

Yeah. He knew exactly who I was. I groaned dramatically. "Please tell me people aren't calling me that."

"Relax. Came up with it all on my lonesome." Miles grinned. I couldn't help but marvel at how good he was at presenting a non-threatening air. There was none of the suppressed danger I'd felt from him during the Transposition. If this were my first impression, I'd probably suspect him of *something*— trying to ingratiate himself to the Merchants' Guild, perhaps, or working some sort of angle, but it'd be far harder to make the connections I'd made during the Transposition with the image he was presenting now.

"Still. It's a hell of a thing you did." Miles spoke casually, as if he was talking about the weather. "I imagine most people are still too relieved that it happened to question how it happened, exactly."

Over-explaining anything at this point would be a dead giveaway that I was either nervous or trying to curry favor. I smiled again. "I appreciate that you helped fortify our region..."

"But you don't know me," Miles finished, almost sheepish at the admonition. "Of course."

The following silence dragged out for what felt like an eternity. I knew what he was doing. Using a break in the conversation to create discomfort and make the other person volunteer information they wouldn't otherwise. Normally, I'd let it backfire. Hold my silence. But "winning" this interaction wouldn't help me. I needed to seem normal.

"Any clue why we're all here?" I asked.

"Yes." Miles stretched his legs out, draping his hands over his knees. "Unfortunately, my lips are sealed. The big man in charge has sworn me to secrecy. But given the timing, you can probably guess the topic."

"The Ordinator," I said glumly.

"Natural that anyone in the Merchants' Guild inner circle would be quick on connecting the dots." He raised an eyebrow. "Though you don't seem thrilled by the idea."

"This feels like an intentional distraction."

"How so?"

I struggled for a moment, deciding how much to reveal or hold back. Talking about Myrddin felt like an obvious tell, but not talking about him when Miles knew he was associated with us would be just as much of a giveaway. Eventually, I shook my head. "The Overseer revealed himself as *the* common enemy to end all common enemies. When that happens, it's natural to overlook differences and consolidate power—not all of us, but most, allying together to ensure we're prepared as possible for the next event."

Miles studied his nails. They were buffed and trimmed to perfection, gleaming in the top-down lighting of the conference room. Had to wonder if he'd done them himself or found a salon crazy enough to open days after the Transposition. "You're ignoring something crucial."

"The event being competitive?"

"Yes."

"I'm not certain that it was."

"Interesting."

"Obviously, I can't speak to what it was really like. And I don't mean to diminish your experience, or the experience of every other User out there busting their asses—"

Miles interrupted, "The hedging isn't necessary. Your life was on the line too. Every civilian was dangling off a cliff."

I propped my chin on a fist. "Think about it. Region 14's receptacle was nearly complete. From what I've heard, the other regions that failed fortification were similarly close. They may have shorted us intentionally, but given the chaos and the likelihood that Region 3 wasn't the only region—or individual Users for that matter—to hoard materials, given the Illuminating Lux's inherent value..."

"Ah." Miles smiled thoughtfully. "Given the variables, if they intentionally shorted the supply, you've postulated the rate of failed fortifications would have been far higher."

"Significantly. Closer to thirty to forty percent." I paused. Something about the way he was filling in the gaps struck me as rote. My uneasiness mounted as I realized Miles had already reached this conclusion. He just wanted to hear me say it. "My guess? They gave us exactly what we needed for each region to fortify. Probably more."

"And how does Myrddin factor in?"

There it was. The trap. Testing how much we knew. Miles hadn't asked about the Ordinator. He asked about Myrddin. There was nothing in the Overseer's wrap-up that connected Myrddin to the Adventurers'

Guild for anyone but the Adventurers' Guild themselves. If I answered as if he'd ask about the Ordinator, he'd have me. If my response was too oblivious given the context of the discussion, he'd have me.

Clever.

I met his eye, unflinching. "You think Myrddin's the Ordinator?"

"It's looking that way." Miles held my gaze, then glanced over at Kinsley. "I already know how she feels about him. If things hadn't come out so publicly, I almost wonder if they would have come out at all. But now, I'm curious about your experiences."

"We didn't talk much."

"With a guild that small?"

Kinsley interjected. "The Merchants' Guild had a shaky start. Several individuals with differing purposes who came together out of necessity. Myrddin wasn't stupid, but he was generally the action guy. Off doing his own thing unless we needed him." I appreciated the break. Holding a conversation with Miles under these circumstances was like fighting a barbed wall. There wasn't much I could do to throw him off-balance, and the chance of slipping up grew higher the longer we spoke.

"Which makes you the, what, tactician?" Miles pointed at me.

"More strategist, really."

"So, even if your interaction was brief, you must have had a read on him. One strategist to another."

I rolled my eyes. Another veiled attempt to gain rapport.

"I'll prove it to you," Miles said, crossing one leg over another. "An average person would be sweating right now, worried about being outcast due to their association with a person who may have caused the deaths of a sizable portion of the population, but you're cold, calm, and collected. Reason being, you've equalized the collateral and insulated yourselves as a byproduct. You had a bad apple, publicly renounced him, then managed to save a region of roughly the same size in a coincidentally dramatic manner that naturally endeared others." He hunched, deep in thought. "Now, I'm not confident why exactly you went for the Hail Mary. Maybe it was to help the Adventurers' Guild. Perhaps it was because you already had an inkling that Myrddin's off-book activities would require something big to sway the court of public opinion in your favor. If the latter is true, you're a bastard, but brilliant nonetheless."

"Any chance you're arriving at the point soon?" I asked.

"The point is, I'm able to piece that together from my brief interaction with you, a handful of accounts from people who interacted with you before the event, and paying attention. So, you must have had some sort of read on Myrddin. Even if the communication between the two of you was limited. And I'm not asking for charity here. Quid pro quo. If you help me out, I'll tell you the working theory."

It wasn't just about painting a connection between us, though he'd done that well. Miles was flexing. Trying to make me feel as if he'd already figured everything out and he was just looking to corroborate what he already knew.

Classic cop tactic.

"If you're asking if he seemed like the kind of person capable of committing an atrocity—"

"I'm not. Just your basic read."

Why was he hammering on this point? Why did my opinion on Myrddin matter to him? He didn't know me from Adam. The only justification I could think of was that he'd gotten wind of how I'd handled the situation with the Adventurers' Guild and the rogue SWAT officer at the open forum. But if they'd been willing to discuss that with him, he was in this deep.

There had to be something I was missing. Miles had felt somewhat responsible for Myrddin's downfall, misattributed the conflict with the probationary Adventurers' Guild, offered to advocate for me at the receptacle, intimidated the members of Roderick's Lodge who'd wanted to kill me right then and there. Why the sudden switch?

"Kinsley was being forthright when she said that Myrddin kept to himself. He was stingy with any details on his class or outside activities. Generally conflict averse." When Miles raised an eyebrow, I continued. "Got the feeling it wasn't for any principled or moral reason, but because he wanted to avoid drawing attention to the Merchants' Guild, and, by proxy, himself."

"You didn't like him." Miles read between the lines.

"I don't like most people. Doesn't mean much."

Tyler passed by us, taking a seat beside Miles. Miles slapped him on the back and leaned in to whisper something, to which Tyler glanced at me and nodded. He looked mostly the same as when I'd seen him last, with one notable exception. A thick eyepatch that covered his right eye. The skin around the patch looked inflamed, veins and blood vessels standing out around the affected area.

Tyler leaned forward and smiled apologetically. "Kinsley told me you intend to raise your level as quickly as possible to catch up once you're up and around."

"Just trying to cover lost ground," I answered slowly.

"We're happy to assist. But recent revelations have changed the landscape. If you're willing, we'd like to split your time," Tyler said.

"Kind of hard to agree to anything with all the cloak and dagger going around," I muttered

"Also, Matt does have a region to manage," Kinsley added.

Tyler nodded, understanding. "You have a full plate. It's understandable you wouldn't agree to anything without knowing why. But I have a feeling, once everything's laid out, you'll want to be involved." Tyler gave Miles a flat look, and the smaller man studied a distant wall innocently. "Also, I apologize for our friend's *unnecessary* drop-in. Your name came up on the short list for a group we're putting together. I put in a good word, but Miles wanted to evaluate you himself."

I stuck a thumb at Miles. "He's assisting?"

Tyler shook his head. "Taking lead. We've gotten to know each other quite well over the last few days. I'm—" he stopped himself, reaching up toward his eyepatch with a grunt. There was a tick in my mind, like emulation telling me he was using a skill, but it wasn't fully firing off. The dry click of an empty revolver, rotating cylinders. "I'll need to focus on administrative matters. Miles is better suited for this sort of thing, regardless."

It reminded me of something I'd almost forgotten in the chaos.

Tyler had nearly died in an ambush that ended in Sara sacrificing her arm to save him. But he'd lost an eye. Obviously their healer had managed to regenerate it, as he'd been back to normal the last time I saw him. However, Talia had suspected the lizards had eaten something imbued with divine energy and infected Tyler with it, to unknown long-term effect.

Something clicked in my mind. That was probably how the gods had justified spoofing his ability, giving him a false negative at a key moment. By compromising it completely, pulling out all the stops to kill me earlier.

But if that was true, the gods had not only failed, but paid dearly for it. Tyler had used the truth-seeing ability sparingly during our region meeting, far more sparingly than when I'd first met him and during the later altercation at the open forum. Add in the fact that he wasn't leading the group investigating Myrddin, considering how much he must have wanted to, it all pointed to a vital realization.

Tyler knew his ability couldn't be trusted.

Which meant if my hunch was correct—barring any monumental fuck-ups—my chances of success had just skyrocketed. I just had to get through this.

The confused murmuring of the conference room had increased as more people arrived, growing into a low roar.

Tyler glanced back at the crowd. "It's about that time." He stood and walked toward the front.

Miles followed behind him and stretched, pausing to turn and shoot me a lazy grin. "We'll chat more later."

I tried one more time. "Not sure what I could even do to help you. I'm just a kid."

"No. You're not." Miles waved behind his back as he walked away.

CHAPTER NINETEEN

I was more confident now that I had Tyler's trust. His wife had been in the region we'd saved, and whatever he and Miles had talked about, I was reasonably sure he didn't suspect me. The man was careful, but he didn't hide his emotions well.

Miles was another story.

I'd watched the way he worked firsthand, knew a fraction of what he was capable of. And that fraction frightened me. Whether he possessed the hubris required to bring a suspect into an investigation was irrelevant. From now on, it was safer to assume that anything he said, any actions he took, were all part of a mind game.

Even if they weren't.

Miles leaned against the wall behind him as Tyler began to speak. His voice was imbued with a unique gravitas that immediately quieted the crowd. "I'd like to apologize for bringing you all here on short notice. It's a time of great hardship for all of us. While there's no definitive number, there are estimates of casualties beyond 200,000. Nearly a sixth of the city's population."

The number made my head spin. I knew it was bad. Toward the end of the Transposition, you couldn't travel a block without seeing a body. Usually more than one.

"There isn't a single person in this room who hasn't experienced a loss of some sort, whether it be great or small." Tyler paused there to study the crowd, let his words sink in.

I angled my wheelchair just enough that my extended peripheral encompassed the crowd. Some looked more crestfallen than others. *Everyone* was tired.

"Most of you saw the broadcasts. The one that occurred before the event, and the follow-up that aired a matter of hours ago."

There was an angry murmur in response. Tyler nodded. "The powers that are driving this seem to view our tragedies as nothing more than setbacks, our victories as the result of their 'gifts.' None of us agreed to be a part of what's happening. No one signed up for this."

A few agreements were uttered.

"Divisions have already begun to form, as have alliances."

"Are you fucking serious?" someone said. It was a man from the Aesir group, Caucasian, with long dreadlocks that extended below his shoulders. His arms were crossed.

Tyler paused, a flash of anger appearing for only a moment before he banished it. Instead, he extended an open palm. "Was there a question in the back?"

"Did you really bring us all here for a pussy-ass kumbaya pitch?"

Surprisingly, the guild leader chuckled. "Speaking of division." A nervous laughter followed, and the Neo-Viking turned red and sat down. "But no. As much as I'd prefer a large-scale alliance—and am willing to consider a smaller alliance with practically any party present here today —that is not the purpose of this meeting." Tyler took a deep breath and looked around, his face stoic. "There's no telling how long this ordeal will last. After less than a month, our losses are catastrophic. If it continues at this rate, less than a year from now, we will be obliterated."

A heavy silence fell over the room.

"Everyone in this room is here because you understand the importance of banding together in times of crisis." Tyler did a slow sweep, surveying the room. "I understand that there are conflicting objectives, differing methods and purposes among our groups. What I'm proposing is not a full-blown alliance. Simply an agreement. That in matters that pose an existential threat—disasters with a likelihood of high casualties —we act as one. Yes?" He pointed toward someone in the back.

A woman in businesswear and glasses in the LRE row lowered her hand. She idly spun a golden pen that had yet to touch the notepad beneath. "We're not opposed to this sort of thing in theory. But if this meeting is about the Ordinator, we're not interested. The Overseer told us practically nothing about them. Not to mention, the footage shielded their appearance. We have better things to do than chasing bogeymen in the dark."

Another murmuring bubbled up from the crowd. Some in agreement, others in dissent.

Tyler reached up, clicking a remote control. The first slide came up on the projector screen. It was one of the stills from Region 6 of me standing in the center of the hellish landscape. He pointed to the figure. "What if I could tell you not only his name, but his objective? Give you access to the tools you'd need to identify him? Would that... hold your interest?"

The woman slowly inclined her head.

"Fair enough. Here's what we know." Tyler picked up speed. "Sometime in the first half of the Transposition, nearly 175,000 men, women, and children died. The surrounding city was transformed into what you see before you. If you're keeping up with the math, that's correct. Most of our casualties stemmed from a single region. There were no eyewitnesses that saw the actual transformation, so we can safely assume it happened quickly. Shortly after, a solo User we'd previously encountered called it in to my associate. This User's name was Myrddin, and as of this time, we believe him to be who the Ordinator was referring to."

"What did he look like?" someone called out.

Tyler grimaced. "We believe Myrddin is in possession of either an item or ability that obfuscates his appearance. The result is subtle but effective. You might see him as tall and stern, while a friend standing next to you might see him as short and Hispanic. Thankfully, this is not limitless. My associate spent a short amount of time fighting alongside him and was able to identify him as the same person, though he looked entirely different."

I watched, in a mix of horror and fascination, as Tyler recounted the events, touching on nearly every interaction we'd had during the Transposition. He was careful to divert blame and suspicion away from the Merchants' Guild when it started pointing that way, stating clearly that every other member of the Merchants' Guild was accounted for. I had a feeling the only reason there wasn't a world of suspicion being thrown my way was my name was on the Adventurers' Guild's roster, accompanied by the NPC class. Tyler was emphatic that there wasn't a feat that could dupe this, with confidence that indicated he must have researched and cross-checked thoroughly.

If that was one of the key reasons I wasn't suspected along with Tyler's personal bias, I needed to find a way to totally absolve myself, and quickly. Because Ellison had managed the same thing with the Merchants' Guild. With over a million people still standing, it was astronomically unlikely we were the only ones. And if that came out before I established an alibi that could somehow clear me after the fact, I was fucked.

The woman from the LRE raised her hand again, and Tyler called on her. "This is all very intriguing. But if Myrddin can change his appearance at any given time, I'm not seeing how it's possible to track him down, let alone catch him."

Tyler glanced back at Miles. "I think that's my cue to let the professional take over."

Miles rubbed his neck in an aw-shucks way as he swapped places with Tyler. He leaned down too close to the standing mic and cleared his throat. "Hi. I'm Miles. I come from a long and decorated history in law-enforcement. No need to get into the details, but I'll be heading up the Ordinator Task Force in cooperation with the Adventurers' Guild."

It struck me that the shyness wasn't an act. Miles wasn't a good speaker. The natural, almost super-human charisma he possessed on an individual level seemed to leave him the moment he started speaking into the mic. Tyler outshone him significantly. It didn't help that the crowd seemed less than thrilled to be speaking to a government official, considering how the government had done approximately fuck-all since the transposition started.

"Tyler did an excellent job bringing you up to speed on the actual events. I'll briefly recount my experience, as it's tied intimately with what I suspect Myrddin is after." Miles struggled with the clicker, and eventually the image shifted to a still from the broadcast: Myrddin stooping to pick up one of the User cores in Region 6. "Not long after the dome became common knowledge, I was reassigned to what the men in charge called the Necromancer Initiative."

Fuck.

All at once, I realized why Miles was so invested in this. Why Tyler felt he could trust him. They had something in common. Myrddin had duped them both.

"There was a certain subset of Users that were killing people en masse. To the extent that local law enforcement picked up on it immediately and notified the proper organization which, in true bureaucratic fashion, pawned it off on us." Miles nodded toward the front-middle row that contained the DPD, Yulia taking up the corner. He flipped through several slides, giving them a much more detailed rundown of the sewer Necromancer he'd described to me.

With one notable exception.

Miles went into detail on a Necromancer's lair. The concept of the lair itself reminded me of Kinsley's sanctuary. According to Miles, the lair served a double purpose as a combined workspace and hideaway for the User. And if the User died, the lair would remain solvent for an hour, then dissipate.

"We'll come back to that." Miles' smirk faded. "Now, I had a feeling there was a Necromancer involved. All signs pointed to it. Before we fully committed to the course, I warned Myrddin about the dangers a Necromancer posed. He'd been nothing but cooperative up to this point, so there was no reason to withhold vital information. Unsurprisingly, this did nothing to dissuade him. I didn't trust him, exactly, but it was in line with his prior motives—protecting the region and minimizing casualties."

Miles paused for a moment as if waiting for questions from the crowd. When none came, he continued. "We got separated during the raid. Our paths converged at the top floor of the building, in the Necromancer's lair. Myrddin beat me there and neutralized the threat. I only got there in time to see the aftermath."

His green eyes flashed in something I couldn't parse in time. It was almost giddy. "This is where it gets *interesting*. I've spent thousands of hours in various interrogation rooms. Taught electives at Quantico on the topic. There's a certain art to it. You can't always get a confession—some perps are too smart for that—but after a while you can easily spot the lies. Everyone has a tell. I say all this so you can understand who exactly we're dealing with. Because nothing about the events Myrddin recounted felt inauthentic. If anything, he seemed genuinely distraught over killing someone, justified as it was. Displayed all the markers of a person who'd gone through a truly traumatic experience."

Miles thumbed the clicker, returning to the image of me standing in the midst of Region 6. "He was so convincing, it wasn't until everything came out at the end of the Transposition that I started having doubts. Those doubts persisted until I returned to the raid site on my own, finding it abandoned."

He thumbed the clicker again, and the familiar image of Vernon's lair returned to the screen. "Seeing is believing. This was taken hours after the Necromancer had supposedly died. I retrieved the alleged Necromancer's corpse and brought it to a colleague of mine, who performed an autopsy. He found that the victim's wounds were inflicted post-mortem and the actual cause of death was due to an overdose consistent with the drugs the Necromancer was using on his victims. Anyone want to connect the dots?"

An uncomfortable murmuring followed as the various guilds conferred among themselves.

Yulia raised a hand. When she stood, there was a clear handprint bruise around her throat and her voice was raspy. "Myrddin was probably already searching for a Necromancer. Part of the reasoning for his actions at Region 6 was to acquire leverage for when he found one. He likely cut a deal with the real Necromancer and killed one of the hostages as a scapegoat."

"Jesus Christ. He already had a region's worth of cores at that point," someone muttered.

"Who would be capable of something like that?"

"This is disturbing and disquieting," the LRE woman said, rubbing the bridge of her nose. "But if you're experienced as you say, and he still managed to elude your suspicions, I'm lost as to how the rest of us are supposed to identify him."

"That's a fair question. To answer it simply, power has limits. I highly doubt Myrddin conceals his appearance at all times. Which is why I called in a favor and had my colleague work up a profile."

There was a rustling of paper, as two stoic-looking users at either side of the conference room began to distribute handouts. An uneasiness grew in my gut as the papers grew closer and closer, each person reading them.

Miles clicked to a bullet point slide. "We're looking for a Caucasian male. Age range between eighteen and thirty. Disadvantaged socioeconomic background, despite being highly educated. It follows that he's mostly self-taught. Charismatic, but not necessarily in a way that makes him stand out. Exceptionally manipulative. Unlikely to form close platonic or romantic attachments. Generally, ruthlessness and an absence of moral compass goes hand in hand with these types, but you already know he's shrewd and exquisitely deceptive. He'll likely be going out of his way to conceal these aspects when he's blending in. But they may bleed through when he's pressed hard enough."

My world began to spin, and I forced myself to take slow, steady breaths.

"It's far more likely that he seats himself adjacent to powerful figures and institutions, rather than in a place of direct leadership, and has a tendency to show up at the right place at the right time, which will likely appear to be nothing more than happenstance."

He knows. I'm fucked.

I reined in the panic strand by strand. Miles didn't know anything definitively. Couldn't know. Half a dozen people in this room alone probably fit that profile. However, our conversation hadn't been a coincidence. He must have already realized I shared some characteristics, though not necessarily how perfectly he'd pigeonholed me.

If I panicked now, it'd be all the confirmation he needed.

"It's unlikely he's an existing guildmate or member. Reiterating what Tyler said, as far as we're aware, the roster system is for the moment ironclad. There are Users who can shield their true class from other Users with identification abilities—" there was a shocked gasp that went over the room. Apparently, that nugget of information wasn't widely known yet. "—but none that we know of that can supersede guild rosters. If you know something we don't, feel free to step forward."

No one did. There was a natural pause, though, and I decided to use it to my advantage. I raised my hand.

Miles raised an eyebrow as he pointed to me, a small smirk playing at the side of his mouth. A silent challenge.

"And if we suspect someone of being Myrddin, what then? This profile casts a wide net. I'm sure you have some sort of plan in mind, considering what could happen if you don't."

Miles cocked his head at me, then looked back toward the crowd. "Matt raises a keen insight. As expected from the newly minted savior of Region 14." I found myself to suddenly be the focal point in of the room, as people glanced at me and whispered to each other. "Make no mistake, we need to handle this issue as soon as possible. If the Ordinator did, in fact, use the chaos of the event as cover for what happened to Region 6, it's likely he'll do something similar when the next event rolls around. Having an amped-up Necromancer in his pocket only exacerbates the threat. However, this is all theoretical. No one has seen Myrddin's face. The last thing we need right now is for this to devolve into a witch hunt." He met my eye again. "If there is someone you suspect to be Myrddin, do not confront them directly. Simply log whatever information you have about the person and forward it to my colleague. Please don't hesitate to add him on your social tab."

The clicker made an audible noise, and the slide displayed a name in large text. Avinash Raju. "He'll be first on the list."

"And what do you intend to do with him?" the woman from the LRE asked. "I don't mean to be callous, but these are desperate times. Someone with the power to level an entire region could be extremely useful, if they were brought to heel."

An opportunist. I made a mental note to get her name from Kinsley later.

"Apprehension is the priority, if we're able to do so safely. That being said, we're not going to take any chances," Miles answered. "The Adventurers' Guild has a method of power suppression, and the ability to confirm that an individual is, indeed, the person we're looking for." He glanced back at Tyler uncertainly. "However, the latter can only be used sparingly. So, we want to be sure before going that route."

My focus dimmed as Tyler and Miles fielded more questions from the crowd and I considered my next move.

CHAPTER TWENTY

The meeting concluded after what felt like an endless round of questions. I intended to make a casual beeline out of the conference center, but I was waylaid by a combination of well-wishers and schmoozers. I handled them as politely as possibly, slowly making my way to the exit at what felt like inches per minute.

<Kinsley: Are you sure we don't need to run?>

She was sticking closer to me now, her jaded facade slipping. Every minute that passed, she looked more like the little girl selling cookies at the end of the world.

<Matt: Miles is a problem. He's obviously looking at me as a potential. But I don't think he's voiced those suspicions to Tyler. He's playing this close until I give him something more to go on. Currently, we're too well positioned and favored for him to take a shot in the dark.>

Finally, we cleared the entryway doors of the Adventurers' Guild's new headquarters and began to head toward the apartment tower.

"What—" Kinsley started, stopping mid-sentence as I cut her off with a message.

<Matt: Don't. You never know who's listening. Until the heat from this dies down, we keep communication on this to an absolute minimum. Text only unless we're in your sanctuary.>
<Kinsley: Fine.>

Kinsley didn't send a follow-up message. Now that we were out in the open, she was walking a few steps away, lost in thought. I wondered if we were thinking along the same lines.

It all came down to an unknowable. The true purpose behind the tragedy of Region 6. There could have been a simple explanation. Maybe a contagion or monster that was meant to be weaker had mutated somehow, its effects far more devastating than the game runners intended. Or they needed to reduce the total population within the dome for some other reason. In either scenario, it made sense they would use me as a scapegoat if the intention was to get me off the board early.

But if that wasn't the case? If the sole purpose was to weaponize the massacre at Region 6 to incite this exact situation?

Then it was my fault.

Not in the traditional sense. I hadn't done anything to directly cause this, other than existing. However, that didn't change the possibility that it had happened because of me.

I had to carry it. And do everything I could to prevent the past from repeating itself. If that meant working myself half to death, or cooperating with people I didn't like, or a straight up Faustian bargain, that was fine.

But I refused to lay down and die.

"That's an interesting look," someone called from the dark. A red ember cherried as Miles took a long pull on his cigarette. He wasn't *on* in the same way as when he'd dropped in on us before the conference. The dark circles around his eyes looked more pronounced.

I leaned toward Kinsley. "Catch up with you in a minute?"

Kinsley nodded, giving Miles a neutral stare. "I'll walk slow."

I wheeled my way over to the trellised bench. A no-smoking sign was etched into the beam that supported the slatted overhang. Beyond the bench was an alley that led to an emergency exit. Miles must have snuck out. It confirmed my earlier thought, that he didn't handle public pressure well.

"The whole lurking-in-shadows, making-cryptic-remarks bit is going to get old fast," I said, unable to hide the resignation in my voice. Miles shoved a blue-green pack of camels in my direction, raising an eyebrow. I shook my head. "I'm seventeen."

"Relax, straight-edge. One year doesn't make that much of a difference." I got the feeling he wasn't talking about the legal smoking age. Miles kept the pack where they were. After a moment's hesitation, I took one. He cupped one hand around the tip and lit it for me.

I took a cautious pull and coughed, trying to hide my disgust.

"It looked like you decided something. Just curious if it had anything to do with what we talked about," Miles finally said.

"You've put me in a difficult position." Absentmindedly, I took another drag. It didn't taste any better, but this time I didn't cough. A light buzz sharpened my mind, building pressure on my temples. "Masks off?"

"Masks off," Miles confirmed.

"You already know I fit the profile. As far as I can tell, you haven't told anyone in immediate leadership, though I'd bet that friend of yours, Avinash—who coincidentally, is about to be extremely well-connected for how insulated he must be—is fully aware. As well as a few others for insurance, if you're overly cautious."

"Considering the power of the individual we're dealing with, it'd be boneheaded not to take precautions."

"Which means I need to keep you alive." I saw Miles lean forward a bit and inwardly smiled. "My guild's reputation is already going to take a hit from what you and Tyler revealed at the meeting. Not a massive one, but a hit nonetheless. It'll be unrecoverable if someone takes you off the board, bringing further accusations to light. I can't contribute much at my current level, but if I'm able to cover ground on that front quickly, the simplest way to ensure that doesn't happen is staying in proximity to you whenever I can."

Miles chuckled. "While I'm touched by your selfless concern for my safety, I've done this before. I don't need your protection."

"But it wouldn't hurt."

"No."

"Which leads to an optics issue." I sighed. "My father told me once about a shortcut the cops used to spot guilt. He said, 'look for the person quickest to help.' Which honestly sounds likes bullshit, and potentially harmful if you run across an honest-to-god altruist. But I looked into it, and apparently it's an actual thing. More than that, it's so common that it's almost like there's a veritable compulsion for guilty parties to insert themselves into investigations into their crimes. They'll drop by the police station, or 'suddenly remember' something important, or just linger around the crime scene itself."

"I didn't know your father was in law enforcement," Miles lied.

"Yes, you did."

He shrugged, shivering at a sudden cool gust of wind that tore through us and shielding his cigarette that had burned down to barely more than the butt. "Yeah. That's a real thing. Though I've always thought it was more of an ego trip than true psychological compulsion."

"You were baiting me with it. Hence, the drop-in before the presentation."

"I was." His green eyes glittered in the dark.

I turned my wheelchair so I was perfectly centered on him. "Cards on the table. I know I'm not Myrddin. So, yes, maybe agreeing to work with you is bad for me short-term, especially if I'm knowingly walking into a trap you've laid out. Still, it seems like the quickest way to clear myself, even if that's going to be uphill for a while. But I won't sign up for this if the reason you're bringing me into it is to clear or confirm your suspicions."

"Because you want to help," Miles said, voice laden with irony.

"I don't give two fucks about helping you." I shook my head. "Or finding the Ordinator, for that matter."

"What then."

I looked off into the darkness. I could see the creeping flesh of Region 6, slowly encroaching in my mind's eye. Joshua Denbrough's hand jutting upward, like a crooked flag pole. "I... can't get the images from the broadcast out of my head. They were haunting. Statistically speaking, someone I knew died there. And I probably won't ever know who."

"My second ex-wife and my daughter used to live in that area." Miles mashed the butt of his cigarette under his feet. "I knew they'd moved. But hearing what happened still nearly sent me into a panic attack."

"That's what I'm saying. It could have been your family or mine. Obliterated in minutes. And if you're right..."

"It'll happen again."

"Unless we stop it."

"So," Miles raised an eyebrow. "you're walking into the lions' den."

Counting the suits, that made two this week.

I hesitated. "Contingent on you not wasting my time, yes."

Miles eyed me, fishing another white cylinder out of the pack. "When I asked you how you felt about Myrddin, you deflected. But you weren't a fan. Before."

The answer took longer to formulate than I expected.

If I was honest, I liked being a User. The feeling of power coupled with the victories and successes was so tangible and real feeling, I couldn't imagine giving it up. I even liked being an Ordinator. The way the class forced me to plan played to my strengths, and I enjoyed being able to control the battlefield.

That wasn't all there was to it, though. My limits were constantly being pushed, to the point I continuously took actions that were natural solutions at the moment, but grew more and more questionable as time went on. My victory over Talia, the betrayal of the spider queen were early examples. More recently, during the standoff with Roderick's Lodge, I'd been fully prepared for them to call my bluff. Mostly to sell the lie—but there was no doubt in my mind I would have followed through, even if it meant the deaths of multiple Users.

Were those actions justified? Probably. In most instances, my life had been on the line, or I'd been acting to protect someone. But that didn't mean I liked it.

"No," I finally said. "There was something about him that scared me."

"Figured."

"Why?"

Miles stood from the bench and rolled his shoulders. "Heard the saying, 'like attracts like?' Personally, I've always found it to be horseshit. More often it's the opposite."

"Like resents like."

"Exactly. Had that issue with my first wife. First, I'm not as convinced it's you as you seem to think. Even if I was, I wouldn't act on it until I had something concrete." Miles rubbed his neck, "Thank my recent crisis of confidence for that. But if you've been truthful, I'm guessing Myrddin didn't like you either. Too many similarities in the way you both think. Which could be invaluable if you can predict his next move. So yes. I intend to use the hell out of you."

Miles was asking me to play a dangerous game.

I frowned. "Never thought we had much in common, but that might be a blind spot on my part."

"We all have them," Miles said darkly.

"So... what now?"

Miles frowned, looking out toward the sky. "This all came together last minute. There's some people I need, if they're available. Or still alive for that matter. I'll also need to cherry-pick a few folks from the Adventurers' Guild to fill the gaps. Probably best to keep this small. Minimize risk." He seemed to release he'd been rambling and gave me a sheepish grin. "I'll contact you in a few days."

Good. There was some time. I breathed an internal sigh of relief. With the final quest floor of the adaptive dungeon tomorrow, and the rendezvous with the suits directly after, my schedule was swamped. And for any interaction with Miles, I'd need to be at the absolute top of my game.

"Looking forward to it."

CHAPTER TWENTY-ONE

It was closing in on two in the morning. Still wired from the meeting, I'd parted ways with Kinsley, finished the last recovery potion, and headed down to the apartment's gym complex. Despite usually being locked around this time, I'd gotten special permission to access it after hours from the landlord—a middle-aged woman with a blonde bob haircut named Dawn, who coincidentally never seemed to sleep. It wasn't the iron I was after, but the adjacent racquetball court.

A handful of Users in the area had converted it to a small training arena. Thick gym pads lined now-scarred white walls.

I'd made the mistake of underestimating the adaptive dungeon the first time. I wasn't about to overestimate my abilities after being mostly wheelchair bound for the last few days.

Carefully, I stood and took a few tentative steps. My muscles ached slightly, but there was no immediate rebound of pain. Feeling slightly emboldened, I jumped up and grabbed onto one of the overhanging platforms that ascended in something of a stairway to a rail-less octagon suspended by a central pillar, and attempted to lift myself up to chest level.

I overshot from the sudden burst of movement, nearly tumbling off the platform back onto the ground, hanging perilously by one arm.

But I didn't fall. Even hanging one-handed, my grip was solid. Surprisingly so.

The sudden dexterity had to be the augmented agility at work. I just hadn't expected it to be this effective. When my stats had been augmented, I'd been completely run down and exhausted. There was a

notable boost then. Now that I was well-rested, the increase felt exponential.

And I hadn't even toggled the **<Operator's Belt>** on yet.

Curious, I tried to lift myself up with one hand. I managed it once, my
chin touching the plexiglass rim of the platform. When I tried to repeat
the feat, my arm began to tire, muscle giving out at the halfway point.

Right. Augmented agility did nothing to boost my strength.

I dropped to the ground in a solid crouch, the wooden floor echoing
with the impact. After considering it and deciding there was no real
reason to wait, I messaged Sae.

<Matt: You up?**>**
<Sae: o-o**>**
<Matt: What?**>**
<Sae: You did not just "you up" me.**>**

I frowned. Was I too short? Or was it that I was messaging her when
we were staying in the same apartment?

<Matt: Figured you'd ignore me if it was too late. Finally out of the chair
and wondering if you'd be down to help me work out the kinks, along
with a few of your own.**>**
<Sae: WTF? Did a horny friend steal your brain interface?**>**

After a quick scan of the conversation, I worded my next message very
carefully.

<Matt: I am currently in the improvised training room adjacent to the
gym. If you're still down to do combat-related activities with me
tomorrow, I figured we could spar and shake the rust off.**>**
<Matt: For the record, "Spar and shake the rust off" is not a double-
entendre.**>**
<Sae: You might be the dumbest smart person I know.**>**
<Matt: In or out. I can help sneak you down here if you like.**>**

There was no response message. Couldn't really blame her. Even
through the viewpoint of **<Born Nihilist>**, I still felt a lingering sense of
horror at the miscommunication.

Still, it made me think. I needed to diverge my maskless life from the
profile. Not all at once—if I altered my behavior drastically, it would be
painstakingly obvious to someone as perceptive as Miles that I was overcorrecting, flagging clear guilt. But if I deviated over time, slowly
painting my altered self in subtle strokes that were different enough to

cast doubt? That could still be an effective strategy, even if he was looking for it.

I rifled through my pockets, eventually withdrawing the wadded receipt from Sam's with the waitress's name scribbled on the corner. Miles had specifically called out that Myrddin would be unlikely to form close platonic or romantic attachments. Bad fucking timing for my best friend to be MIA, but maybe I could do something about the latter.

Even if the thought made me mildly queasy.

The flat white wall of the racquetball court door swung inward. I spun, reaching down toward my hip. Then stopped.

Sae was wearing a dark overcoat. Beneath the sleeves were a pair of gloves that looked slightly oversized but did an excellent job masking her attention-grabbing claws. The chitin around the base of her chin was covered with an orange scarf, her compound eyes concealed by a pair of reflective aviators. The finishing stroke—and, I suspected, the reason for the overcoat—was whatever magic Iris had managed with Sae's legs. Armored augmentation on her legs thickened them, while some clever trickery in the design made her knees appear as if they were bending the correct way. Though considering her uncharacteristic trudge, there was probably a limitation on how quickly she could move and maintain the facade.

It wasn't perfect. Sae still looked suspicious as hell. But no one would mistake her for a monster.

"Iris worked fast."

"Your sister's an angel." Sae took the glasses off, revealing hexagonal-tiled red eyes. "Helped me try it on. It's not functional—she was really beating herself up about that and promised the next version would be, though honestly, I was just happy to not look like a freak—then explained how it worked and passed out on the couch." She paused. "We safe here?"

I nodded. "Should be. Landlady said I was the only one with access."

"Good. First time I haven't been freezing and, of course, I'm too hot." Sae ripped the scarf off and starting dismantling her augments, leaving them in a pile in the corner. I looked away on reflex. While I waited, I plugged the waitress's name into my social, hesitating on the mental trigger to add her.

I blurted out the question before I could think better of it. "How do I ask someone out?"

Sae slowly turned. "Any more hard right turns tonight, and I'm gonna get whiplash, Helpline."

"Forget it."

"You've seriously never done that before? Asked someone out? Flirted?"

I hadn't. For one, it had always struck me as a frivolous waste of time, given my situation. Dating was for people who didn't have to worry about where their next meal was coming from. And I'd never really met anyone I found attractive enough to even consider it.

"Just drop it. Let's do what we came here to do."

"Oh, hell no, now I'm interested." Sae grinned, stalking into my vision. "This Adonis that melted your icy heart."

I crossed my arms. "She's a waitress. And it's nothing serious."

"Huh. Does she know you exist?"

"She made the first move."

"Are you sure?"

I rolled my eyes, despite the fact that I'd utterly missed it at the time. "She wrote down the system equivalent of her number on the receipt."

"Huh. I mean yeah, that's interested. But you have to be careful and consider her motivations."

"Thanks for the vote of confidence."

"Seriously. Maybe it's just hero worship, but from what little I've picked up, you're in a position of power as the region owner and connected to two serious guilds." Sae cocked her head.

I considered it. If the waitress did have an ulterior motive, that was probably ideal in terms of balancing the scales. "Honestly, it's better if she's looking to get something out of it."

Sae gave me a dead stare. "So, you're just looking to..." she smacked a hand against her wrist twice. It clinked, rather than the meaty slap she intended.

That queasy feeling came back into my stomach. "God no."

"So, if it's not sex, and it's not romance, what are you even wanting out of this?" Sae looked completely perplexed. It was a fair question.

"It's an optics issue," I finally admitted, not sure how else to say it. "With this spotlight on me, I need to do whatever I can to look normal. Stop people from asking questions before they start."

"You want to reduce your disquieting, possibly-a-serial-killer vibe," Sae guessed.

I winced. "Okay, hurtful... but yes. That's the general idea."

Sae tilted her head thoughtfully. "I mean, she's already bought in. Short of ghosting her, she'll probably take anything you do as reciprocated interest. How nice is the place she works at?"

"Uncomfortably fancy."

"Fine-dining people tend to be particular about their food. Don't do a restaurant until you know what she likes. Do coffee, or boba, or something."

That was surprisingly insightful. "Should I, uh, wait a certain number of days before reaching out?"

Sae shook her head. "Nah. There are people who play those games, but that's mostly a myth. As long as you didn't start spamming her texts the second you got her contact information, or send significantly more messages than she does, you're fine. Sooner is usually better, to be honest."

I nodded. Slowly, the ridiculousness of the conversation began to sink in and I felt my cheeks redden.

Sae snickered. "To be a fly on the wall in that coffee shop."

"Shut up." Thoroughly ready to forget this conversation ever happened, I stalked to the center of the room, my footsteps reverberating on the scuffed wooden floor. "Your turn in the hot seat. Let's see what you can do."

For the first time, doubt shadowed Sae's expression. "It feels weird."

"Your balance?" I guessed. Her center of gravity had changed significantly.

"I finally looked at my character screen yesterday. Most of the abilities are written in a language I can't understand. But the stats themselves are significantly increased from where they were before."

"Which stats?"

"Strength and agility. Both in the low thirties."

My eyebrow shot up at that. Compared to where she was before, being in the thirties of any stat was an insane boost, even if it didn't align with her class. Sae shook her head. "But that's not the weird part. It feels wrong to take advantage of this. Like..."

"Like you're tacitly approving of what happened to you," I finished.

"Yes. Exactly." Sae peered at me suspiciously. "How can you be so insightful when it comes to psychological shit and simultaneously clueless when it comes to what we just talked about?"

I ignored the jibe. "None of us chose to be in this situation. And sure, there are some monsters that probably prefer this to the world we had before, but they're the minority. Personally, I think there's no shame in using the absolute hell out of any tools you've been given. Regardless of their source. That's just survival. But that's just my feelings on it. What matters is what *you* think."

Sae chewed her lip. "I think... I want that rematch."

I smiled. "Gladly."

CHAPTER TWENTY-TWO

It was better to maintain the appearance of low stakes. A friendly spar of no consequence. Even if, in reality, Sae's performance directly decided whether it was worth risking bringing her into the adaptive dungeon. We'd skated through the trial by the skin of our teeth, and the venture hadn't ended well.

While it was true that, as individuals, we were both far stronger than we were during the trial thanks to her recent stat boost, our combined strength was still probably less than our original group. There was just no easy replacement for the powerhouses we'd lost. Nick and Jinny both.

There was no safety net. No Nick to bulldoze through monsters if either of us were overwhelmed or injured. If I was going to take Sae into the dungeon, she needed to be rock solid.

I took a spot toward the rear of the court. "Sure you don't want to go over your abilities first?"

"I'm sure." Sae's expression was blank as she stared me down. Her demeanor had changed since I'd accepted the rematch, much of the anxiety suddenly absent. The shift in behavior was disquieting, but probably a good sign. "I've worked out what some of them do. You already know what I had before. Not really keen on giving advantages away." She licked her lips in a manner that scared the hell out of me. "How hard do you want to go?"

I hefted a wooden practice saber in my hands. Though light, it was more than heavy enough to cause injuries if I wasn't careful. "It's just a spar."

"Last time we sparred, you almost broke my nose, bashed my head against an armoire, and threw me into a pool." Sae glared at me.

"That was an ambush. I reacted accordingly." I shrugged. "However, point taken. No broken bones." After reevaluating the claws on the end of her long fingers, I added, "Or deep lacerations. Nothing that would do permanent damage or risk causing an injury that would take more than a simple health potion to fix. Beyond that, we want this to be as real as possible."

"You're worried I'll choke." Sae frowned.

"It's just as likely I may be the one to choke," I said. She pursed her lips and I explained. "Seriously, I'm counting on you here."

"Don't patronize me."

I bit back an irritated reply. It was better to be honest, even if showing weakness was something that went against my nature. "Look... I've started experiencing certain issues ever since the event. Everyday noises startle me. And even though I'm probably far safer here than, well, anywhere else, it's almost impossible to drop my guard."

"Post-traumatic stress." Sae connected the dots and her irritation seemed to melt away.

"Exactly. No idea how bad it is. So, this isn't just about evaluation. It's about accountability. I watch your back, you watch mine. If either of us sees anything out of the ordinary, or a glaring issue that wasn't there before, we call each other out on it."

Seemingly mollified, Sae rubbed the back of her neck. "You're making it really hard to be competitive right now."

"Just putting my cards on the table." Some of them, at least.

Sae set her legs in a manner that looked more like a sprinter's stance than anything combat-related. "Ready?"

"Ready," I confirmed, not entirely sure what Sae intended. Did she plan to use her superior strength and speed to plow me over before I could catch my stride? It was a viable strategy, considering the stats, but I couldn't help but be slightly disappointed by the direct approach.

Without looking away, I evaluated and catalogued my surroundings. There were beams in the center of the room, platforms that formed over-sized steps ascending the left and rear walls, where a railed catwalk led to an octagon supported by several beams in the center. I seeded **<Probability Cascade>** on her legs, anchoring the spell to activate when I pressed my index, third, or fourth finger to my palm. Then I anchored a section of heavy looking pads on the rear wall to my thumb, one of the platforms to my pinky. The mana drain was significant compared to the dice, but far less so on the inanimate objects than Sae herself.

Thick crimson fog rose around us, obfuscating my view of her. I felt myself freeze up. This was some variation of the **<Beguiling Gloom>** ability she'd had before. All at once, I was surrounded by red again. I could almost see the silhouettes of figures, shuffling—

<Awareness> screamed, pulling me out of my reverie just in time as Sae emerged like a comet through the mist, glowing blue fist cocked backward.

I threw myself out of the way with no time to think and landed hard on my side, barely managing to salvage the momentum and roll out of it. I sheathed my saber and immediately withdrew my practice bow with **<Page's Quickdraw>**. There was a meaty thump as Sae slammed into the pads on the back left wall.

The fog was dissipating quickly, but if I played this too passive, she'd be able to regroup and try that insanely quick charge again. I nocked an arrow and released it. It *fwipped* into the evaporating mist and hit the floor with the clatter of wood on wood. I pressed a finger into my palm and listened for her to fall, then took another shot, and another.

"Timeout," Sae said.

"Unless you're conceding, we didn't establish timeouts when we went over the rules," I answered, taking another shot in the direction of her voice. There was a loud crack, the feathered tail of the arrowing spiraled out of the mist and landed next to me, sliced in half.

Did she just deflect that arrow with her claws?

"Seriously, wait. I might not be able to control it. It's like I'm constantly peaking. Hard to dial it down."

I considered that, my heart pounding in my chest. The safest option would be to call this off, let Sae drill for a few days until she was fully comfortable with her abilities. But I wasn't sure we had time for that.

"It's fine."

"What?"

"I have the level advantage, as well as more practical experience. And realistically speaking, you won't be holding back in a dungeon. It's better we get a sense of what you can do."

"What if I hurt you?" She sounded small, some anxiety returning to her voice.

"I mean, don't *try* to hurt me, if it's avoidable. But let's play this out."

There was a moment of hesitation. I watched the mist for movement. It stirred back and to the left and I drew another arrow, loosing it in the direction of the disturbance. There was no sound of the arrow bouncing off anything, as if the mist itself absorbed it.

"You dropped this." Sae leapt from the mist holding the arrow I'd just shot out toward me, intent on jabbing the rubber tip into my neck. I let the bow fall and braced. **<Unsparing Fang>** took over, and I used my body as a pivot, deflecting her momentum away from myself.

But she wasn't as light as before, just like all that strength wasn't for nothing. Sae kept her grip on my arm and fell to the ground, pulling me forward and planting a foot on my chest.

Then, with a movement as casual as a kid kicking a soccer ball, Sae launched me. I flew backward, hit the floor, and eventually slid to a stop, trying to shake off the disorientation before it cost me.

She'd knocked me over by one of the platforms that led up to the octagon.

I baited her, waiting until the last possible moment to throw myself forward as she aimed a brutal kick toward my mid-section, her leg hitting the platform behind me instead. It splintered even as she grimaced in pain, and I spun on my back, kicking a leg out from under her and with-drawing my saber in the same motion.

But I'd underestimated how many new tools Sae had to play with. Long black blades formed of chitin emerged from her elbows and she swiveled, driving a blunted edge into my saber, knocking it away. When the follow-up strike came, I was already leaping upward and back, <Operator's Belt> helping me clear the chest-high platform and land on top of it.

There was less than a second to appraise the blades. They were around a foot and a half long and didn't seem to carry much of an edge. More bludgeons than swords. It wasn't a bad setup for her—she could use the elbow extensions to soften and disorient a target, then move in with her claws for the kill.

Problem was, I had no idea how to defend against it. If I was going to win, I needed to figure out a solution. Quickly. I retreated up the plat-forms, Sae chasing behind me. When she reached the seeded platform, I pressed my pinky to my palm and the platform collapsed, dumping her off, following it up with my third finger, making certain she fell.

Without hesitating, I used <Page's Quickdraw> and pulled my cross-bow, firing from the hip as Sae plummeted toward the ground, momentum still carrying her toward me. A feeling of victory rose in my chest. Sae fought well to this point, but there was no way she could avoid a shot at this range.

The arrow struck her and bounced off—but did nothing to stop her heel from obliterating the platform beneath my feet.

She landed hard on her side, and I fell right beside her. My head banged against the wall as I landed and stars exploded behind my eyes. I stabbed the saber toward her blindly, and she knocked it away with an elbow blade, slamming the dull side into my gut before I could so much as blink.

There was a momentary reprieve as we both scrambled to our feet and put distance between us.

I panted. "You're... a lot better..."

"So are you." Sae flexed her wrist suddenly and two thorn-sized black projectiles shot toward me. The double-tap. I delayed my reaction just long enough to insure I didn't dodge into the second. They embedded themselves into the ground a foot away from me. The range wasn't long—probably shorter than my crossbow. But if she intended to use them in conjunction with her poison buff, they didn't need much in the way of range.

She rushed me before I could comment further. I barely fended her off, <Unsparing Fang> working on overdrive to redirect and deflect her attacks as we clashed over and over again. Her strength and speed were oppressive as she threw herself at me, every blocked hit landing like a battering ram.

She'd clearly spent a lot of time thinking about how to use her abilities and managed to put them into execution almost flawlessly. It wasn't just that she was better, though she was. The tentativeness to her movements was gone. As if she'd overcome a mental barrier that'd been holding her back before.

The system had taken something precious from her. Her identity and, to some extent, her humanity. And in return, it had made her a force to be reckoned with.

If I was being honest, I wasn't confident I could take her in a straight fight. Maybe if I was playing dirty, screwing with her head and using both summons, it might be doable. But it was hardly a certain outcome.

That felt like an important reality check. Because Sae was just one User among a sea of hundreds of thousands. And after the Transposition, every single person in that sea—the vast majority of them, at least—would be searching for an edge. An advantage. They'd be leveling and growing as quickly as they could manage, gathering items and artifacts to solidify their power.

And every one of them was a potential threat.

We were both fatiguing now, though I was fading faster than her. I wasn't built for long, drawn-out battles. Even if it was just a spar.

I stabbed out suddenly with my saber, using the final instance of <Probability Cascade>, hoping to catch her by surprise.

Sae recovered from the stumble, swiping my saber away and sending it tumbling to the ground. I reached for my inventory just as she grabbed me by the throat. The sharpened tips of her claws pressed lightly into my neck.

"Tap out," Sae growled.

With a smirk, I glanced down. "Draw?"

She followed my gaze downward and groaned. I'd managed to pull out <Blade of Woe> and press it against her abdomen just as her hand had closed around my throat.

"Ugh. Fine." She released my throat and collapsed to the ground. "Really thought that was a win."

"Almost was."

Sae peered at me suspiciously. In truth, I'd intended to sandbag. Throw the match if it meant building her confidence back up. But that intention hadn't lasted longer than five seconds. She was packing too much power for me to do anything half-assedly. A single lapse in focus would have been my undoing.

I snorted, poking at my bruised ribs. "Let's never do that for real."

Sae raised an eyebrow. "Because we'll both end up in the hospital?"

"Or bleed out in the ambulance."

Silence held as we regained our breath. After we'd taken an adequate amount of time to rest, we started discussing strategy. Sae hadn't used her buffs nearly as much as she could have, the influx of strength and speed distracting her from what were previously her core abilities.

Conversely, Sae gave me shit for my continued lack of creativity.

"We *just* talked about how you need more variety than tripping people." She glared.

"One, it was a spar and there's not that much to work with in here. Two, defending against your onslaught took the entirety of my attention. But yes, you're not wrong." I had been using the power in a more effective way—casting it beforehand and triggering those actions after. Now, I needed to test its limits.

"So..." Sae said. "We're really doing it then. Finding a dungeon tomorrow and getting back to the grind."

That posed an interesting quandary. If it lined up with the trial, the dungeon would probably reset any floor we entered as a party. If my theory held, I'd originally intended to redo the first and second floors as a softball, intending to save most of my mana and strength for the lithid. The lithid itself was still off limits. But now that I thought about everything up to that point, the dungeon seemed to primarily adapt to level first, class and individual second. Which meant Sae would be bringing our average level down while punching far above her weight class.

"Our priority should be getting you to level ten as quickly as possible."

"That's a big jump." Sae opened one eye and looked at me. "Sounds like you figured out what Nick's friend was being all cryptic about."

"The system augments stats at level ten, buffing the two highest you have. From what I can tell so far, it's not necessarily a direct buff—more like getting several feats based around the skill, giving it more utility. Your strength and agility are already a force to be reckoned with, even as they are now. After? You'd be terrifying," I said.

"Good." Sae stared up at the ceiling. "It's better than being weak."

"The plan I have in mind makes sense. It'll help me expand my repertoire with the ability and hopefully boost your level. However, it will require some, uh, flexibility on your part," I admitted.

She shifted, and I felt her eyes on me. "Why do I get the feeling I'm not going to like this?"

CHAPTER TWENTY-THREE

I was perched on the overhead rafter of what appeared to be a large, banquet-style dining hall. Annoyed, I squinted at my scrawled notes. They were a byproduct of trying to cram preparation for the fifth floor in last night after practicing at the training grounds. Not surprising that they were sloppy, considering I could barely see straight by the time I got back to the room.

"So, for a bow, we're thinking either light, water, or divine."

Talia was sitting across from me, dubiously staring down at the hall below us.

"Talia?" I tried again.

"Divine would be best, but from what I understand, such things are rare. And I would not be surprised if the lithid has no weaknesses whatsoever," Talia finally said. Then glanced back toward the floor. "As much as I understand the purpose of this, are we... sure she's alright down there?"

I looked down. Sae was surrounded by goblins and, well, bits of goblins. Arms, legs, torsos were all scattered around the banquet hall. One of them jumped on her back and tried ineffectually to sink its teeth into her chitin shoulder. Sae snarled, grabbing it by the neck and slamming it shoulders down onto the nearby table. The goblin shrieked as Sae bashed her knee into its head, over and over. Two more were trying desperately to tear her off the third. In a howl of rage, Sae sunk her claws into its neck.

"Doing great, Sae!" I called down.

Covered from head to toe in viscera, Sae spun and shouted, "Eat a bag of dicks!" Then flipped me the bird.

"Don't forget to use your magic!"

"Fuck you!"

"See? She's fine." I went back to my notes.

"Matthias," Talia admonished.

"Audrey's down there helping." Even as I spoke, Audrey had seized one of the larger goblins by its hands and legs, holding it steady while Sae —*Jesus*—did extremely violent things to it. "If it starts to go sideways, we'll know immediately."

"I wanted to be the one to help her." Talia glowered.

I sighed. "It's hard to know how she'll respond to you. As far as she knows, you died. Discovering that you survived could throw her off-balance while we're in the dungeon." This was about building Sae's confidence back up. I'd been extremely careful with the first and second floors. When we'd entered the adaptive dungeon as a partied pair, the first floor had reset. But it wasn't the simple puzzle from before. The first floor was absolutely littered with flowerfangs. Sae and I had worked together to clear it. I'd put it a decent effort at first, and when it was obvious she was holding her own and then some, I'd taken a back seat, saving my strength for the lithid fight later on. Much to my surprise and delight, the system had given Sae the lion's share. Which meant she was absolutely raking in experience. "More importantly, there's a visibility issue."

"Visibility?" Talia asked.

"Don't get me wrong. Audrey's fantastic. But you're my strongest, most reliable summon. Hence, I want to utilize your abilities as much as possible." Talia perked up at the praise. I chewed my lip. "Unfortunately, if things keep going according to plan, it's only going to get more difficult to do that."

Understanding lit in Talia's eyes. "That's why you've limited my contact with others. Because the nefarious group you're hunting already saw me."

"And they're not the only ones. Thankfully, we've mostly been careful, and the Overseer kept you out of the recap footage. Hardly anyone knows you exist. Kinsley being the main exception. Still, you could easily be connected to Myrddin if the Adventurers' Guild talks to Jake and the rest of Region 9, though we hit them so fast and hard it's possible your presence went over their heads."

Talia mulled that over. "I see the issue. Our enemies could use me to connect Myrddin to you, while our allies could connect me to Myrddin. It is a complex position you are in."

"Right. If they were coordinating, we'd be fucked." I was momentarily distracted as a dismembered goblin head sailed through the air, tongue lolling out, face masked with surprise. "Thankfully, I can't see the suits working with anyone. Spying, sure. Cooperating is far less likely."

It was a problem I'd been running up against for a while and hadn't worked out a solution. Dyeing Talia's fur was a possibility—if she was amenable, which I doubted—but that wasn't really viable if the suits stayed as quick on the uptake as they'd been so far.

"*Scary!*" Audrey's voice popped into my mind.

I dropped the notebook and drew my bow immediately. The goblins had clustered together. Two larger variants—hobgoblins, unless I missed my guess—were crowding Sae with axes, attacking in tandem, while the smaller goblins took turns stabbing at her back. Another spindly looking goblin was rushing forward with a torch.

I'd tested <Probability Cascade> some earlier. While it was significantly more powerful than spiral, there were some limits that held it back. I couldn't, for example, reach out toward one of the hobgoblins and give him a heart attack, or disable their lungs, or cause acute kidney failure. When I'd tried on previous targets—pale, almost translucent humanoids that lived in a large cave on the second floor—they experienced severe pain that seemed to fade after a short time, but it hadn't killed them. Whatever I inflicted seemed limited to the surface or close to the surface —musculature and otherwise. I'd managed to take one down from a neutral standing position to writhing on the floor with a broken leg. But it had taken a significant portion of mana to do so, and considering the numbers, it wasn't worth it.

Far better to use it on subjects in motion, queuing actions that could reasonably occur within a given timeframe.

And when it came to that? The results cost far less mana and spoke for themselves.

I started casting.

Sae shrunk back, holding both arms out in front of her with a grimace. One of the hobgoblins roared in bloodlust. Then, all of a sudden, his hands went to his throat and his eyes bugged out as he choked on his own tongue.

Letting out a roar of her own, Sae drove her fist into the other hobgoblin's armored head. I managed to preempt the hit and the hobgoblin shrieked, pirouetting in place from the hit, swinging blindly far to Sae's right.

I wasn't close enough to confirm, but if it worked as I suspected it had, the hobgoblin would be seeing double for the rest of its very short life.

That was probably enough, but I wanted to test the ability further. I double cast <Probability Cascade> on an arrow—the first to guide the arrow itself, the second an if-then for when it landed—and nocked it. Then, I exhaled and released the arrow. It shredded through a smaller goblin's temple. Its arms immediately went limp and its mouth hung open as it turned to its fellows and staggered to them for help, clinging desperately to whatever appendage was in reach as they frantically tried to shake it off.

When Sae dispatched the choking hobgoblin and advanced on the second, I returned to my notes.

"Your cruelty grows," Talia observed.

Uncomfortable, I shrugged it off. "I'm being more creative. And they're just goblins."

"They will not always be."

I let that hang, squinting at my chicken-scratched notes. From what Talia had already told me, in terms of physical strength, the lithid wasn't much more powerful than an average human. What made it dangerous were the psychological attacks and foresight. It was capable of skimming thoughts both on the surface and drilling deeper down, confronting the target with their deepest fears via hallucinations and taunts.

The fact that our methods had several commonalities was not lost on me. Given that disquieting connection, I'd done my best to reverse-engineer the methods I would use to take myself down if given the same tools.

The results were grim.

My family was a clear vector of attack. Friends too. Especially if it went after the unresolved cases like Nick and Jinny. Depending on how deep the rabbit hole went, there were numerous instances of despair and desperation in my history that it could call on.

But the real ringer was my father.

I could remember the burning soles of my barefoot feet as I made my way down the sidewalk toward the house his cruiser was parked next to. Seeing people crowded around on their cellphones. Then through the crowd, a door left wide open.

And that was where it stopped. Like a roll of film, sliced in half. Regardless of how much I replayed it.

Textbook repressed memory.

In reality, I'd seen the incident report. I knew what happened. My father made the house call, then died from multiple gunshot wounds. All six shots fired from a revolver over the span of ten seconds. Tragic, but realistically? Not the worst way to go. He was dead before he hit the ground.

His killer was on death row, last time I checked.

I'd made peace with it a long time ago.

However, knowing that and seeing it were two different things. And judging from the memory, I must have seen it. Walked through the door and found him, lying on the floor, bleeding, while some cracked-up wife beater waved a revolver around.

I forced myself to imagine it, along with a plethora of horrific permutations. Uncomfortable as it was, I had to be mentally prepared for the lithid to dig up that memory and throw it in my face.

"Would it help us, if I was able to alter my appearance?" Talia suddenly asked. I looked up to find my summon lost in her thoughts.

"Well... yes," I answered cautiously. "Is that something you can do?"

Talia slid a paw down the wooden grain of the beam, tracing the grainline. "Not at this time. But I feel as if I am on the cusp of something. Stalled at the precipice of dominion."

Now that she mentioned it, my summons did level with me. When I conveyed that thought, Talia shook her head. "I have experienced a minor increase in power each time you've leveled. This feels different. Like a coiled lash in my mind that I may direct, when it finally comes untethered."

It sounded similar to the threshold I'd crossed at level five, when I'd unlocked the conjuration variant of Ordinator.

"There are two possibilities I've been considering based on what happened during the Transposition," I finally said. "Either we find a way to alter your appearance, or I let you go."

Surprise and hurt showed in Talia's expression, and I immediately explained. "Not release you as a summon. Unless that's what you want. Just, I've been thinking about that clash with the Adventurers' Guild. You took the Lux and started racing down the highway. It's hazy, but from what I understand, you made it pretty far. There doesn't seem to be a range limit. Or if there is, it's significant."

"I see. You're considering me as a scout." Talia cocked her head.

"This isn't something I could offer Audrey. Much less the lithid, assuming it drops a core. They're both a short-leash situation. But you're quick, intelligent, and you can take care of yourself. Assuming you operated at night, you could scout, look for dungeons, maybe even clear them yourself if they're low-enough level. Get in too deep and I could just resummon you. You'd have more freedom. Plenty of room to run."

Talia broke eye contact. "There is... considerable trust in your offer. I feel as if I have not earned it, with my actions. With the way I've treated you."

I snorted. "I don't give two fucks about attitude. Just actions. How long did it take you to get those health potions open and down my throat while I was unconscious, bleeding out all over the van again?"

"Silence, whelp." Talia rolled her eyes.

"Point is, it's your decision. I want your help. But I'm aware that we didn't get off on the best foot. You've earned some autonomy. Don't waste that power on something you'd hate doing."

"Maybe I shall use it to develop opposable thumbs." Talia cocked an eyebrow in challenge.

I chuckled. "Not going to lie, that sounds low-key horrifying."

There was a wet splat as a red, dripping organ that looked very much like a liver bounced onto the rafter and splattered red all over my boot. I wrinkled my nose.

"Jesus Christ! Why?"

"Oh, I'm *sorry*, Helpline. Did I get blood on you?" Sae asked, her voice dripping with sarcasm.

I peeked over the rafter and saw Sae staring straight back up at me, drenched from head to foot in viscera. If this was a Carrie cosplay competition, she would have nailed it.

"Uh. You missed one." I pointed to a goblin that was crawling away with only its arms, dragging itself across the floor. Sae stalked toward it, catching up easily. Then summarily drop-kicked it into a wall. It hit with an audible *hurk* and crashed to the ground, utterly still.

"Our pack mate is an excellent huntress." Talia nodded approvingly.

<Adaptive Dungeon, Third Floor has been cleared.>
<XP Reward: M>
<XP Reward reduced for lacking participation.>
<Your party is currently ranked 1st on the Leaderboard!>

"How was it?" Sae asked. Some of her fire had gone out after the last goblin died. Now, she mostly just looked tired.

I slid down the support beam and kicked off three-quarters of the way down, landing squarely on my feet on top of one of the long dining tables. "Do you even have to ask? Look around."

Sae surveyed the bodies. "Yeah, we won. There were so fucking many of them though. Guessing you had to pull plenty of strings for me with that ability."

I blinked. "I lifted a finger exactly one time. When they finally started coordinating and backed you into a corner. And this dungeon is adaptive. It scales. You took out two-Users worth of monsters almost entirely on your own."

At a higher level, no less.

"Oh." Sae perked up at that. "So you're saying I'm better than you."

"Pretty sure I said nothing of the sort."

"It was implied."

"Not on your life."

"So full of yourself." Sae sat down on a bench, swiping through an invisible menu. "Hit level nine. Can actually read this shit now that I've got the translation feat." She glanced up at me, warily. "Might be good to stop soon. I'm dead on my feet."

As much as I wanted her to lock down the augments as soon as possible, it was better that we played it safe. So far, this had been a positive experience. Empowering. And I knew from experience that this was when the dungeon stopped giving a single fuck about fairness. The increase in bullshit from the third floor to the fourth was significant. And if it was particularly harrowing, it could easily leave me too drained to accomplish my primary goal and unsettle Sae's headspace.

"Yeah. Let's call it. We'll stop by the second floor so you can rinse off in the cave's mineral pool, then I'll get Kinsley to door you out when we leave the dungeon."

"If my service has been acceptable, may I ask for a reward?" Talia's voice appeared in my head.

I inwardly groaned, guessing what was coming. *"What is it?"*

"I understand your position. And how this may complicate things. But if what you are saying is correct, this may be the last opportunity. I wish to speak to our pack mate. To wish her well."

It was hard to understand why this was so important to my summon. Nevertheless, it *was* important to her. Whether it was due to pack mentality, imprinting, or whatever else. Which was why it killed me that I had to decline.

"Talia—"

"If I present myself like a spirit guide, as before, it will not jeopardize you."

I cocked my head. That was a possibility I hadn't considered. But I questioned whether it was as simple as Talia implied. Audrey had already been subject to some scrutiny, though Sae was willing to accept my very thin explanation that the summon was Ranger-class related. Considering the circumstances, she was already taking a lot in stride. And I knew from my experience with Kinsley that trust only went so far, even if I'd effectively saved someone's life.

But Talia had never asked me for anything. And Sae could probably use another win, even if it was a small one. And Talia was a decent enough actress. If she did this the way she intended? It was enough of a minor risk that I was willing to chance it.

"Fine."

———

CHAPTER TWENTY-FOUR

I knew there was a chance this wouldn't go how Talia wanted. Of that original group, Jinny was the friendliest toward her, with Nick as a strong second. Sae, by comparison, was a distant third.

It was entirely possible this could backfire completely. People don't always act rational after a tragedy. Looking for someone or something to blame is par for the course, and what better scapegoat than the spirit guide that led us to ruin?

Realistically, there was nothing Talia could have done.

"Elevator's creeping me out." Sae eyed the iron bars warily. "It's got serious cage vibes."

All three floors Sae had cleared were wholly different from my original experience. The elevator was the one aspect that remained relatively unchanged. Figuring it wouldn't do any harm, I briefly recounted my original experience with the dungeon, leaving out the more problematic aspects and altering the story some.

"So, the bear almost killed you, but you took it out on your own. And now you've got the shadow thing left."

"Pretty much."

Before I could say anything further, Sae rounded on me. There was a cloud of anger in her expression. "Why, exactly, are you doing this?"

I studied her. "To finish the quest."

"Does it require you to finish it solo?"

"Well, no."

"And you said getting me to level ten was a priority, right?"

"Yes."

"Then here's an idea, smartass." Sae stuck a finger in my chest. "Give me a day to rest, and we come back and finish this thing together."

There was something beneath the acerbic demeanor. Worry, concern maybe? Still, that wasn't going to happen. "I'm on a timetable."

"What fucking timetable?" Sae held her arms wide. "Feel free to explain it to me, because I don't get it. This dungeon doesn't mess around. By your own admission, it would have happily killed you if you so much as picked the wrong elevator."

"I appreciate the offer, really," I said honestly. "And if things were even slightly different, I'd take you up on it. But there's something valuable to me in the solo-instance. Something I might not be able to obtain if we went that route."

Sae stepped away and crossed her arms, giving me a cold stare. "More secrets. Whatever you're after must be worth it. But I don't understand why you're so quick to put your life on the line when you've already got it made."

"I *don't* have it made. Everything I have is balanced on the edge of a knife—"

"Bullshit. You have an entire region of the city, uncontested, with multiple strong guilds backing your authority. A power that could easily tip the scale of any conflict, as we've so thoroughly seen, and a family that needs you. Yet, you're still acting like you have nothing to lose."

"Uncontested for the moment. And you seem to be under the impression that passivity is an option," I said coldly. "Let me ask you a question. Do you really think the suits are going to just stop at some point? Just sit back and say to themselves, 'You know what? That's enough power. We can dial back on the atrocities, kidnapping, blackmail, and extortion for a bit.' Is that how you think this is going to go?"

"No. But it's not all on you."

"Like hell it's not," I bit back. "I'm not going to sit back in my ivory fucking tower and pretend like things have changed. This is the same dog fight it always has been. The second they took Nick, threatened my family, and killed Jinny, there were two choices. Lay back and let them do what they please, or wipe them out."

Sae backed off. "And I thought I was angry."

"It's not about revenge or posturing." I turned away. "These are people who understand how to take advantage of the flaws in the system. Any system. Elites who soar to untold heights by treading on the heads of those below them. They have no code. And they were killing people by day three. Day-fucking-three, Sae. When everyone else was trying to figure out what the fuck a feat was and deciding whether they needed to go to a psych ward."

"I get that they're bad news."

"And you want them to hurt."

"... Yes," Sae said, her agreement troubled. The elevator doors opened on the third floor, and she stepped out. She was clearly exhausted from the previous ordeal, but somehow she seemed lighter than before. Like some burden weighing her down had been lifted.

While I was glad for her, I couldn't help the flash of envy at that.

She stepped aside to let me pass, and I couldn't tell from her non-directional eyes if she was studying me or staring at the wall. That question answered itself when she grabbed my arm. "Did you mean what you said to me, outside the trial?"

"That the suits will pay?"

Sae shook her head. Her voice was uncharacteristically quiet. "No. About us. Being friends."

"Oh." I stopped, mid-thought, struggling to switch gears. I'd said more than I should have outside the trial, when I was convinced she was dead. Which put me in something of an awkward position. I wasn't much for oversharing. Or sharing, for that matter.

Right now, Sae was adrift. Looking for anyone and anything to cling on to.

"Look, if everything you said was bullshit—if you're just manipulating me? That's fine. Regardless of motivation, you probably saved my life. God, you've done more to help me than my parents ever would."

"It wasn't bullshit," I said quietly.

An expression of relief crossed her face. "I don't think we should back down or let them be. Neither of us is capable of that, I think. But there has to be something after the suits. This can't just be about destruction. Eventually, we have to stop."

I realized what she was getting at. "This is about something that happened in the dungeon. You're different than you were. Like you reached some conclusion or shift in perspective. Did it scare you?"

Sae bit her lip. "Not exactly. It's... difficult to say. And I'm worried what you'll think of me, if I tell you."

"Just say it."

Her eyebrows knitted together. "I mean, I was mostly playing a support role before. Even when there were only three of us. I buffed Nick, watched Jinny's back. Only fought directly if we were completely outnumbered. So, when you told me I'd be taking point to get the majority of the experience, and that you'd only interfere if I was overwhelmed, that was intimidating at first. Then, after the second floor, when those pre-historic humans—or whatever they were—flooded me, I didn't have time to doubt myself. I fell back on my instincts. And after a while..."

Even as Sae trailed off, I understood.

All you really had to do was look at our prior companions in comparison. Nick fought like a classic hero. He dispatched his enemies efficiently and without hesitation. But if there was an opportunity to show mercy, or talk his way out of a situation, he fell back on that as default—the standoff with the spider queen a prime example.

Yet Sae had been different in the adaptive dungeon. There was an undercurrent of brutality to the way she fought.

If Nick was a Knight in shining armor, Sae was a Viking donned in chitin face paint, screaming a war cry at the top of her lungs.

It was alarming to find something like that in yourself. Was it new, brought on by your environment and circumstances? Or had it been lurking beneath the surface, hidden in some line of DNA or strand of neurons this entire time, waiting for the opportunity to show itself?

"It sounds as if the pup has grown into a wolf," a voice called from behind us.

Sae whirled, claws extended, ready to rip the newcomer to shreds. The tension in her body lessened when she saw Talia, but only slightly. "What the fuck is this? You died."

Talia approached with a baleful stare. Then bowed her head. "As a spirit, death is never permanent. I am truly sorry I could not protect you properly. All of you."

A war played out over Sae's features. Anger struggled against happiness, threatening to snuff it out.

Unable to help myself, I came to Talia's aid. "Why the fuck didn't you warn us?" I pressed, letting a simmering rage into my voice. "A short message or warning could have made the difference. You let us walk into a guillotine."

Talia kept her head bowed.

Sae put out a hand and shot me a stern look. "Matt, stop it."

"You're just going to take whatever she says at face value?" I asked, feigning exasperation.

"I get that you're angry. So am I." Sae hesitated as she worked through the issues in her head. "But text chat was offline. And once the trial had started, that membrane went up, covering the entrance. Even if she shouted, we couldn't have heard her. Not to mention, there were twelve of them. Talia wasn't much stronger than us, and you saw how quickly..." Sae trailed off, hands curling into fists.

"Whatever." I walked away, placing my back to a nearby wall.

Talia approached Sae, nosing a clenched fist with her muzzle until Sae relaxed and gently stroked Talia's head.

"At first I had my doubts. But you were all so noble and steadfast. You covered for each other and did not leave your wounded. When you invited me to join you, I was flattered." Real grief filtered into Talia's voice. "Just as I was horrified when that possibility was torn away. With the last vestiges of my consciousness, I watched you disappear back into the trial and thought you gone forever."

Sae was quiet.

"When I regained consciousness, I became aware that you had returned. Not unscathed, but unbroken. A huntress through and through. Pardon the indulgence, but I had to speak to you. Just once. To see you in the flesh and... apologize, for my shortcomings." Talia held her head high. "I will take my leave now."

The story about dying and regaining consciousness, becoming aware of Sae, was all manufactured. But it felt like the emotion and—more surprisingly, regret—that Talia was conveying was genuine. I'd thought she was just angry. She was a summon, after all, there was only so much she could do. However, this exchange was making me realize that Talia didn't see herself that way. She considered herself elevated and strong. And took the responsibility that came with that estimation seriously.

Even now, she'd started to walk away. Sae watched her go, wearing a complex expression I couldn't begin to parse. Finally, she called after the wolf. "So, that's it?"

Talia stopped. "What do you mean?"

"Jinny is dead," Sae said coldly. "We all fucked up. Matt didn't see it coming. Nick immediately lost it as soon as her body hit the ground. And I ran away like a coward. You don't get to martyr yourself and take all the blame."

"You do not have to—"

"I'm not making excuses for you. For any of us. But we all played a part. And if you saw yourself as part of our 'pack,' then why are you running away now?"

Talia studied Sae. Her eyes flicked to me. "I'm unsure how to respond. This is not how I expected it to go."

It made sense now. Why Talia had been so insistent on talking to Sae.

"You wanted her to blame you. To help her move forward by offsetting her guilt on someone she might never see again."

When Talia didn't answer, I offered the only advice I could think of.

"We don't know what's going to happen with the lithid. So, obviously best to not make any promises. Just be as honest as you can."

Talia processed that, waiting a long moment before she spoke again. "Though my death was not permanent, it was not without cost. There are challenges before me. It is uncertain if I will be able to return to you as I was."

Sae strode over and crouched down on in front of her. Talia's tail wagged as she waited attentively. Sae reached out, placing a hand on the wolf's chest, and shoved her gently. "Then hurry and do what you need to do. So you can come back." Sae stuck a thumb at me. "Knowing this guy, things will go to shit soon enough. He might not be willing to admit it, but we need all the help we can get. And when you're back, we'll get you that armor we promised you."

With that, Sae turned to go, leaving Talia behind. I nodded to Talia and followed.

"Even if I can't return, know this. I will be watching over you," Talia called after us.

———

After Kinsley used her power to door Sae back to the penthouse, I made my final preparations for the fifth floor of the adaptive dungeon.

It was a long time coming.

CHAPTER TWENTY-FIVE

Iris sat across from me at a diner down the street from the adaptive dungeon. She'd sent me a message that she was hungry and Mom was MIA. Despite it being well past noon, she kicked both legs out in front of her in excitement as the waiter brought a stack of pancakes slathered in syrup.

It was almost nostalgic. Like the old days.

Only instead of SAT prep, I was perusing Kinsley's store page, racking my brain on how to prepare to fight a creature that might not have any discernible weaknesses. I chased an over easy egg across my plate, brow permanently furrowed, as Iris prepared to dig in. "There's only a fork in here. Give me a knife?"

I passed my roll of silverware over, dimly aware that my own over easy eggs were getting cold.

"Where's Ellison?" Iris asked.

"Hm?" I responded, trying not to lose focus. The waiter passed by again, topping off our water and leaving without saying a word.

"Just, his stuff is gone from your place. And he's not with me and Mom. So, where is he?"

She's trying to distract me, **<Jaded Eye>** *whispered.*

I huffed in irritation, not at Iris, but the title. It was always so grating when there wasn't a direct threat. Which is why I generally leaned back on **<Born Nihilist>**.

That was odd. I'd intended to make the switch later, minimizing the time I'd have the title chittering in my ear. Had I just altered it subconsciously?

Unable to stop myself, I pulled up the title screen and selected **<Born Nihilist>**.

<System Notification: Primary Title cannot be changed until the cooldown is expended. **Time remaining** — 5:34:21>

Apparently, I'd changed it a little over twenty minutes ago. That was concerning. The low-threat dungeon crawling with Sae had gone well—I hadn't hesitated or frozen during the brief time we were fighting together —but that didn't mean I was at a hundred percent.

"Matt?" Iris asked. Her dirty-blonde hair was in a side ponytail and her nails were painted. She looked a hell of a lot better than she had a few days ago.

"Ellison is working some stuff out. And we should be patient with him while he does." I glanced up from the store page suspiciously. "You already messaged him, haven't you."

"Just a few times. He's ignoring me." Iris pouted.

"Yeah. You know how El is. The harder you try with him, the more he pulls away."

"So, nothing happened?" Iris asked. There was an implication in her tone that hinted she knew there was more to it.

I rubbed my eyes blearily. Nothing had shown up on the store page when I searched for divine bows or crossbows. Now, I was going through the flavor text of uncommon or rare items in my price range, looking for anything that hinted at divine association. So far, the search was unproductive. "He's a kid trying to figure out how to be an adult in a world that somehow makes less sense than it already did. He just needs time."

"I guess." Iris carved into her pancakes, making content noises as she shoveled them into her mouth. "It just worries me."

"Why?" I asked idly, mentally turning the page.

"Because he's not as together as he acts. He used to cry at night."

The words immediately broke my focus. An image of Ellison came to mind. He was so strong, so unflappable most of the time. The day he'd been suspended, he came home and explained it in the same sort of tone a person would use to comment on the weather. For a long time, I'd just thought he was stoic.

But as it turned out, the facade wasn't perfect.

I'd snuck back into the apartment late one night a few years ago to the sound of sobbing. A sound so unfamiliar it was almost alien. When I snuck a glance around the dividing wall, I saw Ellison there, clutching his chest like his heart might explode, weeping tears that glimmered on his cheeks in the darkness, folded halfway over like the weight of the world was on his shoulders.

When I opened the door and closed it—louder the second time—the crying immediately stopped. I walked in, poured two cups of water, and sat with him in the dark to spare his dignity. Ellison gave me the typical catty line about being out so late, but it was clear his heart wasn't in it.

I tried to get him to open up. That night and the days that followed. As sure as I was that there had to be something more to it, there didn't seem to be anything specific bothering him. Eventually, I came to the uneasy conclusion that the nights crying alone on the couch were just his way of venting the emotion. Which wasn't great, but arguably better than keeping it bottled until it exploded.

I gave Iris my full attention. "Yeah, he did have episodes. Didn't know you knew."

"But you don't think it's weird?" Iris asked. "That the crying got worse the week before the meteor?"

This isn't an innocent conversation. She has an angle.

My jaw worked as I considered that. Things had been worse than usual, before the system appeared. Our usual avenues for cash had dried up, which was why I was so dead set on getting the tip-sheet from Nick. I'd dismissed it as stress at the time, refocused my resolve on working my ass off so he didn't have to worry as much.

Only, now, looking back at the timing, it went a long way to painting Ellison's distress in a new light. Which begged another question—if he'd known what was about to happen, why didn't he tell us?

Iris was watching me, waiting for an answer. When I couldn't form one, she rested her head on her hand, sipping her water. The waiter immediately came by and refilled her glass, ignoring mine, which was still filled to the brim.

"I think I know what happened," Iris's expression turned pensive. "You pushed him away. Just like you always push everyone away."

"What? No. That's wrong, Iris. I don't push family away," I bit back, raising my voice slightly before I realized it.

"Sure you do." Iris twiddled her straw between her fingertips. "That's why you pawned me off to that architect, rather than helping me yourself."

"With a small fucking legion of mercenaries watching and reporting your every move. You're literally safer now than you've ever been."

"I wonder if that's true," Iris responded.

As I stared at her, my heart raced. This wasn't happening. I wasn't within a hair's breadth of losing both of my siblings, days away from each other. It was up there with some of the worst things I could possibly imagine.

Focus on that thought.

I tried to listen to <Jaded Eye>, but it was impossible to focus on anything as Iris flayed me to my very core.

"It's obvious," Iris said. Her eyes took on a glazed look. "Someone as obsessive as you doesn't just suddenly decide to take a hands-off approach. You're probably hoping Kinsley's people get sloppy." She stared me dead in the face. "I've always been the weak link. Your stupid, overly empathetic little sister. Bleeding heart, disabled, and broken. I barely even had the courage to speak before I became a User. We both know you've always wanted to be free of me."

My mouth was dry. "I've never thought that. *Ever*. If you want me to spend more time with you, I'll make time. Things will be tight for the next few weeks, but after—"

"Always an excuse." Iris rolled her eyes. "I'm going to the bathroom."

As my sister stood to leave, I fought back a storm of emotions. All the while, my title whispered in my ear, slowly eroding the pain. This felt exactly like when Ellison had left. It was almost play for play, point by point. As if it were intentional.

An overwhelming sense of déjà vu swept over me.

Slowly, curtains of stone lowered over my tormented mind, shutting out all emotion as I withdrew something from my inventory and placed it on my knee beneath the table.

<System Notification: You have integrated the following title — **Born Nihilist.** While this title will no longer be available for selection, you will retain a portion of the effects now active regardless of the current title.**>**

Her back was to me as she walked toward the women's room beyond the tables.

"Iris," I called after her.

My deaf sister turned to look at me, showing an expression of utter disappointment.

I pulled the trigger.

The crossbow made an audible twang and the bolt flew out from beneath the table, striking Iris directly in the chest. She wobbled on her feet, staring down at herself as blood blossomed. Iris fell to her knees, helplessly clawing at the bolt.

Someone screamed. Time slowed down as Iris fell backward, and I recounted everything that had led me to this like a mantra.

It wasn't necessarily unlikely that I'd invite my sister to lunch while I prepared for something. That was standard. But today was different. I'd intended to go to the adaptive dungeon. And I'd specifically been preparing myself for the lithid to use my family against me. It was my intention to avoid them until the matter was resolved, leaving early in the morning with Sae. So, it made far more sense that I'd send her to Kinsley's than invite her here. And as much as I was sure Iris was capable of being disappointed with me—maybe rightfully so—she'd never approach it this way. She'd hint at it, or perhaps avoid me entirely. Direct conflict was Ellison's style, not hers.

It was possible that a bad title could alter her behavior. But not this drastically. If this was still the earlier days and Daphne was my only example, perhaps I could have believed that. Yet, the more Users I encountered, the less viable that seemed.

Astrid and Astria's title reflected a sibling dependency turned literal. Like them, each of my titles reflected a part of me that had existed before the system, good or bad.

It was clear by now that titles weren't absolute. They could augment who you were, exacerbate it, even push you toward extremes you'd usually never consider—but they couldn't change you entirely.

The final piece was simple. When I'd called out to Iris as she'd walked away, she'd heard me. Her back was to me, and she still turned when I called. Undoubtedly, it was probably possible for Iris to get her hearing back through some sort of system loophole. Healing, or a boon or reward of some kind. But she would have been so excited, everyone with her contact info would have gotten a celebratory message.

All of this led to one, immutable conclusion: I was already on the fifth floor of the adaptive dungeon.

And the lithid had come to play.

Enraged, I loaded another bolt and stalked across the room to my sister's body. I pointed the crossbow at her forehead. "Are you done?"

There was no response. Through the peripheral of my vision, I saw people exiting the diner in panic, some of them taking off in cars or on foot, while others crowded around the building in a half-circle.

What if I'm wrong?

My resolve began to crumble around the fringes. In the distance, I heard the sound of sirens. I repeated myself once more, my entire body so tight it felt as if I could snap at any moment. "Are you... fucking... done?"

Slowly, as if it was a post-mortem spasm, Iris moved. The movements became less spastic, more guided and intentional. She reached up with one hand and ripped the bolt free, the open wound bleeding freely. Her head rotated slowly until dead eyes stared directly above my head. Her lips parted in a wicked smile. "Oh no. We're just getting started."

The world around us fell away, revealing the dungeon beyond.

CHAPTER TWENTY-SIX

The body disintegrated into dust before I could react.

There was an unearthly shriek as a metal paneled floor pockmarked with dirt and rust replaced the black-and-white diner tile. The booths and tables aged hundreds of years over the span of seconds, the cushioned seats growing a yellow patina of discoloration before eventually turning brown.

A familiar off-white wallpaper speckled with silhouetted flowers spanned the entire wall around a two-storied hall. There was at least double the vertical space than in the diner, maybe triple.

This wasn't good. I kept my crossbow and saber at the ready and forced myself to focus.

If the diner and preparation memories were false, that meant I was missing time. Everything from escorting Sae out of the adaptive dungeon onward was suspect. Meaning whatever preparations and plans I'd made before entering were practically useless if I couldn't buy time to piece them together retroactively.

"Your own sister. And you didn't even hesitate." The voice was harsh and throaty, yet simultaneously quiet. Like it was being inhaled rather than exhaled.

"It was a sloppy imitation. You made more than a few simple mistakes that anyone who spent time with Iris would have easily picked up on." While I ran my mouth, I checked everywhere for **<Broken Legacy>**, finding it hanging on my hip. I could sense that Talia was within the blade, but she didn't seem to be responding to suggestion.

There was no grappling hook, meaning I'd opted to leave Audrey behind—probably because I was worried the lithid could easily tamper with her simple mind.

"A performer... saves their best material... for the finale," the lithid chortled. This time it came from above and behind me. I whirled, seeing only a dilapidated expanse of stoves and appliances that were arranged as if this was once an oversized kitchen.

"Talia," I hissed, trying to wake my summon.

Her barely conscious voice rang in my head. "Barely... any meat on the bones. Let them be."

"What the fuck did you do to her?" I said, slowly rotating in place, looking for any sign of the lithid.

The eerie red glow that permeated the room pulsated as the lithid replied. "The summon bitch? Nothing more than what I did to you. She's even weaker now than she was in the cage. Helpless, even as I feasted upon her tasteless suffering." It cackled madly in a mix of pleasure and raw joy, and I felt the hair stand up on the back of my neck. "Impotent and mired in a past that never happened. She can't bring herself to move forward. It's so trite, so one-note, so stale."

There. I spotted a round, visual distortion on the stretch of wallpaper. I continued my slow pan of the room, waiting until my crossbow was pointed toward it, and activated **<Page's Quickdraw>**, firing a bolt into the distortion.

A scream of agony morphed, modulating slowly into elation.

I swapped weapons quickly as I reloaded so the crossbow was in my dominant hand as I closed on the distortion. The bolts hit the target but elicited no reaction.

Unsure what else to do, I plunged my saber into the distortion. It passed through easily up to the halfway point of the blade, where it caught.

"She's nothing like *you*." A wreathing dark snake with black, oily skin corkscrewed up my blade where it split, lashing around my gauntlet. "An existence willing to cut away pieces of himself, rather than allow the past to have a hold. You are... delectable."

A series of images flashed through my mind. Ride-alongs with Dad, asking him questions about his job with obvious interest. Begging him for stories when I sat on his oversized recliner at night and listening wide-eyed as he grudgingly regaled me with what I asked for.

An audible hissing reached my ears. I glanced down and realized the lithid was burning. The reaction wasn't as definitive or extreme as with the remains of Region 6, but judging from the bubbling black surface, it *was* reacting.

I waited until the boiling reached a fever pitch and I felt its grip weakening to act.

Releasing the sword and yanking my arm clear, I loaded another bolt and, in one smooth motion, pressed the crossbow to the lithid's flesh.

It squealed and unraveled, winding itself back into the wall. Then the wall exploded as a length of darkness the size of a tree-truck emerged from the distortion, slamming into my chest.

I flew backward, my body screaming in pain as I tumbled heels-over-head, springing backward with my fingertips and eventually landing on my feet. A metal clang resounded next to me, and I spotted my saber.

The lithid continued forcing its way into the room in a manner that resembled ground beef from a meat grinder. It groaned loudly. "No... no.... no! The sword is so boring. Give me the knife, Matthias. Give me the knife..."

A needle of fear shot through me. *Give me the knife, Matthias.*

Something about those words resonated.

More than that, for every pound of matter the lithid pushed into the room, the less confident I was that I could handle whatever it would become when it reformed. I looked around, searching desperately for an exit.

There.

Behind the square line-up of dilapidated appliances, in the darkness, I spotted what looked like an opening. A corridor hidden by shadows.

It didn't matter whether this was a complete hallucination or not. If I was able to distance myself from the lithid—regardless of if that was literal or metaphorical—it would buy time to mentally regroup.

I reloaded my crossbow and raced into the corridor.

At first, everything was dark.

Then a single pinprick of light illuminated the hall. It grew larger as I kept up a steady jog until its form became clear. It was a single lightbulb, hanging by the cord from the ceiling. Maybe fifty feet down the corridor was another bulb.

I followed the line of lights, the only sound my own echoing foot-prints and heavy breathing.

My steps slowed as the final bulb in the row expanded, radiating a large, spotlight-like circle of illumination beneath it.

There was a picnic table seated on a bed of grass. And on the picnic table, I spotted a younger version of myself. He was wearing a long-sleeve shirt with a hood. Round glasses that did little to compliment his face. He was sweating as he leafed through a hardback. It was absolutely massive in his small hands.

Curious, I stepped around to the side.

Crime and Punishment.

I was never committed enough to literature to lug a Dostoevsky around in the wild. Which meant, if this was the day I thought it was, I'd picked it out of an immature flare for the dramatic.

Like clockwork, someone in flip-flops with an ankle bracelet appeared across from me.

Her features were cast in darkness, but seeing as how the ankle bracelet was decked out with gold, there was only so many people it could be.

"I'm glad you called. Figured with everything going on, you might not want to see me," Daphne said.

CHAPTER TWENTY-SEVEN

"That's probably for the best. Taking some time apart," the younger version of me answered. I did a double take. Was my voice really that subdued and robotic?

"What?" Daphne asked, her warm disposition unsettled.

"There was a notebook in my bedside table. It's gone."

"Maybe Ellison was being nosy?" Daphne tried.

He shook his head. "Nope. As far as I can tell, it's no longer in the house. Did you take it?"

"I didn't even know you had a journal."

"I don't. It was mostly a series of half-formed thoughts and plans for the future. Some documentation of the trial. And post-therapy notes. Since you didn't answer, I'll ask again. Did you take it?"

Daphne breathed a heavy sigh. "God, you're an ass."

"We're done." I rose from the table and slid the book into a backpack.

"Wait, Matt—"

"With all the legal shit, we shouldn't be talking anyway. Different camps and whatnot."

Daphne stood to her feet, placing her palms flat on the table. "We've been friends for years—"

"During which, you've tried to drive wedges between me and my family, followed me around, and repeatedly violated my privacy. I'd say the friendship has run its course."

I winced at the harshness of the scene. It wasn't that Daphne was a bad person back then. The good always outweighed the bad. But the bad was too substantial to ignore. She was obsessive. I think, if her father had ever been willing to get her tested, she would have easily been diagnosed with borderline personality disorder.

Our friendship started normally, if a bit awkwardly, with our parents constantly bringing us along for lunches and dinners thinly disguised as business meetings.

It was uncommon back then for me to have a friend my age, and as such, I thought that our relationship was normal. The irregularities a more social person would have picked out went entirely over my head. Daphne seemed to always be available and never flaked. She was interested in me, and being an adolescent with very little idea of who I was, we shared that interest. There was some friction—she wanted to invest far more time into our relationship than I did, and had trouble identifying social cues or subtle indicators that I was ready for our interactions to come to a close.

It was only after a few years that the veneer cracked enough to reveal the reality beneath.

In reality, Daphne didn't always have time for me. She just chose to prioritize me over anything else, sometimes to serious detriment.

She got angry and standoffish if I didn't spend enough time with her.

Some of my personal items, including anything I'd so much as scrawled in, began to disappear sporadically.

And it wasn't so much that she had trouble identifying social cues, more accurate that she intentionally ignored them.

It's common for people with BPD to develop a strong fixation on an individual. That fixation can be romantic or, as it was for us, platonic. Occasionally, it works out well enough. Often it doesn't. What it came down to was that Daphne had boundary issues, while I had boundaries in bulk. Even if our history hadn't been recently complicated, it was a terrible fit.

"Matt, stop," Daphne called out to the younger version of myself. In my memory, she'd sounded angrier. Hearing it again, she just sounded sad. "Are you going to tell?"

The inevitable question, and the one thing Daphne cared about more than me. Her secrets.

"Depends." He shot Daphne a bland look. "You planning on making this difficult?"

"No," Daphne said quietly.

"As long as that's true? I have no idea what you're talking about."

Daphne left the younger me standing there by the picnic table. An expression of anger filtered over his features as he watched her go.

Slowly, he turned to me. "How little—"

Before he uttered a word, I slid **<Broken Legacy>** beneath his ribcage.

He coughed once and fell to the ground, his face white. The last thing I was interested in right now was listening to the lithid puppeteer some twisted version of myself. And I couldn't shake the feeling that the more I let it speak, the more power it would have over me.

Still, it was strange. Seeing myself like that.

"*Talia.*"

Nothing. Not even a half-awake response.

For a moment, I considered dismissing and resummoning Talia. Then immediately thought better of it. If the lithid was capable of reading this deeply into my history, it was absolutely capable of reading my more recent memories of how my powers worked and setting any number of traps.

Leaving Talia aside for the moment, I tried to summon Audrey as a test case. Instead of pain, I felt nothing. Like attempting to siphon water from stone.

That answered that.

I took a seat at the picnic table and began to sort through the contents of my inventory. There wasn't much beyond the usual suspects. My bike and weapons still took up the majority of the contents, along with a few healing potions and the rollback charm. The first new additions were a pair of earplugs and what looked like a knock-off Sony recorder.

With little reason not to do so, I pressed the play button as I continued sorting through my things.

"*Your name is Matthias. You are seventeen years old and a senior at Talmont High School. Assuming it ever opens again. In a few minutes, you're about to enter a floor of the adaptive dungeon that contains a creature called a lithid, capable of creating hallucinations and, if Talia is correct, full-blown delusions. You must keep in mind that nothing you're seeing is real, and any psychological effects or distortions you're experiencing are temporary. The same holds true if you can't remember anything at all.*"

My dictation carried on for some time. While I was careful not to make any direct mention of the Ordinator class, I specifically called out the results of the Transposition event, the situation at Region 6, and the recent developments at Region 14, along with my position as region owner.

"*Mom and Iris are fine. Things aren't great with Ellison, but they're mendable if he comes around. Everyone's alive and safe.*"

I stopped rooting through my inventory when I found the bow.

It was made of a dark-gray wood, augmented with tarnished-silver, swirling embellishments.

<Item: Nychta's Retort>

Description: This longbow is enhanced with magical accoutrement in the form of enchanted runes. Some runes reduce the draw weight of the bow, allowing greater range and power regardless of the strength of the User. Others seed the projectile with traces of the divine.

Item Ability: The first shot fired inflicts an additional 200% damage, with a significant boost to critical damage. This effect resets every hour.

Item Class: Epic

< — >

God *damn*. It checked both the boxes for long-range and burst damage, shoring up weaknesses I'd carried forward since the beginning. It wasn't a perfect solution, necessarily—the cooldown left something to be desired—but it was one hell of a start.

Still, I was worried. There was no way the name was a coincidence.

"By now, you've probably noticed the additional items in your inventory and on your person. The bow is of particular interest. Kinsley had no history of it in her records, and as far as we can tell, the entry appeared minutes before you started searching for a bow. It was too good to pass up, and the price was a steal, but I'm all but certain we'll pay more for it later. At the very least, it shows Nychta has a continued interest in our survival."

I hefted the bow, feeling out the weight one more time before replacing it in my inventory. Concerns about Nychta would have to wait until my life wasn't on the line.

"Now, onto the plan. If you've already put it together, stop this recording. If not, I'll lay out the details now. If the lithid is as powerful as Talia expects, it will likely already know what we intend. No point in trying to hide—"

The recording cut out suddenly.

I reached over and scanned backward, replaying the last few seconds. It stopped at the same point.

Panic welled up, and I crushed it ruthlessly before it could overwhelm me. This was par for the course. If I'd thought far enough ahead to make a recording, I must have also known the lithid screwing with it was a real possibility. Which meant, if I'd done this right, it should be possible to piece together my plan from the inventory and Talia alone.

As I continued cataloguing my inventory, the panic slowly faded. That was a good sign. <**Jaded Eye**> was far harder to handle before the integration. Still, I hadn't attained the integration until I was already in the dungeon. The decision to use it wasn't the strange part. What seemed off was that I'd waited until entering the dungeon to use it.

It served as my first indicator that something was wrong. Maybe that was intentional.

<x10 Arrows of Aqueous Matriarch Toxin>

<x5 Bolts of Aqueous Matriarch Toxin>
<Amulet of Eldritch Resistance>
<Weak Poison of Clouded Judgement>
<Goblin Confit>

The arrows made perfect sense. A viable way to use the spider matriarch's toxin at range. They were longer than a standard arrow, with a hammerhead glass tip that contained a green liquid. There was flavor text that indicated this was an ideal projectile to use on a slime, meant to be shot in its path, rather than directly at it.

I was already wearing the amulet, which hopefully stacked with my armor.

But the last two acquisitions had me entirely at a loss. What kind of fucking plan was this? Trying the matriarch's toxin on the lithid made sense—it was sourced from a trial boss, and likely packed significantly more punch than anything you could grab on the open market. Yet, the **<Poison of Clouded Judgement>** seemed like an utter waste. It specifically denoted that it was only effective on low-level creatures or NPCs, unless imbibed voluntarily.

And I had no idea how I'd intended to get a psychic monster to willingly drink poison.

The goblin confit was—well, a disturbing introduction to confit. Supposedly a troll delicacy, it was created by force-feeding goblins an excess of sweet berries for months until they expired from the strain, then slow-cooking them in gilded truffle goat butter.

Which—I mean, what the fuck. I sure as hell wasn't going to eat it.

Maybe the intention was to trick the lithid into eating the confit laced with poison, but again, it being able to read my thoughts made that a tall order with questionable returns, considering that the poison's effects lasted less than ten minutes.

A groggy growl reverberated in my mind.

"*Talia?*"

Talia's voice was drowsy, only slightly more lucid than before. *"What a terrible dream... where are we?"*

A flash of movement from the corridor caught my eye. I scurried out of the spotlight, unsure if it'd even make a difference. "It wasn't a dream. We're on the fifth floor of the adaptive dungeon. The lithid is screwing with our minds. Breaking out of the initial delusion was the first barrier."

"I'll shred it to pieces," Talia hissed.

"You'll get your chance. Are you coherent enough to fight?"

One by one, small shadows emerged from the darkness. Humanoid silhouettes around half my height. Smiling white teeth glittered in the dark. They all held short blades that looked strangely domestic, more like something out of a kitchen knife block than a fantasy equivalent.

"Oh yes," Talia answered, her voice so raw with spite, I couldn't help but wonder what the lithid had shown her.

"Then get ready." I drew **<Broken Legacy>** and threw it directly into the center of the advancing shadows.

CHAPTER TWENTY-EIGHT

The smiling shadows assailed us on all sides. There were dozens of them, the sole saving grace that they didn't seem to have much in terms of health. I nailed one between the eyes with **<Page's Quickdraw>**.

Talia tore pieces off the first few shadows and took several glancing hits from their knives

"Go for vitals!" I shouted back at her. "They're coordinated. They'll keep dogpiling if you give them an opening."

"I resent... that turn of phrase." Talia's voice was muffled as she ripped a chunk out of a shadow's torso. But she listened to the core of what I said and came up with her solution. Venom dripped freely off her fangs as she snapped at the small cluster of shadows that surrounded her, aiming for their arms and legs.

I wasn't certain if poison would work on them, but if it did, they didn't have much body weight to speak of, so the effect would be stronger than normal.

A shadow charged at me, its bright knife angled downward toward my chest as it leaped through the air. I grabbed its knife-hand and neck, pivoting and slamming its lower half onto the spotlight-illuminated park table. There was a sickening crunch that I belatedly realized was its spine snapping. It went limp, dropping the knife and staring up at me, inverted smile forming an eerie frown.

"Join... us..." the shadow whispered, pointing toward the ground where its knife fell.

Out of the corner of my eye, I saw another shadow collapsing to its knees, feebly attempting to remove the bolt I'd fired from the **<Quick Crossbow of the Frost Leech>**.

They're weak to the cold effect too. The only real advantage they have is numbers.

I tried to reach out toward the mass of them with **<Probability Cascade>** and got no feedback whatsoever, even as my mana drained.

Of course. They're not real. More puppets than anything else. I can't direct them because they're already being directed.

I fired my crossbow twice more, taking a page from Talia's book and being less selective about where I hit. Mechanical gears ground as it cocked back, and I nearly loaded another bolt before I saw multiple sets of eyes open around ceiling level.

"Above—" My warning yell was cut off as **<Perception>** flared. The shadow above me dropped, its knife a descending spike as two others attacked from the sides.

I threw myself back onto the picnic table, using **<Quickdraw>** to stabilize the first shot, lodging a bolt into the eye of the shadow that dropped from the ceiling. When the others reacted, I rolled off the table and spun, drawing the bow and firing it instinctively as I retreated backward. Eventually, I felt my thigh brush against Talia's fur.

"Is this it? The lithid's just going to throw numbers at us until we crack?" I sneered, wiping a trickle of blood from my mouth.

"Unlikely. This is just the opening blitz. There's a twist, somewhere."

"All I'm seeing is mindless shadows. Basic pack behavior."

"This is not how a pack hunts. Each is opportunistic, trying to position themselves for the best strike at the expense of the others. More than that, the way they fight feels familiar." Talia's voice was wary.

Don't think about it. Wipe them out.

<Jaded Eye> sounded panicked, as if it was attempting to draw my attention away from something. As it had never intentionally led me astray when the chips were down, I let it refocus my attention purely on the combat itself.

Still, they were multiplying and pressing in tighter. I needed something close range. When I reached for my inventory, dozens of heads snapped around, eyes conveying hungry anticipation. I averted course at the last moment, drawing my saber instead.

Angry cries filled the darkness as they pressed in on me.

"They want something from me," I realized, conveying the thought to Talia. What was it the lithid had said? That the saber was boring?

"Ignore them," Talia answered in my head. She bowled over several shadows that abandoned her to attack me, pausing for a half-second each to nick them with poison and move on.

The shadows fell, one after another, faster than they could replenish. We pushed them back together, out of the spotlight and into the darkness. Nick's saber flashed in my hand in wide, artful flourishes as I used their illuminated eyes and daggers as markers, aiming for necks and arms. It wasn't as second nature as **<Blade of Woe>**, but what it lacked in familiarity, it made up for in range. Talia formed up beside me, snapping at shadows.

For the first time, it felt as if we were winning.

They're luring us away from the light

<Jaded Eye's> warning came too late. As I attempted to relay the warning to Talia and retreat, every marker I used to locate the shadows—eyes, teeth, and daggers—disappeared. Countless invisible hands gripped my sword arm, wrenching at it until the sword fell away.

Simultaneously, the shadows yanked Talia's feet out from under her. She yelped, sections of her body obscured by darkness.

When I tried to help, I found my legs rooted to the floor.

Why are you so afraid of what you are?

A black rage fueled by helplessness rolled over me. I tore my arm free and yanked **<Blade of Woe>** out of my inventory. All at once, the human organs of multiple shadows attacking Talia illuminated the darkness.

I moved.

The blade sang as I ripped through the shadows, eviscerating them. First the ones that clung to me, feeling a dark thrill as I felt them fall away, my fear dissipating as their incorporeal bodies collapsed to the ground.

A sense of cold purpose washed over me, even as I heard them chittering in the darkness, laughing. I hauled one of them off Talia and slit its throat. Stabbed another in the eye. Another across the belly. **<Unsparing Fang>** guided my movements—helped me know where to place my feet and leverage my weight—but the knife work was entirely mine.

"Let her *go*," I shouted. And the shadows trembled. Talia's eye stared up at me widely.

I fired off **<Harrowing Anticipation>**. I wouldn't be able to use it again for the rest of the dungeon, but that was fine if it meant finishing this. The threads that connected the shadows to the lithid became visible.

The beauty of the knife was the efficiency. The brevity of the path from point A to point B.

All at once, the gritty desperation of it all fell away. I danced among them, blade stabbing, slashing, twisting, a feeling of unique purpose washed over me. Every neuron and muscle fiber cooperated in perfect union.

As if this were what I was meant for. Raucous laughter reached my ears, barely identifiable as my own.

The threads from **<Harrowing Anticipation>** led me to the final shadow. It was retreating, casting terrified glances over its shoulder, a gloating smile nowhere to be seen.

I flipped the knife into my off-hand and drew the crossbow with my dominant, using **<Page's Quickdraw>** to fire a bolt into its thigh. It toppled and fell, dragging itself away. I grabbed its hair and pulled its head back, driving the knife into its back over and over.

Something tugged at my pant leg.

I whirled, prepared to plunge my knife into the next target.

"The prey has fallen, Matthias." A wolf I had to concentrate to recognize stood at my side. Her thick eyebrows were pulled together in concern as she stared at the knife in my hand. "I am not your enemy."

"Talia?"

"Are you alright?" Talia cocked her head.

I lowered the knife and ran a hand through my hair, unsettled. "Just... lost myself for a second there. Jesus. My head's killing me."

The shadows fell away, a bright light overhead blinding us. Birds sang, and as my eyes adjusted, perfectly manicured lawns came into focus.

A damning feeling washed over me as I realized not only where, but *when* this was.

"What is this place?" Talia asked.

It was all exactly as I remembered it. The rock yard with weeds that never stopped cropping up, no matter how often it was sprayed. A waist-high iron gate that squealed loudly when it swung open. And a small alcove where I sat to read on weekdays after I'd finished my schoolwork, waiting for Dad to return.

"The last home I ever had," I answered quietly. I turned slowly, toward the end of the road. Identical to the memory I replayed infinitely in my mind, my father's police cruiser was parked at the end of the road. A few neighbors stood at a safe distance from the house, several on their cellphones, either recording or chattering into them.

And I remembered everything.

CHAPTER TWENTY-NINE

Kafka's *Metamorphosis* lay open on my lap, unattended, as I watched Dad's parked squad car at the end of the street. He'd been inside the paint-chipped house for a while now. Ellison was kicking his legs out in Mom's antique rocking chair, the chair emitting a rhythmic squeak as it reached its apex, leaning so far back it threatened to topple at any moment.

"I'm starving," Ellison complained.

"You're not starving. You're hungry," I corrected absentmindedly, still focused on the flurry of unusual activity at the end of the street.

"It's almost six thirty," Ellison said.

"Dad's work is important. Keeps the city safe. Being off-schedule goes with the territory." The same couldn't be said for every cop. You had to either be blind or blatantly ignore the news to believe that. But Dad was old school. All about listening and protecting the community. Putting people first. He talked about them like they were individuals, not some faceless conglomerate. And even if I found him naive at times, it was hard not to respect how much he cared.

A muffled pop reached us. It could have been anything. Car backfire, or an unfortunate squirrel that scurried its way into a power converter.

Then a cluster of five muffled bangs followed, identical to the first.

I slipped from the alcove, placing my back against it. "Get down," I snapped at Ellison. He flopped wide-eyed from the chair to the ground, both of us flinching from the clatter as it fell, one corner banging against the wall.

"Gunshots?" Ellison whispered, his face pale.

"Where's Iris?" I hissed.

"Napping with Mom."

We waited in tense silence for a follow-up. When none came, I peeked over the flowered cushions, exposing as little of myself as possible. A few of the neighbors had emerged from their homes, gawking at the house at the end of the street.

My heart hammered in my chest. It was impossible to tell exactly where the sound had come from, but it was undoubtedly from the direction of the end of the street.

Doubt and fear gnawed at me, along with the screaming need to do *something*. Anything.

"Check on Mom and Iris, then call 911," I told Ellison.

"What are you going to do?" Ellison asked, alarmed.

"Keep watch. Stay low and get moving."

Ellison jolted into action, retreating toward our parents' room in a low crouch.

It's hard to explain what happened next. Put it into words. The best I can describe it is as a scene that materialized in my mind. An image of my father bleeding out on the floor, frightened and alone. It was so visceral and real that I had to confirm it.

Time bled together as I walked out the front door and through the gate in a daze, leaving it open behind me. Asphalt burned my bare feet as I walked numbly toward the house, my pulse vibrating in my neck, vision shuddering with every heartbeat.

Dad had taught me about the bystander effect early on. Given me a slightly sanitized rundown of the murder of Kitty Genovese, a woman who was stalked and murdered over the course of half an hour, even as she screamed for help and dozens of witnesses watched from their windows. The records are spotty, but it was probably more than an hour before the first call came in.

Our so-called neighbors were just standing around, trying to peer through the door at a distance for a better look.

I hated them for their inaction. Hated them with every fiber of my being.

No one even tried to stop me as I walked past. I'm not sure what I was thinking—apart from if Dad was hurt, I wanted to help him, slow the bleeding and buy time until the ambulance got there.

As I stepped through the front door, the scent of mildew and stale cigarettes washed over me, followed by a metallic scent I'd identify far later as methamphetamine.

The walls were bare and undecorated. Soiled carpet stuck to my bare feet.

A woman lay unconscious on the floor, battered and bruised. Her face and upper body littered with dark and purple bruises everywhere her tank top didn't cover. Numbly, on autopilot, I stooped down and pressed two fingers to her neck as my father had shown me.

There was a weak, rhythmic pulse beneath my fingertips. I left her and moved on.

Dad was laid out on the floor next to the couch. He'd fallen backward, likely due to the six gunshot wounds in his chest. His once vibrant-blue eyes were almost colorless, expression locked in a permanent rictus of surprise. As if he couldn't believe someone had actually shot him.

I pressed my fingers against his neck, though there was no need. He was gone.

A wave of grief washed over me and then disappeared, as if it had crossed an invisible threshold and was suddenly snuffed out.

Something cold and foreign took its place.

"Who the fuck are you?" For the first time, I noticed the skinhead on the couch. He was rubbing his head with both hands, the cylinder of a light-metal revolver clinking against his temple.

When I didn't answer, he unraveled further. "It doesn't matter. God dammit. Look what that bitch made me do."

"The woman you beat to hell made you kill a cop?" As the words left my lips, it felt like someone else was saying them. The utter lack of accusation in my voice was probably what saved me. I sounded genuinely curious.

"Fuck. I'm fucked." He rubbed his head vigorously, the revolver leaving red marks on his skin. My gaze strayed from the man to the surrounding scene. There were dozens of burned-down cigarette butts in the ash tray and a bowie knife on the table next to a glass pipe.

It called to me.

This had happened before. Ellison's oblivious bully sitting on the overpass, practically begging to be pushed, was the most recent example. But there had been others. Many others.

I'd always managed to talk myself out of it. Therapy had helped. Talks with my father had helped.

Now my father was gone, and the therapy couldn't help me here. There was no disproportionality to focus on. No unevenness in the scales. And with my father dead, the cops wouldn't look twice before labeling it self-defense. No consequences to speak of.

Still, he outweighed me by fifty to seventy pounds.

"You have to wash your hands. Get the GSR off."

The man stared up at me. "What?"

"Gunshot residue. You're coated in it at this point. You have to wash your hands." I was twisting advice Dad gave me on how to speak to someone in a crisis—let the slightest doubt into your voice, and they'll latch onto it. But if you speak with confidence and authority, they'll cling to your words like a lifeline.

The man stared at me. At first, I thought he might call out my bullshit.

On his long list of issues, the GSR was near the bottom. The murder weapon and empty shells were toward the top, along with the many witnesses who had heard the shots, and if Stockholm syndrome hadn't set in too deeply, the unconscious woman could easily turn on him.

The man stood to his feet suddenly, dropping the gun. "Fuck!" He rushed to the bathroom.

Using a filthy rag from the table as a buffer, I picked up the gun by the trigger guard and popped the cylinder open to confirm he hadn't reloaded. The casings were empty. Good.

With that sorted, I took the knife from the table. The hilt fit snugly in my hand as if it had always been there.

Everything blurred together after I followed him into the bathroom. The next thing I remembered was my mother's face, hovering above me.

"It's okay, baby. It's okay." Tears streamed down her cheeks, ruining day-old mascara. "Give me the knife, baby."

I handed it to her.

Sirens drew closer.

———

"It's a rare thing to lose your husband and son in the same evening. Does she think of that night when she drinks, I wonder?"

Talia's growl of alarm came too late. A sharp, stinging pain sunk deep into my back. I screamed, whirling to face the threat and coming face to face with a mirror.

"No one would have blamed you for it. The sentence would have been light, the situation laden with mitigating circumstances, even if they knew the truth of how it all went down. Why, then, did you run from it, lock it away so deeply that even I can only show you this much?"

The lithid had leaped back several feet after the surprise attack. It had also taken my form, clad in the eldritch armor, a twisted mongrel at its side. Dagger in one hand, crossbow in the other.

"Bastard," Talia said through gritted teeth. "That might be the actual lithid. It looks far more real than the shadows did," Talia said. "Matthias. Can you fight?"

I swooned on my feet, unable to answer her. **<Harrowing Anticipation>** was fading, but from the remnants, this form didn't have threads as the others had. I withdrew a health potion and chugged it, then wiped the residue from my mouth.

"Pretty sure you're on the money," I panted. "We need to end this quickly."

CHAPTER THIRTY

How could I forget something so important?

More than that, I had other memories that directly conflicted with it. Recent memories. I remembered googling the killer's name less than a year ago to confirm he was still in prison.

And Mom was there. She knew. She'd known for years, and we'd never talked about it. And despite the many opportunities she had to throw my shortcomings in my face, she'd never mentioned it, or even hinted at it.

The only times I'd ever been to court was during her hearings.

Another memory bubbled to the surface. Cold water plunging down over me as I clung to myself and shivered, words repeated over and over.

"You're a good boy, Matthias. Listen to me. You did nothing. You wandered in here looking for your father and that monster threatened you. Dragged you to the bathroom and tried to drown you. Everything else is a blur, you understand?"

Had she taken my place?

I wanted to believe it wasn't true. That the lithid's power was just that all-encompassing.

But the dull chill, coupled with the constant pounding in my head, said otherwise.

"Move!" Talia roared, slamming into the back of my knees and dead-legging me. The near-silent whisper of a crossbow bolt sailed over me, directly where my head was. Talia left me to pick myself up as she raced to intercept the mongrel racing toward us—more monstrous mutt than dog. They collided in a horrible blur of claws and teeth and yelps.

Nearly twenty feet away, the lithid advanced toward the clashing dogs, holding its aim and looking for an opening.

It likely had little concern for friendly fire. The thought stirred me out of my daze, throwing me into action. I loaded the first of the poison bolts and spiked it with **<Probability Cascade>**, pulling the trigger and firing it at the lithid. The bolt spiraled through the air and—caught by an errant breeze—struck the lithid dead center as it dodged away.

It hissed and immediately switched targets, its attention entirely on me.

"You hid it away because of how you felt. For the first time that emptiness within you was filled. The knife brought you joy, unfiltered happiness, and contentment. Things you'd never felt before. Things you swore to never feel again."

"Shut up!" I shouted, firing another cascade bolt at the lithid.

It was ready this time. Not bothering to dodge, it raised a hand and swatted the bolt away. **<Ordinator's Emulation>** ticked in the back of my mind, recognizing the ability as **<Probability Cascade>**.

On my left, Talia was losing her clash with the mongrel.

I juked an incoming bolt, using **<Awareness>** to guide me, and rushed toward her.

"Give me an opening, Talia."

Talia reacted perfectly, pressing a paw against her attacker's chin and shoving its head up.

The lithid's smug voice whispered in my mind. "You've spent so long, trying to suppress the monster you've always been. Because society puts people like you in one of two places. Prison or institution. But the world has changed now. You don't have to pretend anymore."

I drove my dagger into the mongrel's side and twisted the blade immediately, withdrawing as it yelped and snapped at me. Talia sunk her teeth into its neck, pressing her advantage.

<Awareness> screamed, and I flung myself backward to narrowly dodge a bolt, catching my weight with one hand and pushing hard against the ground—

A ring of fiery pain blazed through my body, expanding from a second bolt that plunged deep into the nerve cluster between my collarbone and neck.

The lithid advanced, two crossbows in either hand, explaining how the second bolt had come out so fast. It inventoried a hand-crossbow—one I recognized as the shoddy, sightless, repurposed piece of plywood that had been my first weapon—and reloaded the second.

A wave of cold deeper than the frozen wasteland of the fourth floor washed over me.

It copied my face, my abilities, and gear I've owned, including the poisoned bolts.

I slugged an antidote quickly, noticing with irritation as the lithid raised an identical potion to its lips. Then, bracing myself, I tore the arrow out before the heat-drain effect could do any more damage.

My vision narrowed to a pinprick.

"You know the truth. You've always known. The reaction to the system proves it. We've always been teetering on the precipice of savagery. One bad day away from discovering who we really are. But you continue this pointless struggle. When you killed those three Users during the Transposition, you didn't even allow yourself to savor it."

Sensing it was near, I struck out recklessly with the knife, my blood aflame as poison and antidote raged war within me. The lithid countered me easily with **<Unsparing Fang,>** intercepting my rushed attacks and sending me spinning with a savage backhand.

Even as stars exploded behind my eyes, my mind raced.

How was I supposed to beat this thing if it knew every move I would make? I'd gotten a lucky shot off when it was distracted with Talia, but ever since it started focusing on me, it easily dodged everything I threw at it. At this rate, I'd be finished before my summon put the mongrel down.

What was the plan? There must have been one. I had the foresight to make an audio recording in case the lithid trapped me in a hallucination. I must have had something more. Some strategy.

I staggered away as the lithid prattled on, trying to buy time.

"I can free you, Matthias," it whispered. "Give in. Surrender control and bring me to the outside world. Within a day, your burdens will be gone. And I will reforge you into what you were always meant to be."

A harrowing realization struck me. Talia had said the lithid fed on suffering. With the dungeon being adaptive, I'd assumed that suffering would be my own. But that wasn't necessarily true. If I lost here and the lithid invaded my mind and took over as it implied, everyone around me would be in danger.

Focus.

Though our motivations were entirely different, the parallels were significant. Both of us intended to use the other as a weapon in the outside world.

But there was a key disparity that had to do with the nature of the adaptive dungeon. The lithid had been generated exclusively as a monster for me to fight. She'd hinted that Talia's pups had always been dead. Had I entered the fifth floor with someone else, it would have been entirely different.

If the lithid died without dropping a core, my life would continue on as it had.

If I died, however, the lithid would cease to exist.

And it was possibly the only monster in existence with enough self-awareness and external knowledge to piece that together.

It made a critical mistake, telegraphing its intentions. The lithid didn't want to kill me. It wanted to break me.

I took a split second to review my inventory

<x10 Arrows of Aqueous Matriarch Toxin>
<x2 Bolts of Aqueous Matriarch Toxin>
<Amulet of Eldritch Resistance>
<Weak Poison of Clouded Judgement>
<Goblin Confit>

I snorted. The **<Goblin Confit>** wasn't meant to be used as bait. It wasn't meant for anything at all. The randomness of the item was a hint.

There was no plan.

I'd come to the conclusion that if the lithid could read my mind, there was no way to prepare for it ahead of time—that any concrete strategy could easily be used against me if I stuck to it while the enemy was aware.

The **<Poison of Clouded Judgement>** wasn't for the lithid. It was for me. Intended to create an opening the lithid couldn't predict, once I'd gathered enough information within the dungeon to generate a strategy on the fly. My vision more or less returned, save the corona of violet pulsing around the fringes. I wiped the blood from my mouth and grinned at the lithid. It was standing a few feet away from me, a strange expression on its face that looked almost wounded.

Behind her, Talia was chasing the mongrel. It darted between parked cars and trash cans, beating a pointless retreat. She'd have it in a matter of moments.

"You can read my mind, right?" I leered. "Then you know that this isn't a bluff. Because I'll do whatever's necessary to win."

"Wait—" the lithid reached out a hand and rushed toward me.

But it was too late. I swallowed the **<Poison of Clouded Judgement>** and quick drew **<Nychta's Retort>**, loading it with three cascade-infused arrows, and fired them straight up in the air.

It's impossible to fire a projectile perfectly upward. No matter how precise you are, the most minuscule shift will inevitably alter trajectory. I laughed maniacally as the three poisoned arrows reached their apex, and, following the directive of **<Probability Cascade>**, plunged directly toward me.

CHAPTER THIRTY-ONE

There was a bone-jarring impact. My skull collided against the sidewalk as the lithid tackled me to the ground. It outweighed me significantly, and as my lungs compressed, it became nearly impossible to breathe.

Strong arms grabbed me and began to yank.

It's trying to get us both out of the way.

I locked an arm around its neck and kicked its knees out from under it, forcing it into a grapple. I was slower than normal because of the **<Poison of Clouded Judgement>**, but that worked to my advantage. The lithid reacted to my intentions rather than my actions, and I was able to secure it in a clinch.

Its body juddered violently twice as two of the arrows pierced its upper back. I shouted in pain as the third pierced my forearm.

The lithid roared, its version of my mouth opening inhumanly wide as it shrieked.

That's the second dose of the same poison. If I don't get another round of antidote soon, this is over.

My survival instinct kicked into overdrive. I needed to do whatever I could to end this quickly.

I sunk my teeth into its throat. Bilious liquid ran into my mouth and eyes as the lithid squirmed. A chunk of flesh came free, and I spit it out, blindly plunging my dagger into its side, over and over. It swatted at my wrist, and I felt something break.

All at once, it slumped, and I rolled over on top of it, both hands gripping its neck tightly even as pain radiated up my fractured forearm.

"Fucking. Die. Already," I growled, shifting my grip and bearing down harder.

"Matt... it hurts," Jinny said. She stared up at me with terrified eyes, hemorrhaging crimson from the wound in her neck. "You don't have to do this. Anyone can change."

My grip loosened for a fraction of a second.

Three spears of darkness pierced me. Subconsciously, I could feel the lithid attacking my mind. I tried to push it back. The street from my childhood was overtaken with the crimson flesh from Region 6. Jinny's body was still there, lifeless on the ground, as Nick sat beside her, watching impassively as I struggled.

"Hey, man. You have to know I'm probably donezo. I'm not you. Never been good at biding my time." Nick rubbed his head sheepishly. "Probably did something stupid already, and it's not like the suits would ever let that pass."

"And even if he's not, you have me to worry about." Ellison walked in front of me, hands stuffed in his hoody. He studied me impassively as I writhed on the ground. "It wasn't chance that I ended up with a special class that could also disguise itself. They're going to use me against you. And sure, maybe you'll win, but do you really want to deal with the aftermath of killing your brother?"

I felt the lithid's grip on my mind grow tighter.

Miles crouched next to me, peering down. "Sure, you're clever. And you've grown accustomed to being the big fish in a small pond. But we're in the ocean now. I'm more experienced than you. Eventually, you'll make a mistake. And I'll be there waiting."

Estrada rocked slowly, back and forth, in a rocking chair to my left. "You must know where this is going, Matthias. The body count from the first event was astronomical. They speak of correction, but their intent is clear: whittling us down until only the strongest remain." She peered at me through her glasses. "And the list of people you mean to protect grows ever longer. Perhaps it would be wise to stop while you are ahead. The task before you is impossible. You are alone. And you will always be alone."

Next to Estrada, my father's killer idly spun the revolver. He grinned at me, even as he leaked from a half-dozen stab wounds. "You know, I never planned to kill a cop. It just sort of happened. One day, I was fine. The next, boom." He placed the gun on the scarlet ground, barrel pointed at the others. "Guess you can relate. It's only a matter of time before you snap with someone innocent in the crosshairs."

The last of the struggle faded from me as I closed my eyes.

"No," another voice whispered, low and angry. "You said it yourself. The enemy needs Nicholas. Even if he rebelled, they would not cull him so thoughtlessly. Who will save him, if you surrender now?"

"But... Ellison..." I whispered.

"You know neither his mission nor his intent. The wretch is preying on your fear, your tendency to assume the worst. He is an errant pup. Patience and understanding will bring him back to you."

I barely heard her. It was as if the lithid had eroded my mental barriers entirely, and the weight of every burden crashed down on me at once.

A mental shock jolted me, kept me from being swallowed in the flood.

"Your responsibilities are many. That is true. I watched as you took them upon yourself, one after another. And if we were not here, in this crucible, you would not hesitate. Because that is who you are. That is your resolve. It is why I cannot bring myself to hate you, though there are many reasons I should."

"And if I become a monster?"

*"You offered me a choice, before we entered this accursed place. I have chosen. This is my vow. I will remain at your side until the end. And if, in that time, you lose to the darkness, I will stop you. Now **fight!**"*

The hallucinations of my friends and enemies disappeared. I awoke to the clear blue sky—Talia standing over me protectively, and an exquisite pain as gray matter oozed out of my chest. There was a glowing red light in the center of the mass. I spit blood and stared at it until I realized what was happening.

At some point in my unconscious state, I'd grabbed **<Blade of Woe>**. In its haste to overtake me, the lithid had shown me its back. The red mass was a weak spot.

I drove the knife home.

Then immediately fell back, curling up in agony as the gray matter boiled, retreating out of my body and reforming in the shape of a woman —the first form I'd seen it take, what felt like ages ago in the elevator.

"No, no, *no*. I've claimed you!" the lithid shouted in rage. Another dark spear lanced from its side toward my chest.

There was a blur of motion as Talia leapt in front of me, grunting as the lance struck her. She wobbled on her paws, unsettled but still standing. Her voice was a pained whisper, quiet and resolute. "He is mine, wretch. You will not take him from me."

Another spear pierced Talia. I tried to stand, forcing my way to my hands and knees, struggling to stand.

"It's funny. So fucking funny," the lithid seethed. "Those memories you cherish so deeply? Of the pups that suckled on your teats in the dead of winter, as you all huddled in a cave for warmth? None of them are real. You're just like me. A construct of mana that exists solely because this human drew breath. I wanted to reveal that, eventually, once I'd wrung you dry of every drop you had to give. As a parting gift. Those children you mourned were never real in the first place. They were always lifeless corpses in the snow."

Talia roared. Her body exploded, awash in silver flame. The influx of heat was so intense I had to shield my face with my hands. When I lowered them, the spears of darkness were gone. And Talia had changed.

At first, I thought she'd reverted to her original form. She stood nearly a foot taller than before. The navy in her coat was gone, giving her a stark resemblance to the winter wolf I'd fought on the fourth floor. Only, her eyes were golden instead of red. And the reflectiveness of her fur was different. It wasn't white.

It was silver.

"You—" the lithid started

Talia tackled it in the center of its dark, formless mass, driving it to the ground. White flames engulfed the lithid and it shrieked in pain, squirming beneath Talia's paws.

Talia spoke directly to the squirming mass. "It will be some time before I can hold my creator accountable for their cruelty. In the interim, I will settle for you."

I winced as the flames consumed the lithid and it writhed desperately. The display went on for a good minute, the lithid shrinking rapidly to the size of a beachball before Talia stopped to regain her strength, exhausted and panting.

"Why..." even the lithid's voice sounded small. "I... needed the power... only wanted... to be free..."

"Even if they never existed. They were real *to me*," Talia shouted, pressing down on the lithid and burning it around the edges.

"Talia," I called to her weakly.

She spun toward me, her expression a rictus of grief and anger. "*What.*"

I tried to stand and fell back to one knee. "It's your prey. Your prerogative. The lithid needs to die. That much is obvious. But I think, if our roles were reversed, you would advise a clean kill."

Talia bared her teeth. For a moment, her fire burned brighter. Then her face relaxed, expression growing stoic. "Revenge is a distraction. We have to stay focused on the whole."

"Yes."

She turned her stoic gaze down on the lithid. She reached out with a paw, placing it on the center of the dark mass. "Be at peace."

What was left of the lithid burned away in seconds.

CHAPTER THIRTY-TWO

Slowly, the expanse of sky and street below me eroded, leaving a simple gray-paneled room with visible support beams. Even the original dungeon floor was gone. The lithid hadn't left anything behind. I tested my arm carefully and was surprised to find it in working order.

Out of curiosity, I checked my inventory and found that none of the arrows or bolts had been spent.

Everything that happened within the lithid's thrall was undone. Physically, anyway.

Mentally? That was another story.

My hands shook violently until I clasped them together. And I could still feel the tremors. When the shaking subsided, I pulled up my UI and looked at the time.

Only five minutes had expended over the course of what felt like a lifetime.

It was hard to be disappointed with the lack of a core, considering what we'd just been through.

There was too much to unpack and process here. I needed to keep myself distracted for the moment, and the sudden influx of notifications presented a perfect means to that end.

<Adaptive Dungeon, Fifth Floor has been cleared.>
<XP Reward: L>
<Congratulations! You are the first to clear this floor of the Adaptive Dungeon.>
<You are currently ranked 1st on the Leaderboard!>
<Reward: Unspecified Boon — Eldritch Favor>

<Bonus Reward: +2 to Companionship>

I tensed, waiting for a wave of pain from the stat increase.
Nothing happened.
What, was I expecting my companionship muscles to hurt?
Feeling foolish, I pulled up the details on the boon.

<Eldritch Favor: Despite their cruel nature, lithids are surprisingly good sports that delight in finally finding an entity capable of beating them at their own game. Most eldritch creatures you encounter will remain passive unless attacked. Eldritch conjurations or summons will bond more quickly. This effect will be magnified exponentially if the conjuration or summon is a lithid.>

Too bad it didn't drop a monster core. The boon's only half a reward without it. What are the chances of running into another lithid any time soon?
With **<Jaded Eye's>** negativity annoying the hell out of me, I navigated to my title screen.
<Born Nihilist> was grayed out. During the initial clash with the lithid, I'd received a notification that the title had been integrated. I now understood the basic premise of title integration and could appreciate the potential benefits. Most titles had a specific-use case, but the cooldown kept me from swapping between them freely. If I continued to integrate them, I'd eventually reap the benefits of all my titles simultaneously, with a minor loss of effectiveness. But losing **<Born Nihilist>** first was irritating, as it had become something of a crutch.
I reviewed the others briefly.
<Cruel Lens> would be terrible to lean on for any extended period of time. Insightful as it was and useful for digging up secrets, it twisted my perspective far more drastically than the other titles, and I wasn't sure I could stop it from leaking into my personality.
That left **<Jaded Eye>** and—
I blinked. There was a fourth title. One I hadn't possessed before completing the dungeon floor.

<Key Conditions Met: A new title has been unlocked.>
<Scathing Shell — When most would crumble, you push on. Augments the User's existing ability to fight back and retain willpower despite overwhelming odds and significant physical or mental damage. Effectiveness of health and mana regeneration increases the closer the User is to death, at an inverse cost to rationality and awareness. May exacerbate delusions of grandeur.>

Interesting. Dangerous as hell if I used it wrong, but the title's potential as an oh-shit button was undeniable.

And that wasn't even factoring in the synergy with <Vindictive>, which would keep me conscious and on my feet even with severe injuries and major blood loss. I'd considered nixing that feat with the charm the old crafter from my region gifted me—there were situations where it was simply better to lose consciousness. Now, I wasn't so sure.

I added it to the ever-growing list of abilities in need of further testing and returned to the deluge of notifications.

<Quest Complete>
Quest: The Kinsley Accords
Primary Objective Complete — Gain loot and levels as you fulfill your contractual obligations.
Extended Primary Objective Complete — Explore the dungeon, venturing at least to the fifth floor.
EXP GAIN (M)
Reward: Increased relationship with Kinsley, Merchant.
Reward: Progression toward Vocation — Anima Seer
Accept Vocation: Y | N

Fantastic. I'd finally uncovered a vocation.

Just, what the hell was it?

I'd read Jung at some point—recently enough that I knew Anima represented the part of the psyche that focused inward on the subconscious. But the concept was heady and borderline overly complicated on its own. Tack seer on at the end, and who the fuck even knew anymore.

And how was it a vocation, exactly?

Far too many questions for me to just blindly accept it, even though I'd been waiting for a vocation for some time. I focused passed the Y | N text on the vocation name, hoping in vain for a tool-tip.

To my surprise, another window appeared.

<Advisor and Advocate, an Anima Seer forms a connection with a person's soul via brief physical contact. With naturally keen insights, virtuous or profiteering Anima Seers frequently levy their talents to guide Users toward ideal paths of advancement. Less scrupulous members of this vocation may use their ability to act as information brokers, utilizing their connection with contacted Users to spy through their eyes.>

I immediately confirmed the prompt without bothering to read the description twice.

While it was possible I was screwing myself out of a potentially more lucrative vocation further down the line, the ability to guide my allies toward ideal progression was tantalizing enough. Throw in the advantage of being able to widen my perspective to whomever I touched?

Granted, there were obviously limits. There had to be.

Otherwise, I could just walk around the city for a few days, "accidentally" bumping into everyone I met, and gain a borderline omniscient perspective. But there was no way in hell I was turning this down.

<**Level Up:** Ordinator has reached Level 13>

I swiped the level notification away for the moment, too tired to even consider dealing with it.

<**System Notification:** Bond with Eidolon Wolf, Talia, has increased to 9.>

A giant jump from where we were before. Curiously, I looked over to Talia. She was deep in her thoughts, head resting on her paws.

I said the obvious. "That was hell."

"It was."

"It had me, for a moment. Dead to rights. If you hadn't pulled me out..."

Talia breathed out in irritation at the praise. "With a minor eternity spent locked in the clutches of that wretch, I had considerably more practice than you."

"Thank you, Talia."

"We have plenty of time for the sixth floor."

I turned my head and stared. "Did you just make a joke?"

Talia looked away, and I couldn't help but chuckle at how simultaneously awkward and regal she looked. The silver-and-gold form was striking. "So, your new form. Part of the change you mentioned?"

"I believe it is."

"Any changes to your thought patterns, your instincts?"

Talia turned a baleful eye on me. "Apart from the overwhelming desire to slaughter anything that remotely resembles a lithid, no. Though I feel a profound distaste for Vernon and his necromancy I'm reasonably certain wasn't there before. There's also part of me that feels drawn to those poor creatures in Region 6."

"To what purpose?" I asked.

"Absolution."

"Huh." I cocked my head. That sounded almost Templar-ish. "So that flame wasn't just fire. It's probably most effective against both eldritch monsters and the undead."

"There's something else." Talia's brows furrowed as she focused. All at once, she began to shrink, her color darkening, eventually turning black with streaks of brown around her chest. Her chest jutted out, and her pointed ears grew rounded and floppy.

When the change was complete, Talia looked nothing like a wolf. Rather, she resembled the meanest Rottweiler I'd ever seen. "I believe the power read my intent. Or your nature."

"You can change at will?"

"Mana permitting."

Not having to hide her regardless of what role I was playing made things a hell of a lot easier. But, there was still a long road ahead of us. And one more question I couldn't leave unanswered.

"What made up your mind?" I asked.

Talia looked away. "Is the answer important to you?"

"Yes."

My summon took a seat in front of me. "From the beginning, there is much about you that has given me pause. One moment, you seem capable of great kindness and benevolence. The next, you are brutal and cruel. You take great effort to hide these extremes—your kindness, your cruelty. I have spent much of our time together attempting to ascertain which side is the act."

Her expression was indecipherable. "But during our battle with the lithid, I saw much. Of your memories, your life. Your nature. And I believe I finally have my answer."

"You don't have to say it," I cut in, dark shame clouding my mind. If she'd seen the same memories I had, there was no point in dancing around it. She knew what I was.

"Only after did I realize I was asking the wrong question. You are not one or the other, Matthias. You're both. And that is not such a bad thing for an ally to be," Talia finished.

Was that even possible?

I wasn't certain.

Still, I knew one thing for certain. "I'm glad to have you with me, Talia. As an ally." I held a palm straight out, and she pressed her head against it.

"And given the fact that it is bad form to start an alliance with a secret..." Talia reached toward her shoulder and withdrew something.

I stared in shock. Not at the fact that her new form apparently included an inventory—but at the small black sphere in her mouth.

"You killed the lithid. The core dropped for you," I realized.

Talia placed the monster core on the ground before me. All relief I felt at not ever having to deal with or think about the lithid again faded away. She lowered her head and let the sphere drop the last inch. It clinked to the ground, rolling in my direction, before it stalled at my feet.

"You intended to use it as a summon. And while I'm certain this experience dampened your enthusiasm somewhat, our circumstances remain the same. So, the question is," Talia gave me a serious look. "What do we do with it?"

CHAPTER THIRTY-THREE

It always came down to the same question. What, exactly, was I willing to risk for power? My path through the system seemed expertly designed to constantly push me to the brink of what I was willing to tolerate, tossing out little tidbits to reign me back in if I ever drifted beyond that point.

<Eldritch Favor> was a particularly egregious example.

Without it, I had zero interest in the lithid. None. Nada. The psychological trauma it could dole out on a lark simply wasn't worth the risk. Even the idea of being in the same room as Iris made me uncomfortable after what it put me through.

And then there was my mother. If she'd buried what happened in my childhood for this long, this was absolutely, undoubtedly, the worst possible time for me to bring it up to her while she was on the road to recovery. Which meant the poignant mix of horror and curiosity would remain nestled in the back of my mind, positioned to make me doubt myself at the worst possible time.

Putting that aside for a moment, the lithid's potential for collateral damage was astronomical. Far greater than any summon I'd held thus far. If the lithid rebelled—even in a small way—around my friends and family, the harm done from even a brief encounter could be catastrophic.

I could avoid using it around them at all costs, but some crossover was inevitable.

And if I couldn't control it perfectly, and it decided it was hungry?

No. Not worth it.

Enter <Eldritch Favor>. The fact that I was stuck with it regardless of if I selected the lithid as a summon felt as if the system was blatantly waggling sunk cost fallacy in my face, mocking me for even considering the possibility of disposing of it.

Even the description itself felt tailored to me:

<Despite their cruel nature, lithids are surprisingly good sports that delight in finally finding an entity capable of beating them at their own game. Most eldritch creatures you encounter will remain passive unless attacked. Eldritch conjurations or summons will gain bond more quickly. This effect will be magnified exponentially if the conjuration or summon is a lithid.>

It emphasized that the boon wouldn't mindwipe the lithid or perfectly enslave it to my will. Rather that the experience had marked me to other eldritch creatures, and that lithids were powerful enough that they appreciated being bested in battle and would intrinsically know that I'd managed such a feat.

It was a fucking mess, and I was no closer to a decision than I had been fifteen minutes ago, when Talia gave me the core.

"It is rare, to see you this indecisive," Talia observed.

"I can't—it's like bringing a loaded gun into my life that I can only store on the kitchen table. Will it help me defend myself? Yes. Is it powerful? Definitely. Does it have the potential to bite me in the ass? Abso-fuck-ing-lutely."

"It's difficult to believe I am about to say this, but," Talia hesitated. "When you summoned me for the first time, it was clear you were perfectly willing to dismiss me if necessary. You were exceedingly careful, and had I not given you the correct responses, I have no doubt you would have followed through."

"That's different." I extended a hand out to her in frustration. "Smart as you were, you were also pissed. Which made it far easier to read your intentions and motivations. I'm not certain how I'm supposed to feel out a monster with the capacity to read my every goddamn thought and potentially edit my memories."

"It might not be as all-powerful as you're giving it credit for," Talia countered. "Both times it manipulated me, I was pulled into a dream state almost immediately. Same for you, if I understand correctly."

When I nodded, Talia continued. "Then it's possible its abilities may be drastically reduced when we are not in its thrall. Or that they may be entirely different from the creature we encountered. My mind was unaltered, but my abilities—in both forms I've inhabited—have been drastically different from those of my original body."

"Right." I considered that. "The summoning process tailors the summon to the User."

"Now that I consider it, that might make it more threatening, rather than less," Talia hedged.

She wasn't wrong, but I gave her a sour look anyway. "Changing your mind?"

Talia shook her head. "I simply wish to avoid making an instinctual reaction, biased by stirred up strife from the experience we just had."

I hated the idea of it. But Talia was right. This situation was as personal as it got. Any attempt to say otherwise was just lying to myself.

"Okay." I picked up the core and held it out in her direction. "The lithid got us both with its initial hallucination and memory edit, but I imagine it had quite a bit of time to prepare. Once we broke out of it, it more or less focused on me."

Talia's eyes lit up. "Yes. It only attempted to assail me directly after you'd fought it off, and I presented the larger threat."

"It made a few choice comments about preferring me as a... victim. But I can't imagine a being with this thing's capabilities getting tunnel vision. If it were able to, it would have targeted us both. Separated us like it did at the beginning. I think it's more likely that once we actively engaged it, it could only focus its mind fuckery on one of us."

"Then..."

"We're doing this." I squeezed the core tightly, a deep knot of anxiety tightening as I came to the decision. "But there are conditions. We both get a veto before I make a final decision. And we proceed with caution. Both of us."

Talia scowled.

"This isn't what you wanted. I get that. But I don't see another way." I shrugged. "If it's too much, you still have that veto."

"No. No." Talia lowered her head between her paws in a pout. "If we are going to rely on each other, I cannot shirk the parts of that responsibility purely on the basis of finding it dreadful and unpleasant. And disgusting. And macabre."

"Any more adjectives to throw out?" I asked, hiding a smile.

My summon showed a flash of teeth. "I'd prefer to get this over with. When are we going to do it?"

I looked around. Though the room was ordinary and bare, I didn't like the idea of summoning the lithid in its own territory. Even if it was mostly inconspicuous.

"Let's head down to the second floor. I need to make some adjustments beforehand."

———

Matt

Level 13 Ordinator
Identity: Myrddin, Level 13 ???
Strength: 6
Toughness: 6
Agility: 19+
Intelligence: 17+
Perception: 8
Will: 21
Companionship: 3
Active Title: Born Nihilist
Feats: Double-Blind, Ordinator's Guile I, Ordinator's Emulation, Stealth I, Awareness I, Harrowing Anticipation, Page's Quickdraw, Vindictive, Squelch, Acclimation.
Skills: Probability Cascade, LVL 3. Suggestion, LVL 18. One-handed, LVL 16. Negotiation, LVL 11. Unsparing Fang (Emulated), Level 10, Bow Adept, LVL 3.
Boons: Nychta's Veil, Eldritch Favor, Ordinator's Implements,
Summons: Audrey — Flowerfang Hybrid, Bond LVL 5. Talia — Eidolon Wolf, Bond LVL 9
Selve: 50,329 (-100 per week)
Skill Points Available: 0. **Feat points available:** 2.

Not even the tranquility of the lakeside greenery on the second floor was enough to calm my nerves. It didn't help that I was once again dumping my points into willpower—a stat of highly specific usefulness at best—and I still couldn't find anything in the feat list that would allow me to get around the suits' mandatory geas. The geas presented a serious problem, as it prohibited me from reporting my findings to anyone, and more importantly, lying to their leadership.

If I couldn't find a way to circumvent that limitation, the goose was cooked, and any chance of getting Nick out went clear out the window.

After I read through the available feats for the fifth time, **<Jaded Eye>** cackled.

There's nothing here. Same as the last four times. At this point, it's just stalling.

There were a few mages I could go to for help. Astrid and Astria ranked at the top of the list, or maybe an alchemist if I could find one. That was an issue for later, however.

Before I could talk myself out of it, I withdrew the monster core from my inventory and *pulled,* feeling the sphere grow smaller as I absorbed the soul within.

CHAPTER THIRTY-FOUR

Imagine, for a moment, the darkest secret you have. Something that haunts you, lingers in the forefront of your mind like an incomplete shadow. It should be something you are desperately afraid of, something you've managed to live with by shoving it as far down and deep as possible.

You know the one.

Now imagine that your hand has been forced and you're now required to reveal that secret in front of everyone you care for. Despite knowing how their opinion will change, imagining the looks on their faces.

That was how it felt, summoning the lithid. Like fighting through a wave of never-ending shame, reaching the bottom and somehow finding more.

<Summon Slots Available. 3 of 3.>
<Congratulations. You have successfully called a summon. As an aspect of your class, this creature is a unique variant crafted with a combination of your traits and its original abilities. It will level when you level, share a portion of experience earned, and its allocations will reflect yours.>
<Summon added: Abrogated Lithid, Bond Level 20.>

A swirling gray mass of orange and black exploded before me, wind pressure pounding against my armor and knocking me to the ground. The second floor's serene blue sky filled with clouds, a spiraling wind funnel descending to the summon's point of origin.

"It shouldn't be able to attack!" Talia shouted in my mind.

"I don't think it is. Doesn't make sense with how high its bond started," I responded in the same manner, our surrounding environment far too tumultuous for anything more than telekinetic communication. As if to directly contradict me, the wind picked up speed, rampant gusts competing to lift me off the ground.

I looped my arm around an upraised root, anchoring myself to a nearby tree.

"Release it before it's too late!" Talia said, her panic ringing clear.

"If it gets worse. Just hold on a little longer."

When I looked back toward Talia, I saw her clinging to the tree beside me vertically like a squirrel, shooting daggers in my direction. Her claws were dug deeply into the tree, but she was clearly slipping. The wind grew even more intense and one paw came free.

I mentally prepared to release the summon.

Then the wind died. An eerie silence fell over the clearing.

A shadow fell over me, and I looked up.

Less than a foot away, a silhouetted figure towered over me. Where it had once reminded me of viscous motor oil before, its skin was tinted dark blue, its reflective aspect of now bringing to mind a dark ocean, or a moonlit night.

Slowly, it raised a hand and waved. "Hi."

Hi?

The panic in my mind slowly eased as I shifted to my feet, studying the summoned version of the lithid carefully. It had no facial features to speak of, and the silhouette didn't register as female as it had before. It read more androgynous than anything else, its voice equally in between. Strangely enough, it sounded nervous.

"Talia," I called back, refusing to look away from the lithid for even a moment. "You good?"

"Apart from the *several* nails I left behind in the tree? Yes." Talia sounded genuinely annoyed at the loss.

"I'll resummon you later." Subconsciously, I straightened my back. As petty as it sounds, I didn't like that the lithid was taller than me.

Suddenly, it shifted form, legs and torso shortening until it stood half a head below me.

My eyes narrowed.

Now that I was looking for it, I could feel a subtle vibration from **<Ordinator's Emulation>**.

"You are welcome to try. It would take you a long time to learn in your current state and require significantly more mana than you possess." The lithid's statement was oddly candid, stating the reality without rubbing it in.

I waved it off. "That's not—" I stopped. It should have known that wasn't what I was trying to achieve. "You stopped reading my mind?"

"I sensed you didn't like it." The lithid inclined its head toward Talia. "She doesn't either, but as she's also fantasizing about eating me, turnabout is fair play."

"That's a lie," Talia snarled.

Still, this level of cooperation wasn't what I expected.

"Can you isolate how deeply you look?" I asked.

"Yes," the lithid confirmed.

"Read my surface thoughts again."

I braced myself and turned my focus inward. Now that I was looking for it, the intrusion felt like a whisper, a tiny spectator lodged in the depths of my mind. When I felt confident I could detect it again, I told the lithid to sever its connection with Talia and me, and the feeling of being watched receded.

There was an underlying sense of anticipation as it leaned closer.

"Well, you already know why we're here." I leaned slightly away.

The tiny spectator popped into the back of my mind again.

"No," I scolded. The spectator receded immediately, and the lithid huffed in frustration.

"How am I meant to respond correctly when I don't know someone's motivation?" it whined.

"The same way as every other being," Talia growled. She crossed over in front of me as she had during the battle, acting as a shield. "You guess."

"Start by explaining why you seem entirely different from before," I added.

"Oh!" The lithid smiled. Or at least, I think it smiled, from the way its gelatinous cheeks seemed to stretch. "Because I'm not hungry anymore. It's very nice. Before I was a summon, I was starving constantly."

Talia and I looked at each other. I studied the lithid warily. "You're not hungry now?"

"No. Well, I could eat. But it isn't remotely the same."

"For suffering," Talia said flatly.

"Not just suffering. Catharsis tastes far better and tends to be better for the host. But it's harder to achieve, and most hosts break long before we can get to that point." The lithid shifted from side to side and shot me a series of nervous glances.

I sighed. "What?"

"Just, I'd love to know what you thought of my work."

"Your... work?"

The lithid nodded vigorously. "It was more... mean-spirited than it needed to be, perhaps. Because of the hunger. But I was very proud of it. It was some of my best, I think. Pathos, coupled with self-realization and growth. I really let the muse run wild."

The verbiage and persona suddenly clicked.

I felt the vein in my forehead begin to pulse. "Jesus Christ."

"What?" Talia glanced between us, unsure of what she was messing.

"It's an *artist.*"

"Aw." The lithid approached me. When I held out a hand to stop it, it settled for hugging itself excitedly. "It means the world hearing that from you!"

"I'm lost," Talia said dumbly, unknowingly cutting off my scathing retort.

"Explain it to Talia." I stepped aside, not trusting myself to refrain from throttling the creature.

Out of the corner of my eye, I watched as the lithid crouched down in front of Talia's face, planting its hands on its knees. "Ah. Right, a wolf wouldn't have a lot of experience in that regard."

"Don't talk down to me, wretch—"

"Art is a living being's attempt to imitate the objects and events of life. The audience—or rather, those witnessing the art—can experience a variety of emotions and feelings through the eye of the artist. However, some emotions have to be earned. We cannot, for example, simply be told the protagonist is victorious. We have to see them struggle to attain that victory, feel empathy for their pain, to truly feel the magnitude of the victory once they overcome it."

A wave of irritation washed over me.

What an asshole.

It took Talia a second to get it. When she did, her lips pulled back and she unleashed a full-throated growl, taking a threatening step toward the lithid. "You used my pain, my *tragedy,* as fodder for your *art*?"

"I did my best, considering the source material." The lithid shrugged, oblivious to the growing anger of the wolf. "It's difficult to draw water from a stone. The system didn't give you much of a backstory. 'The mother who outlives her children' trope is *so* cliché."

Talia dove forward, claws outstretched, snapping and snarling as the lithid danced around her, shouting in surprise. It dodged around the clearing, swearing loudly as Talia pursued it. Talia was faster, but the lithid was more mobile, creating a chase that looked very much like a matador evading a bull.

It'd be wise to stop it. And I would.

In a moment.

It was easy enough to fill in the blanks. Most lithids probably started out similar to this one. More symbiotic guides than parasites, looking to draw from the release that came from a deep emotional revelation. But when the host died, they turned nastier over time, drawing nourishment from suffering instead, gearing their delusions toward it. As much as I wanted to believe the lithid was deceiving us, it wasn't. If it was trying to ingratiate itself, it was doing a terrible job. Of course, it could know that and be playing it against the grain to achieve the same ends, but I suspected that wasn't the case.

Because I was pretty sure I knew why our bond was so high. Why it was so pleased with my recognition and delighted to see me, even when the hunger was twisting our perceptions. Something Talia said echoed in my mind.

"Enough. Both of you," I said, putting plenty of authority in my voice. The two of them stopped next to the lake, still staring each other down.

"Lithid," I called. It returned to me, glancing backward at Talia as it walked, nearly stumbling over the same root I'd clung to when I'd summoned it.

"She is completely unreasonable," the lithid huffed. It cocked its head at me. "Have you made your decision?"

"Not yet. I still have several questions."

"Ask away." It seemed pleased to be interrogated, somehow.

I held out a finger. "How much of the abilities you displayed have you retained?"

"In a realm of Flauros, most of them," the lithid confirmed. "Simple manipulation and cerebral deep dives are easy enough to perform on the fly. I can possess simple minds easily and use the host as a weapon. Sapient minds are more difficult, scaling to a significant degree contingent on the host's intelligence. The more in-depth hallucinations take a significant amount of preparation, as does detailed duplication of a particular being."

I raised an eyebrow. I'd expected its abilities to be somewhat nerfed, but this made it an incredible asset within a dungeon or similar analogue.

"Outside a realm of Flauros?" I asked.

"This is just my guess, as I've never existed outside a realm. But I should still be able to perform surface level mind-reads and possess less-powerful, non-sapient hosts."

When I thought of Ellison, my mind ticked over a dangerous possibility. "Could you use a duplicate form on the outside?"

"I'm not certain." The lithid mused. "It's unlikely I'd be able to retain the form for a significant length of time. Slightly longer if the host was willing—possession will work similarly."

After processing as much of that as I could, I saved the more outlandish ideas for when I had time for more detailed theory crafting.

I ran a hand through my hair. "Before, you said you were a little hungry. I'm concerned about that. It may have been reset for the moment, with your death and resurrection, but what's to stop it from getting to the point it affects your personality."

"Totally reasonable," the lithid said in a schmoozing tone that grated. "I don't remember much from when I was born, but I do remember the hunger. It was far worse than it is now, and if I do get hungry... well..."

"Spit it out." I barked.

It put two fingers together in an oddly childish gesture. "If you could just... let me dwell within something or someone you're about to kill, that would satisfy me immensely," the lithid said shyly.

I stared at it in horror. Talia made a gagging noise.

"If that's too much—"

Slowly, I put a hand over my face. "No, no, *why not?* You can eat their suffering, then Audrey can devour the corpse! The buffet is stocked for everyone's dietary needs!"

"I've upset you," the lithid realized glumly.

"Leaving that... disquieting.... request alone for a moment," Talia said, "the mechanics interest me. You can dwell within someone without possessing them? In the outside world as well?"

"Of course," the lithid said, as if it was the most normal thing in the world.

"And they would remain unaware of that?" Talia pressed.

"It's very unintrusive," the lithid confirmed.

Picking up on what Talia was driving at, I felt a small surge of anticipation. "And you'd be able to hear what they're saying?"

The lithid suddenly clapped its hands together, making us both jump. "Oh! Yes, I'd be an excellent spy."

"Are you male or female?" I asked suddenly. Talia gave me a questionable look, and I shrugged. It had been rattling around in my head for a while, and referring to human-esque creature as "it" felt degrading somehow.

"Both. Neither." The lithid placed a hand under its chin. "Though I really ought to be male, considering."

"Considering what?" I asked dryly, not sure if I wanted to hear the answer.

"Well, you already have a female summon. The plant is both, but looks and sounds feminine. Add another female to the roster and people might start getting the wrong impression."

"She's a wolf!" I exclaimed.

"He's a human!" Talia said simultaneously, equally put off.

The lithid shrugged. "Doesn't matter. They'll still talk."

"If anyone knows about all three of you at any given time, we'd have far more serious problems," I argued, feeling stupid for how heated I felt.

"Judging from the memories I looked through, a few gods know already. And while the majority are complete degenerates, they've come a long way from the wild days. Wouldn't want to screw yourself out of a boon or favor due to an optics issue."

"Jesus. Just be whatever you want."

"Male," the lithid confirmed. Its form shifted to reflect the change. Its body was slim but muscular, a figure suspiciously similar to my own.

"Talia?" I prompted her.

Talia stared at the lithid with distaste. "As much as I'd like to say otherwise, he is too valuable to turn down."

The lithid hopped up and down in excitement. "Then, I'm in?"

"Not quite." I studied him, dreading giving the question voice. "Our bond is exorbitantly high. Audrey started at one, Talia at zero. I need to know why our bond in particular is so elevated."

"Oh." The lithid shrunk back. "I was going to wait and address that when the time was right. I can't tell you later?"

"Now or never," I reiterated.

"Before I say anything," the lithid hedged, "bear in mind I have a solution for your geas issue."

That got my attention immediately. "And?"

"I'll tell you when the time comes." The lithid bowed his head apologetically.

I gritted my teeth. "Fine. Keep your leverage. Now answer my question."

"The system didn't force me to admire you, or instill loyalty. In truth, I've been waiting to meet you for a long time. But I am, in some ways, a slave to my nature. You had to run the gauntlet first. Even though you... well... you made me." The lithid was the very picture of anxiety, his arms held close to his body, shuffling from foot to foot as he waited for my response.

Foul creatures sustained by hate and regret, formed in the void between worlds when a sapient being commits the unforgivable.

There were plenty of things I wanted to ask about, but I wasn't sure I could handle the answers. I breathed out as the small part of me that still argued for banishing the lithid withered and died.

"Pick a name. We have shit to do."

CHAPTER THIRTY-FIVE

The lithid had chosen "Azure." One degree of separation away from calling itself blue. Since it was—you know—blue.

I shook my head. Creatives came up with the worst names.

"Earth to Matt?" Kinsley prodded me sternly. "You'd give me hell if I was zoning out during prep."

"Can't plan if I can't think," I countered. Realistically, though, she was right. I was having trouble focusing on anything since the lithid encounter. And my hands were still shaking.

We were back at the warehouse I'd found her in. As a hideout, it seemed as good of a place as any. The windows were all boarded up and high off the ground. Difficult to access. Whoever owned it was either outside the city when the dome came down or had abandoned the property, as everything was exactly as we'd left it. Kinsley had been here for nearly a week and no one had found her.

Most importantly, neither Miles nor the suits knew it existed.

"Think later." Kinsley did a slow circle around the facility. "Ditched the computer, shotgun, and everything that could be tied back to me. A few things that probably couldn't, but I got rid of them just in case."

"Fridge is gone," I noted wryly.

"Bought it from the from the store. Not worth the risk, and it's not like you'll be spending that much time here. Hopefully."

"Hopefully," I repeated, barely paying attention.

"Jesus, Matt. Don't sound so confident."

I rubbed my eyes, trying to wake myself up. "Depends on how many resources they're willing to dedicate to vetting me. We should know in the first forty-eight hours how difficult this is going to be."

"It'll be fine," Kinsley insisted. "Anyway, I brought in a cooler and a couch I bought from a few different places. Enough to make it looked lived in."

I had to marvel at the difference between the scared little girl I found here and the guild leader she'd transformed into. Even in a pair of sweats and a t-shirt, Kinsley radiated authority. If she survived the next few years and made the leap to adulthood without cracking, she was going to be terrifying.

I nudged a medium-sized, pink, polka-dotted dog bed positioned next to the bed with the toe of my shoe and snorted.

Kinsley rolled her eyes. "Fuck off. It was the nicest one I could find. The only one I could find. Lotta people picking up dogs these days."

"Oh?" That was either heartwarming or horrifying, depending on how cynically you wanted to look at it.

"Another merchant was talking about it."

"What happened with the group that was giving you problems?" I asked, though I already knew something had happened in her favor. The quest that tasked me with finding more merchants for the Merchants' Guild had been marked completed a few hours ago, despite no action on my part.

"Got tired of the standoff and had them all assassinated," Kinsley said blandly.

I stared at her, my eyes narrowing.

Kinsley gave me a flat look. "Not sure what's more alarming. That you're out of it enough to take that seriously, or that you think I'm capable of it. Whatever. You were right. They folded like cardboard after I walked away from the table. Started reaching out to me individually, trying to cut a deal for themselves."

"A situation you used to pressure the holdouts and play them against each other?"

"Of course."

"Nicely done." I held out a fist, and she bumped it absentmindedly.

"I fucking hate this place," Kinsley said, glancing at the vent next to the shelves.

"Barring some disaster, this is probably the last you'll see of it." I shrugged. "Safer that way. You mentioned the door power had changed? You can use it more now?"

"Once an hour." Kinsley winced. "I've been trying not to lean on it heavily and save it for emergencies, but I *have* been using it. Should still be able to get you from here to the apartment and vice versa the majority of the time..."

"I don't expect you to lock yourself out of a key ability for me. I'll try to give you an hour lead time when I'm coming and going."

"Yeah." Doubt filtered into Kinsley's expression. "Matt, are you sure you don't want me to send some people with you tomorrow? I'd use a proxy to hire them so there's no direct connection. The best guys I can find. People who've been doing this a lot longer than either of us."

I shook my head. "Can't risk it. It doesn't matter how good they are. If they make a single mistake, or there's an ability in play we don't know about, we're blown before we even know their location. Myrddin needs to look like a solo operator on the run, low on resources. Angry, frustrated, with just a hint of desperation."

Kinsley nodded slowly. "It's weird how you talk about him like he's someone else."

"Just compartmentalizing." I spotted a light patch in my shadow, a passing shimmer of blue before it vanished.

Azure wasn't the kind of summon I could just bring in on the spot. Or in the city at all for that matter. The lithid's summoning process was flashy and eye-catching, and probably needed to be done in Flauros if I wanted to keep it completely concealed. So I was in the unfortunate situation of having to keep him summoned and on me. Azure had suggested staying rooted in my shadow as an alternative to concealing him in an implement, and so far, he was mostly invisible.

Kinsley bit her lip. "I'm worried about my dad. He's not built for this. Even if he's prioritizing 'saving' me, he's gotta be running on empty by now. It's only a matter of time before he breaks down."

"Hey. You've taken care of my family. I'll do everything I can to take care of yours." I squeezed her shoulder, trying to impart a sense of confidence without promising anything. If things went south with the suits at the wrong moment, there was a chance Vernon's fate would be out of my hands entirely.

Judging from the sad smile, Kinsley knew the score. "Thanks. I hope your friend's okay too."

A grim silence dampened the atmosphere. Everything was up in the air, and despite my predictions and plans, neither of us could be certain how well this would work out. Hell, if the suits had done the math and worked out that Myrddin was the Ordinator, and ended up being a little more short-sighted or less brazen than I predicted, there was a real possibility they might deem me too much of a liability and kill me outright.

"Oh, I finally got a vocation."

Kinsley's eyebrows shot up. "About damn time, considering how long the system's been teasing it. What'd you snag?"

"Anima Seer."

"The fuck?"

"That's what I said."

As I gave Kinsley the rundown, she pulled up her interface and swiped through several windows. "No equipment for it in the vocation tab."

"Figures."

"I swear, every upgrade you get has a sinister twist. Sounds helpful as hell though. Especially when you start leveling it up—and hey." She grinned. "Even if it's trash, I'll finally have a way to funnel you Selve."

"Can't you use quests to do that?" I asked.

"No," Kinsley said, her expression significantly more grumpy than moments before. "It's stupid. I gave you a quest to survive the Transposition, when you were unconscious, testing a smaller amount first just to see if it worked. It went through, but I received an arbitrage warning for assigning a quest that was too easy and got fucking soft-banned from giving quests for three days."

"Another obstruction." I rolled my eyes. "The system *really* doesn't like handouts."

Kinsley tapped her foot. "Well, come on, you bastard, show me the goods so I can pay you."

There was an awkward silence.

I huffed. "Okay, fine. I have no idea how to access it. There was nothing new on my interface, and the associated abilities weren't on my character sheet."

"Did you check your trade screen?" Kinsley said, like it was the most obvious thing in the world.

That was the one place I hadn't checked, as I'd barely used it since the store had come online. Sure enough, there was another icon shaped like an anvil, intersected with an "S."

I focused on it and a dropdown appeared.

<Vocation: Anima Seer, LVL 1.>
<Vocation Skills: Oracle's Mark, Guiding Vision, Astral Reconnaissance, Contract Generation.>
<Vocation Feats — N/A>

I focused on each of the skills in turn.

<Oracle's Mark: Permanently applied to any individual the User touches.>
<Guiding Vision: Gives the User key insights into another User's class and potential progression paths, so long as Oracle's Mark has been applied, barring interference from certain uncommon feats. The number of charges available scales with vocation level. **Current Uses Available** - 2 of 2.>
<Astral Reconnaissance: Allows the Seer to see through another User's

eyes for a variable length of time, so long as the Oracle's Mark has been applied. This skill will place the Seer into a deep sleep that will last the duration of the scouting period at a minimum. The number of charges available scales with vocation level. **Current Uses Available - 1 of 1>**
<**Contract Generation:** Generates a magical contract for services rendered within a limited scope.>

My dreams of omniscience were crushed for the moment, but the combination of skills and my new summon gave me a hell of a lot more avenues for information gathering than I had before.

I generated a contract for Kinsley, marking <**Guiding Vision**> as the service rendered and leaving the Selve amount blank. When I attempted to activate the skill, her face popped into my mind easily. When I immediately switched gears and tried to pull up Ellison, it drew nothing but a blank. That figured. I'd squeezed Kinsley's shoulder earlier. <**Oracle's Mark**> being retroactive was probably too much to hope for, but I had to try.

Setting that aside, I focused on Kinsley again, waiting until her face appeared in my mind, then fell deeper into the trance.

The resulting overload of information hit me like a tidal wave

CHAPTER THIRTY-SIX

Thousands of lines of text streamed through my vision. It wasn't the void, but I was so blind it might as well be. I staggered on my feet and attempted to catch myself, flailing wildly as rapidly flowing text obliterated my vision. My hand impacted something solid, and I clung to it. I nearly fell several times as I fought an inevitable sense of rotation until it felt as if I was clinging to the handhold upside down, straining against it to keep my feet planted on the floor.

"Matt!"

It took me a second to realize. That was Kinsley, sounding as freaked out as I felt.

Then the floor started to shift beneath me.

"Can't... make anything out," I said through gritted teeth. "It's like it's throwing every merchant ability at me simultaneously. Maybe every ability, period."

"Can you filter it?" Kinsley shouted, her voice unnecessarily loud.

"Don't know," I panted. Thank christ I hadn't tried this on the fly. It would present an obvious point of weakness to anyone who was watching. All they'd need to do was wait for me to read someone and plan accordingly.

"Try," Kinsley urged.

I wanted to, but there was too much white noise to strategize. "What are we even looking for?"

"Uh. Hold on, hold on, let me think."

"Think faster."

Kinsley fell silent, as I experienced the sensation of enduring a rollercoaster without a seatbelt.

"Oh!" she finally said. "I need a way to pad inventory and make it less likely to run out of stock. If that even exists."

At least a third of the text I was reading faded out, the entries rapidly disappearing pixel by pixel. There were still an overwhelming number of entries. They scrolled slightly slower than before but were entirely illegible.

"Be more specific," I said, gagging as my breakfast staged an escape attempt. "I think it's narrowing down the options."

"Um, something that would appeal to crafters."

Nothing changed.

"Too vague," I snapped.

"An ability that would provide a benefit to crafters that sell through me."

The text slowed to a crawl, nearly throwing me off. It was possible to read the options now, though the feats with longer descriptions still slipped past before I could finish them. Still, it was easier to adapt now that my focus wasn't split between reading the options and not falling over.

Slowly, the text began to fade, the real world filtering in. I'd drunkenly clung to a metal trunk across the room from where I'd previously been standing.

Determined not to waste the charge, I closed my eyes and honed in on the text.

<**Knock Off:** A merchant may create duplicated copies of any crafted item. Each copy will erode the quality of the original, along with each cloned copy. Only the original item can be duplicated. Overuse will cause the original item and copies to disappear. This cannot not be used on Legendary items, Artifacts, or currency.>
<**Requirements:** This feat is visible at Level 45 and can be acquired at Level 46. No pre-requisite feats or stat thresholds.>
<**Cost:** 14 feat points>
<**Additional information has been revealed through Guiding Vision!**>
<**Additional information:** This feat pairs particularly well with several feats unlocked within a ten-level range. Under no circumstances should this feat be used on health potions. If this feat is used on a Runebook, only the original copy will retain intrinsic power.>

I rattled off the information to Kinsley as I read, not trusting myself to commit the description to memory.

Gravity seemed to kick back in, and I staggered to the couch, the sense of nausea fading far more slowly than I'd like. Kinsley was still jotting the last of what I said onto a notepad she'd found god knows where.

"Absolutely excellent. Especially if the decrease in degradation is small. *Every* merchant is going to take that, but I have one hell of a lead, and any crafter who isn't an idiot will buy in if I'm not too greedy with the split," Kinsley muttered. "Better to offer generous deals and lock down exclusivity while I can. But hot damn, that's expensive."

I nodded and immediately regretted doing so as the world nodded with me. It was by far the most expensive feat I'd ever seen. I had to wonder if it was due to the obvious benefit of the feat itself, or if the price of feats at higher levels was significantly inflated.

"Not to sound like an ungrateful ass, but was that all?" Kinsley asked, peering over her notepad.

Right. **<Guiding Vision>** was supposed to give me a more profound insight into the class and ideal progression, not just info on a single feat. I vaguely recalled long blocks of text in the original scrawl that were too drawn out to be feat descriptions, but the blocks themselves were utterly indecipherable.

"Just that, I think. Not sure why it shafted me on the rest."

"From what I've heard, and my own personal experience—" Kinsley jotted down a few more notes, then placed the notebook in her inventory. "—Vocations are god fucking awful at the start. And while that might have been somewhat pointless if the feat was cheap—like obviously I'm going to take a perk that good—it's anything but. That one level between visibility and being available for purchase would have screwed me if I didn't know it was coming. Could have taken six more levels to unlock."

I cocked my head. "Yeah, I see how that's useful."

"Is this going to be a Matt thing, or a Myrddin thing?" Kinsley asked.

"Definitely Matt. It'd be wasted on Myrddin."

"Hoped you'd say that. I'm gonna give you 25k for each member of the Merchants' Guild you do this for. Some mercenaries too, if they're willing to extend their exclusivity."

"Give me a second to recover before you start merchandising me," I grumbled.

Kinsley pressed on as if she hadn't heard me. "I'll pitch the Adventurers' Guild on it as well. The more people we get you in front of, the faster you'll level the vocation, and the better off we'll be."

I agreed, though Kinsley was still thinking faster than I could manage at the moment. "Your pricing seems overinflated."

"My ass. It's easily worth that, if not more. You need to streamline the process—maybe get a Q and A document for people to fill in so you can have a specific target *before* you go to ear-infection land—but almost everyone with the means would pay to get some of the system's many blanks filled in." Kinsley squinted. "Hell, tons of people would probably throw money at you just for the additional information section alone on feats they already have. And you should *absolutely* raise the price of that motherfucker when it levels and you gain more functionality."

I said nothing, as my thoughts returned to the imminent meeting with the suits.

"Don't die, Matt," Kinsley said. "Seriously. None of this matters if you screw up and croak. These people aren't messing around."

"Good talk." I staggered to my feet, vision still swimming. "I'm gonna go find a bucket."

"Don't let them get a rise out of you," Kinsley called after me.

"Yeah yeah—where the hell is it? I could have sworn there was one around here."

Kinsley glanced away. "I may have tossed the bucket."

CHAPTER THIRTY-SEVEN

When I'd glanced over the contract I'd read the number as 20,000 and was more than happy with that number, considering we didn't know what the ability did. Somehow, I'd missed the extra zero.

Kinsley and I bickered for a while—I accused her of doing the new-money thing of throwing money around irresponsibly, while she insisted 200,000 was chump change and to consider it a retainer.

I left the majority of my User cores with Kinsley when we parted ways. It was common sense to leave the majority of them off my person, considering their inherent value to the suits.

Back at the apartment, I used my vocational ability once more. Iris had stopped in to visit Sae, and I took my sister aside and ran the ability, with the foreknowledge that I needed to sit down first. She was pushing level 5 already, and there was an upcoming feat at level 7 called **\<Intrinsic Diagnostic\>** that would grant a more detailed understanding of the underlying mechanics of items and structures she created, helping to ground any overly fantastical designs she came up with.

She vented for a while about the sudden entourage of grizzled mercenaries who followed her around. After hearing her main complaint—that they mean-mugged anyone who came too close and intimidated people around her—I tuned out of the conversation and let her vent. Even if Iris didn't like it, it was for the best, and I was glad that Kinsley's personnel were taking the assignment seriously.

I knew that everything that happened in the lithid's clutches wasn't real, but that didn't change the fact that it was hard to look my sister in the eye.

After Iris left, I went to the Adventurers' Guild headquarters and searched for Tara—the waitress who'd left me her name—on the social interface. There were multiple Tara Stricklands in Dallas, but only one who lived in Region 14.

The request pended for less than a minute before it was accepted. I was halfway through writing a meticulously edited introduction message when a notification dinged. Tara had messaged first.

<Tara: Hi <3.>

I stared at the message log, not entirely sure what to do now that she'd beat me to the punch.

<Matt: Hey.>
<Tara: How are you?>
<Matt: I'm okay. You?>
<Tara: Fine. Just getting off work. You're up on the penthouse floor, right?
>

It was common knowledge that I lived here now—a new reality that irked me to no end—but it still felt strange confirming my location to a stranger. So, I did what I always did when a line of questioning made me uncomfortable. I dodged the question, employing some of Sae's earlier advice and keeping it casual.

<Matt: Want to go for coffee this weekend? If you're off. Not sure what your schedule's like.>

There was a long pause between the messages, and I scowled. Somehow I'd managed to screw this up already. Before I could beat myself up more, another alert dinged.

<Tara: ooooor, since we're both in the building, we *could* skip the coffee.>
<Matt: There's always boba or tea if you're not a coffee person.>
<Tara: I do like a little variety ;).>

What the fuck did being in the same building have to do with coffee? And did liking variety mean boba or tea would be a better option? How was I supposed to read between the lines here?

<Tara: Hbu? Do you like to mix it up a little?>
<Matt: I'm pretty flexible.>
<Tara: Mmm. I'll pop into the gym to shower and get ready, then message you, so you can send the elevator down to the lobby.>

What the hell? In something of a panic, I left my room and banged on Sae's door. Sae answered, half-awake. "What—Christ, what happened in the dungeon? You're white as fuck."

I shook my head. "The dungeon went fine. I messaged Tara."

"How'd that go?" Sae asked, her expression a mix of amusement and irritation.

"Not great."

I read the conversation verbatim.

Once I'd finished, Sae stared at me in disbelief. "Bullshit."

"I know. How the hell did we get from coffee on the weekend to 'send the elevator down for me'?"

"You being this naive is the bullshit part. Your girl's down-bad. Wear a rubber. Guess I'll go to the money-grubbing imp's for a bit." Sae grabbed her overcoat.

I blocked the doorway. "That was *not* the intended outcome here."

Sae studied me confused, until her eyes lit with realization. "Oh right, you're a prude. Why did you opt in then?"

"When the fuck did I opt in?" I asked, flabbergasted.

"I mean, it's kind of obvious. You didn't say anything when she offered to skip the coffee, and when she asked if you were kinky, you said you were flexible."

"No one was talking about being kinky!"

"Come on, Matt, what did you think 'mix it up' meant in this context?"

"I—fuck me," I trailed off as I read through the messages again.

Sae snorted. "She will if you send the elevator down."

"Not helping." I didn't like feeling this incompetent. And it wasn't like I was bad at reading social cues. If Nick had come to me with the same string of messages, I would have seen it clear as day. It was just harder to read between the lines when I was a part of the equation.

There was a pause, and Sae's expression softened. "Look, relax. It was a miscommunication. Right now, she thinks you're down for a hookup. And yeah, she's being a little aggressive, but we're in the middle of a sustained crisis. There's probably a ton of people looking to relieve stress. Just don't feel pressured to do anything you're not ready for. If you want to salvage this, just tell her you're wiped out but still down to meet for coffee over the weekend. Also, send that message soon. Otherwise, it'll feel like a flake."

"Okay." I walked away, already working on the reply message. I turned back and looked at Sae suspiciously. "You won't tell anyone, right?"

Sae rolled her eyes. "That your dating game is abysmal? Even if we weren't friends, Helpline, you dragged me kicking and screaming out of the darkest place I've ever been. And I've been to some *dark* places. Your secrets are safe with me."

The contemplative look Sae gave me made it clear she wasn't just talking about Tara. And she wasn't wrong. I'd given her a lot of information for the sake of convenience that painted my history in a questionable light. At first, I'd though she was too absorbed in her circumstances to take the reveals at anything apart from face value. But she had noticed. She was just waiting for the explanation.

"Thanks, Sae. Just give me some time. I'm spinning countless plates right now," I finally said. Sae closed the door and I returned to my room, deep in thought.

I needed to decide—either deal her in as I had Kinsley, or come up with another lie for the pile that would better explain the inconsistencies. The main concern holding me back from the former was that I didn't know what Sae wanted, and there was a good chance, with all the chaos, she didn't either.

Kinsley was safe because of her father. That bond was solid. She'd never leave him behind, and the Overseer had emphasized that only one person could escape the game entirely by killing me. As far as I could tell, Sae hadn't even contacted her parents, and there were hardly any people left in the city she had a real connection to.

For now, it was better to keep the role to myself.

Taking Sae's advice, I shot Tara another message.

<**Matt:** On second thought, I'm pretty wiped out. Full docket for the next few days as well. Still down for coffee this weekend if you are.>

The resulting message didn't come in until I was already in bed, falling asleep.

<**Tara:** No worries. Coffee date sounds nice tbh. Saturday?>
<**Matt:** Saturday.>

———

The day of the meeting dawned. Kinsley doored me from the apartment to the hideout as we'd planned, and I'd walked from the hideout to the park.

I was initially worried that my mask's effectiveness had taken a hit and people might recognize me from the video, but the <**Allfather's Mask**> still worked perfectly in that regard.

There was no need to scout Lakeside. I knew the park like the back of my hand. It was a perfect place to study, plenty of space and greenery, and the lack of a playground meant no screaming children.

I stuck to the rooftops instead and spent the lead up to the meeting time scouting the surrounding streets, scanning faces, and looking for any out-of-place vehicles lingering around the spot. The park was large and winding, with multiple discrete exit points—so if they did intend to ambush me, they'd need more than a few members deployed on the ground.

Only, nothing stuck out. Not a single person, Escalade, or suspiciously parked van. Every random passerby passed a quick scan, even as my title grew crankier by the minute.

An oddly dense section of grass within the park stirred. If <Jaded Eye> hadn't screamed bloody murder, I might have dismissed it as an animal. I pulled out a pair of binoculars from my inventory—a new acquisition from Kinsley's payday—and kept them centered on the oddly shaped mound.

My heart raced as I realized it was breathing. The camouflage was insanely good. I could barely make out a forearm and leg. Everything else was a green blur that blended into the grass perfectly.

I spotted several more similarly dense patches of grass behind it, spread out around the park.

I circled again, looking for anything out of the ordinary.

A thrill of anticipation went through me as I spotted a Silver Benz on the top-level of the hospital parking garage, one street over from the park, ten minutes after noon. Clearly out of place, as there was plenty of parking on the lower sections. The lower levels wouldn't provide nearly as good of an overlook. It must have pulled up in the last few minutes while I was scouting the other side. Two people—a man and a woman in plain-clothes—exited the back seat and discretely shut the doors behind them, descending the stairs and taking the crosswalk across the street, entering the park as a pair.

I didn't recognize them. More importantly, they didn't carry themselves with the same air of professionalism as the Users in the tunnel had. That, combined with the utter lack of surveillance, told me the suits were treating this like a simple meet. Sending lackeys to deliver a message.

My focus returned to the Benz. It was still running, front windows cracked slightly open.

If there's leadership present, they're behind the tinted windows, calling the shots from a distance.

It was time to flex a little.

CHAPTER THIRTY-EIGHT

I kept low and approached the car from the rear and to the right, staying in what should have been a natural blind spot, assuming the rearview mirror wasn't positioned strangely. In case it *was* oddly positioned, I cast **<Probability Cascade>** on the Benz, hearing a resulting click as the car's locks released simultaneously.

The gears ground several times as the driver fiddled with the locks.

Before the spell wore off, I opened the side door and slipped into the passenger seat.

"This my Uber?" I deadpanned.

At which point I realized I may have miscalculated. Because while I'd expected someone higher placed, this was drastically more than I'd bargained for. Gray-hair was sitting in the driver's seat, one hand on the driver-side panel the other holding a half-eaten sandwich, staring at me. A drop of brown mustard dripped from the sandwich and landed on his pleated pants. He slowly lowered the sandwich, placing it on the console, and dabbed the mustard off his pants with a handkerchief, as if I wasn't there.

The Benz's front console displayed a screen showing multiple view-points from body cameras within the park. My eyes narrowed. They did have people in place. If I'd scouted within the park instead of outside, **<Jaded Eye>** would have triggered.

Gray-hair folded the napkin and dabbed his face, staring straight ahead, stone-cold. "Did you break my car?"

"No idea what you're talking about." The application of **<Probability Cascade>** had faded by now.

Gray-hair tested the locks. When they worked, he seemed to thaw a bit, adapting the same casual manner I recognized from the tunnel. "Good. I like this shirt. Getting blood out is such a pain." He laughed as if he'd just told the greatest joke in the world.

"It'd be hell on your upholstery."

"In part. The carpets, for certain. The leather though?" He smiled dreamily. "With a little dish soap and water, it wipes right off. But I'm guessing you've already seen your share of blood. Isn't that right, Ordinator?" He stared straight at me, waiting for a reaction.

So, they had connected the dots. That was unfortunate in some ways, fortunate in others. They were less likely to pull anything if they thought I was capable of leveling an entire region.

I ignored him, looking out toward the park. "This could have been a straightforward conversation."

"If it was up to me, I would have handled it that way," Gray-hair said. "The matter was above my paygrade."

Gray-hair wasn't the leader then. Or, at the very least, not the only one. He reached down toward the console. When I bristled, reaching toward my side, he held eye contact and slowly popped a compartment open. There were two bottles in clear view, dark-glass craft beers with a golden label.

He expected this. Or accounted for the possibility.

The feeling of being out of my depth returned.

Gray-hair picked one up and flicked the cap off with his thumbnail and extended it to me. I took it, inspecting the bottle carefully. <Jaded Eye> didn't trigger. I took a precautionary sip, nearly gagging on the unpleasant, acrid flavor. It was like licking a bitter, yeasty, oak barrel.

"We can still have that conversation," Gray-hair observed as he opened his beer in the same manner. "Main difference being, I hold a far higher opinion of you now than if we'd met on a park bench."

"What was going to happen?" I asked, noticing the lithid's blue shimmer in my shadow again. "If I went to the park?"

"The woman you saw leave my car spent her previous life as an institutional psychologist. We still rely on her talents from time to time." Gray-hair took a deep pull from his beer and let out a satisfied sigh.

"She was going to evaluate me."

"Yes." Gray-hair inclined his head. "If you passed and provided the cores as promised? We intended to hash out a deal. Offer to place you under our protection, should you be so inclined."

Not fucking likely.

"Anything?" I sent Azure a mental prompt.

"Hard to say for sure. I'm getting more emotion than direct thoughts. But nothing to indicate deceit," Azure confirmed.

"And if I failed?" My tone was dangerous.

Gray-hair looked completely relaxed. "If she thought you were insane, or a potential liability? Our civilian snipers would have filled you with enough tranquilizer darts to knock out a horse. Then we would have interrogated you for the location of the rest of the cores, eventually disposing of you humanely once we had what we wanted."

A cold chill went through me. Not from the content of the threat, but the matter-of-factness with which he said it.

"What happens now?" I asked.

"You don't strike me as a maniac, so I see no reason to go to plan B. Everything else is a matter of negotiation. So, tell me." Gray-hair shrugged. "What can our humble organization do for the monster that has the entire city jumping at shadows?"

"I don't need your protection," I said, rejecting his earlier notion. "But I can see which way the wind is blowing. Guilds are the future. Unaffiliated Users will begin to hit roadblocks as guilds soak up more and more territory. Fees, locked-down dungeons, conscription. Eventually, it will be almost impossible to make any progress as a solo operator."

Gray-hair chuckled. "Manifest destiny never left our spirits. Damned as we are."

"I have a few options. But at the end of the day, I'd rather play for the winning team." I leaned toward him, matching his smile.

"And that's us?" Gray-hair asked.

"I've been watching your group for a while. Only seen hints and shadows, though I've been looking. From what I've gathered, your people are clandestine, disciplined, and utterly ruthless in your pursuit of power."

"Many dislike that combination." Gray-hair took another pull and placed his beer aside. "Some placed highly in our very organization. There are those who believe that power held in secret is no power at all. What do you think?"

Further confirmation that there was some sort of internal strife. This wasn't just about recruiting me. He was being careful, trying to avoid bringing in anyone that would weaken his side.

Was that why he'd chosen such an eye-catching vehicle? He'd hoped I would find him so he could evaluate me away from his comrades?

I considered Gray-hair. What I knew about him, how he'd acted in the tunnel. The way he'd want me to respond. His entire demeanor and presentation could be burned down to a single idea. Walk softly and carry a big stick.

"Power is power," I finally said. "No matter the face of it, the real movers and shakers are always lurking in the dark."

"Aptly put," Gray-hair said. Then he stirred, seeming to come to a decision. "You have the cores?"

I withdrew the seven User cores and placed them in the still-open compartment.

"Excellent." Gray-Hair withdrew a manila envelope from the side pocket and handed it to me. When I went to take it, he held onto it for a moment. "I assume you prefer your identity remain anonymous, for obvious reasons?"

"It's a necessity."

"Collecting personal information is a key part of the recruitment process. Leverage and whatnot. Fortunately for you, I find this anonymity you've achieved too valuable to throw away. Maintaining it will take some doing on both our parts. I can shield you from that side of things. But there is a cost." Gray-hair released the envelope.

I opened it and slid the documents out. There was an eight by eleven picture of Buzzcut at the top.

Suddenly, I understood. Gray-hair wasn't just aiming to shore up his faction within the suits.

Gray-hair was cleaning house.

I waited, to ensure my voice was steady. "How do you want it done?"

"His home should provide an ideal staging ground. It's well sound-proofed and isolated."

I wasn't sure I wanted to know the details behind the soundproofing comment.

"Anyone else to worry about?" I asked.

"No. He lives alone." Gray-hair rubbed his head, a single strand of hair coming free. "It's all in the dossier. And this is a selfish request, but if at all possible, don't drag it out? In all honesty, I rather liked him."

I should have kept the question to myself. But I couldn't. "What did he do?"

"Created unnecessary problems that require a solution. Does it matter?"

"No."

"You have a week to prepare. We'll meet here the morning after."

Sensing the meeting was finished, I pulled the handle and opened the side door.

Behind me, I heard the whoosh of a car window rolling down. Gray-hair grinned after me, his teeth overly white. "I'll tell Vernon you said hello."

CHAPTER THIRTY-NINE

I doubled back multiple times on the way to the hideout, alternated moving through both low- and high-population areas.

No sign of a tail. But I'd been wrong before.

Emulation hadn't pinged once during the conversation with Gray-hair. He probably didn't use a skill on me directly, but that didn't mean someone hadn't. Someone nearby, in one of the cars behind us. After returning to the hideout, I stripped off my armor and combed through it for a tracker, specifically focusing on the armor's back, underarms, and legs. I checked the **\<Oracle's Mark\>** list to make sure Gray-hair hadn't made subtle physical contact at any point. He hadn't. Subsequently, I dumped the documents on a nearby table and tore open the manila envelope, searching for anything that resembled a tracker.

Nothing.

Still not satisfied, I changed into civilian clothes and sat down on a bench across from the hideout, **\<Allfather's Mask\>** tuned to provide maximum coverage.

I was looking for drive-bys. Anyone who slowed down a bit too much in proximity of the hideout. Problem was, this was a congested area. Cars slowed down all the time. Some man in a pickup rear-ended a Miata and got out, screaming at the driver, who cowered in her seat.

Annoyed, I used **\<Suggestion\>** to convince him she had a gun on her lap. The screaming driver paled and immediately got back in his car, pickup chugging exhaust as it sped around the Miata and through a nearby stop sign, narrowly swerving around oncoming traffic.

"Considering the task he gave you, wouldn't it make more sense if the suit —" Talia started

"Call him Gray, for simplicity," I said. It was overly terse, even for me.

"If Gray didn't bother tracking you until you accomplished the task?" Talia said.

Azure's bright and cheery voice chimed in, grating. *"Wolf-girl's got a point. He knows where you'll be. Not necessarily when you'll be there, but it's a lot easier to keep tabs on a house than a person—"*

"What the fuck happened with the mind-reading?" I interjected. *"Can you do it or not?"*

"I... I mean... the surface has a lot of interference," Azure babbled. He sounded genuinely intimidated by the question. *"I'm sorry. I tried."*

Trying didn't help me.

But I had enough self-awareness to know when I was displacing anger and managed to avoid directing that thought at the lithid at the last moment. It wasn't his fault. Not to mention with the way he revered me, it'd be disturbingly easy to use him as a punching bag, due to the high bond and the fact neither Talia nor I liked him much.

I needed to be especially careful to avoid that.

Even though Azure had put me through hell, all of my summons had a rocky start. Talia wanted to kill me for the death of her pups. Audrey had every intention of eating me alive.

Azure had done what he was effectively programed to do. Touch a nerve. More stomped than touched, but whatever. Punching down on him for acting according to his nature would be nothing more than bullying.

I rubbed my brow, suddenly tired.

"It's okay. I appreciate the honesty. I'd much rather know you don't have something than think you do and be wrong."

Eventually, I gave up and returned to the hideout. I let out all three summons and sat squarely on the couch, lost in thought.

Azure invited Audrey onto his lap, and when the plant accepted, started feeding her meat from the cooler and petting the flowerfang's head. Out of the corner of my eye, Talia sniffed at the pink dog bed. She looked over at me and the lithid suspiciously. When neither of us paid her any mind, she rotated in a circle and laid down.

There was a new quest in my notification screen.

<Quest Received>
Quest: Blood and Intrigue
Primary Objective — Kill the target.
Secondary Objective — Avoid drawing attention, being tailed, and

accomplishing the Primary Objective in any manner that might blow back

on the quest giver.
Threat Level: (???)
EXP GAIN (???)

Time Limit: One Week.
Reward: Possible recruitment into ??? Guild

"Why even bother filling in the quest name?" I complained aloud. "Just put three fucking question marks in every field and call it a day."

"Big meat bad," Audrey scowled and started to say something else before Azure shoved more ground hamburger in her mouth.

On one hand, I was relieved the quest wasn't part of a chain. On the other, it was entirely possible it was a chain.

"Such a simple mind," I heard Azure whisper. "So much potential for fun."

"Hey," Talia barked, fur on the back of her neck standing straight up.

"Fun?" I asked dangerously.

The lithid wilted. "I mean, you told me not to read you or the dog's minds. You didn't say anything about this one."

Fair enough. He'd gotten both my and Talia's hackles up but pointed out an oversight in the process.

I leaned my face on my hand, staring at the new summon. "Do not mind-read any of my summons, friends, or family except for Ellison. Do not attempt to harm any of my summons, friends, or family. Do not manipulate them. Do not feed on them."

Azure deflated. "What if they're already suffering and I just take a nibble?"

I spoke slowly. "Do not *nibble* on my summons, friends, or family."

"But... why? That's so wasteful." The lithid sounded genuinely distraught.

I pinched the bridge of my nose. "Do you know what a conflict of interest is?"

"Yes," Azure sighed heavily.

"Then you get it. I don't give two shits about our opposition, but I want to avoid putting you in a position where you're incentivized if the people around me are hurting."

"So... you're looking out for me?" Azure asked brightly, bumping his shoulder into mine.

"Obviously, you're my highest priority." I rolled my eyes. "Now scoot over? It's a big couch." The lithid did as I asked with no complaint, seeming in oddly high spirits after our talk. After a few minutes, I understood why. There was a bright light as Azure changed forms into a flower-fang, with red coloring instead of Audrey's purple.

I opened my mouth, then hesitated. Audrey seemed delighted with the development. She interwove a vine with Azure's, and they gallivanted around the room as a pair, doing an excellent impression of the grouped-up flowerflangs from the second floor.

"Azure? This should have gone without saying, but—"

Azure popped back into his human form, sulking. "I promise not to imitate you or your summons, friends, or family." Audrey looked equally disappointed.

I considered the implications, if there was anything I was missing. "The rest, yes. Unless I tell you otherwise. But—" I turned my attention to Audrey. "You know Azure isn't a real flowerfang, right?"

Audrey tilted her head, deep in thought. "Yes. Yet, it's... nice. To see another."

Maybe Audrey was lonely. I sighed, hoping I didn't regret this decision. "You can imitate Audrey."

Azure let out a whoop and shifted to flowerfang form.

"Azure is welcome to a wolf form as well," Talia said. I twisted in my seat to look at her, shocked. "What? If we ever go scouting together, it will be more helpful to have two mobile sets of eyes."

That was shockingly pragmatic, considering what Azure had done to Talia. "Fine. But no social use of Talia's form. Don't use her form to talk to anyone besides us."

"Thank you!" Azure sounded delighted, but his interpretation of a flowerfang's smile looked downright sinister.

"Is there a reason you didn't use him to follow Gray?" Talia asked. *"Azure could have easily slipped into his shadow."*

"Gray's high up. And if my read is correct, he's mired in some sort of power struggle. He'll be taking additional precautions." I glanced at Azure, spinning his newly minted vines in something that resembled a dance. *"And even with the bond, I'm not certain how much we can trust him yet."*

"So he's probationary."

"For the moment."

"Do you intend to carry out Gray's assignment?" Talia asked aloud. Azure parted from Audrey, wandering over to hear the answer.

I began to leaf through the dossier. "I'm not going to kill someone just because some asshole snaps his fingers."

"But it'd be so satisfying if you did," Azure commented.

I put the documents down, studying Talia. "There's more than one way to skin a cat. Due diligence is the name of the game here. As tempting as it is to take Buzzcut out, it's entirely possible that might be the worst option. Especially if Gray is planning to tie up loose ends after we do the dirty work for him."

Talia pointed her nose away with an oddly displeased expression. "Then what do we do?"

I returned to the first page of the dossier.

Buzzcut's real name was Cameron Reed. He was thirty-four. Graduate with honors with a major in economics. But the minor was more interesting.

Criminal Justice

That combination screamed one of two things. Forward-thinking criminal, or law enforcement.

"Research," I answered.

CHAPTER FORTY

I went to the local library for a change of scenery.

As it turned out, Buzzcut was a little of column A, little of column B. The dossier covered his career extensively—he was hired by the Austin City Police Department right out of college. Climbed through the ranks with many accolades and no black marks except a few excessive force complaints that went nowhere. Eventually, he hit lieutenant, at which point he submitted an application to the FBI. The interview went well. All signs pointed to him getting in.

Then, out of nowhere, he was slapped with an Internal Affairs investigation for murder-racketeering and fled to Morocco before he could be brought up on charges.

It was easy enough to read between the lines.

Say whatever you want about the FBI, background vetting is one area where they do not fuck around. They will comb through social media accounts, they will knock on doors and talk to that one friend who passed you a joint freshman year. If you "anonymously" put an edgy manifesto on the internet in middle-school, they'll track it and connect it to you. And if you happen to be a corrupt local asshole who's grown complacent, operating with minimal oversight while playing god, or taking kickbacks, or fist-fucking the civil forfeiture cookie jar, they won't just tell you to jog on.

They'll happily kick everything they uncover to someone who won't hesitate to act on it.

I was guessing, but it was a solid leap. Cameron was dirty as hell, and the FBI uncovered the skeletons in his closet and passed the smoking gun to Internal Affairs.

The question was, what was he doing back here when the dome came down?

There was nothing in the dossier to explain the sudden reappearance stateside. Maybe he ran out of money, but I doubted it. Guys like Cameron always find ways to line their pockets, with or without a badge.

Even the concept of a direct confrontation already seemed like a bad idea before I got to the class information. Then it went from bad to suicidal.

Because Cameron wasn't a recon specialist, as my encounters in the alley and coffee place had led me to believe. He was a Level 19 **<Frenzy Tank>**, with all the capabilities that implied and more. Health regeneration, armored skin, increased damage as the fight went on. From the stats, he could easily out damage me to begin with, and the longer a fight went on, the more dangerous he grew. He had a few odd feat choices geared toward reconnaissance—that would help me if it came down to a fight—making the biggest gulf between us a question of stats, but it also meant if I ended up having to retreat, he had a decent chance of tracking me down.

I dropped the documents in disgust, rubbing my eyes. No matter how I decided to go about it, this wasn't going to be easy.

Out of the corner of my eye, I clocked two people approaching me.

No, two people and a child. I flipped one of the pages I was taking notes on and waited. The woman cleared her throat.

I glanced up as if I'd just noticed them.

"Are you Matt?" she asked, smiling a little too wide.

"That's me." I leaned back and stretched, keeping my body language open and unguarded.

They introduced themselves as residents of Region 14 and thanked me for my intervention. I gave them the humble variation of the aw-shucks-don't-worry-I'm-not-a-tyrant response I'd thoroughly mastered after the first ten times I'd had this conversation. Subtly alluded to the fact that I was just in the right place at the right time and that there was a group of people who lived in the region helping me with the decision-making.

I was getting better at it. I'd expected the regional populace to resent me as a carpet bagger. That might still happen once the warm fuzzies faded, but for now, they seemed to consider me as more of a novelty than anything else.

They chattered on about their previous white-collar jobs for a while. The wife was in talent-acquisition, the husband was in real-estate. I pretended to listen. In truth, the parents were forgettable.

Their kid, on the other hand, was interesting. At first, I thought he was hiding behind his mother. Typical kid stuff. But while he was holding her hand, his body was turned away from her and his head panned from the northeast to the northwest sides of the library.

The same reason I sat here. He's watching the exits.

"Who's this?" I asked.

"Oh!" the mother said, as if she'd forgotten he was there at all. "This is our little warlock, Parker."

"Mom," Parker said. He didn't draw it out, just stated it flatly. Then he looked at me. "Hey."

"How's it going?" I asked him.

"Fine," Parker said. He wasn't being rude, just low energy.

I pried gently into the family's circumstances. It was more or less what I'd guessed. The parents had been trapped inside the region, while Parker was stuck outside. The fact that he'd survived the Transposition alone implied that he'd seen some shit, even if he hadn't strayed far. It was a hard situation, and I had to imagine that the power dynamic in the family had turned upside down overnight.

Still, they hadn't forced him to introduce himself, or corrected him for being short. They didn't seem afraid of him either. All good signs.

In a somewhat awkward transition, I steered the parents toward the topic of vocations, leaving myself an opening to introduce mine. When I offered to give their son a reading, they gladly accepted.

I shot Parker a direct message:

<**Matt:** Do you like fighting?>

The kid's eyes widened.

<**Parker:** Huh?>

<**Matt:** I can steer this in whatever direction you like. If the combat stuff appealed to you, that's fine. If not, I can find another way for you to advance.>

The kid bit his lip.

<**Parker:** Mom and Dad don't have a way to make money right now. Whatever pays the most.>

<**Matt:** That's not what I asked.>

<**Parker:** It was awful.>

<**Matt:** Okay. Let me look.>

I did Parker's reading as his parents stood by. Now that I'd managed it several times, I could keep a straight face even as my equilibrium did backflips.

"So, at level five, you're going to get access to a feat called <**Flauros Resonance**>. Dungeon, trials, anything that lets us slip over to the other side is considered a 'Realm of Flauros.'" I made air quotes. **"<Flauros Resonance>** will highlight those realms within fifty yards. Obviously, you don't want to go in solo. Or at all. They're extremely dangerous. But if you're part of a guild—"

"We're not," the mother said quickly.

I continued on, pretending not to notice the social blunder, "—it's the sort of information Users would compensate you well for. And they'd help with the scouting process, so you'd be safe in the meantime."

"Do you know any guilds that would be interested?" the father asked.

"Mind giving me a minute to check?" I asked. The family nodded and stepped a polite distance away.

<Matt: Got another one.>
<Kinsley: I've had exactly three bites of my macaroni and cheese since the last interruption. Three.>
<Matt: And I've learned that I can't study in a public library anymore unless I want to play small-town celebrity. Just keep eating while we talk.>
<Kinsley: Fine. Give me the details.>
<Matt: Real-estate Developer, HR, and a Warlock who can detect dungeons.>
<Kinsley: Jesus. I was about to tell you to fuck off before I read the last one. Any chance we can lose the other two?>
<Matt: Not unless you want to forcefully separate a kid from his parents—>

I deleted the message and rephrased.

<Matt: No. Warlock's a kid. Probably a package deal.>
<Kinsley: Maaaaaaaatt.>
<Matt: idk what to tell you. I can kick them to the Adventurers' Guild if you don't want to deal with it.>
<Kinsley: I want the kid. And a Real-estate Developer wouldn't be a bad idea, considering our circumstances. But HR? Estrada's already up my ass about swearing.>

I motioned for the woman, struggling to remember her name. "Um, Siobhan?"

She left her husband and son behind and leaned over the cubicle. "Yes?"

"When you said talent acquisition, my mind automatically went to HR."

Siobhan smiled. There was something in the expression that was slightly predatory. "Oh no. My job was a bit more... aggressive than that."

"Aggressive how?"

Siobhan looked up at the ceiling, innocently. "Some might call it poaching."

"Okay, thanks."

As Siobhan walked away, I replayed the entire encounter in my mind. She'd been exceedingly polite. Almost milquetoast, to the point I hadn't bothered learning her name. The kid seemed to be putting up with holding his mother's hand, rather than initiating it. She'd been clever to not hold him in front of her. And while I'd found something of value from the reading, there were plenty of other useful feats he had visibility on that Mom probably would have name-dropped if I hadn't taken an interest in the kid.

Jesus, I had to pay more attention. These people were sharks.

<Matt: It's not HR. More like aggressive recruiting. She's a scary motherfucker and a value add.>

<Kinsley: Nice. But you didn't tell her that, did you? You wouldn't believe some of the numbers people from the region are asking for in terms of salary. Like I'm a walking bag of Selve or something.>

<Matt: That sounds like asshole CEO talk.>

<Kinsley: I pay well, dickhead. A helluva a lot better than most guilds. They're getting boat money, just not yacht money.>

<Matt: Uhuh.>

<Kinsley: My macaroni is cold, Matt. Cold and sad.>

<Matt: Shame you don't have a microwave. I'll send them over.>

Kinsley was taking the age-old approach of expanding while the iron was hot and figuring out the logistics later. The Merchants' Guild still didn't have a building.

I waved the family over and gave them instructions to contact Kinsley, then sent them to the hotel lobby. Dad got foggy eyed. Mom was appreciative, but I could tell she was gloating.

Finally. I reached down toward the upside-down note sheet covering the dossier.

"Why are you looking up non-extradition countries?" Miles asked, leaning over the other side of my cubicle and staring at one of the open books with a quizzical look on his face. "It's not like we can leave."

I jumped. Then gave him a death glare. "Research."

"On?"

I rolled my eyes, keeping my lie as close to the truth as possible. "Background on a new hire for Kinsley. Guy claimed to have spent a few years abroad in Morocco. He was evasive about why he'd left in the first place. Seemed shady."

"Well." Miles popped a mint into his mouth. "Morocco *is* non-extradition. But it also happens to be a favorite for undercovers who need to establish an overseas history on the fly. Something to do with the double benefit of their documents being relatively easy to doctor, and their government being notoriously difficult when it comes to information inquests." Miles shrugged. "Guy's probably shady regardless. Better to steer clear. "

I grimaced, as Miles once again unknowingly pulled the rug out from under me. "Thanks for the tip. Did you want something?"

"Yeah. Got the band together." He stuck his hands in his pockets and grinned. "Figured you'd want to meet them."

CHAPTER FORTY-ONE

My first thought, as I followed Miles to the Adventurers' Guild hall, was how oddly cavalier he was. He'd effectively drawn a target on his own back with the presentation, yet he didn't seem worried.

Correction. He *appeared* not to be worried.

Now that I was looking closer, there was a distinct oblong outline under Mile's dress shirt that was probably Kevlar, and he'd mastered that method of looking while not looking. Turning and walking backward while he talked, glancing up every so often and being particularly mindful of corners.

Out of the corner of my eye, I saw two people keeping pace. No way Miles missed them. We had an entourage.

"Anything?" I asked Azure.

"No." Azure sounded puzzled. *"It's like he's a blank. Like there's nothing there."*

Figured.

"You get everyone you wanted?" I asked.

His mouth turned downward. "More or less."

"So that's a no then."

Miles pointed to a bulletin board as we passed it. The header read "MISSING," with an overstuffed collage of pictures attached to what I assumed to be contact names. The pictures ranged drastically in quality. Some were clearly done by professional photographers for graduations, weddings, while others were low dpi images printed on computer paper. The ages of the missing ranged nearly as much. Adults, elders, and children. On this board alone, there were hundreds, many posted directly on top of each other.

More than a few had emails and phone numbers attached. In case other contact methods came online? I couldn't imagine being that behind the curve.

"Creepy overlords did us a favor in some ways, getting rid of the bodies after they made us run the gauntlet. Morgues would be over-loaded, streets lined with body bags, and you'd still probably stumble across one every so often. Problem being, now we don't know who lived or who died." He cocked his head and looked back. "Abandoned, died in the chaos, or was taken."

"There's not a database?" I asked, surprised. It felt so odd that Kinsley's market was still the only site on the intranet.

"Turns out, not all of us have a genius for a mother." Miles delivered the line smoothly, with a nonchalant shrug.

I felt the world grind to a halt. I'd almost forgotten this happened with <Jaded Eye> sometimes when I was on the verge of a panic attack. Only this time, we'd skipped the panic completely.

I stared at the back of Miles' head and screamed. My voice didn't echo. I panted, waiting for the emotion to subside. Then took a deep breath.

Okay. No one knows who set up the site except me, Kinsley, Iris, Ellison, and my mother herself. Ellison doesn't like me, but he hates authority more. All three kids know how to keep their mouth shut. Which means Miles talked to my mother, or he pulled up her record and did the math. The first would be bad. The second is recoverable. Either way, he wants me to know that he talked to her and that she slipped up and gave him information, whether or not that actually happened. It's what I immediately jumped to, and considering her state, she's the point of weakness. Miles is looking for a reaction. If he did talk to her, this gets complicated. We briefly covered what she needed to keep to herself, but Miles is too fucking good at this. It's better to assume she spilled everything. Meaning he knows that the Merchants' Guild started far smaller than Kinsley and I have been leading the public to believe. That's not neces-sarily an admission of guilt, but it doesn't look good. Have to assume he's aware of the fact that we only brought my family in four days before the Transposition.

Factoring it all together—he's narrowed the original members down to Me, Kinsley, and Myrddin. Or just me and Kinsley.

Which is damning. It's obviously me if he's gotten that far. So, what's stop-ping him?

Kinsley. He'd have to burn a lot of political capital to take me off the board right now, but my popularity is nothing compared to hers. She's a saint. If he's right, Kinsley is either an accomplice or an idiot, and no one who's talked to her for longer than five minutes will think she's an idiot. If he has eyes, he's also probably noticed that she's snapping up every mercenary available on the open market.

Miles can't know that Kinsley would never take it that far, but he's likely worried about open war.

He could just kill me.

No. It's Miles. Everyone was angry and scared at the emergency meeting. He could have whipped them into a murderous frenzy, but he didn't. Advised catch and capture. But we stacked the deck too much between the Region 14-Adventurers' Guild Alliance, and our joint popularity. If he did things the proper way, there'd be too many gaps for us to slip through. Following that philosophy, he's probably waiting for an opportunity to disappear me in the middle of the night and interrogate me offsite away from external interference.

I won't break. But that might not matter. Those comments about doubting himself were real. This is personal for him. Cop guilt displacement. He feels like he evaluated Myrddin and failed, and now it's his responsibility to make it right. No way of knowing whether he'll cross that line, but I can't let it get to that point.

But why hasn't he taken me already? Assuming he talked to Mom yesterday, why not wait to throw this in my face until he has me secured?

Oh.

Oh Miles.

If you just trusted yourself, you'd have me, hook, line, and sinker.

Yet, you can't do it. You can't risk the possibility that I'm not who you think I am.

This was a gambit. From the very beginning. If I'm stupid enough to attack you in broad daylight, you brought Kevlar and backup. Simultaneously, you're making a show of parading me around, knowing that if Myrddin is alive, he'll be keeping an eye on his old guildmates. If it really was just the three of us, and we did have a rocky relationship, he won't be happy that I'm helping your Task-force. You're using me as bait, planning to grab him if he comes after me. And if I do nothing, not wanting the timing to seem suspicious, and Myrddin doesn't show, you'll have the final push you need to tighten the rope.

Now. How do I react?

He was watching me. I could see his eyes in the reflection of a nearby mirror. If Feds were waiting in the Adventurers' Guild hall, I was walking into a tribunal disguised as a strategy meeting. I needed to hit him with something completely unexpected.

I needed to get dirty.

Slowly, I stopped, allowing the massive influx of anxiety to erupt. It was difficult at first, taking the lid off for the first time in a decade. When it got this bad, I crawled under my bed and clung to the slats. My safe space. But my safe space was gone. I was nowhere near the apartments. The anxiety overflowed and didn't stop. Pins and needles shot up my back, to my neck. My head hung on its own, and my upper body began to shake.

Tears streamed freely from my eyes. I crooked my head and tried to look at him, then dropped it again. "I nuh-nuh-nuh-nuh—" I clamped down on the stutter.

Miles grabbed my shoulders. "Kid, are you okay?"

"I nu—fuck. I nu—"

I started to hyperventilate, pressing one hand into my collarbone.

Miles' eyes lit in recognition. "Okay. Okay, I got you, you're having a panic attack."

I groaned and looked around. People from my region were staring.

As usual, Miles was fast on the uptake. I watched from the corner of my eye as he waved his guys away and carted me toward a nearby alley, sitting me down on a milk crate behind a dumpster, hidden from the street. A mix of conflicting emotions went through his face. Probably wondering if he was being played.

He was. But not in the way he was worried about.

Miles crouched down, a safe distance away from me. "What do you need? My thirteen-year-old gets these." He ran a hand through his hair. "Sometimes he wants to be wrapped up in something, sometimes he just needs space—"

"Space," I said, gasping for air.

Miles nodded. But he didn't wait for me to regain my breath, my bearings. "What—uh—what set you off there?" He chuckled. "Last conversation we had, you were stone-cold."

I shook my head, still recovering. Then enunciated each word carefully. "I... know. That you're a just doing your job. My f-f—" I clamped down, waited. "My... father was a cop. You have to investigate. Have to ask questions."

"You can talk to me," Miles encouraged. "I'm on your side."

His "good cop" was perfection.

I pursed my lips tightly, then forced the words out. "Thi-thi-thi-this is the longest my mother has been sober in six years. And there's all this pressure, and I'm doing everything I can, but things keep piling up one after another and everything keeps going wrong and... she always relapses eventually."

The words hung heavy between us.

He would know that everything I was saying was true, if he'd done his homework. And of course he had. Because it was Miles.

Miles breathed a long sigh. "Grow through what you go through."

I wiped my eyes. "You've been in the program?"

He shook his head. "My third wife. Heard that on repeat for about a year. That, and 'One day at a time.' For what it's worth, I think your mom's on her way up. She had her chip out on the table at the café where I tracked her down." He pinched the bridge of his nose. "Drinking a coke."

"Did she... freak out, when she realized why you were asking questions?" I didn't have to fake the concern.

"Nah." Miles shook his head. "Honestly, I'm not even sure she knew it was anything more than a casual conversation. She was so proud of what you all built, even though she was trying to hide it. And she didn't tell me anything directly. About the site. I just pieced it together from what she said." He bit his lip, a flash of guilt across his face. "Let's just... call it a day for now. You can meet the guys later."

I sent a mental message to my summon. "Azure. You said before you could copy me easily on the surface, if needed. Because of our bond."

"Oh, um. Yes," Azure answered.

"How sure are you?"

"One hundred percent." Azure chuckled nervously. "I... may have tried it."

"How long did it last?"

"Five minutes, but I ended it early. From the mana drain, I'm guessing I could maintain the form for at least three times as long."

"Good."

CHAPTER FORTY-TWO

It didn't feel great doing this to Miles. Fed or not, I meant what I said. He was a good guy. But this was about survival now. And survival was where I lived.

"No." I struggled to my feet.

"I'm... not sure if I understand." Miles said.

"You're being very patient with me, but I want this over with." I started to walk toward the Adventurers' Guild building. Miles caught my arm and redirected me down the sidewalk instead.

"Come on, the Five Guys down that way just reopened."

"Not exactly hungry, Miles."

"Yes, you're very determined, I can see that." Miles ignored my complaints and continued to push me toward the restaurant. "But be practical. You look like life punched you in the balls and kept swinging after the count. At least go to the bathroom and wash your face."

"It's fine."

"It's not, Matt," Miles hissed. He checked around us before he spoke. "Look. It took a lot to get you in that room. These guys are pros. If they sense weakness, they're not going to give you the time of day."

It was a good half-measure, seeing that there wasn't an easy way for him to get out of this now. He was giving me time to collect myself and prepare for the bus that was about to hit me. While I was in the bathroom, he was going to message his colleagues, tell them to go easy. Some of them might. But he'd probably spent the last few days convincing them, going over the profile. Their first thought would be suspicion. That I'd gotten to him.

"Sorry." I hiccupped.

"No, kid, *I'm* sorry. I was so gung-ho to fix my fuckup, I nearly gave you a heart attack on the street."

"Fuckup?" I asked curiously.

Miles almost said something, then bit it back. "Not your problem."

He stayed by the door while I power-walked to the bathroom. I turned the water on and cleaned my face, but didn't bother with pressing a paper towel against my eyes to reduce the redness. I wanted Miles to remember, while his taskforce slammed the iron maiden home.

"You're terrifying," Talia muttered.

"Was that panic attack real?" Azure asked, clearly about to gush.

I shot Kinsley a message.

> **<Matt:** GTFO. Sanctuary now. Stay there until I contact you.**>**
> **<System Notification:** The previous message could not be sent.**>**

Fuck.

<Squelch>. Had to be.

Miles was seriously doubting himself, but he was too clever to drop his guard completely.

I held my hand out. The shaking had stopped. "We don't have much time. Talia, I need you on standby in case this goes sideways. Stay ready."

"Done," Talia confirmed.

"Azure—" I hesitated.

"Are they friends?" Azure asked eagerly. And I understood why he was asking.

"The gloves are off. Do as you please, so long as it doesn't tip our hand."

"What's our desired result?" Azure was all business now.

I thought about it carefully. "Radicalize the fringes. Find the ones who are convinced I'm the Ordinator, make them overextend."

There was a pause before Azure answered. "If they're too angry, things may turn nasty."

"We want that. It'll keep Miles off-balance and create tension with the skeptics. Deepen their doubt. Report any pertinent thoughts you pick up to me."

"Split them down the middle," Azure mused. *"I like it."*

"Stay sharp. Both of you."

I switched titles, selecting **<Cruel Lens>** from the dropdown. I'd have to work against it here. Force myself to eliminate any of the title's innate ego and smugness. Play against type.

When I exited the bathroom, Miles was waiting with a white cup in his hands, decorated with red. He held it out to me, apologetically. "Milkshake?"

How nice. He'd even bought me a prop.

By the time we'd entered the Adventurers' Guild and climbed the stairs to the meeting area, Miles looked visibly irritated. To our right, there was a glass panel with an endless line of sparring mats. I caught a glimpse of Sara in workout clothes, doing one-handed bicep curls, and waved.

She smiled, set the barbell down, and waved back, then pulled the towel from around her neck and wiped her face.

Hopefully, she was still here when I left. I couldn't drag Miles directly, but I needed to start laying the groundwork to discredit him yesterday.

Miles had selected a meeting room that was all glass, front and back. It lended further credence to my theory that he wanted Myrddin to either see this directly or hear about it secondhand.

There were four of them inside. Three men and a woman. I noted in dark amusement that they looked nothing like I'd imagined. Instead of the standard Fed suit, they were each in some variety of casual-wear.

And from the look of it, they were already arguing. Perfect.

Miles threw the door open. It banged loudly against the doorstop.

"Glad you could join us," the woman said in a dry monotone.

Detractor.

"We got held up." Miles gave her a subtle glare that last a fraction of a second, then smiled. "Thanks for warming up the projector. Since we're running late, best cut the intros short. From left to right, Foster, Cook, Waller, Hawkins."

I sized them all up behind the guise of a friendly nod.

Foster was a dark-skinned man in a black t-shirt and jeans, his head shaved completely bald.

Skeptic.

Cook never quite outgrew the frat phase and had the kind of face that made him look like he was constantly chewing something. His Hawaiian print shirt was unbuttoned around three buttons lower than anyone would reasonably be comfortable with.

Detractor.

Waller immediately returned to his notes, peering through opaque framed Ray Bans at a yellow legal pad. He wore a vest over his t-shirt that looked vaguely bohemian, all random chevrons and muted colors.

Detractor.

Hawkins, wore a simple tank-top and slacks, her blonde hair framed in a short cut bob.

Undecided.

"Everyone, this is Matt. Our behind-the-scenes correspondent for the afternoon," Miles said.

"Hi, Matt." Hawkins' smile reached gigawatt levels as she turned up the charm. She shook my hand in both of her and her touch lingered. "Thanks for taking the time."

"Always heartwarming when the local celebrities pencil in the little people." Cook smirked, giving me a half-wave.

"It was the least I could do, considering the circumstances." I channeled Nick's casual friendliness. Out of the corner of my eye, I saw Miles flag. That regret he felt for railroading me made him my strongest ally in this room by far.

"Waller." Miles snapped his fingers. "You're the expert here. Want to kick us off?"

Waller peered over his glasses at Miles, then his eyes slid to me. "Given the choice, I'd prefer to start with our new addition."

Miles stopped mid-step, genuine confusion in his face. "That's a little unexpected. Matt is a guest."

"We can theorize all we want, but it's no substitute for someone who knew the man." Waller jotted something down. I focused a small burst of mana on his pen and the tip snapped, spilling ink over the page. "Shit." Waller tried to rip the page free before the ink bled through. Judging from the annoyed look on his face, he failed. Pursing his lips, he glanced up at me. "Is that amenable?"

"Of course." I took three long steps toward the table before Waller held up his hand to stop me.

"There, if you please." He pointed to a single bottomed-out office chair at the window side of the room. The placement was extraordinarily well-thought-out. Anyone who happened to be looking could see me from the outside, oblivious to my state, while Miles and the rest of his people were perfectly shielded. I'd have to look back and between the projector screen and the panel, while they could monitor both my reactions and the screen simultaneously.

And of course, I'd bet every bit of Selve Kinsley had paid me on the office chair being broken, locked in a lower position.

I watched for the telltale shimmer from my periphery as Azure slithered from my shadow into the shade beneath the table. Once he was in, I gave Waller a bemused smile and took a seat on the office chair, standing briefly to pull the lever and raise it.

It worked, but only until I sat down. The chair lowered me slowly to its previous place with a muted hiss.

Miles took his seat at the end of the table, looking mildly sick to his stomach.

Now.

How did I want to play this?

CHAPTER FORTY-THREE

The outcome was already decided. That much was certain.

Their side of the room had something of a frustrated air, as if they were all waiting for a foregone conclusion. Even if the detractors weren't entirely onboard, they'd toe the blue line if the majority decided to pull the trigger.

They were waiting for Miles.

Which meant my only outward advantage going into this—that Miles was doubting himself, unsure of the course he'd put into motion—was somewhat mitigated if they were less likely to listen to him. As expected, this was more trial than inquiry.

Still. There was a sliver of hope.

No conviction is a sure thing. The guiltiest person in the world can escape out from under a mountain of evidence if they create enough doubt in the trial.

My father's words.

And from cursory research in the matter and my personal delve into legal minutia, he was correct. Juries blew bird-in-hand convictions all the time because prosecutors failed to use the bounty of evidence at their disposal to create a convincing narrative. My circumstances here were, in many ways, worse than a fair trial. My judge, jury, and prosecution comprised the same group of people. Which meant, on top of the evidence, there was a mountain of bias that would be insurmountably difficult to overcome.

Alternatively, the advantages were scant. But not insignificant.

It's several magnitudes more difficult to get a conviction for a death penalty case than a multi-year imprisonment. The threshold of proof is higher, the jury acutely aware that any lingering doubt will sit far more heavily once the sentence is carried out.

The same concept applied here to a much greater degree. If they got it wrong, the death of an innocent person would be on their heads.

And sure, it was possible I was overestimating their humanity. That they'd done the ruthless arithmetic and reached the conclusion that the possibility of killing one innocent person was worth the high chance of taking out a monster capable of destroying an entire region and killing hundreds of thousands off the board.

But I didn't think so. If that was the case, I'd either be hanging upside down in some basement while one of them worked me over with a car battery, or dead.

Miles might have been the holdout, but they were all taking a serious risk, questioning me here. Putting both themselves and the Adventurers' Guild in peril. A risk that was borderline idiot if they didn't have some form of countermeasures in place.

A strong suppression ability, or something along those lines?

No, still too risky without knowing definitively it could be contained.

Instance?

It rankled that I still didn't entirely understand what instancing did. I knew it was an uncommon ability that some Users possessed to isolate a selected area from civilians and spying eyes. That it was sometimes used to tidy up bodies or contain volatile powers. And that there was more than one type.

This whole set-up supported that theory—dangling me here by the back window for Myrddin to see didn't make sense if all instances created a visual interference or a pocket dimension. More than likely, this one contained abilities and possibly people.

If that was true, there was a simple enough way to test it.

I drank my milkshake. When I reached the bottom and was noisily sucking air, I made a show of looking around for a trashcan and, finding none, stood and walked toward the door. "One second, let me toss this."

"Wait—" Miles' said.

Before he could finish, I turned the knob. The door didn't budge, a surge of **<Ordinator's Emulation>** indicated the remnants of an ability used on the door that spanned the room. I tried to follow the threads and search for the source.

It wasn't tied to anyone in the room.

They had someone outside set it up. Meaning they're locked in with me, and they know it.

Contingencies on contingencies.

When I turned back, half of them had risen out of their seats. Hawkins seemed to have teleported across the room, now standing within arms' reach, her smile significantly more forced than before. Cook in particular looked ready to leap over the table.

Hawkins touched her hair, prodding it to make sure it was still in place. It was. Was that a tell? "Sorry. Probably should have mentioned this earlier, but with all the potential for counterintelligence, we have a standard operating procedure."

I glanced at Miles.

Miles nodded. "No one leaves the blackout area until the meeting's over."

"Blackout area?" I asked.

"There's a power that restricts outside communication within a certain area," Hawkins explained. "We've found it invaluable. Without it, people could just hop on a voice call and effectively broadcast audio to whomever they wanted."

"Ah. Yeah. That would be a problem." I frowned, as if I was suddenly realizing how many conversations and meetings I'd had could have been transmitted that way. I was walking a thin line here. Furthermore, I needed to come off as inexperienced and somewhat naive, but if I came off as stupid, Miles would realize immediately it was nothing more than theater.

Had to strike a balance somewhere in the middle.

"There's a bin under the lectern." Waller studied me intensely. He was waiting for me to insist, push back, try to get out of the room.

Instead, I nodded to him apologetically and tossed my cup in the trash bin and returned to my seat, doing nothing to give away the fact that this small interaction was enough to confirm my suspicions. Miles, his people, they were still clinging to decency. Bureaucracy. None of them were ready to go full black site without checking their boxes first.

Which meant the sliver of hope was expanding.

As soon as my ass hit the chair, Waller fired off a command. In contrast to Miles, his voice was stern and nasally. Naturally grating in a way that demanded respect. "Take us through the timeline."

"Which timeline?" I looked between Miles and Waller.

"The formation of the Adventurers' Guild, and your first encounters with the individual known as Myrddin," Waller said flatly, staring me down.

Hawkins smiled. "Be as thorough as you can. Even the smallest detail can make a huge difference."

And the smallest fabricated detail you can disprove will give you enough rope to hang me with.

Azure's voice cut through my mind.

"Foster was weathering a midlife crisis before the dome. Male pattern hairloss was already doing a number on his self-esteem, and then his long-term

partner left him shortly after. He was passed over for promotion a handful of times. There's some animosity between him and Waller, though he's not thinking about it enough for me to get anything more specific."

Of course, the only skeptic on my side also happened to be a wet blanket. *"Get more specifics if you can. Next?"*

"Cook hates himself almost as much as he hates you. Which is impressive, considering how they suspect you of literal wholesale slaughter."

"Why?"

"He's doing his best to suppress it, but I'm still getting flashes. They had him in a behavioral analysis unit, reviewing footage. Twisted subject matter, even by my standards."

"Let me guess. Cook found something he 'liked' in the footage."

"A little too much. Can't nail down exactly what it is, but it totally unsettled him. Was on a leave of absence until Miles pulled him back in."

"I can work with that. Keep going. Hawkins and Waller?"

"Hawkins is solid. DEA. She was working with Miles to take down Roderick on a RICO case, stayed with him when the focus shifted to Necromancers. Hawkins might be the only person in the room who doesn't believe you're manipulating Miles to get out of this. They all think highly of him, but she has Miles on one hell of a pedestal.

"So Miles is DEA then? I asked. The Roderick RICO connection was concerning, especially considering their alliance with the Merchants' Guild, but I'd need to pull on that thread later.

Azure hesitated. "No. I get the feeling he was assisting Hawkins in an unofficial capacity. And that isn't unique to her. From what I can tell, Miles has filled in as a pinch hitter for almost everyone in this room. Every one of them owes him. And they're incredibly loyal."

Fucking fantastic. Feds had a well-recorded history of not playing well with other institutions, both at the local level and with other federal agencies. Normally, I could have leaned on that a little, but Miles being a divide-crossing messiah had just nixed that tool from my toolbox.

"Anything from Miles himself?"

"No. Still drawing a blank. But, Matt, he's not the one you should be worried about."

"Waller's a rabid dog disguised as a bean counter. Yeah. I know the type."

Azure sounded panicked. "It's worse than that. That profile Miles blasted out at the emergency meeting? It came from Waller. This is his area of expertise. And he's convinced you're the one they're looking for. He knows—"

I cut Azure off quickly, "Don't tell me the specifics. Whatever he throws at me, my reaction needs to be as authentic as possible. Just amp up his confidence in his findings."

"But... he's going to crucify you."

Let him. The stronger he clung to his profile, the more jarring it would be when I pulled the rug out from under him. I'd interrupted Azure before he could get into the details of the warning, but the context was clear.

I couldn't bullshit my way out of this without falling into one of the many traps Waller had undoubtedly laid.

The best way forward was playing this straight. I looked up at Waller. "Is it okay if I start a little further back, for context?"

Waller inclined his head. "Certainly."

I took a deep breath, my brow furrowing in focus. "I was walking home from school, the morning the meteor hit..."

CHAPTER FORTY-FOUR

I went over all of it with the Feds watching from behind their panel, in painstaking detail. For the most part, I stuck to the truth. Everything from the park where I first met Kinsley to the open forum was mostly accurate, excepting any mention of becoming a User that early. Other elements were subtly tweaked.

The encounter with the SWAT officer was abridged somewhat, making it sound less like a one-on-one encounter, more like a mass-shooting I'd escaped after someone next door was shot. As far as I knew, the officer was still alive, and I didn't want to risk them tracking me down.

To further muddle the scope, I covered my first encounter with the suits in graphic detail—transposing the bounty that had brought me there, to a mysterious text from Nick that took me across town late in the evening. Claimed that I noticed an expensive-looking dagger on one of the bodies, grabbed it, and ran while the Users present were too busy licking their wounds.

Waller steepled his fingers. "So, you saw individuals fighting with fantastical powers beyond your understanding, witnessed a murder, and your first impulse was to rip off the killers?"

I shrunk into myself slightly. "I get how it sounds. But I'd just lost a job, and it looked valuable. When you don't know where your next meal is coming from and there are people at home you're responsible for, you get used to taking what you can, when you can."

Hawkins' expression softened in what could have been genuine empathy.

Waller's eyebrows knitted together, and he was about to ask another question when Miles stepped in. "Let's not get bogged down in that for now. How did this lead you to Kinsley?"

I hid a smile as Waller's second pen apparently ran out of ink and he scowled at it in frustration. Then I told Miles, play by play, exactly how that second encounter with Kinsley had gone. How she'd bailed me out from the suits and asked for my help, how I'd originally shot her down until she offered a solution to the shortage situation. And how I'd gotten the idea for the merchant site early.

"How did you meet Myrddin?" Waller asked irritably, apparently tired of the context he asked for.

I shifted uncomfortably in my seat. "Toward the end of the open forum, a man pulled me aside. I won't bother telling you what he looked like, because as we know, that doesn't matter."

"What was he like?" Foster asked, speaking for the first time. Waller and the rest of the room twisted to look at him. They were too professional to show actual irritation, though their stares spoke volumes.

"Oddly calm." I focused on Foster as I thought back to Gray-hair, how he'd struck me. "*Authentically* calm. That stood out more than everything else. Not sure if any of you were present, but the vibe there was... rough. Like a pressure cooker with a stuck valve. And in the middle of this barely suppressed panic was this person who looked like he was just set apart from the chaos. Unfazed. Like he'd seen it all before."

"Why did he single you out?" Waller asked.

I rubbed my forehead. "The flyers advertising the site. We were being careful, but maybe not careful enough. Ellison—my brother—got them from me and passed them out. I'm not certain how Myrddin knew, but he had one in his hand. He might have been the first outsider to access the site, now that I think about it."

"And how did he approach you?" Waller prompted.

"Casually." I frowned. "With an air of superiority. Like he'd already completely figured out what we were doing and was interested in getting in on the ground floor. He asked a few questions I either didn't want to answer or didn't have the answers to—how many people we had, how we intended to expand."

"What was your impression of him?" Cook asked, with a knowing smirk.

"Suspicious." I cocked my head. "Most people strike me that way, at first. Even knowing that, I couldn't shake it. Something about him put me off. He did me a favor right off the bat though. Pointed out some shady guy walking into city hall who turned out to be one of the shooters from the hospital, and when I left to follow him, told me he'd find me after."

"Why do you think Myrddin pointed out the shooter without intervening himself?" Waller asked.

"Not sure. A test, maybe."

"Moreover, why did you intervene?" Waller pressed, leaning forward.

"Because it felt like the right thing to do? I don't know." I bit my lip. "I couldn't do anything at the hospital. People were dying all around me. The man next door was begging for help before they put a bullet in him. And I just ran."

I thought about Region 6, focused on the harsh reality of it and the tiny skeletal hand grabbing my wrist. Of Iris dead in the lithid's hallucination. My father's funeral. I felt almost nothing focusing on each individually, but rotating through them got a reaction, and my eyes began to water. I ran a sleeve across my face.

Hawkins approached, gave me a sympathetic nod, and passed me a tissue box.

"I'm sure you guys already know what happened with the shooter and the Adventurers' Guild, so I'll spare you." I made a show of blowing my nose, then allowed my expression to harden. "Because after that was when everything went to shit. I met with a friend at this Turkish coffee place. His name was Nick."

"Was?" Waller prompted.

I brooded. "Hopefully not past tense, but it's hard to say. It turned out, Nick was a User, and he'd brought two others with him. They'd found a door to something called a 'trial,' and he wanted my advice on strategy."

"Why would he consult a civilian about that?" Waller said. He didn't roll his eyes, but I could hear the skepticism in his voice.

"Because we were friends, and he often came to me for advice? And hardly any people were organized and connected to experienced Users that early? Not really seeing the issue there." I dulled the retort slightly, but Waller still bristled.

Good. He wasn't unflappable.

Waller tapped his pen against his notepad. "What happened next?"

"I made a mistake." I stared down at the ground. "Myrddin approached me again after the meeting with Nick. He'd followed me from the open forum and pointed out the fact that Nick had a tail. It took me a minute to get a look at him, but it was one of the suits from the alley."

"Yes, yes, your mysterious shadow organization." This time Waller did roll his eyes.

"What was your mistake, Matt?" Hawkins asked, shooting Waller a subtle look of reproach.

I swallowed. "I was already in over my head with the market. The timer was counting down to the Transposition event. I wanted to help Nick without putting myself in trouble I had no business in. Even though I still felt like something about him was off, Myrddin kept pushing to join us, and we didn't have anything resembling muscle to back Nick up. Kinsley sent him to a dungeon on a trial run, and he passed with flying colors. Brought back an ungodly number of valuables and gear and looked relatively unscathed. So, I asked Kinsley to send him to shore up Nick's party before the trial."

"I'm guessing it didn't work out so well?" Waller prompted dryly.

"This is where we get into the weeds a bit." I pursed my lips. "Because I don't know what really happened. Only what Myrddin told me. According to him, the trial itself went fine. It was only after that everything went to shit. They were ambushed by the suits. One of Nick's companions died, the other retreated into the trial itself before it collapsed. Myrddin said, before they took him, that he heard one of them talking about adding Nick to something called the Court."

The table stirred at that. Mile's leaned over and whispered something into Hawkins' ear, and she nodded. Cook and Foster looked at each other uneasily.

"It's working. You've thrown in enough curveballs and referenced events and outside knowledge that their uncertainty is growing. They knew nothing about the suits, but it seems like they've known about the Court for some time. Hawkins, Cook, and Foster are all worried that Waller is about to burn you as a source."

As if he sensed this, Waller looked around the room irritably and the chatter died. His cold gaze returned to me. "Myrddin told you this. And then what?"

I blinked. "Then the Transposition happened. I rode it out with the rest of my region. Kinsley and Myrddin were messaging, but I wasn't privy to their conversation. You'd have to ask her."

"You *know* we can't. She's been stonewalling our inquiries, and I'm guessing that *someone* told her to do so. How were you able to secure Region 14?" Waller dropped his pen.

I shook my head. "That was as much a surprise to me as it was to the rest of you. I have some theories, but they're not pertinent to this."

"Of course they're not." Waller studied his notes.

I glanced at Miles, confused, then back to Waller. "Have I offended you in some way?"

Waller folded his glasses and placed them in his chest pocket. "Let me get this straight. Myrddin never had any interaction with your family. He briefly interfaced with your friends, who are now conveniently either missing or dead, leaving the only people alive who had any meaningful long-term contact with him you, and the politically insulated merchant girl who is accumulating a sizable fortune and a small army. Is that right?"

"There's nothing *convenient* about it. But yes," I said. There was no point in giving him anything more to latch onto. I let confusion filter into my expression as I looked at Miles for help. "What is this?"

Miles glanced away.

"Don't look at him. We're having a conversation." Waller stood to his feet, leaning over the table. He reached in his pocket and pulled out a clicker. The projection screen whirred to life. He motioned toward it. I looked over, sure I was prepared for everything.

I wasn't.

CHAPTER FORTY-FIVE

A picture of Dr. Svelt stared back at me. My therapist for nearly half a decade, before money got too tight and we couldn't afford him anymore. If they had my session notes, this was about to get a lot uglier.

"What the fuck, Miles?" I asked. I didn't have to manufacture the outrage.

"Do—" Waller started

I held up a hand and cut him off. "No. I want an explanation."

Miles shook his head, regret clear in his expression. "You knew we had to look at you. The sooner you answer his questions, the sooner this is over."

"Sure." I held my hands wide, glaring at Waller. "Go ahead. What questions do you have for me about my fucking childhood therapist."

"Several, but we'll start with the obvious. Are you aware of what happened to Dr. Svelt?"

My anger flagged, replaced with concern. "No."

Waller crossed his arms. "Dr. Theodore Svelt was subpoenaed after one of his clients beat a coworker to death on a golf course with a putter. He subsequently lost his license after a series of malpractice allegations arose, centered around a failure to report several clients who, according to his notes, posed an immediate danger to themselves and others."

"I don't understand what this has to do with anything—"

"Then let me illuminate the situation." Waller moved the projector to the next slide.

The profile Miles referenced at the emergency meeting was blown up on the screen as Waller pulled a damnably familiar looking notebook from his bag, decorated with numerous yellow page markers that emitted from the top. He licked his thumb and paged to the first one.

"March 23rd. Matthias referenced homicidal ideation again today, directed toward a juvenile harassing his sister. The ideation is nothing new, with less specificity and focus than previous examples. He continues to grow more adept at warding them off, implementing the exercises and perspective work we've focused on. His innate rationality and knowledge of investigative process and forensics continues to act as a prohibitor despite the absence of empathy. He seems well-grounded, though I do wonder how much of his restraint comes from the understanding that he would be quickly identified as a suspect."

As Waller read off several more entries, my expression grew darker. Eventually, he snapped the notes shut. "There's a lot of psychobabble. But despite the bias Svelt clearly holds in your favor, there's a problematic through-thread, Matthias." Waller studied me. "Your therapist seemed worried about what might happen if you were to find yourself in a situation where you knew, confidently, that you could get away with it."

I spoke to Miles, who was still studying the floor in great detail. "You said I'd get a chance to help. To prove myself." I let pain into my voice.

"And low and behold, his fears came to pass. In the form of Brandon Givens." Waller tossed me a file. I opened it slowly, numbly leafing through a collection of crime scene pictures.

"This wasn't what we talked about, Waller." Foster stared holes in the back of his colleague's head. Both Hawkins and Miles seemed to agree, watching their colleague with distaste.

"Thirty-five stab wounds, supposedly incurred after your mother entered the house and found Brandon attacking you. The lead detective called it self-defense and closed the investigation quickly. Par for the course when a cop killer meets a convenient end." Waller smiled. "The coroner, however, didn't seem so sure. He noted that many of the initial stab wounds were administered at a strange angle. Almost ninety degrees. Your mother would have had to be on her knees or just under five feet tall."

"This has nothing to do with Myrddin," I said through gritted teeth.

"I think it does." Waller shook his head. "Because you never went back to Dr. Svelt after that. I think this was your first. Maybe there were others —there were a few events in your history that are questionable to say the least—or perhaps you were just biding your time. Studying." He bent down to look at me. "Plenty of medical and anatomical textbooks left behind in your old apartment. In our experience, the system has a tendency for revealing who we really are. And I think it handed you the anonymity you've been waiting for."

He's swaying them. You need to do something.

I pulled into myself. "You know, there's a lot I could say. Excuses I could make. About how those textbooks were for work, how I used them as reference for standardized tests. I'm sure you already know that. But you're right." I looked at Waller. "It wasn't my mother. I killed him."

The air of tension grew thicker.

I studied the diagonal threading in my jeans. "Dad was a cop, but he was a pretty understanding guy. He told me, once, that experimenting was part of growing up. That he'd prefer I didn't smoke weed or drink underage, but he understood that forbidding those things was mostly pointless. He just wanted me to be smart about it. There was really only one substance he came down on. Heroin. He said the problem with it was it felt so good that everything else would feel dull in comparison. That 'trying it once' had ruined countless lives, and the high wasn't worth what I'd pay for it."

I stared at Waller defiantly. "They say revenge isn't satisfying. That after it's done, no matter how warranted, or justified, you just feel empty. That's not how it was for me. I felt elated. Overjoyed. Like I'd accomplished something I was meant to do."

"Only it didn't last," Waller tried to lead me.

I shook my head. "When it faded, I realized I'd lost something too. Little things I enjoyed before seemed less significant, less meaningful. Even day-to-day colors seemed less vivid, less notable. Some of that was grief. Some of it wasn't. And ever since, I've been trying to claw that humanity back. The high wasn't worth what I paid for it. Not even close."

"So, you're a good killer," Cook jeered.

I snorted. "No such thing. But I'm not the one you're looking for."

Waller looked visibly unsettled. As if he'd expected me to crack and I had, but not in the way he wanted.

Miles sighed and stood. "I'm sorry this was so invasive, Matt."

"I'm not done," Waller snarled.

"No, I think you are." Foster stood, staring down Waller.

"How is this not obvious?" Waller stalked toward Foster. His voice was pitched low, barely audible. "He's the only viable suspect and literally confessed to a history of violence. You're genuinely buying that two people who fit the profile just so happened to be working together?"

"Or your profile's shit. Maybe you lost your touch," Foster whispered back, apparently finding his backbone.

"You—"

Hawkins stepped between them. "Regardless, we've reached an impasse." She glanced at me sympathetically. "I think we could all use a breather."

They were in a difficult spot. Traditionally, Waller probably had enough for an arrest. This hadn't gone well for me. But Waller had screwed up, pushing this as far as he had, making it clear I was their prime suspect. As I'd guessed before, the threshold of proof was significantly higher considering what Miles intended. Now they were stuck. I'd created enough doubt that they couldn't reasonably disappear me, but as soon as they let me out of the warded room, there was a possibility I'd say fuck-it and go nuclear.

"Can I offer a solution?" I asked. The quiet discussion around me wound down.

"We're listening," Miles said warily.

"Waller."

The man seemed surprised I'd called him. He replaced his glasses. "Yes?"

"You've obviously gone full Will Graham on my ass, so let me ask you a question. Is there anything in your research that indicates I'd be a danger to my family?" I gave him a strained smile.

Waller's lips turned downward. "They might be the only people I'm confident *are* safe from you."

I nodded. "From what I've learned, the situation at Region 6 came on quickly. Essentially, right after the event started. Exploded from a single point and spread to the region limits."

"That's... more or less true," Hawkins confirmed.

"Is this leading somewhere?" Waller probed.

"House arrest," I said, voicing the idea as if I were still mulling it over. "If I was the Ordinator, I wouldn't be able to nuke the region, surrounded by my friends and family. Assuming the Ordinator's even able to do that when an event isn't active. Actually, that's probably the safest place to put me."

"You think he can't manage what he pulled in Region 6 if an event isn't active?" Miles asked.

I shrugged, "If he's capable of doing that much damage on a consistent basis, why the hell are the rest of us still here? He would have used it to deal with Kinsley and I as soon as she kicked him out. Miles too. Innocents in the crossfire be damned."

Waller raised an eyebrow. "You'll allow us to post people outside your door and throughout the building? Kinsley won't interfere?"

"At the end of the day, it's more security. I don't see why not. It'd be hard to monitor my comings and goings otherwise. Then it'll just be a matter of waiting for a sighting."

Everyone looked toward Miles. Even if they doubted his judgement, he was clearly still calling the shots.

Miles's lips thinned to a white line. He looked vaguely nauseous, and I didn't need **<Cruel Lens>** to tell me why. He was already doubting himself. Moreover, he'd made an effort to parade me around publicly. If

Myrddin attacked, Miles would have directly put innocents at risk. Including my family.

"House arrest. For now," Miles said, voice laden with doubt.

———

"I got plenty we can work with," Azure said gleefully.

"Later," I told him.

I was worried about explaining Sae, right up to the moment Cook and Foster cleared her room, finding no one. Cook bumped shoulders with me as he passed, sending a leer my way. "We'll be right outside if you need anything."

"Thanks." I waved him off cordially.

As the door swung shut, I heard Hawkins' voice. "Kinsley in there?"

"Nothing on your end?" Cook asked.

"No. Everyone else is accounted for, but as far as I can tell, the guild leader's—" the door clicked shut.

I pulled up my UI and tried to send a message to Kinsley, returning the same error message, indicating **<Squelch>** was still in effect.

A white doorway appeared in my kitchen, next to the refrigerator. I retreated to my closet and changed quickly, pausing to check my bare skin for any trackers or listening devices. Then I stepped through it without hesitation, my foot barely landing on the soft carpet of Kinsley's domain before dulcet tones reached my ears.

"What the fuck is happening?" Kinsley squawked. "If the lady you sent my way hadn't accidentally tipped me off that you'd left with a tall and handsome stranger, I wouldn't have been able to figure out things were going bad and gotten Sae out in time."

Sae approached, looking equally disgruntled. "There I was, enjoying my mid-afternoon nap, when a screeching midget dragged me into a portal."

"It's a doorway."

"Whatever." Sae quirked an eyebrow. "But she has a point. You're not nearly enough of a celebrity to have your own armed escort."

I glanced at Sae. "You're sleeping a lot."

"I'm depressed."

"Fair." I stared off toward Kinsley's oversized fish tank. The feeling of drowning washing over me once more.

"If this is a coup, we can take them. I have enough mercenaries," Kinsley said. Her hackles were understandably up. This was the closest thing to a home she'd had since this clusterfuck started.

"It's not a coup. And we fuck things up with the Adventurers' Guild if this turns to open conflict." I studied Sae. Despite her frank estimation of her state of mind, she looked far better than she had a matter of days ago. She was rebuilding herself.

"What?" Sae said.

"Can I trust you?" I asked. For the first time, I let **<Cruel Lens>** evaluate her. I didn't like using it on my friends or allies, but that wasn't a line I could afford anymore. It seemed like a kinder alternative than letting Azure root around in her mind.

"Yes, for fuck's sake." Sae glared at me in frustration.

She's still unstable. But she'd also take a bullet for you. Probably more than one. You're the only anchor she has, and she's painfully aware of that. She is as loyal as she is angry, and she's incredibly angry. A dangerous combination.

I bit the bullet. "I'm the Ordinator. You, me, and Kinsley are the only ones who know definitively. Yes, I've been the Ordinator from the beginning. No, I didn't sandbag or avoid using my power during the trial. No, I didn't turn Region 6 into a gory wasteland, yes, whatever's running the system tried to pin it on me, no, I don't know why. The plan was to use that infamy as an in with the suits, but now there are several Users with law enforcement backgrounds who put the pieces together and just press-ganged me into an interrogation, and I'm currently under house arrest. Yes, I have a plan, yes, you play a vital role, and no, you're probably not going to like it."

While they stared at me aghast, I checked my objectives, scanning through until I reached the Personal Objective: Remain unidentified by other Users.

There was no indication that I'd failed it. Which meant it likely referred to my identity as a whole becoming public knowledge.

"You—you—just—you're just gonna tell her like that? After all the hoops you made me jump through?!" Kinsley's jaw worked furiously.

Sae blinked several times, eventually settling into a stoic expression. "Not that I don't have a million questions, but I'm guessing from that info dump that we're at a crisis point."

"This thing with the suits is on a strict timetable, and if this investigation stays focused on me, I can't do shit." I contemplated for a moment, trying to decide if I could afford to prep an extra day. "No. It needs to be tonight. But I get that I'm being a little unreasonable, so if you have anything you can't wait to have answered, shoot."

Sae held up one finger. "First, you sure you're not panicking and jumping the gun here? Doesn't it look reactionary if something happens to clear you right after they pull you in?"

"It usually would," I admitted. "But they dangled me out as bait for Myrddin. It makes sense for him to move quickly on this, before they have their defenses shored up."

"Myrddin being you."

"Yes."

"Got it." Sae considered that, then held up a second finger. "Why is the Ordinator so reviled, exactly?"

Kinsley and I shared a look. I tried to answer thoughtfully. "From what little I know, the Ordinator represents a potential disruption to whatever process the Overseer and his people are attempting to instill. It gains exponential power as long as Ordinator lives, so it's in their best interests to take them out early."

Sae gave me a bland look. "You're disrupting the system."

"Yes."

"The asshole system that turned me into a bug-monster. *That* system."

"Uh. Yes."

Sae held up a third finger, an annoyed expression on her face. "Why the fuck wouldn't you tell me about this sooner?"

Even with **<Cruel Lens'>** reassurance, I didn't like expanding the circle of trust. More links in the chain meant more potential points of weakness. The longer it got, the more likely it would snap.

I rubbed my face and crossed the carpet to Kinsley's sitting room. To my surprise, there was already a whiteboard waiting, complete with a collection of multicolored markers. I picked one up. Azure, Audrey, and Talia all popped into existence and took various places around the sitting room.

"Wait, I don't know this one." Kinsley stopped in front of Azure and peered at him.

"This one would *love* to get to know you," Azure said, dripping fascination.

"Matt. Your new summon is creepy."

"Divine guardian, my ass!" Sae exclaimed.

"That lie was his idea." Talia didn't hesitate to throw me under the bus.

"Matt's always been dodgy. *You* were supposed to be a spirit guide. And why the hell are you white now?"

I sighed and popped the cap. "Let's get started."

CHAPTER FORTY-SIX

I returned to my apartment.

Ironic that I was beginning to finally think of it that way—as mine—now that I was on the verge of losing it, along with everything else.

There was a throbbing hum as Sae stepped through the portal behind me. It was harder to read her these days—along with the physical changes and expressionless compound eyes typically hidden behind sunglasses, she'd become far more reserved than before. Still, the way her shoulders drooped and the way she pulled herself inward was simple enough to read.

"It's not too late for you to bow out," I called over my shoulder as I pulled my social UI and tried to send Kinsley another message, mainly to confirm **<Squelch>** was still in effect.

"That's something you're gonna learn about me, Helpline. I don't back down." Sae stared at me coolly. Still, the bluster fell a bit flat.

"You get that what I'm asking you to do isn't just for me, right?" I asked gently. "It serves a dual purpose."

Sae waved me off. "Yeah, I get it. If I kept hiding forever, my ability to find a solution to this shit—" she gestured to herself "—would be severely gimped. This theater gives me a chance to present myself in a positive light. Not to mention, my usefulness would be limited."

"Sae."

"Fuck off with the mothering. It's just a lot, alright?"

"Yeah."

Sae crossed through the living area and went to her knees, removing one of the lacquered white panels beneath the TV. An adjustment Kinsley had insisted on that seemed extraneous at the time, given our alternative methods of getting in and out unseen. Sae peered in, only to turn and give me a thoughtful look. "Sure you're going to be able to come off as an inexperienced mook?"

I shrugged. "Not long ago, I *was* an inexperienced mook."

She shook her head. "When you're in the shit, you tend to push things too far."

"How so?"

"The first time I got into combat, it was a nothing. A couple of low-level goblins. But I was shitting my pants. Jinny had slightly more experience than me, and she kept shrieking whenever her spells went off. Hell, Nick took to it better than any of us, and he was on the verge of losing his lunch constantly, especially when he cut something open."

My brow furrowed. "You're saying I seemed off."

"Way too comfortable. It didn't matter because Nick vouched for you. But that first ambush? The trial after? I must have wondered a half-dozen times what your background was. Because you just slipped into this analytical combatant mentality, like you'd been wearing it your entire life." She studied the door. "I guess, in a way, it makes me feel better that you were experienced before then. Otherwise, someone might get the impression you're some kind of psycho."

My lips pressed together. As much as I understood that Sae had a point, it was a precarious balance. If I presented myself as too meek and timid, it would seem incongruous in comparison to the type of person who would fight through a forcefield to attempt to save a region. Going too far the other way would arouse suspicion as well.

I opened my mouth to speak, only to be cut off by a sudden explosion of noise.

BANG BANG BANG

That was a cop knock if I'd ever heard one. I snapped my fingers once and pointed to the hole. Sae slipped into the crawlspace, gripping the handles on the reverse-side of the panel and pulling it on behind her. It didn't align perfectly. I helped secure it from the other side until it locked in.

BANG BANG BANG BANG.

More insistent this time. If I made them wait much longer, there wouldn't be a door left to bang on. I grabbed the remote from the coffee table and turned the TV and Blu-ray player on. Unfortunately, the last person to use it had apparently been Iris. A still image of a computer-generated princess belting out a song within the bounds of an ice castle manifested on the vibrant screen. I spent precious seconds scrubbing through the video, looking for anything that resembled a dialogue scene, and pressed play on the first one I found, slowly bumping the volume from mute.

I dropped the controller and headed into the bathroom, kicking my shoes and socks off and mussing my hair, putting a few drops of Visine into my eyes.

BANG BANG BANG—

I threw the door open, revealing both Foster and Hawkins, Hawkins with her fist stopped an inch from the door. She studied my appearance. "Where were you?"

"Asleep," I said irritably.

Foster shook his head. "Told you."

Hawkins shot him a look, then gave me a level stare. "Took you a while to answer the door."

"No, waking up took a while. Answering the door went fairly quickly." I glared at her. I was being intentionally obstinate. Regardless of how in the right they were, they'd turned my life upside down over the course of the afternoon. Being too cooperative would be an obvious tell.

"Should be the last check for the night, Matt," Foster said sympathetically. "Probably being overly careful, but with there's too many new and unknown powers in play to take half measures."

"Glad you're expending so much manpower on watching me, rather than looking for Myrddin."

Hawkins pushed past me and did a lap around the room, sticking her head into each door as Foster waited by the front with me. "You, uh, talking to anyone in here?"

I shook my head, sticking a thumb toward the TV.

"Interesting choice," Foster said.

"Background noise. Can't sleep without it."

"Uhuh." He raised an eyebrow as the animated snowman on screen cracked wise.

"And maybe I like the soundtrack okay—christ. Is she gonna be done anytime soon?"

Hawkins strolled in, as if she'd just gone for a casual walk in the park. "You said you live alone?" I didn't miss the way she eyed the guest room.

"Yep."

"Problem?" Foster asked.

"Just doesn't look that way. More than one toothbrush in the bathroom, couple of mugs in the sink. Blanket in the guest room seems a little odd." Hawkins' eyes slid to me. "Unless you just happen to be a fan of system knock-off Hello Kitty. Surprised you and Cook missed that, Foster."

Along with breathing room to deal with the suits, this was precisely why I needed to redirect the focus of their investigation quickly. None of the Feds were pencil pushers. They all had clear field experience and were extremely perceptive. It was only a matter of time before I made a mistake I couldn't explain away.

"Or," I rolled my eyes, "they were paying attention when I went over how most of my family lived in this suite during my recovery. Given everything that's going on, moving has been something of a scattered process."

"Of course." Hawkins pulled a pot of coffee off the machine and sniffed it.

Foster smiled apologetically. "Anyway. This isn't the Kremlin. Miles was clear. You're allowed to stretch your legs or work out some frustration at the rec center. We'll be rotating out, but I'll be around tonight and tomorrow morning, then back in the PM after I've caught up on sleep."

Smart on Miles' part. Political. He was keeping a sympathetic presence near me by keeping Foster nearby, and making up for any potential weakness that created by making sure there were two of them on my floor at any given time.

Still, it wasn't like he strong-armed Foster into acting this way.

"Thanks, Foster," I said.

'You got it. We heading out?" Foster looked at Hawkins, who'd helped herself to the stale coffee and still had that leveled stare focused in my direction.

Hawkins inclined her head to the door. "I'll be right behind you."

Once the door was shut, I entered the open kitchen and leaned against the counter, facing Foster, making sure to keep my hands visible and my posture non-threatening. "This the part where you tell me *why* you've apparently decided to swap to bad cop over the interim of a handful of hours?"

Hawkins sipped her coffee, then set it aside. "Know anything about work dogs, Matt?"

I blinked, thrown by the non sequitur. "Like, Seeing Eye dogs?"

"No. Drug dogs, corpse dogs, etcetera."

Only a little, but it felt like more of a rhetorical question. I shook my head.

"Lotta controversy around them these days. But they have their uses." Hawkins looked up, as if she was recalling a memory. "A long time ago, before I ended up where I am now, I was rank and file up in Aledo assisting with an investigation. A little boy disappeared. He was small. No more than fifty pounds. We were about a week beyond the first seventy-two hours. Understand the implication there?"

It was safe enough to answer, seeing as how practically every police procedural had blasted this particular factoid out to the public at some point. With every day that passes after the first seventy-two hours of a missing person's case, the chances of success plummet.

"The kid was dead," I said flatly.

Hawkins nodded. "The detectives running the investigation came to the same conclusion. They had almost everything they needed for a conviction. A solid suspect, pieces of trace evidence in the suspect's possession, including the victim's backpack, a shirt, and an iPad. It was damning. All they were missing was a murder weapon and a body."

"Guessing you found the body."

"Not right away. The suspect owned fifteen acres. Canvassing was hell. Foliage so thick you could have walked over a hundred shallow graves without realizing it. Eventually, the DIC stopped being a chintzy bastard and ponied up for cadaver dogs. They have this system, right? The handler and the dogs. They'll canvass an area, and every so often the dog will signal." Hawkins raised her arm and moved a pointed finger in a circle. "False positives are common, so they'll usually wait for both dogs to signal repeatedly. Only we didn't have to wait long. Both dogs signaled almost immediately, ten yards away from the house. Sure enough, there was upturned earth underneath a clump of leaves. We started digging and found…"

Hawkins made a sarcastic magician's flourish. "A fucking buried possum. We dug under it, of course. The killers who *think* they're smart love to hide bodies under animal corpses."

"Was it there?"

"No." Hawkins glanced at her coffee cup. Wordlessly, I held out a hand and she passed it to me. My fingers brushed her skin lightly, and somehow I managed to avoid smiling at the minor victory. With my new vocation ability, I had the means to spy on both Miles and Hawkins now. Three more made a set. I refilled the cup and handed it to her. "But twenty yards to the south, the dogs signaled again. And again. And again."

"He was killing animals and burying them."

"By the dozen." Hawkins looked disgusted. "That went on for at least a week. A week of digging in dirt and finding stinking, mutilated bodies in shallow graves, none of them human. Fatigue set in."

I sighed. "Fascinating as this is, I'm not really seeing the point—"

"I'm getting to it." Hawkins cut me off. "One of the last graves we uncovered was fresher than the rest. A horse. It wasn't even close to dried out, and its stomach had been slashed open, the remains… thoroughly infested. I'll save you the gory details—"

"Those *weren't* the gory details?"

"Trust me." Hawkins shuddered. "It was bad. No one wanted to go near it. Shortly after, some rookie found the murder weapon. A baseball bat tossed into his neighbor's field. DNA did the rest. Matched the traces of blood in the grain to the blood on the backpack. Word came down that the DA was willing to prosecute the case without a body, and we packed it in."

My mouth twitched. "No one bothered to dig under the horse."

Hawkins chuckled. "That's right. Miles said you had good instincts. It stuck in my craw. Even if every other star aligns, prosecuting a murder case without a body is risky at best. And this wasn't the kind of guy who would crack and just give it up, even if the verdict came down as guilty. There was a good chance the family would never be able to bury their son. It kept me up at night. So, I committed the unforgivable sin of jumping the chain of command and brought it up to my lieutenant. Told him everything."

"What'd he do?"

"He was pissed. And instead of laying into the detectives, he grabbed a crime-scene tech, threw three shovels in the back of a squad car, drove us to the property, and marched across the field to the grave. And after a few hours of cutting through filth, and rot, and viscera, we found him."

I dumped the rest of the coffee in the sink, watching it swirl down. "Congratulations. Was this meant to be some thinly veiled parable about how you're not afraid to get your hands dirty?"

"During the interview—"

"Interrogation."

"—interview," Hawkins emphasized. "Waller uncovered something ugly. You didn't bother denying it. Instead, you came clean. Warts and all. But it was a little too easy. I'm uncertain whether we've dug deeply enough."

"It's time for you to go," I said coldly. I needed these people out of my life as soon as possible.

"Sure." Hawkins placed her mug in the sink and approached the door.

Unable to help myself, I called after her. "That lieutenant—the one who believed you and put his career in the line—that was Miles, wasn't it?"

Hawkins paused, her hand on the door. When she turned back, her expression was unreadable. "In the off chance we end up taking this another direction? Whether it's six months or a year from now. No matter how suspicious or mundane the circumstances, if something happens to Miles? You'll find me back on your doorstep. And I won't be as nice the second time around."

"Got it."

"Have a nice night, Matthias."

As soon as the door clicked shut, I sagged, hand pressed to my chest, heart beating rapidly beneath my palm. I previously thought I'd won Hawkins over. Or at least earned her sympathy. As it turned out, I was utterly wrong.

I turned the TV off, set my alarm for a half-hour, and tried to catch some sleep on the couch. If everything worked out perfectly and they bought it, this could all be behind me.

But sleep wouldn't come. The insides of my eyelids felt like oppressive curtains, robbing me of precious minutes.

Eventually, I rolled off the couch and opened the door. Foster and Cook were standing outside.

"Looking a little rough there, champ," Cook sneered. He'd changed from his blue flower-print Hawaiian shirt to a red flower-print Hawaiian shirt. At least the man was consistent.

I ignored him and glanced at Foster. "Mind if I take you up on that rec time?"

Foster grinned. "Sure thing."

A few minutes later, we strode down the hallway. They flanked me professional, Cook behind me and to my left, Foster ahead and to my right. The formation was tight. If I had to do anything physical to alert Kinsley that the wheels were in motion, they would have clocked it immediately. But that wouldn't be necessary.

The solution was the most recent entry in the quest screen.

<Optional Quest Pending>
Quest: Totally Real Merchants' Guild Quest
Primary Objective — Find a dungeon and clear it.
Secondary Objective — Avoid turning Kinsley's hair white before her sixteenth birthday, you bastard.
Reward: 1 Selve
Accept Quest? Y|N

I rejected the quest. With **<Squelch>** blocking direct communications, it was the best alternative we came up with for getting a signal through. Currently, Kinsley and a solid chunk of her mercenaries would be ironing out a highly visible trade deal with merchant holdouts on the far end of the city. This had been in the works for a while, she'd just have a slightly larger entourage than previously intended.

Leaving me, the building, and the Feds coincidentally vulnerable. It was all coming together.

CHAPTER FORTY-SEVEN

We went down to the converted racquetball court area. Foster went in before me while Cook waited outside the door.

I observed them carefully. Other than Miles, I had very little experience with how high-level field agents operated. Cook seemed rusty, reflecting what Azure had told me. He hadn't operated in this capacity in quite some time. Foster, on the other hand, cleared the court almost casually. He was thorough but calm, the only indicator of focus a slight tightness around the eyes. A total reversal of Cook's wound-tight-as-a-coil presentation.

Foster placed his back against the far wall, watching from a distance as I slugged the training bag like my life depended on it, circumventing the mental prompts from **<Unsparing Fang>**. I knew how to throw a punch, and I'd been in a few minor scuffles throughout my childhood, but that was about it. My strategy pre-dome generally boiled down to aiming for something vital and running the fuck away as soon as there was an opening.

Without relying on the gnoll's combat skill, I must have looked green as hell.

"Pivot your back foot and twist your torso," Foster called over.

"What?" I pulled my shirt up and wiped my forehead. It came away damp, dark with sweat.

"You've got decent upper-body strength. But you're trying to just punch with your arm."

Foster crossed the room and demonstrated in slow motion first, then more quickly, slamming the bag with a punch that reverberated like a gunshot against the soft material.

I tried to copy the way he put his entire body into the strike. The first time, I nearly fell over. It was significantly harder to do this without **<Unsparing Fang>**, and I caught myself wishing for the simplicity of a knife.

Still, Foster was patient and guided me with a handful of light touches, manipulating my form until I struck the bag hard, eyes widening at the sound it made.

Foster nodded. "Fast on the uptake. Good. I take it your Page class didn't come with a combat skill?"

"No such luck."

He nodded. "Plenty of classes didn't. There's no small number of people who died during the Transposition because they just didn't know how to protect themselves. I've been hounding both Miles and Sara—you know Sara, right?" When I confirmed that I did, Foster continued, "To get some sort of formal self-defense curriculum going."

"Like a dojo?" I asked. It sounded ridiculous, but I didn't want to shit on his idea for no reason.

Foster made a non-committal grunt. "Nothing out there. Just some classes with experienced instructors open to the public. Practical shit. Brazilian Jujitsu, Krav Maga. Maybe a little Silat for weapons training. And of course, my personal favorite..." Foster launched into a brutal combo that involved a mix of elbows and knees, nearly knocking the bag from its base. "Muay Thai." He grinned.

I was impressed, despite myself. Foster didn't come off with half the swagger of the few guys in high school I knew that brayed about having a black belt, but his skill was plain to see. **<Ordinator's Emulation>** pinged, even though Foster was, assumedly, using a skill he'd honed the hard way, long before we had a system.

"What about Judo?" I asked. It was **<Unsparing Fang's>** closest real-life analogue, and I was curious to hear what he thought of it.

"Mmm." Foster nodded. "It's a solid philosophy, if a bit limited in scope. Good for fighting outside your weight class. Problematic in the context of our situation though. Redirecting aggression and momentum only works up to a certain point. And wearing down your opponent doesn't matter if your opponent has superhuman stamina."

That was true enough. **<Unsparing Fang>** had helped me out of more than a few binds, but there were certain situations where it was of limited use. The offensive aspect was limited, intended to finish fights quickly with brutal capitalizing attacks that left me open if I didn't make enough of an impact to finish things then and there. If I needed to wear something down, I was almost always forced to fall back on my abilities and weapons. And it was almost inevitable that I'd eventually find myself in a situation where **<Unsparing Fang>** was useless, and I was unarmed and low on mana.

"Judo and Muay Thai compliment each other rather well, come to think of it. Striking and grappling covered extensively between the two," Foster mused. For a moment, I wondered if he was baiting me, but he was too caught up in his thoughts for that.

Suddenly, I had a tantalizing proposition for one of my two empty emulation slots.

"At this point, I'd take anything. Even if that means learning it the old-fashioned way," I admitted, smiling internally as I watched Foster's head perk up.

"That can be arranged. Obviously, I can't teach you with things as they are now, but assuming you want anything to do with us after..." Foster trailed off. He looked uncomfortable, as if he felt like broaching this was taking advantage of the circumstances, when in reality it was the other way around.

I sighed. "I'm not... sure about the others. Especially Waller. But I'd be open to staying in contact with you. Especially if you're willing to teach me."

Foster's eyes lit up. "I'd like that."

"Furthermore, I can get you your self-defense program. A cushy spot in either the Adventurers' Guild or Merchants' Guild." I gave him a cold look. "What I need is for you to make all of this... go... away."

Foster's expression darkened. The sound-profile of the training area shrunk to the sound of my heart beating in my ears.

I snorted, then started to laugh.

Foster stared, shocked for a second, then laughed with me. "You son of a bitch."

"Yeah, okay, that was uncalled-for." I wiped my eyes. "Sara's stonewalling you?"

"Not stonewalling, exactly." After the shock, Foster had dropped his guard. He wasn't keeping the same distance from me as he was before. That was good. By the end of this, we'd be the best of friends. "She says they don't have the resources. Given what I've seen, I'm inclined to believe her. It's a hair short of chaos all the way down."

I landed a few more experimental punches on the dummy, emphasizing the technique Foster had shown me. "You're not emphasizing the value."

Foster adjusted my form absentmindedly. "The point is empowering the helpless. Charging a high price would defeat the point."

"The value I'm referring to has nothing to do with money." I gave him a pointed look. "Think about it. Putting the civilians aside for a moment, who do you think the first people in line will be?"

I could practically see the lightbulb turn on above Foster's head. "Magic Users."

"And crafters, and plenty of others with massive potential who just happen to be lacking in direct combat. All brought into the Adventurers' Guild's magnanimous embrace."

Foster grappled with the idea. "Spin it as a recruiting tool."

"They took plenty of casualties during the Transposition. There's no world where they don't jump at the opportunity."

Foster's mouth turned downward. "That just feels so..."

"Cynical?" I raised an eyebrow. "Even if it benefits the guild, it achieves your ends. Altruistic ends at that. Not seeing the downside."

Before Foster could answer, there was a weighty thump against the wall that framed the entryway, punctuated by a strangled curse. We both froze, straining to listen.

"Cook?" I mouthed at Foster.

The agent pressed a finger to his lips and drew a black polymer 1911 from his shoulder holster. He crossed the room, his footsteps silent.

Slowly, he pressed himself against the wall and cracked the door.

Then jumped back, throwing himself against the door as a series of vicious barks and snarls bounced off the walls in multiplying echoes. I saw a few inches of muzzle and yellow, sharpened teeth as *something* attempted to force its way in. Foster strained against the door.

"Run!" he shouted.

"Where?" I said, panicked. "There's no way out!"

Foster turned, bracing his back against the wall, and pointed up toward the observation railing that lined the top of the court. If someone climbed the platforms and made their way into the octagon suspended in the center of the training room, it'd be possible to climb the fencing and slip through. Instead of running, I bolted forward and slammed my shoulder into the door next to foster. There was an audible yelp and the muzzle withdrew.

"Are you fucking crazy? Go." Foster stared at me as we both struggled to hold the door shut as something large and mean-sounding slammed against it, jarring us violently.

Talia was really selling this. Now, it was my turn to do the same.

I drew on every bit of Nick's saccharine heroism I could muster and somehow managed to deliver the line with a straight face. "Screw that. I'm not leaving you."

CHAPTER FORTY-EIGHT

I shook my head, hoping I was projecting the correct amount of terror. "It looked like a monster."

Foster's eyes darted back and forth. Finally, he seemed to decide. "We're not here just to monitor you. Miles thought... he thought there was a chance someone might make an attempt on your life."

"Someone?"

"Myrddin."

"What? Why now? There were plenty of chances before."

Foster looked away.

"Holy shit. For talking to the Taskforce. That motherfucker used me as bait?" I said, outraged.

"Wasn't my idea, didn't like it from the start," Foster said, looking guilty as hell.

I held my silence as the creature slammed against the door. "It doesn't matter. Pointing fingers isn't going to help anyone. How—" the door exploded inward nearly a third of the way, throwing me to the ground. I scrambled to my feet and rammed my shoulder against it, wincing. "How do we get out of this?"

Foster's brow furrowed. "Send for help, barricade the door, and try to get to the penthouse elevator."

I pulled up the social UI and sent a message to the landlord, then to Kinsley. The second message didn't go through. I glared at Foster, furious. "Why are you jamming me?"

Foster looked bewildered. "I'm not. I'm just a civilian. Cook was the User, and the one running **<Squelch>**."

I swore. "Cook's still alive."

The lights cut out, replaced by an eerie red strobe. A voice spoke through a crackly intercom that echoed throughout the building.

We are under attack. The designated authorities have been contacted. All civilians are to lock themselves in their rooms until the danger has passed. Do not answer the door for anyone.

"Cook being alive changes things." I locked eyes with Foster. "You're sure I'm the target?"

"Miles was."

I ran through the scenario in my mind. "Okay. Who's in the building right now?"

"Hawkins and Waller. Miles is running overwatch on an adjacent building."

"You have a way to contact them?" I asked.

Foster held up a walkie.

I nodded. "Tell them to meet us on the penthouse floor. It's defensible, and the elevator requires a card swipe. One entrance, and one exit. Cook is still alive for the moment, but Myrddin doesn't like loose ends. If we just rabbit, he'll finish the job."

"We don't have the firepower to fight Myrddin on our own," Foster shouted back.

"True. Which is why we're not going to fight him. If this works, we get Cook out. But we need that monster out of the way. I'm guessing it's a summon or something along those lines." I glanced at the gun in his hands. "How good of a shot are you?"

"Best you've ever seen."

"Then I'm casting the line." I pulled my hoodie over my head and wrapped it around my arm. Foster's eyes widened in understanding.

Then he smiled grimly. "If we survive this, I'm never letting Cook hear the end of it."

Thump, Thump, Thump—

Timing it perfectly, Foster swung the door open. Then slammed it shut again after a dark mutt, more hyena than dog, charged through, strands of drool hanging from its mouth. Talia skidded on the slick surface as she tried to course correct, giving the vague impression of a cartoon character attempting to sprint on ice.

She gained traction and charged me, barking and snapping. I held my wrapped arm out like a shield and Talia sunk her teeth into the thick material, the rest of her ramming into me, knocking me to the ground.

"Are you sure?" I asked.

"Do it," Talia confirmed.

I strained against her, getting a hand around her throat and, with all my strength, shoved her upward.

A half dozen gunshots rang out in groupings of two. Blood spattered my face as Talia slumped, and I struggled to shove her limp form off me.

Foster had fallen into a crouch, still bracing against the door, the muzzle of his 1911 smoking. I stared at my fallen summon's body. All six shots had landed in a tight grouping at the base of Talia's skull.

A voice spoke, muffled, from outside the door. "First, you and the Oshkosh reject kick me out of the Merchants' Guild. Then you narc on me to the Taskforce. And now you've killed my dog. Never liked you much, Matt, but this is a cut above."

Foster aimed carefully and positioning himself away from any potential ricochet and fired his remaining rounds through the door. The high-caliber rounds punched through the door like it was tissue paper.

"Close." Azure chuckled. Then his voice took on a dark malevolence. "Check on that boyfriend lately, Foster?

Foster's professional stoicism was obliterated in a split second. *"What the hell?"* Foster mouthed, panic in his eyes.

"Kyle wanted to stay in, eat takeout, watch *Fiddler on the Roof* for the fiftieth time—but you went to play super cop and left him all alone. Bad move."

Foster ejected the magazine and reloaded, his expression livid. I caught his gun arm before he could unload the entire magazine into the wall.

"Remember the profile. Myrddin's highly manipulative. He's done his homework, and now he's screwing with you. Trying to knock you off-balance," I mouthed, the words barely more than a whisper.

"What if he isn't?" Foster whispered back, eyes darting back and forth.

"Ninety percent sure it's bullshit. Either way, we won't know until we get Cook to drop **<Squelch>**. You can message Kyle then. Go. I'll meet you at the elevator."

"Are you sure?" Foster looked uncertain. He'd been charged to protect me, and now I was advising him to put me in harms way.

"He's probably a hell of a lot stronger than me, but I have a few tricks up my sleeve." Reaching in my inventory, I withdrew a cylinder filled with golden liquid from my inventory, showing it to him, then replacing it. "I'll be fine. Just get Cook out of harm's way."

We traded places. I braced my back against the door and drew **<Nychta's Retort>**, watching as Foster bounded up the platforms and entered the suspended octagon, scaling the fence and clearing the railing in a feat of jaw-dropping athleticism.

"Getting bored, Matt," Azure crooned. "You're cornered. Either one of you opens the door, or I slice open the Fed and kill you both."

I retreated to the center of the room, nocking an arrow. A few moments later, the door swung open and Azure stepped in and closed the door behind him. He was wearing the **<Allfather's Mask>**, along with my eldritch armor.

I loosed an arrow and it struck the wall next to him. Azure fired several bolts around the room, none of them coming anywhere close to me. Then threw out bags that emitted a foul-smelling smoke that filled the room. Then he knelt down next to the door. His hand dissipated into shadow. *"He's dragging Cook toward the elevator. We're clear."*

We moved quickly. As Azure laid out bolts on the floor, I resummoned Talia, sweat trickling down my brow. Once Talia had reemerged in her silver wolf form, I glanced at her apologetically. "Are you alright?"

"That was... unpleasant," Talia growled.

"Yeah. You took one for the team."

"Considering what you are about to put yourself through, I cannot complain." Talia watched me with concern.

I pointed to the door, "Get moving. Make sure no one sees you until it's time."

"Be careful, pup."

Azure opened the door for her and Talia slipped through. I knelt over the laid-out bolts, casting **<Probability Cascade>** on each of them.

"You had to bring the boyfriend up?" I murmured, keeping my focus on bolts. A single mistake here could easily kill me.

"Like you said," Azure shrugged. "Gloves off."

"Guess I did."

I finished casting the spell on every bolt.

"There may be a problem," Azure said, hesitantly.

"What?" I whipped my head around to face him. He shifted his weight back and forth, projecting nervousness. "Spit it out, we're already taking too long."

"You feel differently to me than other Users. I thought it was our bond. There's a certain resonance—"

"Azure!"

"I felt it again, when I was phasing through the lobby. A presence, similar to yours."

My blood went cold as I slowly connected the dots. "Another unique class?"

"My suspicion as well. I couldn't locate them, though my senses are dulled in my ethereal form. It's possible a third party is taking advantage of this situation."

"Fuck!" I kicked Foster's ejected magazine, sending it skittering across the floor. Then I looked at Azure. "Don't break character unless I tell you."

Azure bit his lip. "This plan already puts you in danger. Adding an unknown variable—"

"Stay on target. I mean it. We either push through this, or we die."

The violet message notification light pinged in my vision, flickering as scores of messages came in. We were out of **<Squelch>** range and almost everyone in my circle had reached out to me, though I was missing some context from previous messages that couldn't be delivered. Mom and Iris were hunkered down in their room. Even Estrada had messaged.

The only person missing from the list was Ellison.

I shot him a message. <Matt: Where are you?**>**

Of course, he didn't answer.

CHAPTER FORTY-NINE

I covered my eyes and threw the cylinder. Even behind my arm, the resulting explosion was painfully bright, leaving a corona of pulsing violet around my vision. I sprinted out of the converted training area, leaping over training equipment and catching a glimpse of myself in the wall mirror, looking mussed and harried.

My side stung. Blood darkened my shirt, the self-inflicted wound bleeding far more heavily than expected.

The lobby was abandoned, pulsing red cast by the eerie rotating emergency lights. A few people called out to me as I ran. Foster was in plain sight, waiting by the elevator, Cook over his shoulders in a fireman's carry. The elevator doors opened. "He's right behind me—"

White-hot pain radiated through me as a bolt pierced my back. I staggered and nearly fell, clinging clumsily to the concierge counter for support. I'd been careful to ensure the bolts didn't strike anywhere vital—the application of **<Probability Cascade>** was the only reason Azure was able to circumvent the summon rules and hit me at all—but it still hurt like hell.

Foster dumped Cook into the open elevator and drew his service weapon. The muzzle flashed three times as he fired, and Azure darted to the side, kicking off a wall and sliding along the tile ground, firing another bolt that struck me in the shoulder.

I swapped into **<Scathing Shell>**. The pain shrunk to an incessant buzz that put my teeth on edge, but it was far more manageable now.

"Come on—" Foster yelled, his shout capitalized by another shot from the 1911. I staggered toward him.

<Perception> flared. I reacted too late. Six thin, surgical-looking knives, barely larger than needles, struck my chest in a semicircle. They didn't pierce deeply—barely more than a half inch—but I felt a strange buzzing that seemed to radiate between them. A familiar figure, short, in black and red armor stepped out from the shadows beside the elevator, his face covered by a chrome mask.

The same person from the cathedral.

The person who was probably Ellison, unless my guess was wrong.

Chrome-mask charged at me, crimson energy charged in his palm.

An image flared of the dead User at the cathedral, with the gaping hole in his chest surrounded by six shallow knife wounds.

Understanding dawned. If he hit me with that, I was done.

Even as my body screamed, I let <Unsparing Fang> guide me, caught Chrome-mask's arm, and stepped in, using his momentum to throw him over the concierge desk. His back struck the counter, and he toppled over, the maneuver buying me precious seconds.

A bolt struck me in the gut. The pain overwhelmed me, and I fell to my knees.

Foster fired twice more, once at Azure, once at Chrome-mask, who ducked back down behind the desk. He pulled the trigger again and the gun jammed. "God *damn* it." He gave up on clearing the jam and pulled a black-metal kukri out of Cook's inventory.

But he was too late. Azure stood over me, casually loading a bolt and pressing the crossbow to my head. "Last chance, Matt. I know either you or Kinsley have the legendary core. Tell me where it is, and I'll end her quickly."

I leaned forward and spat. The wad of saliva dripped down Azure's thigh, and he stared at it in distaste. "Fuck. You."

"Have it your way." Azure's finger tightened on the trigger.

I closed my eyes. There was an audible twang as the crossbow went off, the arrow ricocheting harmlessly off the marble.

Talia tore the crossbow from Azure's grasp. Sae ran alongside her, her chitin feet clicking against the hard surface. She leapt over me and slammed her fist into Chrome-mask's helmet, knocking him back against the desk. He pulled two bludgeons from his back and lashed out at Sae, the weapons glowing with red energy.

Out of nowhere, several civilians armed with baseball bats charged from their hiding places and attacked Myrddin.

Sae grabbed me roughly under the arms and hauled me toward the elevator. "How is it," she grunted in my ear, "I always end up dragging you around?"

"Sae?" I asked, surprise in my voice.

"Who the fuck is that?" Foster shouted.

"Don't shoot! She's a friend," I called back.

Sae pulled me into the elevator with Foster covering us, while Chrome-mask struggled against Talia and Azure incapacitated one of the civilians with a mana garrote. I had to hand it to the civilians. Despite an absence of abilities and a lack of User status, they were giving Azure hell.

Talia slipped in at the last moment before the doors slid shut and the elevator began to rise.

"I thought you were dead."

"Almost was. Would have been, if that bastard had his way," Sae grunted, leaning against the elevator wall and catching her breath.

"Myrddin?" I pulled the six small knives from my chest, wincing as they came free.

"Yeah. He set us up, Matt," Sae seethed. She wasn't a natural actor, but what she lacked in nuance she made up for in intensity. "Been hunting him ever since I got out of the trial. Wasn't sure I could take him, so I've just been following him around. Followed him here and figured he was coming after you, and I couldn't wait anymore."

I grunted in pain as Foster removed the two arrows from my shoulder and back. He looked preoccupied, but I could tell he was listening. "Asshole spun some serious bullshit, said you guys were ambushed when you came out of the trial. That some randoms killed Jinny, took Nick, and that you... retreated into the trial before it collapsed."

"Oh, *that all happened*." Sae scowled. "But Myrddin was with them. Tried to hand us off like a horse trade."

"If you were in the trial before it collapsed, that where you got the dog? And the... uh—"

"Hideous makeover? Yep. System loves twisting the knife."

"Not to interrupt this reunion, but..." Foster looked between us. "Anyone know who that second User was? Myrddin ever mention a partner?"

We both shook our heads. Sae redid her ponytail and gave me a meaningful look. "First I've seen of him, but I've been keeping my distance. Matt?"

"He was always tight-lipped. Far as I knew, he was always flying solo."

There was a groan as Cook sat up. An angry red line from the garrote ran the span of his neck. His eyes focused, and he looked between all of us, then finally to Foster. "What the fuck happened? Whose mutt is that?"

The hair on Talia's neck stood up. Foster spoke before I could. "Myrddin got the drop on you. I was contemplating leaving your ass, but Matt created a diversion for me to pull you out. Then it all went to shit." I kept my silence as Foster caught him up to speed, playing my injuries up more than I would have otherwise. Cook kept looking at me suspiciously, as if he couldn't quite believe what he was hearing.

Once Foster finished, Cook breathed out. "I'll be damned. Miles got it wrong. Or right, depending on how you want to look at it." He glanced at Sae. "Thanks for the assist, bug girl."

Sae bristled. "Who the fuck are these people, Matt?"

Before I could respond, the elevator doors opened. Waller and Hawkins were standing side by side prepared to fire, Waller with a glowing orange spell locked and loaded, Hawkins with a sighted Glock.

"Foster?" Waller asked, his tone laden with stress.

"They're not a threat."

Waller let the spell go, staring at me as Sae looped my arm around her shoulder and walked out. "We need to get him help."

Foster nodded grimly. "Gut shot won't kill him quickly, but the longer it goes untreated, the bigger the problem becomes."

Waller stalked toward Foster and took him aside. "It was Myrddin. You're completely positive?"

"Myrddin, and one more," Foster confirmed. "Ranged-melee hybrid. Where's Miles?"

"Securing our exit," Hawkins said. She looked at me warily, but some of the sympathy she'd shown during the inquisition had reappeared.

In truth, I was barely paying attention to the proceedings. My mind was on Ellison. How had he known when to act? Kinsley and I had been exceedingly careful ever since the Taskforce had formed. Our planning session had taken place entirely within her domain, which was airtight. No one could enter or leave unless she allowed it. Either we had a mole or...

"But you don't think it's weird? That the crying got worse the week before the meteor?"

If Ellison knew in advance about the dome, it was possible that wasn't the extent of his knowledge. If his class gave him some sort of future-sight, it was a reasonable assumption that it reached farther than a week ahead. That would go a long way to explaining why he hadn't bothered to help fortify our region, if he already knew it would be fortified. It also explained why he'd distanced himself, just before I got the ability to spy on anyone I touched. There was a chance he knew everything.

So, why was he trying to kill me?

"The special class disappeared." Azure's panicked voice blazed through my mind.

"Where are you?"

"On my way up the fire escape. He was right behind me, then he just disappeared. Are you sure you don't want me to stop?"

I gritted my teeth, trying to make a decision. *"Keep going."*

"*Wait. I see him. He scaled the wall and just carved through one of the windows of the penthouse floor—*"

Azure's warning came just in time.

I slipped from beneath Sae's arm, just before one of the vacant penthouse doors exploded in a mess of wooden shrapnel.

CHAPTER FIFTY

It's impossible to account for every variable. No matter how methodical your planning, well-thought your reasoning, you'll always leave something out. The best plans always account for something to go wrong, expect proceedings to go off course, and leave ample windows to adjust on the fly. Or at least, that was what I thought.

How the hell was I supposed to account for this?

Chrome-mask was more force of nature than sole combatant. He flew through the wrecked door, so quickly it looked as if he might smash into the adjacent wall, only to land on it, feet first. With a graceless swipe, he hurled three glinting flashes of metal directly toward my face.

Waller stepped in front of me protectively. He raised a protective arm too late. A cry of pain followed—one small blade lodging in his arm, the other two landing in his cheek and just beneath his eye. They dug in less than a half-inch, but given the location, it must have hurt like hell.

"Waller!" Hawkins cried out, bringing her service weapon up to her eye. Before she even lined up a shot, Chrome-mask was moving again.

Time slowed down as Chrome-mask dove off the wall in a trajectory that was almost a straight line, directly at us. Hawkins fired a shot that missed Chrome-mask and shattered the window at the end of the hallway, while Foster finally stirred from his momentary paralysis and swiped out with the butt of his pistol.

Chrome-mask twisted in the air to avoid the blow and something glinted in his hand.

Immediately, I realized what he was trying to do.

I wasn't certain how his power worked yet, exactly, but it seemed to take some setup. A certain number of those thin, needle-like blades in the target before he could use his crimson magic to obliterate the center-point, as he had the Users in the cathedral.

With milliseconds to spare, I dead-legged Waller with a swift kick at the back of his knee, trying to stop Chrome-mask from completing the circuit.

No longer blocked by Waller, Chrome-mask crashed into me with both feet. He was smaller than me and weighed significantly less, but the drop-kick still sent me skidding a small distance down the hallway. I watched helplessly as Chrome-mask scrambled toward the fallen agent, planting the final knife into Waller's forehead.

Then—almost casually—punched through his face, bathing the surrounding hallway in red.

"No!" Foster screamed.

But Sae was faster. Maybe faster than all of us. She grabbed Chrome-mask's head in one clawed hand and picked him up, slamming him repeatedly into a metal doorframe. The top left section of his mask came off, revealing a section of brown hair and a vicious green eye.

Ellison.

My heart sank. On some level, I'd known since the Transposition. But I'd hoped more than anything that I had missed something. That I'd been wrong.

The brother I'd loved since the day he was born snarled in a voice I couldn't recognize as he grabbed Sae's wrist with both hands. He peeled her chitin thumb back, slipping out of the vice grip and pretzeling one leg around her arm for leverage, kicking at her face with the other.

There was a gunshot, and Ellison's head snapped back. He plummeted to the ground and landed motionless. Hawkins and Foster advanced on him.

Talia stood over Ellison, growling.

I moved quickly, straddling Ellison's torso and wrapping my hands around the lightweight material that covered his neck lightly. The bullet from Hawkins' handgun was flattened in the top portion of his mask.

"What are you doing?" I whispered, furious.

From the corner of my eye, I saw Azure climb through the shattered window at the end of the hall.

<Ellison: Listen to me. For once, actually listen. Everything hinges on Iris. Everything. And if your buddies take me captive or kill me, she's as good as dead.>

<Matt: Bullshit.>

<Ellison: Yeah. You always say that. Just like Iris always dies in the second event.>

"We got this, Matt," Foster said, and I felt an arm pulling me free as Hawkins flanked from the side. My expression hardened as I let him pull me off Ellison.

<Matt: What do you mean, always? You tried to kill me in the lobby, Ellison. I can't just let that go.>

Not to mention that he'd killed Waller. This plan was contingent on the Feds making it through—by the skin of their teeth, but alive. The death of my biggest detractor reflected badly on me, no matter how you looked at it.

<Ellison: See how well that justification holds up when the body count gets personal.>

In the past, Ellison always delivered bad news with a similar mix of callousness and apathy. There was a strong possibility he wasn't lying here. A coldness settled over me.

<Matt: No. You're so far over the rubicon, you probably can't even remember what it looked like when you crossed it. You don't get to dictate terms.>

Ellison grunted as Foster and Hawkins hauled him to his feet. His visible eye pierced me, a dark anger emitting from it.

The feeling of wrongness grew thick. This wasn't just about letting him go. If he really wanted my help, all he had to do was threaten to reveal my identity to the public at large. Even if my public face bought me a certain degree of goodwill, someone would eventually make good on the threat. But if he went that route, the bridge between us would be burned to ash. I'd never trust him again.

Instead, he'd brought Iris into it.

<Matt: If I get you out of this, the two of us are going to have a conversation in the near future. Non-negotiable.>
<Ellison: Done. And before you ask, yes, I swear it. On Dad's memory.>

Promises were cheap. But Ellison revered our father in a way I'd never understood. It was, perhaps, the one thing he could have said to convince me he'd follow through. In the distance, the sound of a helicopter grew closer.

I closed my eyes and signaled Azure.

Hawkins and Foster stopped in their tracks as foul-smelling smoke poured through the hallway. Multiple fire alarms went off one after another, each adding to the dissonant keen, wailing like a demented choir. Audrey's vine shot through the smoke and lashed Hawkins' wrist, knocking away the gun. Another grabbed Ellison by the ankle and yanked him from their grasp.

Suddenly unburdened, Foster and Hawkins unloaded down the hallway, firing through the smoke. A bolt struck me in the ribcage, scraping against bone. Sae pulled me out of the way as a hail of flashing knives cut through the air.

Talia charged into the smoke, snarling and growling.

Before I knew what was happening, Miles was standing above me, firing arrow after arrow into the smoke, his face twisted in a rictus of anger. He pointed to a nearby door. "Inside!"

We retreated into the open suite. Foster dragged Cook inside, while Talia, freshly bloodied, slipped in just before the doors closed.

A small family huddled together, staring with wide eyes as our bedraggled group staggered in, slamming the door shut behind us. The sound of whirling helicopter blades grew deafening. A rope ladder banging against the railing on the outside lounge. That must have been how Miles got in. A small assortment of police officers and SWAT unloaded from the helicopter and pushed forward, taking a position beside Miles.

"Waller?" Miles kept his bow trained on the door and glanced at Hawkins.

Hawkins shook her head.

Miles' mouth turned downward. "God fucking dammit. We're leaving. Now. Get in the helicopter. All of you."

Hawkins, Foster, and Sae made their way out onto the balcony overhang. Sae hoisted Cook up the ladder and then dropped back down. When she extended a hand to Hawkins, she ignored it and pulled herself up. She froze and pointed out toward the distance, her voice barely audible over the noise. "Bogey—is that—Myrddin's backup is running!"

Sure enough, I saw a paragliding silhouette approximately the size of my brother making solid time toward the moonlit horizon

My blood dripped freely, staining the plush carpet. I stared at the small family huddled in the corner, a resolute tranquility came over me.

"I can't go."

Miles grabbed me roughly by my hoodie. "The hell you can't. You're bleeding out. He slipped through all your security and literally attacked you where you live. Let the professionals look after your family. It's not safe here."

I glared at Miles. "And whose fault is that?"

Miles released me as if he'd stuck his hands into a fire.

"Nowhere is safe," I pushed. "Everyone in this region is relying on me. If I leave, Myrddin will find a way to make us pay for it. I paid in blood to save them. I can't abandon them now."

I nearly cringed at how painfully valiant it sounded. If it were just us, I would have pushed back with my family's safety instead. But the civilians' presence gave me a unique opportunity to entrench myself in the region further. Solidify that what happened at the end of the event wasn't just a fluke.

Miles studied me through cold blue eyes. "Myrddin fought half a guild and walked out unscathed. Not to mention, he has backup. Fighting him alone only ends one way."

"If he was at the top of his game, sure, but he's injured." Sae took a place next to me. Talia at her side. "And I want a piece of that fucker as much as Matt does."

"Who are you?" Miles shook his head. "Never mind. More importantly, how do you know that?"

Sae glanced at Talia. "Spirit Guardian told me."

Irritation flooded Miles' expression. "Of course. There are Spirit Guardians now."

Foster crossed his arms. "She's solid, Miles. And Hawkins is out of the game, but I'm not. Way I see it, if we end this here, it saves a helluva lot of trouble in the long run."

Miles didn't look convinced. I gave it one last try. "I've been spamming messages to Kinsley, trying to get through. **\<Squelch\>** dropped long enough for me to get a message off. Kinsley's people are on their way. Some patrolling mercs probably heard the gunfire and are already down in the lobby floor. "All we need to do is push him toward the lobby."

With a sigh, Miles steadied himself. He pointed to the arrow emerging from my ribcage. "Foster?"

Foster studied the arrow's placement, then drew a serrated blade, giving me a questioning look. When I nodded and gritted my teeth, he began to saw the shaft, muttering apologies as every vibration sent a new wave of pain from my body. Eventually, I was left with an inch of blood-stained bolt emerging from my hoody.

"Kid should be alright, assuming nothing tears that out. That's the most serious injury. An inch difference and that could have been your heart. Everything else is non-vital. You got lucky." Foster locked eyes with me and inclined his head in tacit approval.

"What's the plan, Matt?" Sae asked.

I considered that for a moment, grunting at a wave of pain. "My guess? Myrddin is leaning on his notoriety from the broadcast. He came here expecting us to run. Engage cautiously, if we engage at all. But no one's that agile without a drawback. He has to be a glass canon."

Miles breathed in sharply. "You want to blitz him."

My expression hardened. "He's been pushing his agenda uncontested from the start. That stops here."

CHAPTER FIFTY-ONE

This was the homestretch.

I'd expected to cover the retreat and was fully prepared to take a few more parting blows from Azure to sell the theater.

What I hadn't expected was the region's reaction. I'd assumed they would cower in their apartments, waiting for the incessantly repetitive emergency message to fade.

I was wrong.

It seemed that many had not taken the events of Transposition lightly. Nearly dying due to their cowardice had not faded from their memories.

Upon exiting the suite, we were greeted with the image of Azure in the midst of a throng of civilians, arms up defensively as they rained down blows on his head and body. Several mages stood on the outskirts with an assortment of glowing wands and staves, awkwardly holding their fire as the civilians shouted obscenities and beat the ever-living hell out of Azure with whatever blunt objects they could get their hands on. Few of them were Users, and fewer still had any real combat experience, so they were doing minimal damage. Still, it had to be accumulating

"Thought you were going to stand outside my family's door and look menacing."

"I tried! They came out of nowhere!" Azure's mental voice sounded oddly affronted, as if he couldn't understand *why* an entire building had taken issue with him.

Miles' collection of DCPD officers in tactical gear started shouting for people to get down on the ground. Only a few headed the warning. Improvising, I reached out and stoked the anger of those still standing, subtly manipulating them into blocking any potential shots from the assault rifles.

One of the cops upfront grew antsy and broke what had to be at least a dozen department regulations, firing his automatic rifle into the ceiling, then screamed again for everyone to get down.

This time everyone listened, laying down and revealing... nothing.

Everyone waited in tense silence, searching the cluster of civilians for Myrddin's form. There was a distinct sound of a door latching shut cut through the quiet.

One of the region mages, now prone, was pointing toward the stairway.

"He's running!" Miles took off, sprinting toward the emergency stairs.

I chased after Miles, outpacing the small stampede of officers easily despite my injuries, throwing open the door to the emergency stairs and chasing after him as he glided down them. Either his agility was significantly higher than mine, or his pre-system training and conditioning pushed him further.

A few steps behind us, Sae vaulted over the railing, straight through the open space of the stairwell like a chitin rocket, plummeting all the way down until she hit the granite floor, stone fracturing beneath her like a spiderweb. "You sold us out, motherfucker!" The scream was filled with so much hatred that it sent a chill down my spine. She was clearly using this as an opportunity to work some shit out.

Miles and I rounded the last flight of stairs, just in time to see Sae hurl Azure through the open doorway.

Azure bounced back quickly and fled into a mix of civilians, Adventurers' Guild, and law enforcement. I amped up both the mages and officers' fear of firing in such a crowded area, but there was little I could do to quell the civilians' rage.

Sae stayed on Azure. I noticed she wasn't using her claws much, and the heavy strikes that could have floored me were absent.

Azure managed to duck under a wild punch. He grabbed a middle-aged woman and held his crossbow to her head. Everyone stopped.

Slowly, Azure backed toward the door.

I noticed a police rifleman standing on the reception desk, looking far too comfortable with the weapon and situation to be an amateur.

"Keep your head down."

Azure ducked his head behind the woman's shoulder. His eyes—gray now, though they'd been cycling through various colors—conveyed utter hate. "Nice makeover. Should have killed you in the trial. Would have been a mercy, considering the end result."

I winced, jockeying for position on the left. They'd rehearsed this, but Sae still had to bear the emotional brunt of the words. Miles flanked across from me, staggering his movements so we didn't hit each other with any potential crossfire.

Sae stalked toward him, advancing at the same rate he retreated, her movements smooth, chitin feet clicking on marble. "Let her go."

"I have minutes. Maybe less," Azure warned.

That would have to be enough. Across from me, Miles' face was a mask of focus, bowstring pulled to his chin, looking for a shot. Azure angled the woman toward him slightly.

"You deserve what's coming. You and the rest of these useless fucks." Azure sneered at me. I frowned. He was missing the mark somewhat, coming off as a little too villainous. Still, the crowd murmured angrily, pushing in tighter. He extended the crossbow out toward them. "Stay back."

<Probability Cascade> washed over my bow. I breathed out. And loosed.

The arrow lodged itself in Azure's crossbow, knocking it to the floor. It clattered to the ground. Azure kicked the woman squarely in the back. Audrey's vines threw open the door behind him and yanked him through.

There was a wave of thundering gunfire outside. Everyone inside hit the deck. I waited, my heart racing in my chest.

"In pursuit. Suspect is fleeing east across the rooftops." The message was blasted over several radios.

A slow cheer went up among the civilians, growing to a thunder. I glanced over at them, surprised. I'd thought they'd be disappointed, maybe even angry. Slowly, the reality dawned. They didn't care about killing the Ordinator. These people had been through hell and come up wanting. And ever since, they'd been seeking an opportunity to prove themselves. Together, they'd driven off a threat and protected me. Just like I'd protected them.

"Thank you," I said, projecting the words so they carried.

Another round of cheers went up. I wobbled on my feet and shook more hands than I could count, blindsided by this outcome. I'd expected this to lose me credibility, not earn it.

This region is a means to an end. Look at them. The last gasp of the wealthy elite. Before you saved their lives, none of these people would have so much as spit on you if you were on fire. They are tools, nothing more, **<Scathing Shell>** *hissed in my mind.*

I struggled against that sentiment. It aligned closely with similar thoughts that had crossed my mind. But that was before all this. Even if my title was right about who they were, they deserved some degree of loyalty for who they chose to be.

Even if none of this was real.

Sae shifted in the center of the lobby awkwardly. There was an unnatural space around her, and while no one was openly staring, they were pointedly avoiding looking at her or growing too close. I hugged her, careful of the arrow in my ribcage. "I'm glad you're alive."

"Getting a weird sense of déjà vu," Sae snorted.

After we parted, the spell of isolation was broken. People approached Sae and thanked her for her help. Asked her questions about Myrddin, her history. I half-listened as she navigated the story we'd agreed on, my attention divided. Because across the foyer, half-shrouded in shadow, Miles watched.

His gaze wasn't hostile, exactly. More like he was looking at a puzzle with a missing piece, trying to imagine how it all fit together. He gave me a half-hearted smile that didn't reach his eyes.

All at once, the adrenaline faded and the pain from my wounds grew overwhelming. Dr. Ansari arrived on site, and I stumbled over to one of the plush white cushion chairs and sat down as she pushed through the crowd and began to open her bag, lips pursed in irritation.

"I am sensing this is going to be a recurring theme, Mr. Matthias."

"You're probably right."

The words from Ellison's message echoed in my mind.

Everything hinges on Iris. Everything.

CHAPTER FIFTY-TWO

THRUM

Bright. Brighter than the birth of the universe.

The crinkling fabric shredded through my ears like a sudden gale of wind. A metal saucer bearing, massive, far too large to be the utensil it resembled, forced its way in my mouth, cracking against my teeth. An overwhelming taste of vanilla radiated through my tastebuds and sinuses, so strong and overwhelming I nearly vomited. The metal withdrew, banging against a molar hard enough that my root nerves screamed.

I watched helplessly as a gigantic fist of flesh manipulated the metal, driving it down into an endless sea of white that split easily as the saucer scooped out its insides.

I—

I—

I—I—I—I

The clock on the trans am's console read 5:00am. Miles took another bite of ice-cream. It tasted like ash in his mouth. He held the pint up and rotated it, gazing at the green and blue label. The brand name was Ben and Harry's, in the same cutesy, copyright-infringing font.

To be fair, it wasn't the system knock-off's fault he couldn't taste it. It wasn't quite the same as the original, but from his previous visits to this particular 7-11, it was a damn good imitation. Right down to the vanilla extract and the shitty little black bits that were supposed to look like ground-up bean. As far as he was concerned, you had to take time to enjoy the simple things in life. The simple things kept you grounded. Reminded you that no matter how dark you delved, there was something waiting for you on the surface.

Of course, that was easier if you could taste it.

Miles scowled at the spoon and proceeded to eat it anyway.

"You're going to get diabetes before you hit forty," Hawkins commented from the passenger seat. She had one knee against the console, an unopened pint of Rocky Road balanced on her knee. The green and red neon lights of the sign illuminated her haggard face, unkept hair, and sizable dark bags under her eyes, foundation and other makeup banished with the cosmetic equivalent of a Brillo Pad. He'd never voice it, but Miles secretly preferred her this way. Not that the makeup was bad. Hawkins was an artist with it, and art should be appreciated. But he'd seen her like this enough to know that something about her sleepless, messy presentation appealed to him.

"Assuming I live to forty. On that note, your hair's going to thin if you don't find a way to manage stress."

"Big talk for a man whose forehead seems to be growing by the year."

Miles toyed with his sideswept hair, pushing it up and inspecting his hairline.

"So, we're dropping Matt. As a suspect," Hawkins asked.

"We are looking in other directions," Miles confirmed.

"Then you're cutting him loose from the Taskforce?" Hawkins asked.

"No."

"So we're not dropping him as a suspect." The pint of ice cream nearly toppled, and Hawkins caught it with a fingertip before it could fall.

Miles fought down an upsurge of annoyance. The problem with working with associates that knew you so well was precisely what it said on the tin. He wasn't sure what he thought. How he felt. About Myrddin, about Matt. About the unknown third party.

His thoughts went to Waller and his chest hurt. Still, taking emotion out of it, the man's death stuck out like a sore thumb. The garrote Miles gave him was an excellent tool for covertly taking down a threat, but Myrddin had every opportunity to kill Cook after he used it. Only, he hadn't. Considering how quickly things had devolved into chaos, the fact that the body count only encompassed a single person was a miracle.

And there was no such thing as miracles.

There was little reason to kill Waller from a rational standpoint. If Myrddin was his own person, unaffiliated from Matt, killing Waller first made a small amount of sense. He'd come up with the profile, which was insulting to Myrddin in too many ways to count. However, it required a degree of pettiness that Miles considered Myrddin to be above. If this was some sort of shadow-play to throw Miles off, killing Waller made no sense at all. If he was smart enough to pull that off, he was smart enough to know that killing the obvious antagonist in the room was stupid as hell.

And Myrddin hadn't even killed Waller. The third party had.

Neither possibility fit.

"This whole thing is a Gordian Knot we don't have time for." Miles dug his spoon into the ice cream, and when it slid off the frozen substance, set it aside. "We have at least three operating Necromancers that we know of. One of which is apparently well-organized with a solid operation, if Matt was telling the truth. Hundreds of Users migrating to Region 5 like it's some sort of Mecca, more concerning that the region is actively encouraging it, and whatever the hell is happening in Region 13."

"Roderick, still living large in Region 2," Hawkins added grimly. "And the cops will never admit it, but they're still struggling to contain the gory, shambling mess that is..."

Miles stiffened.

"Sorry." Hawkins sat back in her seat, placing a hand on her forehead. "It's been a long night."

"Don't worry about it," Miles said quietly. *Just don't say it.*

"Okay, I'm gonna say it." Hawkins slammed her hand down on the console. "You know that Region 6 wasn't your fault, right? By all accounts, it happened before you even meet Myrddin."

"Yeah."

"And Waller wasn't your fault either."

"Maybe not directly," Miles said. His left knee began to bounce. "But I was too slow tonight. It took longer than I expected to pull everyone together. I should have just gone with what I had, but I was sure there was more time."

"You think he knew it was a trap?" Hawkins asked. "Moved preemptively?"

"It's Myrddin. Of course he did," Miles said grimly. "And despite being fully aware of who I was dealing with, I underestimated him."

Miles rolled down the window and threw his half-eaten pint in the adjacent garbage can next to the gas station doorway. A solid ten feet. Then he put the car in reverse and pulled out, turning on cruise control as soon as he hit the thoroughfare.

"Where are we going?" Hawkins asked blandly, as if she didn't care to hear the answer.

"Dropping you off. I think, after all the sideways talk from the Merchants' Initiative, you could use some rest. Thanks for taking the lead with them."

"Not a problem. I mean, we confirmed Kinsley was there most of the night. That they'd scheduled the meeting days ago. That's not nothing."

It wasn't nothing. But it was close.

Miles felt Hawkins' eyes on him. "You did the thing."

"What thing?" Miles watched the road, stepping on the breaks just as a group of Users in robes with torches jaywalked across the highway, chanting something vaguely cultish sounding

"Where you railroad the conversation in another direction and don't answer my question. About leaving the kid in the Taskforce."

"He's well connected, and he's the Adventurers' Guild's golden boy. He also has some sort of connection with Myrddin that we don't fully understand." Miles turned the wheel fully to the right, driving around the trailing crowd of torch-bearers. One of them flipped Miles off. Another grabbed his junk. "We cut him out, it's possible he never talks to us again. And considering how thoroughly Waller scrambled his eggs, I'm not sure we could blame him."

"The legendary user core," Hawkins mused.

"May be a misdirect. Might not be. But Myrddin doesn't run his mouth unnecessarily. Shot in the dark, but I'm starting to get the feeling that payback doesn't really motivate him. Not the type. If they have something he wants, though? He's going to keep coming."

"We sure the Adventurers' Guild has the apartment locked down?" Hawkins looked worried.

"Yeah. Tyler was pissed. He's not taking any chances. And the little girl came storming in with more contractors than I saw over three years in Afghanistan."

Hawkins snorted. "There were *a lot*."

"He's safe. As far as the Ordinator is concerned, we stick to homicide rules."

"A lot of interviews, a lot of sitting on our hands and waiting for Myrddin to make a mistake," Hawkins filled in. "Even if we're dropping him as a suspect—"

"Which we are—"

"I get the feeling *you* aren't." Hawkins held her silence after that, letting the words sink in.

Ten minutes later, Miles pulled in to a small suburban house on the outskirts of the city. If you walked fifty feet further down this road, you could reach out and touch the dome. They'd done that together, at the beginning of all this.

Hawkins got out, then bent down and knocked on the window. Miles rolled it down.

She smiled, tucking a strand of hair behind her ear. "Want company?"

Miles grinned. "Pretty sure that twenty-four-hour chapel in downtown is still open. Want to be my fourth wife?"

Hawkins sighed. "If you drive around brooding until the sun comes up, you'll hate yourself for it."

"Okay, Mom."

"I'm getting mixed signals. Do you want me to be your mom or your wife?"

Miles made a finger-gun and pointed it at her. "Yes."

"Gross." Hawkins rolled her eyes and turned, waving behind her. "See you in the AM."

Once Hawkins was safely inside, Miles pulled out. He drove almost automatically, until he reached the tall blue tarps that lined the outskirts of R6egion . Several people in white hazmat suits had removed their helmets and were smoking at a nearby picnic table. A man in a reflective vest next to a concrete barricade waved a flashlight, indicating for him to go around.

He followed the direction, the numbness returning as he caught glimpses of the flesh-covered buildings behind the barricade.

The core of anger he'd suppressed so well began to bubble in his gut. Waller's face flashed in his mind. Followed by Myrddin's shifting, ever-changing visage. For some reason, the scene of the interrogation, where Myrddin had pretended to waterboard the goon in the Necromancer's operation, flashed in his mind.

It was so easy for things to turn nasty when the stakes were high. If Myrddin had actually intended to waterboard the man with gasoline, Miles might have let him. Instead, he'd been impressed with the man's restraint. The reliance on trickery, rather than brute forcing a situation that could have turned ugly all-too-quickly.

He'd been impressed. With Myrddin's *restraint*.

Miles stepped on the gas, blowing through a stop sign. The white arches of the McDermott Bridge came into view, peeking over the near abandoned highway.

The engine roared as Miles barreled towardsthe bridge, barely stopping on the median that marked the dome's edge, where he stumbled out and onto the sidewalk, gripping the waist-high wall tightly, gazing down into the dark water below as a tingling anxiety ran rampant down his neck, his spine, pressure building until it felt as if his head might explode.

He breathed in and out, waiting for the panic attack to pass.

"Whoever you are," Miles whispered raggedly, searching for his elusive reflection in the water, seeing nothing but darkness. "I'll find you."

CHAPTER FIFTY-THREE

I soared through the sky. Even after ten minutes, the feeling of weightlessness was jarring and alien. In normal circumstances, whatever passed for normal these days, I would have enjoyed this. I was gliding hundreds of feet in the air, getting the sort of million-dollar view only accessible from a helicopter.

Problem was, I'd over-tapped myself last night. Using my vocation ability to spy on Miles was a risk, but the result had paid off in spades. The peace of mind that came with knowing my gambit had mostly succeeded was worth any short-term discomfort I could think of. If I'd just limited my night's activities to that, I'd probably be fine.

But, I'd overextended. Sent Azure out to shore up loose ends.

The problem was Sae. I'd made a mistake, introducing her to my family early. Put her emotional well-being ahead of the all-important rule of compartmentalization. I didn't like the idea of screwing with the minds of people close to me. But I wasn't willing to wager that Ellison was bullshitting me about Iris' life hanging in the balance. And if I was taking that on principal?

The rules could go fuck themselves.

I sent Azure out to modify memories, and ignored his warning that it'd be difficult. He'd need to make multiple trips and draw heavily from my mana to carry it out. If we didn't live in the same building, it wouldn't be possible. The rules for my summons were frustratingly inconsistent. Talia was self-sustaining and could trawl the entire city without me. Azure needed me close by.

It was the only point of weakness left. The last avenue Miles could use to get at me. If he confirmed that Sae was in the building prior to last night? He'd have me.

According to Azure, it was easy enough to edit both my mother's and Estrada's memories. They both had only met Sae a handful of times. I had to thank my friend's shut-in tendencies for that. From their perspective, she simply hadn't been there, and any memory of conversation they had with her in it was edited out cleanly while leaving the core scene intact, not unlike editing a character out of a TV show.

Steinbeck was significantly harder. Sae had made more of an impact on him, as he'd met her in stressful circumstances and accompanied us as we smuggled her into the apartment through Kinsley's door. Azure spent most of the evening editing Sae out of the broadcast memory and giving him a false memory of the previous evening.

Iris, unfortunately, simply wasn't possible.

On top of the work she'd put into the faux armor that made Sae appear more human, she'd kept Sae company far more often than I'd realized. Azure told me she cared for Sae deeply, and excising something so meaningful out of my sister's memories could cause mental scarring at best, irreparable damage at worst.

When Azure proceeded to use that explanation to tell me more about what the people in my life were thinking, I stopped him.

What I'd done was already a gross invasion of privacy. There wasn't any need to delve deeper.

My sister might be the one person I fully trusted to keep a secret. And given what had just happened, I didn't think Miles would seek her out any time soon.

All that to say, I was trying to enjoy the flying. Be in the moment. But the biblical headache, and the way the sun seemed to creep through my eyes and punch every neuron, was seriously cutting into the enjoyment factor.

Someone *bumped* me. I screamed, and any remaining effort to hold onto my lunch was violently ejected onto the ground below.

Hope that doesn't hit someone.

Daron was interesting, for a region leader. The man was wearing a cheap purple vest pushed out so far out from his expansive stomach that in side-profile it nearly formed a cock-eyed J. A pair of white, clearly DIY angel wings ruffled on his back. He flew alongside me, smiling apologetically. "Are you enjoying your tour, Mr. Matthias?" His Southern European accent was thick, and with the wind, his words were barely audible.

"Yes." I wiped my chin.

"'Yes' he says." Daron belly laughed and rotated onto his back, making a show of an unnecessarily flamboyant backstroke. "'Yes.' The air is so clear up here, so clean! How could one not enjoy these beautiful skies?"

Salesman, before. Or a magician? No. Definitely a salesman.

There were a few other people on the tour. All VIPs. But they were some distance behind us. Daron had latched onto me, for obvious reasons. And now my head was spinning, my only point of reference an over-indulgent, dollar-store angel.

The others caught up with us. I took some small comfort in the fact that they all looked similarly queasy.

My stomach turned upside down as I was overcome with the juddering feeling of losing altitude. I looked at Daron in alarm, while one of the other two loudly lost their lunch.

Daron's eyebrows shot up dramatically. "Come, my friends, our time is short."

"Oh my god, we're falling." The man clung to the woman, his face white and grim. The woman panicked and shoved him off.

"We're not falling. We're making our glorious descent with valorous rapidity!" Daron exclaimed.

"That sounds like falling with too many adjectives," I said, having lost any semblance of filter the third time I'd vomited. Now that we were descending steadily, it felt less like we were plummeting, more like the world itself was rocketing toward us. The pointed tower of a skyscraper passed like a thrusting spear.

Daron pulled the tail end of a rope with knotted increments from his inventory. "Take hold! I shall guide us to the celestial plane."

Shall?

I wished I knew Daron was off his gourd *before* I'd let him levitate me hundreds of feet in the air. Lacking any better option, I grabbed the knotted portion of the rope. The man and woman grasped the sections behind me. I closed my eyes, only peeking intermittently to confirm that we were indeed heading toward Region 7 and not some secondary location.

The man behind me was still shrieking, the sounds he made elevated from terror into something that resembled disturbingly carnal bliss.

When Daron announced we were making a final descent, I forced my eyes open. And immediately wished I hadn't. The rock-covered ground of a rooftop was rushing toward us at a velocity that couldn't have been anything other than terminal.

For a moment, my thoughts, my fears, everything blinked out. Just as it had the moment the meteor hit.

Then Daron did... something. He angled his body flat, and a pulse radiated from the charm around his neck.

We crashed into a cushion of air. There had to be some magic fuckery involved, because no matter how soft the landing, that sudden suspension of movement should have been enough to shred our organs.

The cushion remained until all three of us crawled off, then the faint translucent shimmer dissipated. I released the rope, my legs pure rubber as Daron led us toward the door. The others still clung to it tightly, and I couldn't blame them.

Apparently accustomed to this, Daron smiled reassuringly. "Come, friends. Come, come. Your place of respite is nigh."

This was Region 7's claim to fame. The flight charm. It was more limited than I'd hoped, but it still had an insane number of applications and utility.

I doubled over, heaving but coming up dry. Needed to catch my breath. Recenter.

Daron ushered the other two in. I didn't miss the way his hand lingered on the woman's waist, or the way he positioned himself so she had to brush against him as she passed. Two attendants inside the door—both wearing vests, both donning the terrible DIY angel wings—led them down one at a time.

The actions matched his reputation. Now that I thought about it, his refusal to talk to Kinsley directly might be an act of providence.

For him, anyway.

"It takes some time for the charm to recharge," Daron said absent-mindedly. It almost didn't sound like a warning. Almost.

"You didn't teach us how to land either." I frowned. "It's insane that no one's died."

"No one's died, no one's stolen a charm. That's winning, as far as I'm concerned." He gave me a wide smile that amped up my nausea.

"Good for you."

"What?"

I forced myself to stand upright. "That's good to hear."

"Indeed. I look forward to talking business."

"Soon as my head stops spinning."

"This way, my friend, this way." He ushered me in. There was no attendant for me, just Daron himself. We descended a flight of stairs and exited out into something that resembled a spa. Women in string bikinis with dead eyes were giving the previously screeching man a massage. Adonis-like men clad in white towels wrapped around their waists—towels far closer to hand than bath, in terms of dimension—attended the woman.

Both of my fellow tourists looked profoundly uncomfortable.

"What... is this? Exactly?" I had to ask.

"The celestial plane, of course. Where all angels must rest before they take to the skies once more."

I paused. "There's not actually a second round, is there?"

"It's a metaphor."

"Right."

This branding *really* needed some work.

Daron exploded in a belly laugh that startled everyone in the room, including the strippers—masseuses. Whatever. He walked backward, extending his palms flat up to either side of the room. "Now, my young friend, pick your paradise."

I shook my head. "Thanks. But I'd rather get to the point."

He stuck a finger at me. "All business. I like that, I respect that."

He held open the door for me and I followed him down the stairway. There wasn't anything to mark the floors, but I'd been keeping count.

Three floors down, I staggered, placing my hand against the door.

"Stick your chin out more and drop your jaw. Like you've got marbles in your mouth, but not too many," Azure said.

"Clear coms. And stop giving me notes, dammit," I growled back. Aloud, I called after Daron. "Actually, I'm not feeling so well. Mind if I just sit on the stairs for a minute?"

"Of course." Daron smiled. "But I'd never force such an esteemed guest to rest in such an environment. Through the door with you, young sir, through the door."

I followed his direction and entered a floor that looked very much like a corporate office had disemboweled a Precious Moments Etsy shop. Angel wings, angel memorabilia, and motherfucking porcelain angel figurines lined the walls and display shelves. Small cubicles took up the center floor, where people in business casual—mostly men—were seated at desks, talking directly into them.

Despite the plethora of conversation, no one was actually talking to each other. I slowly realized they were all on voice calls.

"I see you resurrected the call center."

Daron pointed me to a plush couch near the stairway door. "Why reinvent when you can reinvigorate?"

I followed his instruction and sat down, still scanning the faces.

Eventually, I found what I was looking for.

I'd missed him because he was hunched over the sink, filling up a neoprene water bottle. Buzzcut turned away from me, his expression bored, neutral. Someone raised a fist toward him as he passed and he bumped it, shooting the man a smile that looked anything but natural on his face.

The flight charm was mostly cover. This was the real reason I'd come.

Now the question was, what was Buzzcut doing here?

CHAPTER FIFTY-FOUR

As if something whispered in the back of his mind, Buzzcut suddenly whipped around. He scanned the room, pausing on me.

I held my breath.

Buzzcut's eyes finally slid off me. He pumped sanitizer into his palm from a bottle on his desk and proceeded to wash his hands intently, working the sanitizer in with practiced ease, paying extra attention to the backs of his hands, going all the way up to his wrists and arms.

I'd found a new functionality, experimenting with the **<Allfather's Mask>** this morning. It wasn't an upgrade exactly—and on the constellation of settings, it was nestled far on the left side. It strengthened the anonymity and memory effect for a single target. Everyone else—Sae, for this morning's experiment—would see me without the mask, while the target would see a person of little importance, who they'd immediately forget after the fact.

Buzzcut was already dialing. Or voice calling, whatever. He looked bored, eyes continually tracking to the bottle on his desk. As he continued whatever rote conversation he was having, he stood and pumped an entire glop of sanitizer into his palm, going through the washing process once more.

He forgot he washed them already. Weird fixation on hygiene.

A few feet away, I saw a faint blue shimmer as Azure navigated the shadows, swimming in the dark places beneath desks and dark lines cast by the wide window divider at the far side of the room.

While Azure did his thing, I made a show of looking nauseous and multitasked. Several quests came in shortly after the showdown at the apartment.

<Quest Received>
Quest Name: Spotlight
Quest Chain Description: Rescue your lost companion.
Current Primary Objective — Assassinate Cameron and gain entry into the enigmatic organization.
Secondary Objective — Find an alternative method to gain entry.
Threat Level: (L)
EXP GAIN (L)
Time Limit: One Week.
Reward: ???

<Quest Received>
Quest Name: Blue Skies
Primary Objective — Secure a flight charm through legitimate means.
Secondary Objective — Open negotiations with Region 7 to obtain a large number of charms for your associated guilds.
Personal Objective — Remain unidentified by other Users.
Threat Level: (S)
EXP GAIN (S)
Time Limit: N/A
Reward: A Flight Charm
Reward: ???

Kinsley assigned the second quest, when I told her I needed an excuse to come here for recon. Figured I might as well kill two birds with one stone.

The first quest was system-assigned, and the timing I'd received it in was interesting. It came in this morning—long after the conversation with Gray-hair—while I was still rubbing sleep from my eyes and utterly at the mercy of the migraine.

It was like the system didn't see the point of assigning me a long-term quest despite the obvious hook until I'd dealt with Miles. Further evidence that Miles was a threat I needed to take seriously, even if he was putting Myrddin on the back burner for now.

More interestingly, it pointed out a potential flaw. The system hadn't bothered to assign anyone a quest during the Transposition event. For the most part, the quest system had entirely disappeared. I'd taken that as nothing more than part of the invisible, unknowable rule set navigating our own personal ship to hell, but given the timing of the situation with Miles and the late assignment, maybe it wasn't that simple.

If it was a question of efficiency? If the system didn't bother assigning quests to someone who was likely to die in the short term to skimp on processing, or something along those lines?

That was hugely exploitable as an early warning.

Of course, there were holes. Counterarguments. The **<Light in the Darkness>** chief among them. My mind drifted to that afternoon in the tunnel and my mouth turned downward. The system had doled out that quest to help Jinny moments before she died. And Buzzcut had been there, standing among them, as Jinny bled out into the gravel.

Azure slipped back into my shadow.

"I know where the suits are," he whispered excitedly.

"Where?" I asked, genuinely surprised, as I hadn't expected to get much from him. We shared the same weakness. Given enough time, access, and information, Azure was a force to be reckoned with. Short-term improvisation was where he lacked.

"Underground!" Azure exclaimed.

I groaned inwardly.

Azure hurriedly continued. "Before you totally disregard that, I saw glimpses of their complex. It's a big operation. Big enough that it's not something they could have manifested themselves in months, let alone weeks."

Huh. "So it's a large underground space that existed before the system. Maybe we can narrow it down. Anything else?"

"Cameron's anxious about going down there. Partly because he's stressing over not getting enough sunlight, partly because he's losing faith in Aaron. Couldn't suss out why, but things are strained."

My eyebrow shot up. That was as close as I'd come to definitive confirmation that Aaron was with the suits.

"And I haven't even told you the best part. The reason Cameron's worried he backed the wrong horse. Aaron almost died in the Transposition. That wasn't cover, that was real. He's a civilian. They had operatives in route to deliver the necessary Lux to Region 14 who suddenly went missing, along with the Lux. It was a coup attempt. Now Aaron's too exposed and people are questioning his authority. It's only a matter of time before Sunny takes over."

The way Azure emphasized Sunny could only mean one thing. Still, I was dumbfounded. *"Gray's real name is Sunny?"*

"Sunny Grounds," Azure cackled in my mind.

"Bullshit."

"I know. But it seems too obvious to be a pseudonym."

"He's got to be a meteorologist." With a name that... unique... it wouldn't be difficult to track him down if he had any significant online presence at all. The library was working on getting an archived version of Wikipedia up on the public computers. Once it was up, I'd have a wealth of information about my would-be employer.

———

I chanced sending Azure out one more time before I was forced to pack it in. He didn't get much more information from Buzzcut's mind about the suits, but he got plenty about Daron and the situation in Region 7. A little too much.

Having gotten wind of our intentions from Kinsley, Tyler had asked me to handle this with care. The Adventurers' Guild leader was as interested in getting our collective hands on the flight charm as anyone. But according to him, Daron spooked easily. This was the first time the man had been willing to sit down and talk to anyone from either guild.

But after what Azure told me, the situation had changed.

Daron's office was on the bottom floor. It was, perhaps, the one place in the building that wasn't decked out in angel theme. If anything, it looked like an artifact from the early nineties. A yellowed pinup poster of a woman clutching her throat who was, apparently, very cold, overlooked an oversized mahogany desk. The desk was executive style and massive. I had no idea how they'd managed to get it through the door.

Through the blinds, a long line of people waited in line outside the front door, while others filled out paperwork at the desks.

Daron closed the door behind him. He absentmindedly reached up and grabbed a string, sliding the blinds closed as he navigated to the other side of the desk and sat down, motioning for me to sit across from him.

I eased into one of the chairs, my injuries from the previous night still giving me no small discomfort.

Daron steepled his fingers and smirked at me. "I'm not giving you our charms."

That was about what I'd expected. Though I hadn't considered the possibility he'd just come out and say it.

It begged an obvious question.

"So why the hell are you wasting my time?" I asked, dropping the faux friendliness from my voice.

Daron smiled wider. "You misunderstand me. I have no interest in selling them on the open market. Their value is in their exclusivity. As a region, we don't have much to set us apart and draw in new residents. A few dungeons, and a handful of mid-size organizations, but nothing compared to the Adventurers' or Merchants' Guild. As a courtesy, however, one region leader to another, I might be willing to extend you the opportunity to buy one."

It took an exorbitant amount of self-control not to facepalm. I hated people like this. People who'd skimmed through *Art of the Deal*, or *Way of the Werewolf*, or *How to Win Friends and Influence People*, and subsequently acted like they'd uncovered the keys to the universe.

"And where, exactly, is this sudden outpouring of generosity coming from?" I asked dryly.

Daron forced himself to hold eye contact, though from the blinking he was having trouble. "I'm always looking to make friends. Specifically, friends in high places." With a flourish, he withdrew a magical contract, placed it down on his desk, and slid it over, rotating the document so it faced me.

I scanned it briefly, snorting when I came to the figure. 75,000 Selve. Quite the sticker shock for a mobility power with such limited utility, considering the short duration and cooldown. It could get you across the city in a fraction of the time, but you'd be walking back.

Talia must have sensed my mood. "Control your temper. As much as I dislike this creature, Tyler wanted us to be diplomatic. And we'll have a charm for Kinsley to study. Just accept his offer and renegotiate in the future."

Despite what Azure told me, I almost considered it. Playing nice for the moment and finding a solution for the Region 7 problem later. But with the way my responsibilities kept stacking up, I couldn't shake the feeling that if I didn't deal with this now, I'd never deal with it at all.

It was Daron himself who gave me the final push.

He leaned over the desk, conspiratorially. "Forgive the intrusion, but I consider myself an observant man."

"I'm sure you do."

"Sex sells. This is the way of things." He tapped a finger on the table, studying me. "Yet I couldn't help but notice how little interest you showed in the attendants upstairs. All those celestial bodies on display, and you gave them little more than a glance."

I smiled thinly. "Never had much interest in strip clubs. Or strip clubs disguised as massage parlors, for that matter."

Daron waggled his eyebrows. "There are many benefits to being my friend, Matthias."

"You're not really my type, Daron." I emphasized his name the same way he'd emphasized mine.

His smile dampened. Still, he tried. "This is a new world. If you're looking for something more, the fantasy of flight is not the only fantasy I offer."

"Matt," Talia warned.

I busied myself with the contract, folding one corner perpendicular to the page. Then another corner. Once I'd fully repurposed the contract as a paper plane, I gave it a gentle toss.

Daron finally broke eye contact, smile dissolving into a scowl as he watched the plane strike the wall behind his calendar and spiral to the floor.

I waited until I had his attention once more. "Let's try again. And maybe, just maybe, we can find a way this doesn't end badly for you."

CHAPTER FIFTY-FIVE

I didn't have the time or the patience to play this nice. In seconds, I was out of my chair and on his side of the room. He flinched, as if I was about to strike him. Instead, I pushed a number of papers and trinkets out of the way and took a seat on the desk, planting one foot on the seat of his chair.

Needed to reset the stakes. Make him think this wasn't really about the charms.

"You know," I spoke idly, "I tend to come off as an asshole. Or so I've been told. As such, I've been making a not-insignificant effort to turn over a new leaf. Sort of an evergreen New Year's resolution to be nicer. If that makes any sense."

"Uh—" Daron started.

"But I find myself constantly placed in situations where being nice just doesn't cut it." I ran a hand through my hair. "Which makes that commitment complicated in situations like this."

"I've been nothing but hospitable," Daron blustered.

"With that?" I pointed to the contract-turned-paper plane. "That was an insult at best."

"How?"

"Because you've been selling flight charms outside your district to the highest bidder." I glared down at him furiously. "That affects the market, Daron. Even if you refuse to take part in it. Hell, especially if you refuse to take part in it."

A bead of perspiration dripped down Daron's forehead as he squinted, deep in thought. "Your vehicle sales—"

"Not just any vehicles," I glowered. "The moneymakers. The not-

Audi's, the not-Lambos, the not-motherfucking-Ferraris. Nobody wants to impulse buy a luxury car when their bougie-ass friends are *flying*."

Daron grew quiet, focused. His eyes flicked to the side, probably trying to pull his social UI and message for help.

I snapped my fingers in front of his face. "Hey. In case you didn't notice? I left a small army of mercenaries outside. Currently, this is a negotiation. You call your guys and this escalates? It stops being a negotiation. Turns into something a lot less pleasant. That what you want?"

I could almost see him carefully closing the screen and turning back to me. "Sorry. I'm— I apologize. We had no intention of stepping on the Merchants' Guild's toes."

"Apologies are cheap. Reparations aren't."

Daron's mouth firmed. "Regardless of what you threaten me with, I cannot sell the flight charm on the open market. That is non-negotiable."

He stared at me, unflinching, long enough for me to realize he was resolute. Which was fine. Daron was right that the exclusivity of the charm was where it drew most of its value. If he let Kinsley sell it, everyone who could afford the charm would buy it—at first. Then the downsides and limitation would trickle into the market discourse, and it would slowly fall out of interest.

I crossed my arms. "Then we're at an impasse. Only, the place you're in looks a lot more tenuous than where I'm standing."

Daron chuckled nervously. "We're both region leaders. In terms of power and authority, we are the same."

"It's like everyone's already forgotten the Transposition," I said. "8 and 9 are average regions at best. Not particularly wealthy. I'm guessing in your rush to lock down 'powerful Friends,' you haven't given them the time of day, despite the fact that they're your bordering neighbors. And of course, there's Region 6 at your back. A convenient chasm for any large-scale attack to push you into. If the next event is even remotely similar, how do you think it's going to play out?

Daron's mouth worked in a silent stammer before he finally found a voice. "Perhaps there's an alternate course."

"I'm listening."

"As I said, it's not feasible for me to sell the charms on the market. But... what if we were to sell a predetermined number of flight charms to both your affiliated guilds, in return for an assurance of support during the next event? Provided, of course, at a significant discount—"

I shook my head and stuck my thumb up, slightly.

Daron frowned. "A small discount."

I repeated the motion.

"At a slight up-charge?" Daron asked, cautiously hopeful.

I nodded slowly. "That would be a step in the right direction."

As much as I didn't like Daron, screwing an entire region out of profit from their only export was unnecessary.

Daron's wide smile started to resurface. I produced a second magical contract, tailored to the terms we discussed, then pushed it over to him. After scanning the terms and finding that everything was as we'd discussed, Daron signed it on behalf of Region 7. Once he'd signed, the rotund man was uncharacteristically quiet.

"Something wrong?" I asked.

"You never wanted to sell the charms on the open market, did you?" Daron asked, disquiet in his voice as the realization dawned on him.

I scooped the contract out from in front of him, signing the corresponding field. "Does it matter? We're both getting plenty out of this deal as it is."

"I guess not." Daron shrugged, shooting me one more suspicious glance before he finally relaxed in his chair.

This was partially why I'd encouraged him to increase his bulk price. He wasn't the brightest bulb in the hardware store, but he wasn't stupid. Even if he realized I'd effectively forced the negotiation toward the outcome I'd intended from the beginning, he'd have the comfort of the money to fall back on.

"Now. About the clip-on angels upstairs."

———

A long line of cars was deadlocked down the street. The waiting motorcade blocked a single lane of traffic, but it seemed as if rubbernecking was the one thing that hadn't changed much. Someone honked and waved at me. I awkwardly waved back, feeling oddly exposed at the attention.

One of the waiting mercenaries popped the door open for me.

"Productive meeting, sir?" Ire asked. The several mercenaries Kinsley assigned me all went by call signs. He had a head and a half on me and was all muscle and tough, sunbaked skin. Overall, the man looked hard as nails, save for the pink chewing gum bubble he incessantly inflated. It never seemed to pop—the bubble. Just slowly deflated and receded into his goateed mouth.

"Just Matt, please."

"You got it, Just Matt." Ire grinned.

I settled in the back seat, feeling entirely out of my element as Ire popped the door and leapt into the passenger side.

Being chauffeured around felt strange and unnecessary. Even if it was for my protection.

"Where to?" my driver asked. He was a humorless-looking man who looked like he'd have difficulty eating, considering the mustache.

With a minor adjustment, I looped my seatbelt over my shoulder and laid down. "Dunno. Need to report to the Adventurers' Guild in the late afternoon. Other than that, we have time to kill. You guys gotta be hungry by now, right?"

Out of the corner of my eye, I saw the men exchange a glance in the front seat.

"We've got calories to spare," Grit—the driver—said. Ire harrumphed and gave him a long-suffering stare. Grit ignored him. "Miss Kinsley was explicit that you were to get as much quality rest as possible."

"You call her Miss Kinsley?"

"Never to her face." Ire snorted.

The irreverence didn't fool me. Kinsley had to be paying a fuckton for this level of loyalty from guys this seasoned.

"I'm resting. I'm comfortable." I plastered over my eyes, blocking out any extraneous light, and indicated toward myself with the other hand.

"Don't look very comfortable," Grit observed.

I shifted in my seat, annoyed at the persistent twinging pain in my ribs. "I got shot last night. As far as comfort goes, this is as good as it gets. Seriously, I spent enough time in the apartment while I was wheelchair-bound. If you want to stop somewhere, just stop somewhere."

"Pete," Ire said.

"No," Grit replied.

"Dude."

"No."

"It's literally ten minutes from here."

"In potentially hostile territory."

"Someone want to fill me in?" I finally said, if only to stop the back and forth. They weren't doing a good job keeping their voices low.

"Grit's a grumpy asshole," Ire said.

"Cautious asshole—*asshole*."

"I knew that already," I said. Grit took a corner at an angle that was probably sharper than necessary, and I grimaced as my head bumped into the side panel. "And generally, I prefer caution to the alternative. But what are we talking about?"

Someone sighed. Most likely Grit.

"Smokey Jon's. First barbecue place to reopen in downtown. With the most glistening, succulent, hard-on inducing ribs you ever did see. System meat's all the same, but the glaze and cooking process? That's where the magic happens," Ire told me.

Grit spoke up. "What Ire's leaving out is that it's in Region 5. Filled to the brim with countless suspicious motherfuckers who won't stop talking about their fucking tower. Bad place to bring a VIP."

I considered it. "Ribs really that good?"

"On my life," Ire promised.

I weighed the potential risk. "I don't think they'll try anything. They're going for a tourist vibe. So long as we stay clear of the dungeon, we should be safe. And I've wanted to get some reconnaissance in for a while anyway. Get a feel for the place."

"Nothing good. That's the feel. All kinds of wrong," Grit insisted.

"You heard the man," Ire grinned.

Grit came to a stop and pulled a U-turn.

"Wake me when we get there." I pulled the neck of my hoodie over my face.

"Roger."

I felt the tendrils of sleep slowly begin to encroach.

There was a chime in my ear. Tyler's name and image appeared on my interface, indicating a voice call.

"This is Matt," I said, not trying to hide the irritation in my voice. Someone chuckled up front.

"Matt," Tyler said flatly, in a voice that didn't sound pleased. "I understand you just met with Daron?"

"Yes. We've got the flight charms. It's all copacetic."

"It was supposed to be initial talks. Kinsley said she was mostly sending you for recreation," Tyler said. Again, I didn't understand why he sounded so irritated.

"There was an opportunity and I took it. What's the problem?"

"I just got off a call with Daron. The man was weeping. He said you strong-armed him. If he reports this to the region council, there's going to be an issue." There was a clear accusation in Tyler's voice. Couldn't afford to brush this off.

"Did he also tell you about the underage girls in swimsuits, acting as post-flight massage attendants?" I shot back.

There was a long pause. "No, he did not."

"For what it's worth, he claimed he didn't know and promised to clean it up."

"You believe him?" Tyler asked.

I rolled my eyes and turned into the seat, shielding myself from the sun. "Do I believe Daron didn't bother asking for ID and he'll probably zip up his image after this? Sure. He doesn't strike me as an always-does-his-homework type of guy. But, Tyler..."

"Where there's smoke, there's fire," Tyler said. He still sounded angry, but not at me.

"I'm not the morality police. Nor am I looking to fuck with anyone's hustle. Just like before the dome, probably more now, there's plenty of desperate, of age people who need to make ends meet and are lacking resources. They need to do that by turning to alternate means? Not my business. Or anyone else's."

"They shouldn't have to," Tyler growled. "We should all be helping each other."

"Maybe. But when's that ever actually happened?"

Tyler hesitated. "I'm tempted to cancel the contract altogether. Give him back his charms and wash our hands of it."

We hit a bump, and I grunted. "Your call. Want my opinion?"

"Shoot."

My brow furrowed. "The question is management. There's a world of difference between someone employing independent contractors and old-school pimping. If Daron's just enabling and taking a nominal fee, or hell, even a house-cut, that's to be expected. But if it's more predatory—if he's actively backing at-risk people into a corner and turning them out? That's a whole other ball game."

A female voice on the other side said something indecipherable, and I waited as Tyler uttered a hushed reply.

After a moment, he spoke. "We're going to have to look into this. No way around it. And it's unfortunate we're already beholden to them."

The seat my face was buried in smelled vaguely of smoke. "We're covered. Daron was so rattled from the negotiation, he barely read over the contract. I snuck in a morality clause."

"Thought you weren't the morality police."

"Only when it suits me. In short, we can sever our connection with Region 7 at any time for conduct unbecoming."

"And keep the charms?"

"We paid for them. Of course, it'd be bad optics to renege on a technicality, unless there's a very public scandal, but that can always be arranged."

Tyler sighed. "Sometimes, Matt, our strategy discussions make me feel like I'm talking to the devil."

"Tell me how you really feel."

"I was mainly calling to ask you to take it easy. It sounded like you were a little on edge. But giving the context, I can't complain. Well done."

"That's what you're paying me for."

Tyler chuckled. "I don't pay you."

"Damn."

"Look. In my opinion, you should be in bed recuperating. From what Miles said, even letting you outside is a risk right now. But since I know you won't listen... do you want in on this? You brought it to my attention.

I can set up a quest. Actually get you paid if you want to look into it yourself."

I thought about it. The image of the dead-eyed sixteen-year-old up in the post-flight lounge, the way she'd looked at me. The ever-burgeoning list of responsibilities and time constraints I already had.

"No," I finally said. "Call an audible if you need me. But there's too much on my plate already."

"Understood. Have a few people in mind, good at what they do. I'll keep you in the loop."

"Thanks."

There was a beep as Tyler ended the call. It felt as if I'd barely closed my eyes before the SUV came to a stop.

"Welcome to Region 5," Ire announced with glee, "home of the best damn barbecue this side of the yeehaw state."

CHAPTER FIFTY-SIX

I had to stop drawing attention to myself as Matt. People were already asking too many questions.

Which was why, as I pushed myself out of the SUV and squinted through the tinted lenses of a pair of dusty Oakley's Ire offered me, I committed myself to doing nothing but enjoying a heaping serving of barbecue.

With that in mind, I swapped from **<Cruel Lens>** to **<Jaded Eye>**. If time used factored into integration, I wanted to avoid integrating the personality quirks that came with **<Cruel Lens>** until it was absolutely necessary.

I reminded myself that this wasn't my region. Wasn't my problem. I was just here for the food.

"God *damn*." Ire slammed his door shut for emphasis. "That smells good."

"Yes, this place serves mana rained down from heaven, we get it." Grit sighed.

To Ire's credit, the sweet, slightly sour scent of barbecue was making my mouth water. I couldn't remember the last time I ate. If the milkshake from Miles counted, it was probably yesterday.

Recalling how close everything that followed had been, my appetite wavered.

Ire slapped me on the back. "You're not going to regret this, trust me." The G36 rattled against his camo jacket as he walked toward a section of strip mall with red lettering overhead that read Smokey Jon's in a curvy font.

"Is he always like this?" I asked Grit.

"Until shit gets real," Grit affirmed, scanning the parking lot. "The shit-gets-real-part's worth tolerating the rest. Mostly."

"I'll take your word for it."

Three people in business casual were strolling down the sidewalk and stopped to wave, all smiles. The one in front appeared to consider approaching us, but glanced at Grit and thought better of it, continuing on his way.

"Weird," Grit said, giving voice to my thoughts.

"Very *Truman Show*. The whole region isn't like this, right?"

"Just the ones we need to worry about," Grit said.

Next to the barbecue place, there was a closed-down Domino's and a defunct donut shop. My mind wandered back to my time at Dunkin's and my old boss. I wondered how he was doing. It'd been weeks now since everything went to hell. Was he still alive?

Ire reached the door first, then turned around to call something back. The childlike excitement in his face died. He swung his rifle out and whistled, pointing two gloved fingers to our right.

Grit was moving to intercept before I even turned my head to look. He pushed a kid—a boy with brown hair, barely older than Ellison—up against a minivan that looked like it hadn't moved in months.

"What the hell?" I called over.

"Little bastard was beelining straight toward you," Grit responded, checking the kid's inventory as he struggled.

"He's just a kid—" I stopped myself. *Ellison* was just a kid. He was also dangerous as hell. Instead of immediately intervening, I took a moment to study the boy carefully. **<Jaded Eye>** didn't flag him as a threat.

"It's okay. Seriously. Let him go."

Grit released the boy. The boy scowled at the mercenary and approached me. His shirt was tattered, covered in dirt, and his jeans were lined with holes.

Self-made holes.

"Sir, I don't know what to do. My mom's sick, and we can't afford any medicine."

"Uhuh, I said.

"My dad went into the Gilded Tower a few days ago," the boy continued. "There's supposed to be a lot of treasure in there." He'd turned to point to a giant structure in the background. It looked more like the remnants of a castle tower than a dungeon, though I knew from experience the inside probably looked nothing like the exterior. "But he hasn't come out since. I'm getting worried."

<Quest Received: A Forgotten Child.**>**

The boy took one look at my growing smirk, then turned and walked away.

"That's it? You're just giving up?" I called after him.

He thrust a middle finger up in the air.

"Come on, give me the pitch at least."

"Fuck you," he called over his shoulder.

The approach had been terrible, but that might have been due to the interference. He was fast on the uptake. Realized the mark wasn't buying it and bailed out early before he got in too deep. While his dirty appearance was mostly self-inflicted, the loose fit of the clothes and gauntness of his cheekbones weren't.

"Are you hungry?" I called after him.

He turned and gave me a wary look. "You a pedo?"

"No."

The kid pointed an accusatory finger at Grit. "*Call of Duty* cosplay over there was feeling me up. He a pedo?"

I glanced at Grit, amused at the way my bodyguard's face was flushing red. "Can't say, just met him this morning."

"No one's a fucking pedo." Grit glared at the kid.

"Just doing his job, making sure you're not a threat." I stepped in front of Grit. The kid didn't look sure, and I couldn't blame him. He was still green. The worst he'd probably gotten was yelled at, maybe roughed up a little. Getting shoved up against a car and frisked had to be a reality check.

"What do you want, exactly?" he called over, still a safe distance away.

"Look, there's no such thing as a free lunch. But plenty are cheap. I just want to hear about the grift. It's a public restaurant. You eat, you talk, you leave. Simple as that."

"Fine," the kid said, giving Grit a wary look. "But I don't want him sitting next to me."

"Done."

———

Ire hadn't oversold the joint.

My middling hunger had skyrocketed the moment a rack was placed in front of me. Even the potato salad was phenomenal, and as a rule, potato salad was almost *always* trash.

After I cleared my plate, I let the kid continue to eat, teasing answers out of him piecemeal.

From what I'd gathered, it was safe to say it wasn't a weird mind control thing, or even cult-ish. The people of Region 7 were being directly incentivized by the region leader to bring Users to the dungeon, and they were compensated for every referral in Selve, scaling depending on the User's level and whether they came with a group.

Civilians were able to give out quests centered around the dungeon, much as the kid had tried to do to me. And despite the obvious initial suspicion, he insisted there was a steady outflow of people.

When I asked him how he'd picked me out as a User, he claimed everyone in Region 7 was capable of differentiating Users from civilians within a certain range.

Once we'd finished, the waitress brought the bill with a color-printed pamphlet displaying a picture of the tower, full of bold, italicized text.

"Hone your adventuring prowess!"

"Untold mystery and treasure within!"

"Raise your level and acquire rare resources!"

It raised more red flags than a bullfighting arena.

I noted that the tower looked smaller in the picture, and the kid confirmed it. Originally, it had been around the size of a three-story building. Now it was—I didn't know. Triple, quadruple that size?

Odd that no one noticed. Hell, I'd been flying above the city and I hadn't noticed.

Ire waited until we were in the car to speak. "Well. We know they're not feeding people to it."

"*Probably,*" Grit amended.

"Grit's right. We don't really know that," I commented.

Ire twisted back in his seat to look at me. "How so?"

"Assuming everything that kid said was true? The scaling rewards. They're incentivized to refer higher-level Users."

Ire considered that. "Rack up plenty of successful lower-level visits as cover to create a consistent track record, a few high-level deaths would seem like a drop in the bucket."

"This is all conjecture," I said. "But it's possible."

I needed to decide how to proceed with Buzzcut soon. Preferably tonight. But getting a handle on what was happening in the city was part of my duties as region leader. And it was only a matter of time before adventurers from Region 14 started heading to Region 7 for free dungeon access.

Decision made, I spoke. "Mind if we swing by on the way back?"

"I'm game," Ire said.

Grit groaned. "Kinsley is not going to be happy."

I snorted. "It's just a drive-by. And if she gives you too much shit, feel free to blame me."

"We'd do that anyway," Ire said cheerfully.

CHAPTER FIFTY-SEVEN

Kinsley and I were going to need to have a conversation about making the orders she gave her men more flexible.

Not far into Region 5, traffic backed up to an excessive degree, forcing us to go on foot. Emphasis on *us*. Ditching Grit and Ire was impossible. When they'd stubbornly refused to let me forge out on my own, I'd convinced them that escorting me around Region 5 in full paramilitary gear was asking for trouble, and they'd ditched the Kevlar and helmets, left their rifles in the car in lieu of the handguns they open-carried on their hips.

They still wore gray-and-white camo pants, but those blended well enough with the general populace. Ever since the Transposition, there was a lot of McMilitary wear going around, even if the typical woodland composite didn't do shit in an urban environment.

I caught sight of them in a reflection of a rear view, doing a not-particularly subtle job of tailing me through the packed area.

If you've ever been to Dallas, you know the city's aesthetic is fairly drab. A menagerie of whites, grays, dark greens, and chrome. Downtown was always the exception, specifically around Deep Ellum at night, where the grays and greens give way to a far wider selection of colorful buildings embellished with neon lights. It's not Vegas, but at the same time, it's not Dallas either. But only at night.

Region 5, which now fully encompassed that neighborhood, brought the colorful nature of the city into the light of day for the first time.

There were banners and streamers everywhere, multi-colored confetti scattered across the ground. Gray, multi-composite storefronts spray-painted in a collage of primary colors that grew more vivid the closer you got to the tower. People—average people—celebrated around grills, air filled with the scent of spiced meat. A bare-chested man in a chrome mask and oddly floral skirt handed me a flyer that read: Destiny.

The *Midsommar* vibes were off the charts.

If it wasn't for the combination of **<Born Nihilist>** and **<Jaded Eye>**, I might have fled. Nothing that looked this good ever was, and the celebratory feel in the face of the recent cataclysm set my teeth on edge.

I climbed the stairs of an elevated walkway that crossed over the backed-up highway and paused at its center, studying the surroundings of the now-in-view tower for the first time.

The massive construction was colossal, most of its surface covered in a shimmering layer of gold so reflective it was difficult to look at. But I didn't care how the tower looked. I needed to see how it functioned in the region's context.

And what I saw raised more questions than answers.

There was a long queue, hundreds of people long. Brass stanchions lined with velvet ropes were arranged in a square maze, trailing a meandering path toward the tower's golden gates. There was a squad of Users at the tower's entrance in heavy gear, covered in a plethora of silver particles and blue, barely visible force field bubbles. By far the most heavily armed and well-equipped security I'd ever seen.

Next to the main queue was a much shorter line. Unlike the bedraggled Users moving at a snail's pace in the square maze, this line moved freely. Users dressed in vivid colors that I'd identified as a hallmark of Region 5 apparel were ushered quickly through the shortcut.

I frowned. Nothing about it felt right, but I was starting to think this wasn't the simple, sinister honey trap I'd assumed it to be.

Something sharp and metal pressed gently against my throat. My eyes widened at the feeling of the dagger. The attack itself wasn't particularly surprising, but the absolute lack of warning was. Grit and Ire had taken up positions on either end of the walkway and hadn't messaged. Even **<Perception>** hadn't given me a heads up.

I kept still but didn't bother raising my hands. "You got me," I said, monotone.

"Looks like the security team could use some work," Miles said.

I turned to face him, letting the blade slide harmlessly across my neck. "There a point to this?"

Miles bounced the tip of his dagger off my shoulder before he sheathed it in a smooth motion. "If I get to you this easily, Myrddin sure as hell can."

Judging from the circles under his eyes, Miles hadn't slept much either.

I smiled thinly. "Where's this sudden, uncharacteristic concern for my well-being coming from?"

Miles grimaced, as if someone had stuck a finger in a festering wound. "You call me out here to gloat?"

I turned from him, leaning back over the walkway railing. Ellison haunted my thoughts as he had since the clash at the penthouse, leading me to the same inevitable conclusions. If I held back from the conspiracy rabbit hole and took everything that happened at face value, accepting that Ellison had extensive knowledge of the future and believing—based on his comments on Iris—that he was acting in a benevolent capacity, the implications presented serious problems.

First, he'd withheld everything from us, despite knowing what was coming. Shouting it to the rooftops would have been his first course. Even if me and the rest of the family hadn't fully believed him, he could have convinced us to leave the outskirts of the city for a short time before the dome went up.

Only, he hadn't. Which meant that leaving either delayed the inevitable, or somehow put us in a distinctly worse situation. Given the meteors and multiple-dome situation the Ordinator implied, that was believable enough.

Ellison was smart. He learned from his mistakes, and he didn't break easily. There was no doubt in my mind that he was actively planning a solution, tweaking it with every iteration. If he was repeating this same situation over and over, it was almost a given.

Which led to the problem. The rift he'd created between us. He'd gone everything short of nuclear to simultaneously hurt me and back me into a very specific corner, where I had little option other than to leave him alone. If he hadn't interfered at the penthouse, I'd likely still be camped in that corner, spread too thin to fully commit to watching a family member who'd made it irrevocably clear he wanted nothing to do with me.

That meant, whatever his solution, he couldn't deal me in, because something undesirable happened if he did. Best-case scenario, it changed the future in a way that undercut his ability to make predictions. Worst-case, I ended up working in opposition to him and created more problems than the help I could offer was worth.

Maybe I couldn't stomach whatever it was he was planning.

Maybe it was worse than that.

Either way, it was hard to imagine and difficult to dwell on.

And if the initial premise was true—that Ellison needed me to remain outside the loop—this repeat was more or less botched. His actions at the penthouse threw that out the window. It didn't matter how many times he'd done this, the way his identity was revealed—a near headshot that shattered an eye in his mask—was too risky to be repeatable. Even with

<Probability Cascade>, a power designed to make the unlikely and borderline impossible possible, I'm not sure I would have risked it.

So, where did we go from here?

"Do you believe in fate?" I asked Miles.

Miles snorted. "That's what you called me here out of the blue to talk about. Fate."

"Just answer the question."

There were near-silent footsteps as Miles took a place next to me. He'd sheathed the short blade but kept a hand on it. "If predestination exists, I'd have a lot of questions about the way things are. Way they were, even. Long before the dome. Exactly what sort of ends justifies the means."

"So no then."

He shook his head. "Nah. I think I'm more comfortable believing we're all just grains of sand in the face of the universe. The alternative is too cruel to fathom."

"That was my thought as well."

Before last night.

"Was?" Miles asked.

I crooked my head sideways to look at him. Miles glanced away. Good. He was still feeling guilty. "I might not believe in fate, but I believe in patterns."

"What sort of patterns?"

"That in times of great strife, there are two groups of people. Bystanders, and movers and shakers."

"Putting yourself in that group, I'm betting," Miles said. He didn't roll his eyes, but I could hear it in his voice. He probably thought I was about to tell him off for putting my family in danger, maybe even threaten him.

"Not just me. We're both entrenched in this. Even if I brought everything to Tyler and did everything in my power to ruin you, I doubt it would take. Your people are too useful and well-connected to waste, despite the misfire."

"And as the man who saved an entire region and is the only living person we know of who fought Myrddin and won, you're mostly untouchable," Miles mused.

"That being said, I have a proposal. With fine print."

This felt like cheating. I already knew Miles had no short-term plans to pursue me. He'd said as much to Hawkins, in the small snippet of his life I'd spied on. But there was a serious advantage in being the first to offer an olive branch.

"I'm listening," Miles prompted.

"Don't get me wrong. I'm fucking angry. You and your people dredged up shit that's haunted me for years. Put my family in danger. Showed up late enough to the party that it almost killed me." I let the words hang.

Miles shoved his hands in his pockets. I waited until it looked like he was ready to walk away. "But we live in uncertain times. So why don't we skip the over the part where I'm angry with you? Where I freeze you out for weeks over the stunt you pulled and create obstructions between you and the Adventurers' and Merchants' Guilds—"

"—And deny our market access?" Miles poked. Good, he'd already noticed that Kinsley had locked him and the rest of the Feds out of the market since last night.

I ignored the jab and forged on. "We also skip the part where we posture and snipe at each other, feeling out weaknesses before the dawn of a larger threat inevitably forces us to work together."

"Just skip straight to cooperation," Miles said flatly, as if he couldn't quite believe what he was hearing.

"Yup."

Miles looked down, then suddenly barked a laugh. "You're unpredictable, I'll give you that. Though given the context, suspending market access feels suspiciously like posturing."

"That was last night."

"What changed?" Miles asked. He gave me that piercing stare again, the one that felt like it could see straight through me.

"I ate breakfast."

Miles snorted. "Okay. Fine. I assume you didn't choose this location for the ambience?"

I studied the queue in front of the Region 5 tower. There was a churro vendor walking the perimeter of the line, exchanging the sugared pastries for Selve.

"Spent much time here?"

"None," Miles admitted. "Though I've heard things through the grapevine."

"Then we're on the same page. I came here expecting a simple honeypot—Region 5 draws in outsiders to die in their dungeon, gain power, or experience, or items in exchange."

"Our first thought as well. It could still be that." Miles looked out over the crowded plaza, his mouth tightening. "But from everything I've heard, that doesn't track. There are level recommendations for floors. Multiple safeguards in place to keep people from wandering into areas they're not ready for. The few casualties were cases of bullheaded Users blatantly ignoring those warnings and getting themselves killed. From the reports, you're far more likely to die wandering into a random dungeon than you are entering the tower."

My eyes wandered to the sign above the entry to the main queue.

TWENTY-FIVE SELVE ENTRY FEE. NO EXCEPTIONS. NON-REFUNDABLE.

"Which begs the question, why are they charging so little? A safe-ish place to level and gear up? That fee is a pittance," Miles noted.

"They want Users. As many as they can get. But they also want them alive. We're missing something." I noted a couple entering the priority queue. A man in civilian clothes with a woman in a sundress in tow, holding a basket between them.

Miles followed my gaze. "Safe enough for a recreational jaunt. The lower floors, at least."

There was a sudden commotion at the exit. The group of battle-ready Users moved swiftly, rotating from the entrance toward the source of the noise, a man in gaudy-looking plate that looked straight out of a high-fantasy novel. He'd bowled over an attendant at the exit line and was now frozen in place, his armor outlined in white.

"What the hell?" Miles muttered.

The armored guard from the front placed a sword against his neck, while a mage readied a massive-looking spell behind him. Though otherwise frozen, the frozen User was loud enough that I could make out snippets of his ranting.

"Fucking crooks... everything I found... paid... fee."

From the way his shoulders were moving, the Wizard was responding, albeit in a much more controlled voice.

Behind them, a tent-like tarp covered the exit line. A woman exited and withdrew items out of the man's inventory, placing them into a black-and-gold box that held far more than it appeared capable of. She pulled a sword from his inventory, along with a series of glowing rocks and a handful of gems, then ran a wand across the man's body. She reached in the pocket of his belt and withdrew an amulet that housed a massive diamond, placing it in the box, then brought the box back into the tented queue.

The man blustered for a while, yelling obscenities, until the woman returned, dumping the box onto the concrete in clear view of the main line. The man gathered his findings, eyebrows furrowed, clearly looking to see if anything was missing and finding, with some puzzlement, that it was all accounted for, including the expensive-looking amulet. He gave the mage and armored guard the finger as he walked away.

"Remind you of anything?" Miles asked quietly.

"TSA," I said immediately. The rout motions, the way they'd scanned him with the wand, resembled security at the airport.

Miles put his back to the retaining wall. "What if we've got it backward?"

The last piece clicked into place.

"They're cataloguing everything that comes out but not taking anything. The point isn't luring *Users* into the dungeon," I realized. "The Users are a means to an end."

"From the look of it, the tower is huge. Too big for one region to do all the groundwork," Miles agreed. "And unless that amulet was very convincing costume jewelry, they're not skimming just anything off the top."

"No." I shook my head. "People hate being ripped off more than almost anything else. Word would spread quickly."

Miles' expression lit up. "Which means—"

"They're looking for something specific. Something they haven't found yet," I finished. "Something potentially powerful enough to justify charging next to nothing for entry in order to crowd-fund the search."

Another wave of people pushed through the exit flap, revealing a row of identical black-and-gold boxes on metal tables before the canvas material covered the exit once more.

"Should we get a closer look?" Miles asked. Going into the dungeon was a logical next step, but there was something off about the question. It felt loaded, somehow.

Miles was testing me.

"Go together to a second location in neutral territory, away from prying eyes. Just you and me?" I crossed my arms and stared at him.

With a long sigh, Miles shook his head. "Even if we're skipping the stupid part. It's going to take a while to build trust."

An idea struck me. I'd intended to spend my evening this way, regardless. One last moment of levity before everything with the suits kicked into full gear. Adding Miles into the mix didn't really cost me anything. "Putting the tower aside for the moment. Why don't we start with a team-building exercise?"

Miles laughed, cutting the mirth off early when he realized I wasn't joking. "Like... a trust fall?"

I reached in my inventory and withdrew a flight charm, dangling the thin chain with a cherub wing in front of him. "Of a sort."

CHAPTER FIFTY-EIGHT

There's something to be said for southern hospitality. I'd never seen the point of it before, but inviting neighbors, friends, and enemies to mingle in a closed setting was a hell of a way to create a sense of unity where none existed before.

Even if that sense of unity was counterfeit.

The location was the old golf course, around twenty minutes east of the city center. With Kinsley's help and a courtesy call to the Region 18 leader, it was easy enough to secure the area as a small venue, with speakers, tables, and chairs quickly unloaded by Kinsley's ever-expanding roster of mercenaries and employees. Grit and Ire arrived shortly after with the catering.

Ire was right. Smokey Jon's was too good not to share.

Sae and Sara chatted over Styrofoam plates nearby. Sae seemed to pick up on Sara's visible discomfort with her appearance and, instead of avoiding her, appeared to be doubling down and chatting Sara's ear off.

A line of SUVs drove onto the green and came to a stop. Shortly after, the rear SUV's passenger door popped open and Iris jumped out. She spotted me and sprinted over, nearly slipping on the grass as she made her final approach, hitting my chair full force and rattling me.

"Are we really going to fly?" Iris asked, her eyes wide.

"After everyone eats and has some time to digest," I answered. Iris looked around, inspecting the various plates present.

"We can't just go now?"

"Patience, kiddo." I ruffled her hair. Then jerked my thumb to Miles, sitting uncomfortably in the lawn chair next to me. "You know who this is?"

"No?" Iris cocked her head.

"He helped save our asses yesterday."

My sister reacted immediately and tackled Miles in a hug. Miles patted her awkwardly, shooting me a dubious look. "Just... doing my job."

I gestured toward my ear, then my sister. Miles nodded in oh-right acknowledgement and waited to repeat himself until he could see her. Before he could, Iris quickly pulled away. "Have you eaten yet?" she asked in excitement.

"Uh. No," Miles said.

I watched in amusement as Iris took Miles' hand and dragged him away. "Come on, the sooner we eat, the sooner we can fly!"

Miles looked back helplessly at me, then followed along as my sister led him to the small line of mercenaries queued up next to the silver serving trays. He'd shown up shortly after Tyler and never seemed to drop his guard until now.

> **<Matt:** Remember. You only met Sae yesterday.>
> **<Iris:** I knooooow. Chat less, fly more.>

Before I could respond, I felt a presence beside me. Mom was there, one hand on my lawn chair, staring after Iris and Miles. "That man. I've met him before."

"Have you?" I asked, clamping down on the immediate burst of irritation.

"He's the one you mentioned, isn't he? Miles? Part of the Taskforce?" Mom asked, visibly working through confusion.

"That's him."

"What a coincidence. We ran into each other at a restaurant, chatted for a while." Mom covered a laugh with her hand as she watched Iris railroad Miles through the serving line. Her wrinkles looked more pronounced than they had weeks ago. As annoyed as I was that she'd unknowingly leaked vital information, it was easy to forget that she'd been working tirelessly in the background this entire time.

"That is a coincidence. Was he nice?" I asked carefully.

Mom sighed. "A perfect gentleman. And look how good he is with your sister."

Hardly. Iris could charm an inanimate object.

There was no mistaking the sigh in my mother's voice. My immediate reaction was to stomp the brakes. Even if Miles *wasn't* a borderline enemy, on the front line of several dangerous situations liable to get him killed, further entanglement with him was dangerous. Then again, I'd created this situation for exactly that purpose. My mother getting... involved with Miles was unlikely to end in anything other than tragedy.

"He's been married before," I hedged.

"So have I." Mom shot me an eyebrow.

"And he has kids."

"Explains why he's so good with them."

I palmed my forehead. "Isn't he a little young for you?"

"Matthias," Mom snapped.

An uncomfortable silence passed between us.

"You're right." Mom gazed down at the green, crestfallen. "Ellison ran away—"

"—He *didn't* run away, he just needs some time," I interrupted, reiterating what I'd already told her.

"I shouldn't be pining like some naïve, star-struck child. Your brother should be my focus right now," Mom finished. There was enough self-loathing in the statement that I hesitated. For the first time in what felt like years, I felt genuine guilt toward her. No matter how spotty our upbringing was, what was happening with Ellison now wasn't my mother's fault.

"How's the system forum coming along?" I asked, attempting to redirect the conversation somewhere more positive.

The pain in her expression lightened somewhat. "Almost have all the kinks ironed out. Should be ready to go live in a few days."

I hesitated. "We lost a lot of people in the Transposition. Makes it hard to keep track of who's alive and who isn't. Miles suggested creating a forum subcategory to gather that information."

My mother's eyes tracked toward the serving line. "That's a wonderful idea."

"Why don't you go talk to him about it?" Saying the words was like chewing glass.

Mom smiled, for the first time in a long time, and waggled an eyebrow. "Is that your way of giving me your blessing?"

"He *is* a cop." I couldn't stop myself from adding it as one final, pointless protest.

"I'll be careful," Mom nodded, overserious, giving me a small wave as she walked lightly toward the serving line, a skip in her step. I scowled as she left, more than a little unhappy with the unexpected turn.

A short figure walked across the green. Kinsley sat on the far end of the row of chairs, as far away from me and everyone else while a small cluster of mercenaries milled around her.

<Matt: Got a second?>

<Kinsley: No. I threw this together last minute, while you waited until the last possible second to add the totally minor foot note that you

happened to INVITE THE FED WE HUSTLED last night, and most
importantly, look at my goddamn plate, Matt.>

Her Styrofoam plate was piled high with a large enough serving of
premium, five-cheese macaroni from Smokey's to feed a small family.
Kinsley continued the dead-eyed stare and slowly raised a fist, middle
finger extended.

Fair enough.

———

Iris shrieked as she flew through the air. I caught her beneath her arms
and sent her flying back toward Mom as we floated together. Mom caught
her, laughing as the momentum pushed them both back, spinning Iris
around in a gravity-defying dance.

On the return trip, Iris flew directly at me, shifting direction right at
the last moment, curving around me and flying out the opposite way like
a slingshot.

"Be careful!" I called after her.

Something clipped my feet, nearly sending me spinning before I
corrected my trajectory.

I glared at Miles. "Really?"

"Fancy a dogfight?" Miles came to a stop with a graceful barrel roll.

"No." I said, moments before I lashed out with a leg and caught his
ankle.

Miles spiraled, the green of the golf course hundreds of feet below us.
"Bastard!" he called back.

"Don't pretend like you weren't asking for it."

When he regained control, he gave me a serious look. "Thanks."

"It was already happening." I shrugged. "Adding a plus one was
simple enough."

"Not just that." Miles surveyed the fliers.

As a whole, the group was dealing with the nausea far better than I
had. Tyler was the only one to lose his dinner. Kinsley was struggling not
to follow in his footsteps. She floated motionless in the air, supine. "It's
fine. No big deal. Just like... floating... in a pool. I'm a cloud. And clouds
don't—" she suddenly writhed in the air and turned to the side with an
audible *hurk,* making the near-fatal mistake of glancing down, slapping
both hands over her mouth and closing her eyes tightly.

"Sure you don't want to turn on your stomach?" I asked.

Kinsley opened one eye and glared at me. "Go away. Let me be a
cloud."

I scanned the sky for Miles. He'd joined my mother and Tyler and was laughing loudly at something Sara had said. Iris swooped around them, and Miles snatched her out of the air, launching her higher. Iris whooped, giggling with a freedom and lightness I hadn't heard in years.

It was so easy to forget how young she really was.

"You okay?" Kinsley asked, one eye open again.

"It's just... I don't know. I can't remember the last time I saw Iris this happy." The words came tumbling out. "Mom too. All I want is this. But the good days are harder and harder to come by."

"It's okay to enjoy them. You get that, right?"

I swallowed. "It's not that simple. I'm underwater. Small chance in hell it's getting any easier. Luck's the only reason I'm still alive. I can reduce risk, take strides to mitigate probability, but in the end, it's down to luck. And eventually, luck runs out. I have to make sure they're safe when it does."

"Jesus. Family outings always make you this bleak?"

"Did you find our makeshift prison?" I asked. I hadn't decided on how to deal with Buzzcut yet, but I needed somewhere to take him if it ended up being less final.

"Yeah. Abandoned building, north end of the region. Basement is solid and securable. Had a few mages reinforce the door and whip up a fancy lock. Added the modifications you asked for. Everything else should be fine as is, unless he can tunnel through concrete." Kinsley avoided eye contact throughout the report.

"Ok. Great. Gonna tell me why cranky's been your default state lately?"

Kinsley looked down at where Mom and Iris had gathered. My sister's braids flew back and up, at an unnatural angle, and Mom cradled her, slowing her downward momentum.

"It's not rational," Kinsley said.

"Doesn't have to be." I shrugged.

"It's not fair to you."

"Things rarely are."

"I miss my dad," Kinsley exploded. "And I know it's unreasonable, and maybe makes me a total bitch, but every time I see you with your family—which is often, us being neighbors—I can't help but think about how my dad is stuck in hell, made to do god knows what. And contrast that to what you have." She tugged at the back of her head. "And yes, I know exactly how shitty that makes me sound."

"Kinsley. You know we'd get Vernon out now if we could."

In the middle of biting her nails, Kinsley said something indecipherable.

"What?" I asked, reaching out toward her back.

"Leave it." Kinsley spat the words, and I pulled my hand away.

Her lip firmed. "Let's just get through the next few weeks. I'll do everything I can to cover on my end. But my dad needs to get out, Matt. As soon as there's an opportunity."

I frowned. "That was always the plan."

"Right." Her confirmation came with a side-eye. "So long as it stays that way."

There was a flash of motion as a pair of dark chitin feet slammed into Kinsley's backside and shoved, sending her spinning, swearing incessantly, toward the opposite end of the of the golf course.

"That seemed like way too serious a conversation for a party." Sae rotated to face me, smoothly shifting herself in a diagonal roll.

"Is everybody better at flying than me?"

"No idea. When are we moving on Cameron?"

I rubbed the bridge of my nose. "That's a lighter topic?"

"Don't get lost in the weeds." Sae prodded me in the ribs. "You said you only have a couple days left."

"We recon this evening. Act tomorrow."

"Really want to push this to the last minute?" Sae's mouth turned downward.

"From the dossier and character sheet, we don't want to go into this half-cocked. Especially if there's an advantage to be had." I smiled widely.

Sae looked slightly perturbed. "Oh?"

"All we have to do is get within range. Azure will do the rest."

CHAPTER FIFTY-NINE

Rain poured, flooding the sidewalk and forming small rivers that followed runoffs to the storm drain. There'd been no warning of the incoming storm, save a few dark clouds on the horizon that overtook the sky in little more than an hour.

Weather is volatile in Texas. Anyone who's lived here for longer than a week can tell you that. But it was different now. There were no more emergency push notifications, no more rain in X minutes heads ups from satellites we no longer had access to. Lightning spiderwebbed the sky, striking somewhere on the far end of the city. In the fading luminescence I caught my reflection from a puddle as I stepped over, jagged lines of the **<Allfather's Mask>** lending my hooded visage a sinister air.

Up ahead, a large-framed man stared anxiously up at the sky from beneath the coverage of an oversized, navy-blue golf umbrella. He held the umbrella in one gloved hand and a calico-colored cat in the other. I barely picked out his words through the storm. "This enough air for you, Shiva?"

The cat wiggled free of his grip. Just a hair too slow, Buzzcut fumbled the catch. The cat plunged straight down and landed with a slosh in a soaked section of grass that lined the sidewalk. It stared up at its master in abject betrayal.

"Oh no, the consequences of your own actions," Buzzcut muttered and moved to cover the cat with his umbrella.

"Meow."

"Going to be reasonable if we go inside now? Stop bouncing off the fucking walls?"

"Meow."

Buzzcut crouched, likely intending to scoop up the cat. I reached out with **<Suggestion>**, directing the cat's attention to the hooded stranger walking in their direction. To its simple mind, I suddenly smelled like tuna and catnip and looked incredibly friendly. It broke from Buzzcut and bounded toward me.

"Dammit. Grab that little shit!" Buzzcut called.

I crouched down and the soaked cat all but leapt into my arms. Buzzcut jogged over to me, half-grunting thanks. "Never calms down unless he gets time outside."

"My dog's the same way."

Talia growled in the recesses of my mind.

"Count yourself lucky you're a dog guy. System litter's all clay based." Buzzcut held his hands out. I awkwardly held the cat out toward him. When he took it, I "accidentally" reached past his glove and contacted bare skin.

"Clay litter is... bad?" I asked. It felt strange, holding a conversation with the man who had hounded me pretty much since the beginning. But saying nothing would be more suspicious.

"Oh yeah. On account of the silica. Numbnuts here breathes in too much silica dust, it's a one-way trip to cancer town." Buzzcut scowled at the cat, which swatted at his nose playfully. "Taking a dip in dirty rain-water after a drought can't be much better."

"Have a good night." I walked away.

"Hey!" Buzzcut called after me.

I stopped, keeping my expression strictly calm as turned back, even as my heart raced in my neck. Even though I'd kept the mask's single target setting, I didn't know when the diminishing returns would kick in, or how quickly. "What?"

Buzzcut pressed a button on the umbrella's grip and it snapped shut. Rain pelted his thinly shorn head. "No telling where he'd have run off to if you didn't grab him. Take it."

I nearly blew him off before I noted the serious expression. This was important to him, somehow. Tentatively, I reached out for the umbrella. "Really?"

"Yeah." Buzzcut smiled. "Hoodie ain't doing shit for this weather, and I got others."

"Thanks."

"Stay safe."

"You too."

I watched from beneath the coverage of the umbrella as Buzzcut carried his cat inside. If that was the only exchange we'd ever had, I might have liked the man. But it was hardly our first exchange.

Buzzcut was a ranking member of the suits. He'd had every intention of killing me in that alley the night of the bounty. While Jinny died, he stood by, watching, just like the rest of them. And he'd taken Nick.

Whatever I did to him was justified.

Once I was certain Buzzcut wasn't watching, I doubled back, darting into the neighboring house with a for-sale sign in the front yard.

I-I-I-I-I-I—

Cameron toweled Shiva off within the confines of the tub. The part of his mind that never shut up reminded him that this was her third bath this week. She hated it, and if he wasn't careful, even the premium oatmeal pet shampoo he stocked up on would eventually dry out her skin.

But with everything being so goddamn dirty, there wasn't really an alternative. He'd need to be more careful with her.

As soon as Cameron loosened his grip on the towel, Shiva leapt over the ceramic wall of the tub and paused in the doorway to yowl at him.

Cameron rolled his eyes. "Right. You've got it *so* hard. You get to fuck off and gnaw on a sofa leg while I'm stuck cleaning up your mess."

"Meow." Shiva flicked her tail and stalked away.

"Whatever."

With a sigh, Cameron set to work. First, he removed the mesh covering that prevented fur from clogging the drain, dumping the contents into a waiting plastic bag and tying it off, tossing it into the bathroom trashcan. He pulled on latex gloves and scrubbed the still-wet surface with a mix of Clorox, water, and vinegar he'd found to be most effective, making even, counterclockwise circles down the right side to the center, where he'd stop, lifting the rag to the opposite edge and clean the left in the same manner, drawing all the filth and grime toward the center. Once it was all drawn together, Cameron wet a new rag and pulled it down the center, feeling accomplishment as the particulates of dirt and dust accumulated at the reflective metal ring before plummeting down the drain.

He repeated the process twice more before he finally felt satisfied.

Standing, he wiped a sheen of sweat off his forehead and washed his hands. When he looked up at the mirror, he froze.

The letters I K N stood out in the fogged section of the mirror.

What the fuck?

Cameron closed the door, then turned the sink's faucet all the way to the left, increasing the temperature of the water. He did the same with the bathtub and walk-in shower, creating more steam.

Only after the mirror fully fogged did the message reveal itself.

I KNOW WHO YOU ARE.

An icy chill traveled the full length of Cameron's spine. What the fuck was this horror movie bullshit? It wasn't anyone from the guild. If someone from the guild was coming for him, it would be direct, extreme, decisive. And they sure as hell wouldn't warn him they were coming.

What would it even mean, anyway? They already knew who he was. Unless—

Cameron shut his eyes. Panicking wouldn't help. Aaron had come straight to him once the dome settled, used Cameron's influence to help organize the jailbreak. If the guild knew who he really was, he'd be dead already.

The most plausible explanation was sleepwalking. He did weird shit in his sleep. It was part of the reason he refused to stay onsite. The quarters segment of the underground compound wasn't much different from gen pop, with the exception of better toilets. Full to the brim with of hungry motherfuckers who would pounce at the slightest sign of weakness, all capable of curb-stomping their own mothers if it meant getting a leg up.

But his subconscious mind was crafty. Before he'd switched medications, he'd often woken up and found himself in places he shouldn't be, in the middle of making food. He'd even found sticky notes scrawled in his handwriting, left in the damndest places.

Looking for evidence that supported his theory, Cameron opened the small metal trashcan at the base of the toilet. Beneath the bag, he found a discarded bottle of rubbing alcohol—still half-full—and a handful of cotton balls at the bottom.

Somehow, discovering the means he'd left the message with gave him some small comfort. Small being the keyword.

There was a dirty smear on the bathtub. Cameron cleaned it one more time. When he exited the bathroom, he pulled the door shut behind him, absentmindedly turning the knob three times.

Click. The latch stuck on the third twist.

"God damn it!" he roared, opening the door and slamming it shut. The latch clicked. Compulsively, he turned the knob thrice more. Once again, it stuck on the third turn.

Cameron stomped down the hallway, throwing open the door that led into the garage, and flicked on the light. For a moment, nothing happened. Then the light flickered on. He stared at the bulb.

Is it just going out? Or is it faulty wiring?

One thing at a time. It was already after midnight, but it wouldn't take long to swap the bulb after he'd finished with the bathroom door. Of course, if the wiring was shot, that was going to take a lot longer to fix, but it was better to cross that bridge when he came to it.

Cameron grabbed the gray toolbox from its place, careful not to upend the meticulously organized contents within, and pulled the door shut behind him. As always, he turned the handle three times, ensuring it latched.

The latch caught on the third pull.

———

CHAPTER SIXTY

"God, that sucks." Streaking violet-and-blue swimmers covered my left eye. I sat up slowly and leaned forward, cradling my head. The nylon sleeping bag's crinkling was absurdly loud.

It took a moment to make out Sae in the darkness. Sae nestled in the nook beside the window, where she pointed toward the house across from us. "No matter how bad you're feeling, I guarantee our friend over there is doing worse."

I stumbled to my feet and leaned against the opposite side of the window, in time to see Buzzcut hauling an entire door into his over-furnished living room. The living room itself was a wreck, covered in manila batting Shiva had emancipated from several now-desiccated couch cushions.

"JESUS FUCKING CHRIST!"

The words were muffled but clearly audible from a house over.

"Not gonna lie, when you floated this idea, it felt very lifetime special." Sae chuckled, watching Buzzcut struggle with what minor crisis to prioritize. Her face grew somber. "But he's seriously tilted."

I closed my eyes, trying to gain my bearings. "Everyone loves to self-diagnose as OCD these days. Doesn't change the fact that the real thing's no joke."

"Especially if your next-door neighbors are *literally* gaslighting you. How'd you know about the OCD?" Sae asked. "It wasn't in the file."

"Negative space."

"Pretend I can't follow your pseudo-intellectual non-sequiturs."

I sighed. "His psych workup. He reads like real type A. Extroverted, observant, thoughtful, and judging. Not the kind to get depressed for extended periods. But the meds told a different story. He's been on Zoloft for the last three years, Paxil and other SSRIs the previous two. Not in I-swallowed-a-bottle-of-aspirin-and-got-admitted-to-the-hospital-for-attention quantities either. Elephant doses."

"So?" Sae shrugged. "Maybe he was ashamed of it or something."

"It's 2024. Everyone's depressed. Regardless, like you said, I got a sense from the paperwork that he was hiding something. And if he was hiding from the suits, it had to be a weakness or disqualifier. Few distinct possibilities, no way of narrowing them down from a distance. So, I dropped by Region 7 and watched him for a while."

Sae whistled low. "One in the morning, and he's bathing those hinges in WD-40."

"Yeah. Azure made them squeak. No idea how. Buzzcut put the plastic down first?" I asked.

"Yep."

"How much you want to bet, when he's done, he's goes straight for the air freshener?"

Sae rolled her eyes. "That's a sucker's bet. First stop's gonna be a bottle of Febreze."

We watched in silent interest as Buzzcut stomped across the living room to the kitchen, pulling a spray bottle from the overhead cabinet. He shook it up thoroughly and squeezed the trigger. A barely perceptible stream of aerosol emitted from the nozzle, then sputtered and died.

Buzzcut shook the bottle and pulled again, drawing nothing.

I felt a sense of stoic satisfaction. Sae's head slowly turned toward me. "You emptied the man's air freshener?"

"*I* didn't."

"Azure again?"

"Yep."

"You're an actual monster."

"It's a balance." I crossed my arms. "Right now, he's just having a terrible night. Obsessive-compulsives are accustomed to this sort of spiraling. They can handle one thing going wrong, maybe even two, but they're fully aware that it gets harder and harder to return to a neutral place the farther down the spiral. As long as we're subtle, he'll stay focused on putting out the fires rather than wondering why they're happening."

"Still..." Sae trailed off, watching Buzzcut move his cat from the couch to the bedroom—surprisingly gentle, considering the turmoil the animal had put him through. "I feel kind of bad."

I frowned. "You realize this isn't going to get any easier, right? These aren't faceless monsters we're hunting. They're not always going to look like bad guys. They're just people."

"People who have it coming," Sae said angrily, more to herself than to me. After a moment of silence, she spoke, her eyes still glued to Buzzcut. "Well? We killing him?"

"Talia?" I asked, letting **\<Broken Legacy\>** fall to the ground. A cloud of dust emerged and faded as my summon took physical form.

"From the glimpse we shared into his mind, it's clear he's hiding something from his betters," Talia said thoughtfully. "I'm just not sure if that's enough to matter. Anything useful gleaned from questioning him could just as likely be gathered once we gain admittance. Capturing our prey puts us at further risk. If it were discovered, or if he escaped, it would compromise you on multiple levels. And as fond as you are of such difficult undertakings..." Talia eyed me. "I cannot help but wonder if, in this case, the simplest solution is best."

"Maybe."

Talia had made several good points. Sunny didn't strike me as the type to fuck around. If he got the slightest inkling I'd betrayed him, it'd be catastrophic.

But I wasn't sure she was right, downplaying Buzzcut's usefulness. He'd been with them since the beginning. He'd have insights into how they worked, how they thought. I still hadn't decided if the stunt I'd pulled to clear my name had been an overextension. It was necessary in the moment, but the repercussions had yet to be seen. Plenty of people had been there, overheard the conflict between Myrddin and Sae.

After some time, Sae whispered. "He's giving up."

Sure enough, Buzzcut was stomping up the living room stairs to the loft, headed toward his bedroom.

"Azure?" I reached out to my summon.

"This is too much fun," Azure giggled.

"Any issues?"

"No. Still blissfully unaware. And so thoroughly, delightfully angry."

"Good. I need to sleep. You'll keep him conscious?"

"Not... exactly." Azure's giggles grew into a guffaw that sounded decidedly evil.

"Azure."

"What?!" He sounded affronted. Like he expected me to curtail whatever he was planning.

"I'm not just gonna fuck off and sleep after you get all maniacal like that. Spill."

"Boo. And here I was, trying to surprise you. Here's the play-by-play. I'm going to let him sleep. Shallowly. Every time he approaches a REM cycle, I'll shove the psychic equivalent of a sliver into his mind. Make sure he stays semiconscious. And in the meantime, I'll pump him full of anxiety and slowly intro-

duce mental images of minor incidents around the house that didn't actually happen. The stove he left on. The fridge he cracked."

I blinked. My intention was as simple as keeping Buzzcut sleep-deprived and unsettled, giving us an edge in the impending confrontation. But if Azure wanted to go the extra mile?

"Just don't tip our hand," I relented.

"Roger! Um...."

"What?"

Azure spoke carefully. "Just hypothetically, it wouldn't be difficult for me to do... something... with the cat."

"Jesus—No. Leave the fucking cat alone."

"Fine."

Our part here was more or less done, though I needed to stay within a certain distance to ensure Azure could siphon mana from me and keep Buzzcut on pins and needles.

"C'mon, let's call it." I gestured to Sae. "Big day tomorrow."

Sae looked out the window one final time, then unrolled her blue sleeping bag, placing it a few feet away, parallel to mine. She opened the zipper and settled in. "This is heavy."

"We can trade bags," I joked.

"You know what I mean."

I did.

"It's not too late to back out."

"Fuckin—the next time you say that to me, Helpline, I'm gonna punch you in the face."

"Got it," I said.

"Good," Sae snapped. After a few moments, she spoke in a much quieter tone. "I understood what I was getting into. In theory."

"What do you mean?"

"I'm not stupid. I knew we were going to get blood on her hands, but. It just sucks. When we first got here, you almost had to tie me down. But after watching him from a distance? Seeing him at home, acting normal? It feels heavier somehow."

I said nothing.

"Nothing's changed. Jinny and Nick, everything that happened to me, it was all their fault. Their fucking fault. And I want them to pay for it," Sae said, the pain in her voice raw.

Again, a response didn't come. It felt like she was struggling against herself, and I was nothing more than a spectator.

Instead of saying something, I reached out from the sleeping bag and took her hand. Sae jumped, then with a hesitance I could almost feel, tightened her hand around mine. Her chitin fingers were icy to the touch.

The tendrils of sleep pulled at me.

"You never said," Sae's voice floated through the haze.

"Hm?"

"Our aim. Catch? Or kill?"

"Haven't decided yet," I murmured, "There's someone I need to talk to first."

I'd been circling this for some time. Searching for any avenue that would allow me to avoid it. Confronting the man who'd opened his home to me. The father of my once best friend, a constant in my life until he threw my mother overboard to drown. And as far as I knew, the tenuous leader of the suits.

Aaron.

CHAPTER SIXTY-ONE

I stared up at the metal beams stretching the length of Aaron's house, supporting the wide-open balcony on the second floor, an adage swirled up in my mind.

"The bigger they are, the harder they fall."

As sayings go, it's horseshit. And that's not even getting into the terminal velocity pedantry. The saying should be: the higher you climb, the grander the parachute. Aaron was proof of that. If he was a normal person, the racketeering trial would have easily ruined him with legal fees alone. Not to mention the damage to reputation, loss of his vocation, and inherent trauma such a drawn-out battle comes with.

It'd taken Mom years to recover from the strain of the trial. She'd only just recently pulled herself out of the bottle, and even now, it was impossible to know whether it was going to stick. Still. If the dome hadn't come down? She'd have no real prospects. Even if it's relatively small, even if you can explain it as a reasonable mistake, a felony is a felony. A steel anvil tethered to any resume, sending it plunging straight into the trash.

If her recovery had legs, she would have spent the rest of her life working for minimum or borderline minimum wage. If Mom got lucky, she'd only have to do so until one of us could support her. And if she didn't get lucky—a much more likely scenario—she'd work until the day she couldn't anymore, or got sick.

With nothing but a guest room as her retirement home.

In terms of contrast, Aaron was doing just fine. He probably made a little less as a lawyer than he had as a hedge fund manager. The house was smaller. Not the massive estate on a hundred-acre plot it once was, but not the smallest residence in the gated community either. When the architect asked him what he wanted, I'm guessing he said something like, "Chic, minimalist, boxy, and post-modern. With a fuckton of glass."

More curiously, he appeared to have almost no security. Slipping past the rent-a-cops at the checkpoint was child's play. Once I was in, Azure confirmed that only one of them was a User, and not a particularly good one at that. There were a few security cameras hidden in various bushes and utility poles, but that was it.

So, what was it? Was he so confident in whatever he and the rest of the suits were running that he considered himself too big to fail? Or was there some other security angle I wasn't seeing, like the camouflaged Users at the park?

It was Aaron. Safest to assume both. Take nothing for granted.

I saw him through a corner window. Aaron's sleeves were rolled up to his forearms, and he held a napkin loosely in his grip. It was one of the few times I'd seen him without a tie. He was leaning halfway over, eyebrow raised as if he'd just told a real gut buster. His audience of one— a woman who must have had an absolute prodigy for a plastic surgeon— guffawed, her joyful laughter creating a strangely macabre image without the accompanying sound. She bounced a baby that couldn't be a day over six months on her knee. Not impressed or not listening, Daphne stared down at her food and poked at it with a fork tentatively.

Aaron slapped her on the shoulder and leaned in conspiratorially. Even as she fought it, Daphne cracked a small smile.

Even with the world on its head, some things had barely changed at all.

They looked happy. Whole. The family looked almost picturesque. Untouched by the dome and everything that came before it. And they'd always looked that way. It was probably what attracted me to them.

I bore down on the swelling heat in my gut. A cool head was the only way through this.

"Azure. Can you get anything from Aaron?" I asked, not getting my hopes up.

"No..." Azure sounded puzzled. "But it's different, somehow. With Sunny and Miles, it was a perceptible blur. Like something was working to shield them—spending significant energy to muddy their thoughts. Meaning, in theory, I could have broken through eventually."

"That's not the case here?"

"It's like there's nothing there. Nothing. No wall to break down, nothing for me to tap into behind it. I'd almost assume he was an empty vessel puppeted by some outside entity, but there's no trace of the astronomical mana required to pull that off."

I shrugged. "He's the leader of a powerful organization. Not surprising that he's taken steps to shield himself."

"This is different," Azure sulked.

"You sure the shield isn't coming from him?"

I had to be sure.

"From everything I can tell, he's just a civilian. Judging from how unconcerned she is, he's keeping his wife out of the loop, but Daphne knows. And she's worried. Wasn't even trying to read her mind—she pretty much screamed it."

"She should—" I bit the rest off. Aaron locked eyes with me through the glass from his seat at the table.

Shit.

For a split second his face was blank, smooth. Processing. Then he smiled widely and gestured toward the front of the house. I awkwardly stepped through the perfectly manicured lawn, circling around to the front to meet him.

"Matthias," Aaron said, warm voice loud enough to announce my presence to the entire house. "So glad you took me up on the offer."

Daphne leaned back to look out into the atrium. "Matt?"

I gave her a small wave and she waved back, grinning. Then the grin died. It wasn't hard to guess what she was thinking about, because I was thinking about the same thing. The last time we'd seen each other.

The tunnel.

"Have to say, your timing's impeccable." Aaron gestured for me to follow him, and I did, my footsteps echoing across the tile. "Council takes up most of my time lately. Too much. Which is why I told them to shove it and took a mental health day. Extra spaghetti on the counter, so help yourself."

I felt physical revulsion at the idea of eating anything that Aaron had cooked. My eyes were drawn to a massive crystal chandelier on the ceiling. "Looks like you all landed okay. After... everything."

"We did." Aaron shot me a pained smile. "It was an adjustment, but we pulled through."

"Glad to hear it," I said, not bothering to hide the sarcasm.

Standing next to the fridge, Aaron's wife had shifted the baby to her hip and waited expectantly. "Who's this?"

"Joyce, this is Matt—Matt, my lovely Joyce, and this adorable bundle of joy..." Aaron kissed his wife's cheek and took the baby from her gently. "Is Olivia."

"Nice to meet you," I said.

"There's parmesan cheese on the counter. Freshly grated. Your favorite," Daphne pointed out, her demeanor still muted.

My hand clenched into a fist. Aaron was playing the perfect doting father, but as he held the baby out toward me, all I could see was him using another innocent as a shield.

"We have business."

"Not at the table you don't," Joyce said, mockingly stern. She gave her husband a knowing look. "No negotiations—"

"—At the family table," Aaron finished. "I remember. So why don't we all—"

The feeling snuck up on me. This tangible, undeniable drive to escape. Even the idea of staying here a minute longer than I had to was impossible to stomach, let alone the time it would take to eat a bowl of Aaron's signature spaghetti.

I would not sit here and play house with the motherfucker who burned mine to the ground.

"No."

"What?" Aaron cocked his head.

"And with a total of one, I'll do you exactly one more favor than you've ever done me. If you're planning on staying in today, don't. Go out in public. Somewhere you'll be noticed, with as many witnesses as possible."

I watched, in some petty semblance of satisfaction, as Joyce slowly crooked her neck toward Aaron. "Babe. What's he talking about?"

Aaron chuckled. "It's an inside joke."

Was she going to buy that?

"Oh. Well, if you're going out to the deck to talk business, eat something. You're too skinny." Joyce dumped a heaving serving of pasta onto an ornate plate and handed it to me.

Apparently she was. Or she'd elevated the practice of looking the other way into an art form.

"Thanks." I smiled tightly. The steam from the fragrant sauce scalded my nostrils.

Aaron waited for me at the back door and I followed him outside. Unsurprisingly, the back had more in common with a botanical garden than a typical yard, with an artificial stream that cut down the center, framed by exotic-looking trees.

"When are you going to ditch that chip on your shoulder?" Aaron said. Now that we were out of earshot from his wife, he'd dropped the overly cheerful disposition. More than anything, he looked disappointed.

It shouldn't have mattered to me. Aaron's approval. But somehow, it did.

"Which chip?"

"The Marx-addled rage that flares up anytime you're reminded that there's people out there who are more fortunate than others." He eyed me.

I bared my teeth. "You're right. I should be more sympathetic. Downgrading from three stories to two must be difficult. Not to mention the reduction in square footage. You're pretty much living on the street."

"How can you not see the hypocrisy?" Aaron countered. The matter-of-fact nature of his voice when he was gearing up for an argument was all it took to hit me with a wave of nostalgia. "You are the one percent. Bonafide Nouveau rich. You maneuvered yourself perfectly, yet you're still stuck in this poor man's mindset centered around the idea that everyone with 'more' is an enemy."

"Save the political shit for someone who cares." I rolled my eyes. Aaron *knew* that wealth didn't even make the top ten list of issues I had with him, but he was pushing this conversation in that direction in order to win. Like this was a moderated debate with stakes, rather than a conversation. "Listen, Aaron. I wasn't bullshitting earlier. You need to be seen today."

Aaron's expression stilled. "Feel free to expand on that. Say what you mean."

"Not yet." I settled down on a bench chair and felt the wound on my back scream in irritation. "No one can hear what I'm about to tell you. Your people or mine."

I guessed—knowing how private he was—that Aaron's house was shielded somehow. Nevertheless, I pulled up my passive skill menu and activated **<Squelch>**.

"You realize, if you try to kill me here—whether or not you succeed, there will be repercussions." For just a second, the mask dropped. And what I saw in his eyes felt strangely familiar.

It's not your time.

I shook my head. "As much as I'd love to rub your nose in it, the old shit between us is buried."

"Really. Just like that?" Aaron's expression turned calculated. "Because it doesn't feel buried. There's so many lies in circulation, Matthias. Hell, even the dreaded Ordinator can't seem to keep his story straight. Rumor has it he claimed to be there that fateful night your friend died. More interesting than that, your friend apparently confirmed it. What was her name? Sae?"

CHAPTER SIXTY-TWO

My hand twitched. It'd be so easy to end Aaron here. My strength wasn't particularly high, but it was still a significant upgrade from a normal person. It'd take seconds to dig my fingers into his throat and squeeze—

"I'd love to get in touch with her. Have a little chat about what she remembers."

<Jaded Eye> crossed the threshold of stress. I stepped back from myself, mentally. Looked back toward the house. Daphne had moved from the kitchen table to the sitting room. She was lounging on a chaise, pretending not to be looking our way. Joyce was tidying up dishes.

Moving on Aaron here—even if my chances of success were good—was worse than idiotic.

It was impulsive.

And no matter how good it would feel in the moment, it wasn't worth the fallout.

Aaron sighed. "Alright. We'll do it your way." He angled away from me and unfastened the clasp of his Rolex, pressing his thumb against a black button hidden within the clasp.

My ears popped from a sudden shift in pressure. A thin, membrane like bubble shimmered around us.

"We're shielded," Aaron explained.

"Where the hell do you keep getting items that look futuristic?" I had to ask.

Aaron gave me a smug grin. "Haven't met a Technomancer yet, I take it."

"No."

"They're infuriating. But incredibly useful. Not even the gods themselves could hear us if they were so inclined. Say what you need to say."

I looked Aaron dead in the face. "Cameron Reed."

Aaron blinked, just a fraction too late. "Who?"

I let out a slow hiss. "Damn. And from what I hear, he thinks so highly of you. Anyway, his number is up."

"If you've come here to threaten the life of someone who may or may not work for me, I think the result may not be to your liking." Aaron didn't bother hiding the threat in his voice.

"On the contrary. I'm here to ask how you'd like us to proceed."

"Us?" Aaron asked.

Like clockwork, Azure hopped the fence. He was wearing my damaged eldritch armor and carried the stench of death with him.

"Can't say I knew what to expect, but this is... something else," Aaron murmured. His body language was still strong, confident. No amount of posturing could hide the sudden paleness in his face.

"Got a vermin infestation on your hands," Azure said. I didn't like what he was doing to my voice. It sounded too gravelly, too pointlessly obfuscated.

"What kind of vermin?" Aaron asked.

"Homegrown. Gray hair. Big smile. Feels like he'd kill you at the slightest provocation. Unnaturally attached to his car?"

"Sunny," Aaron said. He sounded less angry, more disappointed.

"That's the one," I confirmed.

"He said they looked everywhere and couldn't find you," Aaron interrogated Azure directly.

"Technically true. I found him." Azure reached in his inventory and pulled out the dossier, handing it to Aaron. "Which was when he gave me a target."

Aaron leafed through the file and put a hand to his mouth. Then slowly, his face hardened. "Christ. It's hard to believe he'd act so directly."

"Well," I shrugged. "No point in denying it. If it wasn't Myrddin, he'd have pawned this off to someone else. The question is, where do we take it from here?"

Aaron opened his mouth, then closed it. He pointed a finger at me. "Don't do that shit to me. I taught you that."

"What shit?"

"The 'act like you're already a part of a team you want to join' shit." Aaron frowned. "Which implies something I hadn't fully considered."

"Do you want my help or not?"

"Why would you even—" Aaron stopped himself. His expression grew firm. "No. Not until I understand this," he drew an invisible line with his fingertip from Azure to me and stuck the finger in my chest. "And this."

"The Merchants' Guild found some of Myrddin's actions during the Transposition... unpalatable."

"Didn't even bother to hear me out," Azure groused.

I shrugged. "Personally, I don't really care. It takes a lot more for me to throw away someone so useful."

Aaron's brows knit together. "So, the chaos the other night..."

"Feds have been up my ass." I rolled my eyes.

"They thought we were the same person. Nearly crucified Matt for it." Azure chuckled. I shot him a look. That was sharing far more information than necessary.

"We got a little creative," I finished.

"Then the rumor of Myrddin being there was what? A dog whistle?"

I smiled. As much as I hated him, it was always nice how quick Aaron was on the uptake. "Something like that. Figured you'd be one of the few to realize things weren't adding up, making the transition to this moment as smooth as possible."

"None of this explains why you'd be remotely interested in helping me," Aaron said.

I made a vague circle with my hand. "The three of us have something in common. There's only one thing we really care about."

"Power," Azure said.

"And with said power, winning this stupid game," I said. "As much as I hate you, Aaron? You're the one person I'd wager most likely to make it out of this unscathed. And whatever plan you have to do that? I want in."

Aaron crossed his arms and appraised me. "You're different. Not as angry as you used to be."

Just better at hiding it.

"So what." Aaron turned and faced Azure. "You'd enter my organization as his agent?"

"I'm no one's lackey," Azure bristled.

"Myrddin owes me a few favors, but he's his own person," I confirmed. "He needs a guild, and he's obviously capable. You need to clean house and have a Necromancer whose research will benefit significantly from the cores he provides. What's the downside?"

"And in the process, you'll have done me a favor, handed me a special class, and ingratiated yourself as an alley." Aaron nodded slowly. "Not bad. And I'm not saying anything you don't already know. But the fact that the Necromancer in question is Kinsley's father isn't a problem?"

I snorted. "Please. I'm sure you've recognized the similarities between the site and a certain project you worked on a long time ago?"

"It looked like her handiwork, but it was impossible to be certain," Aaron hedged.

I raised an eyebrow. "Well, she didn't want to do it. Not until I twisted her arm. Latent trauma and blah blah blah. If I'm willing to do that to my own mother, you really think I give a shit about some kid I met less than a month ago?"

Aaron glanced over to Azure.

Azure shrugged. "Kinsley cut me loose on a hair-trigger. Fuck her and her people."

"And the losses you suffered?" Aaron asked, scrutinizing me closely.

I kept my voice casual. The words tasted like bile. "Like I told Sunny. Jinny didn't matter, I barely knew her for two days, and what happened was mostly her fault. Sae's alive. And Nick, so long as he's alive and not being tortured—"

"He's not," Aaron confirmed quietly. "All things considered, he's being treated very well."

"Then he's finally out of my hair," I finished. "And yes, the timing sucked, and I really could have used his help during the Transposition, but I survived."

"Okay," Aaron said. He smiled. "Let's do business."

"On one condition." I leveled a stare at him, and for the first time let my anger shine through. "No matter how this ends, Sunny goes down. End of story."

"We're on the same wavelength," Aaron waved dismissively. "Though I'm curious why you are."

"You don't get to make the kind of threats he made and walk away." I remembered in a wave of anger how he'd recited my personal information back to me, then talked in detail about what he'd do if I didn't keep my mouth shut. "He said he'd make my mother bite the curb."

Aaron closed his eyes.

"And that he'd stomp her skull in while my sister watched."

"Jesus." Aaron hissed.

"Guessing he left that out of the report."

"Good fucking guess." Aaron looked genuinely uncomfortable. I had no idea if Sunny's threats had actually disturbed him or if he was playing the reaction up for the sake of building rapport. He was just that good. "Don't get me wrong, if you need someone to send a message, Sunny's your guy. I knew that. But there has to be lines. Obviously it's fine with me."

"What do you want us to do with Cameron?" Azure asked.

"It might be possible to stage something. Whisk him away to a safe-house, if you've got something along those lines," I suggested.

"No." Aaron squinted. "Sunny already knows that's something Myrddin might pull, because of the Necromancer. He'll be more alert to the possibility." He grimaced at Azure. "And he'll probably expect you to bring a trophy."

"He never mentioned it," I interjected, not really wanting things to head in that direction.

"Sunny doesn't always say exactly what he wants. It's been a reoccurring problem." Aaron pulled both hands down his face, giving us a detailed view of the redness beneath the whites of his eyes.

"I have something of a sense for people. And Cameron seems loyal to a fault," Azure said.

It took me a moment to realize why. Azure had enough insight into my mind that he probably knew that killing someone—even if it was someone with the enemy—at the behest of a deranged asshole didn't sit well with me.

That, or he was talking to the tape.

Aaron leaned back against the tall fence, letting his head bang against it lightly. "Mr. Reed is a good man. Professional, despite his neuroticism. He's been an associate of mine long before the dome."

"But?" I prompted.

Aaron looked at the ground, sadly. "He's not steadfast. In what we're trying to do. He's with us because he owes me and trusts me, but he's not committed to the cause. It's only a matter of time before he breaks."

"You realize we aren't true believers either. Partially on the basis of having no idea what you're actually doing," I pointed out.

"In truth, I'm not worried about you, son," Aaron said. "Once you see what I'm building—the endgame—you'll pick the right side. It's undeniable."

It was alarming. Aaron knew the score, knew what we were. What I was. At most, we were friends of convenience, poised to eat each other at any given moment. If I were him, I would have kept me away from whatever secret I was guarding for as long as humanly possible.

The fact that he was still so confident in my long-term support made me uneasy. Aaron was a monster, but he was a patient one. What if he actually had something worthwhile?

"You're advising me to kill him," Azure asked, flatly. "Your own man."

Aaron mulled over the words carefully. "What I'm advising, is for you to follow the directive you were given. There's no telling where Sunny is, and whether he or one of his many followers is watching Mr. Reed's domicile from a distance. It's the safest course."

The fact that Aaron's group was dealing with internal strife, in the grand scheme of things, wasn't particularly surprising. He talked a good game. Had a natural talent for making you think he was above it all, a man set apart. Elevated. But once the polish faded and he was in the shit? He was nothing more than another rat among thousands.

Azure stepped into Aaron's space. I almost directed him to back off—but decided at the last minute to let my summon handle it. Other than a few missteps, Azure had handled this more or less perfectly. "I know what I'm about to say is pointless. That no matter what I say here, people like you don't really get it in their head until their wings are clipped. But sometimes I can't help myself."

I watched as Aaron tensed, ready to send a mental message at a moment's notice.

With a cold smile, Azure leaned in. "I don't share Matt's qualms about pulling innocents into the crossfire. It's the natural order of things. If you ever get it in your head to slip a similarly shaped knife between my ribs, it won't go so smoothly. For you or the people you care about."

"So I've gathered." Aaron gave Azure a nod of acknowledgement and peered at me. "Not the sort of person I'd expect you to throw in with. You always seemed too inflexible for that. Too fixated on some cosmic notion of fairness."

"I grew up."

"Maybe," Aaron said nonchalantly. Then he spoke directly to Azure. "Perhaps a show of good will is in order."

I jumped in, keeping him off-balance. "Start with getting your foot off my people's neck. This only works if I have plausible deniability. All it takes is one weak link in your surveillance network, and it all comes tumbling down."

"Fair enough. Sunny was wrong, threatening you the way he did," Aaron mused. "Done. Though we'll eventually need to figure out where you fit in the organization, that's a long-term issue. I'll find an excuse to lift surveillance in your region."

I had to actively fight myself not to ask the questions that'd haunted me. What Aaron intended. How he'd managed to achieve this position of power as a civilian in such a short span of time. But the longer I spoke to Aaron, the more likely it was that I'd give him an angle. Right now he was on the back foot, and he needed to stay that way.

Those answers would reveal themselves eventually.

"Dad? Everything okay?"

All three heads whipped around to where Daphne was leaning outside the back door. Her face was a mask of worry and concern.

Aaron gave her a strained smile and a polite wave. "All good, sweetie."

There was a gentle whoosh as the door clicked shut behind Daphne, and she disappeared within the depths of the house.

"So, Cameron dies," I confirmed.

"Mr. Reed was special. In a perfect world, I owed him a great deal. That doesn't change the reality that there was no place for him in the grand scheme of things," Aaron said. To his small credit, he actually seemed to struggle with the decision. "And his death will serve a greater purpose."

"Sure he'll appreciate that."

I stuffed my hands in my pockets and began to walk away. Myrddin fell in line behind me.

"Judge me all you want," Aaron called after me. "But we live in a world of problems, Matthias. I'm the only one offering a solution."

"And I'm just following orders," I called back over my shoulder.

CHAPTER SIXTY-THREE

Buzzcut entered his home with all the grimness and gravitas of a man marching to his own execution. He struggled with the bag of cleaning supplies under one arm and closed the door behind him.

With an audible sigh, he hung his keys on the steel hook beside the door, then stopped.

For a moment, he didn't move. Stayed rooted to the spot behind the plasterboard and cocked his head as if he was listening for something.

I'd told Azure to pay special attention to the entryway, make sure we unsettled nothing, avoided setting off any unknown triggers. And my summon had followed through. Absolutely everything was exactly the way Buzzcut had left it, down to every speck of dust, the angle of the doorknob, and the small pile of dust behind the door.

Yet, somehow, he knew.

Buzzcut reached out slowly for the light switch. As soon as he flicked it, **<Probability Cascade>** activated as the leg of one of the hall shelves gave out, spilling out dozens of books as it fell sideways.

Buzzcut dropped the cleaning supplies in his arms and jumped backward with a startled shout.

I waited until the complex black-and-silver sights of **<Nychta's Lament>** perfectly aligned with my target. In the darkened house, the proceeding arrowhead glowed a dull green from Sae's enchantment. It was subtle, only a faint shimmer in the shadow.

At this range, it didn't matter that my skill with the bow was lacking in comparison. I needed the stopping power, and as long as the target was standing still and I'd successfully baited out **<Perception>**, I had him.

I loosed the arrow.

Buzzcut's head snapped to the side and he stumbled back against the door, back slamming into it as he reached up in shock toward where the arrow had pierced his neck. He wasn't bleeding much. A shot through the throat was debilitating enough to make this a hell of a lot easier than it would have been otherwise.

There were precious seconds before his abilities kicked in. Maybe less. I dropped the larger, unwieldy bow and activated **<Page's Quickdraw>**. The crossbow was in my hand in seconds, and I pulled the trigger, aiming for center mass.

Buzzcut threw himself to the side, falling over. The bolt narrowly missed, lodging itself in the wall.

I scowled. **<Perception>** was such a double-edged ability. Fantastic if you were the only one who had it, infuriating when everyone else did.

Audrey dropped from her hiding place on the roof and tangled herself around Buzzcut's upper body, using all her attack and mobility vines to lash his massive arms to his sides. Instead of reloading and risking another miss, I changed tack again, dashing the short distance from the far end of the room and slamming my knee into Buzzcut's face.

His nose flattened like it was made of construction paper, head bouncing back against the wall.

When I tried to repeat the motion, Buzzcut lashed out and kicked my foot out from underneath me. My entire leg felt like someone had hit it with a sledgehammer, and I was suddenly airborne, rotating at a speed more than fast enough to break my neck if I landed wrong. Instinctively, I twisted midair to alter my trajectory and landed jarringly on one knee.

Buzzcut roared. Audrey bit him, sinking her many teeth into the nerve cluster on his shoulder. Instead of running or focusing on the plant tearing his flesh away, Buzzcut forced his way to his feet, bent at the waist, and charged, bowling me over.

All the air went out of my lungs as he landed on me, a few of Audrey's thorns catching my armor and digging into flesh where the armor was torn.

Buzzcut roared again, spittle flying into my face. This time, his voice was more raw, guttural. His shirt strained as his muscles swelled, the fabric growing tauter until it split across the seams, buttons popping free.

I drove the meat of my palm into Buzzcut's ruined nose. He reeled back, sunglasses flying off his head. His considerable weight shifted off me, and I snatched **<Blade of Woe>** from my inventory, stabbing it straight toward his chest.

Instead of sinking in, there was an audible scrape, and I nearly lost my grip on the blade as it recoiled across his body.

Shit. Too late.

I got a leg free and planted a foot against his chest, using all the strength I could muster to dislodge myself. Tile squeaked beneath me as I slid backward. Using a mix of my abilities, I landed two more of Sae's poisoned bolts in Buzzcut's legs.

Whatever protection ability he was using, I'd hoped it followed a logical order. Started around his chest and vitals, but initially left his extremities and lower body unprotected until it fully kicked in.

One bolt bounced off his shin, leaving a deep gash. The other sunk directly into his knee.

Bingo.

Buzzcut howled. His anger was tinged with pain and fear. But he wasn't folding. He bent forward, and there was an audible creak from the vines. A series of explosive pops filled the air as Audrey's vines frayed and snapped, Buzzcut's mass growing more pronounced.

"Now."

A lithe form flew through the darkness. In her altered, feral form, Talia gripped Buzzcut's leg in her jaws, growling loudly. In the short time it took her to join the fray, the magical protection had spread down Buzzcut's body, and Talia's teeth barely sunk in.

Finally freed from Audrey's vines, Buzzcut grabbed Talia by the scruff of her neck and threw her across the room.

"You... have no idea..." Buzzcut wheezed, his voice deep and altered.

Banter was for children. I had no intention of letting him finish.

I raised two fingers and Sae dropped on Buzzcut from the balcony. The same move she'd pulled on me. In some ways, it felt like nostalgic. Only this time, Sae was playing for keeps.

Sae slammed Buzzcut facedown into the ground, hard enough to send a series of spiderwebbing cracks across the tile. He pushed himself onto his hands and knees. I leapt over the counter, landing hard on his wounded leg, feeling the arrow snap from the pressure.

When the blades on her arms failed to do damage, Sae snarled, pinned his head to the ground for leverage, and drove a fist into Buzzcut's ribs repeatedly. There was an odd, echoing feedback that sounded vaguely like a rock bouncing across ice in the middle of winter.

Until the ice broke with an audible crunch. Sensing that the ability that shielded Buzzcut had weakened, Sae's forearm blade extended outward and she cocked her arm, prepared to thrust the blade between Buzzcut's ribs.

In a sudden burst of motion, Buzzcut twisted beneath Sae, driving an elbow into her jaw. The strike caught her by surprise and she hit the ground hard. Even so, honeycombing frost spread down Buzzcut's waist as he struggled to his feet.

At some point, he got his weapons out of his inventory. With his stance, I almost mistook them for boxing gloves. In a way, they were. Only meaner.

The leather gloves were covered with studded metal, while a row of nasty-looking spikes lined the knuckles. Though the spikes themselves were immaculately clean, the leather beneath them was deeply stained. He'd used the hell out of them, and seeing how he was still alive, they'd served him well.

"Don't get hit." Sae was back on her feet but only partially recovered. Her warning sounded obvious until I saw the black, jagged protrusion that stuck out from her jaw where a mandible once sat. Little green sparks kindled on the edges, slowly rebuilding the broken appendage.

Carefully, I took stock. Talia slumped over in the corner on her side, a smudged red imprint on the wall behind her. Audrey dragged herself away from the fight slowly, her mobility vines a fraction of their original size.

Yeah. "Don't get hit" deserved some emphasis.

Buzzcut was still expanding. The panic in his eyes had faded, but the fury remained.

"Move." We split, darting in opposite directions. If he fought defensively, aggressive flanking was the only way to handle this.

Only, Buzzcut wasn't interested in fighting defensively. If he'd waited to go on the offensive, given us time to tire ourselves out, I'm not sure there'd be anything we could do. With my attack summons handled, all he had left to contend with was two Users. We were both strong in our own way, but I'd spent most of my mana setting the stage, and the hit Sae took had visibly rattled her.

In the end, Azure made all the difference. He made sure Buzzcut connected the dots between this ambush and the hellish night that preceded it.

And Cameron was *pissed*.

He didn't even look at Sae as we split, tracking me as I ran in the opposite direction of Sae into the kitchen, trying to put a counter between us to give myself time to reload.

Buzzcut dropped into a crouch and hurled himself at me. The kitchen wasn't massive, and Buzzcut was so big now he had a good chance of tagging me, even if I timed the dodge perfectly.

So instead of trying to evade him, I stopped still, mentally toggled the <Operator's Belt>, and jumped straight up.

My feet barely settled on the top of the massive fridge before he slammed into it full force, the entire stainless steel surface buckling inward, the glass within shattering.

<Probability Cascade> activated, and my arms pinwheeled as the

fridge toppled. Cameron caught it before it could crush him, glaring daggers upward before he ripped the fridge out from under me.

I was already moving, lightly dashing across the countertops as Cameron raged, pots and pans flying everywhere. Tired of my bullshit, he grabbed the counter itself and ripped it from its wooden base with an ear-splitting crack.

Sae walloped him from behind, striking the same spot she'd weakened earlier. Buzzcut turned and chased her, tripping from the unwieldiness of his body and scrambling until he made it back onto his feet.

Like they'd rehearsed it, Sae danced. She threaded the needle throughout the minefield that was now Buzzcut's living room floor, evading him until he reached one of the pre-set traps, raining down blows on him every time he took a misstep and broke through the floorboards.

I watched him try to split the difference—being wary of his footing and his opponent—but Sae was too fast for that, punishing him every time he hesitated or looked away.

Either from the exertion or the poison, Buzzcut was slowing down. I readied my bow and waited for an opening.

With an angry roar, Buzzcut picked up his ruined couch and hurled it at Sae.

Sae slid beneath it, driving a fist into Buzzcut's ruined knee. It cracked, and he fell.

I fired. The arrow sunk into the weak spot on Buzzcut's back.

As if she'd planned it, Sae leapt on Buzzcut's back as he toppled and threaded an arm around his neck, catching him in a blood choke.

But Buzzcut wasn't an amateur. He moved quickly—quickly enough that I had a feeling his abilities didn't offer any protection from that sort of attack—and reached up to grab at Sae's hair. He ripped a handful out at the root and Sae screamed. Instead of knocking her loose, she redoubled her efforts, muscles rippling, her face a sneer.

I reloaded my crossbow and moved closer.

"Feel that? The way your mind's blanking out and your body won't quite respond to anything you ask it to do? *That's* how it felt in the tunnel, you piece of shit," Sae snarled into Buzzcut's ear. He reached up again, trying for another clump of hair, reaching nothing. "And you keep hoping for someone, anyone, to come along and *help* you. Because it can't end this way." Sae chuckled. "But you're alone, Cameron. It *will* end this way. And no one is coming to save you."

The last vestiges of lucidity left Buzzcut's expression. His arms, once struggling to either push Sae off of him or push himself off the floor, went limp.

Slowly, his eyes closed.

Still straddling Cameron, Sae released her hold and leaned back, gasping for air. "Ho-lee shit."

"Good job." It sounded awkward, but I wasn't sure what else to say. Seeing Buzzcut defeated after all the buildup felt strange, somehow.

"For a second," Sae heaved between words, "I thought we were gonna need the tank—"

Buzzcut's eye shot open. It was glowing red—the whole eye, no visible sclera to be seen—and he screamed. Sae tried to grab him, but he threw her off easily, standing to his full height. Between the eye and the dark veins that lined his face, he looked more demon than human now.

Fuck.

Sae was further into the living room, laying smack in the center of the outline where the couch once sat. She was forcing her way to her feet, but her movements were stilted. Either she was stunned, or she'd injured something.

Regardless, she'd be slower than before.

I needed to end this quickly. With a precious few seconds, I studied the kitchen furtively, looking for anything I could use. It was more or less a wreck. The fridge was overturned, and just beyond the fridge, the torn-up marble countertop leaned against a pantry next to the stove like a stone tent. The pieces were all there, but I needed to put them together.

Buzzcut took a menacing step toward Sae.

Lacking a better alternative, I pulled an umbrella out of my inventory and tossed it on the floor in front of him. "Thanks for this, by the way."

Slowly, Buzzcut's head tilted down, not comprehending. Then his mouth widened in a rictus of anger and he lost all interest in Sae.

I didn't bother looking back. Instead, I sprinted into the kitchen and reached toward the back of the stovetop, in the guise of pushing against the wall for momentum. I turned the stove on and redirected myself in the same motion, hoping the ploy wasn't too obvious. I dove into the open space between the counter and the wall.

Buzzcut's footsteps thundered behind me, picking up pace. From his perspective, he'd cornered me.

I covered my ears and shielded my head with my arms.

<Probability Cascade> activated for the last time. The resulting explosion was deafening. I heard something that sounded more like it came from a bear than a human. Bits of marble and pulverized stone rained down on me as the sheet of counter fell to pieces.

I emerged from my improvised shelter to find Buzzcut's once-tidy house a derelict mess. The cupboards and counters were awash in a circle of flame that radiated outward from the stove, where the jagged and blackened remnants of a propane tank sat in the stove's base.

Sae staggered toward me. "You didn't die."

It was a minor miracle I hadn't. Even with the considerable work I'd put in reinforcing the stove's metal interior with **<Probability Cascade>**, redirecting the blast forward, most of what I'd done was theoretical. Something we could fall back on if everything went sideways.

Still, I'd had no intention of being this close to it when it went off. I reached up toward a wetness on my cheeks and my hand came away red. My ears were bleeding.

Buzzcut was slumped over in a pile of rubble. He'd flown clear across the full span of his open-plan home and was half buried in a now-crumbling wall. His face was a mask of blood, his body slowly returning to its original size.

Once I was positive I could walk without falling over, I crossed over toward him, turning back to speak to Sae. "We need to go. That wasn't exactly subtle."

Buzzcut's chest was rising and falling. His breathing was shallow, but he was still alive.

I stood over our target and pointed my crossbow at his head. It would be so easy to pull the trigger. Slowly, I lowered the crossbow and sighed. "Big picture?"

"Big picture," Sae confirmed. She didn't look any happier about than I was, but there was something else in her expression. Relief, maybe.

"Get the curtains."

I pulled up my social UI and sent a message. **<Matt: Door. Plan A.>**

Kinsley's door appeared where the refrigerator used to be.

"You sure about this?" Sae asked. She grabbed Cameron's leg and unceremoniously dragged him toward the exit.

I reached out toward my fallen summons, returning both Talia and Audrey to the void, then went to help her. "More or less."

"Great. Exactly what I wanted to hear right now." Sae glared at me.

"Whether or not he talks, Azure will pull something useful out of him. Eventually."

"It feels like an unnecessary risk," Sae grunted.

"Sunny put a price on his head. Aaron sold him out," I mused. "He doesn't know it yet, but I might be the last friend he has in the world."

CHAPTER SIXTY-FOUR

"This looks more like a bachelor's pad than a prison," Kinsley complained. She lugged a bag of freeze-dried food behind her, readjusting her grip. "And seriously? You're letting him keep his pet?"

I took it from her and placed it next to the litter box and a small basket of cat toys, ignoring Shiva as she clawed at the bag, then surveyed the room. There were a handful of chairs, along with a console connected to a small wide-screen tv, and a long twin bed in the corner. "It plays better this way."

"Because he still has something to lose?" Sae lugged Cameron in like a sack of vegetables, tossing his unconscious body onto the bed. He was blindfolded, and a pair of noise-cancelling earmuffs blocked out all sound. Unceremoniously, Sae shrugged him off her shoulder.

"Not exactly."

Even though she hadn't explicitly stated it, I knew Sae was unhappy with my decision to let Cameron live. I wasn't happy with it either. Sparing him felt like unearned clemency. Still, I was about to enter a Trojan horse scenario where I couldn't trust anyone around me, and I'd inevitably run into unknown variables. Having access to someone with intimate knowledge of the organization would be incredibly valuable.

Cameron probably wouldn't cooperate. The beauty of it was, he didn't have to. There was no need to resort to brute torture or intimidation tactics.

I could just ask him questions and let Azure sieve out the answers from the surface of his mind.

"Hey." Kinsley backed away in alarm. "He's stirring."

Sure enough, Cameron let out an audible groan. He reached his bandaged hand up toward the blindfold on his eyes, but the morphine won out before he reached it and his arm dropped.

Sae turned to me, her mouth turned downward. "If he wakes up and sees me, solid chance he goes for round two."

"Wouldn't want to undo the mercenary healer's hard work." I fished the tape recorder out of my inventory, pausing briefly. With all the magic and Technomancer stuff going around, Aaron hadn't even bothered to consider the far more grounded possibility I'd wear an old-school wire. Less wire than lapel mic taped to the collar of my hoodie. It'd taken a half hour to copy the original message to another device and scrub the original of anything I didn't want Cameron to know. The process was old school—recording over the parts I needed to abridge with dead air. While the result wasn't exactly clean, and a mildly attentive listener would realize there were redactions, what I left painted an obvious truth in broad strokes.

That Aaron had sold Cameron down the river without a second thought.

I made sure the tape was rewound and left the device on the table in the center of the room.

———

Kinsley doored me back to the old safe house. I scrolled past several quest complete notifications and a few messages before finding what I was looking for.

<Meet with Sunny for debrief and entry into ???>
Time Limit: 1:59:21
Location: 3271 Talmont Avenue.

It was a mixed bag. Though I wasn't certain, the continuation of the quest chain likely meant my calling an audible and taking Cameron prisoner hadn't broken the quest chain, or was, at the very least, an acceptable result. The address and the imminent time limit to progress the quest were more difficult right yeah to parse in terms of positive and negative.

On one hand, it saved me the inconvenience of tracking Sunny down, or worse, waiting for him to drop in on me. On the other, that the time and place of the meeting was delivered via the quest in a decidedly non-negotiable way was concerning.

Still, I couldn't back out now. I was committed. Now it was a matter of making sure I was fully prepared.

Matt

Level 14 Ordinator
Identity: Myrddin, Level 14 ???
Strength: 6
Toughness: 8
Agility: 20+
Intelligence: 17+
Perception: 8
Will: 21
Companionship: 3
Active Title: Born Nihilist
Feats: Double-Blind, Ordinator's Guile I, Ordinator's Emulation, Stealth I, Awareness I, Harrowing Anticipation, Page's Quickdraw, Vindictive, Squelch, Acclimation.
Skills: Probability Cascade, LVL 5. Suggestion, LVL 21. One-handed, LVL 19. Negotiation, LVL 16. Unsparing Fang (Emulated), Level 13, Bow Adept, LVL 5.
Boons: Nychta's Veil, Eldritch Favor, Ordinator's Implements,
Summons: Audrey — Flowerfang Hybrid, Bond LVL 5. Talia — Eidolon Wolf, Bond LVL 9. Azure — Abrogated Lithid, Bond LVL 20.
Skill Points Available: 0. **Feat points available:** 2.

The point in agility was obvious. Putting two points into toughness though? Well, it felt like the end of an era. I'd taken too many dings, had too many close calls over the last month to justify the semi-purist approach I'd taken before. I was going to get hit. It was an unfortunate byproduct of my tendency to be in the thick of harrowing situations complicated enough that I couldn't control every variable with my abilities. There was no point in denying it, clinging to the theoretical ideal where I never took damage.

I moved on from the stat allocations to the feats, narrowing my options down to two.

<Hinder: Actively weakens the target and reduces the efficacy of passive abilities. Effected targets will be considerably more susceptible to stealth and surprise attacks and more vulnerable to the psychological toll of inflicted wounds. The latter effect, as well as the chance of detection, increases with each consecutive reapplication of this ability until the ability expires. >
<Escalating Fire: A King's Ranger is the pinnacle of precision. Every bolt, arrow, or stone that lands on the same target does exponentially more damage than the last. As their potency grows, these empowered projectiles require more focus and concentration to aim. The accumulated bonus is lost with the first projectile that misses the intended target or in

the event of the target's expiration. Any ranged attack may be imbued with this ability.>

After brief consideration, I took **<Hinder>**.

So yes, if you wanted to be technical about it, it was yet another debuff skill. But it was still closer to a direct damage buff than almost anything else I had. Automatic shoo-in.

But not a goddamn thing in the world could stop me from taking **<Escalating Fire>** next level.

Enough was enough.

It was time to put some actual cannon into the glass cannon.

The ability had the potential to combine with **<Page's Quickdraw>** in a way I couldn't ignore. This was the advantage of forcing a multi-class, especially when the game system wasn't designed for it—it was possible to string together unintended abilities the creators didn't account for. Some of which could be powerful, borderline broken combinations together if you were willing to get creative.

I locked in the changes and braced myself. It still hurt—but the pain faded much faster than before.

An hour before the meeting time, I left the safe house and headed toward the address.

———

Driving through the city on the cusp of evening felt strange. Given how I caught myself looking toward my UI for a timer that was no longer there, it wasn't hard to pinpoint why. I'd barely touched my motorcycle since the Transposition. My injury and sudden shift in position meant I was rarely driving myself.

Fear gripped me tightly as I came to a stop down the street from the address. It was an old office park, illuminated by dozens of over-bright security lamps, although it was completely empty.

I scanned the surroundings. There was no hint of Sunny or his pampered car. Also, I was all-but-certain the underground facility Azure hinted at *couldn't* be here.

I turned the corner and pulled the motorcycle into my inventory, then turned my mask to full power. With that done, I walked down the sidewalk across the street, watching for any discernible movement, taking great care to check the shrubs and greenery for the camouflaged Users from before, finding none.

From what I could tell, there was nothing out of the ordinary. If anyone was watching me, there was a chance the effectiveness of the

<Allfather's Mask> had already worn off on them. Higher if it was Sunny. I sat at the bus stop on the corner and planned my next move.

"Where are you going?" a monotone voice pierced the silence.

I jumped, turning toward the edge of the bench. A small woman in a robe and hood, her dark hair done up in pigtails, was staring at me. At first I thought she was a child. And I was entirely sure she hadn't been there when I sat down. "I'm not sure."

"You... don't... know?" the girl asked, saying the words slowly.

"I'm looking for my friend."

"What's his name?"

"No idea."

"You don't know your friend's name?" She tilted her head, revealing the left side of her face. It was deeply scarred with crisscrossing red marks, and the milky eye was clearly sightless.

I ignored the question, focusing on the woman. "He asked me to meet him."

"So you know where you're going," the woman concluded with a dreamy smile. Her straightforwardness took me by surprise.

I nodded. "Maybe. I just have no idea how to get there."

"Curious. You do not look at us as the others look at us," the woman observed, then added, "do you know the words?"

"No."

Slowly, she reached out and pressed a hand to my chest. "The mark is undeniable. Her blessing is upon you."

I bore with it, uncomfortable with the contact. As out of it as she appeared, the timing of our meeting was too suspect.

"Any chance you can point me in the right direction?" I asked.

"I will take you to what you truly seek," the woman said. Her sightless eyes glinted in the dark.

I had no idea what the difference was but didn't see any reason not to play along. "That would be ideal. Though I'm curious why you're willing to do so."

"I sense neither avoidance nor repulse in your gaze. You simply see us as we are." The woman held out a gloved hand. Her palm split as she pressed it toward me, an oval pupil, cerulean eye blinked twice and, when it focused on me, the pupil narrowed.

"Grasp the aether." Her hand reached up toward my forehead, taking up my entire view. The cerulean eye darted back and forth, as if it was desperately searching for an escape. Tears leaked from its edges, soaked up by the cloth of the woman's gloves.

"Wait—" Before I could stop her, the woman pressed her palm against my forehead with an audible squelch. I barely had enough time to register that the **<Allfather's Mask>** had voluntarily allowed her hand to pass through before my body twisted and shrunk, my organs pressed together tightly until it was like I could feel them all individually, each about to burst.

My perspective narrowed as my twisted body hurtled through a black space at a speed I couldn't begin to quantify. Every so often, a glint of light would reflect off rounded walls, so darkly red they were almost brown, that led to openings that created what seemed like an infinite number of branching paths and highways.

It looked more organic than constructed, and the way some paths were jagged and never asymmetrical felt reminiscent of a circulatory system on a larger scale.

The darkness gave way to blinding light as I was more sprayed out than shot out—I felt parts of myself that had no business being as far away as they were struggle to return to the whole.

When I finally hit solid ground, I swooned on my feet, struggling to stay upright. My limbs and body appeared to be intact.

"Now, keep your guard up!" a familiar voice called.

"Yes, Ceaseless Knight," someone panted.

"We've been over this, Enid. Drop the title. It's—"

Nick.

CHAPTER SIXTY-FIVE

I couldn't fully comprehend what was happening. I'd fixated so purely on this moment, on every possible painstaking step I might have to take to get to this point, that having it happen so quickly and easily felt strange.

And even though I thought I'd considered every possibility, this wasn't one of them.

I was standing in the center of what was once a large gymnasium, the kind you see in wealthy private schools or anywhere with a serious athletic team. It was kitted out to the nines, complete with climbing walls and folded-up basketball hoops on either side. The center comprised a series of massive mats. Two groups of Users clad in full gear were recovering from some sort of strenuous exercise, possibly a mock battle.

Nick was walking through them, inspecting each person. His classic good looks hadn't suffered in his captivity. Neither had his physique. If anything, Nick appeared even more muscular than before.

He's been leveling.

I didn't like that realization, or the many questions it incurred.

Mind control?

Somewhere in the distance, there was the echo of something massive and mechanical clicking into place. The lights took on a red tinge, and Nick swiped at the air. His brow furrowed. "We have a situation. Everyone, form up on me."

Not only is he out and about unguarded, but he also holds some portion of authority.

One of the two groups of Users in black athletic gear snapped to attention immediately, lining up behind Nick.

A blond man—judging from body language, the leader of the other group—called over to Nick. "What's with the alert?"

"Intruder in the silo," Nick said. "Somewhere in this wing. We need to gear up and get moving."

Fuck. The woman at the bus stop had screwed me. It wasn't supposed to happen this way. In her own words, she'd teleported me directly to what I "sought."

Nick.

And she'd put me in an incredibly compromising position. I'd bypassed whatever screening process Sunny intended and entered their facility directly. Even worse, I was out in the open with nowhere to hide. The only reason no one had seen me yet was a combination of my mask, stealth feat, and that I hadn't moved. If I tried to take cover behind something, they'd spot me immediately.

"There!" a voice said called from behind me. I knew, instinctively, it was directed at me.

Too late.

\<Perception\> screamed.

I stepped to the side blindly, heeding the warning. A blade whistled through the air, carving the space I'd previously occupied in half. It was impossibly long, with a slight curve. The woman wielding it cackled, spinning in place, lashing out artlessly. But the power behind her blows was nothing to sneeze at.

The attacker rotated her blade ninety degrees and swung it in a savage arc toward my neck. I let myself fall backward, barely dodging it, all the while racking my brain on how to handle this. Killing anyone now was a bad look, even if it was in self-defense at no fault of my own. If I surrendered, there was a non-zero chance they'd take me captive but entirely possible that my mask would come off in the process before Aaron or Sunny interceded.

Then there was the problem of Nick. Unlike everyone else present, Nick knew exactly how I fought. What weapons I used. It was an oversight I hadn't considered, because I didn't think I had to. I'd assumed that if Nick figured it out, he'd stay silent. But as much as I wanted to have faith in Nick, faith had never served me well.

I had to operate like he was with them until I received definitive confirmation otherwise.

What would Myrddin do?

What image did I want to present to the suits? Compassion and empathy—hell, even humanity—wouldn't help me here.

These people were hyenas. Any hint of softness would sharpen the knife at my back.

Myrddin was cold. He enjoyed hurting people but was rational enough to understand that impulse could work against him. At this point in his life, he would have worked out exactly how far he could push the limit. What was acceptable and what wasn't.

He was everything I tried not to be.

"A living being seeks above all else to discharge its strength; Life itself is Will to Power," Azure quoted.

Unsurprisingly, my summon was fond of Nietzsche, alongside every other creative on the planet. But Azure had a point. Myrddin had done nothing wrong here and they'd attacked without warning. He wouldn't hold back, wouldn't flinch at his enemy's pain. And if he was in a position where killing was off the table, he'd make damn well sure that the lesson was etched in flesh.

There could be no understanding for mistakes. No tolerance for weakness.

The woman struck again, aiming for Myrddin's head.

A living being seeks above all else to discharge its strength.

I casted **<Probability Cascade>** on my glove and caught the blade between my fingers.

The woman's mouth dropped open in an expression of pure surprise. I pivoted quickly and grabbed her jaw, dragging her down to the ground even as I felt the pressure of her teeth on my armored gauntlet. I pinned her head beneath my knee, cocked a fist, and struck downward.

It was like punching concrete. There was a faint shimmer around her face from where the blow landed, and from the muffled swearing and struggling, she didn't appear stunned.

<Ordinator's Emulation> granted me vague insight into the ability. It was a shield, but not a strong one.

Three more quick strikes and the shield shattered. The woman's jaw snapped like a twig.

"Stay back—" I heard Nick yell out.

To no avail.

Two more charged me in quick succession. Others followed but kept their distance—a bruiser with a strong, ridiculously proportioned upper body that made his head look tiny, and a mage.

They were a step up from the last encounter. Coordinated. The mage kept his distance, methodically tracking the bruiser's movements so he didn't catch the larger man in his crossfire, attacking with thin beams of light from a wand—the magic covered little area, but it felt powerful, like the thin focus point had magnified the potential somehow.

The two Users staggered their attacks expertly, to the point I didn't have time to do anything more than dodge.

I smiled behind the mask. Early on, this would have been more than enough to take me out of the game permanently. But things had changed.

"He's going to hit you any second now, he's going to hit you, he's going to hit you." I barraged the bruiser with **<Suggestion>**, waiting for an opening. The mental bombardment took a toll, because suddenly the bruiser was shooting nervous glances toward the mage.

I faked a stumble.

The bruiser raced forward out of turn, axe overhead, just as the mage was carefully aiming a shot. The thin ray of light *just* missed the bruiser's head, singing his eyebrow.

The bruiser glared daggers at the mage. "Hey! Watch where you're—"

I drove my thumb into his eye. In ordinary circumstances, you wouldn't catch me within ten feet of an opponent like this if I could help it. But as I'd done nothing but avoid their attacks since they'd engaged with me, the bruiser's guard was down.

He dropped his heavy axe with a scream, stumbling backward, blood leaking from the hand that cupped his face. "Motherfuck—"

I sprinted past, the bruiser already forgotten. Mages were the real threat. The only reason this one hadn't already flattened me was that he was a team player, unwilling to hit his ally with friendly fire. I needed to end this before he changed tact.

The mage backpedaled. Several Users behind him brought weapons to bear, but they were too slow to interfere before I reached the mage.

Unfortunately, the mage reached the same conclusion. Instead of attacking, he drew the wand in a tight circle around himself.

I knew what he was doing before **<Emulation>** told me. Creating a barrier.

That wasn't good. If he managed it before I got to him, that would be enough to hold me off until the others stepped in. I could draw a weapon and potentially break through the barrier, but giving away more of my repertoire might tip off Nick.

Damn it.

No. I could still do this. Judging from the faint outline, the mage's shield was forming a bubble. That was smart, as it meant I couldn't simply attack him from the sides, but I knew from my experiences during the Transposition that magical shielding took a small amount of time to kick in.

Pitch-black particles danced across my glove as I fired off **<Hinder>**. Despite its description specifically detailing multiple applications, one use of the ability was incredibly draining.

It slowed the shield's formation, but it was almost too late. There was still a hole, near the top, that would close in seconds.

I toggled the **<Operator's Belt>** and leapt. My enhanced agility guided me, as it had against Cameron, and I narrowly threaded the needle through the opening. I landed squarely within the mage's bubble and knocked the wand from his hand, then grabbed him by the throat.

The flesh around his neck turned white from the pressure as I squeezed, looking around curiously at the still-maintained bubble. A dark chuckle escaped my lips. "Can't dispel it without your wand, can you?"

His eyes grew wide, panicked, as he strained in vain to reach the wand at his feet. When that failed, he struck the arm that held him with wild slaps and punches that carried little force. If I were to guess, he'd probably not bothered putting any stats into strength. As a fellow glass cannon, I felt for him. Though only a little.

Unfortunately for the captive mage, Myrddin would see this as a prime opportunity to show he was not to be fucked with. But how?

Despite their advanced capabilities, I wasn't sure even the suits could fix a serious neck injury. Hence, wheelchairing this guy was probably a bad idea. Flesh wounds were recoverable, unless you accumulated a *lot* of them, like I had during the Transposition.

"Please," the mage begged.

My eyes landed on his rapidly bobbing Adam's apple. I wrapped both hands around his neck, positioned my thumbs against it, and prepared to push.

"Wait," Nick said. He'd moved up next to the bubble, a sweat of perspiration dripping down his forehead. He held both hands palms out, though the non-threatening gesture didn't extend to the rest of his body language.

"Now you want to talk?" I snarled.

Nick nodded. "You're right." He turned to the others. "He's right. Why I keep telling you grumpy fuckers to use your goddamn words before you throw yourselves head first into something half-cocked."

He rounded on the mage. "And why the hell did the both of you decide to engage a potential threat with nothing but your wand and a track suit?"

"... Hurk..." the mage said.

"Do you mind?" Nick asked me.

I loosened my grip slightly.

The mage lapsed into a coughing fit and struggled to speak. "I wanted... to distinguish myself."

"So you rushed, and now you're about to distinguish yourself all over that bubble." Nick gave the mage a hard look.

The mage wilted.

Nick strained to smile. "I appreciate your help, teaching these guys a lesson. A lot of them have some kind of experience, but they don't take the powers and abilities as seriously as they should. Sometimes, it takes a self-serving of humble pie to shake old habits loose."

I inclined my head slowly.

Nick rubbed his neck awkwardly. "Thing is, the idiot in a tracksuit you're about to strangle was placed under my charge. And I take that seriously. His name is Keith. And he might be inexperienced, and an idiot, but I'm responsible for him. The others will live. But if you strangle the life out of him, I'm not sure I can let that go."

Keith suddenly tried to break my grip, and I responded by winding back an arm and slapping him across the face hard enough that my hand hurt.

When Nick tensed, I shrugged. "He was asking for it."

"This is your chance to reset. If you keep pushing, it won't go well for you," Nick warned.

How deep are you in?

"What. You're going to stop me?" I challenged, trying to gauge his mental state. So far, he looked and sounded like the Nick I knew. *Exactly* like the Nick I knew.

Nick blinked. "I mean, I'll try. Can't say how much good it'll do. You put a respectable scrapper out of commission, then manhandled my best tank and mage, all without a weapon. You obviously know what you're doing. The problem comes when you get out of the gym."

"Oh?"

"Oh indeed, buttercup. Because all of us," Nick pointed to the surrounding group, "we're the Z team around these parts. Assuming you clear the room—which is a big assumption, because these guys have put in a lot of work and I'm proud of them—out there?" He indicated the door on the far side of the gym. "You won't make it twenty feet."

A dark-skinned girl with gauges in her ears stepped forward beside Nick. Late teens, maybe older. She spoke with a thick Middle Eastern accent. "There is a woman who can freeze you to stone with nothing more than a glance. A little girl capable of turning your insides to jelly. A man who can pulverize bone with a gentle touch."

"And a unicorn to round out the lot?" I sneered.

The woman frowned sternly. "And as irritatingly modest as my friend here might be, he'll offer far more resistance than you might expect. He is one of our best—"

Nick shouldered passed her. He was still maintaining the sheepish affect, but there was real irritation in his eyes. "*Thank you*, Halima. One of these days we're going to have a little talk about the importance of *underpromising* and *overdelivering*."

Halima didn't look like she got it, but she stepped back just the same.

"They respect you," I realized, saying it aloud before I could stop myself.

"And now that the pre-starting gun jitters are out, they'll stand down if I ask them to. Let's just start over from the beginning." Nick pointed a finger gun at me and grinned. "So, tell me what you want, and we'll see if I can help you out."

So upfront and honest.

Nick wasn't being controlled. If I wasn't already sure, Azure confirmed it. He was under the geas and nothing else. Also, there was no tell, no obvious giveaway that he was doing any of this under duress. If it was simple blackmail, leveraging a random User core and claiming it was Jinny's, I doubted he'd be able to maintain this facade under stress. If it was anyone else, I'd have believed they'd succumbed to whatever temptation Aaron offered.

But Nick *wasn't* anyone else. I'd watched him go through physical therapy so rigorous and draining it was essentially torture in the guise of recovery. I'd watched him struggle as he readjusted to school life. Saw him lose a promising sports career and countless so-called friends.

You can't trust someone you've only seen at their best. Only after you've seen them endure hardships, can you glean an inkling of who they really are.

I was there the night Nick hit rock bottom. Saw the truth for myself.

It was why I hated him. Why I cherished him. Because no matter how many times he got knocked down, how many hardships he endured, Nick served as an eternal rebuttal to my core belief, that people were only as upright as their circumstances allowed.

Nick was earnest, and genuine, and good.

There had to be an angle he was working. It was just a question of finding it.

What the hell are you up to?

CHAPTER SIXTY-SIX

In yet another quirk of inconsistency, the **<Allfather's Mask>** stayed stubbornly impermeable to the blindfold tied around the back of my head. This resulted in a thin strap of cloth fastened around the mask itself, hiding whatever was directly in front of me and little else—the view both above and below the blindfold was expansive.

Seeing how Nick had applied the blindfold himself and his squad didn't seem to notice, I had to assume the mask was projecting a suitably convincing image.

Nick led me through a series of winding concrete corridors. There were several connecting doors that looked as if they could have once been offices.

At the mouth of the hallway, Nick suddenly halted. Playing the part, I ran directly into him, letting out an annoyed grunt.

"Stop," Nick whispered, then he turned back to face me, his back to the larger room, blocking me from view as two civilians with rifles passed by, escorting a tall man idly twirling a double-bladed staff who looked vaguely European. His beak-like nose was pronounced, and the way it framed his narrow eyes gave him a decidedly predatory look. "Laugh like I just said something funny."

I forced a laugh.

Nick's mouth quirked as he gave me a gentle push. As soon as the three were out of earshot, he whispered, "I was thinking more of a light guffaw rather than a maniacal cackle, but sure, that works."

"Not getting why you're helping me," I pointed out.

His brow furrowed. "I'm not. And don't tell anyone I did."

I held my silence, searching for any clue that might illuminate our location. What I saw was almost enough to trip me up entirely. The compound was a series of vertical cylinders, each miles across, with a hole in the center. It was reminiscent of pictures I'd seen of a missile silo—and the more I considered that, the more likely it actually was one—only instead of austere, government furniture, the common areas looked like someone had given an interior designer with a low-key leather fetish an unlimited budget and instructions to "go wild."

Another group approached and Nick pushed me into a doorway, waiting until the group passed to take my arm again.

"That's it. Tell me what's happening or I take the blindfold off." I reached up for the cloth. Nick batted my hand away, then looked furtively back and forth to make sure no one noticed.

"Fine! Fine. Just leave it on," Nick said quietly, maneuvering me through an abandoned section of the compound. "There's a lot of tension around here. Not everyone agrees on how to move forward, and some people are angry. Some of those people would be happy to take their aggression out on a newcomer who breached our security, regardless of why. If that happened, some *other* people would be very upset."

"You're trying to keep the peace," I said, trying to wrap my mind around why Nick would give two shits if this place devolved into chaos.

"Something like that."

"Are you with—what did you say his name was? Sunny?"

Nick snorted. "No. You may or may not know this, seeing as how you weren't on a first-name basis, but he's kind of asshole." His eyes widened. "Not that I'm an insurrectionist or plotting anything, of course."

"Of course." I smiled. Nick was talking to the geas. My friend was still in there. He'd just gotten craftier, better at playing the cards he was dealt.

Or at least that was what I thought, before Nick dropped a bomb I was entirely unprepared for. "Honestly, I'm with the other guy."

Aaron?

I nearly stumbled mid-step. "But you're helping me?"

Nick checked around the corner, reaching back to stop me. He opened his mouth to speak, hesitated. "Look. I saw you fight."

My pulse raced. Was I already compromised?

"And?"

"You're good. Technique is a little..." he made a side-to-side gesture with his hand. "But you're either seasoned and experienced with the system, or a complete natural. You could have shredded Zero-team if you wanted to, but you didn't."

"Would have been a dumb-fucking move," I said bluntly. "And I wasn't throwing softballs."

Nick shrugged dismissively. "Broken jaw, bruised vocal cords, gouged eye. Nothing our healers can't fix in short order." He gave me a knowing look. "Could have been a helluva lot worse if you got vindictive and pulled a weapon or used magic that would have escalated things."

"Didn't get the chance."

"Bullshit. As soon as Katarina got her ass handed to her, you had an opening as large as the Grand Canyon. Regardless, I appreciate it. We're not supposed to get attached to the people in our strike teams, but that's just not in my DNA. A team's a team, you know?"

"What's Zero-team? And for that matter, who is 'we'?" I asked.

"Hm?"

"You said *we're* not supposed to get attached. What differentiates you from them?"

Nick raised an eyebrow. "Sunny hasn't filled you in on that yet, huh? Guess that's a line even he won't cross. Short version, Zero-team is something I volunteered for. As for the rest, we'll talk after you're sworn in."

We approached an elevator next to an industrial-looking keypad. Two guards armed with semi-automatic shotguns stared us down as Nick entered the code.

"What's with the blindfold?" The guard sounded like he'd started smoking a carton a day in kindergarten.

"Sunny's waiting on someone, right?" Nick said, not giving the guard his full attention.

The guard said nothing.

Nick finished entering the code and the number pad emitted a low-pitched beep, rejecting the combination. "What the fuck?"

"Never gets old," one of the guard's snickered.

Nick crossed his arms and stepped directly in front of the guard who laughed. "Gonna explain yourselves? Or do I have to take this up the chain?"

"Sunny's unavailable," the guard said, mimicking Nick's standoffish posture. "There was an incident. He'll be in lockdown until further notice."

"What's your name?" Nick asked me, never averting his eyes from the guard.

"Myrddin," I said. Both guards visibly reacted, displaying varying degrees of surprise for a split second before they returned to their earlier stoicism.

Nick casually extended a hand toward me. "Myrddin here needs to report to Sunny. I'm not sure what Sunny's doing with an outsider—not my business—but as far as I can tell, he's not sworn in. And instead of being routed to the Sieve, he *somehow* got redirected to the facility proper."

Both guards exchanged a meaningful look. One shrugged his shotgun onto his shoulder and punched a quick combination into the keypad. I caught the first few digits before he hunched over the pad, covering it.

Starts with one-nine. Five numbers in total. Could be random if he's smart, but the last combination also started with nineteen. One-nine-four-two-six. 1942, June. Battle of Midway? Didn't take him for a history buff, but it could track if he's fond of melodrama. Assuming I'm not tin foil hatting myself, the new combination could be another year-month combination, with the last number indicating the month.

<Jaded Eye> was sounding more and more like the type of conspiracy theorist I'd walk across the street to avoid, but at least it was a place to start.

The elevator opened, bright overhead light reflecting on the tile. Nick guided me inside, then stepped in after me.

A guard caught the elevator before it closed. "You brought him here. Now piss off."

Nick shook his head. "And catch a stray for leaving an outsider to his own devices? Not on your life. I'll mind my business after I hand him off to Sunny."

The guard looked ready to argue, but must have seen something in Nick's expression that made him think better of it.

The doors slid shut.

There was no telling when I'd see Nick again. My title detected no cameras or listening devices in the elevator. And as far as I could tell, there was no magic or enchantments active in the elevator. No one to overhear us.

I needed to understand what Nick was doing—but even if I was reasonably confident we weren't being watched, I couldn't speak freely. No mistakes. No moments of weakness. I needed to be perfect.

"How the fuck is someone like you even here?" I asked.

"What do you mean?" Nick said.

"Whatever this place is, I know from experience they don't exactly play nice," I said, adopting the affect of someone who was weary but curious. "That's fine with me. In fact, I prefer it. But then you come in—and you've locked down some authority, but you clearly don't belong here."

Anyone else would have taken it personally. But Nick embraced dissent wholeheartedly.

"Because I'm helping a stranger?" Nick raised an eyebrow. "Or because I didn't splatter you all over the training facility as payback?"

"Both. Either."

Nick nodded. The forward momentum that carried him to the elevator seemed to drain out of him, and he relaxed. "You're right that I'm not their usual type. Not that it's a high bar to aspire to, exactly—most of

these bastards would rather kill you than look at you. Sunny's no exception, so be careful. I—uh. They brought me here through a series of events
that wasn't exactly voluntary."

"You were a prisoner."

"I didn't say that." Nick gave me a meaningful look that I took to mean
he *couldn't* say that. "The first few days were rough. They had me isolated.
For good reason. I was... angry."

"Angry enough to do something about it?" I baited.

Nick sighed. "Oh yeah. If I'd gotten the opportunity, I would have. But
they were too buttoned up. My meals were delivered through a slot. Every
day, someone came to talk to me. He was just a normal guy. No cackling or
mustache twirling. The first day, he apologized for the ordeal that
brought me here. Said he made no promises but was working on a fix to at
least right some of the wrongs."

Aaron and the Necromancer grift.

That still didn't explain why Nick was walking around free.

"That's it?"

Nick chuckled. "Hardly. The guy was shockingly upfront with me.
Told me exactly what they were looking to achieve and how I could help.
Even gave me the chance to decline if I agreed to have my memory
wiped."

Other than my own, it was the first time I'd heard of a power capable
of altering memory to that degree.

"Must have been one hell of an offer, if you were willing to bury the
bad blood."

Nick's expression grew thoughtful, probably piecing together how to
say whatever he wanted to express without breaking the geas. "Think
about the direction this is going. There are dozens of domes now, maybe
even hundreds. Imagine if—hypothetically—I told you a there was a way
to end this whole dog and pony show early. Peacefully. Maybe even before
the second event."

I scoffed. "I'd tell you to shove the snake oil up your ass."

Nick laughed loud enough that I couldn't help but jump. "Sorry.
God, you remind me of someone. Anyway, you're right. That's pretty
much what I said. I told him I hated him, and that even if the snake oil
was real, there was no way in hell I was helping his people get a hold
of it."

"What changed?"

"I uh... talked to the snake oil. Jeez, this metaphor really isn't holding
up."

"Hold on. Tell me what you mean."

"Sunny and the other guy? It might seem like they're in charge here,
but that couldn't be farther from the truth. Someone else is pulling the

strings." Nick's smile faded. "And they assured me that once everything was in its proper place, there would be reparations."

Deity. Has to be. No way Aaron got this much of a head start otherwise.

"And you just... believed them?"

There was no way he was falling for such a simple ruse.

"They were very convincing," Nick said, his expression esoteric. "So I had a choice. Go along with it and grease the wheels, use my position to guide things in a less volatile direction until the third party comes into power, or sit there isolated and alone, feeling sorry for myself."

It took a monumental amount of self-control not to out myself right there. I wanted to scream at him for so being so gullible, falling for whatever Wizard-of-Oz horseshit these assholes were pulling.

"Sounds like you have it all figured out," I said, not bothering to keep the coldness out of my voice.

"It's not just for me." Nick's voice was so quiet I could barely hear it.

I rolled my eyes.

Nick smiled a sad smile. "When I first got here, after I was... uh..."

"Not taken prisoner," I filled in, tired of the vagueness of the conversation.

He inclined his head. "All there was to do was wait and sleep. I paced at first, wore a hole in the linoleum. But when I finally ran out of steam and sat down, I realized how *tired* I was. It wasn't the physical exertion—that, I'm pretty used to. But surviving, fighting for your life, it takes a toll."

"The quiet moments are the hardest." The words escaped me before I could stop them.

"I have this friend. Might be the last real friend I have in the world now. He kind of has a monopoly on bad luck. Dad passed away, mom with substance abuse issues who can't hold down a job, two siblings he basically raised himself."

"Sounds like a real sad sack."

Nick's eyes flicked back and forth. "He isn't. I mean, sure, he's surly and has zero tolerance for bullshit—never really stops moving, which always drove me nuts. But when the dome came down, it was like he wasn't even fazed. Like it was just another crisis he had to adjust to. And I realized that was exactly what it was to him. As tired as I was from surviving for days? He's carried that weight his whole life."

My throat felt scratchy. I needed to say something, anything, before Nick noticed the lapse. "Where is he now?"

"Mad as hell, looking for me."

"How do you—"

"I know," Nick said, sounding infinitely more confident than I felt. "That fucker's too stubborn to give up. Always has been."

"Putting that much faith in any one person usually ends in disappointment." I couldn't help but try to temper his expectations.

"Maybe I'm just a better judge of character than you are," Nick shot back.

"Maybe."

Nick smiled thoughtfully. "It's stupid. But imagining him out there, looking for me? That's exactly why I couldn't just crawl into a hole and wallow in my misery. I want to change the world into a place where no one has to suffer. Where life is more than worrying about making ends meet, fighting like hell just to maintain the status quo. And the next time I see my friend, I want to be able to tell him it's over. We won. He can finally rest."

The proclamation echoed in the small bounds of the elevator, so earnest it was almost embarrassing. Nick's cheeks flushed as he likely realized he'd gushed to an unaffiliated stranger. I found myself grateful for the mask's anonymity, yet again. I rarely cared what people thought of me, but somehow, Nick was the exception.

Whatever path this took me down, whatever measures I took to extract Nick and derail the suits, I didn't want the ugliness of my actions to tarnish his image of me.

Even if I didn't deserve it.

I blew air between my lips. "*Christ,* this elevator is taking forever."

"They're made for efficiency, not speed," Nick said.

"Clearly."

"Sorry for talking your ear off."

"It was a good distraction from this snail of a fucking elevator." And to be fair, it wasn't entirely his fault. We'd fallen back into a familiar cadence of argument and discussion that was uniquely ours. Nick had picked up on it subconsciously, though he hadn't connected the dots. It was a reminder that I needed to be careful. Sunny had no idea we were affiliated, but Aaron did, and the lie I'd fed him—that I was glad to be rid of Nick—wouldn't hold up a day if Nick suddenly got friendly with Myrddin.

It was safer for both of us if I distanced myself from Nick as much as possible.

The elevator dinged. "Hold on, always wanted to say this." Nick cleared his throat. "I can only show you the door. You're the one who has to walk through it."

I made a disgusted noise. But I'd missed him, down to his stupid barrage of dated pop-culture references. Nick didn't let Jinny's death break him, as I'd feared. He was misguided. Gullible. But still standing.

I could work with that.

The elevator doors opened to reveal a study. Sunny was standing in the center of the room. He held a bloody paring knife in one hand, muttering something unintelligible. His rolled-up sleeves were soaked in crimson. Behind him were several Users, sitting on a couch next to a bookshelf in varying states of exhaustion.

"Boss," one of them said, eyeing the elevator.

Sunny stared into the painted sunset that hung above his desk, twirling the knife idly in his hand. "Prepare for the delve. Come back with nothing to show for your efforts and there will be consequences. Now get out."

The Users jumped to attention immediately, filing past us into the elevator. There was something in Sunny's posture that conveyed danger in a way I hadn't felt before. He'd come unraveled since our last meeting.

Without looking, he pointed the paring knife at me. "Stay. We have business to discuss."

Reluctantly, I stepped out of the elevator. The doors slammed shut behind me.

CHAPTER SIXTY-SEVEN

Several strategies came to mind, each quickly abandoned. I'd never dealt with someone as explosively unstable as Sunny before. Judging from the unkempt hair, the blood-soaked state of his shirt, and the way he was looking at me, I was seriously reconsidering if ingratiating myself to Sunny was even worth it. And I couldn't lean on Azure here—from the hints my summon dropped, he needed as much mana as possible for the geas.

"You've looked better," I said.

"Okay." Sunny sniffed, hiked up his pants, and approached me casually. But something was off. Something in his expression. I reached for my inventory a split-second before he hauled me off the ground. My entire world exploded in pain as he slammed me head first into the desk. "What fucking game are you playing?" He yanked the back of my head up, his face inches from mine.

"The hell?" The pain and shock radiated through me. My mind raced, trying to parse what he could possibly know that had pissed him off this much. Of course, my first thought was that he somehow knew everything and I'd just walked myself in here like a lamb to the slaughter. "I have no idea what the fuck you're talking about—fuck!"

Sunny pushed my arm behind my back painfully, pinning me to the desk as he went through my inventory. He pulled out my weapons, a manila envelope, along with the bag of User cores I brought, per our agreement. "You just show up in the primary facility as a flex? Trying to make me look bad? Incompetent?"

Fuck this.

I spun, dislocating the shoulder he still held and driving my elbow into his face.

Sunny's head whipped back, and he smiled through bloody teeth.

"Go fuck yourself." I cradled my arm, tense. "There wasn't a directory. I followed the instructions you gave me to the goddamn letter. Which led me nowhere until some lady at a bus stop spouted cryptic nonsense and teleported me into the facility proper. Calm the fuck down."

Sunny pointed the knife at me and took a step forward. "You expect me to believe it's all a fucking coincidence?" He rotated the tip of the knife in a circle. "I give you a little errand to do, then, over the three days that follow, a fucking car bomb nearly wipes me off the face of the planet, and Aaron's suddenly gung-ho about moving up the timeline. But it's all a coincidence, right?"

Aaron wasn't being subtle. And of course Sunny would blame the newcomer. I needed to be careful how I handled this, or I'd end up crushed in the middle.

I snapped back at him. "Blame it on the guy who's been here less than an hour that you can't keep your fucking house in order. Solid leadership there."

My heart hammered as Sunny opened up the envelope and withdrew Cameron's finger, an inscribed picture of a Chinese dragon on the ring. I didn't want to escalate this. But there wasn't a person in the world who would put up with this treatment when I'd effectively done the man a favor for nothing.

"You know what? Fuck this. I don't need this shit. Send me back to the bus stop. I'll take my chances on my own."

"Or what?" Sunny's voice grew dangerous, as if he was daring me to threaten him.

"Or nothing. I did the job and reported back to you. And yeah, I was *hoping* this place would be a good fit, but you've clearly got too much on your hands, and I don't feel like sticking around long enough to bite a bullet I've got nothing to do with."

Sunny placed a damp hand on my throat but didn't squeeze. Instead, he let it slide off my neck, bloodying my armor. "Nothing to do with it? We're passed that. You killed Cameron. Do you have any idea what Aaron would do to you if he found out?"

"You gonna tell him?" I scoffed.

"We're in this together now." Sunny drew a rag from his pocket and wiped the streak of blood from my armor.

A muffled moan sounded from the room attached to his study. We both glanced over, then looked at each other.

"Unfinished business?" I asked.

"Hold on. Just—fucking—stay there." Sunny stalked to the door and opened it partway, slipping inside. There was a terrified scream, then silence. Sunny absentmindedly emerged, fresh blood spatter on his face. I glimpsed plastic spread across the floor and a vacant chair in the center of the room before he closed the door again. "Now it's finished."

"Great."

"You really want to leave?" Sunny asked me, cleaning fresh blood off his knife with a rag.

Not in a body bag.

"No. But I'll tell you right now, I'm not sticking around if you keep waving that thing in my face," I breathed. "Now, I'm missing a lot of context. But it's obvious there's some internal beef, and you're floundering. This guy you're up against, he smart?"

"Thinks he's Einstein. He's not," Sunny evaded. "But yeah."

"And did you say or do anything that could have tipped him off?" I asked. It was a blind stab in the dark, but if Sunny was as paranoid as I thought, he'd come up with something.

"I'm too careful for that. It's not as if..." like clockwork, realization clouded his expression. "Shit."

As tempted as I was to ask *what*, exactly, Sunny had realized, I wanted him to move on from it as quickly as possible, before he poked holes. "Is it recoverable?" In an angry motion, Sunny threw the knife. It wasn't directed at me, but I was still startled by the sudden movement. The knife stuck in the wall beside the door and quivered.

"I'm so tired of this fucker being one step ahead."

"Then improvise. Come up with something he couldn't have possibly accounted for," I urged him. If Sunny folded and ran, my primary avenue of sowing chaos within the group went with him. I needed him here, weakening things from the inside.

Sunny focused, eyes shifting back and forth wildly. "The kid who brought you up here. He say anything to you?"

"He... was helpful." I shrugged. "Seemed to like me, for whatever reason."

Sunny's attention snapped to me. "Wait—really? Could you work him, if you needed to?"

I was missing too much information to piece together where he was going. Part of me wanted Nick as far away from this as possible, but that would only make it more difficult to protect him.

"Given the opportunity, it wouldn't be hard."

"Okay. Okay, I can work with that." Sunny straightened my armor. Suddenly buddy buddy in a way he hadn't been since he gave me the assignment. "We don't have a lot of time. Let's get your introduction over and done with."

Sunny was much better at blocking the elevator password than the henchman before, but I could still get a general idea of the number of inputs. It was between ten and twelve.

Different password than before.

It could have been my imagination, but the elevator seemed to move much more quickly than last time.

The door slid open, revealing an underground area that looked to have been abandoned in the middle of excavation.

Sunny put a hand on my back and shoved me forward, out of the elevator. "Hit the intercom when you're done. And don't doddle."

Before I could ask a question—something like "What the hell am I supposed to do here?", the elevator slid shut.

The underground space was half cave, half smoothed stone, with stalagmites pushing up from the unprocessed areas. Several large, yellow construction vehicles were strewn about the area, covered in a layer of dust and dirt.

More striking was the light-blue glow that illuminated the cavern, light came from iridescent moss that covered the ceiling. As far as I could tell, it was the only lighting the cavern had.

I'd thought, after Region 6, that nothing could faze me. But the other-worldly light got under my skin in a way few things could.

Somehow sensing it was the correct direction to go, I followed the lichen on the ceiling, the unsettling feeling growing stronger the deeper I journeyed into the cave.

Another source of light caught my eye. A woman in robes—one who looked remarkably similar to the woman at the bus stop—beckoned me forward. She stood in the center of a mass of lichen that covered the area. The scarring on her face I'd mistaken as the result of burns was lumines-cent, glowing the same light blue.

"And so, the time has come," she said. She sounded sad somehow, as if my arrival was both a tragedy and a foregone conclusion.

"You brought me here," I pointed out.

"That is not entirely true. I can take no more responsibility for your presence than a grain of sand may claim the coastline it resides upon."

"But it was your responsibility."

The woman smiled, and for just a moment, I spotted a dull glow of blue in the back of her throat. "You've always been here. Just as I've always waited. The result differs, but this meeting has happened more times than either of us can count."

The lichen had piled on top of itself unevenly, creating a static ocean of green and blue. As I drew closer, the outline of a large stone embedded in the back wall grew more pronounced. It was too covered in fungus to make out anything more than an outline

Before her were two kneeling pillows and a single teacup.

"Can we get this over with?" I asked. I'd be lying if I claimed our surroundings, and the woman herself, hadn't unsettled me.

"Are you prepared for the oath?"

"Yes."

The woman knelt and indicated the pillow across from her. "Let us begin."

CHAPTER SIXTY-EIGHT

1. Keep the affairs of the Order of Parcae shielded and secret from outsiders.
2. Answer official queries from Order authority figures truthfully and completely.
3. Limit equipment purchases to the Order's vendors and tradesmen.
4. Report all active system-assigned quests to a member of the Court or equivalent authority within twelve hours.
5. Disclose any outside extracurricular activities involving one or more members of the Order for pre-approval.
6. Place the Advent and associated quests above all.
7. Do not sabotage or bring harm to your guildmates, directly or indirectly, unless doing so directly conflicts with the previous tenets.

Each rule emblazoned itself in the stone between us as the woman recited them. She had an odd, ethereal way of speaking, giving me time to reach one notable conclusion. Either Sunny and Aaron found a way to circumvent the geas, or they were both abusing the hell out of the last two rules. Sunny ordered a hit on Cameron and Aaron let it happen, despite ample warning beforehand. It was possible that their positions granted them a little leeway, but considering how Cameron had effectively nothing to incur it, I couldn't imagine it gave them that much.

No wonder Nick was so damn vague.

The rules were thorough, granting very little wiggle room to play with. All that was missing was some Orwellian edict to report suspicions or witnessed malfeasance from other guildmates—and with the way they set it up, that was almost entirely unnecessary.

"Are you prepared to proceed with the oath?" the woman—Seer, as I'd begun to think of her—asked. On her face, the luminescent blue scarring seemed to pulse in rhythm with my racing heart.

"Not quite. So far, you've only told me what you require. What's in it for me?"

Seer studied me. Just like before, at the bus stop, it was like she was seeing through me entirely, evaluating my every action, past, future, and present. "A chance to start over."

"Isn't that what this is already? The world is unrecognizable compared to what it was only a few months ago. The internet and all the information on it is gone—probably for good, unless some unkempt mongrel in a basement somewhere backed it all up offline. No more background checks, no more Credit Karma. It's all gone."

She smiled, amused. "And that's what you've found? Just like that, the sins of yesterday have vanished, never to haunt us again?"

Miles and the tribunal came to mind, and I looked away.

Seer continued. "Forgive me for making light. Perhaps I spoke in error. A new start calls to mind the image of a man at the exit gates of a prison yard, or a transient who arrives in an unfamiliar city. Their environment, their future prospects and possibilities forever altered. But the person themselves—their actions, their tainted history, their very soul—remain static."

"You're offering to alter my soul?"

She shook her head. "No. Rather, to elevate it. And make you the person you were always meant to be."

I wasn't buying it. But I could see how someone like Nick, or one of the suits, many of whom seemed too adept at organized crime to not have some sort of background in it, would fixate on the opportunity. Nick had taken to self-improvement during his recovery, immersing himself in pontificating audio books and seminars on YouTube. And I'd tried to tell him. That listening to some faux-enlightened, over-educated guru completely out of touch with the modern world wax poetic on the similarities between humans and crustaceans and how the importance of a clean room was a waste of time. At which point he politely told me to get back to my practice LSAT and fuck off.

Seer made an odd noise in the back of her throat. A "hm" that sounded like the cross between an observational tick or the beginning of a laugh. Then she just waited. I knew this tactic well—maintaining an awkward silence, forcing the other party to show their hand—and being on the other side of it, for once, was irritating.

"So, what happens now? Say a few words, swear my allegiance, and you magically fix all my problems?" I asked.

Seer tilted her head quizzically. "People take flight through the sky overhead, illuminate dark streets with magical lights that draw from no earthly source. And our understanding of magic is nascent. Is that so hard to believe?"

"I have a lot of problems."

Her sudden laugh startled me. It was a light sound, as if the idea of earthly difficulty was foreign to her. "It might surprise you. Compared to many who take shelter here, your troubles, your desires, are diminutive. But of course, it is not so simple. We must sow before we reap."

You've certainly sowed.

"Instating the Court as a power center," I said, presenting the guess as a foregone conclusion.

Again, she made that odd sound in her throat. "You see authority as your enemy. Be it a governing body of mortals, or the gods themselves. And why shouldn't you? Over and over, they've promised change for the better. Justice. Peace. False promises that die stillborn once they've achieved their personal goals."

"But not you. You're different."

"I am but a vessel."

"For who?"

"The retainer in violet. Hastur." There was a sudden stirring as she spoke the name, like a breeze rippling through the lichen that surrounded us, though the air itself was dead. The subtle glow pervading the room grew darker, more oppressive.

I licked my lips, suddenly nervous. I'd guessed that the suits had a patron. A deity. It was the only conceivable way of explaining exactly how they'd gotten this far ahead. The combination of **<Nychta's Veil>** along with **<Double-Blind>** and the **<Allfather's Mask>** supposedly granted me some protection from deities. But as I'd seen, that insulation was hardly perfect. And I hadn't expected to come this close to the source so quickly.

"The Court will pass no laws, convene no judgements. They exist purely to guide the whole as they each follow their own path and illuminate the way before them. And if necessary, protect them from those with malice in their hearts."

And the bubblegum and rainbows kept coming. But my feelings on the topic didn't matter. I wasn't here in good faith. If she told me their patron wanted to turn everyone into tiny elves who sat in trees and marketed cookies, I would have accepted that. Because my gut was rarely wrong. And my gut told me that Aaron's plan, and the rosy picture this woman was painting, were mutually exclusive.

No matter how lofty the organization's vision appeared to be, the only person Aaron cared about was himself. It wasn't a question of whether he had an angle. It was only a matter of finding it.

"Are you ready to continue?" Seer asked.

I stalled half-assedly, asking for a moment to review the rules. When she nodded, I made a show of tracing the text on the ground with my fingertip, silently reciting it to myself.

"*Azure?*" I prompted my summon. He'd been uncharacteristically silent ever since the bus stop.

"*You're going to hate me,*" Azure whispered.

"*What? Why?*"

"*For the same reason you don't like alcohol, and have smoked nothing more potent than a cigarette. I knew you wouldn't agree unless you were up against a wall. But I also knew how important this was. And how deeply you'd regret it if you let the opportunity pass. As underhanded as it seems, I did it this way for you. I really did.*" Azure's distress rang clear.

"*If you wanted to talk about it, we should have done that earlier. We're out of time. Now what do you have.*"

"*Do you trust me?*"

Did I trust Azure?

It was impossible to banish the events of the adaptive dungeon from my mind. Azure had opened old wounds and flayed me to my core, exploiting every potential weakness in a manner that was as effective as it was cruel. I understood he didn't see it that way. That his inhuman mind viewed his actions as an artist's depiction of truth, and that there was some element of growth through suffering in his "work." He wanted to watch me overcome the obstacles he created, and when I did, he'd clung to me out of a mix of madness and co-dependence at having that desire finally realized.

Because I'd created him.

Knowing how dangerous Azure could be, I kept him at arm's length until Miles forced my hand. But after the threat had receded, I'd never really reinstated the distance. He'd handled the trial run masterfully and respected the boundaries I'd placed—even if he poked at them from time to time—and he was too useful to keep in reserve.

On some level, I'd been prepared for this. Azure was borderline gleeful whenever he had an idea, no matter how sinister. He didn't have a moral compass, or if he did, it was entirely alien. And considering the lofty pedestal he placed me on, his reticence was derived entirely from my approval, or lack of.

All things considered, I trusted Azure as much as I trusted anyone.

"*Any means necessary. Do whatever you have to do,*" I commanded.

As I continued to trace the text, my finger twitched. It felt too strong to be a muscle spasm.

"You're fighting me," Azure said.

My finger twitched again. "If I am, it's subconscious."

"Just relax your mind."

I did my best to follow his instructions, focusing on my breathing, doing my best to place myself in a meditative state, despite the circumstances.

"I'm ready," I said. Only, I didn't say it. The words, and the way my hand folded over my lap, were all involuntary. I tried to make a fist, and it was like the signal died in my mind before it made its way to my body.

Azure had taken over. However necessary it was, losing control made me profoundly uncomfortable. The only thing keeping me from outright panic was knowing it was Azure in the driver's seat.

The woman dipped her fingers into the small bowl at her side and drew an unfamiliar symbol on my forehead. "Do you accept these mandates as ironclad and agree to be bound by them?"

"I do," Azure spoke through me. A strange buzzing reached my ears.

"Will you submit yourself to the authority of the order and the geas that safeguards it?"

"I will," Azure said. The buzzing grew louder.

"Repeat after me."

Azure repeated the words back carefully. "I, Myrddin, pledge my fealty to the Order of Parcae. To uphold their ideals and protect the weak, to accept the guidance of those above me and foster those beneath me. To follow the guidance of Hastur and reform the city, and eventually the world itself, as a perfect, balanced utopia."

All around us, lichen rippled violently. The blue luminescence grew vibrant, losing color, blue fading to an all-encompassing brightness that burned like white phosphorous. A vaguely humanoid figure covered in coarse lichen struggled to rise. Every inch of his skin was covered in organic green and glowing blue. Gaping holes in the place of his eyes and mouth radiated white.

Suddenly, I was fully in control of my body, scrambling backward. I mentally reached out to Azure and received no answer.

The woman suddenly straightened, still kneeling, her body ramrod straight as she stared at me with astonishment. "The blessed retainer graces you."

Not again.

CHAPTER SIXTY-NINE

The roar of traffic beneath the overpass overtook everything else. I blinked several times, the ferocity of the summer sun oddly intense. Beside me, the super-heated asphalt of the recently repaved road let off the slightly sour stench of tar. The straps of my always-too-heavy backpack dug into my shoulders.

What was I... doing?

Right. I was walking home from the school library. I'd stayed behind for a few hours to get some studying in after class and given up after I'd read the same paragraph five times until I finally realized my retention was failing and I needed a break.

Up ahead, a boy with a scruffy blond mop of hair wearing headphones was sitting on the overpass, flicking pebbles at the cars passing below, smirking at the audible impacts. I didn't know his name, but I recognized him.

For a while, I'd suspected my brother was being bullied. Ellison refused to talk about it. Told me he was fine, that he'd "handle" it. But I saw the way his grades were slipping. The occasional "F — Did Not Complete" on assignments I knew he'd finished.

And when I showed up early, rather than the usual pickup time, I'd watched from a distance as the boy on the overpass tripped Ellison, pushed his face in the dirt and Snap Backed a selfie with my brother as an unwilling participant before he cackled and moved on.

I knew that interceding then and there would do more harm than good. But it hurt to watch.

I drew closer, some part of me waiting for the boy to notice me. He didn't. Beside the line of pebbles at his side, I noticed the rectangular surface of a phone. The chrome around its rounded edges reflected brightly in the sun—the pro version of whatever Apple put out this year.

Maybe I couldn't directly intercede when Ellison was at school. But that didn't mean I couldn't do anything.

The boy was so fixated on tossing the pebbles, and with the headphones on he was oblivious to the world around him. If someone were to take the phone and toss it onto the road behind him, he probably wouldn't notice until the audio cut out, and by then, a dozen tires would have pulverized it.

Was it petty and childish?

Absolutely.

Was I seriously considering it?

Without a doubt.

I drew near him, the fantasy becoming closer to reality with every step.

Seconds away from carrying out the half-assed plan, I hesitated as the boy suddenly grimaced. He reached up to rub his shoulder and pulled up his shirt sleeve, revealing the dark red line of a recently scabbed over cut. Both above and below it were distended white lines of flesh of similar length. Other cuts that had scarred over.

My half-baked intentions faded from my mind as I passed him, mired in a mix of sadness and concern.

Self-harm was common in kids. Sometimes it was just an outlet, an unhealthy way to vent when a person had no one to talk to. But it was also often indicative of deeper troubles and traumas. I rarely involved myself in other people's business, but this sort of thing could escalate quickly. It would probably be best to get the kid's name from Ellison and report it to the school councilor—

A feeling of déjà vu washed over me so strongly I stopped in my tracks, followed by a wave of wrongness that started in my chest and spread throughout my body.

What—

"Betty Botter—blahblahblehblehblech."

I glanced up from my emails on the chunky laptop screen to where Iris sat cross-legged next to the oscillating fan. She pursed her mouth in mild disgust, as if she'd just swallowed a bug, and her forehead glistened as she glared down at the printout. The sweating was probably more because of the typical July heatwave than effort alone, but she'd been at it for hours.

Probably too long.

Idly, I returned to my emails and waved widely to get Iris's attention.

"This one keeps tripping me up," she complained aloud.

"Well, yeah. The Bs have always been a pain point. Take a break." I drew out the consonants automatically for her benefit.

"I can keep going."

That was true. She had the tenacity and perseverance uncommon in a person twice her age. But there was a difference between productive and unproductive work, and after hours of running into a metaphorical wall, she was sliding toward the latter.

I raised an eyebrow and she raised one right back, though her lips turned up and betrayed the stoic expression.

The fan rotated toward her, blowing her hair back for a moment. I squinted, then pointed to the corner of the room. "Try saying it into the fan."

"What?" Iris stared at me blankly.

"Speak into the fan like it's a microphone."

My sister peered at me suspiciously, and I sighed. "It's a trick that helped me control my stutter. You'll be too distracted by the interference to overthink. Plus, the fighting the air makes your mouth and jaw rely on muscle memory."

Iris approached the fan, still shooting uncertain glances my way. It wasn't adjustable and the fixed height was too tall for her to speak into directly, so she grabbed it by the bar and leaned it back, like the world's most unenthusiastic rockstar.

"Betty Botter bought some butter. But she said the butter's bitter if I put it in my batter, it will make my batter bitter. But a bit of better butter will make my batter better."

I closed the laptop screen slowly. Even though the sound was distorted through the fan, it was clear as day. Her eyes were wide. "Did I..."

"You did it!" I punched the air.

My sister did a celebratory dance and capped it off by tackling me with a hug, nearly crushing the laptop. "That tip was magic! Why didn't you mention it sooner!"

I flicked her nose. "Because it was bull."

Iris pulled away. "Huh?"

"The fan thing isn't a thing. Or at least, not one I knew about. You were in a rut, getting frustrated. All I did was distract you from it. The rest was all you, kiddo."

"That was mean."

"Makes sense, I'm a mean person."

Iris leaned her head against my chest. "The worst."

In what felt like seconds, she was asleep. I brushed a bang out of her face. She'd worked so hard for this. I'd told her countless times that her speaking voice was fine, but it didn't matter. Once my sister put her mind to something, she always followed through. A sense of pride welled up in my chest, followed by happiness.

No.

It was more than happiness.

Unlike the first memory, this was more or less exactly how it happened. And when Iris achieved her victory, I'd been happy for her. But this was different. It was like a feeling of warmth and excitement and elevation, so strong and raw and real it felt as if I might burst. It was jarring, because I was certain I'd never felt it before.

———

Stained glass. Black-and-white attire. A cheap suit that fit me like a burlap sack. More cops in attendance than a fire sale at Cabela's.

My father's funeral.

Mom wept unconsolably at the far end of a pew a few rows back, which meant it was my job to stand next to the casket, shell-shocked, listening to the never-ending platitudes of person, after person, after person as I shook each hand.

A woman older than god whose name I didn't know or care to learn towered over me, her stretch-marked bosom on display to a degree that felt mildly inappropriate. Her wide-brimmed black hat threatened to poke me in the forehead.

"It's okay to cry, dear. He was your father."

"Leave the boy alone, Beth." Her husband, a man with a bad combover, rolled his eyes and stepped away.

It was a strain to smile, as if I'd forgotten how. "All cried out, I guess."

Beth pressed her lips together, pity radiating off her like an aura. She reached out toward me, hand stalling when I instinctively moved away. "I know you must feel all this pressure to be strong. You're the man of the house now. But you can be strong tomorrow. No one here will judge you if you cry."

I formed a fist slowly. Beth was rude, but they were all thinking it. Watching my stoic expression. Whispering. Judging. It took every ounce of self-control I had not to scream. To not tell this woman she had no idea what the fuck she was talking about. That I'd spent most of the funeral trying to cry. Hating myself because all I could feel was anger. Angry at my father for taking the call. Angry at the asshole who killed him.

Angry at myself, for being broken.

Can you move on, please? You're holding up the line.

The words died in my throat as hot tears streaked down my face. I would never see him again. We'd never talk long into the evening about his day. He wouldn't be at my high school graduation, or give me long-winded career advice.

That world was gone.

My chest clenched as unadulterated sorrow unrooted me to my very core. It felt like being plunged into a pit, a place so dark and cold and painful that it was hard to focus on anything other than the ache.

I bowed my head.

Finally, Beth seemed satisfied and moved on, a final "Sorry for your loss," her parting shot.

A pair of brown loafers stepped into sight, obscuring my view of the carpet. I slowly looked up. The newcomer wore black, pinstripe pants and a dark-purple vest. His hands rested casually in his pockets. His hair was white, and his long, well-kempt beard and short-cut hair, combined with the rest of the ensemble, called to mind a post-hippie aesthetic.

When he spoke his voice was low, charming. "Quite the turnout. Your father was clearly loved."

"Was there a reason we had to start with this mindfuck?" Those words were all I could manage. Because the pain had given way to anger once more. "Hastur."

Hastur grinned. "It's a pleasure to finally make your acquaintance, Ordinator."

I was fucked.

CHAPTER SEVENTY

Around us, the funeral ground to a halt. My mother's cries stopped. The line of never-ending people froze in place, along with everyone else. Hastur repositioned himself, taking a place beside me. "I've been doing some research recently. You can learn a lot about a culture from their fables, and knowing the full picture is kind of my thing."

"Uhuh."

I reached out for Azure, Talia. When that failed, Audrey.

None of them responded. I was on my own.

Hastur made a vague, circling motion around his head. "One of them stuck. A carpenter—"

"—Jesus." I rolled my eyes.

"Wrong carpenter." Hastur's colorless eyes twinkled. "Anyway, our childless friend builds a puppet to fill the void he feels in his life. Prays to a fairy. Fairy takes pity on him and grants the puppet the most precious gift of all." Hastur made sarcastic spirit fingers. "Life. Next day, the puppet wakes up, suddenly aware and sapient. In a perfect world, that should have been the end. The lonely man has a son, and the self-aware puppet has a father. He's got no strings, to hold him down, to make him fret, or make him frown."

If he wanted me dead, I'd be dead. Need to draw this out. Keep him talking. Everyone has a weakness. Just need to find his.

"It wouldn't be a story without conflict," I pointed out.

"True. Though I dislike conflict for the sake of conflict." Hastur stared through me, then continued his recitation. "The puppet lacks a conscience. But he's not evil. Not at all. His desires are simple. He wants to be human."

"There really are better ways to make an introduction."

Hastur looked oddly apologetic. "I'm sorry. For putting you through this. As much as you hate those words, they need to be said. I couldn't think of a better way to show you."

"Show me what?"

"That what you want—what you really want, hidden beneath a mountain of denial—is attainable."

It hit me like a truck. Why Hastur put me through this. I'd felt real empathy for the boy on the overpass. Joy at my sister's triumph. Despair and grief at my father's funeral. He was showing what my life would have been like, if I was normal.

What is normal?

"You're wrong." I shook my head. "I'm better this way. If I wasn't... like this... I would have cracked a long time ago."

"Then let me pose a question." Hastur smiled. "In a perfect world, one where you were free to pursue your interests, unencumbered by debt, or danger, or existential threats. Would you still want to be what you are?"

"I don't live in a perfect world—"

"But you *could.*" Hastur rested his hands on my shoulders. "In a perfect world, you say fuck MIT. You go to Rice. You major in philosophy and minor in psychology. Because that's where your passion lies. The human condition. What makes us think, feel, breathe. What drives us. The meaning of life. A high calling."

"N-no money in it," I stammered, only realizing after the fact how quickly Hastur had gotten under my skin. Rice and MIT were gone. If they still existed in any capacity, probably within their own dome, they were forever altered.

Hastur shook me lightly. "Fuck the money. It's a perfect world. You don't need money anymore. Everything is affordable. Inflation, corruption, and poverty are gone, artifacts of an ancient past. You teach during your post-graduate, and discover, despite being utterly convinced that you'll hate it, that it's a natural fit. On account of your controversial—albeit brilliant—dissertation on Kant—"

"Kant?" I balked.

"I know, kind of mainstream. If it makes you feel better, you spend most of it ripping him a new asshole."

Somehow, it did.

"It's quite the smackdown." Hastur chuckled nostalgically, as if this wasn't fantasy. As if the dissertation not only existed, but he'd actually read it. Then he grew quieter, more serious. "Rice hires you before you even walk. They send you all over the world. You read things only a handful of people have ever read. You never stop learning, and using that knowledge. You write more papers that are received well. You find you love the travel, something you've never realized because you've always lived in the same place. And in Italy, you meet the woman of your dreams."

I exhaled. I'd been holding my breath without realizing it. He'd been doing so well, only to flub it in the last half.

"She's five years older than you. Accomplished, smart. Smarter than you. She has no interest in a physical relationship, which works out for reasons I'm guessing you understand perfectly. You enjoy all the trappings of a romantic relationship, the comfort and closeness of sharing life with a like-minded person, with none of the expectations. You're happy, satisfied, and fulfilled until the day you die."

"When?" I asked. If nothing else, I was curious what he'd come up with.

"At the ripe old age of 226. Medicine and life expectancy gets a lot better on account of the magic." Hastur's hands dropped off my shoulders, his face suddenly haggard and worn. The funeral attendees, still frozen in place, blinked out one at a time, until only the two of us remained. Hastur sat down on the front row pew, his eyelids drooping.

A wave of calm washed over me, the effect of whatever he'd done to my mind slowly fading. "We lost hundreds of thousands in the first event. You expect me to believe *any* of this is even possible?"

"If the Advent happens before the second event? Yes."

"And you said medicine improved because of magic, which implies that, in this perfect future, the system still exists."

Hastur waved the point away. "The system is only malevolent because the deities behind it have grown twisted and cruel. They subsist on the spectacle, completely ignoring the purpose of the original design. In my hands, it wouldn't be used to drive conflict."

"So that's the plan. Kill the pantheon," I said.

"You say that like it's absurd. But once I regain my power, every potential future exists at my fingertips. I might be the only one capable of winning that fight, now that your patron is on his way out. It's why they keep me weak. They can't kill me without cause, but they can sure as hell stack the deck in their favor."

The last comment resonated. It occurred to me that the sudden wave of tiredness wasn't an act. It made little sense otherwise. This would be the perfect time for him to project strength. Bolster his image. Instead, he looked...

Exhausted.

There was no point in beating around the bush. "You know why I'm here."

"I do." Hastur's lips split in a pained smile. "We've danced this dance countless times before, your predecessors and I."

"Then why am I still breathing?"

Hastur looked me up and down. "For one, that veil of yours is no joke. I couldn't kill you here even if I wanted to—not without breaking enough rules to finally give them an excuse to pull the plug on me. I could... massage the Order to do it, in time, but truthfully, I don't want to."

"Still waiting on the why."

He pinched the bridge of his nose. "Because you're right to be angry. Because I can't fully control the Order in my current state, and they seem more than comfortable using any means to justify the end."

As reasonable and genuine as he sounded, it didn't change what happened. I saw Jinny, struggling to breathe, blood leaking from beneath her hands. "My friend died because they didn't give a shit about collateral. Bled out in seconds."

"I know." Hastur looked nauseous.

"Because of their actions, another friend was changed in the cruelest way possible."

"That's an exaggeration, but I'm aware."

I nearly punched him.

"They were luring Users into a region and killing them for cores."

Hastur's mouth tightened. "Aaron is ambitious. Overly so."

I clenched my fists at my sides. "That doesn't even begin to cover it."

The pew squeaked as Hastur leaned forward. "The Necromancer's research will bear fruit, though you'll need to be patient and finesse him."

"So..." I didn't dare to hope.

"There will be a chance to bring Jinny back. What happened to Sae? That can be undone far more easily, though it will take some doing. The rest... I'll find a way to make it right."

I couldn't trust him. I had no reason to. But hearing him say it, it rocked me.

He rubbed his forehead and suddenly interjected. "Want to guess how many times we've worked together?"

"The previous Ordinators?"

"Yes."

"Few."

"A grand total of zero," Hastur corrected, closing his eyes. The pause was long enough that I almost thought he'd fallen asleep. "Not that there were many of them I would have cooperated with to begin with—they tend to be completely off the deep end. You're not even close to that far gone. Not yet. Of the less... difficult... candidates, most of them died early."

"And the ones who survived?"

"Let's just say the pantheon has a talent for turning them against me." Hastur opened one eye and looked me over. "Returning to your list of sins.

You're correct. There's no excuse. No apology I can offer to make things right. That being said, some concessions are in order, regardless." He opened his hand and a clear, crystal bottle appeared. The liquid, visible through the ornate transparent patterns that decorated the outside, was completely colorless.

I reached for it. It fit snugly in my palm, no larger than a health potion. When Hastur pulled his hand away, someone had dropped a fifty-pound weight in my hand. I fell to one knee, nearly dropping it to the ground. "Christ."

<Item: Asura's Tears>

Description: A collection of tears painstakingly collected from an Asura over thousands of years. These powerful beings slayed many gods over eons of terror before they were finally brought to heel. Few have seen such a marvel. Even fewer still know the extent of the mysteries within. Highly potent. May cause a major cataclysm if dropped.

<Item Class: Artifact.>

After I skimmed the description, I slowly turned to Hastur and glared.

"Probably should have mentioned it was heavy," Hastur said.

"You *think?*"

"Definitely should have mentioned it was heavy."

Carefully, I moved the potion toward my hip with both hands. It slipped into my inventory easily. "The description was useless. What does it do?"

"You're going to want two. I'll give you the second after the advent." Hastur shook his head. "As for what it does, it's best to let you discover that for yourself. You'll want to have a decent alchemist look over it." He hesitated, then added, "Preferably one sworn to silence. Under guard. Completely isolated from the outside world. Did I mention under guard?"

"You did."

The skin beneath Hastur's fingernails was slowly turning black, spreading into his nail bed and up his knuckles. He watched the spread with grim interest. "Drew too deeply for the prediction."

Our time was growing short. I couldn't help but draw the parallel between this and my first encounter with the Allfather. A conversation that left me with far more questions than answers. If it was anything like that encounter, this might be the last chance I had to talk to him.

A dozen questions rotated through my mind before I finally settled on one. "Why me? I'm not a god. And sure, the Ordinator's power grows exponentially, but that's still relative. I'm just a User with a special class. Why are you willing to put so much on the line for a gamble?"

The darkness spread down Hastur's forearm, the blackened skin turning to dust, the top section of his arm disappearing before my eyes. From the way he grimaced, he wasn't impervious to the pain.

"I hate to gamble. But you're already aware of the turmoil growing within the order. Aaron made a mistake bringing Sunny into the fold. One... of many. Now he's paying for it. For as long as they stay entrenched, sniping at each other, the division will spread. Only a fool... fights a two-front war. One of them has to go. It doesn't matter who, but for the future I've forecasted to come to pass, the infighting needs to stop. Quickly."

Another hand, looking to use me as a knife in the dark. My mind was clouded, filled to the brim with thoughts and theories I couldn't even begin to unpack.

"I understand." It felt undignified to stay and watch, so I turned and headed toward the church entrance, an unperceivable weight settling on my shoulders.

"And, Matthias?" Hastur called after me.

I turned. The darkness accelerated and spread quickly, eroding his mouth and jaw. He smiled like the Cheshire Cat, even as his face crumbled.

"You were right. You're not a god. Not yet."

CHAPTER SEVENTY-ONE

I woke up on the floor. Something soft cushioned my head. Before I collected myself, a scathing pain shot down my forearm. I pulled back the gauntlet far enough to see the source—a forking cascade of Lichtenberg figures on the underside of my wrist to my palm contoured by light distended flesh, red around the edges.

Great. Fucker had marked me.

A gloved hand reached out, tracing the pattern. Seer cleared her throat, and when it didn't seem to work, cleared it again. "You spoke to him."

Hastur hadn't transported me anywhere. Our meeting took place entirely in my head. And judging from the lack of soreness and bruises, Seer must have caught me when I lost consciousness. I scrambled to my feet and took a half-step back, reaching a hand toward my face. The mask was still equipped. That didn't necessarily mean anything. She could have easily looked and replaced it during the lapse.

"What the fuck is this?" I asked, pointing to the mark.

"Proof of your allegiance. Evidence of your potential."

"Skip the fucking riddles," I said. With the way my summons all chimed in at once, urging calm, I must have shouted.

Seer leaned back, more surprised than fearful at the sudden outburst. "If it is the mark itself that bothers you, it is invisible to those outside the Order. It speaks to a significance beyond the rank and file. Few are graced by Hastur directly. Those who are, receive a mark. The length of the mark and number of branches directly correlate with the supplicant's potential impact. If—"

"That's enough."

"You don't want to know—"

"We're done here," I cut in.

Seer bowed her head. "Your reaction is unfortunate but not at all uncommon. Coming face to face with a deity can be an alarming and humbling experience. Seek me out when the turmoil has faded. Return the way you came. The elevator will be open to you."

Turmoil was a good word for it. I was spiraling. A profound feeling of uprootedness permeated deep in my mind, threatening to propagate and spread. I needed to reset, recenter, before I did or said something I couldn't explain.

I walked away, fists clenching and unclenching almost entirely on their own. System text scrolled in front of my face as I hurried to the elevator.

<Pivotal Quest Received>

Quest: Fractured Fate

Quest Description: The Retainer in Violet has chosen you as an agent to use the Transposition toward the creation of a utopia. This quest has no visible objectives. Your actions from this point onward will be evaluated on a sliding scale. As you actively contribute to or undermine the Retainer's intent, your standing will adjust appropriately.

System Warning: Pivotal Quests can be hugely rewarding, but are often catalysts for drastic change. Their volatile nature and tendency to affect the world around them can cause other, more mundane quests to become incompletable or lost. The completion of a Pivotal Quest frequently results in serious consequences for the individual as well, such as gaining or transference of patronage and access to exclusive gear, spells, and knowledge.

Quest Difficulty: ???

Time Limit: ???

Quest Reward: That which you desire most.

I swiped it away. This time, the elevator doors slid open on their own and allowed me entry. Once they closed, I retreated within my mind, trying to manage the panic.

Hastur was full of shit. Anyone with power who promised to make things better on the scale he was talking about almost always was. Selflessness, more often than not, is little more than pageantry. Altruism is rarely more than a bedazzled method of stroking your own ego.

Hastur didn't give two fucks about anyone. His endgame, like so many others, was about control. But if—and only if—he was capable of even a fraction of what he claimed, his interpretation of control was...

Tantalizing.

Before the dome, the average person was lucky to make it through life with no major disasters. The lucky ones found a job they didn't hate, a house they could afford. A family that loved them.

Even if you were one of those lucky few, you were still only one bad day away from disaster. Sometimes you didn't even have to make a choice. Sickness, abandonment, and financial ruin were always waiting on the horizon, the three horsemen of the post-modern apocalypse. And if you had any self-awareness, that inevitable realization weighed heavily.

But what if it didn't have to be that way? What if chaos, random chance, and all the other bullshit beyond our control no longer factored? What if someone could just tell you what you needed to do to succeed and be happy?

They can't.

It would be easier to work through this if I was looking at it rationally, but Hastur had nailed me to the fucking wall. When he described my perfect future, I'd felt an honest-to-god stir. A tug of desire I couldn't rationally explain.

His predictions had been so ordinary. The system still existed in the future he'd outlined for me, yet he hadn't even mentioned it.

In Hastur's perfect future, I'd effectively retired from User life, and it was obvious why.

I held my gauntlets palm up and stared at them. They were battle-scarred and torn. Beneath the gauntlet, my arms held scars of their own, connected to a patchwork of close calls inscribed across the rest of my body that grew more numerous almost by the day. There was a twinge in my ribs that ached from sudden changes in temperature. And almost every time I sat down, it was harder to get up again.

I couldn't do this forever.

Too many times already, I'd survived by the skin of my teeth, often on a technicality I hadn't even been aware of. As rational as I tried to be, there was just too much I didn't know. Countless potential threats I couldn't realistically prepare for. I'd thrown myself into it, regardless. Fought like hell. Because the struggle was all I knew. And I thought I'd accepted how it all inevitably ended. That I could be at peace with dying, so long as my family was taken care of.

Hastur had committed the greatest cruelty of all. He'd given me the possibility of hope. Like a bright halo of sun filtering through a curtain.

Almost as bad, he'd given me a taste of what I'd been missing my entire life. How it felt like to be normal. The memories he'd picked all had a powerful emotion attached to them. Empathy, joy, grief. That they weren't all positive and elating only lent more credence to the demonstration. He'd let me sample it all. Even now, the agitation and confusion of emotion felt as if it was being filtered through a pinhole. I had nothing to compare it to before. And now I knew, in painstaking detail, exactly what I was missing.

Throughout my life, I viewed my coldness and lack of empathy as a shield. It protected me from the worst of the storms. The fallout. I'd known on some level that it wasn't free. That the steel blinders that protected me from the lows also robbed me of the highs. But I'd never felt the starkness of the difference until now.

If Hastur had offered to "fix" me and remove the blinders permanently on the spot, I would have passed. As he himself had said, I wasn't sure I'd be capable of doing what I needed to do as a normal person. The fear alone would pose a nigh-insurmountable wall, and there was too high a likelihood of freezing in a key moment.

But after? If the world he'd described was at all possible?

Could I really put the knife down?

Live a normal existence, free of the shadows that plagued me, unburdened by constant conflict?

Too good to be true.

I latched onto the thought like an anchor. Slowly, the false hope drowned beneath a wave of distrust. The gods had given me little reason to trust them farther than I could throw them. Hastur was no exception. His people had been out of pocket from the beginning—and so far as I knew, he'd done little to correct their supposed missteps beyond wagging his finger from a distance and giving me an artifact-level potion like it was a hallmark bereavement card.

He didn't care what they'd done, so long as they were effective. The only reason he was taking action now was to unify the order. Which implied a darker agenda. One that required the sort of people he'd recruited to carry it out. People like Aaron.

It was impossible to strangle the hope completely. Hastur was too compelling for that. I settled for suppressing it, forcing it down into something more manageable.

Maybe Hastur could do everything he promised and more. That didn't matter. Distant theoreticals were irrelevant. Power always came at a price. What mattered was discovering what the Order was willing to pay. And how much, exactly, it would cost the rest of us.

"Azure."

The lithid manifested in my mind's eye, his head hung. "Is it time?"

It took me a moment to realize what he meant. What he must have been waiting for, ever since he underwent the geas. "You think I'm going to release you."

Azure rubbed his arms. "It's the correct decision. My usefulness is limited. I'm bound by the geas now."

He'd answered the lingering question I'd summoned him for, though not with the answer I'd wanted. Once I realized what was happening, I'd hoped the geas wouldn't affect him at all because of his nature. That wasn't the case, and this *was* going to be a lot harder with Azure's hands tied behind his back, but I'd never even considered dismissing him. Probably because he'd just taken the magical equivalent of a bullet for me.

"You're not going anywhere," I said firmly. Azure looked up at me in surprise.

"But..."

"Just, take a back seat for a while. Need to be careful until we know how strict the limitations are." My thoughts went to Nick. He'd given me quite a bit of information, enough that it surprised me he'd gotten away with it without breaching the geas. The more I thought about it, the more certain I was that he probably had. But as far as I knew, it hadn't triggered. It was possible it had something to do with intent. Nick probably hadn't realized how much he was giving away, which, in theory, was why the geas hadn't flagged him. If there was a weakness there, I needed to exploit it.

It was just a matter of figuring out how. Azure looked like he was fighting the urge to hug me. "Really thought I was a goner."

"Not getting out of your contract that easily."

"Thank you, Matt. Truly."

As the elevator doors parted, the sound of raised voices came flooding in. Sunny and Aaron in the middle of what looked like an intense discussion. Sunny towered over Aaron, while the slimmer man stood his ground, unimpressed by the other's intensity.

I fell back into Myrddin.

If I said I wasn't shaken by what Hastur offered, I'd be lying. And if the evidence that supported his claims grew too significant to ignore, I would at least try to keep an open mind. But that was the best I could do. Because I didn't come here to save the world.

I came here to save my friend.

And burn this place to the ground.

CHAPTER SEVENTY-TWO

Sunny loomed over Aaron by at least half a foot, doing the most accurate demonstration of foaming at the mouth I'd ever seen. Despite the intensity, Aaron seemed unaffected, almost bland, hands shoved in his pockets even as Sunny bore down on him.

"It's too fucking soon to move on the tower," Sunny said.

"I'm aware of your opinion on the matter. And if we're bitching about expediency, care to explain the User you just railroaded through the process? The same User who apparently just broke protocol and appeared in the central compound."

Sunny stuck his finger in Aaron's face. A long trail of Lichtenberg figures spanned from his third finger to his forearm. They hadn't been there earlier. Apparently, Seer was telling the truth: anyone outside the Order couldn't see the mark. "I recruit whoever the fuck I want."

Aaron glanced at me, though Sunny hadn't realized I'd returned yet. "An allowance the retainer granted both of us. But I think it's a little odd that the User you bring in last-minute assaults and seriously injures members of the team taking part in an operation you vocally opposed."

Sunny grinned so widely it looked as if his face might split. "They attacked him first. And if I wanted to put some of your people out of commission, Aaron, I wouldn't send a recruit. And he sure as hell wouldn't be unarmed."

Aaron's brow furrowed as he pivoted toward me, directly acknowledging my presence for the first time. "You did all that without a weapon?"

I shrugged. "They were inexperienced. It didn't seem necessary."

"Right..." Like I hadn't even spoken, Aaron focused back in on Sunny. "You see how this looks? And with the timing, there's no way I can know how much you coached him."

"Stop talking out of the side of your fucking mouth. If you want to accuse me of something, say it. We can have it all out in front of the Court and Sibyl and be done with it." Again, Sunny stuck his finger in Aaron's face, a hair's breadth from touching his forehead.

There was enough tension in the room that it felt like either of them could snap at any moment. I was half-tempted to just leave. If I had the elevator code, I might have. Wash my hands of it, take the non-zero chance they might kill each other and save me the trouble. Instead, I unbuckled my gauntlet. When Azure played Myrddin in Aaron's backyard, he'd done so with some cheek. I saw no reason to discontinue the trend.

I held my bare forearm up to the light. "There a trader with ointment? Shit itches like a motherfucker."

Aaron's eyebrows shot up in surprise, while Sunny appeared completely unsettled. From their reactions, I filled in the blanks. Neither expected Hastur to actually talk to me.

"I stand corrected," Aaron murmured.

"Right, uh..." Sunny attempted to regain his balance, though his eyes kept flicking to the mark. "See? Clearly legitimate."

"He who I think he is?" Aaron asked.

"Uhuh," Sunny confirmed.

"Solid get. Though it's unfortunate you were the one to bring him in."

"You—" Sunny bristled and took a step toward Aaron, the tension in the room rising. Aaron held up a hand and placed it on his chest.

"I understand why you skipped the background. That tracks. But you're not skipping containment and analysis. He's not going anywhere for at least two weeks. And once he does, he needs to be observed."

Sunny's eyes narrowed, and he shifted his body slightly. He slowly reached toward his inventory with his out-of-sight arm. Aaron caught the movement and openly smiled, all but daring Sunny to make a move.

There was a part of me that wanted to let him. Watching Aaron be reduced to a bloody smear on the ground was a personal fantasy of mine. But something about the scene was wrong. Aaron was here, unescorted, yet seemed entirely too confident. He had something up his sleeve. Either way, what Aaron was proposing couldn't happen.

I cleared my throat. "Personally, I don't give a fuck, but I'm surprised you're willing to put the research off indefinitely."

The tension flagged as they both stared at me.

"What research," Sunny growled.

"I'd like to know as well." Aaron took several long strides toward me, putting himself in my space. "I certainly hope you don't intend to violate your geas so soon after invoking the oath. The results of that would be... categorically unpleasant."

I cocked my head. That was a subtle warning for my benefit, disguised as a threat. So Aaron wasn't sandbagging trying to keep me tied to the compound. "Is power-leveling the Necromancer tied to the Advent?"

"Not directly." Aaron shrugged.

"Then I'm not violating jack," I said. With all the posturing going on in this room, it was hard to keep my body language neutral, not favoring either of them. "Wasn't exactly keen on joining the Illuminati without a few cards up my sleeve. I only have a handful of User cores on me. Your Necromancer will run through them in less than a week. I stashed the rest somewhere safe. If you want more, well, I'm not really down for twenty-four seven cult life. Hastur seems chill, but I've got my own shit to handle."

"... chill." Aaron twisted back to look at Sunny. "Are we the Illuminati?"

Sunny grunted noncommittally. "Secret society bound by oaths and magic, nascent god, fingers in almost everything?"

"Guess we are," Aaron said.

"Severely lacking in the triangle department," I pointed out. Whatever caused the rift, the rapport between them was still there. I needed to make sure they didn't resolve their differences.

Aaron's smile faded. "As much as I applaud your cleverness, we're still at an impasse. I can't, in good conscience, let a railroaded recruit roam freely. Even if Hastur himself gave his approval."

I breathed out slowly. As I'd always suspected, Aaron was a fantastic liar. There was no trace of deception in his body language or voice. Problem was, he was effectively hemming me in. Either he was doing it on purpose, or he couldn't find a way to let this go in a realistic manner that Sunny would safely buy.

An idea formed. "I'm not sure what he's already told you about me, so I'll just say this. There's only one thing I care about. Winning this fucking game and getting the hell out of Dallas. Short of that, acquiring as much power as possible to make the over-arching goal easier."

"Do you have an alternate endgame in mind?" Aaron's voice changed when he asked. More authoritative and demanding.

I was already answering before I received the prompt from Azure. "Is that an official query?"

"Yes," Aaron said.

"Then no. My patron isn't exactly a bullet-point planner. I originally intended to win the events, carrying a single region to the end, getting to know their strengths and weaknesses intimately in case the final stages get... unpleasant. If Hastur can follow through on his claim—end this before the second event—that won't be necessary."

"Your patron being the Allfather of Entropy?" Aaron asked.

"Yes," I admitted. There was no point in denying it, especially when the lie could be so easily conflicted with all the chatty gods going around.

"Did you get the feeling it's going that way without Hastur's interference? Last man standing?" Aaron asked. I felt genuine interest in the question. Realistically, he'd only spoken to Hastur, who probably revealed little beyond hints and riddles.

"Count yourself lucky," I groused. "The Allfather is infinitely more cryptic than the Retainer. He mentioned nothing to that effect."

"I didn't ask what the Allfather said. I asked what you felt," Aaron corrected.

I considered it. If this was really about reformation, as the Overseer implied, I couldn't see it. The system—and for that matter, the last event —prioritized strength over all.

"They're burning through casualties at an unsustainable rate. At the very least, it's flamethrower eugenics. Within our dome, I could see a few hundred people left at most. The real question is whether this is the semi-finals."

"And the survivors get pitted against each other after the dome comes down," Aaron said thoughtfully. "I've considered that possibility myself."

I silently noted that he hadn't asked me if I was working with Sunny. Either using his authority to inquire directly about a member of the Order with similar authority to his own was off limits, or he knew it was pointless, meaning confirmation that Sunny had found a way to circumvent the geas.

"Putting the theoretical aside, for the moment, I fucked up one of your teams right before an op. That wasn't my intention, and if you want to shift the teams around and find a spot for me, I can more than make up for the three I dropped. Of course, on the condition you drop the isolation requirement."

"What—" Sunny's face turned red.

"I think that's an excellent idea," Aaron said smoothly, all but leering at the taller man. "Anything for the Advent. Isn't that right, Sunny?"

Sunny paused. He seemed to realize why I was going this route. But he didn't look happy about it.

What Aaron said next surprised the hell out of me. "Our high-level teams are well-balanced. In both powers and personalities. There might be a space for you on one of them in the future, but I don't want to fuck with their composition right before an op."

"Meaning..." I trailed off, bracing for it.

"I'm putting you with Zero-team. Make preparations, swing by a vendor if you need to, then report to the Ceaseless Knight. You roll out at sunset."

CHAPTER SEVENTY-THREE

Aaron showed me around and told me a little about the history. Apparently, the entire compound was a retired missile silo. After it was decommissioned, it was privately sold and was in the middle of being converted into some tech bro's apocalypse hideaway when the dome permanently halted construction.

That was annoying. The government didn't make a habit of announcing the locations of missile silos, even decommissioned ones. Outside research wouldn't help me. I needed to locate it another way.

There was a simple vendor square in the center of the compound. Judging from the open plan and alcoves with counters, it had once been a cafeteria. I removed my gauntlet before I perused their wares, and as I hoped, their enthusiasm to help me increased by magnitudes.

Kicking it off with consumables, I cleaned out a thrilled mage of his status-effect palliatives. I already had two of each offered on Kinsley's store but figured having three wouldn't hurt, and there were a few cures for ailments I had yet to see. I paused in the weapon section, swiping through a tablet that all the vendors used. Unsurprisingly, they had an excellent selection, which presented something of an opportunity. I'd been biding my time waiting for an upgrade, intending to fully refresh my collection.

I had a slight advantage, in that everyone and their grandmother seemed to migrate toward hand-crossbows. In a demographic where much of the population fetishized firearms and venues that offered concealed carry courses were more numerous than coffee shops, it was the obvious fallback for a handgun. The downside, of course, was that everyone was buying them. I'd been hunting for a while, but the good ones sold out on Kinsley's store in seconds. And one of my primary weapons—**<Quick Crossbow of The Frost Leech>**—was incredibly recognizable both in appearance and effect. I'd primarily used it as Myrddin, making it a non-issue if Aaron had stuck me with anyone other than Nick, but now that he had, I was in the unfortunate position of having to improvise.

"What are you buyin'?"

I glanced up from the tablet's screen, unsure if the out-of-place reference was accidental, or if the man across from me was invoking it intentionally. There was an apron tied around his waist, and beneath them, knee-high muck boots. He was dour and brooding and sounded like he'd spent his last break setting a carton of cigarettes on fire and breathing in the smoke. There was a silver tag pinned to one arm of the apron that read "Erik."

"Small blade and a hand crossbow," I said, then amended, "a few hand crossbows, actually."

"How many?" The man rumbled.

Uh. "Eight? Actually, nine."

He looked at me like I was the scum of the earth. "You a reseller?"

"No, I—" I stopped mid-sentence to reconsider. I hadn't really been able to talk to anyone about this outside of Kinsley, who didn't have the technical know-how to advise me. Barring some huge, unforeseen outcome, I'd be with the Order at least until things came to a head. And while I'd do everything I could to shroud and mislead them on what the Ordinator's core abilities were, they'd eventually learn the brick and mortar of how I fought. And if this was their weapons vendor, a man embedded with killers who knew their craft, he might have a solution for me.

Briefly, without going into too much detail, I outlined my use case.

By the end, the vendor was stroking his beard thoughtfully. "Got half a mind to tear you a new one for treating any of my creations as disposable, but I can grasp why yer goin that route."

Huh. In my mind, vendors got most of their wares from the system. It made sense that some crafters sold their own work. Though from the look of the catalogue, Erik never stopped working.

He gave me another suspicious look. "Before my wheels spin too quick to stop, I should probably ask. What's your budget? You blow it all at bargain bin potions over there?"

"No. I mean, I'm not looking at buying any artifacts, but it's significant." Even now, it felt strange to say that out loud. Like I was lying, even though it was true.

"Kai!" Erik barked suddenly, his voice carrying across the open space of the cafeteria.

The floor next to Erik turned into a circle of magma and a figure ascended from it, dressed in violet mage's robes. Their face and features were effeminate, and there was a sheen of lip gloss that reflected the overhead light.

"Yes, Erik?" They pitched their voice higher than average but read as male. They sounded annoyed.

Erik slapped the mage's ass with a meaty *thwap,* startling us both. He continued, seemingly oblivious to the mage's growing ire. "Skip the theatrics. I found the market for that enchantment of yours."

"*Which* enchantment," Kai asked irritably.

"The uh," Erik made a vague gesture, "soul-glue one."

Kai threw back their head and laughed harshly, then abruptly cut off. "The binding?"

"That one."

Kai crossed their arms. "The one you waited until *after* I was reduced to a puddle of post-coital bliss to tell me was asinine and unnecessary? That I was spending hours of painstaking effort on something no one sane would waste enchantment space on and that I should—" Kai cast an indignant glance at me, "—and I quote, 'grow up.'"

"That... one," Erik said again, considerably less confident.

"I can come back later," I said.

————

Erik apologized profusely. The big man was clearly embarrassed at having his drama dragged out in the open. We talked it over, and he convinced me to wait on the draw-and-drop idea, suggesting a larger commission that would play to my strengths. Claimed he had a prototype in mind that would work perfectly for my "unique situation."

He didn't charge me up front. Said he was confident I'd like the end product, and if I didn't, he was equally confident he could sell it to someone with a similar ability. Either because of his embarrassment or appreciation that I'd weathered the Kai storm with him, the items he pointed me to in the interim were quality.

He placed one on the table. "For the fights you end quickly."

<**Item:** Crossbow of the Wretch>
Description: Black as the heart of the one who wields it. Because of a confluence of enchantments, critical strikes with this weapon are often fatal, so long as the target loses half their health pool in the initial strike.
Item Class: Rare
Item Value: S42,000

My eyes all but bugged out of my head as I lifted it up and tested the feel. It was full-size, but so light it almost felt hollow.

Erik reached behind the counter again and placed a smaller crossbow on the counter. They clearly made it to look intimidating, with jagged white trappings and an off-white body that closely resembled bone. "For the white-knuckle fights. Figure, when you're in close doing the gunslinger thing, this could be your opener."

\<Item: Hand Crossbow of Pathos\>
Description: Despite its class, this weapon does little enhanced damage beyond the bolt it carries. Its true value lies in the enchantments. So long as the bolt remains embedded in the target, they will find themselves overcome with an agony so complete and exquisite it has the potential to drive the target to madness, should the bolt remain in place for too long.
Item Class: Rare
Item Value: S68,000

"Jesus Christ. They did the enchantments on it?" I stuck my thumb at the corner where Kai busied themself with an assortment of shining gems at the desk in the corner.

Kai twisted in their seat and snapped. "I'm a boy!"

"Sorry."

Erik caught my eye and gave a stoic nod, confirming that Kai was not a person I wanted to fuck with in any capacity. "It's a little twisted, but it makes for a hell of a distraction. And as far as the other one goes, I know you said hand crossbow, but figured you'd reconsider once you held it. Can't help you with the daggers, unfortunately. Unless you'd settle for a small sword."

Kai let out an exasperated sigh and stalked toward the counter. He pulled his outer robe aside and drew one of several daggers on his hip. This one was black with a single line of inlaid ivory, spanning the wide hilt to the narrow tip. "Because you have that mark, and you're commissioning something big, I'll give you a loaner."

"What is it?" I asked.

"It's a knife."

I felt the vein pop out on my forehead. "What does it do?"

"Read the system text, I ain't your daddy." Kai walked back to his place before I could make the mistake of biting back.

When I read the description, though, my irritation faded.

\<Item: Vorpal Gnasher\>
Description: This tooth-like blade can easily carve through common natural and metallic armor types, though it loses sharpness quickly. Once

dull, its original sharpness can be regained through both traditional and magical sharpening techniques only a handful of times before it requires re-enchantment from the original source.

Item Class: Epic
Item Value: ???

"Hold on, *how* much is this worth?" I asked.

"Dunno. It's a spare. Never had it appraised—don't lose it," Kai called over.

It was a clever item to lend. While strong and—I suspected—massively valuable, it required maintenance from the original enchanter, meaning no one could run off with it without eventually ending up with a paperweight. But that old familiar feeling of uneasiness washed over me, the same feeling that haunted me every time a person did me an unrequited favor. I dealt and traded favors daily and knew, on an intimate level, that there was always an associated cost.

Perhaps sensing my hesitation, Erik leaned in and lowered his voice so only I could hear. "There's, uh. A lot of swinging dicks around here. Some are just pricks, others like to throw their weight around. Most of 'em have that tattoo on their wrist. It's not that bad, really. Worked in worse places. But... I guess you could say we're looking to expand our network."

Ah. There it was. Show your worth to the up and comer, help him out early before he hits his stride, and bank on the hope he remembers you when you need it. A simple play, but innocent enough.

"I think I understand." I reached out for Erik's hand. He shook it heartily with enough force that it rattled my teeth.

Then I forked over the Selve, trying not to pay attention to the deep dent in my balance. It'd been too long since I'd delved a dungeon. Bothering Kinsley for a softball quest was always an option if the coffers got low, but considering how much expanding she was doing, I wanted to avoid that for as long as possible. With any luck, this outing with Nick and the Order would be both lucrative and illuminating.

"Heh heh heh, thank you," Erik said.

He had to be doing it on purpose.

CHAPTER SEVENTY-FOUR

In an odd reverse of roles, Nick whiteboarded the op while I mostly sat and listened. Not that the plan was perfect, exactly, but we had a familiar cadence when we brainstormed to solve a problem. So, barring any massive oversights, I held my silence while the others threw bristling glares full of barely disguised hostility.

I wasn't particularly worried. Zero-team lived up to their name. Other than Nick, most of them were a few levels shy of level ten, and nothing about their mix of inexperience and conflicting sense of entitlement impressed me. Keith—the mage who'd nearly had his Adam's apple relocated—could barely look at me.

He'd fold like an eight high when the chips were down. If he even made it that far.

It was difficult to understand why the Order bothered with Users of this caliber. They obviously cared about strength and power more than anything else. Yet they assigned a member of the Court to daycare duty. Power structures were always uneven. The exact reason hierarchies exist. No matter how good you are at something, someone is always better. But the dichotomy between these Users and Cameron—who they'd willingly thrown away—was significant.

The plan itself was quiet. Discrete. Several teams were deploying at the tower in Region 5. The other, more-experienced teams would start higher up. We'd be working our way up the lower levels, clearing the main path. But the real meat and potatoes were the ripples. Nick described them as tiny fractures within the dungeon, small undeveloped sections heavy with magic. They were hidden, but easy enough to identify if you knew how to look. And while they loosely followed the same basic

logic as the tower itself—increasing in difficulty the higher we climbed—
the chances of an aberration, loot and monsters inappropriate to the
levels, increased.

Our target within the ripples were planners. Tiny, near-transparent
entities that shifted form, only identifiable by a pale-white glow, apparently tasked with construction and maintenance on the chambers within
the tower. Nick had a dimensional satchel that could store, in his words, a
"Fuck-ton" of them.

Considering that they repaired damage to the chambers and regenerating monsters, I had a strong suspicion about what Hastur wanted
them for.

For an Order of Parcae operation, it was oddly tame. They didn't
schedule us to kill Users or rip-off someone's inventory. There wasn't
even a kidnapping to speak of. Perhaps because it was also Zero-team's
first official mission.

"Hold up." Nick stared toward the doorway, then back to the small
group, lounging on a series of stools and leather fold-out chairs. "Give me
a second. Review your notes—especially if you're on the four-man. If
you're not, don't distract the people who are. The game starts here,
people." He pointed to his head and walked toward the door.

A small burble of hushed conversation began as Nick walked away,
reminding me of countless classrooms when the teacher was absent.

I ignored them. There was a man of average height waiting by the
door for Nick, but in Nick's presence, he looked completely diminutive. It
wasn't just the contrast. He was almost cowering. His long auburn hair
was glued to his face like he'd just gotten out of the shower, and he made
futile-looking gestures. When he looked back toward me, his expression
seemed to crack, desperation growing by the second.

Holy shit.

It was the guy with the crossbow in the tunnel. The guy who killed
Jinny. And Nick was just there, talking to him. There was nothing in his
body language that reflected he knew who the fuck this guy was.

Crossbow guy said something heated.

Nick offered a lazy stretch.

It was like they were having two different conversations. Only when
he stretched behind his back, his hand clamped down on his arm hard
enough to imprint the flesh—

Someone tapped me. Keith had apparently taken the intermission as
an opportunity to move closer. I dismissed him as a threat almost immediately. There were entire beads of sweat dripping down his forehead in a
stream.

"Hey, man," he said.

Hey man?

"Can I help you?"

"Look... uh. I'm bad with conflict. Terrible, actually. So this is really hard for me." Keith trailed off.

I smiled at him. "I can bring my dog out. If you need an emotional support animal."

"No no. No. Not trying to be rude—would love to meet your dog sometime." Keith laughed and rubbed his neck. "But uh, more of a cat person myself."

"Pity." I was tempted to take it further, but Keith already looked ready to jump out of his skin. Any more and he was likely to go screaming and running out the door. I let my attention lapse and returned to the diagram on the whiteboard. "What do you want?"

"I don't want anything, necessarily." Keith pushed his glasses up his nose. "But since we're going to be on a team together and all, I just wanna check. I do anything to offend you?"

I cocked my head. "Other than attacking me on sight?"

"Yeah. *Awkward,* sorry about that." Keith struggled to continue, like he was wringing the words from stone. "But, like, I wasn't the only one."

"That's true."

"And uh, they got off kind of easy. Where I got the sense that we were a few complex analogue inputs away from a *Mortal Kombat* finisher." His hand went subconsciously to his throat. "Yeah," Keith said, in a voice that almost sounded disappointed with himself. "I just—I wanna know, are we cool? I didn't do something to you, or piss you off somehow more than the others during the fight? Because if I did, I'm—"

"You always talk this much?" I asked.

"He does," Halima said. She stared straight ahead at the corner of the room. Only her head was visible. The rest of her was submerged in a tub of ice on the floor, wedged between two stools. I'd heard of athletes doing something similar. One hell of a pre-game ritual.

In the short time we'd spoken, I'd already gleaned everything from Keith I needed. First, he was a punching bag. Had been for a long time, probably before the dome. He was scared of the team, scared of the man at the door, and, unsurprisingly, scared of me. Nick might be the only person in the base he wasn't scared of. And like any well-worn punching bag, he already knew this sort of approach wouldn't work—anyone dead set on fucking your shit up is unlikely to change their mind if you ask them nicely. But defusing the tension between us wasn't the point. He was testing the waters. Checking to see if I was holding a grudge and if he'd needed to watch out for me in the mission.

I sighed. Offering Keith a little reassurance wouldn't hurt, if it meant he stayed focused on the mission. "They were about to rush me. If our noble Ceaseless Knight hadn't interfered, they would have. I just needed to give them a reason to think twice."

Keith's mouth quirked. "So... it wasn't personal?"

"Yup."

"Thanks, man." he said, oddly elated, then bumped my arm with his fist. "Oh god. Why did I do that—"

"Get your head in the game," I snapped. "We're deploying soon."

"Right." Keith focused on the whiteboard so intently, it looked as if his eyes might pop out.

"Myrddin has the right idea." Nick returned, pointing at me with the dry erase marker.

"What was that about?" I asked, tilting my head toward the door. The bowman was gone.

Nick waved me off. "A family thing. Don't worry about it. Now that the rest of you have had time to ruminate...." he uncapped the marker. "Let's go over this one more time."

CHAPTER SEVENTY-FIVE

Sybil—the woman I previously referred to as Seer—saw us off. The exits were toward the top of the silo in a large cubic room that was littered with narrow stairways that led to various ovals lining the walls, framed by stone. The oval openings contained what looked like a whirlpool of glowing liquid, all draining toward the center from the edges.

There were hundreds of them. Maybe a thousand.

I hung back and studied the scene. Most of the oval portals were slate blue, but several—in rows high above the floor with no access point from the stairs—shone in green, orange. And a single red portal, positioned at the top in the center.

I asked the obvious question. "What are they?"

Nick looked ready to answer, but Sybil beat him to it. Only her mouth moved, the rest of her body frozen in an almost statuesque poise. "The indigo thresholds lead to various locations within the human domain. Only a portion are secured—though their number grows by the day."

That explained a hell of a lot. It explained how the Order remained so elusive. Kinsley's door spell on a grand scale. Even the color reminded me of Kinsley's door. Which led to my next question.

"Did they stay active during the Transposition?" I asked.

Nick tensed. Both Halima and Keith cast concerned glances my way. I couldn't tell if they were uncomfortable with the line of questioning, or that I was interrogating Sybil.

Sybil herself seemed unbothered. "Most of them, yes."

Another unfair advantage. And 'most.' What portals were restricted?

I cleared my throat. "The rest of them—the ones that aren't blue. I'm guessing they lead to Flauros realms?

Nick subtly drove an elbow into my side.

"Shut up," he whispered.

So it wasn't *what* I asked that was making my companions uncomfortable. It was the fact that I was questioning Sybil at all. Which was odd. She didn't seem all that intimidating from my initial impression, and so far, she'd done little other than speak in riddles and act as Hastur's mouthpiece.

Sybil's dreamy expression remained fixed in place. "I cannot answer that question at this time. If you wish to know more, *Ordinator*, come find me on your own."

Fucking Sybil. This marked the second time she'd screwed me.

Keith and Halima both stepped away from me. Keith looked visibly horrified, while Halima maintained a stoic expression, hand reaching toward her rayon-wrapped hilt.

Nick snapped his fingers twice, rounding on Keith and Halima. "Hey! Guys. Myrddin took the oath. Which means?"

"He's... with us," Keith said.

"That's right," Nick said. "What he did? Whoever he was before? None of that matters. The big guy swore him in. If there was a problem, he never would have made it this far."

"Got it," Keith said unhappily.

Halima didn't answer, but her hand dropped away from her hilt.

I considered Nick. Once again, his charisma shined through. But he was too quick on the draw with the intercession. Like it was rehearsed. Someone had already briefed him on who I was—probably Aaron after our initial encounter—and he'd prepared accordingly. I was starting to understand why everyone was so terrified of Sybil. The woman knew things, secrets, and she didn't hesitate to air them out, regardless of who was listening. It didn't feel malicious exactly. More like she didn't see the value of keeping anything on the down low.

No wonder they were cautious around her.

"Is that all, Ordinator?" Sybil asked. The light trace of sarcasm in her voice was probably my imagination.

"I'll find you later," I said.

"Yes, you will."

Nick laughed nervously. "Alrighty. Don't want to take up too much of your time, ma'am. Let's get this show on the road."

Sybil held her arms out to either side. An indigo portal from one of the center bands levitated downward, settling on the ground with a low thrum that vibrated the stone beneath us. A series of atonal chimes followed, and a small portion of the flowing blue liquid within the portal leaked into a rut that encircled the entrance. "The way is unsealed. You may proceed."

Nick nodded. "Halima, Keith, go ahead and secure the perimeter."

Visibly relieved at the prompt, they both hurried ahead. There was a popping noise as they entered the portal, air rushing in to fill the space they vacated as they snapped out of existence.

I waited for Nick to ask what he wanted to ask. He wasn't a lead-from-the-rear sort of guy. If he sent the others ahead, it was for a reason.

Something weighed down on me, like an invisible hand trying to press me into the ground. I grunted and went down to one knee, heart rate spiking, fumbling under the pressure to draw my knife from my inventory. My fingers locked around the handle and I drew it out, keeping the blade hidden behind my back.

Nick stared down at me. A red light shone behind his eyes, his aw-shucks persona entirely gone. He looked cold, and numb, and angry. "This is an official query, under the authority of the Court."

"You're... an official... prick."

"Glad you've held onto a sense of humor." Nick loomed over me. "Region 6."

"That's not a question." I glanced over at Sybil, checking if she intended to interfere. From the amused look on her face, she looked more likely to grab a bucket of popcorn and settle in for the show.

"Not funny, asshole," Nick seethed. "Thousands of people died. All I want to know is if you pulled the plug yourself."

I considered lying. But what was the point? Sybil probably already knew the answer. And if any fragment of Nick's traditionally staunch sense of right and wrong was intact, no matter how twisted, I was pretty certain how he'd come down on wholesale slaughter.

"Maybe." The word popped out of my mouth before I could stop it.

"What the fuck does that mean?" Nick growled.

"It means I don't *fucking know*," I shouted, then regained control of myself. "Something already altered them before I got there. Blood, guts, organs spread out everywhere like some sick painting. There were clothes and cores littering the street. They should have all been dead, but they weren't. They were... still moving. Still alive—reanimated, maybe in some fucked-up capacity. And they were trying to move Lux and cores into their receptacle."

"Why?" Nick asked, mystified.

"That's the great part," I said bitterly. "I stopped them and still don't know. No clue what would have happened if they filled the receptacle. Maybe they would have been fine once it was full. Gathered around a bonfire and sang kumbaya. Or maybe what happened to them would have spread like a fucking wildfire."

Sybil chuckled. It was quiet, almost imperceptible. But I hated her for it.

Something in Nick's posture changed. The sickly red fire behind his eyes burned out. For a moment, he looked like nothing more than the lost kid I ran into in the rehab center. Scared, and confused, and tired. "Not sure I could have made that call."

"Yeah, well, now you know." I stood to my feet

"You, uh—you're not what I thought."

I strode toward the portal. The sooner we got into the tower, the better. I needed to punch something. "Just do me a favor and keep the truth to yourself."

Nick stirred from his reverie. "What, why?"

"Getting blamed for it, regardless. Might as well bank the infamy."

"You... want people to think you're a cold-blooded murderer?" he asked.

Frustrated, I made a spastic gesture, indicating the grim portal room and the silo beyond. "Where the *fuck* do you think we are?"

Nick absorbed this and followed me toward the portal, deep in thought. Out of the corner of my eye, I saw Sybil gently catch his shoulder and lean in to whisper. Turns out, she did know how to be discreet. I lost most of what she said in the portal's hum. It was a struggle to pick out the last few words.

"...cast off the chains that bind you."

CHAPTER SEVENTY-SIX

Kid Rock's muffled, highly processed voice screamed pseudo-rap into my ear. Which led me to the next inevitable question.

What fucking year was it?

With Kinsley's door, there was a sense of movement. Moving from one room to the next. It didn't matter that the rooms were far apart, because you still felt that transition, that forward momentum carrying you from point A to point B.

Traveling through the portal, on the other hand, was disorienting, verging on disturbing. There was no sense of passage. One moment, you were walking into the portal. The next, you were standing still, staring into the yellow-stained porcelain abyss of a broken commode. It felt like blacking out. Losing time.

My thoughts were jumbled, disorderly. I had a hard time remembering what I was doing and why I was here. I couldn't stop thinking about what would have happened if there was someone in the bathroom occupying the same space I just appeared in.

Maybe that's why they sent you to the broken stall, genius.

Oh good. <Jaded Eye> was talking to me again. At least Nick didn't—

I scrambled out of the stall, nearly tripping over my own feet until the open arm of a yellowing, cracked baby changer saved me. I needed to get out of the way before Nick appeared in the same place.

Jesus, I really needed to ask someone if telefragging was a thing.

Carefully, trying to mentally and physically reset, I threw the door open and walked out. The muffled bass grew sharper, but only just, and the scent of mildew, vomit, and liquor washed over me. There was a small bar housing only a dozen stools, with several booths along the lefthand side. At least five heavy-set men in a varying selection of baseball and cowboy hats turned my way. A sixth sat next to the jukebox, fiddling with a handful of quarters. Their suspicious gazes lingered on me for a moment too long, then turned away, settling on where Keith and Halima sat at the bar.

They looked old enough to join the army, but a bit too young to drink. Keith was clutching his wand beneath the bar, his knee bouncing up and down. Halima looked etched from stone.

Nick exited a moment later, nodded toward the door. Keith jumped off the stool immediately and followed him, Halima falling in behind them while I took up the rear.

A notification prompt popped open.

<Guild Quest Received>
Quest: Ancient Blueprint
Initial Objective: Gain entrance to the Gilded Tower.
Primary Objective — Acquire at least twenty planners from ripples on the lower tower floors.
Secondary Objective — Acquire as many planners as possible.
Tertiary Objective — Avoid direct conflict in the tower and keep a low profile.
Threat Level: ???
EXP GAIN (M)
Time Limit: One Day
Reward: Selve, Hastur's Favor, Market Credit (Variable.)

Fuck. What to do? We couldn't fail this mission. Without knowing exactly what Hastur wanted the planners for, it would look bad and draw attention I didn't want. At the very least, we needed the minimal amount. But I didn't like the way the secondary objective was worded. More problematic, there were other teams from the order in play. I didn't know if they were looking for the same thing, or something more critical.

I needed to create problems for the Order on a large scale that didn't immediately point to me, while succeeding in my mission, without succeeding *too* much.

Sometimes, I missed the scantron days.

We pushed open the doors out into the street. Miraculously, it was even louder outside the bar. I'd thought, given the theme park aesthetic, that the party-land bustle of Region 5 would die down some after dark.

Not so much. They just doubled down on the torches.

It had a sweatier, hammering feeling beneath the moon. More like a nightclub than a theme park. Masses of bodies, dancing to a drum-heavy beat. A woman in glowing neon body paint and peacock regalia—an outfit that narrowly dodged blatant cultural appropriation, only by appropriating literally everything into an unrecognizable amalgam— paused as she passed by us, offering a tray furnished with colorful asymmetrical bottles complete with curly straws.

Spiked with 151. Casino tactics. Avoid.

I smacked Keith's hand away and smiled at the woman. "We're fine."

"You're in El Dorado, darlings. Live a little." She pulled an eight ball from her corset and wiggled it in front of my face. The substance within was powdery and clay red. I waited for **\<Jaded Eye's\>** commentary.

Not a damn clue.

I took the bag from her—partially because I was curious, partially because I wanted her to leave without drawing more attention to us. I must have looked confused, because, as a helping hint, she tapped her nostril and winked before she sashayed away.

We took our place in the long queue to the front of the tower. It seemed even taller now than it had the evening I'd scouted the region with Miles, at least as tall as the Bank of America Plaza had been before the meteor reduced it to a smoking ruin. The question was whether it was an optical illusion, or if the tower was actually growing.

I tapped my toe inside my boot, searching for an angle, coming up dry.

Nick elbowed me. "So, uh. You in the habit of taking illicit substances from strangers?"

"Relax, Boy Scout." I scoffed and tossed him the eight ball. He caught it easily, squinting at the bag. "You ever see anything this color?"

"Saw some designer shit once that was bright green. But nothing quite like this," Nick said.

"It looks like strawberry pixie stick," Halima commented, completely seriously. She was standing on her tiptoes, trying to get a better look at the bag.

"You don't snort those," Keith said. He was still pouting, probably because I'd stopped him from taking the drink.

"Were you homeschooled?" Halima asked Keith.

"Seems kind of small time to me. Some girl slipped you a dime bag at a rager. Big whoop," Nick said.

"She's not some girl. She's staff. And I've seen them pass out at least thirty of those bags since. Considering how they're spiking their drinks with rum running around seventy-five percent ABV, I'm curious what exactly they're pairing it with," I said. Probably an upper—any depressant in combination with the rum was likely to zonk out a person with average tolerance—but considering how **\<Jaded Eye\>** didn't trigger, I was guessing it was system related.

Nick raised an eyebrow. "You got a pedigree to go with that bloodhound nose?"

"I'm a fucking sommelier. What's it matter?"

Keith cleared his throat. "I thought sommeliers were wine experts."

I rolled my eyes. "Maybe it's nothing. Maybe it's cocaine stepped on with cayenne. Either way, I want to know where they're getting this shit and how they can afford to give so much of it away."

Nick finally shrugged. "Fair enough. Not sure I see the value, but I'm kind of slow. It's important we stay ahead of the game. More than a few people back at HQ you could pass that off to. Some of 'em might even give you a straight answer. A few might even give it back." Nick passed the baggy back to me and I stuck it in my inventory

Keith looked puzzled. "Is there a liquor version of a sommelier?"

"Why do you always look at me when you have a vocabulary question?" Halima sighed.

I was about to say something pithy about a bartender when a familiar face caught my eye. A man in a Hawaiian shirt was leaning on a pillar next to an old school vendor's cart, biting into a churro.

Immediately, I turned my back to him, my heart pounding.

Cook. Shit.

I snuck another glance over my shoulder. The Fed looked more or less recovered from our altercation, almost bored as he stared out into the crowd, nibbling on the churro with the slow, constant pace of a marathon runner.

Of course Miles had stationed a lookout here. We scouted out the tower recently, and I ran my fucking mouth about how they were looking for something. I told myself it was fine. That Cook was focused on the exit. I'd need to be careful when we made our way out, but he hadn't been exposed to the mask for an extended period. As long as I was cautious and there wasn't a shift change, I'd be fine.

But what if I wasn't?

It all hit me at once. A thousand half-finished thoughts and ideas slid into place, a plan to stick the Feds so far up the Order's ass they wouldn't know what hit them. Simultaneously, a way to create a future exit plan for Nick.

I had a narrow window, but it was there. Couldn't risk it in a public space, with so many people to notice.

\<Matt: Kinsley, are you busy?\>

Several dozen messages arrived, one after another, each berating me for not reaching out sooner or bringing me up to speed. Apparently, Cameron was awake and pissed. He'd tried to muscle his way out and had to be gassed. Kinsley wasn't taking any chances with the containment.

Not long after, Miles came looking for me and she'd fed him a line. According to her, he probably bought it. Probably.

The latter brought up a pain point I still didn't know how to deal with yet. While the three-way altercation between the Ordinator, his unidentified companion, and the Feds had bought me time, Miles was going to get suspicious, eventually. If I could use Azure from a distance—find some sort of mana battery that would let him keep his form for an extended period separate from me—that would more or less solve the problem.

But I'd relay that later. I had something more incendiary in mind.

<**Matt:** I'm selling you a few things in the store. One's low priority. Some chemical compound they're giving out as a party favors in Region 5. The other is a potion. I need an alchemist to evaluate both. Do we have a good alchemist yet?>
<**Kinsley:** Why yes, chronically missing region leader and guild member. We do, in fact, have a master alchemist. Locked down at significant cost by yours truly. In your absence. While you've been gone. Away. Leaving a small child to do your heavy lifting.>

I made a mental note to get that story from her later. I couldn't imagine someone getting that far into a vocation so early in the game, unless they had some sort of specialized background that translated.

<**Matt:** Good. This is the critical part. From my understanding, the potion is priceless. To the extent that any rational person would consider running off and selling it.>
<**Kinsley:** Ooooooh. What does it do?>
<**Matt:** Why do you think I need an alchemist to evaluate it?>
<**Kinsley:** >:(>
<**Matt:** Just assume it's a nuke, or the philosopher's stone.>
<**Kinsley:** ... Okay then. I'm just gonna set up a nice, very well guarded lab in another region.>
<**Matt:** Probably a good idea. One last thing. I need you to forward a message to Miles.>
<**Kinsley:** Sure.>
<**Matt:** From Myrddin.>
<**Kinsley:** WHAT>

I was banking a lot on faith. That Hastur would wait, hoping I would come around despite the disruption. He seemed desperate. And it took far longer than usual for desperate people to cut and run. I could only hope it was the same for gods.

In the meantime, I played the role the Overseer created for me. I crafted the message as quickly as I could, checked it three times, then sent it off. It was like writing an essay. An utterly psychopathic, problematic essay, but when you broke them down to their parts, all essays are the same.

Without missing a beat, I turned to Nick. "Not trying to step on your toes here, but wouldn't it be better if we split up a bit?"

Nick's eyebrows narrowed. "Never split the party—"

"I'm just talking initially. We enter separately, meet back up in whatever this gilded erection has for a lobby, split back up on the exit."

Nick considered that, then nodded. "Smart. Better for optics. Never know who could be watching. Gonna go up front, keep the kids in the middle. You good to take up the rear?"

"Done." I slid back through the line, ending up behind a couple of tough guys who sneered at me when I flagged down a shirtless man in a kilt for one of the festive-looking drinks on his tray. It gave me an excuse to move backward in the line, and to be honest, I kind of enjoyed the potential visual it created.

Then I waited. If Miles was as smart as I thought, he'd figure it out with time to spare.

Twenty minutes later, just as I reached the front of the line, Cook's head snapped up. He dropped the stub of his churro and took several steps forward, brow furrowed as he searched the sea faces with more intensity than before.

Eventually, his gaze landed on me.

I took a tiny suck from the looping straw and flipped him the bird.

CHAPTER SEVENTY-SEVEN

Dearest Kinsley,

I go on to prepare a place for you. Even now, I ascend to find that which you deserve. Along my ascent I found others like me, of which there are many. We are of one mind and soul. We toil and squall and fuck in the fetid mud, while the elites and gods cavort in the skies above, gorging on the fruits of our labors.

Have you enjoyed the clouds, Kinsley? I certainly hope you have, before your wings are clipped.

Now that my anger has passed, I don't blame you for what you did. It was always this way. Society wants to believe it can identify evil people, or bad or harmful people, but it's not practical.

But I cannot look past your hubris. For I am a man of passion. At the orphanage they put me in just before Bush Senior's first term, there were some older boys who caught a horse in a barren field, trapped against the cliff face of a steep mountain. They put kerosene on his tail and lit it and cut the rope. Away went the horse, bombing up the unscalable mountain, stumbling, climbing ever higher to get away from the flame. But the flame went with him. That horse, that's me. The man of passion.

And you set the fire.

I'll continue to climb, kindling this eternal flame you set. For I have found god, and god has found me. I'll search the mountain for the cracks between places, mine the hidden veins of precious metals that exist within the annals of Etemenanki. And I will forge those metals into a sacrificial knife. I'll prepare an altar for you in the shape of an ennea-gram, with an empty shell arranged at each point. After all, a clown can get away with simple murder. I have something more sophisticated in mind.

With love,

Myrddin.

It was the best I could do on short notice. There were a few misdirects that led nowhere: I'd picked an enneagram both because it was less cliche than a pentagram, and if Miles bit and swallowed, it would lead him to the Enneagram personality types, and an assumption that each point of the Enneagram represented the sort of person I intended to kill: The Achiever, the Challenger, and the Investigator would stand out like a sore thumb.

I avoided using my own written voice as much as possible, just because Miles was exactly the sort of motherfucker willing to hunt down old essays and homework once he had a writing sample, so I was cribbing from a combination of Dahmer, Gacy, Bundy, and Fish, paraphrasing at points, referencing indirectly at others, with some conflicting socialist and fascist undertones thrown in to further muddle the message. Along with making the message sound suitably menacing, the references would serve as a dog whistle for Miles. He'd realize I was taunting him—and with any luck, assume I'd accidentally tipped my hand with all the refer-ences to verticality.

It worked. Cook was shoving his way through the crowd, trying to get to me. He circumvented the line, and several region affiliated Users stopped him. He pointed at me, then pulled out his badge and tried to shove past. There was still a mark on his throat from the garrote.

A few of the region Users looked in my direction, but none of them saw me.

I smiled widely, all teeth, and drew my thumb across my neck. Shortly after, someone escorted me through the massive gates.

———

The scent caught me first. Funnel cake, fatty meat, and popcorn hung in the air like olfactory ghosts of a dying past. I went past the small assort-ment of vendors that could have been at home in any festival. At the front, there was a counter that looked a bit like a carnival ticket booth, only instead of small trinkets and plastic prizes no one remembered more than a day, there was a series of swords, axes, and wands. They weren't in the best shape. The top-shelf merchandise was top shelf only in the sense that they were mostly free of nicks and dents. Otherwise, they were basic in their designs and absent the sheen and clarity of good metal.

It was difficult to breathe. Visitors overran the tower, capacity nearly bursting. I spotted Nick. He was standing next to a facsimile of a small medieval village, complete with AstroTurf, speaking to a diminutive-looking man, nodding enthusiastically as the man took "spoke with his hands" to entirely new levels, while Keith and Halima stood off to the side, looking terribly bored.

The peasant reached out to me with an overwrought gesture. "Good ser, are you the last hero?"

Whoever he was, he'd caught me completely flat-footed. "Um... what?"

"He's with us," Nick said.

The peasant raised his hands upward, in one of the most hackneyed portrayals of supplication I'd ever seen. "Praise be to Elphion! The quartet of heroes has formed in the meteor's passing and the ancient prophecy is fulfilled."

Keith cringed, probably too polite to groan out loud. Nick seemed happy to let the whole thing play out. The massive turkey leg he idly nibbled on hemorrhaged grease from its inadequately swaddled backend, directly onto the AstroTurf.

Maybe if none of us said anything, the "peasant" would cut to the chase.

"Do you have a quest—" Nick started.

"A prophecy foretold our arrival?" Halima asked.

I was briefly tempted to throttle her.

"Oh yes." The peasant nodded vigorously, clearly excited at the opportunity to delve into the lore and extend his performance. "Many moons ago, a traveling tinker passed through. He foretold the rise of the tower and the many treasures laid within. He also divined the rise of the four heroes who would climb the tower and unearth the mystery within."

"—three heroes who would climb the tower and unearth the mystery within," someone echoed. Another peasant, a few huts down, repeating the same lines to what looked to be a User couple that had brought along a third wheel. Which meant our current peasant wasn't improvising. Someone wrote this god-awful script.

The man's arm looped through the woman's. I recognized him as one of the pug-faced goons from Sunny's office. But what really caught me off

guard was the woman herself. I knew her immediately, her face permanently etched in my memory since the tunnel.

She was the tail I'd missed. The woman who unloaded the Escalade
with a child in tow and showed up after the trial. Behind them, another,
taller man stood. He was wearing a high ponytail wrapped in leather, his
face a mask of snark.

Gotta be one of the high-level teams.

I was still in the back of the group. The peasant was so focused on
Halima I could probably move freely. I took a step backward, letting the
bustling crowd sweep me toward the second group.

I focused hard, **<Awareness>** filtering the external chatter to a minimum, trying to zone into the conversation.

The woman fiddled with her wallet, retrieving a small golden card
with a dark vortex on the front. Her dark-blue acrylic nails glittered in the
mess of high spotlights.

"You already have the Praetor's Assurance." Their peasant tried to
whistle, but the sound he made was more like wind whipping through a
cave.

"We'd like to fast-pass to the twenty-eighth floor," Acrylics said. She
was the only one looking at the peasant. Pug-face and Ponytail were scanning the room in that laid-back, deceptively casual way that only came
with experience.

Their peasant laughed nervously. "And the Praetor's Assurance allows
you full entry to any floor under thirty. But fair warning, brave heroes.
Past the twentieth floor, the tower grows exceedingly dangerous." He
cupped his mouth and stage whispered, "Floor twenty-eight is no exception. There's talk of vampires afoot."

"Do we look concerned?" Ponytail sneered.

The peasant blinked. "Fair enough." He pointed toward the center of
the room, a mass of people crowded around them. Bright beams of light
illuminated the lifts. Whether they were artificial or actual magic was
impossible to say. "Your writ of assurance provides you with two free
snack items and a discount at the smithery, if you lack silver weapons.
Once you're prepared to embark, head that direction. A tracker will show
you the way."

They all turned at once, walking toward the lifts with purpose. I kept
my head down. Once the high-level team was clear, I scanned the crowd. I
had a minute, maybe less, before my companions noticed my absence.

Need to do this quickly.

I saw my mark. A man wobbling in adventurer's leathers, double-
fisting a pair of blended drinks. My goal was nestled between the index
and second finger of his left hand—a golden-and-black card, exactly the
same as the one Acrylics used to cut the line. I weaved through the crowd,

keeping my focus past the man, and toggled the Ordinator's mask to full coverage.

I ran into him at a brisk walk.

The moment we collided, I used the distraction of the impact to pluck the card out of hand, covering it by making a show of trying to stabilize his drinks.

"What the—" he started.

"My bad. Didn't see you." I slid the card up my sleeve and stepped away.

"No shi... no shit you didn' see me." The man stared at a wet section on his chest with the sort of clouded, confused contempt only a drunk person can manage. I beat a quick retreat toward my group at a brisk walk.

A few seconds later, long after I'd safely disappeared into the crowd, I heard him exclaim. "Where—where the hell'd my PayPal assurance go?"

I still wasn't done. I needed to make sure the card worked and wasn't tied to the User's name. All the vendors had a long line except for one. A guy off to the side who was, strangely, one of the few employees in normal clothes.

"Pink or blue," the man asked, wiping his hands on his apron.

"I don't care."

"Twenty Selve."

Jesus. This really was a theme park. I flashed him the card.

He took the card and marked it with what looked like a piece of gray chalk, leaving a single check mark in the upper-left corner, then reached into the tree of multicolored poofs, handing me a bundle of pink cotton candy and returning the card. "Enjoy your stay in the Gilded Tower."

Good enough. I couldn't know definitively that they didn't have additional security measures in place when you use the card to skip floors, but the interaction at least supported the possibility that they had nothing sophisticated in place.

I toggled the **<Allfather's Mask>** back to the default setting.

The peasant was still talking when I slid back into place beside Nick. "... and so the third age came to pass..."

Nick took one look at me, eyes trailing toward the pink cotton candy in my hand until he looked away, one hand pressed to his mouth, his shoulders shaking.

"What?"

He shook his head, steeling his face. "Nothing at all."

Perhaps—finally—sensing he was losing us, the peasant finally directed us to the lifts. We'd be starting on the second floor. I watched the priority lifts out of the corner of my eye, watching to see how the card process worked. If anything, it was less stringent than the cotton-candy vendor had been. They didn't even bother marking the cards, just glanced at them and ushered the holders onto the priority lift.

A violet message notification lit up in the corner of my vision. I focused on it until it expanded.

Miles.

CHAPTER SEVENTY-EIGHT

<**Miles:** Wasn't sure about the message, but the way you just played that little clusterfuck outside was obvious bait. You clearly wanted me here. I'm here. What now?>

He was probably still outside, making his way through the line.

What now, indeed.

Until I spotted the other Parcae team, the only point of bringing him into this was to draw attention to the tower itself, make things difficult for Aaron, and by extension, Hastur. Hastur had said nothing about the tower, meaning cleaning house was more important to him than whatever the plan was here. Spotting the high-level team and learning their destination presented a rare opportunity.

With Pug-face on the roster, the team was probably Sunny's. Which sent something of a mixed message, but I still wasn't willing to let the opportunity slide.

All I had to do was get Miles snooping around the twenty-eighth floor. He'd gotten here quickly, but there was no way he came unprepared. If it was anyone but Miles, I would have hesitated. I was about to lure him into a trap. The trap wasn't for him, exactly, but it could spring back on him just as easily. But Miles wasn't an idiot. And I got the feeling, seeing him work, that he learned from his mistakes. No matter how rushed he seemed, he'd be fully prepared this time. Best part was, I could be certain neither side would tell the other fuck-all.

<**Myrddin:** Figured I'd do you a favor, since you were nice enough to let

me go after the Transposition. I'll be around floor twenty-eight, waiting
for you.>
<**Miles:** Sorry to burst your bubble, but if you think I'm coming in there
on your terms, you're out of your goddamn mind.>
<**Myrddin:** Sure, you could put people on the exit. Stake me out. But I'm
gonna be honest, your people don't seem that observant, Miles. That's
what, twice now that the idiot in the Hawaiian shirt's fucked the dog?>
<**Miles:** It doesn't have to be like this. No matter how bad things got at
the apartments, I still want to hear your side.>
<**Myrddin:** Let me ask something. Have you had any luck finding me,
since our little altercation? Nailed down any solid leads?>

Miles didn't respond, which spoke for itself.

<**Myrddin:** Then let me state this plainly. After today, I'm about to get
busy on a grand scale. This is your one chance to stop me before that
happens.>

Again, Miles didn't respond. This time, it felt like a minor misplay on
my part. Guys like Miles were used to existential threats. They trained
them to be comfortable with the big scary shit and kind of pressure that
could paralyze the average person, so long as it was abstract. Needed to
make it personal. Break his composure, somehow.
But did I really want to go there?
No choice.

<**Myrddin:** Why didn't you go in, Miles?>
<**Miles:** Because I wasn't born yesterday.>
<**Myrddin:** Not the tower. That I understand. You're a coward, passing
himself off as a hero. I meant, why didn't you go into the house after
Hawkins invited you inside?>

Nothing.

<**Myrddin:** It's a decent place. Suburbs. Edge of the dome. Away from all
the chaos. You would have had a good time. She seems like a peach.>
<**Miles:** Say that to my fucking face, you motherfucker.>

There it was. Hawkins really was the chink in his armor.

<**Myrddin:** Come here and I will. Or don't. Whatever happens next,
though? That's entirely on you.>

I closed the window, even as a cascade of messages came in and the notification light rapidly blinked. No matter how much I'd just pissed him off, Miles was just as manipulative as me, and I didn't trust myself to not get baited into a response.

Miles was biblically pissed. That was both a good and bad thing. My method of provoking him was crass, and it wasn't subtle. But that was fine. I had no intention of meeting him on the upper floor. And if it pissed Miles off enough—which I suspected it had—the Adventurers' Guild, along with whoever else Miles could scrounge up, would trawl around the tower en masse.

It'd take him a while to get into the tower and buy a pass. Once he arrived at the twenty-eighth floor and found it cleared out and empty, he'd backtrack. Reread the message I sent to Kinsley. Eventually he'd figure it out. And there was absolutely no way he'd be bringing any less than the largest group allowed. A full team of five.

His people would catch the high-level team with their hands in the cookie jar and either wipe them out, force a retreat, or capture them.

In terms of the overall goal, it accomplished little more than putting the Order on Miles' radar. But every avalanche started small. As we moved toward the front of the line, I took several deep breaths, trying to steady myself and lower my heart rate.

I caught Nick staring a hole into the back of Keith's head. I elbowed him. "Zoning out?"

Nick jumped, a flash of guilt playing across his features before he settled back into an amiable smile, somehow less authentic than before. "Just... soaking in the ambience. You know what this place reminds me of?"

Wizard Quest.

"Medieval times?"

"Nah, man." Nick looked around as the peasant droned on. "Well, sort of. But no. Couple years ago I was chilling in the Midwest over the summer, hanging with this girl I met at an away game. The entire visit— literal weeks—she kept saying 'We've got to go to Wizard Quest.' And I'm like, 'Do we have to leave the bedroom to get there?' But she's insistent. Like it's this Wisconsin Mecca or something. Anyway, she's obviously excited about it, and I figure, even if it's lame, it'll probably make for a good story."

"Was it lame?" I asked, knowing the answer.

Nick's eyes unfocused, his smile slipping. "Took like two hours to get there, so the drive kinda tapped me out, wasn't in the best mood. We uh, we checked into the hotel. I wanted to linger a bit, settle, but she pushed me out the door. Didn't help that they charged extra to rent tablets that looked like they came out of a Best Buy bargain bin, running a mobile game from 2010."

"So far it sounds lame."

"But then I got inside. And it was a total maze. I found out later it was huge, like half the size of a football stadium. Way bigger than it looked on the outside. There were all these hidden doors, and secret passageways, and mysteries, in the middle of all this art and like, hand-carved statues and miniatures. They had a shire, and like a unicorn sky thing..."

"Volcano biome?" I prompted.

Nick punched me in the shoulder. "Hell yeah, he gets it. The volcano biome was sick. There was this small open-holed mountain there up on a platform, and I'm just staring at it, like 'Is it going to erupt?' Then this grandma in a Slytherin robe hops up on the platform, walks to the top of the mountain, and drops in, like it's nothing. Anyway, bullshit black-light room that took all our 'lives' aside, it really was the best. Made me feel like a kid again. And when our time was up, I didn't want to leave."

It differed from the first time he'd told me the story, back when he still needed two horizontal support poles to stay upright and struggled, sweating and crying, fighting for every inch of distance. A few details had changed, but more than anything else, it felt melancholy. Almost painful. What was happening to him? Was he just tired and nostalgic? Or was there something else going on beneath the surface?

I tried to encourage him. "Dome's not gonna last forever. Maybe when it's gone, you can take a road trip. See it again."

"... Nah."

Alarm bells tripped in my head. Nick brought the place up three times a year minimum, always intending to go back.

"Why?" I asked.

Nick's smile flayed me. "Even if it was miraculously still in one piece and up and running after these aliens, or whatever the hell, are done with us, I like the memories I have of it, you know? And I think, if I went back, it wouldn't be the same. I... I think—"

"Next party of heroes, please step onto the lift." A man in a tunic gestured toward the spotlight. The lift was covered in spiraling circles of runes, each smaller layer more complex than the last. I stepped forward, squinting as the overbright beam of white light poured down on us from above. It had the same effect as a flash-bang, minus the noise. Keith and Halima followed, looking equally discomfited. Nick stepped on last, and no matter how hard I squinted, I couldn't see his face.

"Stay within the third ring and keep your arms to your side. The Gilded Tower is not responsible for any damages to your person or loss of possessions."

I stepped back. As the elevator rose, my stomach plunged. From the grimace on Nick's face, he was thinking the same thing.

I hope this goes better than the last time I took a group into a dungeon.

CHAPTER SEVENTY-NINE

The sense of dread hung over me like the vestiges of a bad dream. I knew, intellectually, that whatever we were about to get into wouldn't be as dangerous as the trial, or even the early floors of the adaptive dungeon. It probably wouldn't come close. But I couldn't shake it. This deeply unsettling feeling that the system could scrub us at any time. That I was malware, cowering in the depth of the system's archives, and bringing attention to myself like this was all but asking for deletion.

When I squinted directly up, through the intensity of the white beam, I could make out the rolling white artifacts of a sparsely clouded sky. "There's no ceiling."

"Get ready." Nick unsheathed his sword and brought his shield to bear, his expression grim. I drew my crossbow, spun the dagger in my hand a few times, making sure of the weight, glancing over Nick's new gear. He'd upgraded since last time. His sword was black and gray, both shorter and thicker than his previous, more heroic-looking blade. Keith drew a wand topped with a stylized golden sun, his face pale.

"Why are we freaking out that there isn't a ceiling?" Halima looked between the three of us, puzzled.

"Dunno," Keith admitted.

Why did the order bother with Users this green? I waited for Nick to explain. When he didn't, I shot Halima a look. "No ceiling means good odds there's not a safe entry point. They're not putting us into a staging area, unless there's some kind of force field—which I doubt. Meaning something could jump us the second we're up there."

Halima absorbed this. Her body language shifted, legs bent slightly. She flicked the guard of her sword with her thumb, exposing the blade around an inch, and placed her other hand on the hilt in a stance that anyone who's watched Saturday morning cartoons for longer than an hour would recognize.

"What?" Halima asked. She didn't look at me, but she raised an eyebrow.

I just hope you have some practical experience and it isn't all from watching Kurosawa films.

I drew **<Broken Legacy>** and dropped it at my side; it collided with the ground, and Talia appeared in her feral dog form. "Asena. Get ready," I told her, using the alternate name we'd agreed on. She heeled at my side, cuing several dubious glances from the others.

Nick gave our distracted members some serious side-eye. "Keith. We talked about this. You need to be welded to the tank's ass every time we enter a new area."

Keith scurried, placing himself next to Nick.

Nick moved on, "And, Hal, as much as I appreciate the level of focus you're putting out, aren't you forgetting something?"

Halima's gaze rested on Talia, mouth quirked in irritation. She released the death grip on the hilt of her sword and clapped her hands together. A sphere of swirling, transparent wind appeared at the steeple of her fingertips. Moments later, a small, quadrupedal creature made of leaves appeared in front of her.

So, Halima was a fellow summoner.

I could see why she was reticent to bring it out. It bobbed back and forth on four, fragile-looking legs. Its eyes were black and beady, mouth high on its face, naturally quirked up in a position that gave it a permanent dumb smile.

It spotted Talia and waddled over, pouncing on the larger summon's paw. Talia raised her arm slightly off the ground and flicked it. The movement and amount of force applied was delicate but still sent the leaf-creature flying across the platform, rolling several times.

"Patta," Halima hissed. "Heel."

Stunned but otherwise unperturbed, Patta ignored his master and waddled back over to Talia, rearing back and pouncing on her foot. Talia was obviously irritated but otherwise let the summon be.

Halima's summon looked useless, but then again, so did Audrey until she opened her mouth. Regardless of why Nick picked these two Users, it was better to disregard them until they proved themselves.

I bumped Nick. "Gonna draw aggro once we're up there. Do some initial damage. Then lead them back to you."

Nick nodded. He was trying to look calm, but the knuckles that gripped his sword were white, his posture tense. "I can do cleanup. Just try not to pull too many."

"Done."

"What about us?" Keith asked, gesturing between himself and Halima

"Support the tank," I answered, hoping that was enough to shut him up so I could hear. The bright white light was fading away, sky coming into clear focus. We had seconds, if that. I cast **<Probability Cascade>** on two bolts, sliding them into my newly purchased quiver.

The sense of dread grew stronger as the platform pushed us up, closer and closer to the destination.

A shadow flitted overhead, round and circular.

I tensed. I'd underestimated the situation. The tower wasn't even going to wait until the elevator landed to throw shit at us.

"Incoming!" I shouted. Nick reacted immediately, spotting the projectile and hefting his shield above his head. A dark-orange glow overtook the shield, offering full coverage to Keith and Halima.

"New plan," Nick growled. "Flank. Take out their ranged."

"Got it." I prepared for impact, hoping Nick could block whatever was coming. Otherwise, this would be like shooting fish in a barrel.

Still obscured by the light, I watched as the object struck Nick's shield—and bounced off perfectly, reversing its trajectory and flying back out of the opening. The deflection method was new to me, a sort of return-to-sender ability I'd never seen him use before.

I smiled. Whatever just tried to sucker-punch us had another thing coming.

The opening was close enough. I dropped low, gathering the strength in my legs, and leapt straight upward, grabbing the rim of the lift's landing point and yanking myself upward, mantling over the edge and rolling, crossbow in hand, ready to take a cheap shot at whatever was waiting.

I brought the sights to bear. Only for a dozen barefoot people in swimsuits to shriek and back away from me.

It took a moment to disregard them as targets. None of them were armed or armored. And they all looked more scared of me than I was of them. There was a tropical vista behind them, full to the brim with people lounging on foldout chairs, many wearing sunglasses, some reading as waves lapped up on the sand.

Instead of some system-created hellhole, I suddenly found myself in the awkward position of being heavily armed and fully prepared to go to war in the middle of a beach party.

One of the few who didn't scatter, a shirtless man with a well-oiled twelve pack and skin so tan it was almost bronze, stepped forward tentatively.

I shifted the crossbow toward him, and he raised his hands immediately, offering me a serene smile. "Welcome to paradise, brah." He pointed toward the sandy ground beside me. "Mind if we get that back?"

I feigned a glance, intending to bait him into attacking if this was all some weird distraction. When he didn't budge, I actually looked.

There was a volleyball a few feet to my right, embedded in an imprint of sand. My mind ran through the last minute, re-contextualizing it and leaving me feeling slightly moronic. A few feet behind more-abs-than-god, a small group of similarly dressed Users waited on either side of a cheap-looking net. We weren't under attack.

"It's clear," I called down the elevator.

Nick, Halima, and Keith arrived on the platform moments later, looking thoroughly confused. I lowered the crossbow and stooped down, scooping up the ball and tossing it to Abs.

"Appreciate you." Abs caught the ball in one giant palm. Then he cocked his head and stuck a finger at me. "First-timers?"

"Something like that," I said.

"Cool. You guys look savage." He looked us all up and down, pausing on Halima. "You even brought a samurai. Or a shrine maiden, or whatever."

A vein popped out on my forehead. "It *is* a dungeon."

"Only if you want it to be." Abs winked. "Monsters on the lower levels are pretty chill. The hardcore climbers rarely spend much time here. You get a HUD prompt?"

I noted the purple notification light in the corner of my vision and expanded it.

\<Gilded Tower Floor 2\>
Tower Assignment: Slay Mandrakes (0/10)
Time: 58:11

"Yeah…" I trailed off, not particularly impressed with the tower so far. "Jesus. Did I stumble into *WoW Classic*?"

Abs threw back his head and guffawed. "Journey and destination, my dude. The objective's personal, so everyone in your party's gotta do it, but if you got a healer or something, you can just let them get the last hit and it'll count. Try not to kill more than you have to. People coming up the lift after you will need them to clear. That's the journey part."

"What happens if we run out of time?" I asked.

"If you take an L, you get sent to the back of the line and gotta pony up the entry fee again."

That was pretty lenient, by system standards.

"And after?" I asked.

Boss fight, maybe? Please?

"You go to the next floor. Or..." Abs grinned and struck a power pose, flexing a bicep. "Stay here and party like the sun's never gonna set. Cause it isn't!"

With that, he ran off, bounding back to his pickup game on the beach. I'd taken everything he said with a grain of salt. But Nick looked like he hadn't been listening at all. Now that I'd switched mental gears, this floor of the dungeon looked more or less conquered. There was even a series of tiki-style thatch huts that appeared freshly built, with multiple serving drinks and refreshments.

Halima and Keith looked mostly delighted with the development. But Nick didn't fully relax until Abs was long gone, and even then, he made no effort to put his weapons away.

Nick forced a smile. "Beach episode?"

"We have a job to do." I watched him carefully.

"Yep." Nick sighed and spun his sword. "Ripples are supposed to start on this floor. Remember, we don't know what they look like, but we know they're here. We're looking for something wrong with the environment. Could be a section of flat grass, or warped tree. Let's get moving."

We moved in a standard formation as Nick proceeded carefully into the green. The original plan was to stay together as we forged through the dungeon floor, away from the beach.

That plan didn't last long.

Halima found the first one. There was a cluster of small white flowers jutting out in all directions I'd overlooked. She dropped to one knee—and for a moment, I thought she intended to smell them. Instead, Halima grabbed the cluster at its singular root and yanked.

The root was large, bigger than the flowers and probably larger than my head—but more than that, it had a face, complete with a gap-mouthed expression as it dangled above the ground and stared at all of us. It slapped its stubby hands against its cheeks and *screamed.*

Halima dropped it, her eyes narrowing, and grabbed her sword. The draw-attack was lightning fast but inaccurate, severing the mandrake's flowers from its head.

The mandrake paused, blinking several times, reaching a stubby hand toward its head to feel for the flowers and grabbing stem instead.

Realization dawned, and it screamed again, the scream crescendoing into a series of shrieks as it raced across the clearing. Its voice was barely decipherable. *"No no no no no no."*

Talia dashed around to cut off its escape. Instead of trying to go around her, or attacking, the mandrake pulled a 180 and dashed directly back toward us, still screaming bloody murder.

Keith stepped forward and mouthed something, then flicked his wand. A purple bolt of energy exploded from his wand. It smashed into the mandrake's forehead, knocking it head over heels. I thought that was it, but the mandrake slowly staggered to its feet, drew in a giant breath, and screamed anew, sprinting off to the side this time, only to be cut off once more and herded toward us.

Nick held his shield limply at his side and watched the scene. "This is just... sad."

I had to agree.

CHAPTER EIGHTY

At this range, I barely had to adjust for drop.

A notification popped.

<Gilded Tower Floor 2>
Tower Assignment: Slay Mandrakes (10/10)
Time: 32:41

I closed the window and turned to Keith. My prior estimation of him had dropped significantly. Accuracy was by far his best quality—it was actually kind of impressive, he could nail almost anything he was looking at, regardless of movement or range.

The problem was Keith's kit was utterly devoid of stopping-power. And when I say devoid, I'm not exaggerating. His performance when we'd found the first mandrake wasn't a fluke. No matter the spell, a magic missile, a wave of fire—it accomplished nothing more than knocking the small monsters off their feet. The three he'd killed had been accomplished by using that knockback to his advantage, then dealing the killing blow with a small utility knife.

And the mandrakes weren't strong. When I snuck **<Blade of Woe's>** hilt out of my inventory to check for weak points, both varieties of mandrakes lit up like a Christmas tree. Literally every part of them was susceptible to damage.

"Done with mine," I announced, spotting another cluster of flowers in the shade of a vine-ridden tree. "Let's finish yours."

Keith followed me, eyes fixed on the ground. "The only reason this isn't a disaster is because these things are weak. We both know it'd be better if we run my timer out."

Probably.

"The Order didn't recruit you out of charity," I said, dropping to one knee in the shade, gripping the flowers close to the root.

"Just good old nepotism," Keith sighed.

That piqued my interest. It smelled like possible leverage and actually explained a lot. The worst monsters in the world had friends, family. People they cared about, even if sometimes their methods of caring were utterly twisted. It made sense that they'd want them on the ground floor of Hastur's utopia, and that they'd segregate them from the larger threats. Maybe that was what Zero-team was. A bunch of golden-parachute recruits stuck together. But if it was true, that begged a bigger question. What the fuck was the Order's leadership doing, putting Nick in charge of them? They were practically handing him leverage. I didn't know what Hastur offered Nick, but it had to be huge, considering they'd effectively placed a colony of rabbits in the lion's den.

I shrugged. "So, you're related to someone important. They wouldn't put you in the field if they didn't think you could hack it."

Keith was staring down at the mandrake, his face drawn, waiting for me to pull it out. His wand trembled in his fingertips. "It's easy to forget that you're new. Everyone contributes. That's how it works here. You contribute, or you die."

"Look, we're not playing league. I'm not gonna prep each one for you and let you finish it. If you can't kill these lemmings, go back before shit hits the fan."

"I know." Keith stared at the ground.

"But I'm gonna make you spend every second of this last half-hour proving to me you can't." I yanked the mandrake free, holding it out to my side and gesturing to it. There had to be a reason Nick brought Keith. It didn't matter what the expectations placed on him were, or what side he was really playing for. Nick wasn't the kind of person to sandbag his team.

Keith pointed his wand at the mandrake, cringing, and mouthed a word. "... *Bolt.*"

The spell landed, shockwave passing over me as the mandrake spun in my grip like a loudly complaining helicopter.

Frustrated, I knelt and stuffed the mandrake back in its hole head first. Its diminutive legs bicycled helplessly through the air. "Okay, no." I ran a hand through my hair. "I've seen someone use that spell before. Concentrated fire. Completely obliterated the target. What's your level?"

"Six," Keith admitted.

Low, but not that low.

"How much INT do you have?"

"Twelve," Keith said.

Again, not low enough for the absolute lack of effectiveness we were seeing.

"Is it your equipment?" I eyed the wand.

Keith looked like he was about to explode. "It's my stupid frigging title." He pulled up his UI in a series of angry swipes and I received a notification.

<**Tread Softly:** Augments and alters the User's magic prowess. Incantations are now the only method of casting. In exchange, spells gain the capacity of being exponentially stronger, depending on the level convictions involved.>

In classic system fashion, it mentioned nothing about spells spoken without conviction being borderline useless.

I raised an eyebrow. "Have you uh... tried..."

Keith's face flushed. He looked away. "Yes, I spent days screaming out my spells like a badly dubbed anime character. No, it didn't work."

On some level, that was a relief, though it didn't fix the problem.

"You were better when we fought."

"When you backhanded me like an afterthought?" Keith asked.

I shook my head. "Still, those spells had more oomph behind them. What was different then?"

"I dunno." Keith rubbed his arm. "I was scared."

"And you wanted to prove yourself."

"Right. And for some reason my magic works better in User duels, anyway. Sparring, at least. The Ceaseless Knight thinks the flavor text is mostly bullshit and my magic abilities don't really kick in until I'm in the shit."

So this was a stress test, trying to draw Keith's abilities out. That seemed uncharacteristically risky for Nick, but I could see him doing it. Several other simpler possibilities crossed my mind that Nick must have been too preoccupied to catch. I settled on one.

"They bring in someone new, pit you against them. Do you ever win the first spar?"

Keith looked up, suddenly attentive. "No."

"Let's try something. What's the worst thing that's ever happened to you?" I asked bluntly.

"My... grandpa died of cancer last year." Keith shifted uncomfortably.

"Hospice or home-care?" I asked.

"Hospice. It was terrible." Keith shuddered.

"Perfect." I nodded. "Now I want you to put yourself in that moment.

Sitting in the hospice room, smelling the antiseptic, looking at your grandpa."

Keith seemed uncertain, but his eyes glazed over and his expression grew somber as he recalled the memory.

I continued. "Now I want you to imagine a cop comes in. He sits down, all grim and resolved. Tells you it's not cancer. There's a cover-up. That a bunch of these *motherfuckers*—" I pointed to the still-struggling mandrake "—broke in and scared the hell out of your grandpa. That he tried to run, but they caught him unbolting the deadbolt and screamed at him, bursting his eardrums and ruining his balance. And once he was down, they swarmed him. Stomped him into hamburger with their stupid stubby feet"

Keith's mouth moved, trying to form words, taking several attempts to do so. "He couldn't run. He was in a wheelchair."

"Then he rolled away, and the mandrakes tipped it over and laughed at him."

"And who was trying to cover up Grandpa being curb-stomped by mandrakes?" Keith asked, but he was staring at the mandrake's flailing legs. His lip curled.

I let my temper flare. "It doesn't matter. What matters is that they did it, Keith! They killed your fucking grandpa, and you know who picked the house? This pathetic screaming motherfucker right here." I yanked the mandrake out of the dirt, switching my grip to the stem and dangling it right in front of the mage. "Are you gonna take that, Keith? Are you just gonna let him get away with it? Or are you gonna *give him what he fucking deserves!*"

A shadow dropped over Keith's face and he set his jaw. I reached into his mind with **<Suggestion>**, amping his emotional state. Keith pointed his wand at the mandrake, his hand steady, his expression cold.

"Eradicate."

<Awareness> shouted a warning last second. I dropped the mandrake and dove out of the way as a black and orange beam larger in width than many of the surrounding trees overtook its body, reducing both the mandrake and the tree behind it to ash.

"Holy shit," Keith said. He turned to me, slack-jawed. "How...?"

"I've seen this shit before." I stood, brushing bits of dirt and grass off my armor. "Titles take precedence over everything. Once you narrow it down, it's just a matter of playing monkey's paw with the wording, trying to figure out what, exactly, the system is using to screw you over."

Keith nodded slowly. The result clearly shocked him. This was probably the peak of what he'd accomplished. He removed his glasses and cleaned them, chuckling nervously. "I uh. I feel like I should pay you, or something."

I shook my head. "Just a favor to a teammate. Nothing more."

Excited to move on, Keith ran ahead, and I followed him, watching as he chewed through the remaining mandrakes in a matter of minutes. He never quite captured the power of that initial blast again, but it was still overkill. Night and day from how he'd been a half hour earlier.

My concern grew.

What I'd left out from my explanation, was that I'd been able to solve the problem so quickly because it wasn't that complicated. Keith didn't strike me as an idiot—a little slow, maybe, but it was more that he was too close to the issue to see the solution. It just needed an outside perspective.

Nick should have seen it.

No. Not "should have."

He *saw* it. And instead of fixing it, fed Keith a line of bullshit.

So, why?

Considering the potential, I wasn't sure I would have helped him at all if I wasn't one-hundred percent confident I could shut him down if needed. **<Suggestion>** was Keith's kryptonite. It helped make him, and if necessary, could break him just as easily. Deaden his emotions. Fog his memories, make them difficult to access. By aiding Keith, I'd created a lowly placed but eventually powerful ally within the Order. One that was easily controlled.

But Nick didn't have my abilities.

Was it that simple? He didn't want to create another powerful User within the Order?

That felt too easy, somehow.

"Hey, guys."

I jumped at the sound of Nick's voice. He was holding back a canopy of vines, surveying the overturned trees and other damage around the clearing. "Jesus. A rampaging elephant come through here?"

I chucked a thumb at Keith, watching Nick's reaction carefully. His face might as well have been carved from stone.

Keith ran over to us, breathing hard. He stopped in front of Nick. "I broke through."

"Good job, kid." Nick fist-bumped him. "With style, from the looks of it. Knew you could do it."

Keith looked away. "Can't take full credit. Or any, really. Myrddin figured it out."

"Thanks for the assist, new guy." Nick gave me the same strained smile, thinning by the second. "Y'all done with your screeching carrots?"

When we both confirmed that we were, Nick pointed back the way he came. "Good. Because I'm pretty sure we found our first ripple."

CHAPTER EIGHTY-ONE

Nick pushed greenery aside as he led us along a small stream that cut directly through the island. It wasn't far removed from something we saw during one of my father's many nature outings—major difference being, this stream didn't feel historic. There was no algae, no accumulation of dirt or evidence of erosion. Just a smooth stone rut that cut through the center of the island.

Up ahead, Halima was kneeling near a section of the stream that dropped off into a stagnant creek. I stared at the ripple. I understood that something was wrong with it, but it took a moment for my mind to stop "fixing" the fallacy. The surface of the water was anomalous. There were no frothing bubbles or ripples from where the stream emptied into the creek.

"It's falling the wrong way," I said. Which made even less sense when you considered the stream was clearly heading this direction.

Halima squinted at the anomaly. "It's hurting my brain to look at."

"Then why are you staring at it?" Keith asked.

"We don't know what the conditions are. If I look away, it might close," Halima answered.

Jesus Christ. I already need a vacation.

I spotted a pebble washed up from the creek and picked it up, tossing it toward the small inverted waterfall. The pebble sunk through the transparent curtain and disappeared.

"Pretty sure it's not going anywhere, Halima," Nick commented.

As they poked and prodded the ripple, a notification popped in my vision.

> **<Kinsley:** I know this probably won't go through, but someone told me the tower was different, so I figured I'd try.>

It shouldn't be possible for Kinsley to message me here. But now that I thought about it, there was nothing in the many handouts for the tower that warned about restricted communications. Either it was common knowledge or the sort of thing you didn't put in a brochure. Another sign that the Tower wasn't a typical Realm of Flauros.

> **<Matt:** It actually did. Shoot.>
> **<Kinsley:** Okay, perfect. I'll just go in order of least to most important. We have a location for a lab outside the region. There's a few regions leasing entire buildings that no one's using anymore for extra Selve, and I landed us three floors.>

Renting multiple floors was smart. Assuming Kinsley intended to keep our business on a single floor, it bought us time to organize if there was a raid.

> **<Matt:** Great.>
> **<Kinsley:** Cameron's demanding someone in charge. Loudly. Pretty sure he's entering the 'anger' stage of grief.>
> **<Matt:** Not great.>
> **<Kinsley:** And surprise, I saved the worst for last. Did you ask some girl who works in our building on a date, then ghost her?>

Shit.

> **<Matt:** ... No.>
> **<Kinsley:** You fucking did. She flagged me down at breakfast, Matt. All sad and abandoned, like a puppy in a cardboard box. The hell's the matter with you?>
> **<Matt:** Kins, I don't have time for this. The Tanya thing was just a cover from Miles, anyway. Can always find someone else.>
> **<Kinsley:** It's *Tara*, you asshole. And what the fuck—I like her, you can't just replace her because you're bad at time management. What kind of message does that send to me, coming from the only role model I have at the moment? What am I supposed to take away from this? Find a nice undependable boy who flakes and uses you as cover from the fuzz?>
> **<Matt:** It wasn't even—whatever. Fine. Jesus. I'll message her when I'm out. Also, if *I'm* your role model, you need to reevaluate some life decisions.>
> **<Kinsley:** K thanks bye.>

I rubbed at my forehead. Things were piling up again.

Nick stood in front of us, tying a coil of rope around his waist. Once he finished, he clapped his hands twice. "Okay. Was under strict orders not to pass these out until we found a ripple. Don't think I really need to say this, but do not, in any circumstances, sell what I'm about to give you to anyone. Especially the open market. It will come back on you. I guarantee it." Nick pulled three plastic cylinders from his inventory and passed them out.

Everyone besides Nick inspected the cylinders. They were glass, with a small flip cap at one end, not unlike what you'd see at the top of a thermos, and the inside was filled with a black, oily substance.

Keith held his straight up and down and popped the cap, giving it a cautious sniff. The dark fluid lurched, strands of dark oil clinging to the lid like tiny hands and evacuating the container, wrapping itself on the bare skin beneath Keith's sleeve in seconds.

Keith yelped and attempted to dislodge the thing, struggling to dig his fingers beneath the rapidly flattening liquid.

Instead of coming free, it absorbed into his skin, and a moment later a visible glowing UI appeared on Keith's wrist.

Nick clucked his tongue. "Great example of what not to do in the ripple. Dangers may not be as obvious as they are out here. As a rule—if you don't know what it is, don't touch it."

"Fine. Now what is this, and why is it in me—Oh. Wait." Keith fiddled with the display, breaking into a smile. "This is sick."

Halima leaned over his shoulder, jockeying for a look. "An advanced interface?"

Nick nodded. "As you've all probably noticed, the system doesn't give us a lot of information in terms of health and status effects, which can lead to some situations where people miss warning signs before everything snowballs. This is your diagnostic, portable doctor, and codex in one."

"Codex?" Halima was still looking at the cylinder with revulsion, but the word had piqued her interest. I was still hung up on the portable doctor comment. Did the Order have these the whole time? When they were back in the tunnel even?

"Not really the star of the show here, but yeah," Nick confirmed. "If you scan your kills, it'll fill in more information about them. Weaknesses, possible drops, and so on."

"Are we centralizing these findings in a database?" Halima asked.

"No." Nick hesitated. "That was supposedly the plan, but some of the higher-level Users and leadership had security concerns. For now, everything is client-side. You can share info with other members of the Order, but both parties have to opt-in. What's more important, this thing can and will save your ass. Hopefully we won't need it, as it only kicks in when things are grim—but if you take a critical hit, or get dosed or overloaded with status effects, it'll synthesize whatever's needed to keep you alive."

"What are the limitations?" I asked.

"It can only do so much." Nick shrugged. "Take a big hit or get poisoned, you're okay. Take a big hit *and* get poisoned—you might be S-O-L. Yellow light at the top left indicates it still has charge. When it's off, you're on your own."

"Does it record anything beyond the User's health?"

"Nah. It can't access your class or title. Which also means it can't factor any passive buffs you have, so keep that in mind."

With a disgusted sigh, Halima popped the cap on her cylinder. The oily entity crawled from the cylinder and absorbed into her skin.

I wasn't sure I believed it. Nick seemed like he was telling the truth, but that didn't mean they'd told him everything. But Hastur already knew too much about me as it was—including my class and abilities. Not to mention, I was pretty sure that regardless of how the device was made, it was eldritch. Which meant I had some power over it. It was a tough call, but so far, the pros outweighed the cons.

Still. I wanted to hear Nick admit it.

"Have they had these for long? Tested them?" I asked.

Nick nodded. "One founder is a bio-enchanter. Been making them pretty much since the beginning."

"Say Keith and I are on our own and he catches a stray arrow, activating his oh-shit button. It heals him enough to get him going, but he panics and tries to run, inadvertently drawing fire. He's slower from the previous injury, so the shooter dials in, catching him in the neck. I'm close by and I haven't used my charge. There anything I can do?"

Nick's blue eyes went cold. "Doesn't take long for someone to bleed out from a wound like that. But yes. Didn't cover it, yet, but these things are modular. You can transfer a charge. Assuming you were fast enough."

"Pretty sure I'd be fast enough," I needled him.

"Getting uncomfortable with how realistic this example sounds," Keith muttered.

"Like I said, hopefully we won't need them." Nick crossed his arms.

I held up a finger. "One more hypothetical."

There was something dark in Nick's expression, almost enough to dissuade me entirely. "Go ahead."

"Great." I smiled. "Let's say Keith *didn't* have the register. He was a VIP, or a contact. Someone we actually gave a shit about keeping alive who got seriously hurt. Could the register make that happen, or is he just fucked?"

Nick stepped in close, looming over me.

"Stop pussyfooting around and say what you want to say," Nick growled.

Halima raised a hand. "I'm... not sure what's happening? But I'd also like to know the answer to Myrddin's question."

Neither of us looked at her.

"You could," Nick finally answered, never taking his eyes from me. "The register would transfer to the wounded party temporarily and return to you after it spent its charge."

"Just making sure we're on the same page," I said.

Nick turned away, casting a weary glance over his shoulder. "Look. I'm an open book. If you—hell, any of you—hear something about me and have questions, just come find me when we're not on a mission. Are we done?"

"We're done." I popped the cylinder's cap and watched the creeping tendrils wrap around my gauntlet. Unlike Keith and Halima, who were both wearing robes, the semi-transparent UI appeared on my gauntlet rather than the skin beneath.

I circled through the readouts. The amount of information on display was impressive, and the interface simple enough to navigate without getting bogged down in endless text—it implemented visuals to create a map of the user's body in three layers. The overall body, underlying musculature, and organs. Most of my display was white, with some light yellow. When I zoomed it to the second layer, there were a handful of yellow splotches showing healing wounds, with information listed displaying the origin and age and a percentile chance of infections.

Out of curiosity, I zoomed one layer further.

There was a flash of orange leading from my lungs toward my heart. It disappeared so quickly I almost missed it. I swapped layers several times, trying to recreate the effect, to no success.

Nick pushed a coil of rope into my chest. He was all business now, the flare of irritation more or less gone. "Hold this. In case we can't hear each other once I'm settled, two yanks means all-clear, come in. Three yanks means hurry the fuck up, because things are hot. Four means I'm stuck or can't move, come and get me. Five plus means I'm panicking and we're boned."

"And... what are we supposed to do in that case?" Keith asked.

Nick shrugged. "Try to tie the rope to something sturdy, so I can climb out if I get clear. Otherwise, cut your losses and report back to the order."

I studied him, looking for any sign of despair, anything out of the ordinary. Nothing in the way he'd presented himself gave the feel of reck-lessness, or a death wish. But such things were rarely obvious.

Too often people presented themselves with tranquility and confi-dence, right before they were gone.

"Sure you don't want me to go first?" I asked. "It's in my skill set."

Nick shook his head and gave me a playful shove. "Stay in your lane, new guy." When that didn't mollify me, he dropped his voice to a whisper and leaned in. "Look, all we know about the ripples is that they're unbalanced and unpredictable. And I feel like we both know how brutal the system can be under normal circumstances, let alone when we're venturing into areas it doesn't want us to go."

When he put it that way, this felt far riskier than I'd considered.

"I could drop into a treasure trove," Nick continued. "Or a meat grinder. There's no way to know for sure. If it goes sideways, just get the kids out." He raised his voice. "If I go MIA, do as Myrddin says."

Halima and Keith were both standing far enough away that they probably hadn't heard us, but they seemed to pick up on the finality in Nick's voice. Neither argued, though Halima looked like she wanted to.

"Good luck," Keith said.

"Just a second." I walked the cord of rope back, looping it around a nearby tree and forming a fulcrum. Now we at least stood a chance of catching him if he ended up falling into a chasm. I wrapped a layer of rope around my forearm and nodded at Nick.

Nick made finger-guns, firing a "shot" at each of us before he blew away imaginary smoke and holstered them. He grinned. "See you fuckers on the other side." He stuck his face in the ripple first, then jumped inside.

No matter what happens. I'm not losing you again.

I dug my heels in and braced, waiting for the rope to go taut. Keith—inexperienced, but quick on the draw—grabbed the rope with his bare hands and did the same.

Halima stood some distance away with her arms crossed, staring at the ripple where Nick had disappeared. "We have nothing to worry about."

"Doesn't hurt to be careful," Keith said.

"Have you ever sparred with the Ceaseless Knight?" Halima countered. "Really sparred, when he's not holding back?"

"No... but..."

"Then you can't possibly understand. There's nothing in this Tower that could put him down, permanently—"

"Shut the fuck up," I hissed. Halima and Keith fell silent. The slack rope was moving, meaning Nick was reaching the end of his lead.

But he hadn't signaled yet. Something was wrong.

Come on, man.

The rope tugged once. Then again, a few seconds later.

"See, he's fine—" Halima trailed off as the rope tugged a third time.

He's sending the signal slowly. Trying not to draw attention to himself.

In a flurry of movement, the rope snapped a half-dozen more times and started flailing erratically. There was immediate slack, which I took to mean that Nick was retreating.

I looped the rope around my waist and continued reeling it in, passing the slack to Keith. Halima was standing stock-still, her mouth open. I shouted at her. "Get in here!"

She started, rushing to take place behind Keith. "What—what do we do?"

"When he went through, he dropped down. He may need help clearing the drop. Get ready to pull your ass off as soon as we hit resistance—" the rope slipped from my hands. I whipped around, back toward the ripple, trying to get a handle on what just happened.

Keith held the end of the rope in shaking hands, black strands fraying from where it was severed.

"Oh... fuck," Keith said.

CHAPTER EIGHTY-TWO

Before

The physical therapy room smelled like lemon pledge and sweat, with a subtle yet distinct undercurrent of feces. I didn't know if they were all like this, like it was some kind of PT signature, but every similar facility in the clinic Nick dragged me to smelled exactly the same.

"*Fuck,*" Nick swore. He was holding onto the two parallel bars in the center of the room, triceps rippling from the effort, occupying the same spot he'd been in ten minutes ago. The only difference was that the back of his hospital gown came undone, flying open like a reverse cape.

I penciled in an answer on the prep book and turned the page.

The supernova event of 1987 is interesting in that there is still no evidence of the neutron star that current theory says should have remained after a supernova of that size. This is in spite of the fact that many of the most sensitive instruments ever developed have searched for the telltale pulse of radiation neutron stars emit. Thus, current theory is wrong in claiming that supernovas of a certain size always produce neutron stars.

Which one of the following, if true, most strengthens the argument?

1. *Most supernova remnants astronomers have detected have a neutron star nearby.*
2. *Sensitive astronomical instruments have detected neutron stars much farther away than the location of the 1987 supernova.*
3. *The supernova of 1987 was the first that scientists were able to observe in progress.*
4. *Several important features of the 1987 supernova are correctly predicted by the current theory.*

5. *Some neutron stars are known to have come into existence by a*
   cause other than a supernova explosion.

I stared at the question. Closed the textbook to check the cover and make sure I hadn't picked up an astronomy prep book by mistake, then opened it again. "The fuck?"

"Fucking what?" Nick asked. Rivulets of sweat poured down his face, and he squinted at me beneath ringlets of soaked hair. He was leaning further forward, looking like a wax mannequin dumped on the side of the road in Tucson.

I uncrossed my legs and walked awkwardly toward him, my foot asleep from sitting in one position for too long, and shoved the book in his face. He blinked several times, struggling to make out the text. "Motherfucker."

I reread the question again, looking for the hook I'd missed, finding none. "Fucking bullshit."

"Pencil in F," Nick suggested, between gasps for air. "For fuck off."

I snorted. "Fucking A. But that was too many words between fucks. You broke the chain."

Still gripping the rails, he extended a finger toward me. "The lawyer shit fits. You're a goddamn shyster."

"Too bad I'm not planning to be a lawyer." Law school was way out of budget. Even if I got a full-ride to both a good college and a solid law school after—which I doubted—the textbooks might as well have been etched in gold. Whatever pittance they offered to cover them wouldn't come close to the final tally. It was too much effort for too little payoff. I dog-eared the page for later research and closed the book. "Can we say that, by the way?"

"Lawyer?" Nick snorted.

"Shyster."

"What's wrong with shyster?"

"Dunno. I think it might be... antisemitic, or something."

"No, it's not." Nick scoffed. A shadow of doubt crossed his face. "Is it?"

I flipped open my burner and pulled up the browser to look it up, only to be greeted by the perpetually spinning circle. "Out of data."

Nick inclined his head backward toward where his phone sat, blasting warring alt-rock over the tranquil spa music that played through the speakers overhead. "Use mine."

I grabbed his phone. He gave me a sort of half-smirk, and I rolled my eyes and focused on the phone screen. The passcode was four digits—meaning he was still using a simple passcode—which made this worlds easier than it could have been. I tried his birthday first.

The phone vibrated, white dots going transparent.

No dice

Graduation year?

Nope.

"Don't lock me out," Nick warned.

"Relax, I've got three more tries." I studied the screen.

Nick wasn't a complete asshole, so it wouldn't be a code I couldn't hope to guess. Or at the very least, he thought I could get it, based on what I knew about him previously or information I'd gleaned in the hospital.

I entered four numbers and groaned, internally, as the phone unlocked.

"Really?"

Nick hee-hawed himself into a coughing fit. He continued to snicker, red-eyed. "A number so magical I had to use it twice."

"Your passcode literally only comprises two numbers, repeated. You're a bellend."

"Gettin' a wee bit British in 'ere, are we?" Nick said, in the worst imitation of a cockney accent I'd ever heard.

"That supposed to be British? Sounds more like a piss-drunk Australian."

Nick opened his mouth, closed it, opened it again. "Before I make the obvious joke, we should probably make sure there's no current pending cancellations in my future. Because I'm pretty sure I may have, possibly, used that word on Twitter."

"Twitter still exists?" I asked.

Nick nodded.

I knew that all this was a distraction. That he was procrastinating. And cancellation a few years from now would be the least of Nick's problems once he was back in circulation. They'd be decent enough until his ration of social pity expired. Maybe a month or two. After that, things would get ugly.

But he was doing me the service of distracting me from my mother, who was probably still wailing her lungs out in the clinic's sister facility.

Least I could do was humor him.

I pulled up Safari and did the research.

"So, you're *probably* in the clear," I finally said.

Nick squinted. "What's probably? Why probably?"

"Shyster is commonly mis-attributed to Shylock, the antagonist from Shakespeare's *Merchant of Venice*. Pound-of-flesh guy was Jewish—and there are still scholars arguing over whether *Merchant of Venice* was problematic as recently as a few years ago. But like I said, it's a misattribution. The word itself predates MoV, and is really only derogatory to lawyers."

"So why am I only *probably* not cancelled?" Nick asked.

"Dubious intent."

"What?"

"Did you say it to a Jewish person?

"No. I don't think so."

"Then you're fine."

Nick was still following through on his wax mannequin act. If he kept heading in this slow, southward direction, he was going to end up on the floor. "Christ. You gotta be so careful about what you say these days, man."

"I dunno—" I hesitated. This was another bad habit I'd developed over the last few weeks. Telling Nick my opinion, something I had, previously, fastidiously kept to myself. He had a talent for drawing it out of me.

"Say it." Nick hoisted himself upward with a grunt, gained four inches, lost three.

I shrugged. "Don't get me wrong. I think there's a lot of problems with the way things are now, with—"

"—*Society?*" Nick drew the word out, making an overly wide, exaggerated clown smile.

"Fuck you."

"Sorry, had to. Go on."

"With... the current climate," I said, taking as many mental side steps around the word "society" as I could. "I think we hyper-fixate on certain issues, while far bigger problems grow malignant and metastasize without ever even making a blip on the social radar. But words have power. It's always been that way. I don't think being mindful of our words —and how they affect the people around us—is that big of an ask."

"Well, now I feel like an asshole," Nick grumbled.

"You told me to say it."

"Like. I know that you're right. I agree with everything you said, I'm just..."

"Just what?"

Nick swiped a sweaty arm across his face and slammed his hand back down. "I know I'm behind on the recovery. And I know what happens if I stagnate. Like, I know. And I'm tired of knowing that and only getting bullshitted in return. The fucking therapist calling it an improvement because I took three more steps than yesterday and managed not to shit myself. They keep telling me I'm doing great. They keep *lying*. And I'm fucking tired of it." The wooden bars vibrated in his grip. "For once, I just want someone to take me to task. Hold me accountable. Like you said. Words have power."

"I mean, your PT's an effete dumbass who probably couldn't wring a genuine moment from Ginsberg's *Howl*—"

"—I understood about sixty percent of that," Nick said.

"—But positive reinforcement is always more effective than negative reinforcement. And that's not societal niceties, or woke posturing. That's science."

"You remember that Junior ROTC program we had, freshman and sophomore year?" Nick asked.

I had to think about it. "Yeah. The drill instructor got fired for putting a student through a car window. School withdrew from the program after that."

Nick laughed. "Sergeant Ross. Not even sure if he was a sergeant, but that was what he made us call him. Dude was such a prick. Plus, I'm pretty sure he had a glandular problem. He had these tight pants and you could see his—well... *anyway*. I was like barely one-twenty, soaking wet."

"Bullshit." The size-difference alone was staggering.

"I was," Nick insisted. "Total noodle. Never stepped in the gym for more than a couple days a week, and when I did, it was mostly cardio. Surprising no one, Sergeant Ross didn't like me much. One day, after drills, he stops me. Asks me why I'm even bothering with JROTC. And being the naïve freshman I was, I told him honestly. I wanted to bulk up for football."

I groaned.

"He uh, he didn't like that." Nick chuckled. "Not one bit. And that motherfucker would not forget it. Every fucking exercise, during drills, laps around the track, he'd find me. 'Look, everybody! It's Talmont's future football star! Peyton Manning weighed two hundred pounds of rock-hard muscle his freshman year. How much do you weigh, fish?' Shit like that."

"Wow. He really was a prick," I said.

"That he was," Nick confirmed. "But he made me aware of the gap. Between fantasizing and actualizing. And instead of discouraging me once I realized how much work I was going to have to put in, all he really did was piss me off. Want to prove him wrong. And it worked. I hit the gym five days a week on top of what I was doing with ROTC. By sophomore year, I made varsity."

I smirked. "Just in time to watch them load that dickhead into the back of a squad car."

"He was an asshole. But he told me a truth I needed to hear. And I—" Nick choked up. "—I know it doesn't work for everybody. But what I need is for someone to tell me the truth. Because as long as I keep thinking to myself, 'It's okay, you made it four steps instead of three,' I'm never going to get out of here. I—" Nick collapsed onto the mat, accumulated sweat flying.

I went to help him, then pulled back at the last moment.

"Is that really what you want?" I asked.

It bothered me how invested I was in his answer. I was getting attached. Another sign that this relationship had run its course. If Nick said yes, it would be as simple as taking my filter off. But I'd found, on more than one occasion, that people who asked for the truth rarely wanted it.

It's why we lie so often.

If I told him the truth, I knew with complete certainty that this odd, cobbled-together friendship we had was over.

"Yes," Nick said.

Well. It had to end sometime.

I looked around the room. This would work better if I had a prop, something I could use to raise the stakes.

Eventually, I found it, blasting alt-rock in the palm of my hand.

"What was your goal for today?" I asked, pressing two fingers to my neck. My pulse was higher than normal. Why the fuck did I care so much?

"I need... I need to make it to the end." He pointed to the far side of the parallel bars.

"And you're healed enough for that?" I checked.

"PT says my leg should be weight-bearing. It just... hurts. But I think I'm done, bro. Can't get over the mental hurdle."

I took no joy in what I was about to do. But if this was the last time we spoke, my last opportunity to repay him for the distraction he'd unknowingly provided, I needed to do it right.

"Hey, Nick?" I said.

"W-what?" Nick sobbed. At some point, he'd started to cry.

"I'm sorry."

I snapped a picture of him, balled up, whimpering, in a puddle of his own sweat and tears. The phone camera made the shutter noise.

"What the fuck?" Nick asked, propping himself up on one arm, expression disturbed.

For the first time in recent memory, I took the mask off. Crouched in front of him. Stuck the phone in his face. "Go on. Look at that pathetic, sniveling shit, mewling about how hard his life is. The one wasting everyone's time. Take a good, long, look at yourself."

Nick lunged for the phone. If he was uninjured, I wouldn't have stood a chance of keeping it from him. As it was, all I had to do was pull my arm back. "Too slow. Just like at the game."

Furious, he grabbed for the phone again. I kept it just out of his reach, and stood, holding the phone behind me so he could see it as I walked to the front-end of the parallel bars.

"You're no Sergeant Ross, Matt. It's obvious what you're doing," he called after me.

"You're right. I'm not your ROTC drill sergeant." I reached the end of the parallel bars and stared at him, disgusted. "I'm the Ghost of Christmas Past, motherfucker. And that—" I pointed to the wheelchair, "—is your goddamn future."

"I'm not doing this." Nick looked away.

"Fine with me." I made a show of scrolling through his contacts. "Let's see. Alexandra, Bethany, Bridget, Bridgette with extra letters, Cassie— Jesus, how many girls do you have in here?"

"Cassie's my mom—What the hell do you think you're doing?" I saw him in my peripheral, watching me with growing alarm.

"Composing a group text. Figured we'd send everyone an update on your progress."

Nick's jaw dropped. "You wouldn't."

"Do I strike you as someone with a robust sense of humor?" I asked dryly.

"Give me my phone back, bro," Nick snapped. His fear, his self-pity, was disappearing. Changing into something feral.

I dropped it onto the mat at the end of the bars. "Come and get it."

He didn't move.

"I don't have to send the picture, Nick. Because pretty soon, that's the only version of you that exists. Everyone will see it for themselves, live and in-person. And Jesus, talking about never getting out of here? What a fucking joke. I don't care how loaded your parents are. PT's fucking expensive. Their insurance probably covers half at most, meaning they're covering the other half out of pocket, meaning—no matter how busy or absent they are—eventually they're gonna be sitting in the therapist's office, getting a status update on exactly how that money is being spent."

"Fuck. You." Nick grabbed the bar.

There you go. Use that anger. Channel it.

I continued, spittle flying out of my mouth. "And sure, maybe the PT milks you for a couple more months. Why give up a cash cow when it's still producing?"

Nick screamed, pulling himself to his feet. His face was gaunt, pale, and he clung to the bars like a man holding onto a life preserver in a hurricane. But his eyes burned.

"Eventually, the therapist will come clean. He won't tell them the truth, exactly. That you're a self-pitying child who won't lift a finger to aid his own recovery. He'll find a nicer way to say it. Like, 'I think Nicholas has made all the progress he can.'"

Nick took a step forward, and another. "You're... a twisted... motherfucker..."

I sneered. "At least I'm honest with myself. Can you say the same? When you're back in school, and all those people are watching you struggle to wheel yourself through the hallways, can you be honest with yourself, Nick? That the only reason you're in a wheelchair is not because you need it—not because the injury was so severe that there was no alternative—but because *you, fucking, quit.*"

"I... am gonna strangle your ass... when I get there," Nick huffed.

"Sure. I'll schedule a time for Friday. Next week," I said. But I was losing the venom. He was over halfway now, moving at a decent clip. Any legitimate annoyance I felt was long gone. Instead, I felt... melancholy. Almost sad.

Strange.

Nick stalled at the finish line, strands of drool dripping from his lips, his teeth. "No—fuck—I can't do it. That's it. I can't do it."

I opened my mouth, fully prepared to launch one final, verbal assault. And found that I couldn't. Instead, I left him there and brought the wheelchair around.

"Yes you can, Nick."

"I *can't,*" Nick shouted hoarsely, his vocal cords fried.

"Just... look." I pointed behind him.

Nick raised his head, slowly, groggily, and gawked at the distance. As I'd suspected, he'd lost track of the progress he made.

I swallowed. "All the way back there—when it took you forever to take a single step—you told me all you wanted was the truth. But if you can look how far you've come and tell me the person who crossed all that distance in such a short time can't close this tiny gap? You're lying to yourself."

"I need a second," Nick rasped.

"Take ten."

Nick closed his eyes and moved. His hand slipped off the end of the bar. I caught him under his armpits before he could fall and grunted. "Got you, buddy. I've got you."

By some miracle, I got him into the chair without dropping him or crumpling like a soda can.

Nick's head lulled back, eyes half-lidded "My... phone."

"Yup." I scooped it up off the mat and deleted the picture. "Pic's gone forever. You're good."

Goodbye, Nick.

Still out of it, Nick tried to put the phone in his pocket, realized he had none, and left it between the chair and his thigh.

His eyes focused on me. "You're... kind of a prick."

It stung, even though it shouldn't have. "Yeah. Just gonna get you to your room, then I'll fuck off, okay?"

Nick held a wobbly finger straight up, like a child with an idea. "When we do this tomorrow, maybe bring it down like a notch. Or like, four notches."

I snorted. Then registered what he was saying. "Are you serious?"

"Yeah, man," Nick swatted at me, annoyed. "I mean forget Ross, you made Gunnery Sergeant Hartman look like Mrs. Doubtfire."

"I got about sixty percent of that," I hesitated. "But I just want to make sure I understand. You actually want me to come back tomorrow?"

"What?" Nick smirked. "Got a hot date you didn't tell me about?"

"*Okay*, don't be a dick."

As far as I could tell, he was serious. I'd definitely hurt him—that was the problem with negative reinforcement, it always left a mark. But he'd forgiven it so easily. We were in uncharted territory now, and I had no idea how to proceed.

Nick's eyes closed completely, and it looked like he was talking in his sleep. "Can we get ice cream?"

"Sure. I can pick up something from the gas station across the street."

"Marble Slab?" Nick asked hopefully.

I rolled my eyes. "We'd need a van with a wheelchair lift again. It's late enough that no one will notice if we borrow one of the clinic's. Shift change is in twenty minutes, could snag the keys from behind the front desk easily enough, but I'm not gonna go through all of that if you're just going to pass out while I'm gone."

"I heard your entire plan, and I am awake and committed," Nick said, forcing his eyes fully open.

"Fine. But you're paying."

By the time I got the keys and returned, I could hear Nick snoring from outside the door.

CHAPTER EIGHTY-THREE

Either he cut the rope on his own, or something cut it for him.

I was already moving before the realization fully registered. Even a half-second hesitation could be the difference between life and death. I needed to get in there. Now.

Reading my intent, Halima placed herself between me and the ripple. Her face was drawn and pale but her mouth was set. "Our orders were explicit."

"Get out of my way," I growled.

Below her, her small bush-with-legs summon looked back and forth between us, collateral caught in the crossfire of a detonating team dynamic. Talia squared off with it and the bush-thing cowered.

"Halima, don't—" Keith tried.

"The Ceaseless Knight—" she cut off, hand gripping her hilt tighter as I ignored her and attempted to walk around, and she shuffled in front of me.

"Move!" I reached out to shove Halima out of the way. Instead of engaging, she danced backward, taking a much more serious stance.

Interesting. Not like Keith. Much more experienced, despite the social naivety. She was fully prepared for this to come to blows.

"Go back to the entrance," I tried again.

"Not without you."

I threw back my head and laughed, then fixed her with an icy stare. "Okay. Fine. We can do this the hard way. But you better be ready to kill me."

"It doesn't have to come to that—" Halima started.

"Yes, it does. For your sake—"

I took another step forward. Halima wasn't much shorter than me, but when you were standing within spitting distance of another person, the inches really added up. She didn't budge, but the fire in her eyes grew uncertain.

"—Because if your little obstruction here costs me the time I need to save Nick? I won't report it to Hastur. Or Sunny. Or Aaron. I won't report it at all. In retrospect, you'll realize what a massive fucking blunder you made. And you'll wonder why there were no consequences. In the meantime, everything around you—your every dream, desire—anything you care about will fail. Everything you touch, turned to ruin."

"You're posturing. Yes, you might be further along and have a special class, but you're just another User," Halima said. It sounded like she was trying to convince herself.

I leaned forward, looking straight ahead, and whispered just loud enough for her to hear. "If you really believe that, why don't you head over to Region 6. Ask them if fucking with me was worth it."

Halima's resolve disappeared. To her credit, she didn't move out of the way. But she also didn't move to stop me as I circled around her.

"What do we do?" Keith called after me.

"Go back to the entrance. Or don't. Your call," I said.

He might have said something else, but I didn't hear it. I splashed through the stream and used the rock alcove for support, lowering myself through the mirage.

Almost immediately, I started falling.

The **<Operator's Belt>** was already on from earlier. I instinctively oriented myself so my feet faced the ground and bent my knees. My eyes took their time adjusting to the darkness, rendering me mostly blind.

<Perception> flared at the last second. I landed in a crouch. My bones jostled from the sudden impact, but somehow I stayed on my feet, maintaining the low-to-the-ground position as I waited for my eyes to adjust.

The chamber resembled a pit more than a cave. All dirt and mud. There were long lengths of tree trunks spanning from the packed-dirt ceiling to the muddy floor, branches and dying greenery squished against the ground.

A bead of moisture touched my cheek, then another. If the tree situation wasn't disorienting enough, floating beads of water descending from the entrance in a chaotic spiral populated the cave, as if gravity lost hold on them once they entered the ripple.

Other than the scattered *taps* of water beads colliding with each other, the cave was utterly silent.

The silence—more than anything else—scared the hell out of me. I'd expected to find Nick entrenched in a life-or-death battle. I knew from the way the rope had spasmed there was some sort of struggle close to the ripple's entrance. Screams, clashing swords, bestial growling and gnashing of teeth, I would have taken any or all of them over the silence.

Because silence, more often than not, meant the struggle was over.

It was so complete that I was startled when Talia landed beside me in barely more than a whisper.

Fighting my instinct to charge blindly into the dark, I activated **<Harrowing Anticipation>**. As the threads spread from my core, the surrounding ground lit up an endless sprawl of glowing red semi-circles, including one directly about two feet in front of me.

Mines?

Probably not, but from the spacing and size, that's what they looked like. I went down on one knee and leaned forward for a better look, prepared to react at the slightest movement.

When none came, I leaned closer.

The color was strange. Off-white. And despite the perfectly rounded hole that ensconced it, the surface itself was bumpy. There was a slit between a pair of parallel protrusions, and to the side of that, a distended knot with two holes—

That's a face.

I breathed out.

Dirt scattered as the face rotated forcefully, parallel protrusions of its mouth parting to reveal flat, horse-like teeth. Still mostly covered in dirt, the mouth snapped several times, its teeth clicking together in a hollow snap.

There was a chorus of snaps that followed from either side, as several surrounding faces replied in kind.

Talia tensed beside me, but after the short echo of chattering, the faces fell dormant again.

Something odd about that response. Felt instinctual, like something an animal or insect would do.

I flicked a piece of moist dirt toward the mouth. Watched it bounce off the creature's cheek. The direct hit elicited no reaction. After a few seconds, a split tongue emerged from its mouth, cleaning the surface of its face in a practiced, clocklike motion, knocking the dirt free.

I replayed the events in my head, coming to an inevitable conclusion. Whatever these things were, they triggered on sound.

I stood slowly, panning the subterranean until I found what I was looking for. A cluster of holes, each big enough to house a small body. As I'd noted earlier, Nick wasn't built for stealth. His armor would have given him away immediately if he was moving. Talia fell in line behind me as we tread carefully, following the trail of holes, noting scuffled footprints in the mud.

We passed by a thick trunk of inverted oak and found the source of the trail.

There were a dozen of them, maybe more. Now that I had a better look, their pale skin looked far closer to the mandrakes we'd killed on the surface than a human's. Still—their anatomy wasn't far off, though it gave the feel of something prehistoric. They had giant hands and feet, and a vicious curve in their spines that gave them the look of something that was always hunched over. And like that first face in the dirt, they had no eyes or indents for them, everything from their forehead to their noses a smooth line of flesh.

Cavefiend.

Several held Nick down. Given the two dead cavefiends, bleeding black blood into the dirt beside him, they weren't taking any chances. Nick was on his back, each arm and leg pinned in place by several cavefiends, an endless number of pallid hands and fingers with too many knuckles keeping him flat against the ground.

One dug its fingers into his throat, keeping him from calling out. Another cavefiend, larger than the rest, stood over Nick. It was trying to pry his mouth open. I solved the mystery of *why* with a glance at the circle of rope hanging on the cavefiend's filthy belt, and the small pieces of pink flesh that hung from that rope like macabre ornaments.

Trophies that looked very much like tongues.

I wasn't able to save Jinny. It was a failure I still carried with me. Her death happened too quickly, the wound too decisive. But this was different. These motherfuckers had made a critical error. Instead of killing their prey immediately, they intended to toy with it instead.

The feeling of helplessness disappeared, consumed by something raw, something visceral.

Something feral.

I snapped.

CHAPTER EIGHTY-FOUR

Time stopped.

My pulse drove a heavy rhythm, and the red strands from **<Harrowing Anticipation>** pulsed alongside it, accelerating. I read the cave like sheet music, every cavefiend a note, the path forward annotated as if clearly marked with a piece of paper. I tweaked the threads with **<Probability Cascade>**, adjusting them minutely until the pitch was perfectly in tune with the vision, pounding in my head.

I was dimly aware, somewhere in the back of my mind, that I couldn't fully accomplish what I intended. I couldn't grasp it. The notes themselves were an unknown quantity—I didn't know how the cavefiends danced. Which left a question of how to fill the gaps. I could go overboard —compose alternate pieces based on how the notes reacted—but it felt like if I did, the threads would disappear before I could use them.

"See?" a voice whispered. Almost reverent. The cavefiends were still frozen in place, but I felt the same presence I felt during the Transposition. A presence that washed over me like a wave of molten iron. "All you had to do was call."

Though I couldn't see her, I was certain. Nychta stood beside me.

Had I called her? I couldn't remember.

"It's... beautiful, but I don't... I don't know how to fix it," I said without words, still obsessing over the trailing threads.

"It's not the grimelings that trouble you. While it's true you're missing information, that's a trivial fix," Nychta answered.

As she spoke, a vast quantity of information filtered into my mind. I understood the grimelings better now, was reasonably confident in how they'd react. They were constructs, the base from which many humanoid monsters formed. This batch was tainted by the only other beings present —the mandrakes—and they were useless now as anything other than guard dogs, shoved within the depths of the ripple.

More important than anything else? They were monstrously strong.

The music reordered itself in my mind clearer than before, but as Nychta had warned me, it wasn't fully clear.

"You can't make sense of it because you've taught yourself that violence is a tool. A dull implement, used only when there's no better option," Nychta whispered. "While the marauder within you wishes for one thing above all others."

"What?" I asked.

"To be *free*."

That felt wrong somehow. I felt a strong desire to argue, create a counterpoint. All I could manage was token paranoia.

"Is there a price for your help?"

Nychta balked. "A price? No, child. I came only to attend the offering you prepared for me. And though your attempts are rudimentary, and the sacrifices you offer only one step above mindless monsters, I see the same potential I always have. The potential that once stayed my hand. Nudging that potential in the right direction to ensure our joint satisfaction is my duty as your patron, nothing more."

"What do I have to do?" I asked. "To see it clearly?"

"Let go," Nychta whispered.

Time resumed.

I slumped the coil of rope off my shoulder and Audrey manifested, scampering silently across the dirt, avoiding the grimelings I mapped out for her, across from the group attacking Nick. She scaled an inverted tree, a handful of vines extending like thin, thorned fingers and smacking against the ground.

Teeth clicked loudly, shattering the quiet. Hands jutted from the dirt as grimelings emerged. But they were vulnerable exiting the ground, and Audrey capitalized, looping her vines around their necks and lifting them into the air, where they struggled and lashed out, attempting to free themselves—but their mouths stayed firmly shut.

I pulled the **<Hand Crossbow of Pathos>** from my inventory and fired a bolt into the center grimeling. It clamped both hands over its mouth, swinging back and forth by its neck from the impact of the bolt until it couldn't hold its silence anymore and screamed. The scream was guttural and terrifying, the sort of sound that haunted dreams and intensified nightmares

The two grimelings hanging on either side of the target immediately seized, reacting as if the noise alone was torture, and grabbed at the center grimeling in a blind panic, trying to stop the noise. They attacked it—punching, kicking, eventually tearing, ripping skin from muscle.

Across from the makeshift gallows, several grimelings among the group surrounding Nick were cringing, pressing their hands against the sides of their head. The big grimeling had stopped trying to get Nick's mouth open and turned around, staring back toward the chaos. It roared once, slapping one of the smaller grimelings when it stepped forward and tried to cover the larger grimeling's mouth.

I reached inside their minds. They had no fear to play with, just irritation and anger. I amped it up, tried to direct it at their companions.

If I had more time, I probably would have turned them against each other.

Unfortunately, that was the exact moment Nick tried to make his escape. He dislodged an arm, only for two of them to push it back down. The big grimeling—having apparently cut his losses—wheeled on Nick, intent on killing him before he could slip away in the pandemonium.

I covered the distance in a dead sprint, instinctively avoiding the burrowed grimelings. Some were rising anyway—teeth clicking, faces grimacing at the noise—but others were burrowing deeper.

Talia got there first and sunk her teeth into the grimeling's ankle, yanking violently until it toppled. Brutish and single-minded, the grimeling ignored Talia and dug its claws into the ground, crawling toward Nick.

Even with everything else going on, I was drawing attention—more attention than I wanted. There were two of them chasing me, and while I was faster, they weren't slow. I didn't have time to line up a shot.

I spun mid-stride and fell, trusting **<Page's Quickdraw>** to guide the shot as I pulled the trigger. The arrow lodged itself in a grimeling's shoulder, and this one didn't get its hands over its mouth in time. It screamed, and the others turned on it immediately. I inventoried **<Pathos>** and drew **<Wretch>** mid-roll, taking aim at the big grimeling that was still wiggling through the dirt toward Nick, waiting for it to pause.

It swatted down toward Talia and she jumped away, giving me the window I needed.

I pulled the trigger. The bolt flew true mostly thanks to **<Probability Cascade>**, dropping vertically while maintaining momentum in a shot that probably wouldn't have passed muster if someone caught it on video. It sunk into the base of the large grimeling's neck, killing it instantly.

But of course, nothing is simple.

With the big one out of the way, the smaller ones were unbound by hierarchy. And they were all hungry. Nick's dark-orange aura flared to life as he struggled, simultaneously attempting to regain his sword a few feet away and knock them off of him.

An icy hand grabbed me by the back of the neck and lifted me up. I'd drawn the attention of another grimeling.

I grabbed its arm with one hand, drawing **<Vorpal Gnasher>** from my inventory and driving it into the elbow joint. The blade stabbed through bone effortlessly, and the grimeling dropped me.

But it lunged forward, teeth snapping, and my leg went out from under me. I still had the knife. I could probably fend it off, but Nick was running out of time—

The tip of a sword plunged through the grimeling's skull, and it went still. Halima stared down at me, looking uncertain. I pointed to the dead grimeling.

<Myrddin: They're blind and hunt by sound. Strong though. Watch your step and don't let them grab you.>

Halima's eyes furrowed. Behind her, Keith incinerated the group of grimelings gathered beneath Audrey in a massive fireball. She banged the flat of her blade off the trunk of a tree, facing off with another grimeling that charged toward her.

<Halima: We've got your back. Go get him.>

I was already running.

CHAPTER EIGHTY-FIVE

I drove my knife through a grimeling's jaw, blade parting flesh and muscle as if it I was tearing through paper.

The second the blade was occupied, two of them—distracted with... *someone*—immediately wheeled and charged me. I pirouetted, keeping the blade in place without driving it home, pushing the wounded grimeling in front of me like a demented puppeteer.

Then I twisted the knife.

The grimeling screamed and its fellows flailed, attacking the screaming grimeling instead. I freed my blade just as they tackled it to the floor.

I stared at them, flipping the knife and catching it easily. The weight differed from **<Blade of Woe>** but it felt right in my hand, like it'd always been there. This was what strength felt like.

"Think carefully, before you deny who you are. Hastur will make you weak. A submissive dog in his sprawling kennel. He'll smooth out the rough edges, removing everything that makes you unique, significant. He'll strangle the warrior within you until only the child remains."

Someone was calling my name. My real name.

They were telling Myrddin to run, insisting that the grimelings were too strong. Someone grabbed at my arm.

I pushed them away.

The lanky grimeling with the loop of tongues advanced on me, two large companions flanking him on either side. One had a scar across his mouth that made it look like he was always smiling, while the other had a slight limp—a broken leg that never healed right.

I cast **<Hinder>** on all three of them with a simple wave of my hand, feeling the distant throb of a headache as my mana drained to dangerous levels.

The repeated uses of my Ordinator abilities cost me. I was down to my weapons and physical prowess, a situation I was dimly aware would have terrified me in normal circumstances. But for maybe the first time in my life, I wasn't afraid.

<Unsparing Fang> worked best if your opponent made the first move. It was tactical—intended to create openings through careful advancement.

Without so much as a second thought, I tossed it away.

Instead, I relied on the pulsing drumbeat in my blood as I sprinted forward, directly at the leader. Lank's mouth twisted, and he opened his arms wide, bracing. I diverged at the last second, ducking low under his outstretched arms before he could catch me in a bear hug, and drove my dagger into the soft tissue behind Gimp's knee-cap. Then pried outward.

Gimp fell, gripping his leg. He had to be in an excruciating amount of pain, but unlike the others, I slashed my dagger in controlled horizontal strikes up his arm, tearing veins open, lingering for just a second too long.

Smiley ran in front of Lank and swiped at me with a backhand. I rolled away, but even the grazing impact across the back of my head and neck was enough to send me sprawling across the ground.

A hard anger welled up within me.

"Show them who you are."

I feigned weakness, staying on my hands and knees until Smiley drew close. Watched as he drew his leg high with every intention of stomping my lights out. I shifted at the last second, whirling to my feet and risking one last use of **<Page's Quickdraw>** to staple his foot to the dirt.

Smiley roared, and I smashed the crossbow's handle into his exposed teeth, feeling an unpleasant crunch as they shattered, and shoved him clear, his foot tearing free of the arrow.

The whole thing had taken seconds. But Lank had no intention of politely waiting his turn.

He gripped the hilt of his crude knife with both hands and drove it down toward my chest. His movements were undisciplined, sloppy. But I was off-balance from shoving Smiley. Dodging wasn't an option.

I dropped both my weapons and caught his forearms. The impact nearly crushed me, slamming me to my knees. Every bone in my body creaked and threatened to snap. He tried to rip the knife free at first, then focused his entire weight on pushing it down until the point of the blade scraped against my solar plexus.

If we stayed like this, he'd break me in half.

Instead, I let myself fall, back impacting the dirt. Lank fell on top of me, single-minded in his ruthlessness, and I felt the blade point punch through my armor and an outer layer of skin. But he'd moved too close to my face in the transition.

I leaned forward, into the blade, feeling it sink in another millimeter, tilted my head to the side for a better angle, and bit down on the soft flesh of his nose.

It tasted like fungus and bile. I bit down for all I was worth and iron filtered into my mouth.

Lank reacted immediately, yanking backward. But all he accomplished was tearing his own nose off his face. I turned and spat it onto the ground, shivering at the taste.

Lank screamed, a bloody opening where his nose used to be.

The reaction was instantaneous. The grimelings still fighting the people I came with—who were they again?—all stood at attention, utterly still.

As one, the majority turned and retreated deeper into the cave.

I cautiously stooped down and retrieved the blade, never taking my eyes from the grimeling. The flesh around the ruins of his nose bubbled, the hole in his face growing smaller. He was regenerating.

Odd. None of the others did.

I charged forward, stopping dead to avoid a horizontal slash, pivoting in place and catching the side of his head with my heel.

Lank jumped backward, knife held in front of him in a forward grip. He was being more cautious now. It tempted me to push my advantage, but something held me back. The rest of these things couldn't see for shit —but Lank could, at the very least, sense me.

I tested the theory, making no audible movement but leaning forward, slashing out toward his face. Lank leaned back, avoiding the blow.

I was right. He was more developed than the others.

Which meant this was a knife fight.

I shifted into an unknown stance on instinct, slapping his knife hand away as he probed my defense, looking for an opening, and landed a glancing blow across his shoulder. The exchange felt rhythmic, and the drums in my mind grew louder.

We repeated the movements again and more of the rhythm grew louder, easier to grasp. Another exchange of blows before we parted. Another glancing wound, closer to his vitals. There was obvious frustration in his sloppy movements, and he put more and more effort into his attacks, eroding his balance. I pushed him back, slowly, feeling the drums grow louder as my enemy panicked.

There was no time to breathe, to think. It was all moving so fast now that the slightest hesitation could kill me.

He lashed out again, and I punished the move, flaying a chunk of pale skin from his knife arm and missing his throat by a hair. He stabbed at me repeatedly, using an absurd amount of power. I danced backward, letting the strange music guide my steps. I knew I was bleeding from a dozen wounds, but it didn't matter.

All that mattered was finishing the dance.

There.

I feigned, stabbing forward with the hilt of the dagger and dropping it into my waiting off hand, driving the blade into Lank's guts, dragging a red line up his torso.

He fell to his knees, gripping my arm with loose fingers. The loop of tongues swayed on the leather circle looped around his waist.

Finish it.

An image of Nick popped into my mind, tied up, helpless. What the grimelings intended to do to him. I locked my fingers under Lank's jaw, prying his mouth open, bringing the dagger forward. His face twisted in realization, revulsion, and fear.

Finish the song, Myrddin.

Someone grabbed at me. I kept a grip on Lank and pressed the dagger against their throat, belatedly turning to look.

A girl stood there, lips parted in a surprised "o."

I strained to remember the girl's name.

"Myrddin. The Ceaseless Kni—Nicholas is hurt," The girl said.

Somewhere, a curtain fell and the drums receded immediately.

As if a fog had lifted, suddenly I could remember her name perfectly. I lowered the dagger. "Halima?"

"Yes." Halima swallowed, rubbing her throat. She pointed to where Keith stood over Nick, helping him stay upright in a sitting position. Blood matted the back of his hair. "He protected us. Saw what you were dealing with and tried to help, but a grimeling struck him in the back of the head."

"Shit." I slammed the dagger behind the grimeling's ear and left in there, in case its regeneration was still in play.

<**You have killed Ancient Grimeling Silencer**>
<**Level Up:** Ordinator has reached Level 14>
<**For killing an enemy far above your level, you have been awarded an additional 3 feat points.**>
<**Congratulations**—for your performance under the patronage of a deity, you have received elevated favor and gained a new skill—>

I swiped the notifications away, hurrying toward Nick. "The codex dose him already?"

Up ahead, Keith shook his head. "It's saying it's empty."

"Probably when they caught him earlier," Halima said.

"Yours?" I asked

"Used it." Halima's hands balled into fists. "I wasn't—they were so strong—"

"Stay focused," I said, realizing with a flare of anger that I was projecting. Divine interference aside—I'd totally lost my head, fighting the grimelings. And Nick was in a bad way as a result. "The Realms of Flauros fuck with you by design. Tear away your defenses, literally and metaphorically. Stay present. Don't think about what could have happened. I may need you."

Halima's eyes widened, and after a moment, she nodded.

"M'fine," Nick said. Tried to push Keith's supporting arms away.

I dropped to one knee and tilted his chin up. One pupil was pinprick small, the other blown to hell. "No, you're not fucking fine." If he fell asleep like this, it was a one-way trip to coma town.

Nick tried to stand and I forced him back down, swiped my codex against his.

<System Notification: User Nick, Ceaseless Knight, is in critical condition. Would you like to transfer Guardian Charge to Nick—>

I selected "yes" before the text could finish scrolling. The oily black band on my wrist pulsed, then dimmed.

I checked Nick's pupils again. The change wasn't huge, but it was there. After a few seconds, he stopped swaying. His hand went to his mouth.

"They... they were gonna cut my fucking tongue out, man..." His eyes watered. For a moment, I saw the old Nick, gripping the parallel physical rehab bars.

I gripped his shoulders gently.

"I've got you, buddy. I got you."

CHAPTER EIGHTY-SIX

We waited for the codex's hold to take effect. Nick shivered, eyes fixed to the ground, paradoxically looking worse the more he healed.

I balanced on the precipice of doubt. As cold as it sounds, this failure was the evidence I needed. Proof that Nick was the same person, that his mind wasn't twisted and repurposed by Hastur, Aaron, or some other unknown party. He wasn't infallible, or perfect, or the model of wise-cracking indifference. That was a mask. One I'd witnessed him don for much of our friendship.

And now that Nick's mask was gone, it was time to decide what to do with mine.

If he wasn't at rock bottom, he was close. Hurt, humiliated, probably a little embarrassed. Completely alone in dark waters, haunted by sharks.

Sure. Revealing my identity was a risk with the geas in place. One I could barely stomach. But Nick needed an undeniable ally, and if I kept my cards too close out of paranoia or stinginess, I could lose him forever.

The defensive wounds on his arms—the least threatening injuries compared to his concussion—finally closed.

"Feeling better?" I asked.

"Sure thing." Nick lit up the room with a false smile that only stayed fixed for a second before it flickered out into a grimace. "Just wish the goddamn ringing in my ears would stop."

"Tinnitus sucks," Keith said. "Scratched under my ear protection at the gun range once for just a second, only for some guy at the far end to unload a AK. It'll get better when there's more background noise. Quiet in here."

Nick leveled a disdainful look at Keith. "I know how tinnitus works."

"Sorry." Keith cringed.

"You were supposed to leave me," Nick said, speaking more to Keith and Halima than he was to me. They both looked unnerved by the blunt statement. Halima took a step back.

"I—" Halima started.

I cut her off. "Yeah. And when I told you scouting was in my wheelhouse, you ignored me in favor of a meat grinder analogy. Guess we all need to work on our listening skills."

Nick was obviously pissed and scared. Looking for someone to blame. And while I didn't particularly care for Keith or Halima, I needed to stop him from punching down and destroying what little unity we had.

He stood up, got in my face. "You've been bucking the chain of command since we met. Popping up in the training center, pushing back on orders, and now this."

I didn't budge. "Oh. My mistake. I didn't realize you were that guy. The leader who only cares about his subordinates 'following orders.'"

Nick's mouth firmed, and I thought he might hit me. Then my words sunk in and the anger drained out of him.

"Guys. Look." Halima pointed toward the end of the cave, where the huge grimeling had fallen. At first I thought it was moving, regenerating despite the knife I left in its skull. The reality was less horrible but far more disgusting. Distended bumps scurried beneath the grimeling's skin.

A tiny translucent claw emerged from the grimeling's mouth, and a small gelatinous crab emerged. It cleaned its eye stalk and looked around, movements sluggish. The eyestalk fixed on our group and the crab's mouth gaped open.

"Is that... what we're looking for?" Halima asked, sounding disturbed.

The crab rotated on six legs, looking for an escape route before another crab emerged from the grimeling's mouth and knocked it off.

Nick pressed the collection bag into my hands, which—now that I thought about it—looked suspiciously net-like. "Let's go fishing."

Catching the crabs was a little like herding cats. Made infinitely easier because Talia's pack hunter instincts pulled their weight and she successfully chased them away from the deeper recesses of the cave, back toward us. Nick helped for the first few catches, then took a breather he never came out of, face white as a sheet.

Handling them up close confirmed my suspicions. They were identical to the crab I'd found in the light pole outside Nick's house a lifetime ago, the night before we entered the trial. But unlike that crab, there was no system warning this time. I wasn't sure why, exactly, if it was because of Hastur's mandate and influence, or because we had a system mission that specifically mandated capturing them, but after what just happened, I appreciated the lack of external interference, which was becoming something of a rarity these days.

Keith bounced back from the near-wipe quickly and was even casting minor spells to slow the crabs and make capturing them easier, while Halima was walking around in a daze, grabbing the creatures when they came near but doing little else.

It was nearly an hour before the notification popped.

<Planners Collected - 20/20. Primary objective complete.>

―――

We scrounged up a few more of the crab constructs before exiting the ripple. Outside, the paradise of the Tower's second floor livened. I was pretty sure I saw a User passing around jello shots, which I pointed out to Nick, who only shook his head.

After a brief discussion, we took a break to recoup, as practically everyone besides the summons had a level-up pending. Nick sank down on an open beach chair and kicked off his boots, resting his head on the horizontal lined rubber straps that made up the body of the chair with an arm over his face. When Keith asked what the plan was after we leveled, Nick told him there wasn't a plan and seemed to sink further into his stupor.

I could understand how he felt, my mind going back to those desperate final minutes when I was alone in the tunnel. He'd gotten his ass-kicked twice now and was probably drowning in self-doubt.

It wasn't his fault, of course. Neither the trial nor the ripple were "standard adventuring fare." But he wouldn't see it that way.

I skimmed the new ability screen first.

<Divine Skill Gained: Twilight's Nocturne, LVL 1.>

And... that was it. Completely absent an in-depth explanation when I needed it most, in true system fashion. At the very least, it was good to have another combat skill, though it was troubling in more ways than one. The most immediate concern was the nature of the skill. While it packed more of a punch than **<Unsparing Fang>**, it affected my focus in problematic ways. I'd tunnel-visioned hard on the grimelings, to the point my friend in danger almost became an afterthought.

The second concern was farther reaching. When the Allfather of Chaos gave me his mask, it was through a loophole: The Shrine of Elevation. There were several coincidences that resulted in a high chance I'd choose the mask—the fact it had to be a common item, how the gnolls' weapons and equipment were unwieldy and poorly suited to me, and my own concerns about staying anonymous. But there *were* other options. I'd chosen the mask, placed it on the Allfather's Shrine, and the Allfather coincidentally blessed it with something that was invaluable to me. So in the end, it was technically "fair." The opposite of Nychta's gift.

Nychta gave me what I needed, when I needed it, her interference much closer to a traditional deus ex machina than a cleverly laid out trail of breadcrumbs.

If it wasn't breaking the rules entirely, it had to be damn close.

Which, again, would be fantastic if I was the only one with a divine edge. There were hundreds of thousands of other Users out there, probably thousands with unique classes. And if gods were giving me freebies —despite the heretical nature of my class—I certainly wasn't the only one.

Deus ex machinas are a boon when you're the only one getting them. When everyone else is, it's just an arms race.

I pushed that concern away for the moment. The gods were a problem, but a distant one I couldn't do anything about, at least in the short-term. I might try to get in touch with Nychta later, see if I could tease more information from her. She had a problem with Hastur. Maybe I could use that.

For now, I needed to do something about my more pressing issues.

I pulled up my pending level and went to work.

Level 15 Ordinator
Identity: Myrddin, Level 15 ???
Strength: 6
Toughness: 8
Agility: 20+
Intelligence: 17+
Perception: 8
Will: 21
Companionship: 3
Active Title: Born Nihilist
Feats: Double-Blind, Ordinator's Guile I, Ordinator's Emulation, Stealth I, Awareness I, Harrowing Anticipation, Page's Quickdraw, Vindictive, Squelch, Acclimation, Hinder
Skills: Probability Cascade, LVL 9. Suggestion, LVL 23. One-handed, LVL 24. Negotiation, LVL 18. Unsparing Fang (Emulated), Level 15, Bow Adept, LVL 5.
Boons: Nychta's Veil, Eldritch Favor, Ordinator's Implements,
Summons: Audrey — Flowerfang Hybrid, Bond LVL 5. Talia — Eidolon Wolf, Bond LVL 9. Azure — Abrogated Lithid, Bond LVL 20.

Skill Points Available: 3. **Feat points available:** 5.

The stat allocation was a struggle.

I'd mostly treated perception as a dump stat up to this point, pumping intelligence and agility to exorbitantly high thresholds. The only time I'd deviated from the course other than the initial tests was raising willpower enough to ensure a solid hold on my summons and putting a few points in toughness and strength when I was in a pinch. It was better to build toward a specific goal than spread points around and end up mediocre in every category. But my circumstances had changed. Putting myself in Nick's shoes, I wasn't sure how much better I would have done, especially if I hadn't noticed the burrows—which had only happened because we were already at full alert. If I was going to take the scout role more seriously and also use my gifted skill, both in a team environment and solo, I needed to accept the reality that I couldn't do all that as a one-trick.

I raised perception by three points.

Still. Acting in a scout capacity didn't mean I didn't need firepower. I bought **<Escalating Fire>** as originally planned, hoping the synergy of **<Hinder>** and **<Page's Quickdraw>** would be as solid as expected.

I nearly bought the upgraded version of **<Squelch>** before I noticed a small asterisk at the end of the stat sheet.

<Multiple branching paths are now available, pending hidden parameters.>

My eyes narrowed. That changed things. It meant there was *something*. I skimmed through the feat list, glancing at Nick. His forearm was still draped over his face, only his nose and mouth visible.

"Hm." I said.

"What?" Nick asked. He shifted his arm, peering at me beneath it.

"At a bit of a crossroads." I reached the bottom of the list and scrolled up to the top again. "Good news is, I leveled. Got bonus talent points for finishing the Ancient Grimeling."

"Great," Nick said. He wasn't sarcastic, exactly, but utterly devoid of the usual enthusiasm.

"There's nothing game-changing in the feat list. Plus, the system's hinting that something might open up soon. And as much as I hate banking resources, a lot of my feats are fucking expensive."

"There's an enormous boost at twenty for sure," Nick mused, emerging from the dark cloud that hung over him. "Is there something at the current level that you want?"

"Nothing I'm not already taking."

"Then bank it." Nick's face darkened. "Or don't. It's not like I have the slightest bit of authority to speak from. I've spent most of my system time free falling from one disaster to another."

Same.

"If we're doing self-pity, I'm pretty sure I have a huntress and or hedonist goddess stalking me."

Nick snorted. "Is she hot?"

"She's *stalking* me," I reiterated.

"Not answering my question."

I blew air out of my lips. "Really? Just—I don't know. She's like a hundred feet tall and I've only seen her legs."

He pointed a finger at me. "But did you want those legs to step on you?"

"What. No."

"Probably not hot then."

Countless stories of The Greek Gods cursing mortals with bad luck for offending their vanity cycled through my mind.

"I *didn't* say that. I am not entertaining or corroborating that. And I have no basis on which to make that judgment." I talked to the tape, in case Nychta was eavesdropping. "Now stop trying to get me murdered, please."

Nick laughed. "So. You get nervous." His eyes trailed to where Halima and Keith sat side by side. Halima was nursing a piña colada, casting worried glances our way as they talked in whispers among themselves. "Sorry for being a dick, before."

"You weren't being a dick. You were coping," I corrected quietly.

"And thanks for saving my ass. I know... how bad that could have gotten. Even though I tried to shrug it off." Nick sighed, wearily staring up into the endless blue sky above. "I really needed this to go well. The kids are losing faith in me. Hell, I'm losing faith in myself."

"They're just worried. If anything, Halima has too much faith in you. She had me half-convinced we should follow orders and you could handle whatever was in there."

He continued on as if I hadn't spoken. "Have you ever had to choose between the high road and the low road? Like had to make a decision that compromised the person you thought you were?"

"Yes," I answered immediately. Though the more accurate response would have been "all the goddamn time."

"What did you do?" Nick asked.

I hesitated. This felt like it was important to him, but I couldn't responsibly give him an answer without knowing why he was asking, and the conclusions he might draw from it. "I've... never given much consideration to compromising myself, to be honest. A way forward is a way forward. Low-risk beats high-risk. Altruism inevitably ends up as self-serving. Cold rationality always wins."

Nick raised an eyebrow. "'Fuck you, I got mine,' huh?"

I nodded. "At least, that was how I thought before. When I was powerless and surviving was the only aim. Before the dome, my best chance of affecting the lives of people around me was to become a politician, or a leader, which was one hell of a long shot I wasn't particularly interested in taking. But things have changed. To maintain that philosophy, now that I have power? It feels..."

"Wrong," Nick finished.

"Pretty much."

"It's funny how we've gone through similar shit and come to completely different conclusions," he said in a tone that gave the impression he didn't find it funny at all.

"Oh?" I prompted.

"You said you never really cared if your decisions compromised you. I envy that." He fiddled with the bandage on the back of his head. "Being true to myself felt like the most important thing in the world. Someone my parents and friends could be proud of. Taking the high road, even if there was every advantage to be gained in diving to the depths."

"And now?" I asked.

His eyebrow furrowed. "Now I'm wondering if I've been bullshitting myself from the beginning."

There were a hundred things I wanted to say to that. But a notification popped, displaying a message from Kinsley. My blood froze.

<Kinsley: Code red. Miles is in trouble.**>**

CHAPTER EIGHTY-SEVEN

My heart raced. Fuck. *Fuck.* I'd all but spelled out in flashing neon that he was walking into a trap. Miles should have been able to handle it. Realistically, he should have gone in prepared with a strong team, equipped to the nines, fully aware of the potential danger.

<**Matt:** What happened?>
<**Kinsley:** I don't know. There's a lot of static.>
<**Matt:** Best guess, Kinsley.>

There was a pause between messages.

<**Kinsley:** I think... Miles's team hit serious resistance, he got pinned down, and they retreated without him, and now they're covering their asses in the guise of sending up a rescue flare. Adventurers' Guild's been keeping a lid on coms, but they sent out support teams which didn't even get to the ripple before they had to abort. They're arguing about whether to send a group-wide alert.>

God dammit. Why didn't he pick his people more carefully?
Because you rushed him. He's only human. As infallible as the rest of us.
I thought of the fast-pass, nestled safely in my inventory.

<**Matt:** Okay. Fine. I can get there, but it's going to take time to slip away without raising suspicions.>
<**Kinsley:** Just... try to hurry. I'm getting mixed messages and a lot of panic, but it sounds apocalyptic.>

<Matt: Is it the suits, or the monsters?>
<Kinsley: Vampires. And, Matt, from all accounts they're *really* not fucking around. Sounds more *Thirty Days of Night* than *Twilight*. Fast. Agile. Strong.>
<Matt: Keep an ear to the ground. I'll do what I can.>
<Kinsley: Sure. Uh. I hate to be the one to say this. Kind of surprised you haven't said it.>
<Matt: What?>
<Kinsley: Again, I feel gross for even writing this out. But. If Miles dies fighting the suits... isn't it... good? For us?>

It took me a second to grasp what she was driving at. The point of contacting Miles and luring him to the Tower was to drag the Order, kicking and screaming, out of the shadows. If they killed Miles, it would arguably shine *more* of a spotlight on them and still accomplish that goal. Save us from the inevitable moment his suspicions shifted back to me. Turn him into a martyr.

<Matt: Just let me know if you hear anything.>
<Kinsley: Okay. Don't die.>

I could decide what to do when I got there. For the moment, the question was, how the hell did I get clear of this without an alibi?

"Everything okay?" Nick asked. He was watching me, and though I'd tried to keep my face neutral, it was possible that something slipped through.

"Yeah. Zoned out." I stood and shuffled the accumulated sand off my armor.

"I can see that."

"Look, we're going to talk about this more." I looked him in the eye, trying to impart how serious I was. "But I realized we were so busy scouring the ripple for planners we didn't really comb it over after. Could be useful resources, items even. Rain check for when I'm back?"

"I'd tell you to watch yourself, but I don't think you need the warning." Nick pursed his lips, then drew the collection bag out of his inventory and handed it to me. "Take it in case you find more crabby friends. Bring Halima if you want an extra pair of hands."

"Thanks."

If what I had in mind was going to work, I'd need to break the line of sight. I focused inward and spoke to Azure.

"*Question.*"

"*Answer,*" Azure chirped back.

"You can't talk to a member of the Order without lying or act against its rules until we know the constraints of the geas."

"That sounded more like a statement."

"You were able to possess me with little issue."

"Still a statement."

"So my question is simple. Could we do the same in reverse, while you're manifested?"

I could almost hear the gears in Azure's mind turning. *"You're talking about swapping places."*

"Hm. Well, technically you can always assume direct control of your summons. Domination is the most basic form of summoning, but it has serious drawbacks. You could make the plant eat a veggie burger, but you'd eventually lose your grip, and she probably wouldn't like you much after."

"Would the actions a dominated being took while under direct control trigger the geas?"

"... No." Azure sounded surprised. *"If you ordered me to do something against the code and I did it, that would trigger it. But if I wasn't in my body, it would be like I wasn't violating the rules at all. Same as when I took the oath in your stead—what kind of three-card monte shit are you cooking up?"*

"Last question. Can I dominate you?"

I squinted after I said it, cringing at my wording, begging any god that happened to be listening that Azure wouldn't make it weird.

"You can dominate me whenever you want," Azure said, an impish lilt to his voice.

Clearly the gods weren't listening.

"Goddammit." I rubbed my forehead. *"Great. Thanks."*

With the rules clarified, I asked Nick if he wanted anything from the bar, reiterated that I'd see be back soon, sidestepped a pair of bare-chested men in swim trunks, and headed toward the one place that probably held the least amount of interest. The bar. There was a growing line filled with weekend warriors, the sort of people who said things like "Work hard, play hard" and debated who in the office had a case of the Mondays. I bumped the internal workings of the mask up to maximum and manifested Azure when I was sure no one was looking.

"What do you think of twinning as a catchphrase?" Azure elbowed me.

Up ahead, some guy with a faux hawk straightened up, doing a vague impression of a meerkat. "Twins?"

"Over there," I stuck my thumb at a group of girls passing by with similar haircuts, and Faux Hawk pointed them out to his friends.

Azure shot me an apologetic look.

"Forget it, how do we do this?" I asked.

We switched back to mental communication, and Azure walked me through the process. The steps I needed to take to dominate a summon weren't all that different from things I'd been doing before. A combination of the methods I used to get the most out of **<Suggestion>** and the out-of-body stuff. I had to imagine seeing the world through his eyes while also commanding him to yield.

Azure stared straight ahead, helping the process while I fell into the summon bond. It felt like slamming my psyche against a wall, and within seconds, I had a headache.

I tried again, this time with more finesse and patience.

There was a noticeable shift, and I realized I'd been thinking about it the wrong way. It wasn't like breaking down a wall exactly, more like my mind was shifting to encompass the wall, mimic it.

Slowly, I felt my mind warp and the throbbing headache kicked into overdrive.

A feeling of displacement roiled my stomach, like I'd just teleported out of existence and back in.

The beach itself hadn't changed, but it was awash in vibrant colors, moving shapes that I slowly identified as people. They were mostly blue, with some greens and yellows scattered throughout.

It suddenly reminded me of the color code we used to refer to my mother's mental state.

"This is how you see the world?" I asked quietly.

"Yep. Or at least, your mind's interpretation of how I see the world." Azure adjusted his hood, making sure his—my—face was hidden before he removed the **<Allfather's Mask>** and handed it to me. Azure himself was almost uniformly blue, the few strands of yellow and green slowly turning to indigo.

I snuck a glance toward where my party was sitting.

Keith glowed with a vibrant yellow aura, bordering on green. Halima was a light orange.

And Nick was entirely red.

If that meant what I thought it meant, I needed to fucking hurry. Every second I wasted here was a second Miles couldn't get back, and every second away was a chance for Nick to slip deeper into whatever struggle he was hinting at.

"Time to bounce?" Azure prompted.

"Yeah. Get lost. Trail us but don't stick too close. Be ready to swap back after I sell Halima the line."

"Roger," Azure said.

The quicker I locked in the alibi, the better.

CHAPTER EIGHTY-EIGHT

"You're sure you don't want me to come in with you?" Halima asked for what was probably the third time.

We backtracked to the creek, just outside of the ripple. The frayed end of the rope was still hanging, abandoned, from the tree, a persisting reminder of how close we'd come. I'd waved Halima over and was doing my best not to squint at the bright-orange aura that surrounded her.

An idea struck me. "Look, let's just be real for a minute. Your fixation on Nick is only partly professional. There's a personal aspect, right?"

Halima froze in her tracks like a deer caught in the headlights. "... No."

Naturally.

"There's no shame in it. He's a likable guy."

Everyone liked Nick, Sae herself the only one in recent memory who deviated from that norm.

Halima shook her head, much more vehement this time. "No. I appreciate his leadership style and his strength. Anything else would be untoward."

"Okay, well, if you felt that way, I'd probably rest easier."

"What? Why?"

"How do you think he's doing right now?" I asked.

This was partly a test to see how perceptive Halima was. I knew he wasn't great—no one would be, after what he'd gone through—but I didn't realize how badly off he was until I took Azure's form and viewed Nick through his shade sight. Halima considered the question for a while, which was a good sign. There was no knee-jerk response filtered through rose-tinted glasses. The muscles in her forearm flexed as she gripped something in her pocket tightly.

"Fucking awful," she finally said, words coming out in a stream. "And what's worse, he's hiding it. Normally if he's discouraged, or worried, he tells us. Let's us know what's happening in his head. But he's trying to play it off like he's fine—which he's clearly not. Which makes this the first time I've had to worry he might do something stupid."

Spot fucking on.

"You have good instincts." I watched, curious, as some of the orange tinting that surrounded her shaded closer to yellow. Was she doubting herself that much? "Which is why I need you out here. I like Keith. Think he has a lot of potential. But you're more tuned into Nick."

Halima's mouth firmed. "What do you need me to do?"

I pointed to a wide patch of shrubbery next to the stream and ripple. "If I find anything decent in there, I'll leave it here so it doesn't overload my inventory. It's a two-minute trek from here to the beach. Check it from time to time. That's our excuse for me bringing you out here and sending you back. In reality, I need you to monitor Nick. Don't tip him off, or try to get a reaction out of him to gauge his state of mind. Just keep watch from a distance. Message me as soon as you feel like something might go wrong."

Halima absorbed the words, then her eyes flicked toward me. "Why do you care?"

"How many decent people do you know in the Order?"

"A few. But you're right that most of the high levels are... unpleasant."

"And how many of those decent people are tanks?" I asked.

"Ah." Halima's eyebrows furrowed. "Just him."

"Exactly. I'll take a mid-level tank I can trust over a high-level I can't any day of the fucking week." I waited for her reaction, hoping she'd buy the deflection onto roles. From the thoughtful expression, it looked like she bit.

"Okay. I can do that. Thank you, Myrddin."

Don't thank me yet.

I turned toward the ripple, putting my back to her and waved.

"What Sybil said..." Halima called after me.

I stopped.

"I won't spread it around," she said, "You're not what I expected. Not at all."

Not knowing how to respond to that, I nodded. Then entered the ripple.

I waited for two minutes, pacing until Azure informed me she was gone. I took the mask off and tossed it up through the ripple.

Then I snapped back into my body, caught the mask, and started running.

———

My agility put in work.

I sprinted to the elevator without stopping, where a small group of Users were waiting to take it down, and took my place in the middle of them. In the meantime, I dialed the mask's power up to a hundred. Our plan was simple. Azure would attempt to find something—anything within the ripple, and collect more planners—while I rushed to floor twenty-eight and looked for a way to pull Miles' ass out of the fire.

We might lose tether before that happened—there hadn't been an opportunity to test how the tether reacted to vertical distance in the real world, and even then, the information wouldn't have been all that useful.

The realms of Flauros rarely worked the same way. It was possible that we'd maintain connection the entire time, or be severed as soon as I took the elevator down. But Halima was so focused on Nick, I doubted she would care if "I" left nothing at the drop spot for her, as long as I returned with something to show for it. It would just strengthen my alibi if Azure could pull it off.

And with the entire tower being a realm of Flauros, I could re-summon Azure whenever I wanted without worrying about his... rather explosive entrance.

The real danger would come from the lobby. By now, anyone who showed as backup would wait there, and many of the Feds and members of the Adventurers' Guild had already encountered me once. Which meant relying on the mask could be a lethal mistake.

I took a breath, cataloged my resources.

There were about twenty people on the elevator down. Most of them were riding bareback, armor with no helmet. There were exactly three exceptions.

Big suited-armor guy with a lance—no go. And why the hell did he have a lance?

Short person with a sword and shield—possible, but not ideal.

The last was a mid-height rogue with a leather hood up, wearing a leather tabard. She read as female, but only because I was standing this close, and I could vaguely catch a hint of strawberry coming from her lip gloss.

Note to self. Increased perception has the potential to vastly increase your creep factor.

I mapped out the lobby floor in my head and started working out a basic plan. Once I had the bones, I reached out with **<Suggestion>**.

"Hey, asshole. Why are you using a lance?"

Lance-guy stiffened and tilted to look at the ridiculously enormous weapon that pointed straight up, towering above the rest of the group.

With the helmet on I couldn't analyze his facial reaction, but his body-language spoke volumes.

Good. He wasn't a weird dual spec build with high int and I was getting through, and he wasn't dumb enough to not doubt his weapon of choice.

I focused on his mind and got a flash of something unexpected.

Huh.

I could work with that.

"Monster Hunter. *Bet you think you're a badass, using the least popular weapon in the game, but let's be honest, you waited until* World, *the most popular entry in the series, to jump in. And I bet you haven't even touched* Rise, *let alone* Sunbreak."

Total cold read, but a statistically probable one. *Monster Hunter World* was a breakout hit, selling more copies than most of the previous entries combined.

And from the way Lance-guy drooped, I nearly pumped my fist.

"*Let's be real. You know it's not working. This isn't a fucking game. Real lances are made for horseback use and are fucking fragile. The only reason it hasn't broken is because you've been using it to bully mandrakes in the dirt. But look at how worn the tip is, just from that. You keep this up and you're gonna get yourself killed.*"

Lance-guy didn't bother to look, because he already knew. Instead, he slowly placed the lance back in his inventory, radiating shame.

"*So you're not a real gamer. What the fuck even is a 'real gamer' anyway. You play what's popular, and that's okay. The only people who would judge you for that are elitist pricks too caught up on glory days of the past that they forget how fucking janky things were back when actual dinosaurs roamed the earth. And sure, it's a game, but there's nothing wrong with taking inspiration from the things you love. So why limit yourself to the poke-stick?*"

Lance-guy cocked his head.

I caught a flash of a comically long katana.

"*Come on, man. Have some standards.*"

Another flash. This time a towering sword, thick and long.

"*Ah. Greatsword. With your physique, that's a solid choice. And you know who has swords like that? The shop at the front. Bet they'd let you hold them, see how they feel.*"

Lance-guy straightened, radiating determination, just as the elevator cleared the shaft, giving us a view of the lobby above. It was still packed, but the feeling was totally different. Instead of the relaxed borderline-party atmosphere from before, people were looking over their shoulders, whispering. I spotted several Feds in the crowd and a few familiar Users I placed in the Adventurers' Guild.

Many were spread out, but there were several standing off to the sides of the elevator.

Perfect.

Shielding most of my body from view behind Lance-guy, I reached out to the Users from the Adventurers' Guild below and emblazoned an image in their minds. Not all of them were susceptible to **\<Suggestion\>**. They didn't need to be.

The stage was set.

CHAPTER EIGHTY-NINE

They know what you did, during the Transposition.

You thought no one saw. That you'd just get away with it.

But now it's over.

You think they'll take you prisoner? No. Maybe in the old days, but we don't live in the old days anymore.

And now—the fuck?

With the elevator still suspended twenty feet above the ground, the rogue hauled ass, vaulting the guard railing and landing hard. She took less than a second to recover before she set off running at an absurdly fast clip despite the limp, arms pumping, pushing people out of her way, moving like hell itself was chasing her.

I stared after her, gobsmacked along with the rest of the elevator's population.

I'd clocked her gear and presence, guessed she was a rogue type and that her gear looked too expensive to be a new User's, and made the connection from personal experience that most sneaky-rogue types probably hadn't gotten out of the event clean. She also had some int, which made reading her harder.

So mostly, I was throwing darts blindfolded.

The rogue bowled over Hawkins, flipping over her and dead legging her on the way down. Every present member of the Adventurers' Guild converged, far more than I realized. While their armor and robes were still wildly varied depending on class, there were small colored patches on their shoulders that varied. Probably indicating squad and rank.

Smart.

They'd figured out that something screwy was going on during our previous encounter and planned accordingly. Organized better. Having this intel helped. I needed to keep in mind I wouldn't be able to run circles around them like last time.

They quickly hemmed the rogue in. She drew twin pearlescent daggers, but as soon as she stopped moving, there was an explosion of sound and a net entrapped her from the knees up, sending her tumbling to the ground. I'd meant to make her nervous in hopes she'd crack and act more suspicious. Not... *this*.

What the hell *had* she done during the Transposition?

Many Users and Tower employees alike gathered around the display at a distant circumference, rubber-necking. That was a mixed bag. It meant more visual interference closer to the chaos but also left the path from here to the fast-pass elevator as bare and open as a wholesale store after a fire sale.

Lance-guy gave the pandemonium a quick scan, apparently deciding that getting a closer look was less important than his come-to-greatsword moment, and took long lumbering steps toward the store, clinking as he walked.

"No, wait—"

I met immediate, mind-numbing resistance. He was *dead-set* on visiting the store. So much so that I wasn't sure I could have talked him out of it with hours to do so.

Swearing under my breath, I kept pace behind him, angling myself so he blocked me from view, slowly increasing the distance between us. My heart pounded in my throat. The further I grew from him, the less coverage he provided. All it would take was one savvy person at the far edges to turn around and spot me, and things would get a lot more complicated.

After what felt like an eternity, I reached the fast-pass elevator. The attendant was up on his toes, trying to get a look at what was happening between the gawking crowd.

I grabbed his arm and forced the card into his hand. He jumped and looked at me with a foggy expression anyone who's worked a twelve-hour shift would recognize. "Sorry. Um, floor?"

"Twenty-eight."

A conflicted look came over him, his attention split between me and the chaos. "Oh, uh, be careful, fair hero, vampires—"

"I drink vampire blood for breakfast, let me pass," I snarled.

"Kay." The attendant swiped the card and stepped aside, his warning and my presence as good as forgotten. "Jesus, what's with the vampire craze all of a sudden?"

I was so fixated on getting onto the elevator clear of the lobby that the last muttering didn't sink in until the elevator was already moving. "Wait. How many people are on the twenty-eighth floor?"

"Good luck vanquishing the Dark Lord, hero." He gave me a wave without looking back.

"How many people?" I hissed, trying to keep my voice down even as the elevator rose higher.

"We await your victorious return."

"*You fucker!*"

But unless I started screaming at the top of my lungs, he was already out of earshot.

———

I knelt in the center of the elevator. My heart was still racing, for an entirely different reason. I had every intention of entering a ripple on twenty-eight. One of the highest the Gilded Tower would allow you to jump to. There was a reason I hadn't dared push farther into the adaptive dungeon. The more difficult system content didn't screw around. I'd nearly died fighting Azure in his corrupted form.

There were unknown variables in the ripple. The high-level team and Miles' group, along with the Adventurers' Guild's rescue team made three, but the attendant made it sound like there were more. If the Adventurers' Guild sent in a second rescue group, that made four, but I wasn't sure if they would when, according to Kinsley, the first was trounced so soundly.

And unlike the adaptive dungeon, there was no guarantee of a possibility of clutching this out.

Talia paced back and forth. Even Audrey, shifting back and forth on her vines, looked profoundly uncomfortable.

"Azure. You still around?" I tried.

"*Yes. Not only is our alibi ironclad, I found some useful stuff. Valuable stuff, anyway. Did you know these grimelings have gems deep in their ear canals? Like oysters or something. I know they're supposed to be screwups, or spares, or whatever, but what exactly is the purpose of that—*"

"I want to hear this, Azure, I really do, but I'm about to walk into a floor filled with vampires, and a ripple filled with meaner vampires or worse. You already told me how to deal with basic vampires, but we didn't have time to talk about what I might deal with in the ripple."

"*It could also be easier?*" Azure said. But he didn't sound convinced.

"Assume it's not."

"*Okay. Okay, let me think. If we're taking the grimeling mandrake situa-*"

tion literally, while different, they had aspects that were the reverse of each other. The mandrakes screamed, and the grimelings hated sound. So, could be a minor K'uei? They're little frog demons that inject blood, rather than drink it. You should be able to handle them, though you might pick up a few diseases. Nure-onna's another possibility, though they stick closer to shrines."

At this rate, we were going to run out of time. "Give me the absolute worst-case."

"Nosferatu," Azure said instantly. "They'll look like a normal vampire, but paler. You can really only tell by the expanded ability set. If you see them shape-shift into something functional or literally disappear into shadows, don't even try to fight them. Just get Miles and run. And if they're red—like have red spiderwebbing throughout their bodies—forget about Miles, turn around, and get out."

"That bad?" I asked. Azure was a lot of things, but he rarely exaggerated.

"Matt," Azure said, concerned. "A single Crimson Nosferatu could level this city if something transported it here before the dome."

"And now?"

"A high-level User would take it down, eventually. But..." he hesitated. "They could take out a region easily, if one say, escaped at night."

"Great. Keep in touch."

"Stay safe," Azure said.

That wasn't the type of power I could fight, in any circumstances. It didn't matter how much backup I had, that was the sort of overwhelming power that won. Period.

I swallowed, trying to still the shaking in my hands. Pulled up the store page and paid fifteen thousand and change for a common silver dagger—all that was currently available—and two dozen silver-tipped arrows.

I flipped it in my hand and frowned, finding the weight completely off. We really needed to do something about Kinsley's stock issues.

"This is absurd," Talia growled. "Miles made his den when he made you his enemy. What is the point of placing him in harm's way if you come to his rescue regardless?"

"I thought he could handle it." He *should* have been able to handle it, if his team didn't maroon him like Kinsley suspected. Ran afoul of the Order and gotten out if there was too much of a power differential.

"Then cut your losses and abandon this foolishness." Talia rounded on me, her muzzle inches from my face.

"Big... meat," Audrey said.

"You wanted to be partners," I said. "If you're regretting it, take the elevator back down."

"I'm *worried* about you!" Talia shook her head. "About *us*. That you're about to throw everything away to put a sword in your enemy's hand—"

"Big meat," Audrey said again, more insistently. She reached out with her vines and snagged Talia's tail.

"Release me, you simpleton!"

But Audrey didn't let go, just hung on, stubbornly maintaining her grip as the other summon spun in a circle, trying to throw her off.

Big meat.

"She's right," I realized.

Talia slowed, looking at me like I'd lost my mind.

"Miles hunts Necromancers. And by doing so, probably saves hundreds, maybe even thousands of lives those Necromancers would take when they come to power. But it's not just that. It's easy to forget with all the noise that Miles isn't the enemy. Or the Adventurers' Guild, or the Order, or anyone else. The enemy gave me a class that made me public enemy number one. Created a situation tailor-made to turn everyone in fucking Dallas against each other. Killed a hundred thousand during the Transposition event."

"Revenge is a distraction," Talia said slowly. It was becoming our mantra.

"Yes."

Her hackles were still raised, but eventually she backed down with a huff. "It's getting increasingly harder to keep sight of the whole."

"You're not alone in that," I admitted. "I'm... struggling. Which is why I need to deal Nick in, consequences be damned."

"And if he sells you out? Or gets compromised?"

"We run," I said. "Use Kinsley's abilities to get the innocents out and lay low. It's not ideal. I wanted to wait until we had a definitive solution for the geas so the chances of him getting compromised were smaller, but I don't think he's gonna last if I do."

"He was an admirable member of our pack, but I'll admit, I don't understand why you're willing to go so far for him. The path you've taken to get here was not an easy one," Talia said. She cocked her head. "Why is that?"

I answered honestly. "I don't know."

Talia circled around and plopped down next to me. "So. We gamble."

"I mean, we might not even have to." I chuckled. "If we stumble across a Crimson Nosferatu on our way to Miles, it's probably all over."

Talia's lips pulled back, revealing her teeth. "If we find such an enemy, I have no intention of slipping quietly into the aether."

"Same." I held a fist out toward her. "No guarantee it will, but if it comes to that? We'll put on one hell of a show."

Instead of pawing my fist, as she had before, Talia placed her head underneath it and left it there. As I stroked her coarse fur, a wave of calm washed over me, all the fears and unknowns slipping away.

For some reason, I thought of Jinny's title.

Half as long.

Twice as bright.

CHAPTER NINETY

I stepped off the elevator. Compared to the beach-party atmosphere of the second floor, the atmosphere here was night and day. It was cold, and instead of vibrant tropical faire, I was treated to a wasteland of gray brick and gothic architecture with a tall ceiling, scattered with bright splashes of red.

A catacomb. How quaint.

Whatever battle took place here dyed the image, spattering its cliche-but-reserved creepiness with grindhouse red, bodies and trails of blood soaking into the ground. Judging from the bodies, the only time I'd seen this many monsters in one place was during the Transposition.

"Looks like we missed the fun." Talia heeled at my side. While her tone was calm, her hackles were raised, the beginning of a growl in her throat.

"Fan out. Look for casualties," I murmured.

Audrey got vertical, moving cautiously at first, scaling the wall effort-lessly with her vines until she hung from the ceiling, traversing it with spider-like grace. Talia went the opposite direction, moving at a silent jog. I almost told her to slow down until I saw her pause at a corner, carefully peek around it, and move on.

I bent down, staring at the multitude of footprints at the entrance, stupidly hoping King's Ranger came with some sort of innate tracking ability. It didn't. I tried to count them, but there were so many going both directions it was impossible to get a solid headcount. Someone who'd lived in a rural area might glean more. Even with my enhanced percep-tion, the most I could nail down was that the footprints were probably human. Or at least, humanoid.

I left a little room for doubt, as they drastically ranged in size. There were footprints big enough for me put both feet together and stand in the center of them, and some small enough—

Wait.

I leaned far down, putting out a hand to catch myself. There was a small set of footprints in the mud, heading deeper into the catacombs. Too small.

Human Adolescent. Between nine and fourteen. **<Jaded Eye>** *filled in the blanks.*

I frowned. Highly specific deductions were par for the course with the title, even early on. It could divine a sidearm a civilian was carrying from the bulge in their waistband or outline in their clothes. Shame it couldn't do the same with a User's inventory, but the point was, it probably wasn't wrong.

Which begged the question. Who the hell brought a kid in here?

Tyler and the Adventurers' Guild weren't the type to use child soldiers. The Order was capable of it, but there wasn't a kid in the three-man squad that came up here. The woman with them had a kid—unless she'd pulled an *American Sniper* and carried around a fake baby as a prop —but unless she'd been feeding it something nasty, admittedly a real possibility with all the dodgy magic in play, the kid wasn't with them.

Which meant either some ballsy kid made it up to the tower's twenty-eighth floor, or there was a third party in play.

I grimaced. I needed to pay more attention to peoples' shoes.

There was a looping shadow on the ceiling, and I nearly reached for my dagger before I sensed Audrey, sending me feelings of calm and serenity.

Audrey dropped from the ceiling and landed with a wet plop, wiggling gleefully in the mud, stopping only when she noticed my expression. "Problem?"

"I'm guessing from your reaction that the floor is empty?" I said, attempting to tamp down my irritation at the ruined tracks.

"Many dead biters," Audrey confirmed.

"Anything taste good?" I asked idly, watching Talia slink her way back. From her expression, she didn't share the plant summon's cheer.

"Biters always taste worse than foragers." Audrey said it like it was common knowledge.

Talia gave the plant a pointed look. "Feasting on the fallen is best reserved for after we know we're safe. I nearly tore you open."

"You tear open." Audrey stuck a vine at me. "He bring back. My turn to tear you open."

I looked between them, confused. "You guys ran into each other?"

Talia stopped snarling at Audrey long enough to look at me. "As dungeons go, it's rather small. All vampire corpses, except the body of a human I didn't recognize that looked like it was here for a while."

"Was it a kid?"

"No, he was man-sized." Talia cocked her head.

"Any sign of the ripple?"

"Few possibilities, none I wished to risk sticking my head into, considering the situation we just escaped from. Why did you ask about a child? I can't imagine a child surviving in here."

"Tracks at the door. And I feel the same way, but why do you?" I was curious to hear her reasoning. I didn't have the most generous view of humanity, but Talia's view was more brutal than mine.

"Because what this floor lacks in size, it makes up for in cruelty. Considering the number of bodies, I'd wager a guess the vampires were all hiding in the crypts lining the wall. More nefarious, the circular layout creates a perpetual flank. It'd be next to impossible for a small group to get through without being surrounded. A child would last minutes, if that, before they were picked off."

A chill went through me. The Order's group were likely the first to go through. Meaning they dealt with an upper-level ambush and came out unscathed.

Talia approached the tracks, circling them once before she bent down over a singular small track Audrey missed, nostrils flaring in a precautionary sniff. Not satisfied, she bent down further until her muzzle was nearly pressed to the mud. Then huffed.

"Something you don't recognize?"

Talia slowly shook her head, eyes still fixed on the tracks. "More like it was never here at all. No scent at all."

"Could be too old."

"Track hasn't been walked over. It's at least somewhat fresh."

"What does lack of scent mean?"

The wolf summon gave me a grave look. "Either a being highly versed in stealth—which begs the question of why they were sloppy enough to leave tracks—or someone particularly powerful."

An uncomfortable idea proliferated in the depths of my mind. As it hardened into suspicion, I pulled up my direct messages and fired off a query to Kinsley.

<System Notification: Message could not be sent. Messaging is restricted above floor twenty-five.>

Well, that confirmed why communications had been such a clusterfuck. I pinched the bridge of my nose and tried to center myself.

"What is it?" Talia asked.

No point in holding it back.

"There's a chance my brother is in there," I finally said.

Talia took a long time to respond. "That's... bad."

If anything, that was an understatement. Not that he was in danger. If Ellison was being truthful during our cryptic conversation, he probably knew exactly what he was walking into, which put him one over on the rest of us. The problem was I didn't know what he wanted or what he was after. But I could guess. He'd killed Waller without hesitation, taken a shot at me in the apartment lobby. I'd spent a decent time in denial on the latter point. Just because he was running his own game didn't make him hostile, maybe he was helping me sell it, making it look good for the cameras.

But the longer I mulled it over, the less likely it seemed.

His power was lethal. Waller and the massacre at the cathedral was proof of that. And maybe he knew I had **<Awareness>** and expected me to dodge, but that was a gigantic risk for a small payoff. The opposite of how Ellison preferred to operate.

There was a reason he was being so cagey with information. I couldn't imagine working against him, especially with Iris's safety in the balance as he alleged, but if something about Ellison's "plan" was too horrible to stomach, I had to admit it *was* possible. My best guess was that he tried for a Batman gambit. The lobby and Feds on my ass presented an opportunity for a free shot. Either he killed me or helped sell it. If I survived, his plausible deniability was intact.

Either outcome worked for his purposes.

"Squeeze that fist any harder and you'll break it," Talia warned.

I hadn't even realized I was doing it. Slowly, I uncurled my fingers and let my hand hang loose at my side.

"If our paths cross, should we consider him hostile?" Talia asked gently.

I shook my head. Then shook it again.

"No." My voice was raw.

"Very well," Talia said. She knew me well enough by now that she was aware how sensitive this was. She didn't push as she had in the elevator, but she also didn't move. Just waited expectantly.

"If Ellison's here, there's a good chance whatever's happening inside the ripple is crucial. That's the rub with other people knowing you have future knowledge. Downside, he probably knows we're coming. And if our paths cross," I repeated her wording numbly. "There's a good chance he'll approach us. He'll probably seem friendly. May even want to cooperate."

Talia bared a smile. "Which of course we'll reject."

"No," I muttered. "I've been thinking about it a lot, and the only reason he hasn't come at me again is because it hasn't been convenient.

Ellison's about the long game. Always has been, even to a fault. Blinds him on the here and now. Right now we're not worth dealing with, and it needs to stay that way. The more oblivious he thinks we are, the better this will go. We play along. For now. Which is why I need you both to be eyes in the back of my head. Don't make it obvious, but I need at least one pair of eyes on him at all times."

A heavy silence hung between us. Talia spoke the words I didn't want to consider.

"And if his entire reason for being there is because this ripple presents another opportunity to 'deal with us?'" Talia asked. "What then?"

I ignored the question. Not because she was wrong to ask, but because I couldn't bring myself to answer. Instead, I walked around her, treading deeper into the catacombs, stepping over vampire bodies strewn all over the circular path. The carnage was the definition of overkill. Some corpses had gaping holes large enough to see through, while others were literally ripped apart.

Something ate one vampire from the head down, leaving only a torso with a bouquet of severed entrails. I looked closer and found thousands of tiny bite marks.

Audrey insisted it wasn't her handiwork. Which meant we had something new to worry about.

The ripple was in the bed of an empty sarcophagus large enough to be a giant's last resting place. It looked around a foot deeper on the inside than it was on the outside, and when I lowered a loop of rope into it, the rope fell straight through.

I fixed the rope to an iron loop on the wall that looked like it secured a prisoner's manacles. Keeping in mind that this was apparently a resting place for vampires, I tried not to think too far into it. It was probably just window dressing.

With anticipation and nausea warring in my stomach, I lowered myself down into the sarcophagus.

As soon as my head cleared the ripple, there was a chorus of malignant screams. A long scroll of text popped up before I could so much as look down.

<System Notification: You are entering a high-traffic realm with high-level Users and monsters. Ordinator interface—>
<System Error: Ordinator is a null object. User is entering a Planner realm. Terminate bonus—>
<System Error: DMANFOANETR INTRUDER DETECTED PENDING—?>
<System Error: GO BACK—>
<Local User Notification: The difficulty of this realm has increased due

to unplanned circumstances. Retreat will not incur a penalty. The last
User standing will receive an artifact as compensation.>
　　<Administrative Override: GREETINGS, ORDINATOR. THE
PARAMETERS ARE MET. ORDINATOR INTERFACE IS ONLINE. EVERY
USER DEFEATED IN THIS REALM YIELDS DOUBLE XP. EVERY LEVEL
ATTAINED RETURNS INCREASED REWARDS. HAPPY HUNTING.>

CHAPTER NINETY-ONE

Hell looked a lot like California.

The towering basalt formations below were like pictures I'd seen of the Devil's Postpile monument, only warped by nightmares and blown up to a hundred times the scale. A sprawling wasteland of hexagonal red beams bigger than redwood trees formed treacherous, uneven paths that frequently plunged downward, some coming to abrupt dead ends that plunged into black chasms.

Battle sounds.

I paused, the mental equivalent of my finger on the button to access the Ordinator interface. What stopped me was the local message that promised an artifact, combined with the personal message that promised increased XP. The system had tried to incentivize killing Users before, during the trial, an option I'd easily turned down.

If push came to shove, I'd use it, but it was better to wait until I had a better grasp of the situation.

It was tempting to head directly down the main path. Miles had called for help some time ago, and in a fight for your life, every second counts. But I needed to scout first. Get a measure of the situation.

I looked upward, searching for a vantage. Around a hundred feet up, there was a thin pathway only three or four posts wide that hung over the stone platforms. I stared at it for a little too long, looking for movement, anything to betray that the pathway wasn't as empty as it looked, or for <Jaded Eye> to warn me.

"Audrey," I whispered and held my arms out.

Audrey hopped up onto my back, fixing her vines around my waist and beneath my arms in an impromptu harness.

I glanced at Talia. "Gonna get up there. You want to scout on your own or hitch a ride?"

Talia peeked over the edge and balked. "I'll stay here. Multiple perspectives could help."

Her reaction struck me as off. "You realize if I fall to my death, you die too?"

She gave me a dirty look. "Yes. But I'll die peacefully, rather than screaming into the void."

Fair enough.

"Stay low, stay smart."

"Always do."

Talia took off down the descending platforms, timing her run perfectly to avoid tripping on the uneven terrain. As she ran, her fur rustled, taking on a muddy red hue that blended in with the environment not unlike a chameleon's natural camouflage.

Given the daunting verticality of my destination, I almost envied her. I'd used Audrey to maneuver during the Transposition to great effect, as there were a wealth of crags and ledges she could easily hold on to.

This would be harder.

"Any ideas?" I asked.

Audrey bobbed, considering the gap and our impending climb. Then she turned toward the ground and stabbed the platform below our feet. Her hardened vine tip pierced several inches into the platform. She tugged at it and it didn't budge. Which meant we had a way forward. Just one that left a queasy feeling in my stomach.

"Sure your vine won't snap?"

The plant summon leveraged the tips of three vines toward me. "They should be... enough. Yes. But, belt. Just in case."

Taking heed, I toggled the **<Operator's Belt>**. Then walked to the edge of the platform, gauging the distance. Every part of me wanted to use the flight charm instead and skip the high-wire act entirely. But there's nowhere to hide when you're flying around in the air, and I was counting on it for an emergency escape if I ran into anything I couldn't handle that could outrun me.

Or saving me if I fell into an endless abyss.

I backed up to the far edge of the platform until my heel was almost hanging off the edge, then got down into a runner's position.

"Onward, steed!" Audrey commanded, shattering my concentration. She turned away innocently when I looked at her.

Dammit. I was stalling. I looped the flight charm around my arm as a final precaution and focused on my goal. Clearing this gap.

It was nothing. Just a little jump. Angle was important, because hitting it straight on with all the momentum from the jump was a quick ticket to concussion town, assuming I didn't break my arms. But if I jumped too wide, Audrey might not punch through at all.

I pushed off, sprinting toward the ledge, arms pumping, gaining as much speed as possible before I leapt. Air rushed past my face, ruffling the fabric of my armor as I reached the apex of the jump and plunged.

Shink!

Audrey's vines took purchase, makeshift harness jarring me as they halted the downward momentum and I swung upward, bouncing against the segmented posts hard enough to rattle my teeth. Two more vines shot upward, anchoring into the formation and lifting me higher. Audrey pulled her three anchoring vines free and repeated the maneuver until I could reach out and touch the ledge.

I grabbed it and hauled myself up, breathing hard. The ordeal took years off my life, but it was worth it. The winding paths were far easier to discern from above.

Audrey snacked on a strip of raw sirloin I'd pulled from my inventory as I moved on, staying crouched—giving nothing to anyone who was looking up. The last thing I wanted was a vampire's attention, let alone one of Sunny's people.

"Any sign of Miles?" I reached out to Talia.

"No. But I found the Adventurers' Guild. And Tyler is here." Something in Talia's tone sounded exceptionally worried.

There was a clustered column blocking my view of the direction she'd gone. I hauled ass down the path until I had a vantage. And what I saw made my heart drop.

The Adventurers' Guild had assembled in mass. There were at least twenty of them, maybe more. They'd either abused the hell out of the four-man team, splitting up in quads and reassembling once they ascended, or the Gilded Tower's leadership made an exception. The group was both large and cohesive, full of high-level Users, Tyler at their front.

And they were still getting shit on.

Vampires railed against a small assembly of heavily armorer Users, all snarls and guttural screams, literally throwing themselves against shields and swords, pushing the tanks back. That wouldn't have been a problem if they had an effective back line—but small red creatures wreathed in flame flanked their casters. A few spellswords and hybrids had pivoted to fight the imps—Sara among them, but they weren't tanks. Any second now they'd break, crushed beneath between the two.

Fuck it.

I opened my UI and tabbed into the Ordinator Interface, hoping for a quick solution.

Instead, I found a staggering list.

<**Ordinator Interface**>
<**Dungeon Level:** ???>
<**Rewards:** Random Allotment>
<**Traps:** Unavailable>
<**Monster Directives:** (All) Seek and Destroy>
<**Monster Behavior:** Aggressive>
<**Monster Placement**>
<**Boss Directives:** ???>
<**Win Condition:** Boss Clear, Last User Standing>

Not every option was active. Dungeon level, rewards, traps, monster placement, and win condition were all grayed out and unresponsive. Monster directives, however, had a dropdown longer than the fucking bible. I scanned it, looking for keywords. Inactive, catatonic, cowardly, and terminally suicidal were all frustratingly absent from the list. Lacking a better option, I picked **Assign**, hoping to find Users in the dropdown list.

Again, it was extensive.

Assign to Boss
Assign to Entrance
Assign to Territory
Assign to Ordinator

Oh.

Not what I had in mind, but there was no way in hell I was turning it down.

<**WARNING:** The current selection will result in terminal mana drain. Narrow Selection or Continue?>

I ground my teeth and opted for not dying, narrowing the selection. "Vampires" weren't present on the list, but "Nosferatu" was. Selection called up a percentage slider, which I lowered by increments of ten percent, heart dropping as the percentage grew lower and lower. When it hit twenty percent, the selection finally went through. A mind-splitting headache hit me like a hurricane and I fell to my hands and knees. The world seemed grayer, drained of color, the once-dark red basalt below me a muted wine.

With considerable effort, I raised my head.

At first glance, nothing changed. The Adventurers' Guild was still beset on both sides, struggling against an endless tide of monsters. Imps on one side, vampires on the other. But a small portion of vampires, scattered throughout the seething mass, were completely motionless. They stood still, arms limp at their sides. Like they were waiting for something.

And they were staring directly at me.

I reached out, as I did with Talia and Audrey, directing my thoughts to them.

"Fall to the back of the group, discreetly."

The vampires didn't give any sort of confirmation they'd heard. Instead, they carefully waded backward through the melee, until they stood at the rear of the battle.

"Now. Kill your friends."

CHAPTER NINETY-TWO

One of the controlled vampires rammed a pointed hand into the back of a smaller vampire in front of him, ripping out a red chunk. It was impossible to see at this distance, but given the location, it was probably a heart.

A few others carried out the order a split second later, felling twice their number.

The Nosferatus' ruthless efficiency chilled me. Azure was right. If even only a few of them cornered me, or drew me into an ambush the way the grimelings had, it would be over in seconds. And not because I won.

I laid flat and withdrew my full-sized crossbow, loading the silver-tipped bolts. As I prepared, Talia leapt from her hiding place, all teeth and claws as she attacked the imps from the opposite side. At my direction, she aimed to disable, ripping out tendons from the back of legs, inner thighs. An imp leapt on top of her, only to be blasted by a wave of divine energy. It looked odd, coming from her Doberman-like form, and probably wasn't as effective as it would have been on something eldritch, but it still flattened the imp long enough for Talia to tear its burning throat out.

Meanwhile, the members of the Adventurers' Guild moved with every intention of capitalizing on their sudden luck, though they were still confused and recovering. Tyler charged in, swinging his massive sword at the vampires. The blade caught one of the distracted creatures in the mid-section, bisecting it. He yelled something over his shoulder and several of his tanks rotated backward, facing the imps instead.

Good. Tyler's truth-sight ability might be compromised, but losing an eye hadn't slowed him down. If anything, his situational awareness was better than it was during the Transposition.

But now that the jig was up, my assigned vampires were in trouble. One's head was ripped from his shoulders, another was dogpiled by the unaffected vampires. They pinned his arms and bit him repeatedly until tackling him to the ground.

Shit.

It was only natural that mine were getting picked off. I'd assigned twenty percent to myself. Discounting the Adventurers' Guild, they outnumbered my forces five to one—slightly less in this battle, after the sneak attack, but slim odds just the same.

Fall back. Hit and run when their attention is on the humans.

I repeated myself several times before they listened, their hesitation costing me a couple more casualties. One of them struck out at an AG member displaced in the chaos who—thankfully—dodged just in time.

No.

The vampire turned, straight up stopped in the middle of battle, and hissed at me.

Obey.

Another hiss.

Jump off a cliff then.

The vampire scowled and spun around, digging his fingers into an unassigned Nosferatu's chest, leaving a crater. I realized he'd reverted the previous command.

Okay, so my control over them wasn't perfect. It made sense; they weren't summons, didn't have a bond or attachment to me. I held some sort of authority, but any monster I directed was disinclined to go against their base instincts. It was a little like **<Suggestion>**. Far broader and more powerful, but situational and harder to control.

"*The imps are replenishing!*"

I glanced at Talia's side of the battlefield in time to watch a User with a war hammer knock a fiery humanoid into orbit. It pinwheeled into the chasm, emitting a distant shriek. A dozen more of them scrambled on top of each other to get to the User, scratching at his armor and faceplate. And he wasn't the only one. Even with the rotated tanks in play, that side of the battle was going far worse than before.

"*Regenerating?*"

"*No. Every time one falls, another takes its place.*" Talia hesitated. "*Comes around the corner back behind the outcropping. And they don't feel demonic. They feel artificial, somehow. Not unlike that useless creature that follows Halima around.*"

They're not native to the ripple.

The information completely reframed the conflict. If Talia was right, it meant another summoner was in play. An opportunistic User who saw the Adventurers' Guild engage with the vampires and hung back, using their summons as proxy to attack from afar.

Sunny's group aiming for the artifact. Had to be.

Below, the unassigned vampires broke ranks and ran. The last few tanks and melee Users rotated toward the back, engaging the imps. But as Talia said, the imps were growing in number, keeping the Adventurers' Guild from retreating. It didn't leave me with much of a choice.

Either abandon them and potentially lose allies, or take out the summoner.

A few more vampires arrived from farther out, coming around the corner and looking directly at me. With a simple thought, they rushed up beside Talia and engaged the imps fearlessly, despite a clear weakness to fire that left their wounds black and angry.

I jumped down to a lower platform, landing lightly and breaking into a run.

I got them into this. I'd get them out.

———

I spotted the summoner's hiding place immediately. There was a wide circular platform defended by palisades that looked built on the spot, cobbled together from materials that looked identical to the red stone that made up the posts. It was at the far end of a long, winding trail.

Problem was, the trickle of imps never stopped. I couldn't help but wonder where, exactly, the summoner was getting so much mana. The imps were solid fighters and capable of speech, which put them at least on the same level as Audrey. They were obviously far higher level than me, and intelligence increased mana capacity, but intelligence was my second-highest stat. Even if my intelligence was doubled, I doubted I could summon Audrey more than a dozen times consecutively.

Maybe there was a distinction between a traditional summoner manifesting generic mobs—even discounting that some of them were resummons, I couldn't imagine she'd found a monster core for each one—and my bonded summons. Dodging the imps on the open path was hard. Even with my stealth skill, they had caught me in the open more than once, and as far as I could see, there was only one route to the platform. Probably why the summoner chose it.

I still couldn't justify using the flight charm, so Audrey and I took the low route. The imps were ferocious but not observant. We gained ground at a snail's pace, using Audrey's vines to hang from the side of the posts every time a patrol came near.

We finally neared the barricaded dead end. Audrey dropped us off the side and we made our way around the back.

In the middle of the final ascent, the rhythmic beating of leathery wings passed directly behind my head, startling me.

I drew my crossbow in a hurry. Three bats settled on a small outcropping I was about to use as a foothold. Their behavior was off. They'd landed this close. And their heads were all turned to the side, the black beady eyes behind their pig-like snouts boring holes into me.

Waiting for orders.

I told them to stay, wait.

Instead of acquiescence, I was hit with a wave of ravenous hunger. It came from the center bat, which was shimmying back and forth. In more than one way, it reminded me of Audrey.

Feed soon, I promised, hoping I'd be out of the dungeon before they could hold me to it.

Another wave of hunger blasted me, but it felt more like a reminder rather than a demand.

Audrey hauled me as high up as we could reasonably go without someone hearing her movements, then hurled me up to the top. I caught the ledge with both hands and carefully pulled myself up.

If it was Sunny's people, I'd pass myself off as backup. If it was a monster summoning the imps, I'd keep it busy long enough for the Adventurers' Guild to get clear.

I thought I was prepared for whatever I found up there.

I was wrong.

CHAPTER NINETY-THREE

Blood everywhere. Bodies strewn across the ground, limbs and arms overlapping. Armor reduced to chunks of metal and gaping flesh. A twin blade forged of dark iron and silver edges was cast aside, familiar.

She knelt at the center, both hands poised to compress the big adventurer's chest. His head lolled off to the side, his eyes lifeless. But the woman didn't move. Almost like she was petrified. Her dark hair was wild, eyes wide, seeing everything but seeing nothing.

Thud

Thud

Thud

It felt familiar in a way I didn't like. A way that invoked a tunnel and another lone survivor, their world shattered, grasping at the threads to keep going and coming up short. Her hands glowed blue and an imp manifested outside the palisades, blind rushing down winding the path I'd just taken without looking back.

"Come on come on come on fucking die already just fucking die-" Barely audible words came out in a ceaseless ramble that never fully stopped.

The adventurer the woman tended was on his back, while the other two were on their stomachs, heads angled away from her, nothing before them but a sheer cliff. One's arm extended upward, hand and fingers curved, as if he'd tried to crawl away.

With all the powers, and flight charms, and fancy apartments, it was so easy to forget. That the odds were against us and, more often than not, this was how it ended.

Obliteration.

I hated the Order for what they'd done. To Jinny. Sae. And this woman was there. I saw her, loading her kid out of the Escalade, and later, when she did nothing. The next step should have been as simple as checking a box. Crossing a T.

Maybe it was a holdover from whatever Hastur had done to my mind, but I couldn't bring myself to do what I'd come here to do.

An alternative solution presented itself.

"The Adventurers' Guild still holding at the bridge?" I asked Talia.

"Yes."

"Status?"

"Without the vampire pincer they're stable, but not making progress. None dead. Some wounded. Probably why they're not pushing forward. Hoping whatever's manifesting the imps will run out of juice."

"Yeah. I'm dealing with that."

"Then deal with it quickly. They've noticed my presence and are letting me be for now, but that could change at any moment."

"Noted. Play it safe."

Good. That meant this could work. But I needed a plan B. I sent a brief mental prompt to the vampires below and received an answer. One I needed but didn't want.

Another imp manifested beyond the barricade.

I unlaced my gauntlet, revealing Hastur's mark, and placed it in front of the woman's face. She took a full second to look at it, then screeched, falling flat on her ass and scampering backward toward the barricade. Magic flowed down her arms and she prepared to cast.

One hand went to my inventory, and with the other I extended my palm out toward her, taking a few careful steps. "I'm your backup-"

"—W-who the hell are you?" she said.

"Your backup," I repeated evenly, making sure she could see Hastur's mark on my arm. "We need to make tracks. Imps are pushing the other users back, so we have a window to the exit."

"Stay the fuck away from me!" she screamed. The magic in her hands pulsed.

I stopped in my tracks. Fought through her mental resistance and soothed a portion of the black, raging anxiety in her mind with **<Suggestion>**. The current still ravaged her. I tried again.

"What's your name?" I asked.

"Maria." Her voice was small.

For the first time, recognition flitted through her eyes. "Sunny sent you? My messages got through?"

"Yes," I lied. If the Adventurers' Guild picked her up at the chokepoint, it wouldn't matter. They wouldn't be letting her go until she spilled, and she literally couldn't spill.

"Shit. *Shit.*" Maria released her spells and pulled at her hair until several frazzled strands came loose. She slapped the ground, tried to stand and failed, chest heaving, lungs pumping overtime. If I didn't calm her, she'd hyperventilate.

I crouched in front of her. Snapped my fingers and pointed to my eye. "Look here."

She looked.

"Deep breaths." I breathed in deeply, held it, then breathed out.

She breathed. Short panicked gulps slowly subsided, and clarity bubbled up to the surface.

"You're here. I'm here." I took on a zen cadence. "You went through something traumatic. That's normal. But backup arrived in time. You have an exit. Everything will be okay. But I need you to come with me."

For a moment, hope filtered into her face, and I thought I had her. But her mouth set.

"No." Maria shook her head, matted hair trailing behind the motion in a zigzag. She pushed herself back up on her knees and crawled to the downed adventurer, placing her hands on his chest. A few seconds later, he seized, and another imp manifested beyond the palisades. I monitored it, but like all the others, it scampered down the path without looking back. Then I scanned the grounded adventurer. Was he still alive? Was she draining him of mana, somehow?

Had she done the same thing to the other two?

"Need to stay," Maria said.

"Why?"

She reached into her inventory and tossed me a mesh bag. I opened it and found several near-translucent crabs in the bottom. But somehow less than we'd found in the grimeling cave.

"Didn't finish the quest." She was still rambling, but it was easier to make out the words now. "Not even close. Little bastards kept dying or running away to where we couldn't reach them. Then that fucker showed up."

Miles?

"This User? He was alone?"

Maria shuddered. "The rest were trash. We would have shredded them in seconds if it was just them. *Him*, though? He was a goddamn nightmare. Took hit-and-run to another level." She pointed to one of the downed adventurers with long hair, the smarmy one carrying around twin blades. Not so smarmy now. "Just fucking look."

I walked over to him and lifted the bandage on his lower back. There was a jagged wound big as a pool ball in diameter. Bastard didn't need a bandage, he needed a new kidney and a staple gun. No wonder he bled out.

Maria spoke through gritted teeth. "Whatever his class? Whatever gear he was using? Arrows hit like a goddamn fifty cal. And he was fast, too. Impossible to pin down."

Definitely Miles.

"Still alive then. He going to cause us problems?"

She scoffed. "With any luck, he died screaming. Vamp food. There was a wave of them that got between us. Fucked up both sides. We got pushed to the fringes, he and his got pushed further in."

Good chance Miles was still alive then. But none of this explained why she wasn't leaving. If I kept harping on that point, she'd sense the agenda behind it. I switched tact, tried for rapport.

"You a vet?"

Maria just looked at me, startled.

"Small number of people know what a wound from a fifty cal looks like. And it sounded like you were speaking from experience," I explained.

"Marines. Semper-fuckin-fi. Did a few tours. Don't bother thanking me for my service." Her eyes gained a far-off quality. "You know they screw you on VA benefits if you bag a DD? You can be a perfect little stone-cold soldier for years, but break down at the wrong moment and do one little thing at the end they don't like? Forget accounting for PTSD, or the mental toll. You're done. Fuck your health insurance, fuck your kid's health insurance, fuck *you*. And now I'm fucking here." Bitterness gave way to melancholy and despair.

"Lot about the old world made little sense," I said, mainly to keep her talking.

"Were you in?" she asked, giving me a curious side-eye.

"No."

"Fine. Don't tell me."

I pushed past it, trying to get through. "If you saw combat, you know that retreating isn't cowardice. It's tactical repositioning."

"Not about that."

"Then what is it about?" I ran a hand through my hair.

She hesitated. Grimaced. Then gestured to the men on the ground. "My... title... lets me absorb life-force and convert it to mana."

"...Ah."

So she *had* drained them.

She spoke faster, trying to justify herself before I drew my own conclusions. "They were all wounded. One was already unconscious, the other passed out the second he put him down. First one, I didn't know it would kill him. Never took it that far. Second one... I guess I did."

Maybe she hadn't known, definitively, but there was no way it hadn't crossed her mind.

"And now it's big boy's turn," I finished.

Her face turned dark. "Just go. Get out of here."

"I'm trying to *help* you."

Maria snapped back. "If I go back to the Order, they're not just going to pat my ass and give me a better-luck-next-time-champ. Sunny's gonna ask. And because of this geas bullshit, I can't massage the facts." Her eyes trailed to the bag in my hand. "If I come back with next to nothing and have to explain what happened here? I'm fucked."

"In that case, aren't you boned anyway? For doing this to members of the Order?"

She shook her head. "All they care about is results."

"So, what's the alternative?"

Her face was hard. "This position's defensible. Hold out until everyone on this floor is gone or dead. Bag the artifact, grab as many planners as I can. Get out."

"Just that?"

I hammered her with **<Suggestion>**, poking as many holes in her strategy as I could. I felt her mind harden, shoving away the doubt until I couldn't influence her at all.

With that, I watched Plan A crumble to ash.

I stood. "You've been honest with me, so I'll level with you. I'm the Ordinator."

Her jaw dropped. "I heard the rumors but thought they were just people spinning bullshit. Sunny really brought you in?"

I continued before she could regain her wit. "Look, I saw what you're up against. Whoever they are, they're here in number. And they're not just going to give up. But crowd control's my specialty. If you can keep them distracted, I can finish them. Then I'll see myself out and you can claim the artifact."

Maria's eyes narrowed. "You'd do that."

"Of course," I looked to the side. "For a few favors to be named later."

"I'm not blowing you."

"Not the sort of favor I'm interested in."

I watched her think. Consider her circumstances. Eventually, she nodded. "Okay. You gonna do to them what you did to Region 6?"

"On a smaller scale. But it's still difficult. Takes time to set up, otherwise things get... unpleasant."

"I can do that. Buy you time." Maria shivered. Her eyes flicked, navigating something unseen, and a few seconds later I got a prompt.

<User Maria has invited you to join a team>

I accepted the prompt. As I navigated the team screen and searched for her level, I prayed. Prayed to no one in particular that she was the baby of her group, low-level enough that I could justify guiding her into the Adventurers' Guild without putting them in danger.

<LVL 26>

Fuck.

CHAPTER NINETY-FOUR

"Ordinator. No listed level. So you weren't bullshitting. Bout time I had some luck, you're really saving my ass here," Maria looked up from her screen. She dusted herself off, and for the first time, she smiled.

"I help you, we both help Hastur, eventually we all end up in a better place," I said. The words tasted like ash.

She looked around at the carnage and her mouth tightened. "What about the bodies?"

I circled around, studying ponytail guy's corpse. "Can't take 'em with us. Should probably salvage what we can. Anything else would be wasteful. He have anything good on him?"

"Uh, maybe—" Maria tripped as she walked toward me as the application of **<Probability Spiral>** I'd set before revealing myself finally fired.

I caught her. "Careful."

"Sorry..." she trailed off, gazing down at the blade in her chest like it was an alien object. Something that made no sense.

I'd intended to finish her quickly, before she even knew what happened, but judging from the location, the blade missed her heart by a quarter-inch.

Her mouth worked. Quivered. "I... have a family."

"I know."

I said it without animus or pity. Because there was nothing else to say.

"Die," she whispered. The ground beneath us trembled. Maria grew pale as a ring of blue light expanded outward. Her entire body glowed as power ripped through her.

I leapt backward, the circle expanding, consuming more of the platform as it chased after me. It defied sense. She shouldn't have enough mana for this. A few minutes ago, she was draining her team just to summon the imps.

Unless she's draining her own life-force.

This was what I was worried about, given her level. Mages were dangerous enough as it was. If I handed her off to the Adventurers' Guild and she pulled this shit?

It'd be a massacre.

The feeling of power grew more oppressive, unbearable, and the ground cracked under my feet. Then suddenly, the circle stopped.

Maria hadn't moved from where she stood, but her head was turned to the side, her eyes flitting back and forth. Slowly, as my eyes adjusted, I saw the vampire draining her. She struggled for a moment, and it shook her, not unlike how a wolf would shake another to show authority.

After another moment of struggle and another shake, Maria stilled.

"She won't turn?" I checked.

Not unless she bites us. It chortled in a way that made me profoundly uncomfortable.

"And there's no pain," I said. "I have your word?"

The vampire nodded confirmation. From the scrambling mental message he'd sent me earlier, they incurred most of the violence capturing prey. Once captured, their bite had an anesthetic effect. Another bat flew up from the crevasse and latched onto her opposite shoulder. I looked inward, for just a moment, trying to gauge what I was feeling, finding only a void.

I reached into Maria's mind with **<Suggestion>**. She was completely susceptible now. So it was easy enough to create an image. The subject of the image was a struggle, because I didn't fully understand her.

I created what I would have wanted to see.

Maria wasn't in the ripple. In the dungeon, or the Tower, or even the goddamn south. That was a long time ago, and she'd won, taken her spoils and moved as far north as she could. A warm blanket was wrapped around her waist, and the ceiling fan kept the temperature perfect. She was reading a book, a cozy mystery where the main character could stop getting herself in trouble, but always, eventually, got herself out of it.

Was it a little boring?

Sure.

Did she want something more stressful?

Hell no.

Because she'd survived. And at the end, she'd found that after all the fighting, stress, and heartbreak, there was hope in the world, peace. She could feel it in the blanket, in the cheery atmosphere of the house she bought, the rural surroundings outside. She'd fought like hell to get there, but she'd finally found it.

And she had every intention of reveling in it.

Her eyes blurred, text growing less legible by the second. She'd stayed up too late watching TV the previous night. She frowned. What time was it? Her kid would be home from school soon, and she'd need to throw something together.

Eh, fuck it. There were leftovers in the fridge. She had time for a nap.

Right?

Probably.

Slowly, Maria closed her eyes.

And then, nothing.

———

A level-up notification popped, as well as a few others I couldn't bring myself to look at.

I'd gathered whatever I could quickly grab and stuffed it into my inventory. Then left without looking back.

Audrey kept us vertical, pushing farther into the spiraling maze of bridges while Talia sprinted beneath us. She'd had to circle around a few clusters of vampires that were beyond my influence, but mostly they didn't seem interested in chasing her. Maybe because Talia was a summon.

She'd reported that the Adventurers' Guild had retreated to the elevator, and as much as I could have used the help, it was one hell of a relief.

To say I was second-guessing myself was an understatement.

On one hand, this was the path before me. The path I'd chosen. I'd taken out an entire squad of Sunny's high-level Users without firing a bolt, outed the order in front of the Adventurers' Guild, and, assuming I found Miles alive, managed the outcome so the casualties on my side were nonexistent.

An acceptable outcome.

So why didn't it feel that way?

As much as I didn't want to admit it, the Maria situation gnawed at me. It wasn't like she didn't have it coming. They'd all stood around, watching Jinny die after their shooter jumped the gun, when all it would take to save her was a single one of them lending a codex, or their healer stepping in. But the look on her face...

I tried to spare her. It didn't take. In the end, I just... expedited the process and limited collateral.

I reiterated the thought over and over until the queasiness in my gut lost its edge.

"Those bodies... dead bitey ones?" Audrey's mental voice interrupted.

The observation startled me from my stupor and refocused me on the ground. Below us, there were dozens of ash piles strewn around the rocky ground. I checked with Talia to make sure the ground was clear, then descended.

Once we were on the ground, I tried to clear the doubts from my mind and pay attention.

Judging from the large swath of vampire bodies, arrows, and several sections of cratered ground, an enormous battle had happened here. One that resulted in monster casualties but, from what I could tell, no Users. There was some blood—trails of it leading back toward the outcropping where the Order Users made their last stand—but none leading any other direction.

I studied the ground, trying to make sense of what I was seeing. "If this is the spot Maria was talking about, where they got ambushed and driven apart, Miles got out clean," I said quietly, studying the ground.

"Not quite," Talia said. She was at the far edge of the carnage, her nose was hovering above a dark-red splotch.

"That's him? You're sure?" I asked.

"Unless another human smells exactly like him? Yes."

I crossed the clearing to Talia, stepping over bodies until I reached her. With some relief, I noted that the initial spatter was probably where he was wounded. The trail of blood lightened after that, leading up an incline. He'd kept pressure on the wound.

And the blood had yet to dry.

I reached out to both summons. "Okay. Goal is extraction. But this is Miles we're dealing with. Hyper-vigilance. Non-verbal communication only, assume everything that strikes you as odd is a trap. Don't ignore any detail. We're almost home free."

They both nodded.

I steeled myself as Talia followed the trail.

Whatever state Miles was in, somehow, I doubted he'd be happy to see me.

CHAPTER NINETY-FIVE

The trail of blood led to a small alcove beneath a rock formation reminiscent of an overpass. There it stopped, a small puddle forming on the ground but no Miles.

"Stopped here to rest? Patch himself up?" I mused.

"Or something picked him off," Talia said. Like she was hoping it had.

Either way, it looked like a dead end. Miles retreated, dragged himself to cover, and judging from the streak of blood on the rock wall, slid down it to rest. But there was no trail of blood leading away. If a monster attacked him, there would have been more blood in the proximity.

Talia walked a short distance away, nose to the ground. Then doubled back and did the same thing again in another direction, and another.

"His scent is everywhere," she complained. *"Like he couldn't decide where to go."*

It painted a grim picture. And not one that helped us.

<Jaded Eye> ground out a warning. Unlike practically every other time the title helped me, this warning was vague and unspecific. It sensed that something was wrong but couldn't tell what.

I absorbed it without reaction, careful to keep my face neutral giving nothing away, and gave the surroundings another once-over. It was around two hundred yards of flat ground. Very little cover, beyond a craggy perimeter. Now that I was looking carefully, what bothered me was how exposed the position was. It wasn't the sort of place Miles was likely to choose unless his hand was forced, or—

Shit.

Heart racing, I went through the tactics Maria described. Miles used his squad to draw fire and floated, taking opportunistic shots and flanking while still protecting his group. If he thought I'd brought Maria's group in, it had absolutely occurred to him I could do the same thing. Hanging back. Hunting.

If I was him and misled my target? Made them think I was more wounded than I actually was? This was the exact play I'd make.

I stayed perfectly still, staring at the bloodstain.

"Talia, keep sniffing the ground and stay as far from me as you plausibly can. Audrey. Scale the wall. Act like you're looking for something. "

The plant summon did as I asked, picking up on the urgency in the message.

Everything in me screamed to move as I crouched down, feigning interest in the trail.

Then leapt straight up. Audrey's vines yanked me upward, onto the cliff as the stone below devolved into a magmatic pool of fire, hot enough that I felt my skin burning within my armor. There was an explosion above and Audrey's vines snapped, her presence vanishing from my mind.

Seconds away from plunging to my death, I kicked off the wall and twisted, landing on my feet, barely clearing the pool. **<Awareness>** screamed, and I dodged the blur that passed inches from my face and exploded against the wall. Off-balance but predicting the double tap, I straightened, every nth of focus within me directed toward the series of craggy formations and cast **<Probability Cascade>** on myself.

The blur came blisteringly fast, rocketing toward my chest.

Can't dodge.

My intent wavered, and in a lapse of sanity, all focus went to my gauntlet.

I caught it.

The arrow lacked a point. Instead of a tip, it had a dark flathead with a round body large enough to carry a payload. It was tempting to send it back as a warning shot, but this being Miles?

I pulled back my arm and threw it as far as I could.

The arrow exploded before it hit the ground in a sphere of blue fire.

My heart beat like a drum in my ears. I scanned the rocks for him. "You got it wrong. I came to rescue you—"

A half-dozen arrows answered, one after another. The first few went wide, the last shots directed at me with laser precision. They exploded almost randomly as I weaved between them, catching the far edge of more than one shockwave.

I advanced as randomly as I could, zigzagging across the open space. It was far more dangerous than if I was up against an enemy I could see— I couldn't affect his accuracy. Upside was, he couldn't exactly reposition without giving himself away.

Every time **<Awareness>** was off cooldown, I focused on the craggy rocks, trying to pick him out. Finally, I saw it. A small, unnatural looking thin rock, pointed at an angle.

Not unlike the shaft of a bow.

There you are.

I beamed the location to Talia and dodged to the right, leaping over her as she hauled ass directly toward Miles' hiding place. I pulled a hairpin turn and sprinted directly toward him. Maybe twenty feet behind Talia, but she was faster than me, and the spacing between us was widening.

<Jaded Eye's> warning came just in time, and I skidded to a stop just as the rock floor before me bubbled, dissipating to nothing, and threw myself to the side as another arrow whistled by my ear.

Talia fumbled through the air, plunging straight downward. I reached out, balanced on the edge, and Talia returned to implement form, **<Broken Legacy>** zipping back toward me out of the void. Just before I caught the knife, Miles fired another arrow. This time at my feet, and an explosion shook the rock, sending **<Broken Legacy>** spinning off course, off into the void. I had to move. It would keep trying to return to me, but without a good angle on the opening, it—and Talia—were trapped beneath.

"Asshole," I hissed.

"Prick," Miles called back. "Knew something was up with that fucking knife."

He wanted to talk. Probably stall while he cooked up another contingency. Fine.

I drained what little mana I had, casting **<Probability Spiral>** on the conspicuously body-shaped rock until my vision swam.

If possible, I needed to distract him without making his view of me worse than it already was.

"How much Selve did you burn on this?" I called over. "Between the traps and the arrows, couldn't have been cheap."

There was a long pause before the answer came. "A lot."

"Save yourself some cash and talk to me."

He snorted. "Yeah, never heard that one before."

"Maybe you have. But I haven't returned fire. I'm unarmed."

"Really. You came in here without a single weapon on you?"

I paused a beat. "Well. No. But I'm not holding one."

"Okay smart guy. You want to talk?" Miles threw out his bow first, then emerged from behind a rock. He looked much as I remembered him from the Transposition, but he'd upgraded. His leather armor was reinforced with metal, painted matte black.

And there was pure, unbridled fury in his eyes.

Something held me back, some wariness in the back of my mind. He was being too cooperative, considering the absolute lethality he'd pursued me with just moments before.

I kept my answer short. "Yes."

"What exactly do we have left to talk about?"

Clink.

<Broken Legacy> bounced against the lip of the chasm and dropped back down again. It was getting closer to where I needed it to be.

His arm twitched, and when I reflexively went for my inventory, he smiled a false smile. "Uh-huh. If you wanted to talk so badly, why didn't you come and find me after the Transposition?"

"After the Overseer blasted me all over the city? Just waltz into your domain with all that fucking heat? Come on, Miles. We both know how that would have gone down."

"'Blasted.' Like you didn't fucking do it." Miles paced, but his hand never went far from his side.

"It doesn't matter what I say. You won't listen." Something occurred to me. I cocked my head. "Was your team retreating a gambit to lure me in?"

"Got it in one." Miles chuckled. "Took a minute to realize you were winding me up, sending amateurs to do your dirty work, but unfortunately for you, I've seen it before."

"Listen," I started.

"Did you massacre Region 6?" Miles asked, point blank.

Clink.

My fist tightened. "No. It was already fucked before I got there. Everything else was the Overseer pulling strings, throwing me under the bus. He seem like the truthful sort to you?"

"And the attack on the apartments? When that short-stack of yours iced *my fucking friend.*" He struck his chest, emphasizing the last three words.

"No one was supposed to die. All I wanted was the Legendary User Core. The guy who backed me up was an unknown quantity, someone with future knowledge. And frankly, I'm pretty sure he has it in for me too."

Miles rolled his eyes. "Putting that massive convenience aside for the moment. You had no intention of killing Matthias to silence him. Really."

I snorted. "Matt's the type of motherfucker who memorizes the A section of a dictionary and calls himself a genius after. Not even close to as smart as he thinks he is. Whatever he knows, it can't hurt me, and I don't give a shit about anything he could spill. I just wanted the core. And it was going to get a lot harder to get it once you all locked him down."

Miles made an "ahah" gesture. "Of course. The Legendary User Core, along with most of the cores of people in Region 6. All for that Necromancer you 'saved.'"

I hesitated. He had me there. Any denial would read as false. "Yes."

Clink. I saw it fall this time. I'd have it soon.

"To what purpose—no, don't tell me. See, this is our key problem." He scratched the back of his neck. "You say all that, and despite all evidence to the contrary, I'm inclined to believe you. Like I believed you during the Transposition. You're the best goddamn liar I've ever seen, and trust me when I say that's a high fucking bar. I'm sure if I give you a room to spin something, you'll have my head spinning like a top, chasing after all manner of bullshit. Which'll eventually leave me slack-jawed, dick in my hand, when the next grand tragedy hits."

He paused, stared at me curiously over the gap. "You like westerns, Myrddin?"

The sudden change of topic threw me. "Never dabbled."

Miles inclined his head. "Right, I forget how young you are. There are some modern ones that are decent. *Hostiles, Hell or High Water, 3:10 to Yuma.* But the old ones have a certain clarity, a—how do I say it—a purity of focus. White hat, black hat. The clashing of ideals. Good versus evil. And more often than not, it all comes down... to a draw."

His hand stirred by his side.

I stiffened, ready to activate my Page skill at a moment's notice.

What the hell was he thinking? He'd seen me fight. He was more technically proficient and better trained, but with getting a weapon out of my inventory, the only User who could match my speed was probably another Page.

"Don't do it," I snapped.

He gave me a look that was almost sad. "The most fucked up part, kid? I really did like you."

"Don't—"

Miles drew.

CHAPTER NINETY-SIX

The movement was blazingly fast and perfectly controlled. Only Mile's wrist and forearm moved, his shoulder motionless as he pulled something black and carbon from his inventory and pointed it at me.

Time slowed down.

Muzzle flare flashed three times.

It was likely only due to **<Probability Cascade>** that the first few shots missed. Something too fast to perceive struck my shoulder armor and knocked me off-balance.

Simultaneously, there was a metal blur as **<Broken Legacy>** freed itself from the pit and shot toward me.

I activated **<Page's Quickdraw>** mid-fall. My hand crossbow leapt into my grip and I aimed for the meat of Miles' thigh. Then squeezed the trigger.

He screamed and fell. We hit the ground moments apart, but the hand crossbow's pain effect didn't stop him from leveling the shaking muzzle of a stockless submachine gun directly at my head.

Blackness overtook me. Smothered me.

And for a moment, I thought it was over.

But the gunfire continued, and the blackness that covered me emitted a harsh growl, radiating pain and anger. Rage overtook me as my mind caught up with my body. Miles had brought a fucking machine gun to a crossbow fight. He'd be penalized if he killed me with it, same as I almost was at the beginning. And now Talia was paying for my shortcomings, shielding me with her own body.

"*No!*"

"Stay," Talia rasped. Her body shuddered as she took another bullet.

An unbearable rage welled up from my core.

I'm going to kill him—

I felt the breath of her muzzle as she nipped my ear. "Don't... get distracted... pup."

The meaning of her words hit like a bucket of ice water, bringing everything back into focus.

"Okay. I'll bring you back as soon as I can," I said, my voice hoarse.

Click. Click. Click.

Across the gap, Miles swore, and there was a loud clatter. From the grunts of pain, he'd run out of ammo. Was trying to get the bolt out of his leg and failing. I forced myself up on an elbow and peeked over Talia.

Sprawled out on his ass, Miles leveled a Glock at my head, and I ducked back behind the wolf just before he fired. Staggered, panicked footsteps trailed away from us. Talia's body dissipated, leaving me with a clear line on Miles, hauling ass deeper into the ripple. A series of notifications popped.

<Local User Notification:>
Rogue Bounty at the Gilded Tower, Floor 28 and 1/2
Threat Level: High
Time Limit: Until a condition is met.
Conditions: Neutralize or Terminate.
Reward: EXP (L), S100,000 - 200 Rare User Cores
<Notification End.>

God fucking dammit, Miles.

He'd tried to kill me with a blacklisted weapon. Put it all on the line. Instead, he'd "harmed" me and killed Talia, which was apparently enough for the system to flag him. The bounty was no joke. Now, if I left him injured and running scared, I might as well be signing his death warrant.

If I said it didn't tempt me, I'd be lying.

But looking at everything from a purely rational perspective, nothing had changed. The trap he'd laid had failed, and he was in more trouble now than when he was pretending to be.

Don't get distracted.

I set after him, running at a slow jog. The injury would slow him down. Now it was just a question of how many bullets he had left.

———

The answer was many.

Many bullets.

I followed from a distance, exposing as little of myself as possible. He tried another ambush, but the pain from the bolt had unsettled him. Mostly he just ran, limping painfully with every step.

I'd picked up a few vampires in the interim, used one to keep watch and the others to pull away the attention we were drawing. So far, it was just vampires on vampires.

I took cover behind a cluster of beams and called out, "Getting tired yet?"

A bullet answered. It went far wide, glancing off the stony ground and ricocheting off, meters away.

"Guess that's a no."

I staggered as a soul-rending screech, loud and unbearable, chilled me to my core. A massive shadow flitted overhead, and I instinctively ducked. Seconds later, an impact large enough to be a bomb shook the entire dungeon, sending bits of detritus skidding past where I lay prone, my entire body shaking.

Every vampire in my awareness blinked out.

Once rife with the noises of monsters and squalling, the ripple fell silent.

Fear coursed through me, fear more raw and real than any I'd felt before. Fear that made me feel like I was a child who just discovered how terrifying the world really was.

I forced my eyes open.

Nearby, one of the overhanging bridges collapsed, crumbling into the abyss. It'd been shredded in half. Hole running clear through it.

And far off, in the direction Miles was running, there was an angled crater. Miles was a bloodied mess, facedown, motionless. And above him a lone figure stood, completely still. Its skin was crimson, its body sleek and thin, with arms that ended in claws.

A voice that slithered and pervaded everything, coming from everywhere all at once, filled the ripple.

"You... want him? Come... take... him."

The Crimson Nosferatu matched Azure's description perfectly. My body trembled. And somehow, with monumental effort, I pushed myself up to my knees. It hadn't moved an inch and didn't seem to be in any hurry.

I reached out to Miles with **<Suggestion>** and felt significant pushback.

It was confirmation he was still alive, still conscious. Didn't solve the problem. The Nosferatu felt absurdly powerful, but that didn't mean it was intelligent. Maybe I could influence it. I reached out with **<Suggestion>**—

The connection snapped, and my vision dimmed to almost nothing. When it returned, I felt shell-shocked, hollow.

Numbly, I tried to mentally review the resources I had, placing them on the ground in front of me.

The common silver knife and the arrowheads.

My crossbows, bow, and potions.

My mana was dry.

GET OUT.

No. I could come up with something. I just needed a plan. Some way to distract it long enough to grab Miles and get out.

How. It's faster than you. Smarter than you. If you're lucky as hell, maybe it'll even let you go.

The Crimson Nosferatu's voice silenced my inner thoughts. "How long do you intend to make me *wait?*"

Helplessness overtook me. The same helplessness I'd felt in the tunnel. Maybe Kinsley was right. Maybe we were better off with Miles gone. He'd come within seconds of killing me, and this thing had manhandled him like he was nothing.

Another voice radiated in my mind. One I hadn't heard in a very long time.

You have to choose what you want to be. And you have to keep making that choice.

For perhaps the first time, I listened to my father's words. This didn't feel like a fight I could win. Everything in my rational mind was screaming at me to run. But if I ran, my actions spoke for themselves. I would have pulled Miles into a situation he couldn't handle and abandoned him when it got hard.

And maybe it was Hastur's revelation of what my life could have been, or maybe I'd changed. I didn't know.

Regardless of why, I gathered my things and stood. Crossbow in one hand, dagger in the other.

The Nosferatu cackled and its aura pressed down on me. "Finally. I hope... your power... exceeds... your stature."

That was an odd taunt. Power aside, it was half a head taller, if that.

Someone cleared their throat.

I started and turned, blinking several times, unable to believe what I was seeing.

Ellison was standing next to me, his arms crossed. His stoic face held a hint of a smile. "Sorry you had to find out this way, Matt. But it's not *always* about you."

CHAPTER NINETY-SEVEN

Ellison looked...

I swallowed down the swell of emotion and tried to shake it off.

Kids are small. That's obvious. But you don't truly realize until you take responsibility for one, how slowly they grow. Maybe it wouldn't feel so painstaking if they grew up protected in a vacuum. But they don't. The world swirls around them, tearing at their unknowing hearts, shredding them with a debris of endless collateral they had nothing to do with. Hurting them for no goddamn reason, when they did nothing to deserve it. And you can't help feeling that eventually, the storms and gusts will tire of toying with them and rip them from your arms entirely, carrying them away.

Because as much as we'd like them to be, kids aren't protected by some common law of decency, or God, or trivial plot convenience. They get hungry and gaunt when there isn't enough food to go around, fall victim to outside influences and grow cynical, and in the end, die like anything else.

So, as much as we'd like to wish the opposite, we are so often left wishing for something many would consider cruel.

Grow up and grow up quickly. Please. Before the world throws more hurt your way than I can protect you from.

Ellison's physical characteristics had changed little. His arms were bigger, the clavicle at his neck more pronounced, his shoulders broader. He still held his trademark, all-knowing smirk that was his default expression when he wasn't scowling.

But his eyes had aged a thousand years.

His metal armor reflected a warm blue, a fiery indigo bird etched into his chest piece, wreathed in blue flame.

Behind him, maybe twenty feet away from us, a man with long curly hair, wreathed in cloth bandages that flowed freely behind him despite the absence of wind in the cave, stood. He was gazing at the Nosferatu in the crater but seemed entirely too relaxed, considering the strength of the enemy at hand.

Belatedly, I realized Ellison was talking. "... and now I'm waiting for you to pay attention again."

I blinked.

"There it is," Ellison said. "What I was saying—before you drifted off to poignant nostalgia land—was that there were... quite a few things I needed to grab to prepare for this. And I knew you could handle it. Nine times out of ten, you pull that victory out of your ass. That's why I couldn't help more during the Transposition." He trailed off and his gaze grew distant. "Still. I know the toll it took on you. What it cost. And I'm sorry I couldn't help more."

I *wanted* to talk to him. There was nothing I wanted more. But the Crimson Nosferatu didn't seem like the type of creature polite enough to let you pause for an aside.

I inclined my head toward it. "Is—"

"He'll wait," Ellison finished. "He's ornery, but his perception of time is different. Hell, he's older than most of the population of Texas combined. Also, he's a pompous geriatric fuck who likes to let his prey come to him."

"And Miles?"

"Stable. The collateral looks bad, but the amount of control that thing has is absurd. It knows I want to get Miles out, and there's nothing more useless than a dead hostage."

Something ticked in my mind. An inconsistency. "The vampire. Did you mean he *thinks* he's older?"

From my mostly guesswork understanding, monsters generated in the realms of Flauros were synthesized at the behest of something greater. Probably by the planners. Their previous life memories were fabrications —the only life they truly lived was whatever they carved out for themselves in the dungeons.

Ellison slowly shook his head. "Not... exactly. This really what you want to talk about?"

No. It wasn't.

"Your ability. The future knowledge. How does it work?"

A dark shadow flitted across Ellison's face. "Time loop."

"Progressive or self-contained?"

"Self-contained."

"Any carry over of abilities, items?"

"Not a damn thing except this." Ellison pointed to his head and scowled. "And even then, I don't get the full package. My memories fade like anyone else's. They're more or less consistent, unless shit goes really bad early and post-traumatic stress gets out of control, then my memories from that loop are fucked."

I slowly connected the dots. There was a problem with time loop fiction that always stuck out to me, in that the protagonists go through several life-times' worth of trauma and mentally age dozens, if not hundreds of years. Realistically, any normal person who went through that would be reduced to a gibbering mess of insanity by the end, and the accumulated anxiety, depression, and angst the constant futility would incur.

"They reset your fucking mental state," I hissed, barely able to believe it.

"You always have such a visceral reaction to that," Ellison mused. "But yes. Hell, half the time I wake up at the beginning. As soon as I think about the shit I've done in the previous loops, it inevitably ends with me purging in the bathroom."

I gritted my teeth. As far as the average person went, I'd done a decent job taking things in stride. But going through something like this once had been hard enough. Losing all the progress I'd made and, despite that, knowing all the horrors in store? I couldn't imagine.

It was all I could do to stay calm, fists clenched at my side. "If you'd told me earlier, I..."

Ellison quirked an eyebrow. "You... what? Would you even have believed all this shit at the beginning? The guy who watched someone with powers out of a Marvel movie get eighty-sixed in an alley and went to work at Dunkin's the next day?"

He knew about that. The way he was talking, he'd been in the loop for a while. I had to assume he knew everything, keep deceit to an absolute minimum.

"Fair. But I'm not that person anymore. Let me help you *now*," I argued. "Deal me in. I won't undercut you, or muscle in, or try to steer things in a direction I want. You're on point. So fucking delegate."

"To be fair," Ellison continued as if he hadn't heard me, his expression softening. "You catch on pretty fast. Faster than most people. There were a few times, mostly earlier on, when I woke up and I just couldn't handle it. What happened before. Couldn't get out of bed. Couldn't eat. And when I... broke... it was like you knew exactly what to do. You scheduled a shrink appointment we couldn't afford—date always set after the dome came down, but it was the thought that counted—took off work, and let me cling to you like a stupid child. You even read to me. Though I'll be honest, the book you usually chose was, uh. Not the greatest, considering."

There was a *lot* to unpack there, and in the meantime, my mind seized on the last thing he said.

I pinched the bridge of my nose and sighed. "Please tell me it wasn't Vonnegut."

"*Slaughterhouse 5,* baby." Ellison grinned, but the grin was hollow. "'All moments past, present, and future, always have existed, always will exist.' When you first read that passage I burst into tears—confused the hell out of you. The second time, though, it was actually kind of comforting. That time is static. Realized. Every decision we will or won't make already etched in stone."

Ellison had confirmed what I'd suspected. He'd been resetting to a scant few days before shit hit the fan. Given that, there was no way he hadn't tried to leave. Either with us in tow or on his own.

"I take it outside the dome isn't much better?" I asked.

"Outside is different. Fewer monsters and powers, more supply issues, starvation, and garden variety people losing their minds in the face of the apocalypse. Sweeping everyone we give a shit about outside the dome is the same as prematurely breaking open a cocoon. It cripples us when it counts."

"And?"

Ellison gave me an even look. "We die, Matt. Every one of us. So far that happens inside the dome too, but at least the system gives us a fighting chance."

An icy chill went through me. I'd never been overly positive about our prospects, where things within the dome were going. Having it confirmed felt different.

"What happens after the citywide game?"

"I can't tell you that."

"What's the purpose of the Ordinator class?"

"Can't tell you that either."

"Why is Iris so important?"

Ellison feigned confusion. "Because she's our sister?"

"In the greater scheme of things."

"Oh. Definitely can't tell you that."

"Well. Why the fuck not?" I finally asked, barely filtering the hurt and hostility out of my voice. Addressed the elephant in the room that'd been present ever since I guessed his abilities. That up to a certain point, he knew everything that came to pass and made an informed choice to keep me out of it.

Ellison paused for the first time. Before, his responses were like mine every time Nick regurgitated the Wizard Quest story. More or less on auto-pilot. Now, he was thinking about them. Why? I'd almost certainly asked him this before. Was he considering giving me a different answer? Something real?

He flexed his jaw, seeming to decide. "I know what you're thinking. Probably how many things you'd do differently, if you were in my shoes. It's not that easy. Time, the order of events, it's all so much more finicky than it is in the stories. There's no set track, no predestination. The smallest changes end up altering things for no goddamn reason, and sometimes things change regardless of what you do. Ghosts in the machine."

"The butterfly effect."

"More or less. I tried warning everyone. Telling them what I know. Tried it more than once. Want to guess what happened?" Ellison asked.

I thought of how the Overseer had cranked up the difficulty of the Transposition in response to an abnormal amount of User advancement. "It changed everything too much. You weren't able to make viable predictions anymore, and while maybe we cleared some of the initial hurdles with no issue, the eyes in the sky kept throwing curveballs and we eventually got blindsided."

"Yep." Ellison scoffed. "God, I hate how quick you are on the uptake. It took a lot of blood, tears, and wasted time before I even considered that. Point is, I've switched tactics. These days I help people who need to stay alive exactly when they need it, kill people who need killing, disappear, avoid explaining anything. Problem is, there's still a laundry list of giant variables I don't know how to control."

I didn't want to ask. But I had to. "Am I someone who needs to stay alive? Or…"

For a moment, Ellison looked shaken. "Doesn't matter. I'm here for Miles, same as you."

Then, a beat later he added, "Guessing you caught on to what happened at the apartments."

"More or less," I said, trying very hard not to think about how casual my brother was on the topic.

"Truth is, I don't know what you are." Ellison struggled, searching for a way to say whatever he was thinking. "Ever. You're the biggest variable there is. Sometimes, you're the best resource I have. Sometimes, you're my worst fucking enemy. I've tried dealing you in, obliquely pointing you in the right direction, abandoning you entirely, and a bunch of other shit not worth repeating. No matter what I do or how many times I try it, the outcome is completely unpredictable."

The cold arithmetic of it chilled me, as the events of the apartment snapped into context. When I looked at it abstractly, Ellison was being honest, insofar as me not falling into either camp he'd described. I wasn't a threat or an ally. Instead, I was a variable.

And the best way to deal with a troublesome variable is to remove it entirely.

Ellison waved an arm. "That being said, this iteration of you is unique in a few ways that caught my eye. The uh, last breakfast we shared, I gave you a lot of shit for being a hypocrite—mainly as a vehicle for getting you to leave me the fuck alone."

"I remember," I said, only a little bitter.

"Well, it wasn't bullshit. You are a hypocrite."

"Thanks."

"But I don't think that's necessarily a bad thing."

"Really—"

The Nosferatu hissed loud enough to fill the dungeon, startling both of us. Ellison fell silent, his smirk fading to stoic neutrality. The significance of the fact that it still unsettled him, despite running into it multiple times before, wasn't lost on me.

Apparently, the conversation was over.

Ellison cleared his throat. When he called across the crystal clearing to the Nosferatu, he almost sounded like a comic book hero. "I'll meet you in combat, crimson one. But if you wish for a genuine test, you must give me time to make preparations."

"Then make *haste*," the Nosferatu hissed.

I processed what had happened, slowly. "That actually *worked*?"

"Uh-huh," Ellison said. "The higher-level monsters develop a lot of quirks. Some get nastier, more deviant, others gain certain preferences. It's all about drawing out their values, figuring a way to use it against them. But you already know a thing or two about that. Can't speak to where this motherfucker got the *Dragon Ball Z* fight logic from, but I will not complain."

He took a knee and drew various metal pieces and cylinders out of his inventory. One by one, he assembled them with practiced ease, the pieces coming together to form a tripod. Slowly, the device took shape. Once I realized what it was, I couldn't help but snort.

"A ballista."

"I call it the anti-armor, magic-deterring, cyber-influenced, magic-implosion ballista. Or AAMDCIMIB."

It was a terrible name with an equally terrible acronym, but somehow, knowing that despite everything my brother must have endured he still held on to some of his old quirks, was a minor comfort.

"You are a fool, small one. No mortal weapon can wound me," the Nosferatu called over the clearing.

"Every time you mention my height is another five minutes you'll suffer before I kill you," Ellison muttered.

He pressed a tiny object, similar in size and shape to a roll of lipstick, to the far end of the ballista's bow. As he pulled it back, a luminescent blue beam of light emerged, tethered to the bow. He held the object far from his body and stepped over the miniature ballista's body, attaching the beam to the other edge and stepped away, ballista complete with the requisite string. Then he fiddled with the gear-like mechanisms of the ballista, pressing his head against its body before returning to the adjustments, dialing in the range.

"To answer the question you didn't finish—the 'really, being a hypocrite isn't a bad thing' in an unnecessarily sarcastic voice," Ellison said quietly, "I'm not talking about flip-flopping, or punching down on someone for doing something you do regularly. I'm talking about the big shit. How many wars do you think could have been averted if the drum beaters at the top were introspective enough to stop buying into their own propaganda?"

"You're not wrong, but I'm not seeing how that applies here," I said.

Ellison shook the ballista, then banged his forearm against it. There was a click of something falling into place.

"Cold rationality and self-interest are an effective mix for survival. There's a reason so many assholes make it to the end of the world. But there's a limit to how much that can help you before it does the opposite. And from my observations, you, in particular, can reach far greater heights of power, the more people you're trying to protect—almost out of pure necessity. Our family. The Adventurers' Guild. Kinsley. Nick. Sae. Miles." Ellison paused, as if deciding whether to mention something. "Jinny."

"Is—"

"I can't answer that. What I can say is that, excluding the last name, this is the first time they've all been alive simultaneously. Mostly because you helped them. Other things I can't talk about are also going uncharacteristically well. Which is why... I did what I did."

It stung, but I understood. "Tried to remove the variable before it skewed the results."

"Exactly." For just a second, Ellison looked ashamed. "I've obviously reconsidered, which is why we're having this conversation. I can't fully deal you in, but I don't think this deviation from you is an act, and if I don't take advantage of it now, I might never have another chance."

"What do you need from me?" I asked.

"First and foremost, I need space to work. If you follow me, try to figure out what I'm doing, or use your vocation ability to spy on me, we're done."

"Got it."

Ellison loaded the ballista bolt. Or at least, that was what I assumed it was. It was forged from pure shadow, and despite the decently lit environment, it almost convinced my mind there was nothing there.

"Secondly. I need you to do what I ask, when I ask. For the immediate future, that's grabbing Miles while I'm keeping Mister BBEG over there busy. Don't back me up, don't even take a parting shot." Ellison scratched his nose with his third finger—the signal to ignore what he'd just said. With the timing, he wanted me to prioritize getting Miles out but wouldn't turn down any help I could give him on the exit. "Once you're in the elevator, I need you to pass on a message to Miles, from you, in this exact wording. 'For someone so concerned about the good of the people, you really ought to look into what Waller was doing in his free time.'"

"What—you can't tell me that," I finished before he could speak.

"Now you're getting it." Ellison smiled. A genuine smile, not a smirk. It slowly faded. "I'll let the Fed fill you in after he's not jammed up with a bounty and investigates. Waller needed killing. It seemed like a solid opportunity, but now that we're working together, it could make your life a lot more difficult. You need Miles off your back. Trust me. The guy is relentless."

"Figured that one out," I muttered.

"Once the ball is live, you need to hurry. If you take too long with Miles, you may miss something else. Something important."

Nick? Or something else. It's all so goddamn vague.

"Also, be careful with the Order of Parcae," Ellison continued. "I'm guessing you've figured out we need them in some capacity, but their management leaves a lot to be desired. You've handled them well enough, and I think you're heading in a good direction—dragging them out into the spotlight with this stunt, not shooting Aaron in the face the first time you saw him, keeping body count to a minimum before you know all the players. Just again, be careful. I've never seen this exact scenario, but as you know, they're not fucking around. The Order turns nasty on a dime."

"Hastur?" I asked.

Ellison shook his head and pressed his lips together.

"How long has it been?" I finally asked. "Since the first loop?"

Ellison's voice was tired. "At one point I kept track. Wrote the number down on my journal as soon as I woke up and stared at it until I was confident I'd committed it to memory. But now? I can't even remember the number I gave up on."

The image of Ellison I was trying to hold on to—my impression of him as a moody, clever kid who would hopefully brighten up after his teenage years—finally faded away, and I saw him for what he was. A soldier who had been at war for far too long.

I opened my mouth.

"Yes," Ellison cut me off and pulled a hand down his brow, contorting his face. "Assuming I survive this, I'll come to dinner. Might even stay and watch a movie."

"Great." In that moment, that was all I wanted.

"Lastly. You've got a thirty-second window before this thing grows its head back." In one smooth motion, Ellison reached down and fired the ballista.

CHAPTER NINETY-EIGHT

There wasn't thumping release, or a twang, or even a blur of motion. The glowing blue "string" returning to its original position was the only sign the ballista fired, and even then it looked like it must have slipped the catch rather than ejected the bolt.

FWOOM

A shockwave knocked me to one knee, jarring my arms and wrists as I came dangerously close to face-planting on the crystal cavern floor. I searched through the haze of the aftereffect just in time to see an outline of a human torso flying through the air. Slowly, my mind connected the dots and I realized what had just happened.

The Crimson Nosferatu—a creature Azure described as so powerful it could level cities—was cleaved in half by the shadow bolt.

"Holy fuck," I murmured, at a loss for words.

Ellison didn't cheer or celebrate, his face a mask of barely contained panic as his armor extended from his neck, wrapping around his head and forming a helmet. "God dammit, too low. Damocles! Get the head—"

Before he even gave the order, the man sprinted forward almost too quickly to track, lugging a massive great sword behind him until he reached the Nosferatu and brought the sword down in a massive overhead strike, again and again, each impact ringing out like a sledgehammer on iron.

"Go, get Miles out *now*." Ellison shoved me forward. As I ran, he called after me. "Make sure he leaves the ripple first!"

Why?

There wasn't time to ask. Miles was up, staggering away from the crater. From his movements he was stunned, or injured, or both, but from

prior experience, it wouldn't be long before he was up and running, dragging us both into more bullshit.

Off to the side, Ellison's companion—Damocles—was still smashing
the full weight of his sword across the creature's throat, over and over like
a lumberjack splitting wood, while Ellison bound its legs and arms with a
silver wire, swearing loudly and shouting instructions.

I pulled my hand crossbow with **<Page's Quickdraw>** and fired a
torment bolt, aiming for the creature's exposed entrails, watching with
grim satisfaction as it struck home and the Nosferatu writhed.

Right on cue, Miles' head lolled in my direction and his eyes fixated on
me. He drunkenly turned and lurched away from me.

I wheeled him around before he gained momentum and, pulling the
blow at the last second, struck his nose with the meat of my palm. Carti-
lage buckled under my palm but didn't break, and Miles' head snapped
back, his eyes hazy and confused.

"Use your goddamn brain. I'm trying to save your life. We all are," I
shouted, hoping I'd finally gotten through, and chanced looping his arm
around my neck for support. This was a vulnerable position. If he had a
mana garrote on him, it'd be child's play to slip it around my throat. His
feet dragged, slowing us down. "*Run,* motherfucker."

"Jesus Christ," Miles muttered. He was staring at the Nosferatu, which
—despite being bound, shot, bludgeoned, and losing enough blood to kill
an elephant—had already regrown its legs and was slowly but consis-
tently breaking free of its restraints. Finally, Miles seemed to conclude
that even if this was some kind of con, getting out of the Tower was the
best course of action. His grip tightened around the back of my neck and
his legs pumped, movements still clumsy and uncoordinated.

Eventually our movements synced, and we made decent time as we
raced across the clearing.

"Felt like—" Miles' devolved into a series of coughs. "Getting hit by a
bus. Twice. Didn't even hear it coming."

"Might be your ears, considering all the goddamn gunfire," I said.

"What is it?"

"Bad fucking news—*Shit!*"

Bad news got worse as **<Awareness>** screamed and I ducked, dragging Miles with me, barely clearing a crescent wave of red. The Nosferatu's claw-like hands pointed toward us, ignoring Ellison and company
entirely as it shrieked in an alien tongue with a voice full of rage.

Not good. If I had to guess, Ellison's joint attack broke its rules of
engagement, and now it had every intention of taking the slight out on
the hostage.

We started running again at a slower pace, dodging the crescent
blades of magic as they came. With every passing second, the Nosferatu

seemed closer to escaping, more binds snapping free as it recovered its power.

As soon as it freed itself and had access to even a fraction of its mobility, we were done.

Flight charm?

Using the charm would be an automatic tell. Miles would have almost definitive confirmation that Myrddin was connected to the Adventurers' Guild, and it would undo everything I'd done to throw him off. I'd use it if I had to, but...

Maybe there was another option.

"That thing breaks free, we're S-O-L. Anything in your back pocket that could help? Teleport spell, speed acceleration, anything at all?" I tried.

Miles thought hard, then his expression grew conflicted. "I... don't think so."

I held back a litany of expletives and let him reconsider.

Come on, Miles. Think about it. It would have been so easy to let you burn, but here I am, dragging your ass out of the fire.

Another beat. Another nothing from Miles.

Fuck it.

I reached toward my inventory and prepared to grab the flight charm.

Before I could, our feet left the ground, crimson crescent passing beneath us as we elevated into the air. We rose vertically, about ten yards in the air until we plateaued and bobbed treacherously. Of course. They'd designed the flight charm for one person, not two.

Careful to mask the movement, I reached into my inventory and activated my flight charm. The turbulence ceased, and we smoothly rose and rocketed toward the exit.

Miles' face was hard. But he didn't shake me off, or attempt to throw me into the fathomless depths around the platforms below. Instead, he spoke. "Much as I hate to admit it, I was out of my depth."

Same.

It made a certain sort of sense, though I couldn't imagine doing the same in his shoes. I saved his life; he saved mine. That was the person Miles was. Unshakably fair. Even after everything he thought I'd done, and the fucked-up things that happened between us, and absent a single witness, he refused to change.

Maybe that was the reason I couldn't stomach the idea of hanging him out to dry.

I loosened my grip and slipped down a little as we approached the exit, maneuvering myself so I could follow Ellison's directive and exit the ripple a split second after Miles. We rocketed out of the ripple and back into the main floor, veering to avoid the opposite wall and crashing into the mud, sprawling awkwardly across the ground.

A stream of notifications scrolled before me.

Beyond the text, a small ember of golden light etched an ornate white ring that seated an amber stone into existence, almost like it was 3D printed. Just as it finished forming, I snatched it before Miles—still shaking off shock and slowly rising from the mud—could notice.

<Level Up: Ordinator has reached Level 17. As the hidden parameters have been met, a new Ordinator branch is now available.>

In ordinary circumstances, the advancement would have thrilled me. But I couldn't tear my eyes away from the wording of the final notification.

<System Notification: Congratulations. As the last User standing in the designated area, you've received an artifact.>

Either Ellison was dead, or he wasn't a User at all.

CHAPTER NINETY-NINE

Before

Ellison was particular about schedules. Timing. I'd left him at the library, and he'd instructed me to pick him up at a quarter to seven. So I shifted my schedule around, made sure Russ—my manager at the laundromat—knew I'd be leaving exactly at 7:30, and arrived like clockwork.

That was nearly an hour ago. Night filtered in through the broad library windows, and much of the overhead lighting around the outer edges of the library had already shut off, giving the main section of broad tables a spotlight feeling. Ellison was bent over a younger girl's textbook, pointing at a section of text, his expression strained. He'd say something, and the girl would shake her head, and Ellison would cross his arms, lost in thought, before he spoke again. I recognized his body language similar to instances where he was trying to figure out how to explain something to Iris.

Finally, the girl nodded, and I felt an internal sigh of relief.

She was the last of three similarly confounded middle-schoolers, all of whom I'd watched Ellison help since arriving on schedule. Like the rest, she shut her book, shoved it in her backpack, gave Ellison a weapons-grade nuclear smile, and left with a hop in her step, passing by me on her way to the exit without so much as a glance or a look back.

Ellison, alternatively, looked rumpled and fatigued. He gathered his things in an uncharacteristically unhurried fashion and nearly ran into me.

"Study group?" I asked.

Ellison blinked several times before his bleary eyes fully focused on me. "Oh, hey. What time is it?"

"Nearly nine."

From his aghast expression, I might as well have told him the sky was yellow.

"Well... shit," Ellison finally said. Then, after he had a second to think about it. "Didn't mess anything up for you, did I?"

"No," I lied. I had a helpline gig lined up for after I took him home, but it paid little and wasn't time-sensitive.

"How long were you waiting?"

I shrugged. "Not too long. Got caught up at Maple's."

Ellison half-nodded, hooded eyes squinting at the clock on the wall as if he couldn't quite bring himself to believe it was really that late. "Sorry."

"No worries."

We started toward the exit, earning several irritated looks from the few remaining evening staff who were probably hoping to leave early. I passed him a bottle of water and pulled a tiny container of Tylenol from my bag, shook it at him. Ellison took it quickly, unscrewed the cap and poured two into his hand, then downed them, draining almost half the bottle. Afterward, he shot me a suspicious look.

"How the hell do you always know?" he asked.

"I'm your brother. It's my job to know things."

"Pretty sure most brothers aren't psychic," Ellison grumbled.

I shrugged. "The good ones are."

We walked in silence for a while. From the number of screwed-up expressions Ellison was cycling through, I could tell he needed to talk about something. But trying to pry it out of him never worked. So I let him stew as we traveled through the library double doors and approached the bike rack. I pulled my keyring from my jean pocket and undid the chain lock, grabbing the handlebars and hefting the front wheel of my bike free from the rack.

I raised a questioning eyebrow. "Ride? Or hoof it?"

"Let's walk for now," Ellison said, "at least until the Tylenol kicks in."

It'd take us longer to get home on foot, but that was fine. I wheeled my bike alongside us and pulled my burner from my pocket, flipping it open and shooting a quick text to my helpline client, letting them know there was a blip and I needed to reschedule. A response came almost immediately, but I didn't look at it. The library was on the edge of a decent area of town, but the closer we grew to home, the more alert we needed to be.

We passed a small group of homeless men lounging at the mouth of an alley, one of whom was familiar.

"Hey, Greg," I waved.

"Hi, Greg," Ellison parroted.

"Lo, boys." Greg grinned a wide and gap-toothed smile. He was looking better now that summer was over and we'd moved more deeply into the autumn months, and his tomato-red complexion had faded to a warm scarlet. "How's the static this evening?"

Translation: any cops around?

"Pretty clear," I said. Then peered deeper into the alley and frowned. They'd done a good job obscuring their various hodgepodge sleeping accommodations, but Greg's eternally overfull cart was sticking out a little, along with a sleeping bag housed within a cardboard box. "May want to drag that dumpster over a bit."

Greg turned to study the alley, immediately saw the issue. "Golden, golden. Good lookin' out. 'Preciate you both."

"Have a good night."

Once we were out of earshot, Ellison finally boiled over.

"I know it's stupid," he said.

I played dumb. "What's stupid?"

My brother sighed. "The study group. You've told me at least half a dozen times that the best way to study is by yourself."

I made a show of considering that and tried to come up with the best way to respond. Things were so much easier between us when I could be direct with him, but those days were long since over. "How many times a week are you meeting?"

"Once."

"And how many people?" I asked, though I didn't need to. Unless a large contingent had left before I arrived, there were five other kids.

"Six in total," Ellison confirmed.

"And they spent most of the time studying? Not chatting or goofing around?"

"We didn't even have time to chat," Ellison's voice rose, and he ranted. "They're all so fucking behind. All the teachers care about is getting us ready for the standardized shit, so that gets all the attention in class, and they expect us to study for the other tests entirely on our own."

I resisted the urge to get into a drawn-out venting session about the public school system, because while he wasn't wrong, that also wasn't the core of his problem.

"Ah," I said.

"'Ah' what, head ass?" Ellison gave me a small shove. "Come on. I know you have an opinion, you always do. Why can't you just give it to me straight like you did to Greg?"

Because Greg's happy to take all the help he can get.

I blew out air. "Do I believe the best way to study is on your own? Yes. Do I also understand that solo-study can get monotonous as hell and an occasional change of format can help you refresh, and that infrequently teaching someone else the material grants a differing insight that helps you understand it better? Also yes."

"Oh," Ellison said.

I swatted him lightly across the top of his head, mussing his hair. My brother recoiled and toyed with his bangs, scowling until they fell back into their usual place.

"Obviously, I get it. So curb the attitude and stop acting like I'm out to get you." I nearly said more but didn't want to push my luck. Instead, I took the indirect route. "My opinion doesn't matter. What matters is that despite going to the efforts of organizing this on the down-low and having a seemingly successful session, *you* seem less than happy with the results."

"Because it sucked!" Ellison shouted. He quickly brought his volume under control, but the irritation remained. "I didn't mind teaching at first. Like you said, it reinforced things, helped me internalize them. But then I had to do it again, and again. And now my head hurts and I just feel... drained."

"How many kids in the group are further ahead in their studies than you?" I asked, careful to circumvent the word "smart."

Ellison stared down at the sidewalk as we walked, lost in thought. "None of them, I guess. Dia's pretty quick, but she's 'gifted' and doesn't really spend that much time studying—come to think of it, most of the smart kids wouldn't be the first to sign up for a study group."

There you go.

"Mmm," I answered noncommittally.

"And it's not like I know everything. It'd be a pain to get them there, but even if I only snagged one or two, I wouldn't constantly be playing unpaid substitute and there'd be someone to teach me for a change—" Ellison's eyes narrowed and he glared at me suspiciously. "That was some Socratic, bamboozling bullshit."

"No idea what you're talking about."

CHAPTER ONE HUNDRED

Loss, despair, and a tiny flicker of hope all tore at my mind, burning any semblance of cognizance to ash. Nothing mattered. Not the order, not whatever overcomplicated bullshit I was trying to accomplish here. None of it meant anything if Ellison was gone.

Was he? He knew. Had to. Somehow concluded that, once we were out, the system would reward an artifact and made sure it went to me—did he know that because he was aware he and his companions weren't traditional Users and were therefore exempt from receiving the artifact? Or because missing the Nosferatu's head was a critical mistake and he'd lose, and what kind of fucking time loop was it for fuck's sake? If Ellison died, did everything reset? Or were there quantum elements in play, and every time he died he moved to a new timeline?

Too many fucking unknowns.

Crack

I put my fist through a stone coffin, barely feeling the impact. It fractured in a series of spiderwebbing cracks and collapsed, spilling out desiccated bones and dust. It barely registered that the coffin was nearly an inch thick and I shouldn't have been able to break through it.

The panic blew the lid off, growing more sharp and pronounced, a tingling, fraying ache that threatened to paralyze me. I put my fist through another coffin, and again, the stone obliterated as if I'd struck it with a hammer. It hurt more this time, and I felt a pulse of pain in my fist that granted a moment of clarity before I plunged into a never-ending pool of anxiety.

"Myrddin."

Someone was calling out to me. Someone I didn't care about.

Go back go back now you have to know for sure you have to see go now go now GO NOW!

"Myrddin." Miles caught my shoulder before I could jump back in the ripple.

I pivoted and swung a blind backhand that hit nothing, trying to get around the interference so I could—

Do what, exactly? Save him? If the worst had happened, Ellison was already gone. Go anyway and bet on the astronomical odds he'd dropped a core? The Nosferatu would pick me off as easily as breathing. And I'd seen its power firsthand. Payback was out of the question.

At least for now.

Slowly, I stopped moving. That old familiar feeling of helplessness overtook me, rooted my feet in place.

The tunnel vision faded, and I stared down the threaded barrel of a Glock, dimly realizing what happened. I fucked up. And in my brief lapse of sanity, Miles had taken the initiative and now held the advantage. His right eye aligned with the sight, his expression emotionless and cold.

When I spoke, my voice was so twisted and raw I barely recognized it. "You got a memory loss issue, Miles?"

"Stay. Back," Miles said.

"Because you had ample fucking opportunity to throw me into an abyss a few minutes ago and let it slip through your fingers." I growled and took another step forward.

Miles retreated, keeping a constant distance of around five feet between us. A less experienced shooter harboring the same level of anger might have pressed the gun against my head and made for an easy disarm, but Miles never missed a beat. "That was before you started punching through stone. And just because I overlooked half-pint backing you up again in the moment, doesn't mean I am now. Not without one hell of an explanation."

I gritted my teeth and tried to banish the image of Ellison that popped up in my mind. "If you want answers, get the goddamn gun out of my face."

A mental recoil sent a wave of pain through my neurons. It felt similar to when I tried to cast **<Suggestion>** on a target with elevated intelligence. Only I hadn't.

Miles' grimaced and lowered the gun. He didn't inventory it, just gripped it at his side, and when I tried to walk past him toward the elevator, he still retreated as before, staying between me and the elevator.

"That bounty notification probably went out to everyone at the Tower. It's possible the Adventurers' Guild is playing interference, but if some actual monsters down there in the line decide they want a shot at you, there's only so long the guild can hold them off. All of which means we have a tight window to get you out." I glared at him. "Make up your fucking mind."

Every part of me wanted to abandon this course altogether and rush back into the ripple. Even before the dome and the Transposition, I had trouble trusting Ellison, probably because of the many similarities we shared. What I'd missed was how that lack of trust frayed our relationship, slowly wore it down and fostered resentment. Maybe he had just been trying to get some space that last breakfast at Sam's, but the only reason his words cut so deeply was because they were steeped in truth.

At some point, I'd lost sight of who he was and just saw the parts of him that reminded me of myself.

If I wanted to make a change—for Ellison to trust me again—I needed to return the favor. There was no faking the tiredness in his voice. He'd been doing this for a long, long time. And he'd specifically told me that if I took too long getting Miles clear, it would make things harder in the long run.

For now, I'd believe. It didn't come naturally and directly conflicted with my tendency to think the worst. But I'd believe just the same. Ellison wasn't dead. He just wasn't a User.

Because—let's face it—if I looked at all this in terms of game balance, a time loop ability was completely overpowered. And another layer of system fuckery was pretty much par for the course at this point.

Having worked through his own inner conundrum, Miles inventoried his weapon. He stared at me, as if expecting a sudden attack at any moment. When none came, he finally seemed to relax.

"Now. You said something about answers." Miles raised an eyebrow.

———

I multitasked, checking in with Azure and chatting with Kinsley as soon as we came back into range. The situation in the lobby wasn't great. The Adventurers' Guild had acted quickly, leveraging their influence to protect Miles and suspend elevator entry as soon as the bounty notification went out, but things were deteriorating quickly. They weren't able to stop anyone inside the Tower from using the elevators, so I instructed Azure to disguise himself as a random adventurer, go down to the lobby, and report to Sara as me. After some convincing, I let my summon handle explaining why I'd missed what must have been a never-ending mess of red-alerts and all-hands-on-deck. It was difficult to take a hands-off approach for once, but Azure's talent was crafting narrative.

Getting Miles out was an outright pain in the ass, largely because the Tower was protected. I dropped a hint for him to coordinate with Kinsley and see if there was anywhere in the Tower she could door to, while I coordinated with her from the other side. Once he was out, she'd immediately spirit him away with her sanctuary ability until we could figure out next steps.

While the lower floors of the Tower weren't blocked from communication, they had a hell of a lot more protections in place to protect from unwanted entry and teleportation. Kinsley went through, painstakingly testing each floor and failing to find an entry point until she landed on the fourth floor. She warned me it felt unstable, that the Tower's security seemed almost intelligent and she didn't think she could open a door inside the Tower again.

Which meant me, Nick, and the rest would be on our own.

I just took that in stride, because I had my hands full just telling Miles the truth.

Or at least, doing so without giving him enough rope to hang me with.

It was a mostly undeveloped theory. One percolating in the back of my mind for quite some time since the Allfather revealed himself as my patron, and was reinforced every time a god interfered.

"They're cheating," Miles said aloud, as if wrapping his mind around the idea.

I nodded. "It's the only thing that makes sense. The Overseer's public statements imply they've been doing this for some time. And while I can't exactly show hard evidence for this, the Allfather's, Proctor's, and Nychta's comments all seem to imply these inquisitions have been going on for a staggeringly long time. My class. *Your* class—unless I'm completely wrong—and the way they screwed with Tyler's truth-sight ability right when it would have the most devastating outcome. Now, granted, all of those prior cases have justification. I'm guessing you answered questions within the void before your class was assigned, just like mine?"

Miles nodded, his mouth tight.

"And divine-tainted monsters wounded Tyler, which is a little more borderline. But Hastur is running his own fucking guild, and more problematic, Nychta outright granted me something I needed at the perfect moment."

"Things are devolving," Miles finished.

"Right now they're running a proxy war. Using third parties to snipe at each other, jockeying for position, all while maintaining plausible deniability. Remind you of anything?" I asked.

Miles looked troubled. "Might as well be pulling directly out of the spook playbook. Fund the ragtag resistance against the regime you don't like, arm and back them—at least until they either crumble, overthrow the regime, or do something you don't approve of—then call it a day."

"Rarely ends well for the resistance. Even if they win."

"That's a goddamn understatement," Miles said, rubbing his chin. Then he caught himself and reentered his focus on me. "Though all this spitballing is feeling like a distraction."

"How so?"

"None of it explains what happened in the tunnel. Or why you waltzed into a goddamn death camp and spared the Necromancer running the show."

I winced. Largely because he wasn't wrong. That was what I'd done. And sure, it looked far worse from the outside, but there was only so much I could tell him without putting Kinsley in hot water. This was a critical pain point with Miles. I couldn't deflect or blow it off. Whatever he believed or disbelieved, this was what he needed to buy in more than anything else.

We were in dangerous territory now, specifically regarding the tunnel. I was technically safe for as long as I was a member of the Order of Parcae and the geas remained effective, but when Miles found a way around it and also happened upon someone who could unequivocally confirm what actually happened that day, I was fucked.

And he would, eventually, find a way.

Which left me with two alternatives. Make myself so critical and valuable to both the Feds and the Adventurers' Guild that eliminating me wouldn't be workable when the news broke.

Or eliminate every witness from the Order in attendance that night.

Both felt flimsy—the more contact I had with Miles, the more likely he was to connect the dots. And the second option...

"I have a family."

I squeezed my eyes shut and tried to banish the voice, then centered myself, piecing together the best version of what to tell Miles. When I opened them, he was still standing across from me on the elevator, his arms folded.

"The Order of Parcae approached me early."

CHAPTER ONE HUNDRED ONE

Miles' eyes bore into me. It wasn't like during the panel with the Feds, where he was already doubting himself and willing to give me the benefit of the doubt. If he caught a single inkling of deceit, there was no question. He was gone.

I continued. "I'm not sure how they knew, but I suspect it has something to do with their patron."

"Hastur," Miles filled in.

"They didn't really pass the sniff test, even that early on. Watched them steamroll a bounty like it was nothing. My abilities were far more limited back then, and given the more understated, slow-burn nature of my class, my first instinct was to avoid large groups. At least until I got a better handle on where this was all going."

"And they really formed that fast?" Miles prompted.

I nodded. "Within a day of the dome, maybe less. I'd put money on it. Nobody mobilizes that quickly unless they have an outside line—again, divine interference. So, they court me, I'm unsure, they get a little more aggressive than I'm comfortable with, which ends with me getting the hell out. For a little while, it's radio silence. I fall in with Kinsley and the nascent Merchants' Guild by chance. Matt tells me his friend has a lead on some special dungeon—"

"The trial," Miles said.

"And while I don't feel completely comfortable with the idea, one of them caught my eye. Some girl that went to school with them. Jinny."

Miles scoffed.

I waved the scorn away. "Not like it sounds. Not exactly. Might be the only thing you got right in the profile. She had a title that granted her significantly more stat and feat points with every level. As a mage she was already strong then, but over time?"

"Yeah." Miles nodded slowly. "Would have been a monster by now."

I grunted confirmation. "Only the Order shows up, waiting for me outside the trial. From their perspective, it looks like I've rejected them wholesale and formed my own group—and I already have enough experience with them to guess how they'll handle that."

"Not well."

He's still working you. **<Jaded Eye's>** commentary nearly threw me off. I grimaced. Even if I was editorializing somewhat, it was still difficult enough to recount the events without interference. But it didn't matter if Miles didn't fully believe me, all I needed to do was to create a wedge of doubt.

"Tried to play it off like I'd been doing them a favor. Scouting. Figured if I could get the Order to spare them, that was a better alternative to catching them in my collateral, and eventually, I could get them out. Nick and Sae weren't much to write home about, but Jinny was one hell of a sweetener. I..." I trailed off, swallowed. "I betrayed her trust and revealed her title. Figured that would clinch it."

"Only it didn't go that way," Miles said.

"Jinny didn't take it well. To be clear, it wasn't her fault—if there was anyone to blame, it was me. But... she took a shot at me, then they took a shot at her. Their aim was better. She bled out in seconds and everything went to hell. Sae panicked and ran back into the ripple, they captured Nick—"

"Why?" Miles asked pointedly. "You just said he was nothing to write home about, why would they take on deadweight?"

"The Court," I answered reluctantly. Originally, I'd meant to bring up the Court and keep Nick out of the spotlight, but Miles was too sharp not to pick up on the inconsistency. "I'm still working on figuring out the details, but it's one of the Order's side projects. There are Users with hierarchical classes similar to a historical monarchy. Barons, Kings, Queens, Knights, and they seem dead set on collecting them. Whatever the overarching purpose, Nick's a Court Knight. So they bagged him."

"Sounds like they *weren't* just there for you," Miles observed. His accusation was so subtle it almost flew under the radar.

I gritted my teeth and pressed on. "I didn't react well. To Jinny's death, or the way they put innocent people in the crosshairs to strong-arm me into joining them. It felt wrong to just give in. Like they'd have too much leverage and I'd be stuck doing their bidding. I used my abilities to disappear, which wasn't hard. The Transposition started shortly after and, as you know, all hell broke loose. Tried to help the Merchants' Guild with their region, and you already know how that went."

"Get to the Necromancer," Miles growled. He felt like we were running out of time.

"There were two reasons I spared him. One personal, one broad. I'll start with the second. I'd just gotten back from Region 6, and I was in shock. Not to mention angry as hell, only to find out that someone was picking off our people and they probably had an excess of Lux. Made sense to kill two birds with one stone. I imagine you went for the same reason. But when we got there, I recognized it as an Order operation. Everything else was more or less on the level—I wasn't even sure what I was going to do until I found the Necromancer."

Miles groaned and pressed a hand to his forehead. He'd already guessed where this was going.

I finished it anyway. "He wasn't... what I expected. Not at all. There was no maniacal laughing or gleeful hand rubbing. He was just some guy, trying to level up his abilities and eventually bring his daughter back to life. The Order was effectively holding him hostage—which sure, might have been bullshit, but I didn't get the sense he was lying, and for the Order, the hostage tactic was completely on brand. Considering the sheer volume of cores I gathered from Region 6, everything fell in place after that. Join the Order with the cores as collateral and simultaneously work to undercut them and prevent the wholesale slaughter of Users. It all just sort of clicked into place."

"And the second reason?" Miles asked.

I slowly reached back and withdrew Jinny's core, holding it out in the palm of my hand.

"Ah," Miles said. Then the look on his face grew so frigid I caught a chill. "Must be nice. Getting the chance to bring a friend back."

I swallowed. "I talked to him—the kid—before we saved you. And for someone so concerned about the good of the people, you really ought to look into what Waller was doing in his free time."

A shadow of doubt crossed Mile's expression, and I whispered a silent thanks to Ellison.

The elevator arrived on the fourth floor. The floor comprised a sprawling autumn forest, and leaves crunched under our feet as we walked towardsthe spot Kinsley mentioned. Miles was utterly silent as he absorbed what I'd told him. It'd be a lot for someone who didn't have skin in the game, and Miles had more than most.

"Look," Miles finally said. "Let's say I believe you. In that case, your goals are good. Noble, even. If it's anything like the first, stopping the second Transposition event could save countless lives, and any intel we can glean on a potential war between these asshat patrons of ours gives us options we'd otherwise lack. And the judgment call to leave the Order intact while ousting their leadership can't have been easy, considering your history."

"It wasn't," I said darkly.

Miles shook his head. "Still. This game you're playing at? I've played it for real. Hell, I was a natural. Sometimes I even enjoyed it. And I still wouldn't go back for all the money in the world. Undercover work takes a different sort of toll. It's a meat grinder. A lot of good cops go in, and nearly half as many broken train wrecks come out. And that's discounting the casualties who die or start playing for the other side, which isn't a small number. They're all thoroughly informed on the risks. You wanna know why they still sign up?"

I nodded.

"Hubris. They all think they're the exception. That they have what it takes to end up on the good side of the coin flip. In the end, a coin flip's exactly that. Each and every one of them is trained to the nines, evaluated, has a handler, a support team, and enough backup to turn over the whole goddamn city if they go missing. All resources you lack. And they weren't dealing with gods, or powers, or some skin-and-bones asshole putting enough heat on their cover to melt tungsten. I don't mean to take away from what you've accomplished. But you've already made a lot of mistakes."

"Like?"

He studied me. "Sure. I'll give you one. What was your plan, if you let mister-just-trying-to-resurrect-his-daughter-go and the Order decided you weren't worth the trouble?"

"I—"

"Did you even create a contingency to take that Necromancer off the board if the Order told you and your cores to shove off?"

"There wasn't time," I protested, despite myself.

"Too bad. Because if he *was* their only Necromancer and your plan fell through, you gave up an opportunity to take a mass murderer out of play for *nothing*. And that little horror show they put on during the Transposition would have repeated itself. Only the next time, they'd be smarter about it."

I stopped in place as Miles continued onward, heat crawling up my neck. But I wasn't angry because he was being unfair, or that he'd said anything incorrect.

I was angry because he was right.

Miles called behind him. "If even a fraction of this yarn you've spun checks out, you've earned a cease fire. But you're in this up to your neck, and the water's rising. Call it and come in with me before you drown."

The situation with Vernon was more complicated than I'd let on. I couldn't end him in good conscience, considering his relation to Kinsley.

But he owed me his life. I probably *could* have coordinated a contingency to meet with Vernon if the worst happened. The Order was squelching his communications, but if I was clever enough, it was possible to bait him out. And all I'd need to do to neutralize his future body count was engineer a situation where I could talk to him long enough to tell him the truth: his daughter was alive.

But I'd assumed success and ignored the gamble.

A blue glow caught my eye. Kinsley's door appeared in the trunk of a large tree.

"Yes, I've made mistakes. Yes, there are things I could have done better. But I can't just throw it all away."

"Your funeral." Miles reached for the knob and didn't bother looking back.

I set my teeth. "Anyone who kills me gets an all-expenses paid ticket out of the dome. And while I can't say what goes into clearing that bounty on your head, I'm guessing you'll have your hands full for a while. You really think you can protect me from every goddamn User in Dallas and deal with that at the same time?"

Miles hesitated.

"So, teach me."

Miles stopped. Turned and gave me an are-you-fucking-serious look.

I crossed my arms. "You said it yourself. You're a natural."

"No."

"Cards on the table. With you as my handler—"

"No."

"—I'd have the oversight I'm lacking, and everything I uncover goes to you first, in regular, organized reports."

"For fuck's sake, how many times do I have to say it," Miles snapped. When I said nothing, he boiled over. "You're completely untrained, compulsive, and what's more, I'm pretty sure you enjoy this shit, all of which makes you exactly the wrong sort of person for the job, not to mention I literally shot you less than two hours ago—"

"—it didn't take—"

"And most important, I don't fucking trust you."

"Trust has to start somewhere," I said quietly.

"Then drop the goddamn magic and show me your real fucking face," he growled.

A long silence stretched between us. Unfamiliar birds flitted from tree to tree, chirping out odd cadences. A cool chill ruffled our clothing. There was an uncanny feeling of an impasse, an insurmountable obstacle. Miles couldn't justify working with me until he had some sort of leverage. And I couldn't take the mask off until I knew, unequivocally, that we were on the same side. Too many people knew as it was, and even if that wasn't the case, Miles wasn't the sort of person I could gamble on.

"Need to get going and figure out how to deal with this bounty," Miles finally said.

"Yeah."

Disappointment washed over me. For a moment, I'd seen a different future. One where Miles and I were allies, not just enemies working towards the same goal.

"Guessing it'll be a tremendous pain in the ass."

"Could have just shot me with an arrow."

He rolled his eyes. "We both know how that would have gone."

I shrugged. "Maybe."

It was as good of a time as any for Miles to leave. But he didn't. Instead he seemed distracted, troubled. "After that, I'll poke around. See if that Waller comment holds any weight."

I held my breath.

"If it does..." Miles sighed. "We'll meet in Kinsley's sanctuary. That's probably the closest we're going to get to neutral ground."

With that, he was gone.

I took a minute to absorb the victory. It wasn't ironclad, and I wasn't willing to discount the possibility that Miles was acting his ass off and working an angle. But, for maybe the first time, I didn't get that impression. His advice to me, and his warning, had both felt genuine.

Only time would tell.

For now, I needed to level, look over the artifact Ellison apparently wanted me to have. And finally, square things with Nick.

CHAPTER ONE HUNDRED TWO

<Hidden parameters fulfilled. A new Ordinator branch can now be accessed.>

Something from the ripple activated the parameters.

I nearly focused on it before realizing that the last time I'd done so—for the conjuration branch—it resulted in a sprawling multiple choice that took a considerable amount of time to sift through. With no immediate conflicts and the rest of my team lounging beachside, it was tempting. I put it off, not wanting to rush advancement while I was still off-balance. Instead, I fished around in my inventory for the artifact.

And found nothing.

I summoned a health potion to ensure my inventory hadn't failed, then tried to withdraw the ring again.

Nothing.

Panicked, I checked my pockets, the small, mostly unused pouches on the **<Operator's Belt>**, anywhere I could have accidentally stuffed it in the heat of the moment and found nothing. I was double-checking everything, a hair's breadth from dumping out the entirety of my inventory onto the elevator, when I felt a slight pressure on one of my fingers. Something unfamiliar.

I removed my gauntlet. And swallowed.

There, crowning my third finger, was a simple band of silver metal. There was only one explanation. A ring I was utterly sure I'd placed in my inventory had somehow equipped itself.

Despite that, it pulled free easily. Cradled in the center of my palm, its weight was so light it felt like I wasn't holding anything at all.

<Artifact: The Devil's Share>
<Item Description: This seemingly innocuous ring is a source of untold power for any mage or ability-dependent User. While worn, the User may cast any appropriately mastered ability reflexively. Spells and abilities cast reflexively cost far less mana to use and may be invoked in a fraction of the time.>
<System Warning: Contingently bound item. After five uses, this item binds to the User.>
<Uses remaining: 2/5>

Insidious.

Over every other adjective rolling through my head—unbalanced, broken, overpowered, game-changer—the word *insidious* screamed inside my mind like a signal flare.

The concept of a bound item was alarming enough. I'd heard enough horror stories about cursed weapons and items in fiction to balk at the idea of an item that bound to my person. At best, it would forever take up a potential item slot and become literally irreplaceable. At worst—

Well, that wasn't a small list.

I stepped off the elevator with barely enough foresight to check that no one from my Order team was nearby. There was an abnormally high number of people in line for the elevator, all of whom were in considerably lower spirits than earlier. News of the chaos in the lobby had probably reached this floor by now, so they either planned to gawk or get clear of the Tower in fear the elevators might shut down.

After giving the crowd one last scan to ensure none of my team was present, I retreated into the floor, away from the elevator and toward the ripple.

My scattered thoughts returned to the ring. Specifically, its name. *The Devil's Share.* Its accompanying system text claimed it required two additional uses to bind. At first that seemed like an error, or perhaps a holdover from a previous user. If someone had it before me, maybe they'd used it a handful of times before throwing it away.

That felt wrong.

I worked my way backward, reviewing every event that followed the system awarding me the artifact. Shortly after I received it, I'd thought Ellison had died. Rationally, that made little sense—even less so now that I had some distance from it. He sounded like he'd been doing this for a long time, and therefore it stood to reason that a person in his position was capable of affecting large-scale change. Whatever impact saving both Miles and myself might have, we wouldn't cast a shadow to the sort of paradigm shifts Ellison could achieve over a loop. Throwing all that potential away to save two Users was more than sloppy; it was downright stupid. Stupid in a mewling, sentimental way that was entirely out of character for my brother, even before the dome.

Still, I wasn't thinking rationally. Emotion took over, and I'd obliterated two stone coffins with nothing more than my fist.

How?

I pulled off my other gauntlet and flexed my fingers out, inspecting my knuckles for damage. They were pristine.

Did I cast **<Probability Cascade>** without even realizing it? I looked inward and found that my stores were regenerating at their normal pace, bordering on half. The last fringes of a headache still plied at my temples. When I broke the coffins my mana was low, bordering on depleted. A normal cast could have easily blacked me out.

If I had cast reflexively, the comparative drain was almost nothing.

But it was the ease with which I'd used it that chilled me. I reviewed the moment again and again, trying to find some element I was missing. Some mental prompt or ideation that the ring translated as a desire to use the ability. The closest I found was that I hadn't tried to strike the surface of the coffin. I'd tried to strike *through* it.

The same thing happened with Miles. I hadn't even considered using **<Suggestion>** to persuade him, because as opposed as we were, that was thoroughly outside the rules I'd set for myself, but the mental pushback slammed against me as if I had.

Was that all it took? *Desire?*

I fought the urge to throw the artifact as far as I could.

If my theory was right, the mere existence of intrusive thoughts made the ring a do-not-fuck-with proposition of the highest order. Sure, in a general sense it let you punch far above your weight class and chuck significantly more fireballs before you needed to rest. But what about later, when there was no threat, and some entitled asshole cut the dinner line in front of you?

Like duct taping a loaded firearm with a hair-trigger to the hands of someone with no concept of gun safety.

And if a normal mage lost control, started attacking neutral parties and allies, that specific situation would inevitably equalize itself. The guy obviously raining down magic indiscriminately eventually gets clipped. Natural order. But if an *Ordinator* lost control?

No. I *needed* to get rid of it.

But...

The Crimson Nosferatu's harrowing visage appeared in my mind, along with the heart-stopping power it radiated. I'd managed getting Miles clear and even landed a parting shot, but I hadn't been able to do anything to help with the heavy lifting. Not really.

Considering that Ellison had gone through this so many times he'd lost count? The casual manner with which he'd made preparations, all the while bringing me up to speed? The Nosferatu probably didn't even rank all that high on his list of priorities. Things were going to get worse. Like the events that led to the **<Allfather's Mask>**, it all came down to the same sobering equation. The prisoner's dilemma. Any power I left on the table was power someone else would take. Either directly—finding the ring, putting it on—or indirectly, by gaining a similarly powerful artifact while I surrendered mine. And Ellison made sure it had ended up with me, instead of Miles.

I wavered.

There was no point in using it if it crippled me, but there was only one way to get definitive confirmation that it would.

My breath grew shallow as I pulled up the ring's description, magnified the text so that **<Uses Remaining: 2/5>** overlayed a large swath of my vision, fully prepared to rip it off the second the number decreased.

Nothing happened.

More testing was in order. I went a little deeper into the forest, parallel to the line for the elevator. Not so far that I couldn't make them out, but far enough that they'd have a difficult time spotting me, and dialed the mask up to full power. This test was hardly scientific. Hell, I couldn't even repeat it. If uses remaining decreased, I'd look for the closest thing to Mordor. But if it didn't? If I could keep the intrusive thoughts in line through discipline and self-control, and be reasonably sure I could use the ring safely?

The possibilities were limitless.

CHAPTER ONE HUNDRED THREE

I searched the faces of the crowd, trying to find an appropriate target. Someone cruel or angry, someone who would test me through nothing more than existing. Leaving them be, without accidentally using **<Probability Cascade>**, or **<Suggestion>**, or even **<Hinder>** would serve as a test of my self-control with the ring equipped.

And yes, I know how that sounds. I've always seen other people as the enemy, the other, the competition. If they couldn't trade favors, influence, or be useful, they were nothing but the potential to hinder—and I was better off stepping on them than over.

It should have been easy to find a target. Someone. Anyone.

But I couldn't. As I scanned the tired, worried faces, I couldn't single anyone out. Which should have been impossible with this crowd. The best of them were people who gained User status post Transposition. Everyone else was a slacker, a nothing, an idiot waste of space frittering away precious hours before the next event hit. And when it did, they'd be worse than deadweight.

So why didn't I hate them?

Maybe because their once-smug and carefree faces were laden with worry, but it didn't feel that simple. It felt... systemic. As if something within me had shifted. It wasn't Hastur. His influence on my mind had long since faded. It was something else. The people in line were just that. People. They got scared, and didn't manage their time properly, and fell back on vices and empty comforts when they had nothing else.

When did I change?

I shoved the troubling line of thought down, sidelining it for later when I had time to consider it properly, and disappeared further into the forest.

/////

After a few minutes of walking, I found it. An oval clearing in the trees, still partially covered by canopy above. At least a half-dozen abnormally long sprouts of green stuck up out of the ground, scattered around the fringes. Mandrakes.

The Mandrakes themselves weren't particularly threatening. Even in a larger group, I doubted they'd do little more than scream and run away. But we'd dealt with them one at a time for a reason. The few times we'd gotten hasty, their screams had grated together, combining into a stomach-churning screech with an effect that was more exponential than additive. And seeing as how I only had a single chance to get this right, I needed as much sensory overload as possible.

<Uses remaining: 2/5>

Nothing yet. Good. Now the actual test.

I braced myself. Then leaned down to grab the leafy sprout at the root and yanked it out of the ground.

The mandrake squealed immediately. Its grubby fingers latched onto my gauntlet and tried to free itself. I briefly considered using **<Suggestion>** to silence it, then checked the "uses remaining" and found them unchanged. I repeated the process again, uprooting another mandrake with my free hand and feeling my gut tighten as their shrieks ground together.

It was worse than I remembered. The pitch and cadence varied, mixed in with words, but they were always discordant to each other, and the discordance swelled in volume until I could barely hear my own grunts of discomfort. This would probably damage my hearing, but considering the sheer amount of deafening chaos during the Transposition and my hearing's currently undamaged state, it was a given that a health potion would mitigate damage, as long as I took it immediately after.

I placed the second mandrake alongside its neighbor, taking small satisfaction from watching them smack together as the sprouts on their head formed a strange, flowerless bouquet, and pulled the third.

Again, the volume grew exponentially. But despite the pounding in my head and the growing pain in my ears, the increase wasn't nearly as bad as I'd expected. It occurred to me that there might be a safety cap on how much impairment the mandrakes could cause. This was the first floor of the Tower—and while I could hardly classify the system as lenient, the early Tower floors seemed like a significant step down from anything I'd faced in the adaptive dungeon.

With that disarming notion in mind, I yanked at the largest of the remaining roots. It took several attempts. Eventually, a large clump of earth came free, yielding a plump mandrake, nearly double the size of the rest. It stretched in an exaggerated yawn and its beady eyes blinked open, looking around in lazy bewilderment until its gaze finally settled on me.

It opened its mouth.

Pure white agony shot through my mind. I'd been through a lot since the dome came down, experienced more than my share of injuries and pain, topping out with the divine damage I'd taken forcing my way through the barrier around Region 14.

If I compared the two, the divine damage was still worse. But it wasn't *constant*. Not like this. The mandrake quartet screamed in coordinated discordance, sending the profoundly excruciating jolts that accompany a broken bone through my ears and mind and throughout my entire body. My presence of mind and sense of self shattered.

All I wanted was for it to stop. But my hand wouldn't open, paralyzed in place. I opened my eyes to slits, searching for the fourth mandrake in the bundle. If I could shatter its focus with **<Suggestion>**—

My vision was gray.

I searched for the overlay in a panic.

Then there was a sickening pop as my eardrums blew simultaneously.

The world upended itself and I lost my balance, stumbling face-first into the grass. I fought an endless wave of vertigo as I watched the three normal mandrakes beat a hasty retreat in opposite directions, completely uncoordinated in their mad scramble out of the clearing.

Alone now, the large mandrake planted its hands on its hips and screamed once more, though I could barely hear it. Realizing it wasn't having as much of an effect, the mandrake pulled its leg back and kicked my gauntlet—making no more impact than a thrown pebble—then jogged away at a relaxed clip.

"Fuck you too," I mumbled after it. Then searched again for the overlay.

<Uses remaining: 2/5>

Relief washed over me, despite the pain. My mana was low, but I *hadn't* casted. And despite wanting, no, *needing* them to stop, now that I was aware of what the artifact did, I managed not to use it. The mandrakes scream must have had a mana-draining effect. When we were dealing with them one at a time, it must have been minuscule, but like the screams, the effect was exponential when there were more of them.

I swallowed two health potions. Eventually, the pain faded and the hazy underwater quality of my hearing sharpened, fully restored. As shaky as I felt, the memory of the pain still lingering at the forefront of my mind, I had to remember that this was a win.

It wouldn't break me, or render me dangerous or out of control. The ring was usable. There was a part of me that still wasn't sure if it was worth the risk, but I was leaning more toward equipping it than casting it away.

There was only one last piece of housekeeping left.

I pulled up my class information, fully prepared to face a gauntlet of vague multiple-choice questions.

None came.

<Ordinator has enhanced Conjuration Branch with Puppet Master Augment>
<Safeguards removed>
<Conjuration enhanced>
<Conjuration-acceptable targets widened>
<Divine shielding enhanced>
<Mental shielding enhanced>
<Relevant feats added>
<Default ability added>

That was... a lot. More than I could even process. The notification centered on increasing my shielding from the divine concerned me. Because the system wasn't exactly big on handouts. If it was giving me increased protection, it was out of necessity. And from prior experience, it wouldn't come close to adequate. I drew up my ability list, checking the default ability first.

<Subjugation, LVL 1>

I read the description once. Then again. And again. A cold lance of fear pierced me, chilling me to the bone.

Slowly, I pulled **<The Devil's Share>** free from my finger and secured it in my pocket, testing to make sure I could feel it through my gauntlet's padding. Its circular outline stood out clearly. I'd need to check it constantly until I could properly secure it.

Especially now.

From the beginning, it was difficult to understand why the Ordinator class was so singled out. If anything, it felt underpowered and had a highly specific use-case, sacrificing almost all offensive potential for the promise of eventual power creep. The details were spotty, vague. And while everyone alive in the dome saw the same footage of Ordinators wreaking havoc, my predecessors had clearly reached their endgame. And it stood to reason that there were more than a few other carry classes—

such as Necromancers—that didn't fully come into their own until endgame.

Why were gods themselves seem so keen to take me off the board? I'd wanted an explanation more than almost anything.

And now, I had one.

CHAPTER ONE HUNDRED FOUR

<New Ability Unlocked: Subjugation. This ability allows an Ordinator to enthrall any mortal entity within specific parameters: A target entity must be absent mental shielding and lack active divine protection, not exceed more than 110% of the Ordinator's current level or 130% of their current intelligence stat, or have been previously subjugated. After successful enthrallment, the target entity will carry out any command the Ordinator gives to the best of their ability. On expiration, the target will feel as if they acted of their own volition. **Duration**—24 hours.>

<**Warning:** While the target entity will do its best to reconcile actions taken during enthrallment, if these actions create too much cognitive dissonance, the target may reject absolvement entirely.

<**Warning:** While this ability technically has no cooldown, it requires an astronomical amount of mana and mental strain. Use with caution.>

This was so far beyond the pale I couldn't even remember what it looked like when I passed it. Laughter exploded out of me, harsh and strained. It all made so much sense now. Putting the ethical and moral concerns aside —of which there were a fuckton—no wonder they wanted me dead. No wonder Ellison couldn't trust me. The ability was completely broken, and this was only the baseline of the Puppet Master augment.

And **<The Devil's Share>** offset the ability's biggest downside—the mana cost.

It was beautiful. It was *fantastic.* And I wouldn't have trusted Gandhi with it, let alone myself.

If I got this earlier, would I have even tried to convince Miles? Or would I have just waved my fucking hand after he shot me and made it happen? And if I really wanted to be a normal person like Hastur implied, a concept I was still wrapping my head around, was there even any coming back from this?

It was everything I ever wanted. All the control, all the power, all wrapped in a neat package of technicalities and faux-downsides that could probably—eventually—be eroded away through upgrades. The more I leveled, the higher-level Users I could affect.

But.

I could have made Tyler believe me. Or influenced enough people around him until he at least considered the possibility I was telling him the truth.

I could have stopped the crossbowman.

And killing Maria would have been completely unnecessary. If my level was high enough to bring her within the target range, I could have simply ordered her to surrender herself to the Adventurers' Guild and tell them everything they wanted to know.

I knew what was happening. I could feel myself trying to justify it, even now. And making those justifications was only going to get easier, every time I used it.

<Suggestion> was just training wheels for the real deal.

<Subjugation> was the answer to everything. It was how I would win. It was my undoing. And it scared the goddamn hell out of me.

Fuck. I couldn't trust myself here. I needed to talk to Nick. As soon as possible.

It took far too long to notice the violet notification light of a new message.

<Halima: Myrddin.**>**
<Myrddin: Yes.**>**

The cheery ping of a voice call came seconds later.

"What?" I answered irritably

If Halima picked up on my tone, she completely ignored it. "You're out of the ripple?"

"Yes."

"And you told me to trust my instincts, right?"

I paused. "With Nick. Yeah, that's what I said." There was heavy breathing on the other side and the sound of footsteps crunching through greenery. "Are you running?"

"I think—I think I fucked up." Halima's voice was raw.

"Fucked up how? Are you in trouble?"

"No. Not me. Keith. And maybe Nick, or because of Nick, I don't know." Whatever it was, it sounded bad.

"You're not making sense," I said, trying to keep my voice calm.

"They're gone, need to find them." Her breaths grew more panicked, short, clipped.

I stood, goosebumps rising on the backs of my arms. "Halima, are you somewhere safe?"

"Yeah, but—"

"Great. Now *sit the fuck down.*" I put every ounce of authority I had into the command.

Silence. A rustling of grass. I gave her a full minute.

"Tell me what happened."

"Nick was fine. Everything was fine. I mean—he was still down, and scared looking, but he was fine." Her voice was more composed, though the panic still rang clear.

"And then?" I prompted.

"He just stood up, out of nowhere. Stared out into the ocean for a while. Scared me. I mean, he doesn't seem like the type, but what if he just walked out into it—"

"—but he didn't," I said, trying to redirect.

There was a rustle on the other side of the line. "No. He apologized. Said he was tired of brooding and wanted to explore around the island, look for other ripples. I figured that was a good thing, you know? But he said it was better if we kept working in pairs, that he'd bring Keith and told me to wait for you. Then he smiled at me. At both of us."

"What kind of smile?" I asked.

"What do you mean—"

"—Describe it."

"Uh. Tight, no teeth. Squinty. And it—it didn't feel warm. Didn't feel like him. I think something's wrong. Really, really wrong. Maybe that's stupid."

"It's not stupid," I said quietly.

Something flickered in the back of my mind. A memory from a hospital room just after he got the worst news of his life.

"It's alright. This was always a possibility. And you know what? They're gonna give me a cane. Won't play ball again, but I'll have all the swagger in the world." Same smile. Same expression. Cold as the goddamn arctic.

A choked sound echoed from the other side of the call. "Maybe I'm overreacting."

She wasn't. Something was wrong. He wasn't the type to kill himself, but he was absolutely the sort to go out in a blaze of glory. But no, that didn't fit. Why bring Keith? The mage was harmless, bordering on a civilian. He'd pack a lot more of a punch once he got a handle on his title.

The obvious problem Nick had sandbagged him on.

Why? Think, goddammit.

Hastur had mind-fucked me in a big way. I had to assume he did the same to Nick. Offered him something that both profoundly unsettled him and was an offer he couldn't refuse. I could see Nick working with the Order, but not after what they did to Jinny. Not with how he felt about her, not with what he lost. The only way I could remotely see that happening was if Hastur offered him something big.

What did Nick want? What the fuck did he want?

Whatever he wanted, Hastur had placed him as the leader of Zero-team. Put him there for a reason. Zero-team comprised Users who were primarily—

Oh fuck.

I spoke rapidly. "Who got Keith into Zero-team?"

Halima hesitated. "I don't—"

"Don't bullshit me here, Halima. If you actually care about Nick, or Keith, you need to fucking level with me. The nepotism is obvious, I just need to know who."

"His brother. Darren," Halima whispered.

The name meant nothing to me. "Description."

"Sort of pasty. On the short side of tall. Long red hair."

Keith's brother was the fucking redhead with the ponytail. The one who'd pulled Nick aside moments before we left on the mission, and it looked like he was begging. The one who shot Jinny.

"Okay, good," I said, bringing my voice down, projecting a calmness I didn't feel. "Any idea where they went?"

"East along the beachside, but their footprints led into the forest, which is where I lost them. I'm sorry—"

"It's okay." I pushed my fingers back through my hair. The cardinal direction narrowed it down, and I'd made physical contact with Nick when I gave him my healing charge. "I have a way to find them."

CHAPTER ONE HUNDRED FIVE

I-I-I-I-I-I snapped back into my mind with a gasp, vision fish-eyed and scratchy. What was that? My seer sight worked fine every other time I'd used it—but a single attempt on Nick left me feeling drained, ill.

Fuck.

In retrospect, it made sense. Whoever Nick's patron was, he didn't seem like the spin-the-world, then-go-out-for-cigarettes type. It was possible he had some sort of ongoing divine protection. Though that they apparently cared more about shielding Nick's thoughts from prying eyes rather than keeping his tongue in his head irked me to no end.

Okay, fine. Keith then. Not what I wanted. He'd lack any insight on what was happening in Nick's head or what he intended, but he'd still have the most important detail—location. I'd try to glean the rest from context.

———

Lumpy yellowing fingers the size of logs curled downward, countless knuckles interspersed in a tight focus that grew blurry around the circumference of the finger, craggy skin set deep with lines that wound creeks and fissures around a brownish core. My-my-my-my-my-my-my—

—Keith plucked a cluster of fruit in the air, squinting at it. As odd and bizarrely shaped as it was, he was pretty sure this specimen was a non-system fruit. His parents used to buy them from the commune by the pound, justifying their purchase by grinding them into a sour-bitter paste, which they then slathered on everything.

With a frown, he turned the fruit over. They were supposed to be looking for anything out of the ordinary.

"Leave for two seconds and come back find you grabbin' nuts." Nick's sudden reappearance startled Keith, and the tamarind pod flew from his shocked-open hand. The older boy bent down and picked up the pod, then cocked his head. "Throwing together some trail mix?"

"They're not native. Most of the fruit and greenery on this floor are pretty tropical, to the point it could almost pass for South America. But this is an entire continent removed. Could be a sign of a ripple."

The words entered his mind and nearly escaped before a gray miasma of doubt strangled.

What if I'm wrong? What if this finally sets Nick off and he requests a transfer? What if he thinks I'm wasting his time and hates me more than he already does?

Nick was better at hiding it than most people.

There was something about Keith that put most people off. He'd never quite nailed down what. Maybe it was the slight nasal timbre of his voice, or his timid nature, or his occasionally obsessive interests, but he'd gone to great efforts to alter and hide all that, and while sometimes it took longer, the result was always the same.

For a brief, cruel moment, Keith had thought that Nick would be the exception. The so-called Ceaseless Knight looked like the exact sort of person who frequently took issue with Keith, so he'd prepared for the worst. But instead of the expected hazing or ostracization, Nick spent just as much time working with Keith as he did with the more promising members of Zero-team. He'd even openly shared details of his personal life, confiding in Keith about how he could barely walk before the system. It felt like a non sequitur, and Keith had been laying in his barracks bunk when it finally hit him why Nick told the story.

The new team leader was reaching out to him. Empathizing. In a way almost no one ever had. For the first time in forever, it felt like someone actually cared.

Keith woke up bright and early the next day, almost vibrating at the prospect of going to the training facility and sweating his ass off, and tried to suppress the tiny pinprick of hope growing in his chest. The possibility of a new start. This, of course, made it all the more devastating when right before training was about to start, he caught Nick's expression in a mirror as the team leader watched his warmups with the same disgusted apathy as anyone else.

That hurt. More than Keith cared to admit. But it was also fair. He *was* worthless, as a person. Weak, and not really smart enough to do anything other than occasionally talk over peoples' heads. His parents ground that into him first, every time he got back a report card or injury, then his brother and their grandparents. That many people couldn't be wrong. If anything, Nick was gracious in being slower on the uptake than the rest of them. And even if Nick had now course corrected and distanced himself, he was still willing to give Keith opportunities most wouldn't—picking him for the mission, for example, despite there being plenty of other better candidates in Zero-team.

Which was why it was very important that Keith say and do nothing to make their relationship worse.

"They're tamarinds." Keith's mouth went on auto-pilot. "Closer to fruit than nut. Just thought it was kind of weird to see stuff from the outside world in a place that's supposed to be a fantasy realm."

"Really?" Nick peered at him, then back at the cluster. "There were banana trees by the elevator, man. Unless they were a weird fantasy copyright infringement. Right color, but kinda big."

Plantains.

"Sorry," Keith said.

"Don't worry about it." Nick rubbed the back of his neck. "We rolled out of the elevator in a hurry. Just, like, try to mind your surroundings and shit."

"I'll be better," Keith promised himself as much as Nick.

Nick rolled his eyes. "Don't take everything so damn seriously. And stop apologizing like it's your job."

"Sorry."

"The hell did I just say?" Nick muttered.

They walked in silence then, proceeding through the shadowed greenery of the forest toward the bluffs. Nick had spotted them from a distance and extrapolated it was worth checking for a ripple. Something about points of interest. Keith didn't really follow the logic, but he wasn't about to question it. Even if their search yielded nothing, the bluffs overlooked the vast ocean on a mostly unoccupied side of the island. In more casual circumstances, Keith would happily make the hike for the view alone.

The trees thinned, growing sparser and further apart until they disappeared entirely, a verdant green incline stretched out and upward before them.

With the end in sight, Keith wanted to rush ahead and scramble up the hill, eager to take it all in.

But Nick had stopped moving. He looked distracted, far away.

"Everything okay?" Keith asked.

Instead of answering, Nick reached in his inventory and withdrew something that resembled a knotted stick with a handle. A wand. Though its appearance didn't hold a candle to some of the more expensive—and frankly gaudy—wands Keith frequently saw around the Order. Nick held it gingerly, as if it was precious despite its appearance. "Uh. Don't spread it around, but they've given Zero-team a line of credit at the vendor. When you're 'ready,' I'm supposed to help you guys upgrade. Thing is, most of the others are already kitted out."

It made sense, Keith thought glumly. Most of the Zero-team had higher-level Users with plenty of resources looking out for them, while Keith suspected his brother viewed the assignment as little more than the teenage version of free childcare.

"Should be an upgrade from that rat-poker you've been waving around. Here." Nick stuck the wand out to him with zero fanfare. He looked away, grimacing slightly as he waited for the mage

Keith sucked in a breath. The system text read **<Wand of a Thousand Cuts>**. It was graded rare, which put it on a higher tier than pretty much anything he owned. But he hesitated, not wanting to appear too eager. "Are you sure? Seems like it means something to you."

Nick's jaw worked. "Yeah. It's fine. It uh, it used to belong to a friend. Found it in the vendor's stock and paid a pretty penny for it. Meant to hold it for her in case she needed it. You know, when she came back."

"And she doesn't need it anymore?" Keith asked, trying to temper his own expectations. Even if the wand was a loaner, he'd be fine with that. It meant more that he'd been considered at all.

Slowly, Nick shook his head. "No. And even if she did, with the way I am now? I'm pretty sure she'd want nothing to do with me."

"I'm sorry," Keith said. He was racking his mind, trying to come up with a reason someone would actively dislike the Zero-team leader and coming up dry.

"Me too." Nick wiped his face with his sleeve. His voice muffled through the fabric. "Been putting this off a while, if I'm honest. But holding off before I went into the ripple turned out to be a massive blunder. Just sentimentality welling up to bite me in the ass. As always." Again, he pushed the wand toward Keith.

This time, Keith took it. It was heavier than it looked. He held it the same way Nick had—as if it was made of glass. Given the soberness of the exchange, he tried his best to hide his excitement. "Thanks. For trusting me with something so valuable. I'll take good care of it and swear I won't let you down." Keith looked up from the wand. "And it's not like I'm going anywhere. If you ever want it back, or just want to hold it or something, I totally get it."

Nick suddenly looked away and coughed, his shoulders bunching in silent hacks. When he turned back, his eyes were red around the edges. "Appreciate that, buddy. I... really do. Tell you what. We'll probably end up searching the entire area, but I'm not really particular about where we start. Any ideas?"

"How 'bout the top of the bluffs?" Keith said, verbalizing his earlier thought, studying the path to the top. "Incline's pretty steep. We'll need to climb in a few places, but there are plenty of handholds. And even if the ripple's not up there, we'll have a good vantage on the rest of the area."

Nick nodded slowly. There was something in his grimness that felt resigned somehow. "Sure. Not sure I trust my city-boy ass to navigate that, so why don't you take point?"

"Really?"

"Yeah. Lead the way."

This wasn't a good day, exactly. There were too many close calls for that. But with his earlier breakthrough thanks to Myrddin, and Nick's generosity, it was still shaping up to be one of the better in recent memory. Keith set his shoulders and prepared to march up the incline, the sound of waves beckoning him onward.

Something nagged at the back of Keith's mind. A promise he'd made. He pulled up his interface and tried to send a party message. When it failed for the second time, he looked over his shoulder at Nick. "Been meaning to keep Halima updated on our location, but nothing's going through."

For just a second, Nick froze. Then shrugged whatever it was off just as quickly. "Probably just the realms of Flauros being unpredictable. Could be some sort of interference. Let me give it a shot." After a few seconds, Nick nodded. "Still working for me. Halima and Myrddin are on their way. From the sound of it, they're gonna be a while."

"Should we wait?"

"Nah. There's a good chance it's not up there. Might as well save them the climb."

"If it's not, can—" Keith hesitated. "Can we hang out while we catch our breath? Grab a bite to eat and talk?"

Nick nodded. "Sure, kid. Whatever you want."

———

I couldn't believe it. Refused to believe it.

The ability faded, and when I opened my eyes, my vision was woozy and gray. I stood upright too quickly and nearly fell, stumbling forward and catching myself on the limb of a nearby tree. Maybe I was being my usual, cynical self. There was a chance I was wrong. That this wasn't what I thought it was.

While I waited for the dizziness to fade, I called Halima.

She picked up on the first chime. "What happened?"

"Heard anything since earlier?" My voice was raw.

"No," Halima said. "Nothing going through from me either. Just errors every time I try to send them a message."

"Any possibility something came in while you weren't looking?" My heart pounded. The answer was written all over Nick's face. The cold, carefully restrained *intent* that Keith was too naïve to recognize.

"Myrddin, I've been glued to the goddamn UI since the last time we talked, waiting to hear something. I'm looking at it right now. There's nothing," Halima said.

God fucking dammit, Nick. This isn't you.

"Now what?" she asked, sounding scared again. "What do we do?"

"Stay put. I'll reach back out when I find them." With a few mental presses, I disconnected the voice chat before she could argue.

And ran.

CHAPTER ONE HUNDRED SIX

Low-hanging branches snagged against my armor as I ran. Every upraised bramble, root, and vine threatened to trip me, send me stumbling off course or into the unforgiving trunk of a tree as I split my attention between watching my footing and checking my progress against the coastline.

Is the Tower itself trying to stop me?

It was a paranoid thought. A stupid one. The Tower, along with the surrounding region, had bigger agendas of their own. And while I was certain the higher levels of the Tower would be more in line with the malevolence I expected from dungeons, this was little more than a tourist floor.

No. The actual source of turmoil was my rising panic. Even now, my mind warred with the reality of what I'd seen. Created excuses. Sugarcoated. Like, maybe I'd read Nick wrong and there was nothing sinister happening at all. Maybe because I was so laser-focused on him, I was misattributing trauma to malice. Maybe they really were just going for a fucking picnic.

The maybes were seductive, because the alternative meant a much larger error in judgment. That Nick wasn't who I thought he was. And I'm not sure I'd ever gotten something this critical so utterly wrong.

There had to be a reason. A justification. *Something* to explain why Nick was even considering this. People were running around, spewing fire from their hands and summoning fantasy creatures out of their bodies. It was possible there was mind control in play, or mental reprogramming, or hypnosis, or NLP, or a god damn shapeshifter.

Because Nick wouldn't do this. He wouldn't.

A mandrake screamed up ahead, and my lungs burned as I sprinted around a small group of three, smacking the small root creatures around with dull-looking weapons.

"Hey!" One of them, a guy still sporting Oakleys, shouted after me. Could be he was just asking for directions, but we were deep in the forest. I couldn't take the risk that someone might take issue with my abrupt departure and follow me. Every second counted, and there were already too many variables. A slight miscalculation and I'd be too late, if I wasn't already.

I chanced the side effects from a low-mana cast and barged into his mind with **<Suggestion>**, sending him the mental equivalent of an amber alert, drawing attention to the blood on my armor and not-so-kindly amplifying the concept of minding his own fucking business. Oakley sputtered something in a higher pitch as the blues and browns that had returned to my vision retreated, leaving my view of the blurring trees and overgrowth almost entirely monochromatic.

Which of course, made it almost impossible to differentiate the rock from the ground.

THUNK

The bones in my foot crunched as I went down hard, catching myself in a half-assed tumble that took me down a small slope. A sap-stained tree took up my entire vision, its rough bark mere inches away.

I pulled myself to my feet, favoring my left leg until the pain faded enough to be confident there wasn't a break. My mana was lower than I'd thought, judging from the easing headache and partial restoration of vision. **<Suggestion>** was an efficient skill compared to the rest, and it was probably better that I'd found out this way rather than gone in ignorant.

Still, I'd lost time. And with most of my abilities inaccessible, I needed a summon.

Without giving myself a chance to overthink and consider the reality that this was exactly how people in stories ended up stuck with cursed or bound items, I tore off my gauntlet and hesitated for just a second before I placed **<The Devil's Share>** on my finger.

Now it was just a matter of deciding which.

Azure had the most utility. He could distract Keith, delay Nick, and since we were in a realm of Flauros, batter everyone present into daze-eyed submission if it came to that. But he was still carrying out orders in the lobby, and using him in a manner that the geas considered hostile could cause it to trigger.

Talia was the fastest of my summons by several orders of magnitude and would probably at least agree to give me a ride if I asked. If she kept her original form—the hulking, raging arctic wolf that still haunted my dreams—it might have been an actual option. In her current form, however, she wasn't much larger than her real-world counterparts, and there was a reason humans rode horses instead of dogs. Even if she was willing, there was no point in trying it if her back gave out at the wrong time and launched me as a byproduct.

So. Audrey then.

As soon as I decided, I felt the beginnings of the usual cuticle-pulling sensation and braced myself. But instead of getting worse, it stopped, and Audrey popped into existence a few feet away. The cast took maybe a tenth of the time it usually did.

<Uses remaining: 1/5>

"Ah! Was nowhere. Now somewhere. So quick and... odd." Audrey looked around, bewildered.

"On me!" I shouted behind me, not bothering to slow down.

Audrey lashed to my arm and reeled herself in, bounding awkwardly across the ground. "Where—are—we—going?"

"Forward." I double-checked the coastline through the trees on my right, then pointed straight ahead. "Fast. Speed over everything. Doesn't matter if I get banged up a little. Use the trees to stabilize us and try to avoid hazards."

"Swing?"

"If there's a clearing."

Six tough-looking navigation vines shot out from Audrey's body, extending in all directions. Her grip around my shoulders tightened, and it felt as if I was hardly touching the ground, my weight reduced to almost nothing. It took her a moment to adjust to the new environment, then our speed picked up to the momentum of the sort of breakneck sprint that would have winded me in minutes. The trees blurred by so quickly they were almost indistinguishable.

"You're... afraid." Audrey's voice was just audible over the wind whistling in my ears. "Is it bad?"

Bad didn't cover it. Nick was my touchstone. He could be pragmatic, but he was also stalwart, and loyal, and kind, even though the world had done nothing but kick him in the teeth for it. That tenacity, that refusal to change, made him a rare breed. Authentic. And despite our opposing views on almost everything, his authenticity somehow placed him as the person I used to measure tough decisions I couldn't trust myself to make. The person whose opinion mattered most. I needed him now more than ever.

And he was about to do something so heinous that even I couldn't imagine it.

You take someone I love. I take someone you love.

And I couldn't shake the feeling that, if he followed through, my friend would be gone forever.

The trees thinned, golden light emanating from up ahead. With fewer obstacles to contend with, Audrey positioned us low to the ground in a slow swing, my boot catching bits of dirt and detritus on the zenith, then warned me right before she let go. I kept the momentum and hit the ground running. My vision washed out by the eternal sunrise. As my eyes adjusted, I searched the towering bluff, hoping to see two lone figures, still climbing their way to the top.

My heart sank as I spotted movement up at the top. It looked like the back of someone's head. If Keith was still alive, it wouldn't stay that way for long. Nick would want to do it quickly. Before he lost his nerve.

Do I even make that?

I forced my legs to keep pushing forward, even as a curtain of despair descended.

There was at least a hundred yards of clearing between me and the bluffs. Audrey could help with the climb once we got there, but there weren't enough trees along the way for her to close the initial gap more than she already had. The flight charm was still offline for at least another day. I had two pending levels, and there was probably a feat in the King's Ranger tree that could help, but I didn't have time to take five and read descriptions—

The skill points.

There were eight available. I'd only gained two levels in the ripple, so the number seemed wrong until I remembered the event's multiplier wasn't limited to experience. It promised increased leveling rewards as well. In the chaos of the self-equipping artifact and the terrifying new Ordinator ability, I'd overlooked them.

This was going to suck.

"Keep us moving. Drag me if you have to," I said.

"*Why?*" Audrey asked, alarmed. But her vines had already pierced the surrounding ground in response.

I slammed all eight points into agility and hit confirm. The muscle spasms started, and I ground my teeth together hard enough that I could feel them moving. A charley horse from hell obliterated my calf muscle, and Audrey awkwardly hefted me upward and forward before I could fall to my knees, moving like a giant spider as I writhed in her grasp.

After thirty seconds that felt like infinity, the pain subsided.

The exhaustion that had seeped into every muscle was gone, replaced with a strange glowing energy that radiated in my chest, begging to be set loose.

"Drop me," I said, staying focused on the ground.

My summon lowered us to the ground, bits of dirt flying toward us as her anchored vines tore free. I realized, with no small wonder, that I could pick them out individually, see the trajectory of each tiny incoming projectile, and know intuitively how I needed to move to avoid them.

I crouched low and sprinted forward in an explosion of movement.

Audrey shrieked into my ear as we shredded down the hill at break-neck speed, blades of grass quivering as we shredded through them. And almost before I even realized what happened, my palms slapped against the stone base of the bluffs.

It was so easy to forget the difference stats made. They were incre-mental by nature, and after the initial distribution, when the number of points awarded dropped and those few points were often spread out among several attributes, it was easy to forget exactly how huge the cumulative sum was.

I climbed, praying that the slipshod level-up had bought me enough time.

And prepared for the absolute shitshow that would follow if it hadn't.

CHAPTER ONE HUNDRED SEVEN

Golden-hour sunlight sliced across the top of the bluffs and obscured my vision as I pulled myself up and over the summit. Scaling it had given me time to think, to come to terms with the worst that could happen. What was likely to happen.

I was always too late. Despite every effort to the contrary, every painstaking effort to get ahead of things before they happened and a lifetime of chronic overthinking, that's how it felt. I could manage a small- or mid-sized crisis, but the big ones had a way of sneaking up on you in a manner too rapid and devastating to account for, and then suddenly, instead of acting, you're reacting, dumping smoldering ashes into a cinerary urn. Pivoting and moving on become default states of being, simply because it feels better than dwelling, and reveling, and assigning fault.

I guess, in the most literal sense, surviving is coping.

Which is why, as my eyes adjusted to the light, that sense of acceptance disappeared. Because for once, I wasn't too late.

Keith stood at the edge of the bluffs looking out over the ocean. Shivers radiated through his shoulders, his legs, and his core.

Someone who resembled Nick stood behind him. I say resembled, because considering that I'd known him for years, he was almost unrecognizable. A blood-red aura—reminiscent of the golden aura I'd seen him use frequently—occluded him in a red fog you had to squint to see through. His shield was still on his back, and the double-bladed sword in his hands pointed downward, sharpened tip grazing carelessly across the rocky ground.

"It's like you don't care," Nick said to Keith. His voice was monotone, utterly devoid of fluctuation.

Keith shook his head, refusing to look back. Nick couldn't see Keith's expression. From my angle, beneath the terror and the confusion, he had the practiced tiredness of someone who was used to being routinely disheartened.

"Your life's on the line!" Nick shouted, emotion filtering in. "But you won't fucking fight. Won't lift a goddamn finger. And you don't even want to know *why?*"

There was a sheer physicality to Nick that gave me pause. He dwarfed Keith by comparison, but at six-and-a-half feet he was taller than most of the population. It was more than that. Before, with the grimelings, there was a timidity to him. A built-in flinch that stopped him from being the absolute wrecking ball I knew he could be.

That was all but gone now.

If it came to blows, I wasn't sure I could take him.

Need to work quickly.

I circled around them counterclockwise, putting my back to the drop and placing myself out of reach and firmly in Nick's peripheral.

"Maybe he's not answering you because he's scared shitless." My voice was scathing. "But I'd love to know what led to this look-at-the-flowers moment. Wanna break it down for me, Nick?"

Nick didn't start, a testament to how deep in this he was. Instead, the eyes that slowly panned to me were cold, calculating. He was sizing me up in a way he hadn't before. "Thought you were supposed to be in the ripple."

I blew air out through my mouth. "And you left out summary execution on the docket today. Guess neither of us have been entirely forthcoming."

"I have to do this," Nick said, ignoring the prod. It sounded familiar, like he'd recited the words a thousand times before speaking them out loud.

"Really? This seems like the sort of thing you really don't have to do." I played up the abrasiveness of my voice, trying to shock him out of whatever state he was in. "And I'm not seeing how this factors into your goal. Was the line you fed me about wanting a better world a lie? Or are you just partially full of shit?"

He shook his head slowly. "Aaron mentioned you might be a problem. And that I could deal with you, if necessary."

"Sure." I nodded in mock understanding. "So, first you kill the kid—who despite his inexperience rushed into an unbalanced pocket realm to save your goddamn life. Then you kill the witness who, not to toot my horn, actually saved your life. Then maybe Halima puts two and two together. You gonna kill her too?"

"I—"

"Admit it. Whatever this is, you're *not* cut out for this shit. And you're only considering it because someone put a metaphorical gun to your head." I was trying to pull him back from whatever hypothetical Hastur had floated him, bring him back down to earth and ground him in reality.

But from the way Nick's expression hardened and he wheeled on me, it was exactly the wrong thing to say. "This is none of your fucking business. Turn around, climb back down the bluffs, and keep your mouth shut about what you saw here."

I made a show of contemplating that blandly as my mind raced, looking for a way to stall. "Hm. No."

"That's a direct order," Nick tried again.

"Oh, is it? Didn't realize. Unfortunately, still a no."

His brow furrowed. "I've seen your mark. You're bound by the geas, same as me. You can't refuse a direct order."

I shrugged, ignoring the insight. "It's easy to imagine how you're feeling. Trapped. Hemmed in. The cards are on the table, and now that everyone's seen them, you've let yourself believe that the only way out is through. But you're wrong. There's another option. All of this can go away."

Nick rolled his eyes but hesitated. His hand tightened on the hilt of the sword. "That so?"

Playing along. Not completely closed off. I have a chance here.

I held out a hand, palm up. "I'll explain the rest in private. Just put the sword down and walk away."

"I-I-I won't tell anyone," Keith mumbled, terror in his voice.

Nick studied the ground at his feet, his expression obscured in shadow and aura. When he looked up again, the tight smile on his lips set off a chorus of alarm bells. Despite the smile, Nick gripped his sword tightly, point rising slightly off the ground. "Okay."

It took every ounce of self-control I had to not shift into a combat stance. His reaction registered as inauthentic immediately. And for good reason. It was the same damn tactic I used. Giving the appearance of coming to agreement or alliance, only to immediately—and violently—snap back on it, gaining an element of surprise.

The sunset behind Nick grew increasingly golden by the second and the red of his aura was more vibrant, less washed out than before. I had mana. Not a lot, but enough to do something. Especially if I used the artifact.

I could... command him to stand down.

This was **<Subjugation's>** purpose. He was lower level than me, or at the very least, within the target range. Hell, Nick himself wouldn't even realize what happened. It would intrinsically plant the decision to spare Keith in his mind, assimilated as if that was a decision he'd made for himself. Using it was the most reasonable option. Anything else would lead to a fight I wasn't sure I could win, and a fallout I wasn't sure I could survive. And as a result, it would preserve the person I knew. The touch stone I needed.

Would it really, if you made the choice for him? Would you even be able to trust him? Or would that just slowly eat away at any concept of a rekindled friendship?

Just as I predicted, Nick suddenly spun, raising his sword, fully prepared to bring the blade down on Keith's neck.

CHAPTER ONE HUNDRED EIGHT

"What I need is for someone to tell me the truth."

I switched targets at the last second.

My body boiled under the strain, most of the mana I'd regenerated draining away.

All at once, I understood Keith in a way I'd never truly understood anyone. Fully grasped every neuron of his psyche, as I parsed through what made him tick, what drove him, the struggles he'd gone through and the utter absence of self-confidence, all tied to a hundred different threads that were just waiting for someone to come along and pull them.

Dodge backward.

Keith did, in the process doing what I'd pictured rather than following the command to the letter. He leapt away from the edge and Nick's descending blade, and stumbled a little. The movements were significantly smoother than standard-Keith, but it was clear his body couldn't quite keep up with his mind, and I needed to account for that.

Frustrated by the unexpected resistance, Nick roared and charged at Keith, sword stabbing out toward his chest.

Redirect his momentum.

Keith grabbed Nick's sword arm and pivoted, sending him stumbling awkwardly across the bluffs.

Nick reeled back a few steps, then leaned and spit, his face dark. The surrounding aura swelled out like crimson wings. I'd hoped that Keith's sudden shift would snap Nick out of the rage, or at the very least confuse him enough to contravene his tunnel vision, but it wasn't working. If anything, the sudden difficulty made him more motivated to follow through.

As Keith didn't have the baked-in experience of Audrey or Talia, I micro-tasked, puppeting him through a series of short direct commands and, together, we evaded Nick's onslaught.

But this was just delaying the inevitable. Spinning a stalemate into a loss.

I needed to separate them. The question was how.

Ideas cycled through my mind until I landed on one. Something dangerous that I'd never consider in less dire circumstances but all I could come up with on the fly.

I directed Keith to run a wide circle across the bluffs. As Nick chased after him, I scrambled toward the ledge and looked down, mind running through several calculations. There was nothing but ocean below, most of the rocks on the far-left side.

With a fragment of a plan, I sent Keith the silver bullet.

Keith ran to the far end of the cliff, then threw his hands in the air and shouted a name.

"JINNY."

Nick halted dead in his tracks.

I false-started, stopping to watch. All I'd done was send Keith a redacted image of Jinny's death, along with instructions to shout her name. But now, Keith was continuing on his own. "That was her name, wasn't it?" he asked breathlessly, withdrawing the wand from his inventory. "And this was hers, right?"

Nick hesitated, color gone from his face.

"And you gave it to me because you feel like tainting her memory is the only way to get through it. Because you *know* she wouldn't want you to do this. You're a good guy, with a good heart. That's why she loved you."

I could have slammed a sledgehammer into Nick's gut to less devastating effect.

His face scrunched up, his teeth clenching. "I don't *want* to be the good guy. The guy who gets stepped on, fucked with, and fucked up because he's not mean enough. I'm *tired* of being the good guy."

Again, Keith shook his head, speaking entirely of his own volition. "We can't help what we are. At our core. We can hide it. Disguise it. Push it so deep it might even take an entire lifetime for it to resurface. But you are what you are. Nature always wins over nurture, in the end."

Nick shook his head several times, then set his teeth. He raised his sword arm.

Too slow.

I crouched low and took off like a rocket, supercharged agility flinging me forward, eyes fixed on my target—Nick's torso.

He saw me coming out of the corner of his eye and shifted suddenly, trying to alter his positioning to intercept me. But I was too quick. I snared his torso with both arms and let the rest of my weight slam into him.

Nick grunted, swearing up a storm as I pushed him back. Then the ground disappeared beneath us and his eyes widened in realization.

Doing this for your own good, Nick.

Now in free fall, we plummeted toward the water. Audrey's vines snagged on a few outcroppings and slowed the fall. My feet hit the water and Nick plummeted past me, leaving a trail of bubbles in his wake.

Shit. His armor.

I swam straight down, tearing through the water until I caught up. His eyes were open and urgent, but he wasn't moving, arms spread out at his side. Probably still stunned from the impact. I tore off the **<Operator's Belt>** and pulled it tight around his waist. Immediately, his direction reversed, and with urging he shot upward. I kept a hold on the belt, riding the buoyancy up to the surface.

We barely breached the surface before a heavy gauntlet struck me across the temple. I spun in a mess of bubbles and fury, struggling to right myself, ready to give as good as I got.

When I burst through again, though, I'd misread the aggression. He flailed in a panic, the top section of his armor pulled down by gravity, constantly threatening to upend him as he slapped at the water. Given what he'd almost done, it tempted the spiteful part of me to let him flail for a while.

I spotted Keith.

A dark shadow flitted beneath us. Something brushed my leg, too quick to make out.

Given that—whatever it was—was out here, on the outskirts of the dungeon floor proper, I wasn't overly worried, but I knew better than to tempt fate. I glanced over my shoulder and spotted a sandy bank a short distance away, hidden in the alcove of the bluffs.

Near decade-old rescue and CPR lessons came back to me piecemeal, and I did my best to follow what I could remember, starting with not approaching a drowning person from the front. Instead, I treaded water until I was behind Nick and grabbed him roughly under the arms.

Crack

The back of Nick's head smashed against my mask with enough force to stun me and nearly loosen my grip.

"Fucker! Stop! There's something in the water—"

THUNK

This time, when Nick curled inward and threw his head back, I was ready for it. I tucked my chin, and the back of his head bounced painfully off the stable upper section of my mask. He stopped struggling and I tightened my hold, propelling us toward the sandbank with haphazard kicks.

Out of the corner of my eye, I spotted the shadow. It was bigger than I'd originally thought.

"Audrey. Can you swim?"

"Nooooo." My summon's mental voice sounded utterly miserable, and I realized that from where she clung to my back, her head was probably well below the surface.

"Can you at least breathe?" I asked, monitoring the circling shadow. Now that Nick seemed to be panicking less—maybe he'd finally realized I wasn't actively trying to drown him—I reached back, kicking and treading with one arm. Faster, but not fast enough.

Audrey sent back a complex reply, a composite of words and images. I gathered she didn't need to breathe regularly, though being underwater was unpleasant, and if we submerged her for too long, it would kill her.

I felt bad for doing it—between Miles, the Crimson Nosferatu, and the grimelings, this outing had been stressful on my summons—but I sent Audrey a picture of a net and an image of her zipping toward a generic shark and wrapping it up.

Her response was reticent. *"If I catch it..."*

"Of course. Dig in. Assuming you can even eat that much. From the size, it's probably hundreds of pounds—"

The dark shadow made a second pass, and there was a tangible relief as the vines released from my shoulder. As the shadow retreated, a much smaller shadow followed it.

Good. Audrey snagged it. Assuming she could distract whatever it was for even a few minutes, we were probably in the clear. I'd need to compensate her later, especially if whatever was out there inevitably got the better of her. Something fancy. Sushi, maybe.

As soon as there was enough sand underneath us to stand on, Nick pushed me away. I let him go, crawling up onto the sandbar and heaving for breath.

<Awareness> shrieked. I rolled away just as Nick buried a massive knife into my imprint in the sand. His aura returned full force, spite radiating from it.

"Are you insane?" I scrambled backward, trying to keep away from him as he advanced. Now that the crisis was over, a dark curtain of anger descended over me. But Nick wasn't listening. I wasn't even sure if he was hearing me. He stomped across the sandbar like a malevolent automaton, his eyes dead, nothing left of him but rage.

I'd been more or less in hiding since the Transposition started. Maybe even before that, if I was being honest. It'd kept me alive. Kept my family safe. But I was tired of hiding.

I took the mask off.

CHAPTER ONE HUNDRED NINE

"Matt?" Nick's jaw hung open, and he stared agape. Slowly, the dark-red aura that was so reminiscent of the Crimson Nosferatu's drained away, until he finally resembled Nick again.

I didn't know what to say. Despite knowing this was a possibility, I hadn't planned this far, and at the moment, came up empty.

"What the fuck." Nick passed a hand through his hair, his face conflicted. "No. No, no no. This is a trick. Hastur's testing me."

"We met in the rehab center. You were there for your leg, I was there for my mom."

Nick shook his head vehemently. "No—"

I went down the list. "The passcode on your phone is six nine repeating. Your favorite game is *Resident Evil 4*—the original, not the remake, seeing as how, in your opinion, they cut too much of the campiness. You'd pick Waffle House over IHOP any day."

"Shut up."

"You say your greatest fear is being alone—but I'd argue it's not actually that. I think given the excess of flings you try to keep on as friends, and how tightly you've clung to me, I think your greatest fear is being irrelevant, but more than that, being unloved. And until today, *if someone put a gun to my fucking head and asked me to pick out the one good fucking person in the fucking world, I would have pointed at you.*" I realized, belatedly, that I was shouting. And I didn't care. "Past *fucking* tense."

The punch came quicker than I expected, and the entire left side of my face went numb as Nick's fist slammed into my jaw. I spun like a top and went down. Nick stood over me, his fist trembling. "Fuck *you*, Matt. You have no idea what it was like."

"Then tell me." I gestured at myself wildly. "Because I'm right goddamn here, and personally, I'd love an explanation for *that*. Because that wasn't you." I pointed to the cliffs.

This was it. The last chance. If he was being manipulated or controlled through profound means that even Azure could not detect, this was where he'd offer a rational explanation. Something that was well-thought out and made sense. Some premeditated bullshit about a mental break, or a Macguffin, or some trumped-up needs-of-the-many equivocations. Anything.

Shame and anger warred on Nick's face. "Where were you?"

You did not just ask me that.

"While I was neck-deep in the deepest, darkest hole imaginable, *where the fuck were you?*" Nick shouted, spittle flying. "Cause from where I'm standing, it looks like all you've been working is spinning that class I gave you into something better. Glad you could run around touring the Flauros realms playing swashbuckling rogue and advancing while Jinny and Sae rotted and I fended for my fucking self."

In ordinary circumstances, I might have understood. He'd lost someone he loved and was held prisoner by the people who took her from him, and he'd been through a series of traumatic experiences one after another.

"I-I-I-I—" I clamped down on the stutter, hating myself for it. "No. That's what you think of me. Okay. Great. Glad we're clearing the air." A thousand biting rebuttals cycled through my mind, but in the end, I said nothing, just reached in my inventory and withdrew an object.

"Is that?"

"Yeah." The User core glinted violet in my gloved hand. Nick took a step backward. When I spoke, my voice was monotone. "Snatched it off her while you were busy ruining any chance we had to de-escalate." I tossed it underhanded, and Nick caught it. He stared at it, cradling it in his hands, his anger replaced with sadness.

I removed my dagger and crossbow first, stripping them from my belt and tossing them aside.

His eyes narrowed as he watched me. "What are you doing?"

"Giving you what you asked for," I muttered, dark anger still coursing through my veins.

"The hell?"

"Back at the house, you said you wanted to see what I could do in a straight fight." I finished unbuckling my gauntlet and tossed it into the sand. Then undid my other gauntlet and continued removing my armor piece by piece until I was down to my hoodie and jeans. "And you're spoiling for one. So, now's your chance."

For a second, I thought Nick would argue. Instead, he stood, pocketing the orb, and followed suit, removing his sword from his belt and placing it onto the sand. "No weapons, spells, or active abilities?"

"Yep," I confirmed.

"Anything else?"

"I'll do my best not to break anything."

A dark cloud overtook his expression—only to be immediately replaced by confusion and pain as I threw a fistful of sand in his face. "You *bastard*—"

I weaved under his flailing arms, venting all my frustration, anger, and fear, and drove my elbow into Nick's chin.

He stumbled backward, trying to right himself.

I advanced. "You have no fucking idea what I've been through, trying to get to you. And you know what's funny? I was about to tell you. Couldn't do it right away, as I wasn't sure if you were being influenced and still hadn't figured out a way around the geas, but if you'd kept it together for just one more fucking day—*Oof.*"

Nick's body blow hit hard enough to lift me off my feet and leave my stomach a writhing knot of pain and spasms. I ducked under the follow-up haymaker. He panted and sneered. "Must be nice up there in that ivory tower you judge the rest of us from."

I defended myself as well as I could, using **<Unsparing Fang>** to turn away his heavy blows. "I've never judged you."

"No. You just never said it out loud." Nick jabbed at me twice, testing my reaction. Now that the element of surprise had faded, he'd settled into something that resembled a boxing stance.

The first few blows had comprised wild swings, fueled by anger and fear. But it'd gone on long enough that we both fell back onto experience, and the fight settled into a rhythm. **<Unsparing Fang>** thrived on capitalizing when your opponent over-committed, and Nick—despite his anger—did a devilishly good job maintaining an iron defense. Ordinarily I'd change tact, go on the offensive, but I couldn't do that when every strike he threw packed enough individual power to put me down. By the same token, with my enhanced agility, Nick couldn't land a solid hit.

Unstoppable force met immovable object. Neither making any real headway as the wind rustled our clothes, sodden sand glittering beneath advancing and retreating feet beneath a sun that would never set, until we were both staggering and our movements grew sloppy in the unrelenting tide of push and pull.

There was a sensation of mana discharging, draining color from my vision. I panicked for a moment, terrified I casted something accidentally, only realizing shortly after that the drain came from far to my right, beneath the ocean's surface. Audrey had used an ability. My summon was still tangling with whatever was down there.

But the split-second lapse was all it took to tip the balance.

Nick charged forward, lifting me up by my legs and slamming onto my back, pinning my shoulder with one arm and cocking his fist back. I closed my eyes, bracing for the blow.

It never came.

"Why... did you have to stop me?" Nick choked out. When I opened my eyes, there were tears streaming down his face. "I know you. If the tables were turned, if Iris or Ellison died in that tunnel—you wouldn't have stopped at his brother. You'd make him radioactive. Shred through everyone he cared about until there was no one left."

Nick deserved the truth. Not something I thought he needed to hear. So I let myself think about it. Really consider it. "If someone killed my brother or sister—or hurt them to get to me—I'd spend a very long time driving home how profound of a fuck-up that was before I let it end."

Nick's expression grew more confused.

"So, maybe you've got it right," I murmured. "Maybe I would do that. But *you* wouldn't."

Slowly, Nick pushed himself up and collapsed on the sand beside me, expression defeated. He looked like he'd aged ten years in an hour. "Yeah. *Yeah.*" He leaned his head back and stared at the sky. "Would have regretted it, no matter what Hastur said. And of course I went and screwed it all up before I figured that out."

"Not... necessarily," I hedged, feeling tangible relief at Nick's confirmation that Hastur had a hand in this unexpected turn.

Nick peered at me. "With the geas, he won't have any choice in the matter. He'll have to report it."

"Not if he's convinced he nodded off on the bluffs and everything that happened after was a dream." That, and the directive to find Halima, were the last orders I gave Keith, and he'd accepted them with no issue. I neglected to mention that Nick being forced by Aaron or Sunny to make a report now that he knew my Ordinator role was just as much, if not more, of an issue.

"As if." Nick scoffed. When I didn't laugh, he gaped openly. "You can actually do that?"

"There's a lot I can do," I deflected. **<Subjugation>** was order of magnitudes more powerful than **<Suggestion>**, but without testing— which was problematic in its own right—I had to assume the same rules applied. The biggest limiter was immediacy. If I'd waited hours after the altercation with Nick to give Keith the order, it was entirely possible the command would fail or Keith would reject it outright. There was no point in telling Nick anything if he wasn't stable and I might need to use **<Subjugation>** to wipe his memories to obscure my identity. As much as I hated it, that *was* the simpler option. If he kept his memories, we'd need to either quickly find a solution to the geas, or abandon the Order entirely and bunker Nick down somewhere with constant **\<Squelch\>** coverage so he couldn't receive orders or be forced to report.

Before I decided anything, I needed the piece I was missing. "I'll tell you everything. But first, I need to know what happened with Hastur to put you on the warpath. The whole truth, Nick. This is important."

Nick suddenly looked very far away. "Might as well. Got nowhere else to be."

CHAPTER ONE HUNDRED TEN

Before

A puff of air stirred Nick's eyelashes and he grimaced, letting out a groan and pressing the side of his head deeper into the pillow. Hazy tendrils of exhaustion pulled him back toward the throes of unconsciousness as sleep prepared to take him once more.

Another puff, lower. He wrinkled his nose and blindly seized a pillow, placing it over his head.

A thread of merry laughter banished the haziness in his mind. He blinked away the sleep, a pair of deep-blue eyes slowly shifting into focus. Jinny stretched forward, and soft lips kissed his forehead.

"Good morning, sweet prince."

Nick blinked several times, memories of the last day slowly coming back to him. "... Hi."

Jinny snorted. "Hi, he says."

The more the memories came into focus, the less sense they made. "Sorry." Nick pushed himself up onto one elbow and looked around. They were at his aunt's house, which lined up with the last thing he remembered. But... "Uh. I'm a little disoriented."

"Sure," Jinny said. Nick had always thought she was beautiful, but it was her presence—her wisdom, the way she talked to you like you were the only other person in the world—that utterly enthralled him. And now that presence was close enough that it was making his head spin.

Well, it was going to sound stupid no matter how he phrased it.

"Are you a wizard?"

Jinny laughed, and despite his confusion, Nick chuckled with her. "Did we really go out for ice cream, wake up in some dingy maintenance tunnels and fight actual goblins with fantasy weapons, come back here and call everyone we knew, only for them to call us insane, then passionately consummate our relationship? Or did I get a serious concussion somewhere down the line?"

"Wow." Jinny cushioned her face with a hand. "I can't believe ice cream and passionate consummation ranks higher than the obvious." She pointed toward the foot of the bed.

"Obvious what?" Nick asked. He peeked under the covers. "Welp. I'm definitely naked."

"Your *leg*."

Oh. *Oh.* Nick shuffled off the covers in a hurry and gaped at what had once been a source of never-ending hardship. The muscles of his bad leg were no longer atrophied and shriveled. The only remaining evidence was several patches of scar tissue, the badges of several surgeries. He took a deep breath.

And stood.

No pain. Not completely convinced, he walked in a small circle. Again, it didn't hurt. He hopped in place several times, waiting for the telltale ache.

Nothing.

"It's real. It actually happened. And—what?" he asked. Jinny had covered all but a single eye with one hand, her face and neck flushing increasingly red. Her one visible eye flicked down.

Nick snatched the duvet from where it fell on the ground, quickly wrapping it around his waist. He rubbed the back of his head sheepishly. "Sorry."

"It's fine. I'm fine." Jinny fell back into the mattress, staring at the ceiling. "We had... quite the day."

"Yes we did." Nick sat on the edge of the bed, his mind sputtering to take it all in. It was easier than the previous day, but there was still a part of him that wondered if he was going insane. He glanced at Jinny, uncharacteristically at a loss for words. "Did you, uh, hear from anyone?"

Jinny shook her head. "No. Caught up on a few of my group chats this morning, but the meteor's still all anyone's talking about. Nothing about goblins or lizard people. And..." She wrinkled her nose.

"What?" Nick asked.

"It's stupid."

"It's not stupid if it's bothering you."

"Yes, you're very smooth." Jinny tilted her head and gave him the most sultry look he'd ever seen in his life. Nick caught himself just shy of falling off the edge. "But it feels petty to talk about in the wake of everything going on."

Nick shrugged. "Considering how batshit insane the last twenty-four hours have been, I feel like we could probably use some normalcy. Even if it is petty."

"Fine." Jinny sighed. "We were spotted leaving school together, yesterday."

"Even a comet doesn't stop the rumor mill, huh?" Nick joked, but the joke fell short. He was worried. Jinny was one of his oldest friends and one of the few who remained. And they'd crossed the line last night in a big way. There were mitigating factors, of course. Neither of them were in a good state of mind by the time they'd worked through their contact lists, and after she'd kissed him, everything that followed was frantic and primal, two people desperately trying to make sense of a world that had gone completely off the rails.

These things happened. But in Nick's experience, that excuse didn't prevent previously functional relationships from being altered or sometimes damaged when sex was involved.

"Uh." He rubbed his shoulder, suddenly cold, searching for words beneath Jinny's insightful gaze. "Everything... got a little crazy. We were both freaking out. All things considered, I wouldn't blame you at all if you —you know—wanted to forget that this happened."

Jinny blinked. "I set a giant centipede on fire with my mind. Not sure there's any forgetting that."

"I meant... the naked bits."

"Oh," Jinny said. An awkward silence swelled up between them until it was almost too much for Nick to bear. "I'm alright with it being a one-time thing."

"Of course," Nick said automatically, doing everything he could to hide the disappointment that crashed over him.

"I've always thought we were pretty compatible. But you started dodging me after your injury, then I met someone..."

"Definitely compatible. Wait. What?"

"And now there's meteors and magic out of nowhere—"

"—when did I dodge you?" Nick interjected, struggling to keep up.

"—and if you look at everything altogether, it seems like a decent chance this is the start of something big. Hopefully not bad, but big, so it's probably not a good time to start a relationship," Jinny finished thoughtfully. "Not to mention, my mom would kill me."

Again, the awkward silence. But this time, Nick understood why. He'd done the same thing dozens of times. She was giving him an out. In case it really was a one-time thing, or he got caught up in the moment and regretted it after.

Only, he didn't regret it. Not even a little.

Feeling slightly manic, Nick laid back down beside her, taking care to make sure his blanket-wrapped waist stayed covered. "Counterpoint?"

"Go ahead." Jinny hid a small smile.

"If we both think we're compatible, and this *is* the start of something big... wouldn't it be great if we started it together?" Nick asked, floating the idea as casually as he could manage.

For a moment, Jinny said nothing. "As much as I'd like that... I've got some baggage."

"Same."

Her voice took on a serious air. "I mean it, Nick. This might not end well."

"And won't you tell me what it is? The baggage?"

Jinny shook her head.

"That's fair." Nick thought about it. "What sort of damage could it do? To us?"

"Let's..." Jinny blew air out through her teeth. "Let's just say—hypothetically—"

Nick nodded.

"—I had some sort of health condition. And I could be fine and live forever or be a complete dumpster fire and die tomorrow. Would you... still want me? Even knowing what I might put you through?" Jinny looked down, a curtain of hair obscuring her face.

A surge of worry shot through Nick. She just looked so unsure and crestfallen. He wasn't worried for himself, of course. More concerned about her, mainly because whatever she was hinting at seemed serious, nothing like what he expected from these sorts of conversations. He remembered her visits to the rehab center, and to his aunt's house after. Long nights of hanging out in the living room watching movies and being comfortable in her presence, no expectations, no self-consciousness, no anxiety.

"Girl." Nick sighed. "I'd swipe right on you if you were pushing a hundred and I had to break you out of the retirement home every go-round."

Jinny choked a laugh. "You can't mean that."

"Damn straight I can." Nick took her hand. "Hell, even if we just had tomorrow, that'd still be worth it. Every day I get after that, I might as well be winning the lottery."

Nick wrapped his arms around her as Jinny pressed her head into his neck and kissed him lightly on the collarbone. "Promise you won't regret it?"

He promised.

/////

Nick started awake, the pain in his chest seizing. He grimaced, grasping at his shirt, rocking back and forth until it receded. They'd thrown him in here days ago. A bare stone room with a slot at the base of the door, where his food was delivered. He'd refused to eat and drank as little as possible, though despite the austere nature of the prison, the food itself smelled quite good. That worked for a while, because the pain in his stomach distracted him from the hole in his chest, the near-literal manifestation of loss.

His surroundings shifted and blurred. When they came back into focus, his prison was cylindrical, rather than square, a circle of desiccated soil beneath him, decrepit, crumbling bricks formed the rounded surface that rose all the way to the open top.

He was in the well again. The same well he fell into as a child, when his parents had moved from Oregon to Dallas, shortly before their divorce. He'd found his way out on his own back in middle-school, only to fall back in after the doctors told him he'd never walk unassisted again. The walls had been taller than the first time then, and they were even taller now.

"Well," a voice said from nowhere. Nick started, turning to take in a thin, well-dressed man with a ponytail. He was wearing dark dress-pants and a black button-down shirt with the sleeves rolled up, accented by a light-purple vest. His head tilted upward, and he studied the opening of the hole with detached interest. "A little on the nose, but accurate enough."

"Who are you?" Nick licked his parched lips. They felt like sandpaper against his tongue.

"Have you ever tried just... climbing out?" the man mused, continuing on as if he hadn't heard. "In your head, I mean. Wonder if that would work."

"No. Sometimes I get close. Sometimes I can hang on, close to the top, but I always fall, eventually."

The man turned to Nick with a quizzical look, pointing upward. "You know there's medication for this."

Nick shook his head. Everything he'd tried either didn't work, worked for a little while and stopped working, or had side effects worse than the symptoms.

The man inclined his head. "Okay. Fine. Then what's the plan, Stan? You're too stubborn to kill yourself, but if you keep refusing food, that's gonna happen anyway."

Something about how casually the man was talking about this rubbed Nick the wrong way, though he couldn't explain why. And just as quickly, any irritation he felt ebbed away to nothing. It didn't matter. Nothing mattered here.

"I'm tired," Nick said, hoping the man would take a hint and leave him alone.

"I know." The man looked at him with sympathy. Not pity. Sympathy.

"Who are you?" Nick asked again.

"You're not gonna like it," the man warned.

"Who are you?"

"The Retainer in Violet. Or Hastur, if you prefer. The de facto patron of the Order of Parcae. You... know them as the suits."

Nick breathed in sharply. He hadn't minded the man's presence before, but now that he knew, a numb stab of anger grew within him like a sliver under a fingernail. "Get out."

"See, *this* is why I didn't want to tell you."

"GET OUT," Nick bellowed, the sudden harshness of his voice echoing, bouncing upward toward the opening. Rather than move, or react, or argue, Hastur shoved his hands in his pockets and waited.

Hours passed, dragging into what felt like days. Any anger Nick felt slowly drained away into numbness, and he felt the slightest tinge of spite.

"Do you enjoy this—"

"—No," Hastur interjected.

"Lording over some pathetic fuck, reveling in your own superiority?"

"Think you've got me confused with *your* patron, but I'll let that go—"

"Fuck. *You.*" Nick spat, a glob of saliva that landed at Hastur's feet.

"What happened to your friend, shouldn't have happened," Hastur said. Wary, Nick searched his expression for any glibness or condescension, finding none. "And if I could bring her back right now, I would."

"Coulda woulda shoulda." Nick laughed. It was a harsh sound.

"Fair enough." Hastur extended his hands to his sides and let them drop. "Good intentions mean little in the grand scheme. And I should know. After all, my intention was to derail the entire initiative before it got this far." Regret played across his face.

"Before your people started murdering innocent people in tunnels?" Nick snarled.

Hastur blinked several times. "Well, yes. But not what I'm referring to. Right, we brought you in before the first event even started." The god snapped his fingers and suddenly the well disappeared.

The walls of the well were replaced with a blood-red skyline. They were levitating hundreds of feet in the air, and below them was absolute chaos. Nick gawked, trying to parse it all. Below them, a dozen Users were fighting a giant with all the effectiveness of ants taking on an elephant, their blows and attacks just as effective. The giant stomped down, flattening four of them in an instant. Beyond them, other Users were scuffling with smaller monsters, a few of them fighting amongst themselves. There were so many bodies.

"What is this?" Nick whispered, fearing the answer.

"Not a vision, or a potential future, if that's what you're thinking."

Hastur shook his head. "This is happening as we speak. It's barbaric. Sickening."

"If my friend's still alive—"

"Who, Matt?" Hastur nodded. "He's still out there. Doing his thing."

Nick closed his mouth, trying not to give anything away.

"But he won't last much longer on his own. And no matter how bad this looks, it's nothing compared to the second event. As hard as it might be to believe in your current state, the purpose of the Order is to instate the Court—and as a side effect, stop all this from happening."

Nick's attention snapped to him. "You're right. I don't believe you."

Hastur studied him briefly, then looked away. "Would you like to know why the walls keep getting higher?"

"What walls?" Nick asked, confused by the sudden shift in conversation.

"You're already aware of this on some level, but since humans are uniquely adept at ignoring things they know to be true, I'll do you the courtesy of spelling it out," Hastur mused, his calm voice radiating authority. "It's a defect. Most beings are products of their environment. Their circumstances. You touch a hot stove, it burns you, you pull your hand back. Next time you'll avoid touching the stove at all. Action, reaction, acclimation."

He chuckled and rubbed at the scruff lining his jaw. "You should have learned, very early on, that the world is not a kind place. Or a fair one. Your father imparted that lesson well."

Nick froze, a needle of fear worming its way into the base of his neck. "Don't—"

"Relax." Hastur shifted his head back and forth. "Point is, you should have learned then. Most people would have. But instead of accepting that the wall was just a wall, a natural boundary that simply was, you kept throwing yourself against it. Slicing yourself open and bleeding love and kindness into a world that wouldn't give a rat-fuck if you disappeared tomorrow."

"So. I only have myself to blame." Nick laughed. If he was understanding this so-called god correctly, the sentiment was crueler than anything he could have imagined.

Hastur shook his head. "To reiterate. It's a defect. One that I'm willing to address as part of your compensation."

A burgeoning silence grew between them. Hastur had to know he wanted to ask. And Nick had spent enough time around manipulators to know when he was being baited.

It was Nick who broke first. "Compensation?"

Hastur smiled and reached out to take Nick's arm. The pain in his chest ceased, like his emotions were sound waves strangled with an anechoic chamber. Nick pulled his arm free and stepped back. He was feeling panic, but it was more muted than usual, less sharp and distracting. "What the hell did you do to me?"

The god put out a soothing hand, palm out. "Alleviated your pain. And presented a modicum of what it would feel like, if you let the ungrounded optimism and idealism go."

Nick tried to ignore it. The voice in his head that told him this was the first time, possibly ever, he'd felt grounded. Unflappable. Even thinking about Jinny didn't hurt as much as it had. The pain was still there, but there was more anger than anything else. It felt...

Good.

"You're still human, of course. Tragedy will still hurt you. The highs will be lower, but the lows will be higher. And you'll never have to scale the walls again."

As much as he hated himself for his own weakness, Nick wanted it. He was tired of being let down, disappointed, going through the agony of piecing himself back together for it to happen all over again.

"What's the purpose of the Order?" Nick asked.

"In the long term, to achieve a perfect future," Hastur answered easily. "In the short term, to end the initiative before the second Transposition event."

Ending the "initiative" wasn't an issue in Nick's opinion, but the second part gave him pause. "Perfect by what metric?"

"Perfect to each individual human, for most of their lifetimes."

"That's impossible." Nick shook his head.

"It's unlikely," Hastur agreed. "That's where I come in. Along with the Order, until they're superseded by the Court. In the meantime, I'll need to clean house. There are tensions within the order, which has led to aggressive, dangerous mandates. That's part of what I'd like your help with. Reforming the order into a kinder, more benevolent version of itself."

"Thought that was a bad thing." Nick's lip curled.

Hastur shook his head. "I don't think kindness and benevolence are aspects of weakness in the grand scheme, Nick. But they're destroying you from the inside. They always have. And if you take advantage of my offer, some part of you would still keep them. They would just be... tempered. Manageable."

Nick thought for a long time. "And if I told you to take your offer and shove it up your ass? That I'm not interested in joining your little cult, and if you're doling out compensation, all I want is Jinny back and nothing else?"

"Then I will respect your wishes," Hastur said. A moment later, the feeling of despair flooded back, full force, and Nick clutched at his chest, gasping at the pain. "With a warning."

"What... warning," Nick asked through gritted teeth.

"I can see the threads of different worlds—though you'd probably call them timelines. Your friend. Jinny? She had little time left even if she lived through the tragedy. Two months. Three at the most, assuming Metia spared her. And while the order will eventually have the means to bring her back, it won't be long before you're back here. In this place." Hastur ran the tip of his finger across a crumbling bricking, brushing his fingers together and watching the dust as it faded away. "And the walls will be ever higher."

"You're lying."

"What reason do I have to lie?" Hastur asked

Nick tried desperately to hang onto the anger from before. Anything to distract him from how he was feeling now. But what Hastur was implying lined up with what Jinny hinted at a little too well to be coincidence. "Maybe... you're right. Maybe I've been an idiot this whole time. Maybe the world is shit, and you're the only way it's ever going to get better. Fine. But I want the crossbowman gone. The one who killed Jinny. I want him fucking dead."

Hastur's eyes lit up. "Revenge? Certainly. You'll do that yourself, with my blessing. He'll see no protection from me. But first, I need to know that you're committed. That you want what I'm offering."

Nick hesitated. He wasn't expecting Hastur to agree so easily. It seemed too easy somehow, like there was a trap he'd missed. "Can I think about it?"

"Certainly. But you'll need to stay here until you decide. This isn't a half-in, half-out situation, I'm afraid."

With that, Hastur left him.

And he didn't come back. As the walls grew taller and the pain metastasized, Nick slammed his head backward into the brick wall. Eventually, even the physical pain didn't help. He screamed for Hastur and received no answer.

Finally, after what felt like eons, Hastur returned.

"I can't." Nick whimpered. "I can't take it anymore."

"Tell me what you want," Hastur prompted. He was going to make Nick say it.

Nick's stomach churned, and he blinked away tears. His mind turned once again toward Jinny, then to the images of the Transposition. "If... I accept your gift. In this perfect future... will it actually make a difference? Make me better at helping people? If I can just turn it all off and do what needs to be done?"

He jumped as a hand settled on his head, cold and comforting in equal measure. "My dear boy. With my help you will save more lives than you can count. I'll hone the power within you and forge a blade sharper than any sword. A hero's blade. And you will forge your own legend."

"What do I have to do?" Nick asked. He'd do almost anything if he didn't have to feel this way anymore.

Hastur's voice was soothing, almost hypnotic. "First, you must harden your heart. Set fire to the bridge at your back and spare no thought to retreat."

"And how do I do that? Kill the crossbowman?" Nick asked, feeling uncomfortable at the idea now that it was very real.

Hastur shook his head. "Killing the one who wronged you isn't enough. You must even the scales. Dirty your hands in a manner that symbolizes your transformation. Only then will you be free."

The god leaned down low and whispered into Nick's ear. "The real threat is not your target, but his brother."

Nick jerked in surprise and stared at Hastur. "What?"

"This initiative is far sloppier than previous iterations. That an Ordinator was assigned at all is evidence enough. But the crossbowman you loathe so dearly is kin to a User who represents a far more egregious oversight."

"You're saying his brother is a threat," Nick asked, already feeling completely over his head.

"In his current form, he is harmless. Which I suspect will pose more difficulty for you than if he was a monster in human form. But the way his title interacts with certain abilities he will receive, further down the line? He will be a threat to everyone. Even the gods." Hastur shook his head slowly.

"What's his name?" Nick swallowed, his mouth suddenly dry.

Hastur chuckled. "You never asked the 'crossbowman's' name. I wonder why that is." When Nick didn't respond, he gave a half-nod. "His name is Keith. As ordinary as his appearance, I'm afraid."

"And you're certain?" Nick asked. "That he's as big of a threat as you think?"

Hastur's eyes were fathomless. "The question is whether you can become the man you wish to be. Capable of abandoning your childish idealism and placing the needs of the many over the needs of the few. Dirtying your hands, for the sake of the people you care about."

There were a million reasons to say no. There had to be. But at that moment, Nick couldn't think of them. The pain in his chest throbbed, intensifying. And beyond Hastur's patient gaze, he saw the walls growing ever higher.

"If you need more time..." Hastur began.

Nick answered before the words fully formed in his mind. "I'll do it."

CHAPTER ONE HUNDRED ELEVEN

This was the problem with planning in a vacuum. Hastur had struck me as more genuinely well-meaning than most of the gods I'd encountered. He wasn't actively trying to kill me, didn't pass around any classes or abilities that immediately made me a target, and was relatively straightforward about what his goal was. It was a low bar, but I'd still taken some small solace from it.

Now, though? That solace was gone.

Nick's account changed things. Maybe I was wrong and Keith was a genuine threat, but it felt too tidy. Too convenient. It reeked of manipulation, gaslighting, with threads of psychological torture and brainwashing. Which was ironic as, now that I'd thought about it, he'd used similar tactics with me. I hadn't recognized them for what they were because he'd been so damn positive in his delivery, almost edifying.

Probably why he'd gone that route.

Despite having everything in the world to say about his experiences, my temper had flared, and I didn't want to get it wrong. So, instead, I spent most of the next hour telling Nick everything. And I mean everything. It took longer than I expected, spanning from the story of my father and the man who killed him, then jumping ahead to the first encounter with the Allfather of Chaos, to what really happened those first few days, to my encounter with Hastur and my side of things in the Tower—including the artifact and ability I'd gained.

His reactions were mixed. I could tell it hurt that I hadn't shared my history, though he understood. When I admitted to withholding my User status in the early days, he tried to keep his face neutral but anger showed through. He was still angry when I told him about the events of the Transposition, but it felt as if that anger was no longer targeted solely at me. As I went on, detailing the astronomical amount of trouble holding the Ordinator class had put me in almost by default, his anger faded. When I told him what happened to Sae, tears welled up in his eyes. And by the time I finished outlining my abilities, including the new acquisition, he looked uncomfortable, maybe even a little scared.

Nick whistled a low pitch. "Well... based on everything you've said about it, guess it's a good thing it was you who ended up as the Ordinator instead of some megalomaniacal asshole."

I gave him a pointed look.

"I mean, you're only an asshole sometimes," Nick protested, and I couldn't help but snort. "And you're *way* less of an asshole than you could be, all things considered."

"Thanks."

"Seriously." Nick's expression was grave. "Think about what would have happened if the wrong person ended up with your class. Someone like Sunny."

"Or Aaron."

Nick shifted uncomfortably. "You've dropped bits and pieces about the trial over the years, but I didn't know he was *that* Aaron."

"Not really where I expected to find him either," I admitted, sieving a clump of sand between my fingertips. "Bigger problem is... there's a solid chance I *am* the wrong person. Or worse, the right one, if that's what the Allfather's going for." Nick seemed to take issue with that, and I pressed ahead before he could cut me off. "Come on. I just told you my history."

"Far as I'm concerned, the Givens asshole had it coming. He killed your fucking dad," Nick snapped, oddly vehement. An incongruity struck me.

I studied Nick carefully, filtering out any accusation from my voice before I spoke. "I never called him by name."

"Who?"

"The shooter."

Nick opened his mouth, closed it, opened it again. "You uh, must've at some point—"

"No. I didn't," I said.

"Fuck, fine, just chill with the third degree." Nick massaged the bridge of his nose. "You went super cold the first time I asked about your dad, and it made me wonder if there was something more there. I might have gotten curious and looked him up when I was in the hospital with too much time on my hands, which eventually led to the discovery that not only was he dead—there was a puff piece in the telegram about a certain hero mom 'defending her children.'"

I couldn't believe it. Not what he was saying, but the subtext. "You already pieced it together."

"No." Nick shook his head, looking more than a little guilty. "I mean, not at first, anyway. Not until I met your mom and saw firsthand how timid she was while you were on the other side of the table, cold, calculated, and withdrawn."

"And you still wanted to be friends?" I asked, more than a little dumbfounded.

"Course I did." Nick shrugged. "And while it was harrowing to hear you tell it, I still feel the same way. I guess it's an extreme example of what I've always admired about you. If you get it in your head that something unpleasant needs to be done, you don't wring your hands or obsess over what might happen, or feel sorry for yourself. You just get it done. God. I *wish* I could do that. I really do."

"Nick…" I started.

"Point is, so long as you're being careful, the Ordinator class is in excellent hands," Nick said, matter-of-factly.

I shook my head. "As much as I try to be vigilant and stick to my own rules, slipping is only a matter of time. With Suggestion, I originally meant to keep it on a short leash, only using it on monsters and explicit threats. That didn't even last through the Transposition."

"How so?" Nick asked.

Even with everything I'd already told him, I was ashamed to tell the story. "When I was heading home with the first haul of Lux, I'd just been jumped by those civilians in Region 9. I was scared, paranoid, hyperfocused on delivering the goods before someone took them from me. And there was this guy—more balls than brains, acting pseudo-alpha as a way of coping with his own fear—you know the type."

Nick nodded.

"He got in my way, and I just… skewered him." I grimaced. "Stripped his mental defenses and broke him down. No hesitation. It was almost instinctive. Didn't even realize what I'd done until after."

Nick's eyebrows knitted together. "Which is why the suspiciously convenient pairing of the Devil's Share and Subjugation scares the fuck out of you."

I shivered. "It'd be so easy to go off the deep end if I got used to it. Start snapping off orders to anyone in earshot, for any reason. Literally manifest what I want to happen."

"You can only use it on each person once, right? You'd run out eventually," Nick tried, but even he had to know how weak that sounded.

"There's a million people still trapped in the dome. It'd take a while," I mumbled.

"As much as this idea sucks, you could just… not use it?"

I squinted out over the water. "Maybe."

But I knew exactly how likely that was. I'd had countless chances to walk away from power, questionably sourced and otherwise. I never had.

"It's what I would do." Nick shrugged. "But that's my problem. When I'm dealing with something difficult, I get so caught up in ethics and hypotheticals that more often than not I end up just passively hoping for the best. And then I have the gall to be shocked when it bites me in the ass. Like a fucking idiot." The self-loathing in his voice was so poignant it was almost painful.

"Fuck Hastur." I spoke before I fully realized what I was going to say.

Nick laughed nervously. "Thought you, uh, didn't want to piss the gods off. And..." he trailed off, oddly small looking for his substantial frame. "On some level, I thought you'd agree with him."

The words hit me like a slap in the face.

"What the hell?"

"I mean—" Nick spoke with his hands. "You've made it clear plenty of times you think I'm immature and naïve."

"—I never said that."

"But you've implied it." He pointed a finger at me and raised an eyebrow. "Wouldn't it be better, on some level, if we were just always aligned? If I didn't push back every time you considered doing something I was uncomfortable with?"

That was wrong. And it was obvious how much Nick needed to hear the answer. I searched for the best way to put it into words, taking my time with it.

"Believe it or not, I used to be a lot more cynical. I thought I was enlightened, that my circumstances gave me special insight into the way the world really worked. That I had it all figured out, and anyone who had hope — genuine hope, for things to be better or different—was either lying to themselves or naïve idiots spinning fairytales. That the only reason they felt that way was because they hadn't looked behind the curtain and seen the world for what it truly was. And that if they had, they'd be every bit as miserable and bitter as me."

Nick wedged his feet into the sand. "What changed?"

"I met you."

"Bullshit." He rolled his eyes but didn't look at me.

I ignored the denial and moved on. "I watched you lose things I never even had. Watched you lose *everything*. But despite what you went through, all the bullshit you endured, you were always so quick to help others. Even when it drained you, or ended up being a massive pain in the ass, you did it anyway. Somehow, you never stopped caring about people, no matter how badly they disappointed you."

"Sounds idiotic." Nick mumbled.

"No." I shook my head. "It's just your nature. You're a good person, you've always been. And anyone who tries to smother that is a fool. We *need* people like you. Now more than ever."

He stared down at the sand. "I'm not sure that's true anymore, Matt. Not after what I did."

"You didn't do shit."

"I was gonna—"

"You didn't do shit," I repeated. "And maybe I forced your hand, and you picked wrong in a moment of panic, but you had all the time in the world to end him before I got there. So no, Nick. I didn't use Subjugation on you for a reason. Because I don't want to change who you are."

Despite the somber nature of the discussion, Nick smiled. "Sing my praises all you want, but you can't preach being true to myself if the same doesn't apply to you."

I looked away. "It's different."

"It's not." Nick punched me in the shoulder. "If our roles were reversed — trust me, I would have tried like hell — but I don't think I would make it here. Christ. You made some hard fucking calls. Maybe I get a few of them right, but not without turning into a whimpering sack of trauma potatoes on the floor. You were making these calls, and spinning a dozen other plates, all while drop-kicking the wolves from the door."

"Too many metaphors," I grumbled.

"Point *is*," Nick let the word hang. "I wouldn't change you either." A cloud darkened his bright expression. "Though all this has me wondering where we go from here."

"There are a few possibilities." I sighed. "At the very least, I need to get Kinsley's dad out. No clue *how*. Considering the extent everything's spiraled out of control, we're basically blown. But our best bet after that is probably to run. Keep squelch active 24-7 until we find a way to..."

Deal with the geas.

"You know," I finished.

Nick frowned. "But... it's weird."

"What is?" I asked, only half-listening as I'd already started working how much of a pain in the ass getting out of the Tower and dodging the Order was going to be.

"The Order is full of killers, people with pre-dome combat experience. So it tracks that Hastur would want to harden up his less-experienced members."

"Uhuh."

Nick winced. "Uh, I realize what I'm about to say is probably pretty rude."

"Just say it," I said, drafting a message to Kinsley.

"Why the hell did he want you to change at all?"

"Because..." I trailed off, simultaneously seeing what he was driving at and finding myself completely clueless.

Huh. I hadn't thought of it until now, mostly just chalked it up to offering me an incentive I hadn't known I wanted, but Hastur had essentially tried to force a transformation with a result that would leave me and Nick in opposite spaces. A net zero. That was strange. Implied the existence of an angle I had yet to consider.

When I said as much, Nick jumped to his feet and nearly stumbled in the sand, eyes all but bugging out of his head. "Holy shit."

CHAPTER ONE HUNDRED TWELVE

Nick had yet to give me an answer. He'd walked across the sandbar back toward the bluffs in a hurry and was going over the stony wall with a fine-tooth comb, eyes furrowed as he ran his hands over any irregularity.

"What are we doing?" I asked.

Nick accidentally pulled a piece of craggy stone free and casually tossed it aside. "You said it'd be a net-zero."

"If we both accepted Hastur's deal?" I hurried to keep pace with him as he shuffled along the stone base, wildly looking back and forth.

"Right. You become the man who feels too much, I become the rational, unfeeling bastard." Nick glanced at me. "Sorry."

I shrugged. "Doesn't matter. Still not following you."

"Thing *is*." Nick pried another piece of rock free with a grunt and tossed it aside. "It's not actually a net zero. Think about it. Even if I suddenly had your mindset, I'd lack your experience, your history. It'd be like giving someone a gun with no safety."

It finally hit me. "And I'd be learning to manage a shitton of interference. You're right. It's not net zero. It's suboptimal."

Apparently not finding what he was looking for, Nick started knocking on the bluffs. "Uh-huh. And you're the problem solver, so you tell me. Why would a being with god-tier foresight—especially one obsessed with creating 'a perfect future'—make a gambit with a suboptimal outcome?"

"Maybe he only needs one of us," I tried. "Or this is his way of making sure we're beholden to him."

Nick shook his head. "What do we know about Hastur?"

"He's an asshole."

"Okay, yes, but I meant what does he want?"

"Supposedly? Peace." I frowned and went down the list. "To end the Transposition. And he's unhappy with the state of the order to the point he's willing to spill loyal blood—holy shit." My jaw dropped. "He should have foreseen the conflict between Sunny and Aaron. So he's not actually omniscient. Or at least, his ability to see the future is far more compromised than he's led us to believe."

"We're off to see the wizard, Toto." Nick reached inside a crevice, then grunted and withdrew his hand, still frantically moving down the face of the bluffs. "Hastur's throwing shit at the wall and seeing what sticks. But it's not all parlor tricks. He has power, actual power. Question is, how much?"

I remembered, in a moment of discomfort, exactly how appealing the future Hastur described to me had been. How there was a part of me that still longed for it. Then how quickly his power and lucidity had drained away. "He's insightful enough that it has to be significant. But it's not perfect. More like he has an idea of what one person's future will be, and how to change it, but can't guarantee that any action he takes will bring about his ideal ends. He has to make a change, then look into the future and see how it all pans out."

"Wanna guess how many people he talks to?" Nick glanced at me, raising an eyebrow.

"Few. One in five?" I guessed.

"Closer to one in twenty," Nick said. "So, it's not just bullshit. He needs us for something. If I—" he stopped suddenly, some of his energy draining away, looking vaguely nauseous. Then seemed to gather his courage and started again. "If you didn't get to me before I... went through with it. With Keith. How would that have affected you?"

"Not well," I admitted. "Bare minimum, I'd put off revealing my identity. There'd be a lot of lost trust, and an upswing in self-doubt. I've already been questioning whether I can play the Ordinator role without going off the deep end, and if I saw *you* go off the deep end... I'd be much more likely to take Hastur up on his offer."

"Exactly," Nick said.

"But that's only one potential future." The pieces fell into place. "He had to know he was putting us on a collision course. And if so, then..."

"He knew damn well that this could happen," Nick finished. "And I'm betting he accounted for it."

The thought chilled me, and I shivered despite the tropical warmth of our surroundings. But it didn't seem to bother Nick. "For fuck's sake, what are you looking for?"

"A ripple." Nick paused. He'd run out of wall and gone down on his knees, searching where the sandbar met the bluffs. "Or a secret passage.

There has to be something he wants us to find with this specific outcome."

"Nick." I grabbed his shoulder and stopped him. My friend turned to look at me, a sheen of sweat on his brow. "All you're doing is strengthening the argument for us to run. Look at what he's doing to Aaron and Sunny. The knives at their backs. If Hastur's aware it could play out this way and we might turn against him? *Then we are running out of time.*"

"I don't want to turn against him," Nick mumbled. I processed that in silence, as small waves crashed onto the sandbar and receded into the ocean.

"What?" It was all I could do to keep my voice neutral.

"We're important, in the grand scheme. That's why he chose us," Nick insisted.

"After everything he did—"

"So, when a god's the one who fucks with people and does morally questionable shit to try to achieve a better outcome, then suddenly it's not okay anymore," Nick snapped.

I took a step back.

"You... can't know what he really wants. No one does."

Nick smiled, the expression so painful it hurt. "When Hastur told me he didn't want me to suffer, I believed him. When he said he wanted a better world, a *kinder* world, I believed him.

That doesn't mean shit.

"Even if Hastur's well-meaning, Nick, he's still..." but I couldn't bring myself to say it. To point out that Nick was being naïve, foolish. Not after what he'd just gone through. That ground was shaky as it was.

"Calculated." Nick gave a quick, grim nod. "Which is why I think there are two possibilities. Either he's fully prepared to squash us the second we come out of the Tower—or this exact possibility was accounted for." He pointed up to the bluffs. "You confront me up top, defend Keith, blitz me into the water, and we end up here."

I let my more prominent pushback go for now and instead focused on the obvious fallacy. "Okay, sure. But why are you so fixated on this location? If some god coordinated all this, aren't we just as likely to find something walking back, or meet someone important on another floor of the tower?"

Nick shook his head. "*No.* This *has* to be it. I never felt more strongly about anything in my life."

It felt more than desperate. Like he'd already shot the dealer and was flipping cards, trying desperately to come up with an ace.

But.

His fixation wasn't entirely irrational. On the off chance I'd beaten him in a direct confrontation, or used subjugation to bring him into line, there were few alternative scenarios where we ended up down here, if any. And considering the surrounding geography, the sandbar was vaguely crescent shaped, pressed up against the bluffs in a hidden alcove, all but invisible from the summit and surrounding beaches. Anyone searching the area without going for a swim would probably miss it. Hell, I'd missed it. We might find nothing, but if Aaron and Sunny intended to deal with us in the biblical manner, there was no reason to risk aggravating leadership in this region further by sending teams in after us when they could just wait outside. All that said, we needed to do this right.

"Okay. Both the ripple in the forest and the ripple on floor twenty-eight were in plain sight," I called over my shoulder and crunched through sand, crossing to the opposite side of the sandbar and peering into the water. "If there was something in the bluffs—especially something we're 'supposed' to find, you would have found it by now."

Finally, Nick stopped futzing with the rock wall and stood at my side. He glanced at me, then the water, and eventually back to me. "Right... but don't you hate swimming?"

"Yep. Which is why I'm delegating."

I reached out a hand to summon Audrey—and found to my surprise that I didn't need to summon her. Her consciousness was so weak I thought she'd died, tussling with whatever was below the surface.

Nick chuckled nervously. "You about to part the Red Sea over there?"

"Just give me a second."

My eyebrows furrowed. Audrey's mind felt more sluggish than usual. She wasn't dying, but I had probably submerged her for too long. When I asked if she wanted me to release and re-summon her, I got a dramatic response as scattered, shotgunned feelings that culminated in a vehement negative.

Okay, then come to the sandbar.

Audrey didn't answer. Twenty feet offshore, there was an explosion of white bubbles.

"What—" Nick started. But before he could finish, dark-gray flesh breached the surface, water cascading down it on both sides. "—the actual fuck."

I reached for my crossbow even as a stream of mist sprayed up into the air. It took a second to register the familiarity of something I'd only seen in YouTube videos and ocean documentaries.

It's a blowhole.

Nick unsheathed his sword just as a soaked, miserable-looking plant broke the surface, her vines looped around the creature's sides forming half-reins, half-saddle. I caught his arm, signaling for him to wait as I held the crossbow at my side.

"Audrey? You uh, catch something?"

My summon released her hold, and with nothing to keep her balanced, slid down the whale's rubbery flesh and slapped into the shallow water. I waited long enough to observe the creature's behavior. It seemed more or less passive, though no less imposing in terms of sheer mass. Once I was mostly sure Audrey's impromptu mount would not turn around and eat me, I waded in and fished her out of the water, never taking my eyes from the creature as I carried her up to the shore.

"How the hell'd you pull that off?" I muttered, more than a little impressed.

"Made... new friend." Audrey coughed—ejecting a ridiculous amount of water back into the ocean as we waded back to Nick.

"Again. How?" I reiterated.

"Simple mind... easy to subjugate," Audrey said.

I was so shocked I nearly dropped her. When she'd said she'd made a new friend, she wasn't being coy. She was being literal. A unique aspect of my summoner class was that my summons sometimes shared my abilities, and it seemed like Audrey had won the lottery in that regard. Before I could make a comment, Audrey wrapped a vine around my back, using me as leverage to raise herself high enough to look over my shoulder. "Stay close. Eat tiny fish. Be happy," she barked at the whale with a surprising amount of authority.

A tail bigger than my entire body raised and slapped down on the water in response, sending up a geyser.

Despite myself, I chuckled. "Always full of surprises."

Nick was waiting for us at the edge of the sandbar, eyebrows raised high enough that it looked like they were trying to jump off his head. "Uh. I keep cycling through one-liners, but I think I'm actually at a loss for words."

I snorted. "My plant summon mentally wrangled a mammal that outweighs her by a hundred tons or so and bent it to her will. Just business as usual."

"Uh-huh."

"No bending," Audrey protested. "He was scared. I made him less scared."

There were a thousand questions I wanted to ask her. But only one that really mattered.

Once we reached the sandbar, I praised her first, patting her head and pulling a raw cut of beef from the icebox in my inventory. She scarfed it down and looked somewhat restored.

"Now." I crouched in front of her, waiting until I had her full attention. "What was the whale scared of?"

CHAPTER ONE HUNDRED THIRTEEN

Of all the many possibilities I'd accounted for before embarking into the tower, riding a whale wasn't one of them.

"This is some real Studio Ghibli shit." Nick's face was white as a sheet as he clung to the long coil of rope encircling the whale.

"You were the one all amped on following fate," I growled, not feeling much better. Just being in the open ocean put my nerves on edge. We'd waited an hour for my mana to regenerate, and a quick internal check put it at just over half, which was hopefully enough. Assuming we didn't drown, which was probably the worst that could happen.

"What if we get the bends?" Nick whispered.

"The what?" I asked.

"What do you mean, 'the what'?" He grinned. "Oh my. Do I actually know something you don't?"

"Shut up."

"Sourpuss. My uncle told me about it when we went scuba-diving," Nick answered, reciting the information. "You dive deep enough, atmospheric pressure compresses stuff in your body. But if you come up too quickly, it can get released in the wrong place, like your bloodstream."

"Great." I felt the blood drain out of my face. Audrey was up front, closest to the whale's head. "Audrey? Any chance your thrall told you how deep we're going?"

Audrey cocked her head. "No. I ask." She leaned down and did... something. I wasn't sure if she was using **<Suggestion>**, or if they had some other sort of connection because of **<Subjugation>**. Either way, she seemed keyed into the whale in a similar way that I'd keyed into Keith.

From what she'd said earlier, the whale was terrified. Not of a sea monster or something worse, but a fissure deep below the surface. There was a crack in the stone wall of the bluffs far beneath the surface exuding something Audrey translated as "gross" that made it difficult to see. More notably, the fissure was pulling in seawater indiscriminately, sucking in any ocean creature that drew near. It was impossible to say whether the anomaly was a ripple or something else, but it fit the bill if Nick was right and there was something for us to find in these exact circumstances.

After Audrey's stunt, I was beginning to wonder if he was right.

"Deep." Audrey cocked her head as the whale let out a low, moaning rumble. "Less deep than deep deep." I groaned, Nick echoing me a second later. The system helped with translation at certain points, but apparently not with specific metrics.

"Did he tell you how to avoid it?" I asked Nick.

Nick mulled that over. "Exhale slowly as you rise and don't come up too fast."

"Is it even an issue if you're free-diving? Not breathing from an oxygen tank?"

"Dunno." Nick shrugged.

I rubbed the bridge of my nose, suddenly exhausted. I'd decided to— at least in the short-term—follow Nick's lead and go with the flow. If there was even a slight chance he was right, it was worth looking into. Even if every fiber of my being was screaming to back out.

Better to just get it over with.

"Okay. Audrey, if I tap you, it means I'm at my limit and we need to go back to the surface," I said, wrapping my mind around what we were about to do.

"What if I'm at my limit?" Nick asked nervously.

"Then tap me, and I'll tap Audrey. For now, deep breath." I elbowed Nick, then gripped the rope with both hands. "Audrey, tell her to take us down."

The whale jerked into motion far more abruptly than expected, plunging us into warm water that quickly grew cold. My ears popped shortly after, the speed with which we were moving making impossible to see the dark blue of the surrounding ocean through more than a slit.

The little I could see grew darker and darker still, as the depth and pressure increased. Above, the scattered reflection of the sun was still visible, though watching the glowing amber above grow more faint exacerbated my anxiety by the second.

I counted down from sixty slowly, trying to keep track of the time even as my lungs burned.

Darkness seeped into the surrounding water, dyeing the dark blue an inky black. The feeling of a current streaming past ceased as the whale stopped in place. I reached out blindly, trying to belay panic as my fingers brushed nothing but unyielding stone. Right when I was on the verge of signaling for Audrey to return to the surface, my hand landed on something slimy, almost membrane-like. I pushed through up to my shoulder and felt the icy chill of open air on my fingertips on the other side.

Bingo.

I reached back and grabbed Nick's arm, placing his hand on the gap in the surface. Once he realized what he was feeling, he kicked off the whale and swam head first into the opening. I extended my arm through the fissure and waited, heart racing, lungs burning. Much longer and I wouldn't make it back up to the surface.

Strong hands closed around my arm and unseated me, dragging me into the fissure. I had a moment of panic but didn't fight and allowed myself to be pulled.

In complete disorientation, I broke the surface with a gasp, taking long pulls of stale air as my vision adjusted to the darkness. I'd gone through sideways and somehow came out right-side up, and it took a moment as my mind reconciled the conflict. Nick pulled at me, still tugging upward after I was well clear of the gap.

I twisted out of his grip. "I'm through already."

"Shh," Nick hissed. The urgency in his voice banished the fogginess from my mind, and the surroundings slowly came into focus. I let him pull me to my feet, still ankle-deep in the stinking liquid.

Ornate marble pillars loomed in the distance, cloaked in shadow. We were at the far end of a long rectangular fountain, though maybe fountain was the wrong word. It was a long square rectangle of dark water, little spouts bubbling up every few feet. Across a wide ream of plush-red carpet, there was another matching rectangular water fixture framing the walkway. The carpet itself extended toward a set of stairs.

And at the base of the stairs was a stoic Knight in full plate. His plate glimmered in the low light, and he held a broken bastard sword loosely in one hand. His head was tilted downward, as if he was staring down into the carpet itself.

Motion caught my eye. Something flitting around in the shadows that surrounded the walkway. Multiple somethings. Whatever they were, they seemed to move in quick, sporadic bursts.

That we were mostly on our own stuck firmly in my mind. I focused and started to summon Talia.

Then froze, as the disheveled Knight straightened and raised his sword arm, extending the jagged point directly at me.

CHAPTER ONE HUNDRED FOURTEEN

Raw danger flagged in my mind. The lone figure had an ancient, primal feeling, not unlike the Crimson Nosferatu from the higher floors, though that encounter was so oppressive it made it almost impossible to think. Still. Now that I had a better look, the grim "T" shape that bisected the Knight's helmet was unnaturally dark, as if the sourceless light radiated from apparently nowhere. I let the unfinished summon slip from my mind and instinctively took a step back. The broken point of the Knight's sword stayed trained on me. When I didn't use any of my abilities or summon Talia again, there was a creak of metal and the broken pointed shifted to Nick.

A voice resonated from within the helmet, metallic with a hint of mockery. "Why are you here?"

Still soaked to the bone, Nick glanced over at me, probably looking for guidance. For once, I didn't have any for him. This—us being here, discovering this place—resulted from Nick, following his instincts. Unfortunately, that meant we were improvising.

And even as he stepped forward, sword untouched in its sheathe, shield unstrapped from his back and held loosely in his off-hand, I could see how scared he was. Scared and uncertain. From his perspective, he'd been daisy-chaining from one failure to another since the opening act of this shitshow.

Come on, Nick.

"A reasonable question, good Knight," Nick said. There was a trace of the LARP-speak he'd used before the trial to talk to Talia, but it was more downplayed, reserved. Almost Shakespearean. He smiled, mouth closed. "I seem to have lost my way."

Skittering feet echoed off the marble behind us and I spun, looking for the source, finding nothing. I was careful to not do *anything* that could be misinterpreted as aggression, but I angled myself with my back to a fountain so I could both watch behind us and help Nick if things degenerated.

The suit of armor creaked as the Knight cocked his head. "Perhaps it is best that you arrived here. At the simulacrum, rather than the whole."

"And where is this?" Nick asked. "Or rather, what is it meant to be?"

The armor exhaled a tinny rasp and spoke, equal parts reverent and bitter. "A pale imitation, failed and discarded. Avalon."

Something about the name was unbearably familiar. But I couldn't place it.

As the Knight threw back his head and cackled, the shadows around the edges of the room grew darker, pressed inward. "The cruelty is immeasurable. We were found imperfect, and he threw us away. All his creations. Yet graced the likes of you with his boon?"

Nick's eyes flicked around, searching the shadows. "Only gods and crazed old men speak in riddles, friend. Declare your meaning plainly, so we may reach common ground."

The Knight's voice grew angrier the more he spoke, building to a crescendo. "Are you truly so ignorant of the potential you squander? The favor you hold? You are unworthy of the legacy of *Pendragon*."

With that last word, it clicked. *Arthur* Pendragon. As in Arthur of the sword-in-the-stone variety. This Knight—and potentially the surrounding creatures lurking in the shadows—were cribbed from Arthurian lore. But none of this seemed productive. The Knight was clearly addled, a more refined version of the failed experiments we faced in the first ripple, but just as mad.

Or at least, that was what I thought.

Nick's face was stricken, pale. "I never asked for any of this. For my title."

What the hell?

The Knight laughed that bitter laugh once more. "Your table is vacant, your queen reduced to a fragment that may never be whole again. And even here, in this godforsaken place, you can't say his name."

Nick's arms went slack, dangling limply at his side. "Afallach chose the wrong person."

His anguish resonated deeply. Echoed similar thoughts I'd had about my patron, time and time again. That the shoes he wanted me to fill were too inconceivably big, and giving me the Ordinator class was an irreconcilable blunder.

Slowly, the Knight lowered his sword to a ninety-degree angle, pointing it to the ground at his feet. "Then submit yourself to my judgment, so he may iterate once more." Capitalizing the finality of the statement, two more suits of armor stepped out from the shadows behind the Knight, flanking him on either side. They felt less ancient than the first but looked powerful. The shadows pressed in, tightening the circle into a stranglehold. I could almost make out the creatures within—glimpses of long limbs, and teeth, and claws.

Nick straightened his back, set his shoulders. "If I do as you ask, will you let my friend go?"

After brief consideration, the Knight nodded.

"What are you doing?" I caught his shoulder.

He gave me a half-hearted sigh. "Look at them all. You were right. This was a dumb idea."

"I never said that."

"Seeing as how I keep pulling you into my shit, the least I can do is get you out of it."

"A god missed a box on his checklist and somehow you got the bag. Who gives a damn if you're the right person," I snapped. "None of us asked for any of this. This clusterfuck of patrons, and powers and abilities and tragedy and mind games and knives in the fucking dark. We're survivors. Not the fucking devout and chosen. And *you*." I rounded on the Knight. "No wonder your god abandoned you."

The sword switched targets again, the Knight's movement incredibly fast. "Do not speak of matters you cannot possibly understand—"

Just like the Crimson Nosferatu. The ones that think they're older are more personality driven. They'll cream you in a fight but have exploitable quirks.

I snarled. "Keep whinging, you recyclable motherfucker, but I have a damn excellent memory, and nothing you say is going to change the facts. Honor itself is an ancient concept, but the Arthurian Knights of the Round made it their own. Yet here you are, a coterie of half-baked failures attempting to pass judgment on the genuine article through ambush and trickery."

All three of the Knights stepped forward, their body language brimming with anger.

"Uh. Matt," Nick tried to cut in.

"I'm not fucking done." I pointed at the center Knight, still advancing with the broken sword. "Because if this colossal dipstick had an atom of his creator's essence, gave two dog-squatting shits about what his patron wanted, he would have found an honorable way to prove you unworthy."

Take the bait, dammit.

I stood there impassively, giving nothing away even as the Knights advanced and my heart hammered in my throat.

Almost begrudgingly, the broken Knight ground to a halt, the others pausing beside him. I felt something staring at me through the T of his visor, radiating hate. "How mirthful, for one such as you to speak of honor."

I showed my teeth. "None of this has anything to do with me. It's all his show. I'm just along for the ride."

"If that is what you believe, you have not been paying attention." With that cryptic statement, the Knight returned his focus to Nick. He held his sword out to the retainer on his left, who held it point down while the Knight held his arm up and unstrapped his gauntlet.

Nick leaned over and whispered in my ear. "What the hell is happening?"

"That should be my line."

"Matt."

I shook my head. "Just... listen. He's strong. Don't know how big the gap is, safe to say it's substantial. But you can do this. You don't have to win. Just stay on defense, drag it out long enough for me to find an angle. I've got your back. Just buy me time."

Before Nick could ask what was probably one of many pointed questions, the Knight removed his gauntlet and cast it on the ground, where it landed and bounced with a resounding clang. The same dark shadow that formed the creatures swirling behind us made up his arm and clawed hand. When he spoke, his voice echoed through the chamber, resonating power and authority. "Usurper of Pendragon. I challenge you to a duel."

CHAPTER ONE HUNDRED FIFTEEN

As Nick observed the gauntlet on the ground and understanding dawned, his tired eyes returned to me, a wave of calm settling over him. The well-worn exhaustion in his face cleared. Ever since we'd unexpectedly reunited within the suits' compound, he'd felt unhinged, untethered, as if he was overcompensating for a piece of himself that eroded away.

He patted my shoulder gently, then pushed me away. "Nah."

My eyebrow shot up. "'Nah?' What—" I looked at the Knight, his shadow arm still on full display as he waited for Nick's answer. "What in the ever-loving fuck do you mean, 'nah?'"

"The way you operate. Protecting the people you love no matter what you have to do to achieve that outcome, I respect it. I really do." Nick shifted his head from side to side, stretched his arms, bent his leg, and grabbed the ankle of his once-crippled leg, pulling it backward in a runner's stretch. "But you can't fight all my battles for me. And I can't be the person I want to be if I fold into the fetal position and let you dirty your hands every time it gets hard."

"What are we even talking about right now..." I trailed off, bewildered, as I turned to look at the Knight, slowly putting the pieces together. "Because of him? The only goddamn reason he stopped is because I turned his psychology against him. They're just monsters in armor, Nick. Monsters with rules."

"Is Audrey just a monster? Talia? Azure?" Nick raised an eyebrow. "From everything you've said, they seem pretty human to me."

The flippant comment caught me off guard. And as much as I wanted to reject that on pure technicality, Talia and Audrey had both grieved their families and bore scars from the loss, in a manner that was uncannily similar to human grief. At some point, I had stopped thinking of all my summons as highly intelligent animals and started thinking of them as people. Over the last few months, they'd both performed far above their station and saved my ass more times than I cared to count. On top of all that, they'd questioned their own existence, and wanted answers for why they were created. That was as human as it got.

Before I could rally, Nick continued. "I'm not the same fighter I was. I've learned a lot. Trained. Gained new abilities I'm restricted from even talking about. This guy has a legitimate grievance. He believes I've stolen something I wasn't meant to have. He might be right. And even though you talked him into it, he stood down and chose fairness. It's only right that I give him a proper shot."

Nick was going to die. After everything I'd gone through to save him, he was going to fucking die.

"This isn't a game. You're not getting paragon points for this shit. Don't be stupid," I snapped.

Nick's smile faded. "Yeah. Guess it's a little much, expecting trust after the trail of fuck-ups that got me here."

The words lined up like beaded sights.

If you'd listened to me in the tunnel, instead of losing yourself in rage and self-righteousness, we'd be in a helluva better place than we are right fucking now.

I couldn't pull the trigger.

Nick already knew he'd made a mistake in the tunnel, he'd all but copped to it. If I let the bolt fly, it would still end him, just in a different way. Still, letting it go was like breathing glass.

"No. I trust you. More now than ever." I pushed him forward. "Knock 'em dead."

His eyes widened, the dimming light returned to his expression full force. He held out his fist and I bumped it, numbly watching as he approached the center Knight.

For whatever reason, Nick had decided this was a hill he was willing to die on, and I needed to respect it. At least for now. If push came to shove and things turned dire, I wasn't sure I could stop myself from intervening.

But that didn't mean I had to make it easy for them.

Nick drew his sword and hefted his shield. The central Knight held his sword at the ready, and the tension in the room grew viscous, the shadows almost palpable.

"What the hell are you doing?" I snapped, going for a mix of enraged, irritated, and condescending.

"Uh," Nick said, staring at me awkwardly.

The central Knight said nothing, but I felt his murderous gaze turn toward me once again.

"Him I get." I chucked a thumb at Nick. "Lack of myth knowledge, probably a little CTE sprinkled on top—"

"Hey!" Nick protested.

"—but you?" I stood directly in front of the central Knight, cutting between them. "You should know damn well how duels work."

The murderous gaze turned downright fatal, and for a moment I thought he might cut me down where I stood. Enough so that I got to the point, rather than waiting for him to ask. "There's always a second, and there's always a brief period of negotiation where the seconds negotiate acceptable terms."

"It is a duel to the death. That is non-negotiable," the Knight said flatly.

"If that's the only territory you think we have to cover, the ripple really has addled your brains," I shot back, listing on my fingers. "There's acceptable weapon usage, acceptable item and magic usage, whether the combat will be broken up by recovery periods or if it's a marathon to the finish, conditions to be followed if someone's weapon breaks—"

"A pretender does not retain the right to a second," the central Knight growled.

My LSAT prep popped into my head as I recognized the fallacy. "That's the entire point of your duel, isn't it? To establish his legitimacy. Denying him a second by taking the result of a duel as a foregone conclusion seems clearly unchivalrous, if not outright malfeasant, don't you think?"

My attention derailed as one of the flanking Knights muttered something, only for the central Knight to hold out a hand, swiftly silencing him.

Did he just say 'Fucking Merlin?'

I ignored it and moved on. "For the moment, the assumption must be that he is a Knight. And as his Page, I am his second by default. To deny me this role is to deny the basic tenets upheld by the round table, that you and your like sacrificed lives to defend."

Slowly, the central Knight looked at Nick, and in a voice that sounded like he'd aged a thousand years, asked, "Do you wish to designate this one as your second, ser?"

With that hurdle cleared, I gave Nick a full-toothed smile, the one that generally made people profoundly uncomfortable.

"Yep," Nick blurted. "Second. Sounds good."

———

I'd made several ridiculous initial demands, giving myself as much time as possible to engineer a solution with the highest chance of getting us out of this alive that wouldn't rain on Nick's hero moment. First, I requested that the surrounding circle of shadows receded, as they were a source of intimidation that would affect Nick far more than it affected the local Knights. That took more effort than I'd expected, as the shadows didn't seem compliant, and it took a small army of shadow men in tabards to push them back, which provided valuable intel—though it showed this ripple was far more populated than I'd hoped. The possibility of fighting our way out in the worst-case scenario grew more and more bleak.

Next, I asked for a table and two chairs as setting for the negotiation and spent an absurd amount of time arranging them, then asked for the shadow servants to bring out racks of weapons for our champions to choose from, and spent an absurd amount of time arranging them.

They didn't let me run ramshackle over them, drawing the line when I requested a small selection of food for the negotiations, but saving that, with their honor so blatantly called into question, they more or less bent over backward to achieve fairness and be generous to the challenged, so long as I could justify it. And while he'd hovered over me at first, the central Knight had eventually thrown up his hands and given up supervising me and taken a place in the corner next to Nick.

Nick, naturally, chatted him up, and the last time I checked on them they were examining each other's weapons and seemed to be in the middle of a spirited conversation. Or argument. Either way, they were distracted, which was exactly what I wanted.

By the time my plan fully formed, every person in the room had distanced themselves from me for fear of another demand, and when I placed two sheets of paper on the table, no one was paying enough attention to notice.

I withdrew a pen from my inventory and pressed it hard against the top page, then lifted the corner to confirm.

With a deep breath, I leaned back in the seat and let myself relax. Then announced, "I'm ready."

"Oh?" the central Knight called over. "Our hospitality finally meets your standards?"

I nodded, fiddling with the pen beneath the table, trying to force myself to relax.

"Then I will call my second."

The withdrawn shadows had revealed a stairwell at the far end of the room, their destination still shrouded in darkness. Somewhere in the black, there was a rhythmic clank as armored feet descended, revealing the long body of what was possibly the tallest man in armor I'd ever seen.

Like the rest of the Knights, his helmet covered his face.

Despite his long, almost awkward frame, he slid into the chair across from me with a sinewy grace I found disquieting and towered over me in torso height alone. The lower section of his reflective breastplate ground against the table. He reached down to move it, blatantly overcorrecting and shoving the edge of the table into my gut.

"So. This is the whelp who wants to negotiate terms? Doesn't look like much." The sneer I couldn't see carried in his voice.

Despite myself, I smiled.

A bully. I can work with that.

CHAPTER ONE HUNDRED SIXTEEN

I slowly looked back over at Sir Stonewall, as I'd come to think of him. Stonewall was still conversing with Nick in the hall's corner, his lackeys— as they were mostly identical aside from a slight difference in circumference, I'll refer to them as Pot and Kettle—posted up against the wall at attention some distance away.

The tall one sitting across from me I thought of as Dent, on account of the baseball-sized crater in the side of his helmet.

I fought my initial impulse to swap titles to **<Cruel Lens>**. It would have been better for the negotiation, but if things went badly I needed **<Jaded Eye>**, and if it all went to hell in a handbasket, reserving the option to switch to **<Scathing Shell>** could be a literal lifesaver.

Dent had crossed one leg over the other and was leaning to one side, seeming to relish in how his weight abused the wooden chair beneath him, intentionally forcing it to creak. Stonewall chose him for a reason. I'd expected someone craftier, less direct, but in some ways this worked better for my intended result.

"Are there any rules to this negotiation?" I asked.

"Aren't you old enough to know that in the real world, there aren't rules?" Dent's smarmy voice echoed from within his helmet. "Maybe—"

Thanks for the green light.

<Subjugation> flared from my outstretched fingertips beneath the table. A chunk of my mana drained away, but I estimated it was less than half, closer to a third. Dent stiffened, twitched once, then stilled. I sucked in a breath, surprised by the absence of backlash. There was no reaction from the rest of the room. It'd been a calculated risk with caveats. If anyone had noticed or cried foul, I'd simply point out that Dent had literally just told me there were no rules.

I hit him with **<Suggestion>** before he could say anything to give us away.

"Continue with this negotiation as you would have before. Anything I say out loud should be reacted to according to your personality and previous predisposition, while any commands you receive in this manner should be considered law."

"Maybe what?" I prompted.

Dent resumed his snide commentary. "Maybe things are different where you come from, out there with the savages."

"Anyone who exists outside the realms of Flauros is a savage?"

"It's more—one could say—an educated guess." Dent drummed his fingers on the table, feigning boredom. Then pointed at Nick. "If he dies, you know what I'd like?"

"What?" I asked, completely fine with taking a passive role now that I held an advantage.

Both of Dent's hands slammed down on the table, and he leaned forward in a snakelike motion. "I'd like to put my thumbs through your eyes. Nice and slow. Scramble them around a little until there's nothin' left but jam."

This was why he was chosen. He clearly wasn't the smartest of the bunch, or **<Subjugation>** would have failed. Dent was the type that preferred strong-arming his way through a discussion, using shock tactics and nastiness to throw the other party off-balance.

I leaned back, considered it. "A life is not a small thing—"

"Oh, I'd leave you alive."

That was chilling.

"Fine. My sense of sight is not a small thing. In fact, I value it quite highly." I leaned back and picked out some gunk between the outside knuckles of my gauntlet. "As the challenging party, there would need to be equal concessions from your side."

"Like what?"

"For starters, the duelists need to be using similar weapons."

"Swords, of course," Dent said, a little too carefree.

The intended deceit was obvious. It didn't surprise me. As of now, the only order I'd given Dent was to act how he normally would, and in this situation, he'd be acting in bad faith. I remembered the way Nick fought during the trial. How powerful Stonewall felt. If Nick didn't have his full defensive kit, that was a problem.

"Swords and shields," I corrected.

Dent huffed. "Makes no difference. Just a question of how long we draw it out. Minutes, rather than seconds. What else?"

"The swords should be of similar make, rarity, and power."

"Should we have the craftsmen construct a bassinet for a mid-duel nap while we're at it?" Dent guffawed.

"Do you have crafters?" I asked, genuinely curious.

His laughter trailed off. "Eh. No. They died."

"This is non-negotiable." I tapped my cheek. "If you want my eyes."

That shut him up. He shifted his head from side to side, considering. "Mm. Fine." He nodded toward the racks of weapons in the center of the room. "But he's gotta use one of ours. Not the other way around."

"Done. Final pre-requisite for your condition. I'd like to summon my familiar."

Dent lost some of his devil-may-care attitude, irritation flaring. "Don't think I'm ignorant of what happens when your ilk gets left to their own devices. To what purpose?"

I sighed. "Look around. We are the challenged party, yet we're surrounded by your men, your servants, your..." I glanced disdainfully at the swirling ring of shadows, further back than before but still ever-present. "... Creatures. If anyone in your camp had a problem with the direction the duel was going and others came to their aid, there's likely little I could do about it, with or without my familiar. Regardless, I'd prefer the extra security."

"And what manner of monster is this familiar?" Dent asked cautiously.

"A dog. Slightly larger than average, unexceptional otherwise."

Dent went through the mental calculations of what chance a dog had against heavy armor and apparently liked the result. "Done," he said, with a smile in his voice. "Such fun to be had. With you, me, and your over-grown mutt."

I ignored him and jotted down the three conditions we'd established, pressing hard. I added a subsection for "results," adding an entry for what would happen should each contestant win, and inscribed Dent's demand lightly, letting the rolling tip of the pen do most of the work.

I'd barely finished when Dent leaned against the table, forcing the edge further into my gut. "There'll be no magic. No spells of any kind."

Huh. Unless things had changed, Nick didn't have any magic besides the defensive barrier spell, but there was no need to give that away for free.

"Why?" I asked.

"Because I know better than to judge a man on his appearance," Dent growled. "And even if he's just a sword, there's a chance you'd cast somethin' on him to tip the scales in your favor."

I considered that. As the conditions went, it was severely double-edged. It'd deny Stonewall from using anything nasty he was holding in reserve but would also severely restrict my ability to meddle in the duel itself. If Stonewall was drastically more powerful than Nick, there was only so much I could do from the sideline compared to whatever bullshit ripple magic Stonewall could be hiding. If the power divide was too drastic, I couldn't be blatant with **<Probability Cascade>** without Nick or the Knights noticing, neither of which would end well. Pushing back was an option, using my influence over Dent to force him to rescind the condition. But if the terms were too one-sided, the Knights would have ample reason to suspect foul play.

It was a net gain at best, a net zero at worst.

I voiced my displeasure and argued, eventually letting Dent wear me down and conceding, pressing firmly as I jotted the condition down.

"What do we do in the event of a breach?" I asked.

"A what?" With his accent, the "what" sounded like "wot."

"If either side interferes with the duel," I restated.

"Well." He rested his chin on his fist. "If you interfere—and by interfere I mean squeeze out even the tiniest spurt of magic—we kill you. After I put your eyes out, of course."

"Of course. And if your side interferes? You'll all honorably put each other to the sword?"

Dent snorted. "Never going to happen. Come up with something else."

"Sounds fair to me, considering that if I so much as 'spurt' magic onto the ground, my life is forfeit."

He crossed his arms. "Your life isn't worth a single Knight of the Round, let alone the lives of every being in our domain. *Come up with something else.*"

I mirrored his posture, stalemating us for a time and buying myself time to think. I looked toward the swirling shadows, circling like a tornado from hell. When Stonewall had removed his gauntlet to challenge Nick to a duel, his arm comprised the same shadow.

"Argue, but eventually comply with my next request."

I sighed dramatically. "We've already established that if your camp goes back on their word, we stand little chance. Compensation, then. Any man who interferes will be punished by forfeiting his armor and arms, which will be relinquished to me."

"The armor alone would be far too heavy for your scrawny form."

"Doesn't matter. I'd sell it even if it fit."

Again, Dent audibly choked, trying not to laugh. "Madness. Your friend is about to die, and you're here, divining a method to make a profit when he does."

"Those are my terms," I said coldly.

"You know what?" Dent chuckled. "Sure. You can have the arms and armor of any Knight who breaches the rules of engagement."

"Any *being* who breaches the rules of engagement," I clarified.

"Aye." Dent slowly nodded. "Any being."

The rest of the negotiations went smoothly. Dent seemed pleased with the apparent outcome. As pleased as I was with the actual outcome. I signed my name, and once I explained the custom, he signed his where I'd underlined.

Sir Kay.

"Here. Your copy." I handed him the top sheet and removed the sheet at the bottom, placing it in my inventory before he looked at it too closely.

He watched me in confusion. "Magic?"

"Just triplicate," I said, but he was still staring at the page. "Carbonless paper that passes the ink down to the bottom copy. Saves me the annoyance of writing everything out twice."

"Watch yourself, Wizard." He didn't seem pleased, but I suspected the displeasure was out of suspicion of magic itself, rather than anything more specific. He stared at me, then seemed to disregard it as foolishness and walked with loud, clanking footsteps across the hall toward Stonewall.

With the negotiations settled, I let out a breath of relief, trying to ignore the feeling that I'd dropped the ball. I'd done everything I could to safeguard us while still technically abiding by Nick's wishes. If the Knights' so-called code was pure aesthetics and they made a move, we'd have a shot.

But aside from doing whatever I could to establish a fair competition, I'd done precious little to tip the scales of the duel itself in our favor. Everything else was up to Nick.

CHAPTER ONE HUNDRED SEVENTEEN

"I'm gonna crap my pants," Nick said.

Somehow, I didn't strangle him.

After the terms were finalized, a handful of shadow people escorted us to the square open area at the end of the hall, pushing and prodding if we moved too slowly. The wide ream of royal-red carpet bisected the square, which I eyeballed at about twenty-five square feet. There was ample flat terrain, more than enough for a simple duel.

"And *why* are you crapping your pants?"

"I thought the Knights of the Round Table were a myth." Nick ground his teeth, leaning forward a bit to sneak a glance at Stonewall, who was conversing with Dent. "But that guy has seen some shit. Like 'Battle of the Bastards' level shit."

"No, he *thinks* he's seen some shit."

"*I* think he's seen some shit." Nick pointed at his own chest for emphasis, on the verge of panic. "He fought the Romans and won, Matt. As in the Roman Empire? As in the dudes went to war in skirts and, despite that, still somehow *conquered almost everything?*"

My mind ticked. "Okay, one, the Knights of the Round Table are fictional. The Roman Empire wasn't. They never actually fought, and if that guy comes from a version of Arthurian lore where they fought the Romans, it was probably some sort of weird 12th century British propaganda."

"How does that help me when fictional-propaganda-man is standing *right there?*" Nick hissed.

I rubbed the bridge of my nose. "Just, chill. Give me a second."

"He's so casual about it. Cool. Like he's the real deal," Nick said, genuine admiration in his voice.

I peered at Nick. "Do you want to fight him, or marry him?"

Nick extended his arms, "Where's the 'none of the above' option?"

"That's the one where you don't tell me, confidently, that you want a fair duel, only to crumble like a house of cards shortly after," I snapped.

"Fuck," Nick said, loud enough that the heads of several nearby shadow people turned our way. *"Fuck."*

Need to head him off before he spirals.

"Listen." I took him by the shoulders and forced eye contact. "Putting aside the fact that he's a fictional character, there are plenty of reasons this could go in your favor. One, his memories are artificial, same as Audrey's and Talia's." I left out Azure, for obvious reasons. "Remembering battles and war campaigns might make him self-assured, but there's no guarantee his memories will directly correspond to ability and skill. They probably won't."

"Sure you're not just blowing smoke up my ass?"

"Certain. Because he's not even the final product. Said it himself. His god threw him away. He was a failed experiment, just like the grimelings. Meaning that even if there is a version of him out there in the Tower that can back up the Roman-spanking, this one probably can't."

Nick squinted at Stonewall again and seemed to accept that as a possibility. "Okay, yeah. You're right. Just got intimidated by the stories."

"Never happened."

"Right, he just thinks it happened." Nick paused, taking several deep breaths. Slowly, his prior confidence returned. "Just... on the off chance he ends up nuking me from orbit, look after this, okay?" He placed Jinny's User core in the palm of my hand. "And if you manage to bring her back, tell her I'm sorry, and stuff."

I glanced next to Stonewall at Dent who, despite his helmet, did an excellent job of giving the impression of leering. He made a gesture that resembled a man forcing his thumbs into two overripe tomatoes. "Yeah. Probably gonna need to train Talia to see for me and go cane-shopping while I'm at it, but after I get my bearings, I will."

"What?" He gave me an odd look. "The hell are you talking about?"

"Don't worry about it."

The concern in Nick's expression grew. "What did you do?"

"Crawl out of my ass, I did what I had to. That's the way this works, right?" When the answer didn't satisfy him, I sighed and rubbed the back of my neck. "The negotiator had a specific... request. A condition to be satisfied if you lose. I was able to spin it into better terms for us."

"What request?" Nick's voice was stone cold.

I sighed. "If you lose, Arthurian Psycho over there gets real up close and personal with my eye sockets."

Golden aura flared around Nick's shoulders, reflecting off his metal armor. He stared daggers at the tall Knight, hefted the blade he'd selected, and spun it at the wrist. "And if I win? Do you get up close and personal with *his* eye sockets?"

"No."

"Then I'm fighting him next." And with that Nick walked away, toward the center of the square.

"Wait," I called after him, "We need to strategize—"

He didn't even bother to look back and didn't stop until he reached the center of the square.

I rubbed my mouth and hid a smile behind my hand. The truth was, Nick didn't need a tactics session. He needed motivation. And sure, I could have mentioned the fact that I'd taken Dent as a contingency, which made the ocular threat approximately as dangerous as a safety cone, but why deny Nick the fuel? I hadn't forgotten how he sprung into overdrive when I'd been captured by the spider during the trial. He'd gone from capable-but-inexperienced fighter to absolute wrecking ball.

Talia's eyes bored into me from where she heeled at my feet. "I'd ask if anyone's ever called you a bastard, but the answer is clear."

"Uh-huh." I glanced at her. "Was I right?"

Talia looked away, toward where Nick stood at the center. "Not entirely." She switched to nonverbal communication, voice echoing in my mind. "They are only eldritch in part. The mana in these ripples is aberrant to begin with. That, combined with their abandonment and subsequent bitterness, tainted their souls, compounding until they drew too deeply on the wrong sort of mana."

"Is there enough eldritch in the mix that you could do serious damage?" I asked.

"Perhaps. But I do not know if my purification abilities alone will be enough to turn the tide."

That was fine. If Nick could deliver the goods and everything stayed above board, it might not even be an issue. I settled in at the edge of the circle, across from Dent. He was doing something with his thumbs again, trying to get in my head. I ignored him and took in the situation. There were Knights on both sides of the circle. Some were obviously keeping tabs on me, but most were on Stonewall's side of the arena, murmuring amongst themselves. From the body language, they weren't exactly worried, but they weren't thrilled either. And unless I was reading it wrong, several of them seemed to be overtly glaring in Dent's direction.

Not happy with the terms of the duel. Something in there hurts him. Good.

Stonewall didn't share their concerns. He'd crossed his arms and conversed with Nick at the center, though Nick seemed a lot less interested in conversation than mean-mugging Dent. His mouth was a straight line, his eyes cold, and for a moment, I could guess why Hastur wanted Nick emotionless and free of guilt.

Because if he ever looked at me that way?

I'd start running.

Having grown tired of all the preamble, Stonewall took a few loose steps back and stopped, lifting his sword in simple salute. Knights and shadows alike fell silent.

Nick returned a deep nod that was almost a bow. Then brought his weapons to bear.

CHAPTER ONE HUNDRED EIGHTEEN

The chamber was dead silent, the shuffling of the combatants' heavy boots underpinned by running water. Now that the duel had started, every observer—even Dent, who I'd half-expected to resort to crass jeering—stood motionless and quiet, the occasional grind of metal and shifting of weight the only indicator they were alive.

Stonewall gave off the feel of a rattlesnake. He had half-a-head of height on Nick and extended reach to match. As Nick circled, he positioned himself at the outer limits of the tank's range, simple, practiced footwork keeping him there.

It felt rote. Methodical. Like the motions of a chess master who had played this opening thousands of times and performed the routine with otherworldly patience.

It worried me enough that I wondered if I'd made a mistake, not negotiating for a duel by proxy and attempting to take Nick's place. While my friend's abilities were better suited for this in theory and he had a respectable number of monsters under his belt, he'd sat out the Transposition. Other than the brief, violent encounter at the end of the trial, he lacked the exposure to User on User combat, which in my experience, was a different animal entirely.

A bead of sweat dripped down Nick's forehead. His mouth turned downward. In a flash of motion, he rushed forward, catching the edge of Stonewall's shield on his own and flinging it to the side, driving the point of his glowing blade at the armpit gap in Stonewall's breastplate.

There was a split second of metal grinding on metal echoing across the grounds. Maybe it was wishful thinking, or the ferocity of the blow, but for a moment I thought Nick had ended it in one strike. Then

Stonewall pivoted. Shield still out of position, he flicked his sword under and up, knocking Nick's blade away with a dexterous maneuver more appropriate to an Olympic fencer than a Knight.

Even off-balance, the counter delivered enough force that Nick stumbled backward, barely holding onto his blade until he found his footing and brought his shield up. His eyebrows furrowed.

Stonewall's echoing voice was unbothered, detached. "If you survive this, a word to the wise. Informing your opponent that you are self-taught cedes an unnecessary advantage."

Nick smirked, though his eyes were still cold. "That would have bought me—what—thirty seconds of caution before you figured it out? Plus, I guess I wanted to get to know you better."

Does he think he's a fucking shounen character?

That seemed to catch Stonewall's attention. The Knight's helmet tilted to the side. "To what purpose?"

I had no idea what they'd talked about, but against all odds, Nick had managed to get inside Stonewall's head. Now all he had to do was leave the question unanswered, let it needle at his opponent. Against someone as disciplined as Stonewall appeared to be, it probably wouldn't add up to much, but it was still something.

"Dunno," Nick said, and I fought the urge to facepalm. "You seem like an interesting guy. If that was gonna be our only chance to talk, guess I wanted to pick your brain a little."

Stonewall nodded. "There is value in knowing one's opponent. But familiarity is nothing in the face of true power."

He raised his leg and kicked Nick's shield.

Nick saw it coming and braced.

It didn't matter. That simple motion resounded like a hammer on steel, imparting enough force to send Nick flying backpedaling across the ring where he slammed into several Knights, bouncing off and landing painfully on his side with a mighty clang. The ring of shadows that surrounded us appeared to bend inward, tendrils of oily smoke reaching toward Nick's armor. Kettle—the first Knight to reach him—bent down, apparently intending to grab him beneath the arms and hoist him up, but seemed to struggle as the tendrils drew closer.

Not trying to keep the action moving. Sandbagging. Intentionally exposing him to whatever that shit is on the perimeter.

Careful not to make visible motion, I broke through Kettle's mind, amplifying already present feelings of disgust and self-loathing.

Kettle pulled back as if he'd been burned. Two Knights took his place, lifting Nick to his feet and shoving him forcefully back to the center.

Pot and Kettle were part of Stonewall's retinue. Of course they had more of a personal stake in his victory. It didn't bode well, but it wasn't dire. A few feet to my left, Pot was obviously monitoring me, which meant I only really needed to watch Kettle. The shadow cyclone was more of a problem. As Nick shakily rose to his feet, I reached inside my inventory and gripped **<Blade of Woe's>** handle tightly. Hundreds of tiny red weak points glowed from within the indecipherable mass. Which meant, at the very least, we could kill them.

Meanwhile, Nick turned his head to the side and spit. "That... all you got?"

I fought another urge to facepalm. Why was he making this harder for himself?

Naturally, Stonewall took this as a signal to go on the offensive. He pressed forward, never fully lowering his guard, systematically battering Nick's shield with powerful strikes that reverberated through the shield and my friend's body. Instead of retreating, or changing tact, Nick barely moved, electing to block every blow, even those he could have easily side-stepped.

Doubt clouded my mind. Unless I was missing something, Nick was performing *worse* than he had before. In the trial, his versatility and improvisation were enough to make me revisit my decision to go it alone. Now, this was the first time he'd held a shield. Reactive, panicky, and entirely on the defensive. Where was the warrior who bulldozed through a swamp full of monsters?

Had I read it wrong? Had everything that had happened broken him, traumatized him to the point he'd entirely regressed?

Stonewall slammed a vicious overhead, aiming for the shield itself. A terrible metallic pop resounded. Nick screamed, falling backward, a straight-line dent bisecting his shield, centered exactly on where his arm was strapped in on the other side.

Enough.

I brushed Dent's mind, preparing to give the man an order that would break the rules of engagement. It was possible it wouldn't trigger the magical contract in my inventory, if I was the one telling him to do so, or even register that I'd been the one to break it. But when I'd written out most of the consequences for our side on the triplicate, I'd pressed lightly. Meaning the ink hadn't carried through to the contract paper and we'd face no repercussions whatsoever beyond what the ripple itself could dole out.

"Matt. This thing with Jinny."

I shook my head. "It's gonna get out one way or another."

"Sure." He bit his lip. "But if it doesn't, promise you're not going to help it along?"

I gritted my teeth, withdrawing from Dent. Throughout our entire friendship, I'd never been fully honest with Nick. Not until today. And when I'd told him it was important that we were different, that we held different beliefs and different rules, I meant it.

Idealists are frustrating. Infuriating as they are inflexible. They hold impossibly naïve positions, and equivocate, and split hairs, and get lost in pointless hypotheticals—often as the world burns down around them. And much as they'd like to believe otherwise, they're anything but perfect. If anything, they're more susceptible to despair and discouragement than the rest of us.

It's that detachment from reality that makes people like me necessary in a crisis. The pragmatists, the mathematical monsters, the coldhearted bastards who believe good ends justify almost any means. The necessary evils. But if you take that as a license to smother the people who resist, who dare to hope, who wholeheartedly uphold the conviction that we don't have to become monsters to destroy monsters, and genuinely, perhaps even stupidly, believe that things can be better?

When the crisis is over and the smoke fades, evil is all you're left with. Necessary and otherwise.

And if I interfered now and denied his wishes, the bond of trust we'd started to build would be null and forfeit. Even if he never knew it. I'd just be using him as another tool to meet my own ends.

Stonewall, tired of the drawn-out duel, attempted to end it. He drew his arm back and swung the blade at Nick's neck, perfectly on target. Nick raised his shield too late, and the force of the coup de grâce landed entirely on the top of his shield, driving it into his forehead.

Nick somehow managed to roll away from the follow-up, awkwardly shoving himself up to his feet and teetering backward, barely regaining his balance. It was almost convincing.

Until his eyes flicked to the shadows at his side.

My jaw dropped.

Playing into Stonewall's expectations of an untrained fighter. Faking it. But only to an extent. He still took one hell of a beating. Why?

All at once, it clicked. He'd done something similar before when we were fighting the swarms during the trial,

"Enough," Stonewall said. He pointed his sword at Nick, still swaying on his feet. "The outcome is obvious. Yield and submit to judgment."

"No point in surrendering a duel to the death," Nick huffed, wiping blood from the corner of his mouth.

Stonewall studied him silently. "You are no Knight of the Round. Let alone worthy of Afallach's inheritance."

"So... you keep... telling me."

"That being said. You fought against a superior opponent with bravery, honor, and integrity. And while you might not be one of us, you share, at the very least, a piece of our essence. It would bring no pleasure to slay you." Stonewall looked up, observing the hall. "The terms are simple. One of us must die. But this place will not last forever." He indicated the swirling shadows. "It is already coming undone, though it will be some time before we greet our final rest. Remain here with us and greet the void. That is the only courtesy I can grant you."

"Sure. I get a nice quiet end, while Andre the Giant over there gets to finger paint with my friend's aqueous fluid." Nick glared at Dent with open contempt.

Stonewall did a long-suffering slow turn, holding a long look with his second that implied this was the first he'd heard of it, then announced, "Fulfilling such a brutish and dishonorable agreement won't be necessary in any circumstance. Will it, Sir Kay?"

Dent looked down and away in an odd, sheepish manner that clashed with his considerable height. "Just having some fun, Gawain. Didn't mean nothin' by it."

"I'm sure." Stonewall turned back to Nick. "And there you have it. Now. What is your answer?"

Nick seemed to recognize he was being offered genuine kindness. He nodded and took a moment to regain his breath. Then spoke. "Thanks. But... this is the first time in a long time I've felt like myself again. Even if it hurts, and it's hard. I'm only here because people put their trust in me. Believed in the person they thought I was," he glanced at me. "Fought like hell to save me from myself." His eyes grew distant. "Loved me. Despite my flaws."

Jinny's shadow, the darkness that had clung to him ever since we'd reunited, ebbed away. A tear traced down his cheek.

"I don't know if they're right. Or hell, if I even deserve a fraction of it." He looked up at Gawain. "But I owe it to them to try."

"You... wish to continue the duel?" Gawain asked, as if he couldn't quite believe what he was hearing.

The golden aura receded, coalescing into his shield, concentrating into a single white orb that was so bright it lit the entire room. I smiled despite the gravity of the situation. As always, I'd underestimated him. He'd worked within the rules of the duel and pushed a passive ability to the absolute limit. Every impact he'd weathered, hit he'd blocked, and lick he'd taken had been absorbed by the same ability he'd used in the trial— to tank the axe hit from the giant swarm and redirect the force back on the wielder. It was different now, an evolution or significantly advanced form of the original ability, and considering how it spread over his entire armor, it probably wasn't limited to one blow.

Nick wiped the trickle of blood from the side of his mouth.

"I didn't hear no bell."

CHAPTER ONE HUNDRED NINETEEN

The friend I'd once watched struggle to walk, flew.

His feet barely touched the ground as he closed the gap to Gawain. At the last second, he flicked his shield arm out, loosened straps sliding easily from his arm as the shield skidded off to the side. He gripped the sword with both hands, swinging it more like a baseball bat than any martial weapon. Metal clashed with metal, resonating a deep hum as Gawain recoiled, shield going wide, leaving him open.

Nick spun around, his once-clumsy movements fluid and graceful as he guided the blisteringly fast follow-up strike into the gap at Gawain's thigh.

"Mmf."

Gawain staggered back, off-balance for less than a second before he corrected his form. Shadow hissed freely from the fractured metal armor in a steady stream that formed small clouds, advected by the swirling gale of air between the two combatants. Tendrils of smoke from the swirling shadows that surrounded us snaked toward the clouds formed by Gawain's wound, absorbing them quickly.

The exchange grew fierce, as Gawain tried to meet Nick's sudden flurry of aggression in kind, but Nick didn't give him an opening, every brutal two-handed strike flowing smoothly into the next.

It felt like I was witnessing the birth of something monumental. Something that only happened once in a lifetime.

Which made it all the harder to stop watching.

Because while Gawain himself seemed honorable enough, given his refusal of Sir Kay's proclivities, one of his Knights had attempted to sandbag Nick while he was *losing*. It stood to reason now that he was turning the tide, things were going to escalate.

Most of the Knights were still viewing the bout impassively. There were plenty of clenched fists, and angry mutterings, but no sudden movements or hands reaching for swords. But Kettle—the Knight who had tried to sabotage Nick—was nowhere to be seen.

I looked around in a panic and realized Pot was also gone moments before a sharp point pressed into my back and an armored forearm looped around my throat.

"Don't," Pot whispered.

Talia growled and bent low, ready to pounce.

Why—shit. The contract hasn't been activated because he hasn't hurt me yet. Same with Kettle.

I held out a hand to still her.

Not yet. Need to time this right.

"Wow," I carefully turned my head, ensuring he could hear me while still monitoring the duel. "You guys really are the defects."

"Keep your voice low," Pot growled, and the point pressed harder into my side.

"Have you ever *not* been a follower, Pot? Don't answer that. It's rhetorical." I ran my mouth, still buying time. "Not to mention obvious. That's all you are. Worse, you're not even a good follower. A dressed-up, trumped-up sycophant who will do anything for the person they follow, even if doing so directly conflicts with their wishes. Because, apparently, a stupid motherfucker like you knows what's best for them."

"On second thought. Shut. Up."

"Must be a real burden to Sir Gawain, with a snake like you coiled in his satchel."

"Saxon *filth*—"

Nick's battle cry cut him off. Gawain was half-stooped over. My friend bellowed at the top of his lungs, bringing the blade down directly on Gawain's head. His helmet split open and shadow spilled from the wound, spreading out, becoming fog. The last of the retaliatory power faded, and Nick took a half-step backward. He was drenched in sweat, heaving.

Kettle reappeared from the crowd and raced into the circle, approaching Nick from behind, brandishing a nasty-looking war hammer in both hands.

Now.

I sucked in a breath and shouted, "Nick! Behind!"

Everything happened at once.

Nick whirled, exhaustion forgotten, then watched dumbfounded as the previously villainous Sir Kay leapt forward to defend him.

Pain enveloped me as the blade at my back dug in a quarter inch—then disappeared. The arm around my neck loosened as the armor itself disappeared.

Credit to Kinsley. The contract paper worked.

Subconsciously using **<Page's Quickdraw>**, I pulled my hand crossbow and aimed it backward, over my shoulder. The shadow that was once housed in a suit of armor reeled backward, bolt stuck where its face should be, struggling to maintain its form. I lashed out with my heel. The strike landed at chest level and the shadow stumbled backward.

Tendrils, thick and hungry, extended out from the swirling circle, dragging Pot into it even as he screamed and struggled to escape.

<Awareness> warned me just in time, and I ducked beneath the long horizontal sweep of a longsword. The Knight who attacked me was advancing, one of several. They'd witnessed the end of what just happened, but not necessarily the why.

"Traitors!" Sir Kay bellowed, suddenly heroic and completely out of character, delivering the lines I'd fed him. He fought side by side with Nick as they both worked together to push back Kettle, Sir Gawain motionless behind them. "Traitors to the Round!"

Some Knights turned, but it was deafeningly loud, and several appeared to not notice.

Not enough. Need to stall until they get a read on the situation. If they attack me under the impression they're defending themselves, the contract may not trigger. Me on flat terrain against multiple guys in heavy armor would not go well.

I sent Talia an image and a question.

After responding with an affirmative, she raced away from the dueling square toward the swirling shadow perimeter, returning to her wolf form, white fur overtaking brown and black as her muzzle extended. She opened her mouth and howled, purification magic extending out in a small crystalline radius that covered both of us. The shadows shrieked as twisted, barely perceptible forms frantically crawled over each other, trying desperately to get away. They didn't seem capable of complex thought and were torn between maintaining the barrier and staying the hell away from Talia's purification magic, forming a gap large enough for both of us to escape into.

As we advanced, the shadows slid back into place, muffling the sound of the melee. All light faded, and fear turned to rage and hunger as tendrils sparked, recoiling as they clashed with Talia's magic.

"How long can you hold it?" I asked her.

My summon's expression was hard to read at the best of times, harder now that I had to pick it out between flashes of repelled tendrils. If I had to guess, she looked strained.

"Not... long. Will need to recover after a minute," Talia growled. A feathery knife of darkness flashed, bouncing away from my neck. "Did you have this planned the entire time and not tell me?"

I shook my head. Then realized that she probably couldn't see it. "Kind of making it up as I go."

Nick was a bad influence.

"So... what... now?" Talia grunted.

"Now?" I looked around. Despite the hostility of the environment, I felt oddly comfortable. The unformed shadows posed as much of a threat to the Knights as they did to me. So long as I had Sir Kay defending Nick and could buy Talia enough time to recover, it provided the perfect environment for me to do what I did best.

Hit and run.

I grabbed <**Blade of Woe's**> hilt and couldn't help but chuckle low in my throat as dozens of splashes of yellow and red appeared beyond the barrier of the dark. "Now, we hunt."

CHAPTER ONE HUNDRED TWENTY

I emerged from the shadows, thrusting my dagger forearm deep into the gaping hole of an errant Knight's armor, feeling resistance as the blade slowed, then release as something severed. I should have been terrified, scared shitless, but there was no fear, no hesitation.

Gawain radiated rage. He seemed to understand what had happened —the betrayal of his men—but despite their poor judgment, Gawain himself walked the talk. As soon he realized they were targeting Nick, he dropped the duel to defend my friend, mowing down all who interfered. Judging from the carnage, the shorn-through armor that freely leaked smoke from fallen Knights, limiting magic usage for the duel might have saved Nick's life.

A Knight wound up to swing his war hammer, more behind him turning by the moment.

I tried to influence him directly and nearly died for it, hammer smashing into the ground inches from my feet.

Intelligence is too high. Need to unbalance him.

Talia bit at the Knight's boot, momentarily stopping his advance. Sir Kay broke from Gawain and Nick, bowing forward at the waist like a bull. He bowled into the war hammer Knight, knocking him a few steps forward. **<Probability Cascade>** fired, sending the Knight careening across the ground, the floor itself unnaturally slick.

If there was more breathing room, I might have taken a second to appreciate what just happened. **<The Devil's Share>** had responded to my subconscious intentions, casting **<Probability Cascade>** on the marble ground the moment the thought had entered my mind. I'd need to watch the mana usage—even with the reduction, it'd be incredibly easy to tap myself out that way—but other than that, it was a hell of an upgrade.

I pirouetted out of the way of an errant blade, quick-drawing my crossbow and letting my abilities take over. I pulled the trigger and the pain-bolt rocketed forward, threading the needle of the stumbling Knight's visor slit.

It wouldn't do much beyond pissing him off and obscuring his vision, but that was fine. As far as I could tell, the Knights only had two weaknesses. One was in the upper left quadrant of their chests, the same location as a human heart. The second was the armor itself. When Pot and Kettle intentionally broke the contract, it had whisked their armor into my inventory, and the smoke that had filled the armor was violently pulled into the circling black ring that still enveloped us.

So far at least, they hadn't reformed.

Unfortunately, a large contingent of the Knights didn't seem to be in on it. Rather, they'd witnessed the duel turn into a melee, two of their own die, and taken it all rather personally. It was an unstated rule of the contract I'd been unaware of. As long as the terms weren't being knowingly violated, the Knights' armor remained their own.

Which meant I needed to get creative.

The war hammer Knight roared, bolt shaft and fletching still sticking out from his visor. He charged, pulling the hammer back, his run a half-stagger. I wedged the toe of my boot beneath a fallen spear and lobbed it toward him. He paid it no mind until the last second, when the spear tip continued its rotation, lining up perfectly with his throat. He flinched and ducked his head.

The spear tip bounced harmlessly off his helmet, spinning off to the side. By the time he looked up, I'd already repositioned. He swung the hammer at me, fully committing even as his footing betrayed him.

The hammer itself was on target. He was *fast*. Even a few days ago, it might have been enough to hit me. Bruisers were supposed to be slow, manageable so long as you didn't get hit. But there'd been a line of exceptions to that rule. Thankfully, I had the experience of fighting Buzzcut to fall back on, and because the situation had forced my hand, my agility was reaching absurd levels.

I sidestepped, touching the hammer and correcting its course, watching with no small satisfaction as the war hammer Knight slammed into a cluster of his fellows, toppling several and obliterating one with a wild swing.

"Drop!" Nick roared over the chaos. He'd abandoned his place in the center and was racing toward me, slowing only momentarily to retrieve his shield from the ground. <Awareness> flared. I dropped to one knee immediately, bending low. Nick soared over my head, full plate and all, and I twisted to watch as he brandished his shield, absorbing a handful of clanging blows before he turned it sideways. It shone golden light as he swung it like a glaive, cutting several Knights off at the knees.

Others pressed in on him from the side, threatening to surround us. I grabbed his shoulder and pulled him back, firing a few more bolts, landing enough that they hesitated to pursue.

"Why the fuck are they still attacking?" Nick yelled over his shoulder at Gawain.

Gawain shook his head. His right arm was reduced to a smoking stump, and he was now managing almost entirely with his left. That he was still fighting so well regardless of the handicap was a testament of his skill. "When I said this place was coming unraveled, I wasn't just talking about the ripple itself. Look at them." He stared out at the Knights, swarming in the chaos, and cut one down who dared to press him. "Some retain their faculties, but many are further gone than I realized. There's something else at work."

"Well. That fucking sucks," Nick groused.

"Stay your blades, men of the circle!" Gawain shouted.

There was a hesitation, a lull that felt entirely too temporary.

I reloaded my crossbow as quickly as I could, pushing bolts into the auto-loader one at a time, trying to stay on top of things despite how outnumbered we were. A single mistake here could be fatal. "Gawain, I get that you're pumped to make a fatalistic stand here and all, but the rest of us need a plan. If this turns into a slugfest, we lose. Honor besmirched. Only a matter of time."

He kept his blade trained on the advancing Knights and hesitated, visor turning toward the ring of shadow. "Find the Wizard. I sense his hand in this. He's stoking their anger, suppressing their reason."

There's a fucking Wizard?

"Where?" I asked.

Gawain indicated the wreathe of shadows with his blade, grimly. "In the depths. Finish him with dignity, if you can. He was not always this way."

Shit. The ring itself didn't cover that much surface area, but it was entirely opaque. If I only had myself to worry about, I could probably find the target fairly easily. But it would take time and focus, meaning I'd be leaving Gawain and Nick entirely open, with only a handful of loyal Knights and Sir Kay to cover them.

I looked down at Talia. "Recovered yet?"

When she nodded she had, I checked my mana stores, swore, then asked Sir Kay a silent question. I'd gotten lucky that he was within the level-range for **<Subjugation>**, but if I kept relying on luck, I'd end up drained and vulnerable with nothing to show for it, if not worse. I needed

Knights who were talented but inexperienced—if the ripple followed any logical order, they would be low-level enough that this would work.

Sir Kay pointed to two separate Knights. One wielded a halberd and seemed to champ at the bit, ready to charge us. The other was stiff, almost robotic, wielding a mace and shield.

I subjugated them one after another, nearly swooning as the mana drained away, leaving me with a fifth, if that.

Both Knights stiffened.

As with Sir Kay, prying into their minds after subjugating them was almost too easy.

You serve the round.

There was resistance. Gray tendrils that grasped their minds and pushed back. But it felt too lazy to be an organized defense. If the source of the resistance was the Wizard Gawain mentioned, managing every Knight on the battlefield had spread him too thin.

I slipped through the cracks, maneuvering until I reached the minds within.

Report to Sir Gawain, defend your guest. Do your duty.

My invisible enemy made a mistake. He seemed to find my command amusing, and I felt him laughing, somewhere behind us. When the time came, I had a place to look.

With a shudder, the Knights obeyed, pushing through the crowd and taking a defensive position next to Nick and Gawain. I was ready for Gawain to comment, but he said nothing, just shifted to the side, giving the newcomers space to position.

Nick gave me a worried glance but said nothing. Probably thinking about what we talked about earlier. Instead, he offered caution. "Remember. Tap me in if you need me. No hero shit."

I smirked. Despite the gravity of the situation, Nick of all people warning me not to be a hero was too much. "The hero shit's your job."

Whatever time Gawain had bought us dwindled, and the Knights charged. Gawain readied himself with his men, Sir Kay, and Nick doing the same a moment later. With Talia sprinting ahead of me, purification magic emitting from her in a translucent sphere, I plunged back into the wreathe.

Not long after the shadows closed in behind us, a snarling voice emanated from the gloom.

"So... the Ordinator himself seeks an audience."

A lance of gray energy cut through Talia's shield and curved away from her directly toward my eye, too quick to track as anything other than a blur. **<Awareness>** sounded a warning that was entirely too late.

CHAPTER ONE HUNDRED TWENTY-ONE

I twisted frantically, dodging the lance of gray energy by only a hair's width. It disappeared behind me with a speed that made me shudder. That was entirely too close.

Talia's shield fended off the worst of the shadow gale, protecting us from the lethal, face-melting effect the eldritch magic might have had. But it did nothing for the windstorm of pressure that swirled around us, continuing to build.

My summon pressed forward, head low, teeth bared as she struggled to advance. It was all I could do to keep a hand on her and manage my footing without being uprooted and swept away.

"How much longer?" I asked, stealing a glance to the side. With **\<Blade of Woe\>** in hand, I could still see the vitals of Nick, Gawain, and Sir Kay still holding the same formation. For now, at least, they were still standing. We needed to hurry.

"Hard... to say," Talia grunted. Her nails scraped on the marble ground as the wind blew her back a few inches, and I went down on one knee to brace and steady her. A light-blue eye acknowledged me. "Thank you." Her attention returned to the gale. "When we first entered the circle, it was more focused. Unyielding. It seems far more scattered now."

"Any guesses why?"

"Unsure."

I squinted, trying to make out anything in the darkness. There was nothing but swirling shapes, lines that almost formed discernible characteristics, only to vanish into malevolent mist. The only constant was—

Tendrils?

They were almost tangible. Not in the shadow itself, but the negative spaces. There were dozens of them. They reminded me of the threads, the connective tissue for everything when **<Harrowing Anticipation>** was active.

Suddenly paranoid, I checked my abilities to confirm. **<Harrowing Anticipation>** was still in deep cooldown from when I'd used it in the first ripple against the grimelings. There'd been no accidental cast.

"Can you see them?" I murmured to Talia.

She searched in the direction I was looking, then turned back to me with a worried expression. "See what? There's nothing but darkness."

Intrigued, I picked one out and traced it to its exit point. It swirled and wound a path of nothingness, all the way to the edge of the mist. They all did, each lining up with the glowing vitals of the Knights beyond.

My true-sight ability is on cooldown. Talia can't see them. So why can I?

There was one just outside the shield. Nearly in arm's reach. The rest seemed to be intentionally avoiding it, moving quickly, barely discernible spaces that moved with an unnerving serpentine grace.

I withdrew **<Vorpal Gnasher>** from my inventory. The dagger's sharpness was fleeting, but it could punch through steel. If I was attempting to cut through something almost intangible, it was the best tool for the job.

With a deep breath, I swung the blade outside the barrier, directly toward one of the translucent tendrils, aiming for its center. The dagger passed through it with no resistance—but the tendril snapped away, severed portion emitting an audible squeal.

Bingo.

But the reprisal was swift and furious. A dozen smaller tendrils wrapped around my wrist before I could withdraw it into the shield, too fast for any warning, coiled tightly enough to cut off my circulation almost immediately. "Tal—"

I cut off mid-sentence as it yanked me out of the shield, into the black.

Darkness washed over me, frigid and complete.

Something pressed in on my mind, building pressure in my skull. I got an arm free, only to have it snagged by another tendril seconds later, grip significantly stronger than before. Whatever it was, it wasn't trying to kill me yet. But **<Jaded Eye>** whispered that it'd be more than happy to break me if I kept struggling.

"Be still," a voice commanded, abrasive and sibilant.

I went limp, playing at surrender. When I acted, it needed to be decisive. The tendrils grew thicker, closer together. The pressure in my mind grew, degrading Talia's panicked attempts to reach me into nothing more but noise.

Getting closer to the source.

The pressure intensified. **"You will serve me."**

"I will serve," I answered.

"During your tenure in my service, you will obey my commands and destroy all enemies of the Round."

"I will obey." I could almost see him now. He struck an unimpressive silhouette in the gloom, almost half-skeletal. There was a void where his nose should have been, the flesh that surrounded it withered and black. He smiled widely, gums receded, teeth discolored and long. His chest was caved in, and a dozen tendrils emitted from his sternum.

"Once your tenure is complete, you will host my soul and deliver me from this godforsaken place."

I maintained a blank expression. Between Gawain's assertion that "the Wizard" was the one driving the Knights to violence, and the nature of the commands he was giving me, it was obvious. He had powers similar to mine. They weren't working, but he had to think they were. Probably the only reason I was still alive.

He brought me closer, making a show of inspecting me, leering. "Out of every candidate in the cosmos, the Allfather chose you? Some honorless whelp?"

"I am unworthy," I said, placating him.

"I'll enjoy wearing your skin, boy. Correcting every flaw, erasing the weakness. Destroying any potential attachment that could lead you astray. Creating the perfect vessel."

I suppressed the rage. Bottled it. I'd use it soon, but not until the perfect moment. I could feel Talia, struggling to close the distance, getting closer.

He drew me inches from his face. "Oh, the fun we'll have." Suddenly, his gleeful expression faltered. "What—"

"Now."

The effect of Talia's purification shield was immediate, and the wizard screamed, his leathery skin bubbling. The tendrils loosened as I fell with him, twisting in the air so my knee aligned with his chin, my full weight crushing his jaw against the floor. I wielded the vorpal blade like a scythe, slashing through the tendrils at his mid-section, hacking through the ghostly apparitions, trying to sever as many as I could before he could rally.

Even through the roar of the storm, I heard seemingly endless clanging as multiple Knights collapsed to the ground. Once the tendrils were gone, I put the blade to his throat.

He laughed a wet, blood-filled cough, uncaring as his throat bobbed against the blade, drawing beads of red. "Thought I smelled it on you. The lithid's touch."

"What about it?" I growled.

He raised an eyebrow, grinning through broken teeth. "If you've already met one, you're more damned than I realized."

Belatedly, I realized it was Eldritch Favor that saved my ass, preventing the Wizard from enslaving me. If we got out of this, I needed to shore up my mental defenses. Talia's shield flickered. She warned me silently that she couldn't hold it for much longer.

If the shield goes, we're probably back where we started.

There was no time. Still pinning the old man down, I drove my dagger into the nerve cluster in his shoulder, bracing him as he screamed. "Only chance. Tell me something useful, and I'll make it quick. Why do you have powers similar to mine? Are you an Ordinator?"

He giggled, halfway between delirium and agony. "You have no idea—"

I twisted the knife, backhanding him to shorten the resulting howl. "What about 'only chance' don't you understand?"

He panted, his breaths small moans. Eldritch Favor was keeping me alive, but I could see the holes and tears in my armor slowly and steadily being eaten away, consumed by the shadow despite multiple layers of protection. As with any pure magic User, it was only a matter of time before he got to me.

"Did you think you were the only one? So childish. So impossibly naïve." He coughed twice, then fixed me with a blank stare. "The slow plunge into dark waters, unknowing and uncaring of what lies beneath. Who are you doing this for?"

Still fixated on the first thing he said, I could feel the blood draining from my face. "There are other Ordinators?"

"Sickly daughter. Lover in dire straits. The family—" he smirked. "There it is. Yes, I think so. The *family*."

I growled subconsciously, deep in my throat. "Think I've never seen a cold read before, asshole? This isn't getting under my skin. All you're doing is making this harder on yourself. Tell me about the others!"

"You're jaded." The old man nodded. "That's good. Hold on to that. You'll need it."

"Last. Chance," I reiterated, putting more weight on the knife.

"Then..." the man grunted. "I'll tell you a secret. How strong you are? The power and influence you hold? None of it matters."

"Myrddin." Talia was calling my name. But the faraway look in the old man's eyes transfixed me. So unfathomably vast, filled with bittersweet regret.

He spoke slowly, as if every word aged him. "Even if you bring the world itself to its ancient knees, it won't matter. Because no matter how careful you are, the core flaw remains the same. The people you're discarding your humanity for? They're as damned as the day they were born. You can't save them. Because you can't protect them from yourself."

An icy chill went through me. I refused to show any reaction, make any movement to give away the distress that rampaged through my psyche, but he'd gotten to me in a way so few people could.

"Matt!" Talia roared.

Somehow, I came back to myself just in time. The old man's eyes caught fire, violet flame transforming them into a charred ruin as he opened his mouth, violet illuminating his throat.

Suicide attack.

I gripped his head tightly with both hands and snapped his neck. Gouts of flame escaped his mouth, singing my fingers, and I leapt off him as the fire consumed him from within. In a matter of seconds, his tattered robe and the flesh beneath was consumed, leaving nothing but a blackened corpse.

Well. Almost nothing.

There was a glittering at the center of his chest, refracting the light of the last few embers of his body that had yet to burn out. At first I thought it was a monster core. But the shape and color were both wrong. It was a trilliant cut gem, the color of an amber so dark it was almost black.

I reached down tentatively, ash crumbling around my fingertips as I gripped it and pulled. It was hot to the touch, even through the thick material of my gauntlet. As soon as the gem came free, the swirling shadows thinned and dissipated, revealing the chamber beyond.

<Level Up: Ordinator has reached Level 18.>
<Level Up: Ordinator has reached Level 19.>
<Legendary Material Acquired: Essence of Merlin (Incomplete)>

CHAPTER ONE HUNDRED TWENTY-TWO

The essence I'd received was even lighter on detail than usual. It was like some higher power had created the drop but hadn't bothered filling in the description field. It was a crafting material, but I had no way of knowing what it did or how good it was from description alone.

I wasn't happy about it, but it tracked, considering the nature of this place.

Unfinished.

As the shadows that drove them dispersed to nothing, the corrupted Knights of the Round fell.

Some slid to their knees, propping themselves up by their blades with breath-like shudders until they stilled, while others seemed to pass on instantly, their armor clanging to the ground like puppets with cut strings, pieces scattering across the ground.

Nick stood at the center of the chaos, bemused. He spotted me and nodded, stoically. Tension flooded out of me. Nick was safe. We'd made it. We were both still alive.

Gawain and his contingent were still standing, though there were only a half-dozen, far less than before, and judging from their sluggish movements and difficulty standing, it wouldn't be long until they followed the others.

With the threat handled, my eyes traveled downward, pouring over the charred corpse at my feet. It really was a shame I had to kill him. The similarities of our power sets were undeniable. There was little question in my mind that Merlin was an Ordinator—or at the very least, a failed copy of one. And from what he'd said, he wasn't the only one. If he'd been more agreeable, less hellbent on using me as a vessel, we probably could have helped each other.

There was a sluggish clanking as a lithe suit of armor took its place at my side.

"You cook 'em like that?" Sir Kay asked, more curious than anything else.

I shook my head. "Cooked himself. I just got out of the way."

He leaned over the corpse, bent at the waist, and spit. A small wad of dark liquid landed on Merlin's charred cheek. "Good riddance."

"Not a fan, I take it."

"Always thought he was better than us. Too good for the Round Table, yet ordered us around like he was Arthur himself." At the mention of Arthur, Sir Kay glanced over to where Nick and Gawain were conversing quietly. "Him though? He's the real thing. One of us. No matter what Sir Stick-up-his-arse says."

"Nick?" I asked.

"Yeh. Saved my bacon more than once, despite me being a right shite to you at the beginning." Sir Kay shook his head. "Don't understand people like them."

Same.

Suddenly, he grabbed my shoulder and pressed down. My blade was in my hand before I could react on a conscious level, and I nearly lashed out. Then I realized what was actually happening.

Sir Kay was fading. The shadows still visible from gaps in his armor were graying out, and gravity itself turned on him. His legs trembled, and as he sank to his knees, I caught him under his armpit to steady him. Even his voice sounded static, less clearly defined. "Don't... think I'm gonna be useful for much longer."

I didn't know what to say. If it wasn't for **<Subjugation>**, he'd likely have fought for the other side. But he'd given it his all. And even if he was an asshole, he'd fought like hell. Protected Nick. Given me time to find Merlin.

This was all so surreal.

"You did everything I asked of you and more." I searched his visor, trying to approximate eye contact. "Conducted yourself with honor."

His barked laugh sounded like a distant hiss. "Honor my arse. We both know I only did it cause you made me. But... I did my best. And..." his voice grew far away. "It felt good. To crack heads alongside Gawain again."

"Is there anything you want?" I asked. The way he sounded, he didn't have long. "Anything I can do for you?"

Sir Kay's helmet rotated toward Merlin. "Well. His eyes are already gone. Wed his face for me?"

I cocked my head. "You mean—"

"Do it myself, but it don't come out right no more."

I snuck a glance back over at Nick and Sir Gawain. They appeared to be having a much less coarse conversation. Gawain offered Nick his sword. From the tears streaking down Nick's face, and the way Gawain was trembling, he was on his way out as well.

"Uh. Sure. Might wait a while, if that's alright."

Sir Kay nodded. "Fewer witnesses. I understand."

"Anything else?"

"Felt nice... having a purpose again." All strength went out of him, and I leaned him back, straining a little to keep his head from hitting the floor. His visor turned toward Nick. "He important to you?"

"Yeah."

"Like a brother?"

"In everything but blood."

A choking noise emerged from Sir Kay's helmet. "Had a brother once. Self-righteous, arrogant, always had all the answers. Hated the prick."

"Constantly in your business, looking over your shoulder..."

Sir Kay nodded weakly. "Aye. You know it well. We mended things for a while. Even tried his way of doing things. Worked for a while. But eventually, it all fell apart again. Distance grew. And when he needed me most, I wasn't there. Only realized how much he mattered to me after he was gone." He reached up and braced a hand on my neck. "Don't make the same mistake I did."

I nodded slowly.

Sir Kay's heavy gauntlet slid off my neck and clattered to the floor.

He was gone.

I stood slowly. All the Knights were gone now, reduced to human-shaped piles of armor on the floor. Every ache and pain I'd been ignoring flared, new wounds and scars alike making themselves known. For the first time in my life, I felt old.

Can't keep this up forever.

Nick rubbed furiously at his face as I approached, trying to erase the evidence of emotion from his conversation with the fallen Knight and failing. He sheathed his sword and scowled at me. "Go ahead. Say it."

"Say what?" I asked.

"'Dude wanted to kill you and you're crying over him,' or 'See, we should have done it my way,' or 'Stop being a giant piss baby.'"

I said nothing. Waited.

Slowly, Nick let the conflicting emotions go and seemed to center himself. "Thanks. For waiting to step in until they made the first move. I know you prefer to be proactive, and my nattering forced you to be reactive." He reached out to Talia. The wolf summon sniffed his gauntlet, then pressed her head into it. "And thank you for helping him."

"We are a pack. It is my role and my duty," my summon said, staring up at Nick with kind eyes. "I worried for you."

I'd hoped Nick had something to show for the bond he'd forged with Gawain. But he seemed cagey, aloof. We checked the rest of the chamber, looking for any doors or hidden passages that might lead deeper into the ripple, finding nothing. As we scavenged the remains of the battlefield, gathering as many intact sets of armor and weapons as we could carry, the glow of victory faded.

Nothing had changed. We were still in danger from the Order. We had a lot to sell, more than enough to potentially cover our escape and a life on the run, but other than that, our circumstances were still dire. Better to grab more than we needed then come up short.

At the top of the throne room, nestled between two thrones, there was an empty pedestal. The brass plaque beneath it read "Guardian of the people, servant to the needy." Nick sat in the larger throne—presumably the King's—while I pried decorative gemstones out of the golden backing of the thrones themselves. **<Vorpal Gnasher's>** increasingly blunted tip was still more than thin enough to fit between most of the larger gems and the base.

An eye-catching ruby, slightly smaller than a fist, was giving me more trouble than the rest.

I paused, short of breath from the effort, and looked at him. "Gonna say anything or just stew over it? Also, if you wanna help with this, feel free."

"Any jars need to be opened while I'm at it?" Nick asked.

"Fuck you." I tossed the dagger to him hilt first, watching with small satisfaction as he fat-fingered it repeatedly and it bounced off his grip twice before he finally caught it and glared.

Nick went to work on the ruby, mouth set in a thin line. "If we walked out of here right now with nothing to show for it, how fucked would we be?"

There was something he wasn't telling me. I thought through it.

Even if we left now and somehow got clear of the Tower, me and everyone else in my sphere were on the wrong side of the hourglass. Hastur might have more important things on his plate, but I doubted Aaron and Sunny had any intention of letting desertion slide. Hell, Aaron had ordered the death of someone who'd been more or less loyal to him because it served his purposes and he didn't seem to think Buzzcut could hack it in the end. We'd use Kinsley's store to offload as much of our loot as we could, pump and dump, then close shop before the Order made the connection and came after her. But there were only so many places in a city to run. Eventually, our luck would run out.

And if Merlin wasn't just screwing with me and there were other Ordinators out there, everything was about to get a lot worse.

"Probably a solid four on the fucked scale. Only thing downgrading it from a five is that we have the initiative."

Nick nodded. He'd already known the answer. He just wanted to hear it out loud. "Myrddin. Why that name?"

Of all the questions I'd expected, it wasn't this. "Uh. I needed something to go by during the Transposition. Figured you know—wizard, pulled strings from the shadows, played the long game. Popped into my head and I went with it. Seemed à propos."

"So Merlin was a little too on the nose, and the rest was coincidental. You could have just as easily picked Elminster, or Severus, or whatever." There was a whinge of metal as Nick got the ruby free.

"Something like that," I said. But as I spoke, I knew it was too easy. There were too many odd coincidences with this ripple, lining up with Nick's theory that Hastur wanted us to find this place. But we'd hit a dead end.

He tossed me the ruby. I caught it and stuffed it in my inventory. When I looked up, his arms were crossed, and he looked uncharacteristically irritated. "I'm just a guy."

"And I'm a socially awkward asshole. Why are we stating the obvious?"

"You're not hearing me," Nick started, and I sensed the beginning of a rant. "Everyone thinks I'm something I'm not. It's always been that way. All these expectations get put on me and I just smile and nod, even though secretly I've got no clue what they're smoking. Up to this point, I've just sort of accepted it as an opportunity to fake it until I make it."

"But this is different," I filled in.

"There's so many layers that I'm not sure what to believe." Nick rubbed the back of his neck, then pulled out a statuette of a red dragon. Its body was snakelike and armless, its roaring mouth filled with endless rows of teeth. Given the context, the Knights of the Round, its meaning was immediately apparent.

"The Pendragon." My eyes slid from the statuette to my friend, shifting uncomfortably as he waited. "Gawain gave you that?"

"He started muttering in old English and, before I knew it, this just popped into existence."

There were a lot of implications to unpack there. But the statuette's base was perfectly circular, and when I checked the pedestal, it looked to be a perfect fit.

"It doesn't have to mean anything," I muttered, talking to myself as much as Nick.

"Uhuh," Nick said.

"And even if it means something, there's a high possibility we're being manipulated. The Tower can generate anything, and it seems to want to be climbed."

"Right. Dungeons are dicks, no matter how tall they are."

"This one in particular," I emphasized. "We have no idea what its agenda is, other than that it seems to *want* to be ransacked, which in and of itself is suspect."

But we have to look.

I took a deep breath and placed the statuette on the center of the pedestal. There was a deep rumbling that reverberated through the chamber as the ground itself seemed to vibrate. The wall behind the thrones shook, kicking up a cloud of dust as it receded into the ground. A wave of fresh, humid air washed in.

The dust settled to reveal a moonlit lake, vibrant blue waters reflecting a starry sky. Beneath the water's surface were dozens, if not hundreds of planners. And in the center of the lake was a stone outcropping. The stone itself was crested by a dark silhouette in the shape of a T that cast its cross-like shadow over the lake.

"Is that?" Nick asked.

It had to be. The weapon behind the myth.

Excalibur.

CHAPTER ONE HUNDRED TWENTY-THREE

We cleared the surroundings methodically. Nick and I searched opposite sides while Talia moved much quicker, looping around the entire lake, nose to the ground. There wasn't much to it beyond the glowing lake and a starry sky above. The beginning of a rocky embankment and tree trunks were harshly cut off, nothing but void beyond them.

Like a game world that was only half finished.

I was tempted to reach off the edge—how often do you get to interact with an utter *absence* of matter—but **<Jaded Eye>** screamed at me the moment the thought popped into my mind.

So much for that.

Talia returned to me, her gait slower than normal, exhaustion clear in her face and posture. "Nothing of note." She hesitated, glancing back in the direction she'd come. "Unless a portal activates and spews monsters everywhere."

I raised an eyebrow. "That seems... highly specific."

Talia inclined her head, and I followed as she padded toward the section that might have once led to a forest. There was a tree unnaturally bent in the shape of an upside-down U, oddly free of bark and branches. "The scent of magic is almost overwhelming here." She gave me a queer look. "You really can't smell that?"

I shook my head. "Smells like a tree." I took in a deep breath and wrinkled my nose. "And fish."

Talia looked over past where Nick was approaching, to the body of water at the center of the clearing. "I suspect that is the lake."

"Aren't they constructs? Why would they keep the smell?"

"Why would any of this be happening?" Talia gave me a cautious look. "This feels too convenient. Manufactured."

"I know." My mouth tightened.

The lake full of planners was likely more than enough to buy us back in to Hastur's good graces. But if he'd known it was here, why hadn't he told us himself? Where was the catch?

"You guys find anything?" Nick called over. He'd relaxed somewhat, but still looked more than ready to raise the shield at his side at the first sign of trouble.

"Magical tree." I chucked a thumb back at the deformity.

"Oh good. Matches the magical sword," Nick said.

"Nothing on your end?"

Nick shook his head. "There was a circle in the grass. Looked a little like a half-built elevator similar to the one we rode to the second floor, but definitely wasn't functional." He paused, stopping directly before the upside-down U. Then stepped through it before either Talia or I could grab him.

"Fool," Talia hissed.

"You are literally the asshole who reads out of the creepy book at the beginning of a horror movie and gets all his friends killed," I snapped.

"Worked out in *Army of Darkness*." Nick chuckled from the other side, then winced. "Sort of. Eventually. Gotta say though, the tree doesn't seem very magical." He frowned.

Talia turned her nose up. "Things of this nature are rarely as they appear."

Nick nodded thoughtfully, then looked at me. "You're the closest thing to a mage we got. Sense anything?"

I grimaced. He knew damn well I wasn't a mage. Lately, however, I'd been able to see hints of the threads that tied the realms of Flauros together. It wasn't consistent, and the only reason I even recognized them was due to <Harrowing Anticipation> which, of course, was still on cooldown.

Feeling foolish, I stood in front of the bent tree and closed my eyes, holding out a hand toward it.

"What is he doing?" I heard Talia whisper to Nick.

"Shh." Nick hushed her, "He's beginning to believe."

"Reference quota. You've damn well reached it," I snapped, keeping my eyes shut.

"Aw."

This wasn't getting us anywhere.

But before I gave up, I noticed a heat from within my gauntlet. <The Devil's Share> was unnaturally warm. When I moved my hand away, it quickly cooled. When I did the opposite, reaching in further, it grew hot again.

"Uh. Matt?" Nick called out nervously.

I ignored him. A bead of sweat dripped down my forehead. Just as the heat grew almost unbearable, a bright scarlet thread lanced across the inside of my eyelid. And another. And another. They all led to a center point, bright enough to leave an afterimage. I grabbed it.

<System Notification: You have discovered a waypoint. Once a waypoint is bound to a central hub, it will fortify its surroundings and provide an expedited method of travel.**>**

<Would you like to bind this waypoint to a central hub? Y|N>.

Almost immediately, I hit "Y." If I was understanding correctly, this was a potential backdoor into the Tower. We'd been told the ripples didn't last forever, but if the bit about fortifying its surroundings was accurate, maybe this ripple would last longer.

Either way, there wasn't a chance in hell I was going to wager that the system would interpret "No," as "No forever."

I studied the lump of magmatic rock in my hand. It was spiderwebbed with orange, and despite looking hot enough to incinerate everything below my wrist to ashes, was only slightly warm.

<System Notification: You have received a Waystone.>**

Off to the side, Nick and Talia were still watching, though they appeared to have taken several steps back.

"What?" I asked.

"You just summoned a lava rock and grabbed it like it was nothing," Nick said slowly. "Maybe it's the edgy outfit, but... that was some dark lord shit."

"It was... mildly distressing," Talia agreed.

I rolled my eyes and explained what the system text had revealed. Nick's face lit up halfway through my explanation.

"The Order's portal room. That's gotta be a central hub, right?" he asked.

"Pretty sure," I confirmed.

"Then we're back in." Nick grinned. "With all the bargaining power in the world. Aaron and Sunny can't do shit if we come back with a boatload of planners and a backdoor into the Tower to show for it."

"This is feeling more and more like a trap," Talia repeated, sounding more frustrated than before. Nick—who probably wanted to take our stroke of luck at face value—turned to argue with her. I clapped once, cutting them both off before it escalated.

"Talia's right," I said. "The timing is suspect. We don't know what this is, or why it's being handed to us. That goes double for the planners in the lake. And the sword," I shifted my gaze to where the blade still glittered atop the boulder, glinting with starlight. "The system is infinitely more likely to fuck us over than help us. Even if a ripple has different rules, we need to be on guard."

Nick's mouth turned downward. Probably wasn't happy about it, but I could tell he took the warning seriously. He knew all too well how quickly victory could turn to ash.

With the perimeter secured, there was only one thing left to do. I stepped into the lake gingerly, the facade of water only about ankle deep. Despite natural fears to the contrary, the planners remained pacifistic, scurrying out of the way and doing little else beyond keeping their distance.

"Seems alright so far," I said over my shoulder.

There was a splash as Nick followed me, trudging through the water.

I'm not sure what I expected to feel as we approached the stone. Anxiety. Dread, maybe. But for the first time, a feeling of curiosity struck me. Of discovery. If Talia was right, we'd been directed to this place for a reason. Something was guiding us here, maybe Hastur, or something else.

I'd spent so long afraid of whatever came next, that having that fear overshadowed by curiosity felt strangely freeing. It was like a glimpse into what could have been. Me, and Nick, and Jinny, and Sae, adventuring into the unknown, leveling, exploring the realms of Flauros and bringing the bounty home. If the Transposition hadn't been so damn bloody. If I wasn't the Ordinator.

If Jinny hadn't died.

We pushed forward slowly, cautiously. There were so many planners that we couldn't see the uneven floor beneath the surface. It could have dropped off at any moment, but it didn't.

After a matter of minutes, we reached the rock outcropping at the center. I scaled it easily, hefting myself up and reaching back down to help Nick, groaning as he nearly ripped my arm out of its socket pulling himself up.

The item embedded at the center was indeed a sword. Its innate silver hilt had a swirling wavy pattern reminiscent of Damascus steel.

Nick panted from the effort, transfixed on the sword as he spoke. "You know, I keep thinking about what happened in the throne room."

"Yeah?" So had I. "What about it?"

Nick smiled. "If we'd gone in the way I wanted, assumed the Knights would hold up their end of the bargain—Merlin and the corrupted

Knights would have killed us. And if you rat fucked them out of the gate, I don't get Gawain's respect, and he doesn't give me the key to this place."

It made sense. The only reason we'd gotten this far was because I'd let him play it out. Taken precautions, been ready for it to go sideways.

"We got lucky," I said, after a moment's hesitation.

Nick caught my arm. "That's not it, man. It wasn't luck. The shit you were saying earlier, on the sandbar? About how you always go to the nuclear option? And how it's not naïve to want things to be better? You trusted me to bring it home. And I trusted you to have my back with a giant fucking stick."

He must have read the skepticism on my face, because he crossed his arms. "Yeah. I'm not stupid. You only stall like that when you're machinating. I just... hoped whatever you were doing was insurance. And it was. That's what I'm saying. It works. We just have to trust each other."

I sighed. "There'll be friction. Times where we disagree. I may do things you don't like, things you may hate me for."

Nick shook his head. "Dislike? Sure. Question? Absolutely. But hate? Never going to happen."

I wanted to believe him. Wanted it more than he could know. Unfortunately, there was no telling where this rabbit hole led. How bad things were going to get. What he was saying felt childish, but like Nick himself had said, I was inclined to think that way.

Now, to the elephant in the room. I reached down and flicked the hilt of the sword, resulting in a resonant thunk. "Well, Pendragon? You gonna pull this thing out, or we just going to stand up here and chatter?"

Nick glared at me. "Don't call me that." Then he eyed the sword. "Looks pretty stuck in there. Come on, man, you did the work to get us here. Sure you don't want to give it a shot?"

I briefly considered the possibility. Then disregarded it. "Nah. Too cliche for me. Swords are your bag. Not to mention, non-zero chance that it'd crumble to ash, or get corrupted by my dark lord shit."

"Ha-ha." Nick smirked, then did a cautious double take. "You'd uh, tell me if your class had some nefarious long-term goal right? Give a dude a heads up?"

"Of *course* I would."

"Great." His eyes narrowed. "Wait. That's exactly what you'd say if you had some nefarious long-term goal."

"No. I mean yes, but I'd be less sarcastic about it."

"Dick."

"Brainlet."

Seeming to summon his courage, Nick grabbed the hilt of the blade. And pulled.

CHAPTER ONE HUNDRED
TWENTY-FOUR

A loud crack echoed out across the water, followed by the vibrating hum of metal. Nick stared at the sword in his hand with an utterly inscrutable expression. Then raised his head and bellowed to the heavens. "Come the fuck on!"

Before I knew what was happening, laughter poured out of me in a crescendoing wave, growing to a guffaw. Most fictional depictions of the sword in the stone comprised the sword sliding out freely, as if it'd been sheathed there. This result was likely far more realistic, if not entirely anti-climactic. As Nick slowly turned toward me, utterly furious, I tried to clamp down on the laughter, snickering instead. "Let me guess, this has never happened to you before?"

"Yuk it up, edgelord." Nick brandished the ruined blade at me threateningly. It had snapped clean in half at a jagged angle and rose to an uneven taper at the end, giving the supposedly mythic blade a toothpick-like appearance.

I raised my arms in exaggerated surrender. "Please, ser. Don't prick me to death."

"Show you a prick," Nick muttered, holding the blade horizontally and studying it in disbelief. "What the actual fuck, Gawain? I thought he actually *liked* me."

Something Gawain said came to mind. "The way he talked, it sounded like this place was originally meant to be a Tower floor, but it was abandoned and left unfinished. If that's true, it kind of makes sense."

"FuuuUUuUUUUUuuUUuUck!" Nick reeled back as if to throw the blade clean across the chamber, thought better of it at the last moment, and swung it downward instead, swiping impotently at the air. The end caught an uplifted section of rock and shattered, taking another few inches off the sword as the fragments ricocheted and bounced, skittering across the stone and into the water with a series of plops.

I clamped a hand over my mouth. Nick was silent as a funeral. Slowly, he attempted to replace the sword into the gap in the stone. For a moment it stood upright.

Then fell over. The gemstone in the hilt shattered.

"I'm done!" Nick threw up his hands.

Somehow, I managed not to laugh. I bent down and picked up the sword. It didn't even register as an item. No feeling of magic either, but the heft and weight felt fine, about average for a sword its size. "Okay. Obviously, there are some flaws with the metal."

"You *think?!*" Nick raved.

"Might be a structural issue. That'd be on theme, flawed and unfinished like the ripple itself." I shifted my head from side to side. "But the metal itself might be valuable. If we find someone to melt it down, might be enough material left to reforge a spearhead, or a dagger."

"Right! Great! Let's melt down Excalibur!" Nick rambled. "Actually, why even make it a weapon? We could just gussy up a couple of grails while we're at it. Get into the grail-trading business."

"Probably not enough metal for that. If you factor in circumference, thickness, the base, and the rounded edges, there isn't enough for a single grail, let alone..." I trailed off, as Nick looked about ready to have a heart attack. "Uh. There might be enough for a small grail?"

He squished his face with both hands, accentuating his reddening cheeks. "Just. Gonna take five."

"Yeah. Catch your breath."

Maybe the real Excalibur was the friends we made along the way.

I snorted, wisely keeping the joke to myself as I inventoried the sword, gathering the smaller metal fragments scattered around the rock as well. It probably wouldn't add up to anything, but I'd consult Erik and Kai first. If they couldn't do anything with it, I'd dispose of it quietly. The less said about it after today, the better.

On my stomach, I could see a glint of metal from deeper in the hole. Maybe if I loosened the rocks around the edges and came back with the proper tools, I could get the rest of it out.

"Matt," Nick called, the beginnings of alarm in his voice.

I stood and brushed myself off, walking to where he stood at the edge of the outcropping, looking down into the water.

The planners were moving like ants in an overturned anthill. They were scrambling over the top of each other, water above them boiling as they moved in circular patterns, going everywhere and nowhere at once.

"Did taking the sword out piss them off?" Nick asked.

"Hard to say." It was a classic setup—grab an item in a suspiciously safe area, only for the innocent creatures that surrounded it to take issue —but that didn't feel right. They weren't trying to climb toward us or even pushing up against the rock. Rather, they seemed ignorant of us as they went about their business.

A clearing formed off to the lefthand side, the planner crabs spreading out and illuminating the dark floor beneath. There were many vertical rectangles scratched into the dirt, spaced out in an oddly familiar setup I couldn't place until I spotted the tail of a clear comet above them.

"That's the skyline," Nick said immediately, his brow furrowed.

Another clearing formed. Then another. And another.

The second was a clear representation of the tunnel. And while the hieroglyphic figures lacked detail, it was easy enough to tell who was who. Sae, retreating into the gate. Jinny, immobile on the ground. Nick, depicted with a black wound on his heart, crouching over her, a crown-like aura radiating around his head. Me, my face hidden within a cowl, standing off to the side.

They took us through every subsequent major event that centered on Nick: his suffering in captivity. His temptation. Then to the current moment, where he held a broken sword aloft atop an outcropping in the center of the lake. Judging from the glinting metal in the otherwise dirt scrawling, it was a safe guess that they'd used the sword's metal that had fallen into the lake.

"What are they—" Nick started.

"Shh." I held a finger to my lips.

Like clockwork, more clearings opened, continuing to create a circle around the rock. These were less familiar. More abstract. Meant to represent the future rather than the past. While the meaning was more shrouded, they seemed to depict Nick, climbing to the top of the Tower with me at his side.

The second to last pictograph was like the one that depicted the current day. Only this time, the sword in Nick's hand was whole. And with the luminescence from the planners, it seemed to glow with an almost radiant light.

And the last picture portrayed Nick, sitting on a throne. I stood off to the side, a silent guardian as he reigned over several individuals too detailed to be generic subjects.

"That's the Court, I think," Nick said.

Suddenly, everything clicked. I nearly reeled at the scale of it, the unbelievable vision. Hastur's reason for sending us here. The nature of the order. How he intended to pull one over on the pantheon, all of whom seemed to be interested in little beyond reveling in blood.

Every con starts with a story. A fiction tailored to your mark, presented so confidently that they want to buy in. If you do it right, they'll want to believe you, no matter how unlikely the story is. I had more in common with Hastur than I realized. Because unless I was completely off base, he was in the planning stages of a con on the grandest scale imaginable.

With Nick in the starring role.

Meanwhile, Nick was still fixated on the final drawing. The figure sitting on the throne beside him. I'd missed her entirely, too focused on other parts of the mural to notice. With the basic drawing style, she had no definable characteristics. But she looked exactly like the representation of Jinny from the pictograph of the tunnel.

He turned to me, face downcast, shimmering eyes reflecting the light of the crabs below. "It's all bullshit, right?"

"I... don't know," I answered honestly.

"Come on." He wiped at his face, his mouth tight with anger. "A *prophecy?* Really? And not only that, a prophecy that cribs its mythos from your pseudonym and just so happens to center around climbing the Tower. A Tower we've already established wants to be climbed."

I still didn't have an answer for that. The Transposition was too high stress, nonstop, and as much as I tried to remember the exact thought process that led to the name, details escaped me. All I recalled was the name popping into my head and sticking there.

"Is it bullshit?" I chewed on that for a moment. "Probably. But not for us. We're not the marks here."

"Then who is?" Nick asked.

There was only one answer. "The pantheon."

Nick scoffed, but I pressed on, the theory becoming more concrete the longer I spoke. "Think about it. The gods are bored. It's impossible to say for sure, but I think they've been doing this a very long time. To different worlds, or realms, or whatever. Maybe making people eat each other and releasing the survivors, only to move on to the next world was exciting once, but after doing that countless times, it's rote. Which makes any deviation noteworthy and interesting, instead of a threat."

"I'm... not following," Nick said. But he was paying attention.

"Hastur's not cribbing from Arthurian legend. He's taking parts of it, but what he's really stealing is its structure. The monomyth. Which lends itself to some of the best stories every told." I pointed to the first pictograph that displayed the comet. "Dome comes down. You wake up in the underground, and suddenly there are goblins everywhere. That's step one, the 'call to adventure.'"

"Okay," Nick said slowly. "But I wasn't exactly keen on it, at first. Until we were completely backed into a wall, we were basically just running away."

I smiled. "Step two is 'refusal of the call.'"

"Bullshit." Nick's eyes widened.

"Read The Hero's Journey and tell me I'm wrong. But that's step two. Wanna guess what step three is?"

"Go back to your aunt's house and destress in a biblical fashion?" Nick guessed.

"What—No. Gross." I wrinkled my nose. "It's 'supernatural aid.' The hero receives help from a guide or spiritual being."

"Which never happened," Nick said confidently.

"Really? What did Talia call herself, when you met?"

His confidence flagged as he turned to look at my wolf summon, still resting at the edge of a lake. "A spirit guide. Holy fuck." He glanced over his shoulder at me. "You make her call herself that?"

I shook my head. She'd come up with it on her own. "Next, the hero crosses the threshold, leaving their known world behind as they enter a new and dangerous realm."

"The trial."

"Immediately followed by the belly of the whale. Where the hero undergoes a transformative experience, usually a brush with death." I softened my voice. It still hit him like a brick wall, and I waited for him to recover before I continued. "Not saying it was meant to happen. Or that it was anything more than a tragedy. I've never believed in predestination, and I don't intend to start. He's using it as framing. Hastur likely has multiple paths to his perfect future, potentially including one where you killed Keith and went entirely off the deep end."

"Then what's the point of going along?" Nick asked. Shame flashed across his face at the mention of Keith. "If it's all bullshit?"

"Because Hastur is using us to tell the sort of story that doesn't happen in reality. Something that will give the gods pause, make them curious to how it will all play out. If he sends one of his more powerful Users into the ripple to get the planners and scram, it's less interesting than if he plays it this way. It's a misdirect—for what, I don't know. But what's important is that he's conning them, not us. And you're his protagonist."

Nick looked unsteady as he sat down, legs hanging over the rock's edge. "What if I can't? I'm fucked up, man. Have been for a while."

I wanted to encourage him. The Nick who had risen to Gawain's challenge and nearly beaten him wasn't a man trying to be a hero. He simply was one. But it had to be his choice. "Then we run, and Hastur can go fuck himself."

"You'd do that?" Nick raised an eyebrow. "Just throw all this away, knowing what we know?"

I hesitated. "The monomyth structure doesn't lend itself to a comfy story, Nick. Depending on how closely Hastur sticks to it, you'd go through a lot of shit. You'd win eventually, but you'd... suffer. Worse, it can be cyclical. So you might get through all of it, only to start it over again. Your friends and family would be in an elevated amount of danger, just looking at the most common examples. And every victory would come with a cost. Your choice, whether you want any part of it."

He looked down at the roving crabs below. "What step are we at now, if you had to guess?"

"This is probably the 'meeting with the goddess,'" I said. Then snorted as Nick balefully panned the area. "It's not always literal. It just refers to a moment of sudden inspiration tied to either the divine or the hero's higher self."

"So Hastur's the goddess." Nick looked disappointed.

"Kind of a letdown."

"No shit." He was quiet for a long time before he spoke again. "I get it. Having a god in our pocket would give us a lot more backing than we have right now. We'd need to figure out what his endgame is, but if he commits to me as his leading man, my survival is in his best interest. It'd give us time."

"Leverage," I agreed.

"Jinny's gone, Sae's disfigured, you're public enemy number one, and as far as everyone else goes, a tenth of the city's population died in the first Transposition. Everyone I care about is dead or already in danger. Stopping the second Transposition event is the best chance I have to protect everyone, even if it puts them in more danger in the short term."

I nodded. "And it's not like we'd be sitting on our hands. We'll take steps to protect any potential targets. Get ahead of the game. Split our time between handling things in the city and climbing the Tower." I surveyed the lake and the opening to the throne room beyond. "And I'm betting the authentic version of this floor is toward the Top, if not the highest. They want people to find it, but no one's made it yet. Guessing that's why they check everyone's gear coming out of the Tower. Everyone wants the mythical sword."

He looked up. "You'll be there? To help?"

I nodded slowly, thinking back to what he'd said earlier. "Every step of the way. I go low, you go high. We play it smart."

Slowly, the resolve from the duel filtered back into his face. "Okay. We're doing this."

It felt monumental. A moment we would look back on. I held out a fist and Nick bumped it, then pushed off the rock, splashing back into the water below and headed toward the throne room.

I landed behind him a few moments later, water splattering my clothes. I took off my mask and wiped it. Up ahead, directly in my path a section of planners cleared, revealing another pictograph below. I nearly called out to Nick before I realized what it was depicting.

A chill radiated through me as I stared downward. It was the throne room from before, but the figures meant to represent Nick and Jinny were gone, along with the rest of the court.. In their place, the cowled figure that represented me stood alone at the apex of the stairs, hundreds of figures at the base of the throne forming a faceless army.

"Coming?" Nick called back to me. "There's too many to fit in the bag. They can gather up the planners once we open the portal."

"Yeah. You're probably right." I scraped my foot along, erasing the mural with more force than was strictly necessary.

It wouldn't end that way. I'd make sure of it.

———

Getting out took some effort. Basic compared to what we'd gone through in the tower itself, but it wasn't nothing. Nick wore my mask, renewing its effect on the many members of the Adventurers' Guild milling about, waiting for "Myrddin" to emerge. I donned a horrifically heavy suit of armor, including a helmet, borrowed from one of the fallen Knights. Azure replaced an attendant and escorted me behind a curtain, and I made a show of taking the armor off and putting it back on, making it appear as if he'd done his due diligence.

From there, I sold the Waystone to Kinsley for a single Selve, and Nick and I took the long walk to the bus stop where we'd first met Sybil. As I'd hoped, she—or one of her facades, I wasn't entirely sure how her power worked—was waiting.

"Greetings, Ordinator," she said, directly to me.

"Can you take us straight to Hastur?" I asked, keeping my tone clipped. Theoretically, **<Awareness>** and **<Jaded Eye>** would notify me of any danger or potential traps, but the lack of visibility through the helmet slit was bothering me.

"Something wrong with the front door?" It sounded like a joke, but considering the predicament she put me in last time, it got my hackles up, regardless. I nearly snapped at her before Nick stepped in.

"We have something." Nick leaned in to whisper in her ear. "For Hastur. It's sensitive."

For the first time since I'd known her, Sybil tensed up. "Is it really so urgent? He is... indisposed."

"Pretty sure he'll be more angry if you make him wait," Nick pressed.

"Very well." Sybil waved her hand, and the rollercoaster feeling from before roiled through me as I snapped back into consciousness in the expanse of the underground excavation area and an overwhelming force bore down on my shoulders. It was all I could do not to fall to my knees. Nick, beside me, didn't seem to have any such problem.

Hastur was in the middle of something. His desiccated body was submerged in the water of a porcelain bath, the tentacle-like mycelium that covered his body extending out from the tub, giving him the appearance of an overgrown potted plant. He hadn't bothered opening his eyes and appeared serene, despite the pressure on my body.

Nick looked between me and Hastur, worriedly. "Is there a problem?"

"The problem..." Hastur's natural voice was guttural, harsh. "Is I told this one to clean house. Which he seems to have misinterpreted as a directive to douse it in gasoline and light a match. The casualties were expected, but short of brute forcing things, it will be nigh impossible to access the Tower now."

This was always going to be the hard part. Justifying why I'd made it harder for the Order to access the Tower. I'd intended to place blame on the Feds, use them as a scapegoat. It wasn't my fault they'd tracked me down, after all. But with our new bargaining chips, I didn't have to.

And despite the overwhelming pressure, I couldn't help but smile. We were right. Hastur didn't know everything.

"Let him go." The booming voice was so powerful, so authoritative, for a moment I thought someone else had entered the room. Nick took a menacing step forward, hand resting on the pommel of his sword.

Hastur opened a single eye, looking over him with interest. "Someone found their courage."

All at once, the pressure that weighed me down released.

"A less charitable deity might find your directness rude. Or worse, a threat," Hastur said, both eyes open now, completely focused on Nick.

Nick didn't falter. "Not a demand. A request. The first of several."

"Fascinating." Hastur stroked his chin. "You barge into my chambers unannounced on the tailcoat of failure with... requests. Or perhaps your failure wasn't such a failure after all."

Nick didn't take the bait, his expression easygoing now that Hastur wasn't trying to grind me into the concrete. It was like somewhere between here and the Tower he'd flipped a switch. All things considered, he was doing exceptionally well.

"Dormammu, I've come to bargain," Nick announced.

I facepalmed. "Jesus Christ."

"Not your best." Hastur frowned. "But elaborate on this bargain, and why I should be interested."

Nick counted off on his fingers, undeterred. "You'll remove my geas. If you want Matt to clean house, I can't be beholden to the current leaders. There's a good chance they'll try to use me against him, once they figure out we're working together, and potentially compromise his identity.

We'll also need resources, people who aren't amateurs assigned to us. A permanent position in the Court."

"And why would I do that?" Hastur countered.

"Because you want a backdoor into the Tower. A discrete way for the Order of Parcae's Users to come and go," I said.

"A metric fuck-ton of planners," Nick added.

"And, just spitballing here, but I'm guessing you might want the legendary sword at the top of the Tower that the people who run it are looking for. And a hero to wield it." I smirked.

That it took Hastur a moment to connect the dots was disquieting. Highlighted the reality that the way forward Nick and I had found was truly one of many. When he finally got it, however, his smile was full.

"I see. This is the path you've chosen. If you were aware of how astronomically unlikely this outcome was, you'd understand my reticence," Hastur said. I could almost see the calculation in his expression as he focused on Nick. "You were so angry, so lost. While I'm glad to see you back from the brink, I can't help but wonder. Will you regret it?"

There was an audible scrape as Nick ground his teeth together. I put my hand on his back and it stopped.

"Maybe," Nick finally admitted. "But looking at it from both sides, I'd regret the alternative more. No matter what's fair, or just, or whatever. Keith's brother was the one who pulled the trigger. And if I start taking everyone who wrongs me to task, it'll be impossible to focus on the big picture."

"Inspiring." Hastur nodded thoughtfully. "Surprising, but inspiring. I'm not terribly fond of moral victories, but it would have been a travesty to lose a disciple with so much potential."

"Then why offer him up like a lamb to slaughter?" Nick growled. "It would have never crossed my mind if you didn't put it there."

"Yes. It would have," Hastur retorted, imparting a certainty to his words that was undeniable. Nick looked away as he continued. "Eventually. To answer your question, it was a matter of triage. The Order is on the verge of fracture, to say nothing of the Court. Losing him cost me less than losing you. And while this might sound monstrous, I have lived too long to allow naivety to blunt the blade of reality. An uneven trade is always preferable to an outright loss."

His frigid eyes snapped to me, and I felt a fraction of the weight from before. "And you. You are certain you wish to remain as you are?"

I shifted under the weight, keeping my expression stoic. "Yes."

He pointed at my gauntlet. "That recent acquisition of yours will prove a challenge. A boon, to be certain, but a challenge. And while—as you've both guessed—my current state limits the extent of my gaze, and the Tower itself is well protected, I witnessed your encounter with a certain caster. One in Mr. Fields Camp."

Maria.

Her surprised expression popped into my mind, as she looked down at the knife in her chest.

"From a technical standpoint, it was brilliantly handled. Outmatched, worn down, and you still emerged victorious. But in the aftermath, your soul... trembled. You've killed before, but not like that. And if you remain on this path, serving as the Ceaseless Knight's dark vanguard, she will not be the last." Hastur's voice was forlorn, almost sympathetic. "He doesn't know what he's asking of you. But I do."

Did I want to be normal? To walk into a room without immediately looking for an exit route, meet someone without the automatic mental calculation of what they could do for me and how I could best use them, and the most efficient way to kill them if they turned on me?

Of course I did.

But...

Nick grabbed my shoulder. There was nothing but concern and understanding in his expression, a silent question in his eyes. He'd support me no matter what I decided. And somehow, knowing that made it easier.

Our world was about as far from normal as you could get.

Maybe it always has been.

The things that made me different also kept the people I cared about healthy and alive.

It was time to stop fighting that. No more hand wringing. If we made it through, there'd be time to work through my issues. Maybe go back to therapy. Find a kinder way to live. But the best chance of that happening —returning to a semi-normal, semi-functional world—was ending this before the next Transposition event wiped out another massive swath of the population. I needed to keep **<Subjugation>** in check. Everything else was fair game.

"I'm sure you'll find a more lucrative way to compensate me," I finally said.

Hastur blinked, then laughed. "Opportunistic as always. How fitting. Make no mistake, my young friend. When I reach my zenith, you and yours will want for nothing. I will respect your decision." He smirked. "But if you ever wish to know the truth of your nature, you need only ask."

It was clear bait, placed before me with no effort to disguise it. He was still working an angle. The question was why.

Before I could think on that further, Nick stepped forward. "So?"

Hastur raised his arm and drew a lazy circle with his finger. Nick grunted. When he unfastened his gauntlet, the Order's mark was gone, and presumably the geas with it.

The desiccated god closed his eyes and relaxed, sinking deeper into the bath until his shriveled face was the only visible part of him. "The Ordinator and the Pendragon. Old and new, joined as one. Yes. It'll be different this time. Mark my words, and mark them well. We're going to do great things together."

———

The story will continue in Double-Blind 3!

THANK YOU FOR READING
GILDED TOWER

We hope you enjoyed it as much as we enjoyed bringing it to you. We just wanted to take a moment to encourage you to review the book. Follow this link: Gilded Tower to be directed to the book's Amazon product page to leave your review.

Every review helps further the author's reach and, ultimately, helps them continue writing fantastic books for us all to enjoy.

———

Also in Series:
DOUBLE-BLIND
GILDED TOWER

———

Want to discuss our books with other readers and even the authors? Join our Discord server today and be a part of the Aethon community.

Facebook | Instagram | Twitter | Website

You can also join our non-spam mailing list by visiting www.subscribepage.com/AethonReadersGroup and never miss out on future releases. You'll also receive three full books completely Free as our thanks to you.

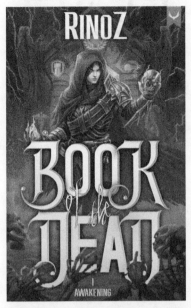

—

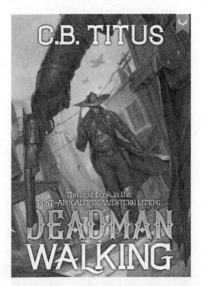

*A broken body. A mysterious world. **It'll take all his Intelligence to survive.** After close brush with death, Garrett realizes that he's in a new world. And worse, he's missing an arm and paralyzed from the waist down. A fact that doesn't deter the brutal gang lord whose floor he's crashing on from wanting to throw him out into the street. The only thing standing between Garrett and a cold death at the mercy of the city's scavengers are his own wits and a plucky young woman. Armed with a System that gives him experience for exploring his new world, Garrett is determined to do whatever it takes to keep himself safe from the threats closing in all around him. Even if it means becoming a villain. But the inn and city are far from what they seem. Terrifying creatures lurk around every corner and there is no weapon that can stop them. A strange lucid Dream world hovers on the edge of Garrett's consciousness, and it isn't content to stay a dream. When it starts bleeding into the real world, Garrett realizes that the hostile gangs around him are the least of his worries... **Don't miss Book 1 of a new Fantasy LitRPG Series by Seth Ring, bestselling author of Nova Terra and Battle Mage Farmer. Join Garrett as he uses hisintelligence and talents to make himself useful in a harsh reality, proving it takes more than just muscles to be strong. About the Series:** Mixing light horror elements with epic fantasy action, mystery, magic, intellectual maneuvering, guild building, and a grim fantasy world where monsters are everywhere waiting to devour the already disabled protagonist, this LitRPG/GameLit series is perfect for readers who enjoy exploring rich worlds and complex characters.*

Get Dreamer's Throne Now!

———

For all our LitRPG books, visit our website.

Made in the USA
Las Vegas, NV
10 November 2024

11533072R00395